Terror from Above

As Miri glanced up to see three bat riders circling overhead, the four Bottom Dwellers sprang at her. Miri fired wildly, hitting one of them. Another grabbed Gythe and tore her from Miri's grasp. Miri rounded on him, trying to break his hold.

Another bat rider threw Miri to the ground.

One of the bat riders landed on the ground, the Bottom Dweller carrying Gythe ran to the bat and flung Gythe to the rider, who dragged her onto the back of the huge bat.

Miri ran after Gythe, trying to catch hold of her, but the bat flapped away, evading her grasp. She watched in horror as the bat rider carried Gythe into the air.

The dragons were still there, wings spread, watching the fight. Miri ran toward them, shouting and waving her arms. Her words came out in gasps.

"I know you understand me!" she told them. "You saw what happened! They took Gythe. She played her music for you. She sang to you! Help me get her back!"

Miri pointed to the bat carrying Gythe, dwindling in the distance. She spread her hands, entreating the dragons. "Please! We don't have much time! Help me save her!"

The large male folded his wings and looked at the female, who quit hissing and looked at her male sibling. He lowered himself to the ground, inviting Miri to fly.

Now there was hope. . . .

"Multifaceted action and well-drawn characters will keep any fantasy fan's excitement at feverish pitch."
—*Publishers Weekly*

STORM RIDERS

MARGARET WEIS
AND
ROBERT KRAMMES

TOR®
fantasy

A TOM DOHERTY ASSOCIATES BOOK
NEW YORK

This is a work of fiction. All of the characters, organizations, and events portrayed in this novel are either products of the authors' imaginations or are used fictitiously.

STORM RIDERS

Copyright © 2013 by Margaret Weis and Robert Krammes

Dragon ornament copyright © 2013 by Jeff Easley

All rights reserved.

Maps by Ellisa Mitchell

Edited by James Frenkel

A Tor Book
Published by Tom Doherty Associates, LLC
175 Fifth Avenue
New York, NY 10010

www.tor-forge.com

Tor® is a registered trademark of Tom Doherty Associates, LLC.

ISBN 978-0-7653-6952-9

Tor books may be purchased for educational, business, or promotional use. For information on bulk purchases, please contact Macmillan Corporate and Premium Sales Department at 1-800-221-7945, extension 5442, or write specialmarkets@macmillan.com.

First Edition: July 2013
First Mass Market Edition: August 2014

Printed in the United States of America

0 9 8 7 6 5 4 3 2 1

To Tom Doherty
for being my friend

—Margaret

For my family:
My Mother
My brother, Jim, and sister, Sue
Nephews: Chris, Elbee, and Jimmy
And always, my beloved Mary
And my late-night helpers, Shackelton and Mew

—Robert

ACKNOWLEDGMENTS

In discussing theology with Saint Marie, Father Jacob happens to be thinking along the same lines as Descartes. The quotes are from Descartes' *Meditations,* Meditation I, "Of the Things We May Doubt."

The opening quotation in chapter forty-two, on the playing of baccarat, is from the article "Why Baccarat, the Game of Princes and Spies, Has Become a Target for High-Tech Cheaters" by Andrew Rosenblum, Popsci.com.

We would like to acknowledge the contribution of Chris Pierson in creating background for the characters of Sir Henry, Admiral Randolph Baker, and Captain Alan Northrop in the Dragon Brigade novella, "The Affair of the Orb."

The verse from Gythe's "Song of the Pirate King" is adapted from the traditional pirate song "Captain Kidd."

We would also like to thank Chris Rahn for his work on the cover art, bringing our vision to life, and to thank Jeff Easley for the dragon art in the interior.

Rosia

Dragon Lands

Milosceau

the Dragon Duchies

Dragon Lands

Duchy of Cadrea

Caltreau

Duchy of REINHOLT

Estadel

Winter Ho-Grech River

Port Grese

Mountains

Ciel-el-terre

Ho-Grech River

Westfirth

County ALTON

ELLIE PROVINCE

DEFOR

OSBANIA MOUNTAINS

St. Agnes

Long River

Jennis River

MARTINI PROVINCE

Bay of Saighn

Duchy of PIESTE

Chaudrun River

Lake Fulmeau

Vailpointe

Easguard

Royal River

New Evreux

Duon

Duchy of ALMICE

County BRIGHAN MARJOLAINE

DEFT FULMEAU PROVINCE

EVREUX

PROVINCE

Drie Mountains

Duchy of OSSAE

Eudaine

County CHENUYAT

Duchy of BOUELET

KHARUN DIR DESERT

Capione

Argonne

Fe WILDES

County GALIAR

Strait de Domcado

Braffa

1

A play should never be too long. If bored, the audience may walk out, choosing their own ending.

—Sir Walter Maidstone,
Freyan playwright

In the bedchamber upstairs in the elegant house in Freya's capital city of Haever, the child of Sir Henry Wallace was coming into the world. Sir Henry was downstairs in his study, listening in agony to his young wife's moans and screams. Sir Henry sat and paced and sat again and paced again, alternately cursing God or praying to Him. For the first time in Sir Henry's long, illustrious and, many would say, infamous life, he was helpless.

He had done all he could. He had hired the best physicians, healers, nurses, and midwives, including the physician who attended to Her Majesty, Queen Mary of Freya. His wife's bedchamber and the long hallway outside were crowded with illustrious medical practitioners, midwives, and healers, who got into heated arguments with the physicians over the best course of treatment. But as one of the midwives said with a shrug, "Babies will come as babies will come and there's only so much a body can do."

His wife's labor had been so long and difficult that Sir Henry, appalled at the terrible sounds emanating from her bedchamber, had already once attempted to force his way through the door. The physicians and midwives, healers and nurses had united to wrestle him out of the room. Expectant fathers were considered a nuisance, if not a downright menace.

Sir Henry, the most powerful man in the kingdom of Freya, was forced to retreat, taking refuge in his study. He tried to read a recently published book, an account of the Blackfire War written by an eminent Freyan historian, but when he realized he'd read the same paragraph six times, he tossed the book to the floor.

Going to the window, he stood staring moodily into the street. The summer evening was gentle and warm; he shed his coat and threw off his cravat. The mists of the Breath on the distant horizon were fading shades of delicate pink and orange. As night's shadows closed in, lights gleamed in the windows of the city homes of the Freyan noble lords.

The lamplighter would be coming soon, Sir Henry thought. A particularly loud scream caused him to shudder and break out in a cold sweat.

Preoccupied with his fears and hopes, he paid only scant attention to the wyvern-drawn carriage rapidly descending from the twilight sky to land on the street outside the house. Sir Henry assumed this was yet another doctor. He was about to turn away when he caught sight of a tall, heavily cloaked yet extremely familiar figure descending from the carriage.

Sir Henry uttered an exclamation of joy. He left his study in his shirtsleeves and went to the door himself, nearly colliding with the shocked footman who was supposed to attend to such duties.

Sir Henry yanked open the door, startling Mr. Sloan, who had his hand on the bell.

"Come in, Franklin, come in," said Sir Henry, quite forgetting himself and addressing Mr. Sloan by his given name. He took hold of Mr. Sloan's hand and gripped it tightly. "It is good to see you."

Mr. Sloan was taken aback and much affected by his master's unusual warmth. Flushing slightly, he murmured that he hoped he found Sir Henry well.

Sir Henry recovered himself and stepped back to allow the footman to remove Mr. Sloan's cloak and hat and take them away. Mr. Sloan, with a worried glance, indicated his concern at the number of carriages parked in the street, many decorated with the coats-of-arms of well-known physicians or healers.

"My lord," said Mr. Sloan, "is everything—"

"The child is coming," said Sir Henry.

Another moaning cry from upstairs proclaimed the truth of this statement.

Mr. Sloan did the unthinkable. He clasped Sir Henry's hand as fellow man to fellow man, not as secretary to his employer, and pressed the cold hand in warm sympathy.

"I will pray to God for your lady wife and the child, my lord."

"Thank you, Mr. Sloan," said Sir Henry. He turned away, cleared his throat, and then said in his usual formal tone, "Have you dined?"

"No, my lord," said Mr. Sloan. "I came straight from the ship. Captain Northrop sends his regards, by the way."

Hearing another cry, Mr. Sloan hesitated. "If this is not a good time, my lord, I can return—"

"No, no," said Sir Henry. "I need something to distract me. I have not dined either. I fear I cannot offer you a proper meal. The doctors have the kitchen staff boiling water and doing God knows what else."

"A bite standing is all I require, my lord," said Mr. Sloan.

"I believe we can do better than that," said Sir Henry with a faint smile.

He rang a bell and gave instructions to bring a collation of cold meats and cheeses, bread, nuts, and fruit, a bottle of wine for himself, and a pitcher of ale for Mr. Sloan, whose strict religious views permitted the consumption of ale, but not wine.

The two men retired to the study, where they did justice to the food and then settled down to discuss Mr. Sloan's recent trip to the city-state of Braffa, and the momentous events that had occurred in Mr. Sloan's absence.

"I was not expecting you for another week, Mr. Sloan," said Sir Henry. "I judge by your hasty return that you have important news."

"Indeed I do, my lord. King Alaric has withdrawn the Rosian fleet from Braffa."

Sir Henry was in the act of raising a glass of port to his lips. He stopped midway to stare, then set the glass down untasted.

"The devil he has! What has he done with the ships?"

"Ordered them back to Rosia."

"He's terrified because of the attack on Westfirth," said Sir Henry.

"So one would assume, my lord. Have you received any information from your agents in Rosia?"

"Not a word. Few ship captains have been either brave or foolhardy enough to venture out into the Breath since the attack on Westfirth. I can't say I blame them. I saw King Alaric's pride, the *Royal Lion,* explode and sink in flames—a terrible sight, Mr. Sloan. The enemy fired only a single shot—a green beam of contramagic from a cannon the size of a popgun. And yet it sank a sixty-gun warship."

Mr. Sloan appeared suitably impressed.

Sir Henry sighed. "I suppose I should have celebrated the Rosian defeat, but I could not bring myself to do so."

"No, my lord," said Mr. Sloan. "Understandable. I myself saw those demonic creatures when they attacked your manor house. Do you fear Freya is next?"

"I'm not sure what I fear, and that makes me even more afraid," said Sir Henry. "By the way, I did not at first give credence to your account of the bat-riding demons. My apologies."

"None required, my lord. I found it difficult to believe my own eyes," said Mr. Sloan.

He sat forward in his chair and, despite the fact that the study was heavily protected by magical constructs that dampened the sound, he lowered his voice. "You mentioned a beam of green light. I am reminded, my lord, of the cutter *Defiant*, and a certain woman . . ."

"Eiddwen. Yes," said Sir Henry, his face darkening. "She is involved, of that I am certain. She tried to have me assassinated in Westfirth, just prior to the attack."

"Good God, my lord!" said Mr. Sloan, shocked into blasphemy. "You were not hurt—"

"I escaped unscathed and, as it turned out, I gained some immensely valuable information. Eiddwen laid an ambush for me and my old nemesis, Father Jacob Northrop. We were attacked by demons in an alley. Father Jacob saved my life." Sir Henry gave a grim smile. "And I saved Eiddwen's."

"My lord?" Mr. Sloan was bewildered.

"Not of my volition, believe me," Sir Henry said drily. "She disguised herself as a sailor and stowed away on the merchant ship I had hired to smuggle myself and the journeyman, Alcazar, out of Westfirth. Eiddwen either knew the demons were going to attack Westfirth or she was the one who ordered the attack. She needed to leave before she was caught in the assault."

"You are certain she is connected to these fiends?" Mr. Sloan asked.

"I am. She used the demons to try to kill me, first in my own house and, failing that, in Westfirth."

"If so, my lord, that means . . ." Mr. Sloan paused.

"That means that whoever these people are, *I* helped fund their infernal green beam contramagic weapons," said Sir Henry with some bitterness.

"You speak of them as people. I assume you do not believe the fiends are minions of the Evil One, my lord?"

"I saw one of them shot dead, Mr. Sloan. I think it likely a true demon of hell would be able to withstand a mere bullet."

"An excellent point, my lord." Mr. Sloan appeared relieved. "What about Mistress Eiddwen? You speak of her in the present tense. I gather you let her live."

"I had no choice," said Sir Henry with a grim smile. "Much as I would have liked to have wrung her lovely neck, there were too many witnesses on board the ship. She had chosen the battleground. That made me cautious. We drank a toast to our mutual destruction."

"So what did you do with her, my lord?"

"Nothing I could do, Mr. Sloan, except deliver her to some godforsaken place on the Rosian coast. She disembarked, and that was the last I have seen or heard of the woman. I did tell her that if she ever attacked me or my family again I would track her to the hell where she was spawned, chain her to the devil's gridiron, and pour boiling oil on her."

"What was her reply to that, my lord?"

"She laughed. She said that her reason for trying to kill me had been merely to tie up a loose end, and that events had been set in motion that I could not stop."

Sir Henry finished the port. Rising to his feet, he walked

to the door, opened it, listened, shook his head, slammed the door, walked back to the table, and sat down. He poured another glass of port for himself, but did not drink. He merely sat, brooding, and gazed at the carpet.

Mr. Sloan thought it expedient to turn his master's thoughts to a more pleasant topic.

"How is Alcazar progressing with his invention, my lord?"

Sir Henry looked up with a smile. "Quite well, Mr. Sloan. He has produced a vast quantity of the magically enhanced steel. Tests have proven that the magical constructs he placed on the pewter tankard work even better on steel, as he theorized. A cannonball fired directly at a plate of the magically enhanced steel bounced off, leaving scarcely a dent."

"Excellent news, my lord," said Mr. Sloan.

"And I made an important discovery, Mr. Sloan," said Sir Henry. "This is news I have shared with no one, not even Alcazar. Or should I say *especially* not Alcazar—the man leaks like a punctured balloon. Alcazar's steel not only deflects bullets and cannonballs." Sir Henry paused for dramatic effect, lowering his voice. "The steel deflects the demonic green beam weapon's fire."

Mr. Sloan's eyes widened. "How did you make this discovery, my lord?"

"You know that I carried that blasted tankard with me in a leather satchel the entire time I was in Rosia. When Eiddwen's demons shot their green fireballs from their long guns at me, I flung the satchel up to guard my face. The contramagic fire hit the satchel. The leather disintegrated. The tankard inside was untouched. As was I, fortunately."

"God be thanked, my lord," said Mr. Sloan in solemn tones.

"I did thank Him, Mr. Sloan. Of that you may be certain. I have set Alcazar and his workers the task of manufacturing large plates made of this magical metal, which I will have installed on a gunboat. Given your news, it appears I may be making a journey soon to Braffa. If I encounter any of the demons along the way, I should be protected."

Sir Henry raised his glass. "Let us drink to the confusion of our enemies, be they demons or Rosians."

Mr. Sloan took a sip of his ale, and Sir Henry downed his entire glass of port. Another scream came from upstairs. Sir Henry swore under his breath and mopped his head with a handkerchief. Mr. Sloan rose quietly to pour his master another glass of port. Sir Henry thanked him with a look, accepted the glass, and resumed their conversation.

"I have one concern, Mr. Sloan."

Mr. Sloan might well have said, "Only one, my lord?" Instead, he merely inclined his head to indicate that he was listening attentively.

"A brief preface to this tale. When I was in Westfirth, I discovered the son of my Rosian counterpart, the Countess de Marjolaine, had found out about Alcazar and his invention and was trying to prevent Alcazar and me from escaping to Freya. Captain de Guichen is a gallant soldier, but he lacks his mother's skill at intrigue. I was able to not only give him the slip in Westfirth, but to take his best friend, one Monsieur Rodrigo de Villeneuve, hostage to ensure my safety. I took Monsieur de Villeneuve on board my ship, letting Captain de Guichen know that I would most certainly kill his friend if he attempted to stop me."

"What became of the captain, my lord?" Mr. Sloan asked, concerned. "I trust he is not still pursuing you."

"No, Mr. Sloan, Captain de Guichen and his friends are currently languishing on a remote island in the Breath, thanks to a cannonball fired from Admiral Baker's warship. The captain is not what concerns me. During the voyage on the *Raven,* Alcazar and Monsieur de Villeneuve discussed the magically enhanced steel. I paid no heed to their blathering, for they were going on about theorems and postulates and whatnot. Unfortunately, their discussion occurred before I knew Eiddwen was on board. I think it most likely she eavesdropped on them."

"That *is* unfortunate, my lord," said Mr. Sloan. "Do you know whether she overheard anything about this new steel?"

"I fear so. The two idiots were talking openly of contramagic in regard to the magical steel. I ordered them to shut up, but she would have undoubtedly found their conversation most interesting."

Mr. Sloan shook his head. "Most disturbing, my lord."

"Indeed. I had not mentioned to Alcazar or anyone the fact that the steel is resistant to contramagic. Although I have no doubt the clever Monsieur de Villeneuve will soon arrive at that conclusion."

"Why do you say that, my lord?"

"Because when we parted and I sent him off to join his shipmates on their deserted island, I gave Monsieur de Villeneuve the pewter tankard as a gift for my old enemy, the Countess de Marjolaine."

Mr. Sloan was in the act of drinking ale when he received this startling news. He swallowed the wrong way, choked, and spent several moments coughing into his handkerchief.

"I beg your pardon, Mr. Sloan. I should have waited until you had finished."

"Please give the matter no thought, my lord," said Mr. Sloan when he could speak. "If I could inquire as to why you would—"

"—give an immensely important military discovery to our enemies?"

"I am certain you have good reason."

"I do, Mr. Sloan."

Sir Henry rested his elbows on the arms of the chair,

brought the tips of his fingers together, and placed his two forefingers on his narrow chin. He gazed in silence into the empty grate for long moments while Mr. Sloan sat quietly, waiting.

"The demons attacked a stone guard tower not twenty miles from where we are sitting, Mr. Sloan. When you and I inspected the site, we saw how the magical constructs that strengthened the stones had been completely erased. That attack on Freyan soil was both a test and a taunt. The attack on our Rosian enemies in Westfirth was the same. As Eiddwen said, events have been set in motion. These fiends are letting both nations know that they are coming and there is not a damn thing we can do to stop them."

Sir Henry was once again silent. Leaving his chair, he went to the window. Darkness had fallen. The lamplighter had been and gone. A gentle mist wreathed the shining lamps in ghostly halos.

"I foresee a time, Mr. Sloan, when Rosia and Freya will be unwilling allies in a war against this demonic foe, whoever or whatever it is. I want my ally to be as strong as myself. That is why I sent the pewter tankard to the countess. She will understand."

Sir Henry started to say something else when he was interrupted by the sounds of a great commotion upstairs: feet pounding, muffled voices, an agonized scream, and then silence. Then raised voices and more pounding footfalls.

Sir Henry paled. He and Mr. Sloan looked at each other. Sir Henry put his hand on the back of the chair for support and stood staring at the closed door.

There was a knock. Sir Henry tried to speak and failed.

"Enter," said Mr. Sloan.

The footman opened the door and announced the royal physician. He came into the room, smiling expansively.

"A son, my lord. Congratulations."

Sir Henry's grip on the chair tightened. "My wife?"

"Your son was born without complications. Lady Anne is young and healthy. I venture to say she will bear your lordship many more children. When I left her, she was already sitting up and asking for a cup of tea."

"Praise God," said Mr. Sloan.

Sir Henry muttered something and turned his back. He blinked his eyes, wiped his nose, and offered a heartfelt silent prayer. Regaining his composure, he then expressed his thanks to the royal physician and insisted that he partake of a glass of port.

The royal physician, knowing the quality of Sir Henry's port, was only too happy to accept. The gentlemen were toasting Sir Henry and Lady Anne when the nursemaid entered the room, carrying a large bundle.

She curtsied and said, "Lady Anne sends her regards, my lord, and asks if you would like to meet your son."

The nursemaid lifted a fold of the blanket to reveal the young lord, who was notable for being extremely red, wrinkled, and bald. He was screaming lustily, his small fists flailing, his eyes squinched tight shut.

Sir Henry regarded the child with pride and dismay. "He's quite ugly, isn't he, Mr. Sloan?"

Mr. Sloan gave a discreet cough. "I was about to say he resembles you, my lord."

2

The rift that split dragonkind dates back to the fall of the Sunlit Empire. The dragon noble families do not speak of what caused the schism, though historians say it had to do with their friendliness to humans. The wild dragons took their reasons and their anger with them, disappearing into the uncharted places of the world.

—Count Suldrigail,
historian of the dragon clan Blumont

The Cadre of the Lost was living up to their name. Their houseboat, the *Cloud Hopper,* had been ambushed by a Freyan frigate lying in wait for them near a deserted island. The ambush had been orchestrated by Sir Henry Wallace, Freyan diplomat, spy, and assassin. Concealed behind the island's only mountain, the frigate had opened fire before anyone on board the houseboat knew it was there. The *Cloud Hopper* had gone down in flames, crash-landing on one of the multitude of deserted islands in the Chain of Pearls.

The island was far from the shipping lanes, which meant there was no hope of rescue. Stephano had not even bothered to light signal fires, knowing it would be useless. No one would see the light or the smoke. If they were going to escape, they would have to do it on their own.

This day, the thirty-second day of their maroonment, as Rodrigo termed it, he and Dag took their seats at what was jocularly known as the dining table—a wooden plank from a cargo box balanced on two tree stumps. The sun had set behind the mountain, spreading darkness over the campsite.

The members of the Cadre were eating their main meal late to take advantage of the cool evening breeze that provided some relief from the stifling summer heat. Their chairs were logs, cut and planed smooth or at least as smooth as Dag had been able to make them. Rodrigo still complained about splinters in his posterior, but these days he complained about everything.

Miri carried dishes to the table. Since the crockery had all broken in the crash, they were eating out of tin cups and off tin plates. She plunked these down on the plank. The pewter tankard, given to Rodrigo by Sir Henry, was accorded a place of honor in the center.

"The tankard is inscribed with the magical constructs Alcazar developed to use on steel," Rodrigo explained to his comrades. "According to Alcazar, bullets bounce off the metal. You can pack the tankard with gunpowder, blow it up, and perhaps cause a dent or two."

Stephano asked Dag to test the tankard, and Dag obliged, firing his blunderbuss at point-blank range. The blast sent the tankard clanging and bounding over the ground. When Stephano retrieved it, he found to his amazement that there was not a scratch on it.

"Wallace risked his life to kidnap Alcazar and this tankard," Stephano said. "Why would he give it to Rosia—his most hated foe? He must know that we will figure out how to produce the metal."

"Especially since *I* was the one who developed the theory

behind it," Rodrigo said. "As for why he gave it to me, that has to do with the Bottom Dwellers."

"The demons? What have they got to do with magically enhanced steel?" Stephano asked.

"I am not certain," Rodrigo answered. "All I know is that prior to the Bottom Dwellers' attack on Westfirth, Sir Henry was going to kill me. After the demons blew up the *Royal Lion,* he wasn't. He gave me the tankard and said I was to give it to your mother."

Thus the pewter tankard had earned its honored place on the table. Today, Gythe added a few decorative sprigs of goldenrod.

"Stephano told me not to wait for him," said Dag, lowering himself gingerly onto the log that served as a chair. Dag was a large man and somewhat ungainly, and he had to balance himself carefully on the log or else end up on the ground. "He and Gythe are still trying to befriend the dragons."

"Useless," Miri said curtly. "I've told Stephano as much. These are wild dragons. They are not like the noble dragons he knew on Rosia. These dragons left their homes centuries ago because they didn't trust humans. They're not likely to change their minds. He needs to give up this foolish dream that he's going to start his own Dragon Brigade."

She slammed an iron pot down onto the table. "Eat up. Fish stew."

Rodrigo peered at the contents—bits of cut-up fish and wild vegetables—and blanched. "I can't."

"Can't what?" Miri demanded.

"I can't eat fish stew," said Rodrigo plaintively. "Not again."

"We had squirrel stew last night," said Miri.

"That's worse," Rodrigo muttered.

"Are you saying my cooking is bad?" Miri put her hands on her hips.

"I'm saying the fish stew is bad. The squirrel stew is beyond bad. The bread, however, is almost edible. I will make do with that."

Rodrigo reached for a hunk of bread that Miri had made from ground millet and wild yeast. She rapped him on the knuckles with her spoon, causing him to drop it with a pained yelp.

"Get up from my table, sir. This instant. If you don't like my cooking, you don't have to eat it!"

"But Miri, you must understand," Rodrigo protested, snatching back his bruised knuckles. "I have a refined palate—"

"You're going to have a refined skull unless you do as I say!" Miri cried, grabbing a knife.

"Go ahead. Kill me now," said Rodrigo glumly. "Put me out of my misery."

Miri blindly flung the knife at Rodrigo, missed, and nearly hit Dag. She was going for Rodrigo with her fists when Dag caught hold of her around the waist and dragged her back. With her red hair standing up like the fur on an angry cat, Miri kicked Rodrigo in the shin, then gathered up her skirts and ran back to the *Cloud Hopper*. She disappeared belowdecks.

"Now look what you've done!" Dag said angrily to Rodrigo, who was examining his leg worriedly to see if she'd caused a bruise. "Miri spends all day fixing meals: gathering vegetables, fishing, setting snares, and picking fruit, and all you do is complain!"

"I said the bread was edible," Rodrigo muttered, and reached for the loaf.

"Oh, no, you don't!" Dag yelled, and moving to stop him, overturned the plank table, sending plates, bread, stew pot, and stew onto the grass.

Doctor Ellington, the large orange-striped tabby, strolled

over and sniffed at the pot. He sneezed twice and walked off. Rodrigo gazed down at the mess.

"See there. Even the cat won't eat it."

Dag glared murderously at Rodrigo. He was saved by the arrival of Stephano and Gythe, emerging from the woods. They had been with the wild dragons, and judging by their appearance, today had not been a good day. Stephano walked with his head down, his shoulders slumped. Gythe held her harp close to her chest, finding comfort in the instrument where there was comfort nowhere else.

Stephano took one look at the overturned table, the scattered dishes, and Dag standing with clenched fists ready to pound Rodrigo and sighed. "What happened now?"

"Fish stew happened," said Rodrigo. He rose to his feet. "I'm going for a walk."

"Take a long one," Dag advised, scowling. "Off the edge of the island."

Miri leaned out a window of the *Cloud Hopper* to shake her fist and shout something in the Trundler language.

Stephano shook his head. "I don't know what she said, but it didn't sound good. Gythe, go see to your sister. Rigo, get back here and clean up this mess. Dag, give me a hand with the table."

Gythe hurried to the houseboat, Dag helped Stephano lift the plank and replace it on the tree stumps, and Rodrigo picked up plates, cups, and cutlery. The fish stew was not salvageable.

The three sat down; Dag was grim, Rodrigo maddeningly nonchalant, and Stephano discouraged.

Rodrigo picked up the loaf and brushed off the dirt. "Bread?"

"I'm not hungry," said Stephano. He looked around, suddenly alarmed. "Where's the pewter tankard? We can't lose that."

Rodrigo located the tankard in the grass and replaced it on the table, flowers and all.

"Any progress with the wild dragons, sir?" Dag asked.

"None," said Stephano, running his hand through his sweat-damp hair. "Gythe plays her harp and I tell them stories, but the three dragons just sit there and stare at us."

"I was hoping someday I'd have the chance to ride a dragon, sir," Dag said.

"Doesn't look as if any of us will have the chance," said Stephano gloomily. "Every day the dragons come to the field around noon. The same three. I swear they're listening and that they understand what I'm saying. Why would they sit there if they didn't? Wild dragons lived around humans for centuries. They learned our language, the same as their civilized cousins. Even if it was long ago, the elders would remember it. These three don't give any sign that they understand—not the blink of an eye or the flick of a tail. And yet they come back, day after day."

Stephano rested his elbows on the table and lowered his head into his hands. "Sometimes I think we're never going to get off this goddamned island."

"Relying on wild dragons was always a bit of a long shot, sir," said Dag.

"I wasn't relying on them. I thought it would be . . ." Stephano shook his head and fell silent.

"Like old times," said Rodrigo. "Your own Dragon Brigade."

"I suppose I did," said Stephano. "What a stupid notion that was! How are the repairs to the *Hopper* coming?"

Fire had destroyed the galley and all their food stores. A piece of shrapnel had punctured one of the lift tanks, allowing the precious gas that kept the ship afloat to leak out. Cannonballs had punched a few holes in the hull and torn up the balloon and sails.

"I shored up that support knee and replaced most of the decking in the galley," said Dag. "The main deck and galley are finished. I've cut the rest of the planks and should have those in place soon. The hull is structurally sound. We can nail canvas over the holes to keep the weather out until we reach port. Miri's been patching the sails and the balloon. With one remaining large lift tank and a full reserve tank, Miri's confident that we will have enough lift to sail the boat off the island and back home."

"That's good news," said Stephano, brightening. "Rigo, what about the magic?"

Rodrigo answered with a snort.

"That is not very helpful," said Stephano.

Rodrigo was Stephano's childhood friend, a loyal companion, dearer than any brother. Brilliant, witty, talented, a favorite of the ladies, fond of fine clothes and fine wine and fine silk sheets shared with a lovely companion, Rodrigo was convinced he was stranded in hell. And he seemed determined to make life hell for everyone else.

"I don't know what else to tell you, Stephano," Rodrigo answered. "Gythe and I can repair the Trundler magic. The problem is the damage done by the green fire that hit the boat when the Bottom Dwellers attacked us at the abbey. Wherever the green fire hit, the magical constructs Gythe and I laid over that area are unstable. They weaken and break. Which means they can't be repaired."

"Why is this happening?" Stephano asked.

"I have no idea," said Rodrigo with a shrug. "I don't understand contramagic. And that is what is at work here."

"I don't think you should talk about . . . that foul magic," Dag said, glowering. "It's evil."

"Contramagic is *not* evil," said Rodrigo. "As I've told you before, contramagic is neither good nor evil. It is simply the opposite of magic. Just as air is neither good nor evil, or fire or dirt, for that matter."

"The church has proclaimed such magic evil," said Dag, his face growing darker.

"That's because the church is a bloody ignoramus—"

"Stop it, both of you!" Stephano ordered sharply.

They all sat in silence for a moment, not a comfortable silence as between friends, but an angry, disheartened silence.

Dag was bare chested in the heat, except for the suspenders holding up his trousers. He wore a kerchief around his forehead to keep the sweat from dripping in his eyes as he worked.

Stephano was in shirtsleeves and trousers. He kept his blond hair cut short.

Rodrigo would have as soon run naked through the woods as appear without a shirt. He would occasionally take off his lavender coat, if the day were especially hot, and even then he insisted on retaining his weskit. He had been reduced to doing his own laundry after Miri and Gythe had both flatly refused. His linen was as clean as beating his clothes on rocks in the lake could make them.

He broke the silence. "I can't think about magic when I'm starving."

"You are not starving," said Stephano shortly.

"Fish stew, night after bloody night when the island is teeming with deer—"

"We've been over this," said Stephano. "Dragons live on deer meat and it takes a lot of deer to feed a clan of dragons. If the dragons think we're competing with them for their food supply, they'll eat *us*."

Dag sighed loudly and glumly ate bread. Rodrigo tossed his share to the cat. Stephano regarded his friends with concern. As their commander he was responsible for keeping up their spirits, even on days when his own spirits were dragging on the ground behind him. Stephano was worried especially about open warfare breaking out between Dag and Rodrigo.

Stephano had first encountered Dag when they were on opposite sides during the battle known as the Siege of the Royal Sail. Dag was an expert shot, coolheaded and courageous in a fight. He was accustomed to living in rough conditions, making the best of a bad time.

Dag had tolerated Rodrigo, but never liked him. A man of strict religious upbringing, Dag considered Rodrigo a wastrel and a libertine. Rodrigo professed to like Dag, and then treated him in a patronizing manner that was worse than outright enmity.

The three men once again fell silent. A slight breeze stirred the leaves. The songs and calls of birds were cheering sounds in the evening.

"Look at it this way, Rigo," said Stephano, trying to raise his friend's spirits. "With all the weight you've lost, you'll have to buy an entirely new wardrobe."

Rodrigo managed a wan smile. "I can add the cost to the expenses and give the bill to your mother. We were doing a job for her, after all, when we were shot down."

"A job we failed. Wallace escaped with the journeyman we were supposed to save. Alcazar is undoubtedly producing this magically enhanced steel for our enemies."

Stephano gave the pewter tankard a flick with his thumb and forefinger.

"The countess can hardly blame you for the fact that we were attacked by the Bottom Dwellers," said Rodrigo.

"No, but she will blame me for being stupid enough to fall for Sir Henry's ruse and actually helping him to safely escape Westfirth."

"Not to mention shooting the confidential agent of His Eminence, the grand bishop," said Rodrigo slyly.

"That was an accident," Stephano protested. "I only winged Monsieur Dubois."

"Bourgeois little man," said Rodrigo.

"Bourgeois or not, he and my mother have the same job, just different masters. The countess spies on people for the king, while Dubois spies on the same people for the grand bishop."

"And Sir Henry Wallace spies on both," said Dag.

"While they spy on him," said Stephano.

"Who's watching who's watching who's watching whom," said Rodrigo, using one of his favorite expressions.

"That about sums it up." Stephano gave a rueful laugh. "Sometimes I wonder why I want to go back to that life. Look at how peaceful, how beautiful, how quiet it is here on our island . . ."

"I did *not* hear you say that!" said Rodrigo, appalled. He rose to his feet. "I'll go apologize to Miri."

"Let her cool down a bit first," Dag suggested. "Or we'll be burying what's left of you beneath that tree."

Rodrigo sat back down and began running his hands over the table as though he were playing a pianoforte.

"You were starting to tell me about replacing the magical constructs," Stephano said.

Rodrigo brought his hands down in a silent, crashing chord. "I'm baffled. The contramagic devours any construct I try to lay over it. I need to find a way to negate it, but I don't know that much about it."

"Can we set sail without any magic?" Dag asked. "I know the magic's useful . . ."

"The magic is not 'useful,'" said Rodrigo reprovingly. "The magic is necessary. Among other things, the magical constructs that charge the gas in the lift tanks that keep us afloat are regulated by the magical constructs on the helm." Rodrigo fixed Stephano with a stern eye. "We've been over this."

"I know, I know," said Stephano. He rested his head in his hands. "I keep hoping something will change."

"Here comes Miri," said Dag warningly.

Miri emerged from the *Cloud Hopper* with Gythe. They were carrying towels, going to the lake to bathe.

Miri McPike and her sister, Gythe, were Trundlers, a nomadic people who belonged to no nation, swore allegiance to no king. They sailed the world in their houseboats, whose trundling motion in the air gave them their name. Miri was the oldest, in her thirties. She had raised Gythe, who was about ten years younger, after their parents were murdered by the Bottom Dwellers. The *Cloud Hopper* was Miri's boat, the only legacy most Trundler children inherit.

Miri was a striking woman, with green eyes, hair the color of a forest fire, and a temper to match. She had met Stephano years ago. The two had started as friends, then became lovers, and were now friends again. Miri had told Stephano weeks ago, when the *Hopper* had been sinking in the Breath, that she had fallen in love with Dag. Stephano had given her his blessing then, but he wasn't sure how he felt about such a pairing and he was starting to think Dag wasn't sure how he felt about it either.

Gythe had strawberry-blond hair that was fine as cobweb, more the color of clouds at sunset than flame. She was winsome, fragile, and had never spoken a word since the day she had discovered what was left of her murdered parents. The Trundler healers could find nothing wrong with her physically. She could still sing the older Trundler songs, still sing her magic. Words were gone.

"If she talks, she fears she will have to speak of the horror she saw that day," Miri had once told Stephano. "I don't think she can bear it."

Both women normally wore traditional Trundler garb, consisting of an ankle-length skirt over loose trousers that tied at the ankles and a linen blouse that buttoned up the front with long sleeves to protect from the sun. Whenever Trundler women had to climb the rigging of their houseboats, they would take off the cumbersome skirt, wearing only the trousers. In the heat, they wore the skirts and blouses only.

Miri held her head high and refused to look at the men. Gythe cast them an unhappy glance as they passed. Gythe was upset whenever anyone quarreled.

"Do you have your pistol?" Stephano asked, as he always asked.

Miri did not answer, except to pat the stowaway pistol that she had tucked into her waistband. Stephano had decreed that no one leave the campsite without a weapon. The exception was Rodrigo, who may have known which end of a gun to hold, but not always where to point it.

Stephano wondered if he should try to mollify Miri. Gythe saw him open his mouth and shook her head emphatically in warning. The two women, accompanied by the cat, Doctor Ellington, who was apparently not speaking to the men either, walked the path that led to the lake and disappeared into the brush.

Stephano rubbed his temples. The oppressive heat was making his head ache. He went back to discussing the magic.

"You said Gythe was a savant, someone extraordinarily skilled in magic, like that priest, Father Jacob. Gythe covered the boat in Trundler protection spells. Maybe she can do something about the contramagic."

"Gythe is what one might term 'magically illiterate,'"

said Rodrigo. "She never had any formal training. She makes magic intuitively, the same way she plays the harp. She can't read music. She can't 'read' magic. Unlike Father Jacob, who knows all the rules and theories and equations that deal with magic, Gythe flings magic about like rice at a wedding. Repairing the magic is up to me, I'm afraid."

"If that's the case, we'll be marooned here for life," Dag muttered.

"Rigo's been there when we needed him before," said Stephano with a smile, remembering years ago when Rodrigo had risked his life to rescue him when he was near death on the field of battle.

Rodrigo only shook his head and played a silent dirge on the table. Dag rested his chin in his hands, leaned his elbows on the table, and gazed at the stars, perhaps dreaming of riding dragons. Stephano sat glumly in the dark. In trying to cheer his friends, he had ended up depressing himself.

The air was fragrant with the smell of night-blooming jasmine. Birds whistled a few last notes as they settled into their nests. The breeze strengthened and, in the distance, lightning flickered among the clouds.

Stephano roused himself. "Dag, you better go fetch Miri and Gythe. There's a storm brewing—"

"They're coming, sir," said Dag. "I can see their lights."

Miri carried the lantern, letting it swing back and forth as she walked. Gythe was entertaining herself with her magical "fireflies," sparkling flares of colorful, winking magical light she cast up into the trees and scattered along the path. Dr. Ellington always tried his best to maintain his dignity and refrain from batting at them, but when one flitted past his nose, the temptation proved too great. He pounced, catching the light, then watched in annoyance as it darted away.

Miri sat down on a tree stump and placed the lantern on the table. The light flowed over them, gathering them in its friendly circle. Dag picked up the cat, set him on his knee, and stroked him. The Doctor purred, a low, throaty rumbling. Gythe, whose long, strawberry-blond hair fell in sleek, wet waves around her shoulders, began to carefully comb the tangles from Miri's wet, curly hair.

"Miri," said Rodrigo, "I'm truly sorry. I didn't mean to upset you."

"I know," Miri said with a half smile. "It's the heat. We'll all feel better in the morning. The storm will cool the air."

The lightning was striking closer. Thunder rumbled and a few raindrops began to fall. When one hit the Doctor on the nose, he jumped off Dag's knee and made a dash for the *Cloud Hopper*. His human friends followed, leaving the dishes and the pewter tankard on the table to be washed by the rain.

Dag had repaired the fire damage done to the *Cloud Hopper*, making the houseboat once more livable, if not yet ready to fly. Miri and Gythe retired to the cabin they shared, while Rodrigo and Stephano lay down in their sleeping hammocks suspended from the overhead. Dag had a mattress on the floor so he could keep a pistol near to hand. He remained on deck, having volunteered to take first watch.

Outside the boat, the storm raged. Lightning flashed, thunder boomed, and the rain lashed the deck where Dag had taken shelter beneath a canvas awning they'd formed out of a sail. Stephano, lying in his hammock, could hear Dag's feet pacing the deck restlessly, heedless of the rain.

If we don't get back home soon, Stephano thought, there'll be murder done.

"Rigo, you asleep?" he asked.

"No," said Rodrigo. "Water's leaking somewhere. That infernal drip is keeping me awake."

"Mind if I talk?"

"So long as you don't drip, I am amenable."

"This is all my fault. My mother warned me about Sir Henry," said Stephano. "Father Jacob warned me. Me and my damn arrogance. I didn't listen and here we are, trapped in this godforsaken place."

"My dear fellow, you're becoming as monotonous as that drip. I hear this from you every day. You didn't shoot us down. Sir Henry Wallace shot us down."

"I can't wait for the next time I see him," said Stephano.

"And here I thought you'd learned your lesson when it came to that nefarious bounder," said Rodrigo. "What's done is done. Look at it this way: because of you, we have in our possession a pewter tankard that will revolutionize warfare. And now, if you'll excuse me, I'm going to plug my ears with candle wax."

Rodrigo shut out the sound of dripping water and was soon asleep.

Stephano lay awake a long time, listening to the rain.

3

I have been trying to understand contramagic, but at this point, I am at a loss. More than thirty days have passed since we were attacked by contramagic weapons and yet the residual effects of the contramagic still prevent me from replacing the magic. I feel as if I am trying to draw a construct on a piece of paper that someone keeps moving. And if I don't find the answer, I fear we will never leave this godforsaken island.

—Journal of Rodrigo de Villeneuve

The next day dawned, or so Stephano supposed. He could not prove it by the sun, which had yet to make an appearance from behind the heavy clouds. He and Dag inspected the repairs done to the *Cloud Hopper* and then spent the rest of the morning oiling and cleaning the boat's cannons and checking their weapons.

Gythe crawled nimbly among the rigging. She had been born on a houseboat and had worked on one since she was a little girl. Stephano loved watching her, for she was as graceful and skilled as any circus acrobat, though sometimes he watched with his heart in his throat. The deck was a long way down.

Miri often related how her uncle would hold races for the children to see who would be the first to climb the rigging to the top, touch the balloon, and slide down again. The winner was rewarded with small cakes known as ginger nuts. Gythe almost always won those races. Miri also told how the children would dare one another to jump from boat to boat when they were sailing, leaping across the vast empty expanse of sky to land breathless and laughing on the deck.

"Only when our parents weren't watching," Miri added.

While Gythe worked among the rigging, Miri went to inspect her traps and snares. Rodrigo took one look at the weather and decided to stay in bed. Doctor Ellington, wet and miserable, crouched under the table and sulked.

The rain continued into midday, then stopped. The clouds remained, gray and wispy, hanging to the ground. Stephano said it was too wet to go see the dragons today. Gythe signed with her hands, pointing to the field where they met the dragons, that she was going. Miri had returned with a brace of rabbits, which put her in a good mood. She told him he might as well go with Gythe. There was nothing for either of them to do around the boat.

Stephano and Gythe walked in silence to the field. The rain dripped from trees, landing with dull plops on the ground. Over the past month the two of them had worn away the grass in places and they squelched through the mud and puddles. Gythe had on her trousers that tied at the ankles, not wanting to dirty the hem of her skirt. With an oilskin coat over her clothes, she was drier than Stephano. He wore, as always, his uniform coat from his days with the Dragon Brigade. The coat was embellished with dragons, the tales he told the three wildlings were all about dragons. He kept hoping he was impressing them, hoping they would allow him to ride them.

He had always dreamed of starting his own Dragon Brigade, of being able to thumb his nose at King Alaric. He had hoped this was the start of his dream, but that hope was gone; a foolish dream, a pipe dream. Rodrigo would figure out the magic and then there would be nothing keeping them from flying home and leaving the wild dragons behind.

When he and Gythe reached the field the three dragons were not there. Stephano waited for an hour, by his pocket watch, and still the dragons did not arrive.

"Well, that's that," he said. "We should be going back."

Gythe made a disappointed face and picked up her harp. The two were about to return to the boat when they heard the rush of wings. The three dragons flew out from the clouds.

As Stephano gazed up at them, his heart beat fast at the magnificent sight. The dragons always flew in from the west, the direction of the island's lone mountain, leading him to guess the dragons lived in the mountain's caverns.

The noble "civilized" dragons of Rosia had left their mountain caverns long ago. They had built elegant mansions similar to human palaces, but uniquely adapted to dragons' needs and lifestyle. Stephano had heard rumors before he left that the noble dragons had abandoned their humanlike dwellings to return to the mountain fastness. He had no way of knowing if these rumors were true. He had not visited the dragon duchies in a long time. Being with his old friends, reliving the old glory days, was too painful.

The three dragons landed one by one in the clearing. The female dragon landed first, as usual, with the two males following her. By this, Stephano knew that the female was the leader. One of the males was her clutch-mate, her brother. Both had the rare and beautiful bluish-purple scales much prized among dragonkind. The third dragon was the first they had met after they had crashed on the island. He was larger than the other two, with scales of dark green.

Stephano suddenly felt reckless. After all, he had nothing

to lose except his life and the way he was feeling, his life didn't count for much.

He did not know their names. He had asked them, but the dragons had not responded. He had named them himself, calling the green dragon "Verdi," the purple female "Viola," and the purple male "Petard," because this particular dragon appeared to have a volatile nature judging by an event he had witnessed.

Viola, his clutch-mate, had once dragged a deer into the field and was preparing to devour it when Petard snagged the carcass with his fangs and tried to gulp it down before she could stop him. Viola lunged at her brother, bit him in the back of the head, and pinned his neck with her claw. The bite was not severe, merely a warning. She snarled and showed her fangs. Petard meekly relinquished the deer.

Viola then tore the deer apart and ate it in front of Stephano. He knew dragon behavior and he understood that Viola was deliberately eating the deer in front of him for a reason, perhaps trying to shock him.

Stephano had seen dragons feeding before and he was not in the least shocked. In fact, he'd told Rodrigo he'd seen worse table manners in the officers' mess. He watched Viola rip up the meat and took the opportunity to talk about how certain dragons in the Dragon Brigade were assigned the task of hunting to keep their comrades fed.

The wild dragons were smaller than their civilized cousins, with a sleek build that made them faster in flight. Over the centuries, the noble dragons had grown too large, in Stephano's estimation, equating heft and bulk with strength and power. Stephano and the other officers in the Dragon Brigade had often argued the point, some preferring a dragon who could batter down a stone wall with claw and tail. Others, like Stephano, preferred maneuverability and speed in flight.

He recalled Sergeant Hroal, the dragon he'd met fighting Bottom Dwellers at the Abbey of Saint Agnes. Hroal was seventy feet long and when standing on the ground could have poked his snout into the cathedral's steeple. Hroal was so heavy he had difficulty taking to the air. The sergeant was what was known as a "common" dragon; not a member of one of the noble dragon families. Some of the noble dragons were even larger—eighty feet from snout to tail, weighing God only knew how much.

Verdi, the largest of the three wild dragons, was perhaps thirty-five feet in length. Petard was slightly smaller, and Viola even smaller than her sibling. They were all fast, able to dart and dive, more like barn swallows than their ponderous dragon cousins. Stephano often imagined what it would be like to ride on the back of one of these fast youngsters.

Stephano liked Viola, who was the steadiest of the three. He pictured the two of them diving out of the clouds, taking revenge on the Freyan naval frigate, the *Resolute,* that had shot down the *Cloud Hopper.* He pictured Viola's claws raking the balloon, tearing it to shreds; the dragon's lashing tail snapping the yardarms in passing.

A dream—all a dream.

The dragons settled themselves in a line, with Verdi to Stephano's left, Viola in the center, and Petard on the right. The dragons were at their ease with their front legs tucked beneath their chests, their tails curled around the back legs, their long, graceful necks curved, heads down. Their spiked manes relaxed and folded back on their necks. They were in a resting position, but their eyes were wary, alert.

Gythe and Stephano had taken shelter from the spatter of raindrops at the edge of the tree line. Gythe started to walk toward the dragons, to play her harp for them as usual. Stephano stopped her.

"Stay here under the cover," he said.

Gythe regarded him with frowning disapproval, the same look Miri would give him when she was certain she wasn't going to like whatever he was proposing.

"I'm going to try to approach the dragons, see how close I can get," said Stephano.

Gythe grimaced and patted her stomach.

Stephano smiled. "If they were going to eat me, they would have done so before now."

Gythe latched on to his arm, indicating she was coming with him.

Stephano gently detached her. "You stay here, play your music. Let them know I'm not a threat. Sing the song about the Pirate King. They seem to like that one."

Gythe rolled her eyes. As far as she could tell, the dragons didn't like anything she sang. She sat down on a fallen log, placed her harp in her lap, and began to sing the old Trundler song that told in a great many verses of the adventures of the Pirate King, a Trundler hero, even though in the end the nations of the world had come together to sink his island base.

I steered from sound to sound, as I sailed, as I sailed.
I steered from sound to sound, as I sailed.
I steered from sound to sound, and many ships I found,
and most of them I burned, as I sailed.

As Gythe sang, accompanying herself on the harp, Stephano began to walk toward the dragons. He held out his hands to show he was not armed. He walked slowly, deliberately, smiling and calm on the outside, even if he was not particularly calm on the inside. He kept close watch on the dragons.

The three seemed at first puzzled by this break in the routine they'd established over the weeks. Stephano walked closer and the dragons' puzzlement turned to suspicion.

With their spiked manes bristling in warning, they raised their heads and dug their back claws into the ground. As Stephano moved ever nearer, Petard's head reared up. He half spread his wings, a clear sign to Stephano to back off. Viola watched Stephano intently, making no overtly threatening gesture, yet giving him no encouragement either. Verdi gazed down his snout at Stephano. The green dragon's eyes narrowed.

Stephano slowed his pace, creeping nearer a small step at a time.

"I want you to trust me," Stephano called to them, having no idea if they understood him or not. "I want you to know that I trust you."

Petard heaved himself to his feet, wings spread fully, his head lowered, his jaws slightly parted. His tail thumped the ground. His lip curled, showing his fangs. Viola rose, not as dramatically, moving fluidly, with an effortless grace. Verdi shifted, half rising, poised and ready for flight.

Stephano stopped. The message was clear. He gave a rueful smile and shrugged.

"Sorry," he said to them. "I guess I've failed."

He backed off. Petard continued to flare his wings. Viola had a glint in her eye. She seemed more amused than frightened. Verdi settled back down. When Stephano reached his usual place in the field, near the stump on which Gythe usually sat with her harp, Petard finally relaxed. The dragon folded his wings and returned to his recumbent position. He continued to keep a wary eye on Stephano.

Gythe came out from beneath the shelter of the trees, carrying her harp. She sat down on the tree stump and prepared to play another tune.

"Not today. Let's go back to the boat," said Stephano, dispirited.

Gythe cast him a pleading look.

"It's no use, Gythe," said Stephano. "The dragons don't trust me. And if they don't trust me, I can't trust them."

He looked back at the dragons.

"We won't be coming to the clearing anymore," he called to them. "We have work to do to repair our boat. But we both have found pleasure in knowing you. Thank you for visiting us."

He bowed formally and Gythe made a graceful curtsy, then the two walked back to the tree line. When they were in the shadows of the trees, Stephano cast a glance over his shoulder.

The three dragons remained seated in the clearing, staring after them, expressionless.

Gythe and Stephano returned to find Rodrigo sitting at the table. He was attempting to draw constructs on a board that had been part of the *Cloud Hopper*'s deck before it was damaged by a beam of green fire. He had placed the four-foot plank on their dinner table and was trying unsuccessfully to restore the ruined constructs. He was deep in concentration, muttering beneath his breath. Stephano, seeing his friend shake his head in frustration and then rub out the constructs he'd drawn, had no need to ask how things were going with the magic.

On board the *Cloud Hopper,* Dag and Miri were testing the workings of the two air screws used to steer the boat. Miri operated the screws from the helm—a brass control panel inscribed with magical constructs. When Miri touched a construct, the magic flowed from her into the construct and from there along cables made of braided leather that led to the screws. Miri touched one construct and the air screw began to whirl. Then she touched another. Dag walked to the opposite side of the boat, peered down at the air screw.

"Nothing," he reported.

"Is the cable connected?" Miri asked.

"Yes," said Dag patiently. "For the tenth time, the cable is connected."

Miri shook her head in exasperation. Her red hair was damp from the moist air, red curls clinging to her cheeks and forehead. She dragged her hair back.

"It's the magic. It's not working. So damn frustrating. I always took the magic that powered this boat for granted. Never again, let me tell you!"

Disheartened, she walked over to the table where Rodrigo was working.

"How is your repair work coming along?" she asked.

"It isn't," Rodrigo answered dourly. "What makes this problem so baffling is that we sailed from the Abbey to Westfirth and from Westfirth to wherever we are without any problems. The contramagic must have been eating away at the magic all this time and the damage from the cannon fire exacerbated the situation. We might well have sailed along for months without ever knowing the extent of the damage until we simply dropped out of the sky. Observe."

When he drew sigils on either side of the damaged portion, they stayed where they were drawn. But in the section affected by contramagic, the delicate lines of the sigil shivered and slowly warped even as he drew it, rendering it useless.

Rodrigo was glaring at the plank in frustration when Doctor Ellington came strolling out of the woods. Seeing Rodrigo and Stephano seated at the table, the cat thought it was time to eat. He jumped up and landed in the middle of the plank, treading all over the useless sigils.

Rodrigo swore, and both Miri and Stephano made a grab for the Doctor. Stephano dragged the cat off the table. Rodrigo stopped swearing abruptly.

"A flash!" he cried excitedly. "There was a flash! Did you see it?"

"See what?" asked Stephano, struggling to hold the hissing, squirming cat. "Ouch! He's scratching me!"

"Set the Doctor down on the board again. Right in this spot. Hold him there."

"He doesn't want to be held," said Stephano grimly.

"There! I felt it!" Rodrigo said at the same time. "Did you feel that? Oh, sorry, I forgot. You haven't a magical bone in your body. Miri, did you see? Gythe! Come look!"

Gythe came running to see the magic. Dag came running to rescue his cat, who was pinned to the table. The Doctor's howls could likely be heard for miles.

"Ouch, damn it! He bit me. Dag, take your cat!"

"Miri, see . . . Wait, it's not happening. Dag, pick up the cat and put him down again in the exact same spot."

"Are you experimenting with my cat?" Dag demanded irately.

"I'm fairly certain this won't hurt him," said Rodrigo.

"'Fairly certain'?" Dag repeated, glowering.

"I think the Doctor might be the key to getting off this island," said Rodrigo.

Dag glowered, but he picked up the Doctor and, looking grim, gingerly set the cat down on the table. Miri and Gythe hung over Rodrigo's shoulder, watching intently.

"There! Did you see?" Rodrigo exclaimed, triumphant.

Miri gasped. Gythe put her hands over her mouth.

"What? What did you see?" asked Stephano, staring down at the table.

"A flash of light arced between the two sigils in the far construct," said Miri, awed. "The magic is flowing through the cat over the part damaged by the contramagic, forming the connection. But how is that possible?"

"At the moment, I don't know," said Rodrigo. "I will have

to study the matter, but it would appear that Doctor Ellington is a bridge. The cat must be a natural channeler. I wonder if all animals are natural channelers or is this just unique to the Doctor? Or maybe unique to cats? I will make that a part of my study, perhaps write a treatise . . ."

"Rigo!" said Stephano sharply. "What about the damage?"

"What? Oh, yes. The cat's body connected the magic that connected the sigils. The magic flowed through him as magic flows through Miri when she touches the constructs on the helm. Just for an instant, mind you. The Doctor could not do channeling on a regular basis."

"Damn right he won't!" Dag said firmly.

Rodrigo smiled broadly at the cat. "I could kiss him on his little flea-bitten head!"

Doctor Ellington, looking deeply offended at the notion, wriggled out of Dag's grasp and fled into the woods.

"I'm sorry, but I don't see how having a magic-channeling cat helps us," said Stephano.

"The problem has been that any new construct I tried to draw across the contramagic area shriveled up and disappeared. These constructs are necessary because they don't just act as protection magic for the hull plank here, they transmit the commands from the helm along the leather cables that run to the lift tanks, the balloon, the air screws . . ."

"And if I can't control the magical constructs in the balloon or tanks, they won't work," Miri added.

"When the cat was a bridge, I could keep the magic flowing over the damaged area to the construct on the other side."

"But I thought you couldn't draw a construct through the contramagic," Dag said.

"I still can't. I'm not drawing a construct. Watch: I place an energy sigil here on the undamaged part and a sigil on the other side," Rodrigo explained, demonstrating. "You see the energy flowing between them over the bad part."

"Some of us can see it," Stephano said grimly. "And some of us can't."

"I can see it and it works. This means we can jury-rig the magic," said Miri excitedly.

"We can place bridging lines between the constructs that were not hit by contramagic, using them to bypass the parts of the boat damaged by contramagic. This will keep the magic flowing. It won't be easy," Rodrigo added more somberly. "Gythe and I will have to renew these energy-generating sigils during the flight to keep them working. And there is, of course, always the distinct possibility the magic could fail . . ."

Stephano shook his head. "I don't want to know what could go wrong. Tell me this . . ." He looked from Rodrigo to Gythe to Miri. "Will this repair get us home?"

"I think it might," said Miri.

Gythe nodded her head and smiled.

Stephano breathed a deep sigh. "How long will it take?"

"Shouldn't take long at all," said Rodrigo. "A day, maybe two."

"Oh, Rigo! I could kiss *your* flea-bitten head!" Miri cried.

"Even I could kiss him," said Dag, smiling broadly.

"Kiss me instead," Miri said, smiling up at him.

Dag blushed, but he did give her a peck on the cheek. Gythe began to sing and clap her hands. Miri tugged at Dag, who hesitated, then began to shuffle his feet and at last broke into a lumbering stride.

"He looks just like a bear in the circus," Rodrigo remarked to Stephano under his breath. He held out his hands to Gythe. "May I have this dance, mademoiselle?"

Gythe laughed and the two went spinning gracefully over the grass.

Stephano stood apart, watching his friends with affection so great that it threatened to overflow his heart, spill out of his eyes. For a long time, he had refused to allow himself to think of home. Now he relaxed and let himself remember with fond longing his old retainer, Benoit, griping about his aches and pains; the smell of the leather-bound books in the library; the small area in the backyard where he practiced his fencing; the kitchen where the Cadre gathered to make their plans. Within a week or so, depending on how far they were from Rosia, he might be sitting in that kitchen with his friends, reminiscing about the time they had been marooned on a deserted island.

When everyone ran out of breath and stopped dancing, Rodrigo, Miri, and Gythe went back to the *Cloud Hopper* to start work on the bridging constructs. Doctor Ellington returned from his jaunt, jumped up on Dag's shoulder, and began kneading with his paws.

"He's never going to let us forget that he saved us," Stephano observed.

"Do you mean Rigo or the cat, sir?" said Dag, petting the Doctor.

"Both, unfortunately," said Stephano. "Whenever I try to avoid going to court with Rigo he will sigh and say, 'How soon you forget! If it hadn't been for me, you'd still be stuck on that wretched island.' And I'll end up having to put on a cravat to go have tea with some infernal duchess."

He and Dag boarded the *Cloud Hopper* to find Rodrigo talking breathlessly to himself as he scrawled magical sigils and lines on the lift tank. Gythe and Miri stood close by, watching him intently.

"There, it's finished," Rodrigo said, standing up. "We should do a test, send the magic into the tank or whatever it is you do to the tank to see if it works."

"At the same time, we should fill the tank so that we can check to see if it leaks," said Miri.

"All we have left is the gas in the reserve tank," said Dag. "If the gas in this tank leaks out, we'll have only one full lift tank."

"Can't we sail with one lift tank?" Rodrigo asked. "We have the gas in the balloon as well."

Gythe giggled, then caught her sister's stern eye and put a hand over her mouth.

"No, Rigo, we can't," Miri said. "When I send the magical charge through the gas, the amount of lift increases as the internal pressure of the tank increases. That's the advantage of the lift tank over the balloon. The lift tank is much smaller than the balloon and provides the same amount of lift. We have to have pressure enough inside the tank to hear any significant leak. And we have to see if your magic works. If it doesn't, it won't matter if we have a hundred lift tanks."

"The decision is yours, Miri," said Stephano. "The *Cloud Hopper* is your boat."

Dag was unhappy. "I wish I could be absolutely sure those fixes I made will hold . . ."

"None of us can be sure of anything," said Miri briskly. "We have to fill the tank sometime. Might as well be now."

Miri opened the valve that released the gas in the reserve tank, sending it flowing into the lift tank. She bent down to keep watch on a small metal bump on the tank known as the "wart." Inside the wart were several pieces of leather covered with extremely detailed constructs designed to react to slight changes in the internal pressure of the tank. Reading those changes, Miri knew to shut the valve off when the tank was full.

Miri hurried to the brass helm, where she touched the construct that sent the magical energy flowing into the lift tank. Everyone waited tensely to see if the bridge Rodrigo had created would work. Nothing happened for several heart-stopping moments, and then the starboard side of the *Cloud Hopper* began to rise.

"We're going home," said Rodrigo.

4

I made a discovery today with the assistance of that wonderful cat, Doctor Ellington. A bridging construct that routes the magic through a conduit can bypass the damage done by contramagic. Gythe and I will have to work day and night to keep the magic flowing by constantly renewing the constructs, but I believe it should work.

—Journal of Rodrigo de Villeneuve

Miri stopped the flow of magic and the *Cloud Hopper* gently sank back to the ground. While everyone else was congratulating one another, Dag cautioned them not to get too excited.

"We have to make certain the tank doesn't leak. I'm still not sure about those repairs I made . . ."

"Only one way to find out," said Miri.

The tank was built into the bulkhead beneath the starboard wing. On Miri's orders, they all crouched down near the tank, their heads cocked, straining to hear.

"We must look like a bunch of lunatics," Rodrigo remarked. "Squatting here staring at a tank."

"Quiet!" the others all said, glaring at him.

Miri shifted her glare to the Doctor, who came over to

remind them with loud meows that it was time for dinner. Gythe hurriedly grabbed the cat and scratched him under his chin. He purred and shut his eyes in contentment.

"I don't hear any hissing," said Stephano, after several moments.

"I don't either." Miri smiled at Dag. "You did a wonderful job."

"Might be a slow leak," Dag said. "We wouldn't hear that."

Miri shook her head at him.

"Dag will fret over his repairs all the way home," she said to Gythe. "Let's fix supper."

Rodrigo turned to go below. "I'm going to start packing."

"Supper and packing can wait," said Stephano. "Rigo, you need to finish the rest of the bridging constructs. Gythe, you start placing your protection magic over Rigo's bridging constructs," said Stephano.

"Protect the constructs from what? Mosquitoes?" Rodrigo asked, slapping irritably at his neck. "Never mind dragons, I think we could ride the mosquitoes back to Evreux."

Stephano was adamant, however, and Rodrigo was forced to postpone his packing. Gythe enjoyed weaving her magical web of protective spells. Singing softly to herself, she drew the constructs so swiftly that Rodrigo was enthralled.

"I've seen her create constructs all over this boat," he said to Stephano. "And I still have no idea what she does or how she does it. I think it has something to do with her singing. Miri sings when she whips up that yellow healing goo of hers, as well. Does the singing help her to remember the constructs? Or does the singing work as a construct itself? Do all Trundlers sing when they cast magic or is this unique to the McPike clan? I have no idea."

"You're watching to make sure she doesn't cocoon the

boat in protective magic, right?" Stephano asked. "Like she did the time we almost sank in the Breath?"

"Oh, yes. Gythe understands now. Although her layers of magic did prove to be useful when the demons attacked. She kept the contramagic from breaking down our constructs quite so fast. She's only placing a couple of layers this time."

"But if we're attacked again—"

"My dear fellow, this boat is being held together by a stew pot and one of my silk shirts. Magic—her magic, my magic—can only do so much. A child with a peashooter could knock us out of the sky."

That night, as they sat down to supper, everyone was in a good mood. Rodrigo even complimented the meal.

Miri outlined their plans for the next day.

"Gythe and I will finish patching the balloon. Once that's done, Rigo can add his magical constructs. Dag and Stephano, we need to stock up on food for the trip and fill the water barrels. I figure we should be ready to sail for home in two days."

The next day dawned clear and bright, though not noticeably cooler. Everyone was cheerful, however, and set to work with a will. Dag thumped the lift tank and was relieved and pleased to announce that the gas had not leaked out. Everyone knew this already, because they'd heard him thump the tank at intervals throughout the night.

Miri and Gythe completed stitching and patching the balloon, then handed the voluminous bundle of gaily colored, red- and yellow-striped silk over to Rodrigo to repair the magical constructs. The balloon was chambered, each chamber holding its own quantity of gas so that if the balloon was damaged, one chamber could leak without causing the other chambers to lose the precious gas.

Gythe and Miri rewarded Rodrigo for his work by offering to wash his clothes. Carrying their basket piled high with shirts and skirts, pantaloons and underdrawers, they walked down to the lake. Doctor Ellington accompanied them, his tail moving from side to side in a slow and graceful wave.

"Do you have your pistol?" Stephano called out.

"Yes, Papa," Miri returned, laughing and flourishing the weapon.

Dag and Stephano hauled water in buckets from the nearby stream to fill the water barrels that were located belowdecks. As Dag carried his buckets down the stairs, Stephano stopped to stare at Rodrigo, who was bent over backward pressing his hands into the small of his back.

"Whatever are you doing?" Stephano asked.

"Muscle cramp," Rodrigo grunted, gazing up at the sky as he twisted and turned to ease the pain. "What a beautiful day. Only one cloud in heaven's vault."

He paused. His eyes narrowed and he said in a puzzled tone of voice, "That's very strange behavior in a cloud."

Stephano squinted at the cloud. Rodrigo was right. The cloud was receding and then swelling and then receding again.

"Look at that cloud," said Stephano to Dag as he came up to the foredeck. "Have you ever seen a cloud behave like that?"

"No, sir," said Dag.

"I need the spyglass," said Stephano.

Rodrigo ran to the helm to grab the spyglass they kept in a cabinet underneath. He brought it to Stephano, who raised it to his eye.

"Bloody hell!" Stephano swore, and handed the glass to Dag, who peered through it, then lowered it.

"Bloody hell is right, sir. Those are Bottom Dwellers."

"You mean the demons? How could a cloud be demons?" Rodrigo gasped.

Stephano didn't answer. He looked through the glass again. He could see clearly the huge bats of the Bottom Dwellers, their leathery wings dark against the blue sky, and their riders: men in demonic-looking armor perched on the backs of the bats, sitting comfortably between the head and the wings.

The Bottom Dwellers did not fly in formation, as did dragon riders. They flew in a swarm that, at a great distance, could be easily mistaken for a cloud constantly shifting position. They were flying at a leisurely pace. Several bats occasionally broke off from the main group; some swooping down low over the treetops.

Dag had gone below to fetch his own spyglass and he was watching alongside Stephano.

"If it didn't sound crazy, I'd say they were a search party, sir," Dag said. "But what could they be searching for?"

Stephano felt his gut tighten. "They're looking for us."

Rodrigo gaped at him. "For us? How could they know we're here? No one knows we're here except Sir Henry—"

"And the crew of that merchant vessel and the crew of the frigate that brought us down. I hope to God I'm wrong, but better to be safe than sorry. Dag, mount one of the swivel guns. I'll tend to the other."

The swivel gun was a small cannon that could be mounted on a swiveling stand on the ship's rail. The *Cloud Hopper* had four swivel guns, two four-pound cannons, and one cannon known as the "frog," for its squat body and large mouth, that could fire a twenty-four-pound ball. The swivel gun had proven effective in fighting the Bottom Dwellers because, unlike the cannons, the weapon could be quickly swiveled in its mount by the gunner to find the best target. The swivel gun was also faster to load, using chambers preloaded with powder and grapeshot that could be swiftly switched in and out.

Stephano picked up a swivel gun from where it lay on the deck and mounted it on the stand at the bow.

"Sir Henry wouldn't spy for them," Rodrigo argued, trailing after Stephano. "The demons tried to assassinate him, remember? They attacked his ship. He loathes them as much as we do. I guess it is possible that someone on board the ship was a spy . . ."

"I don't have the answers, Rigo," said Stephano, fumbling at the bolts that held the swivel gun in place. "And I don't have time to argue about it. Go below and bring up the bags with the canisters, plus Dag needs a shirt and his armor. And I'll need my flight coat. You'll find it—"

"I know," said Rodrigo, and he disappeared into the hold.

"I'll do this, sir," said Dag, taking over the swivel gun. "You keep an eye on the bastards."

Rodrigo came up the stairs, dragging the heavy sacks containing the canisters. At Dag's direction, he dropped one sack by each gun, then went back down below for the armor and the flight coat. Stephano watched the bat riders. They had re-formed, now flying in more or less a straight line spread across the sky.

"They're moving slowly, taking their time. They're definitely searching for something. Fortunately the boat's hidden—"

"Sir!" Dag cried. "The balloon!"

When the *Cloud Hopper* had been hit by cannon fire, Miri had managed to guide the burning boat into a small clearing, keeping them from crashing into the trees. The boat was partially hidden by a canopy of tree branches. The gaily colored silk of the balloon, spread out on the deck for patching, made a bright red splash among the green.

Stephano turned around so fast he nearly tripped himself. He and Dag worked feverishly to gather the yards of silk in their arms, bundle it up, and shove it into the hold. Down below, Rodrigo caught the silk and pulled it through the door. He came back up on deck lugging Dag's shirt, his metal cuirass, and Stephano's flight coat.

Dag's cuirass was a breastplate and a back piece made of magically enhanced metal that fit over the shoulders and rested on the hip, protecting the torso. The cuirass had been damaged by the green fire in the fight with the Bottom Dwellers in Westfirth. He'd spent considerable time on the island repairing it.

"I drew some magical constructs on the armor," Rodrigo said, handing it to Dag. "I hope you don't mind."

"What sort of magic?" Dag demanded, scowling.

"I just added a few constructs I thought might help withstand an attack from the contramagic green fire," said Rodrigo. "They're similar to those Gythe cast on the boat. I'll be interested to see if they work."

"You mean this is an experiment?" Dag asked, eyeing the cuirass with suspicion.

"The theory is quite sound," said Rodrigo. "I did the same for my lavender coat. Ever since that demon tried to kill me, I have been determined that I will never again be unprepared."

"Thank you," Dag said gruffly.

"You are welcome. I did the same for you," Rodrigo said, handing Stephano his flight coat.

The calf-length flight coat was made of the finest quality leather, padded, with a high collar and a mantle that covered his shoulders. Two dragons made of contrasting colors of leather had been appliquéd on the coat, one over each breast. The cost of the specially designed coat had been quite dear, having required him to hire a crafter to inscribe the leather with magical constructs meant to protect against bullets, shrapnel, and the like.

Stephano hoped Rodrigo was right and that his theory was sound, and that the constructs would protect against the balls of green contramagic fire blasting from the Bottom Dwellers' weapons. Watching the flying demons closing in, he counted at least twenty.

Stephano thrust his arms into the sleeves and settled the coat around his shoulders. He would melt in the heat with the heavy leather coat on, but that was better than roasting in green fire.

"You'll need the pistols, sir," said Dag. "There're two beneath the helm, already loaded. You'll have to load the ones in the weapons locker. Miri was going to—"

Dag stopped talking. His face blanched.

"Miri! She and Gythe and the Doctor! They're down at the lake!" Dag picked up his blunderbuss. "I'll go after them—"

"No," said Stephano tersely.

"You going for them, sir?"

"No one's going," said Stephano, keeping watch on the Bottom Dwellers. "No one is leaving the boat. The bat riders are too close. They'd see you."

Dag glared at him in anger. "Miri and Gythe are out there alone, sir!"

"The Bottom Dwellers haven't found them. They haven't found us yet either. If you run out in the open, the bat riders will spot you for sure. Miri's armed. She and Gythe will take cover."

"Not if they don't know the demons are coming!" Dag snarled. He eyed Stephano, stood irresolute for a moment, then he headed for the gangplank. "The hell with you, sir. I'm going."

"I gave you an order, Sergeant," said Stephano sharply. "Return to your post."

Dag kept walking.

Rodrigo said with quiet urgency, "You both need to keep perfectly still!"

The three froze and looked up into the sky. The line of

Bottom Dwellers was passing overhead. The majority of the demons were south of the *Cloud Hopper,* flying east, toward Rosia. One or two of the bat riders had broken away. They were going to fly quite near.

Even if they couldn't see the boat, they could see signs of human habitation in the clearing: the table where they ate, the cauldron over the cook fire, the small tent used by Miri to smoke meat. It would take just one bat rider to glance down at the right moment. Dag and Stephano stood immobile. Rodrigo crouched behind the helm.

The bats soared over the treetops and flew past. Stephano drew a relieved breath, only to see one of the bats veer off and circle back around. They heard a shrill whistle, sounding the alert, summoning the others. Stephano let out his breath in a curse.

"Damnation! Dag, man the swivel gun!"

"No, sir. I'm going after Miri," Dag returned, striding down the gangplank.

Stephano ran after him and grabbed him by the shoulder. Dag rounded on him angrily, raising his fists.

"Let go of me, sir, or by God I'll—"

"Listen to me, Dag! This is Miri's boat," said Stephano. "The *Cloud Hopper* is her life! What do you think *she* would want you to do? Would she want you to go rescue her when she doesn't need rescuing or fight to save her boat?"

Dag looked away toward the lake. His jaw tightened. He looked back at Stephano and struck aside his arm.

"If anything happens to them, sir," Dag said in a low voice, his eyes fixed intently on Stephano, "God help you."

He came back up the gangplank to take his place behind the swivel gun.

"That was a threat," said Rodrigo.

"He's upset," said Stephano, as he hurried to the first swivel gun and maneuvered it into position.

"Ready, Dag?" he called.

Dag's answer was a grunt. He stared, stony faced, at the bat riders, who now were all converging on the *Cloud Hopper.*

Bats began to drop out of the sky, flying at the boat. Their riders were lifting their weapons—long guns firing the devastating balls of contramagic that utterly destroyed any magical construct they touched.

"You and Gythe laid down the protection spells again," said Stephano to Rodrigo, who was hiding beneath the helm. "Will they hold?"

"For a short time," said Rodrigo.

Stephano cast him a sharp glance. "How short?"

Rodrigo shook his head. "Short."

"Can you fix the constructs if they're damaged?" Stephano asked urgently. "Replace them, strengthen them, keep them working?"

"They're Gythe's constructs. *And* they're Trundler constructs. Only Gythe can do anything with them."

Stephano swore under his breath and crouched behind the swivel gun, preparing to take aim.

"The water buckets are full. Be ready to put out any fires," he told Rodrigo, who was not permitted to handle a weapon. "Here they come."

Rodrigo raised his head slightly and peeked out over the helm. He was about to duck back down when he stopped, transfixed, staring at something in the open field in front of the *Cloud Hopper.* An expression of horror contorted his face.

"What?" Stephano cried, alarmed. His first thought was of Miri and Gythe. "What do you see? What's out there?"

"The tankard!" Rodrigo gasped.

Stephano had no idea at first what he was talking about, and then realization struck. "Rigo, no, you can't—"

He was too late. Rodrigo had jumped up from behind the helm and was running for the gangplank.

"Wait! Rigo, stop!" Stephano shouted.

Rodrigo paid no heed. He kept running.

"What's he doing?" Dag roared. "He's going to get his fool head blown off!"

"The pewter tankard! We left it on the table!" Stephano yelled.

The Bottom Dwellers were swooping down over the tree-tops. Spotting Rodrigo running out into the open, several shifted their attention to him, leaving others to attack the boat. Dag and Stephano opened fire with the swivel guns, taking care to keep their aim high to avoid hitting Rodrigo, who was racing across the campsite toward the table on which stood the pewter tankard, filled with flowers.

A ball of green fire burst near him, causing him to stumble and almost fall. He managed to stay upright and keep running. The bat swiftly flew off, giving its rider time to reload the weapon.

Another demon was there to take its place, diving down on Rodrigo. Stephano targeted this demon with the swivel gun and fired. He and Dag were using grapeshot—balls of lead, slightly larger than a musket ball—that spread out in a cone when fired. He must have hit the bat a glancing blow, for suddenly it veered off, taking to the sky and nearly dumping its rider, who had to drop his weapon to cling to its neck.

Dag fired and shot one bat out of the sky. The creature landed on the ground in front of the *Cloud Hopper,* clawing and screeching in its death throes. The rider was nowhere to be seen. Stephano was firing the swivel gun as fast as he could load in the canisters. He hit one of the riders broad in the chest, knocking him off his bat. Balls of green fire struck the tree branches above him, setting them ablaze.

A bat rider swooped down on Rodrigo, who had almost

reached the table. Dag fired, striking the bat rider as he fired at Rodrigo. The fireball struck the wooden table, which burst into flames. Rodrigo tried to brave the fire to reach the tankard, but the heat was too intense.

"Rigo!" Stephano shouted desperately. "Get back here!"

Rodrigo ignored him. Fanning away the smoke, he stared into the flames that were consuming the table and the tree-stump chairs, trying to find the tankard. Stephano fired at a riderless bat that was diving at Rodrigo from behind. Stephano missed, and the bat struck Rodrigo, knocking him down and digging its claws into his coat, ready to tear him apart.

Rodrigo flailed at the bat, kicking and fighting to escape, as the creature tried to bite him in the neck. Stephano left the swivel gun, intending to run to his friend.

Dag jostled Stephano aside. Drawing his pistol, Dag yelled, "Cover me!" and dashed out to save Rodrigo.

At the lake, Miri, dressed only in her trousers, blouse, and corset stood over the washtub, stirring the clothes in the soapy water with a stick. She shoved them under, poked and prodded them. When she was satisfied they were clean, she hauled the soapy clothes out of the washtub and gave them to Gythe, who rinsed them off in the lake and then wrung them out and spread them on the tops of rocks or draped them over the bushes to dry. Gythe sang while she worked, a Trundler song women sang to ease the monotony of laundry day. Miri joined her in the chorus. Both were in a good mood. They were going home.

Doctor Ellington observed the proceedings from a safe distance. He objected to laundry day, which was far too wet for his liking. He sat on a boulder near where the women were working, keeping away from Gythe, who would mischievously flick water at him.

Miri was wiping the sweat from her face when she realized Gythe had stopped singing. She had been on her hands and knees, dunking her blouse in the lake and now she straightened, looking around nervously.

"Did you hear that?" she signed to Miri.

"Hear what?" Miri asked. "I didn't hear anything."

Gythe shaded her eyes with her hand to look across the lake. Miri paid little heed, thinking that perhaps the dragons were coming or maybe Rodrigo was going to play one of his silly pranks on them. Then she noticed Doctor Ellington had also heard the sound. The cat was staring fixedly at something in the sky. Miri followed the cat's gaze.

"Bat riders! Run before they see us!" Miri said urgently.

Gythe flung the blouse into the water, jumped to her feet, and ran for the shelter of the trees. Miri hurried after her and found Gythe crouched in the shadows, her hands over her ears.

"Gythe!" said Miri. "We have to go back to the boat!"

Gythe shook her head. "They want my help."

She kept her hands pressed tightly over her ears. Miri gently touched Gythe's cheek and Gythe slowly lowered her hands.

"Are the Bottom Dwellers calling out to you?" Miri asked. "Like they did at Westfirth?"

Gythe nodded. Her face was strained. She made the sign for the *Cloud Hopper*. "They've come to find us."

Miri gazed at her in bewilderment. "That doesn't make sense. How do they know we're here?"

"She told them."

"She? What she?"

Gythe spread her hands. "Someone called 'Eiddwen.' "

"Never heard of her," Miri said, rising. "We have to warn Stephano."

Gythe pulled her sister back down.

"They'll see us. We have to stay here!" she signed.

Miri spent an agonized moment deliberating. The Bottom Dwellers had spoken to Gythe before. She claimed she could hear their voices in her head. They said terrible things to her, accusing her of having left them to die, telling her they were coming to take their revenge on those who had tried to destroy them. One of the Bottom Dwellers had actually boarded the *Cloud Hopper* to try to abduct her. Rodrigo theorized that perhaps the Bottom Dwellers targeted Gythe because she was a savant.

"The same way they targeted Father Jacob," Rodrigo had said. "He is also a savant and he said they came for him, as well."

These thoughts ran through Miri's mind. If the Bottom Dwellers had come looking for the *Cloud Hopper* seeking Gythe then the last place she and Gythe should be was with the *Hopper*. As she was trying to decide what to do, Doctor Ellington appeared, looking irate, under the impression he'd been abandoned. Gythe grabbed hold of the startled cat and held him close.

Miri made up her mind.

"We will stay here. We should keep out of sight."

Miri reached for her pistol, only to remember she had removed the gun so as not to get the powder wet, and placed it on a boulder. Hunkering down in the shadows of the trees, she peered through the branches. The bat riders were flying past, heading in the general direction of the *Cloud Hopper*. Miri decided to make a run for it. She dashed out into the open, grabbed the pistol, and ran back to Gythe and the Doctor.

"They flew north. I don't think they saw us," Miri reported. "But we need to go deeper into the woods."

Gythe rose to her feet, still holding on to the cat, who was always content to allow someone to carry him. Miri led the way, her pistol drawn. Gythe suddenly stopped and turned, pointing.

Miri fearfully raised the pistol. Gythe shook her head and indicated the field where she and Stephano went every day to meet the dragons. Although Stephano had told the dragons he would not be back, the three dragons had apparently not understood him. They were there, waiting for them.

At that moment the dragons saw the bat riders. Their heads tilted, their necks stretched. They sniffed the air. One spoke, the female, and the other two responded. They sounded angry, but not shocked or surprised. Their manes bristled, their wings flicked. Their tails thumped the ground.

Dragons were extremely territorial. Even among their own kind, dragons would follow strict protocols when one dragon ventured into the territory claimed by another. These dragons were definitely not pleased to see interlopers flying over their island.

Miri hoped the wild dragons would either attack the bat riders or at least drive them away. The dragons kept an eye on the Bottom Dwellers, but when the bat riders did not bother them, the dragons appeared content to let them fly off. The three dragons settled down to wait for the songs and stories.

The bat riders were no longer in sight. Miri waited tensely. She didn't hear anything and she began to relax.

"They've gone—"

The sound of gunfire cut her off.

Gythe held fast to the cat. Miri looked around. They were still in the shadows of the trees, probably as good a place as any to hide. She checked to make certain the pistol was loaded, though she knew very well that it would be. Dag loaded the pistols every morning. Miri rested the pistol on the ground and drew the stowaway gun from her corset. She made certain it, too, was loaded and then tucked it away.

She had two shots and that was all, for she hadn't brought any ammunition or gunpowder. She carried the weapons to protect against an attack by a wild beast—a wolf or a mountain lion. A single shot would frighten away a predator, but a single shot wouldn't stop one of the Bottom Dwellers.

Miri looked back at the dragons. At the sound of gunfire, the three reared up, coming to their full height. They were staring in the direction of the *Cloud Hopper,* which was only a short distance away. They must be watching the fight, for they appeared interested, intrigued.

"Do something to help, you stupid beasts," Miri told them.

Gythe grabbed hold of her sister, warning, "Keep silent!"

"Are the bat riders looking for you?" Miri asked, trying to still the quiver in her voice.

Gythe nodded.

"How can they hear you?"

Gythe touched her head. "My thoughts."

The sound of an explosion from the direction of the *Cloud Hopper* made Miri flinch. Her beloved boat was under attack, her sister was in danger, and she had only two shots.

"How can anyone hear your thoughts?" Miri asked softly, crouching down beside Gythe.

"You don't believe me."

"I do, Gythe!" Miri protested. "It's just so . . . It doesn't make sense."

Gythe put her hand over her sister's mouth, entreating her to keep quiet.

"You have no magic," said Gythe. She stared into the shadows, then made a small sign. "And I have too much."

Smoke drifted among the trees. Miri could see the flames. Her boat was on fire. She grasped the pistol in one hand, the stowaway gun in the other, and waited.

5

Supposition: Magic and contramagic are opposing primal forces that exist throughout the world. Question: How can someone use a primal force such as magic to contain and control a second primal force such as contramagic, when the two negate each other at contact? How do the Bottom Dwellers use contramagic in their weapons without the contramagic devouring the steel? They may well destroy us before we find the answers.

—Journal of Rodrigo de Villeneuve

Dag was a deeply religious man, and he did not approve of Rodrigo's licentious lifestyle. Rodrigo's moral standards made the tomcat Doctor Ellington seem a model of virtue. Dag considered Rodrigo to be a fop, a dandy, a coward who had never bothered to learn to use pistol or sword because he knew someone else would always protect him. Dag had never been able to understand how Stephano—a man of honor, a courageous soldier—could be friends with the dissolute Rodrigo, who mocked Dag's beliefs and always seemed to be looking down that long aristocratic nose of his.

Dag was therefore amazed and grudgingly impressed to

see Rodrigo risking his life by rushing into a throng of demons to save the pewter tankard.

"He has more guts than I expected," Dag said to himself, grabbing his blunderbuss and two pistols. "More guts and less brains."

Some of the bats were landing; their riders dismounting to launch a ground assault against the *Cloud Hopper* while their bats harassed the boat's defenders from the air. One of the bat riders came straight at Dag as he was running down the gangplank. He fired the blunderbuss and the bat rider seemed to disintegrate. Dag threw the blunderbuss into the grass and drew his pistol.

A second bat landed on the ground near Rodrigo and began hobbling toward him. The bats were lethally graceful in the air, awkward and ungainly on the ground. The bat used both its feet and wings to walk, pulling itself along by digging the tips of its wings into the ground. The grotesque sight turned Dag's stomach.

The bat already perched on Rodrigo's back was pecking at his neck, tearing his flesh. Blood covered Rodrigo's coat. He'd lost consciousness. Dag lifted his pistol, aimed, and fired. The bat flapped, screamed, and toppled over. The second bat flew away.

Dag stuffed the spent pistol into his belt and drew the second. Green fire flared behind him. He could feel the heat. Stephano kept up near continuous fire with the swivel gun. Judging by the sounds of screams and screeching, he was doing some damage.

The bat riders were converging on the *Cloud Hopper* and for the moment, Dag was in the clear. He grabbed Rodrigo and turned him gently over. Rodrigo's face was covered with blood from a gash on his forehead. His hair was singed, as were his eyebrows. The dandy's beloved lavender coat was ruined, the fine fabric torn, black with soot, red with blood. Parts of it were still smoldering.

Dag took hold of Rodrigo by the shoulders, glanced behind him to get his bearings, then began to drag Rodrigo toward the *Cloud Hopper.*

Green light seemed to flare constantly now. Smoke filled the air, making it difficult for Dag to see. He had gone only a few feet when a bat rider emerged from the smoke almost directly in front of him. The Bottom Dweller was so close Dag could see the man's eyes in a hideous helm made to look like the face of a fiend from hell. The bat rider seemed as startled to see Dag as Dag was to see him. The demon raised his cannonlike weapon.

Dag dropped Rodrigo, grabbed his pistol, and fired before the bat rider could bring his long gun to his shoulder. The bullet hit the Bottom Dweller in the mouth. The man flung up his arms and went over backward.

Dag took hold of Rodrigo again and once more started to drag him along, heading for the *Cloud Hopper.* Stephano shouted a warning and Dag ducked as a bat dove for him. The swivel gun banged and the bat was gone. Dag didn't look to see what happened to it.

He had almost reached the *Cloud Hopper* when Stephano shouted urgently, "Down! Get down!" Dag hurled himself on top of Rodrigo. The green fire struck the cuirass, hitting him in the small of the back. The last time he'd been hit by the green fire, the blast had destroyed the magical constructs on his cuirass, nearly roasting him alive. This time, the new magic on the cuirass saved him. He felt like he'd been kicked in the back by a wyvern, but at least he wouldn't spend a week lying on his stomach covered in Miri's yellow goo.

"Guess you're of some use after all," Dag grunted, once more grabbing hold of Rodrigo.

Stephano left the swivel gun and, armed with two pistols, ran down to cover his friends. Two bat riders were trying to run up the gangplank. Stephano shot at one. The bat rider collapsed and rolled on the ground in pain. The second had his weapon aimed and ready to fire.

"Drop the pistol, sir!" Dag yelled.

Stephano let go of the pistol just as a ball of green flame burst from the demonic gun, enveloping the pistol. Constructs on the pistol crackled and sparked. The pistol exploded in midair. The bat rider retreated to reload.

Dag scrambled up the gangplank, hauling Rodrigo with him. Behind him, he could hear Stephano swearing—a good sign. At least the captain was alive. Dag hauled Rodrigo to the helm, which was protected by a windscreen and would offer some protection. Dag bundled him underneath the brass plate control panel.

"How is he?" Stephano shouted, running back to the swivel gun.

"He'll live," Dag yelled back. "He won't be quite as pretty—"

Rodrigo tried to sit up. "The tankard . . ."

Dag pushed Rodrigo back down. "Stay there and don't move."

Rodrigo groaned and closed his eyes.

Dag returned to his swivel gun as three bat riders flew down from the sky, targeting the boat. Green fire from their cannons struck the wing and the exposed portion of the lift tank. Snaking trails of blue light from Gythe's spells flared, protecting the tank from the contramagic.

Another blast struck the lift tank, a direct hit. This time no comforting blue light flared. Dag and Stephano exchanged grim glances. The protection spells had been breached.

The bat riders soared into the air and came around for another pass. Dag braced himself, but this time the Bottom

Dwellers didn't aim at the *Cloud Hopper.* They fired at the bodies of their wounded and dead, causing them to burst into flame. The demon Stephano had shot in the leg died in the fire, writhing until the flames ended his agony.

Dag watched dispassionately, wrinkling his nose at the stench of burning flesh. The bat riders flew off. He and Stephano both stayed at their guns, scanning the skies. They waited several moments, but no more Bottom Dwellers appeared.

"That's damn odd," Dag stated, staring into the gray clouds. "They could have finished us off."

"They might be back," said Stephano. "I'll stay here with Rigo. Reload your weapons and then go fetch Miri and Gythe."

Dag flushed at the recollection of his angry outburst. "I'm sorry about that, sir. You were right. Miri and Gythe were safe, seemingly, and we did manage to save Miri's boat."

"You were right to worry about them," said Stephano. He reached out his hand to Dag. "All forgotten."

Dag started to shake, then stopped.

"Your hand's bleeding, sir," said Dag.

Stephano looked down. His hand was burned and bloody from the blast that had destroyed his pistol.

"Thanks to you I still *have* a hand," he said ruefully. "I'd forgotten that contramagic and gunpowder don't mix. We'll shake on it later."

Stephano knelt down on the deck beside Rodrigo. Dag hurried down the gangplank to see what had become of his favorite weapon, his blunderbuss.

"How are you feeling?" Stephano asked Rodrigo.

"Never mind me. What happened to the tankard?"

"Dag's checking on it," said Stephano evasively.

Dag was relieved to find his blunderbuss had escaped the assault unscathed. Picking it up, he looked over at the large patch of blackened grass and the smoldering ashes of what had once been their dining table. When he was back on board he caught Stephano's eye and shook his head. He began to reload his weapons. Rodrigo saw the expression on his friend's face.

"The tankard's destroyed, isn't it?"

"We don't know—" Stephano began. He stopped, then whispered, "Hush!"

Dag looked up, alarmed, to see Stephano staring at the lift tank.

"What's the matter?" Rodrigo asked groggily.

"Keep quiet! Listen!"

Dag froze in place. Rodrigo propped himself up on his elbow. No one spoke. They all could hear quite clearly the sound of hissing. Dag laid the blunderbuss carefully on the deck and hurried to the tank. Stephano was there before him. Rodrigo limped over to join them, peering over their shoulders.

The brass tank was dented and ruptured and in some places the metal looked as if it had melted, as though it had been splashed with acid.

"That hissing noise means the gas is escaping!" Rodrigo said, his voice rising in panic.

"We know," said Stephano grimly.

In its natural state, the Breath of God provided a small amount of lift. Once the Breath was refined and "cleaned" as the refiners termed it, the gas was pumped into a lift tank where it could be magically charged to provide the lift needed to sail the ships of the world of Aeronne. Without lift gas, a boat as heavy as the *Cloud Hopper* would never leave the ground.

"Then do something!" Rodrigo shook his friend by the shoulder. "We can't fly without the gas. You have to stop it! Plug up the crack! Put your hand over it! Do something!"

Stephano looked at Dag, who shook his head.

"Maybe a crafter skilled in metallurgy—"

"Oh, God!" Rodrigo groaned. He sank to the deck, his head in his arms.

Dag went back to reloading his weapons.

The sound of pistol shot echoed through the trees.

Miri could hear the battle raging around the *Cloud Hopper*. She was in agony, afraid for her friends, afraid for her boat, afraid for her sister. Gythe pressed her face into Doctor Ellington's fur. The cat was quiet, his eyes golden slits. His ears twitched. Flashes of green light and orange flame flared from the direction of their boat. Miri could hear the swivel gun firing, bats screeching.

Then, abruptly, silence.

Miri caught her breath. "The firing's stopped."

That could be good *or* bad. Either her friends had driven off the foe or they were all dead.

Gythe looked up. Her eyes widened. "They're coming!"

Sticks snapped, branches creaked, weeds rustled—the sounds of men moving through the heavy underbrush.

"It might be Stephano," said Miri.

Gythe shook her head. "They're coming for me."

Doctor Ellington hissed and leaped from Gythe's arms, scratching her. His tail furred out, he ran into the forest.

"Leave him!" Miri ordered, catching hold of Gythe. "Stay quiet."

Gythe crouched beside her sister. Miri gripped the gun and tried to keep her hands from shaking.

The Bottom Dwellers were coming closer, the sounds growing louder. Miri knelt in the brush, in the shadows of the trees. Whoever was out there was almost on them. Miri raised the gun.

Five bat riders came into view, moving through the trees. They had fanned out, walking in a line like a search party hunting the woods for a lost child.

Miri picked out a bat rider moving slightly ahead of the others. Miri judged he was the commander. He motioned to the others, telling them to spread out. She aimed the pistol at his chest, the largest target. She wasn't a particularly good shot, but at this range she could hardly miss.

The commander drew closer. He walked with his head cocked, listening, again motioning the others to alter course. They were converging on Miri's location, drawn to Gythe as iron to a lodestone.

The commander was not expecting trouble. He carried the long gun slung over his shoulder. Perhaps he could sense Gythe's terror and assumed his quarry was helpless, unarmed.

He wants to take Gythe alive, Miri realized.

Her fear almost suffocated her. She had to force herself to draw in deep breaths. She had only two shots and five bat riders. Her plan was to drop the commander. Dag and Stephano said you always aimed for the commander. His death would leave the others rattled, confused. They would have to stop, try to figure out what to do. Hopefully that would give Miri time to escape with Gythe, make a run for the *Cloud Hopper*.

A tree branch blocked the commander's path. He stopped to haul it aside.

Miri rose and fired.

The bullet hit the commander in the chest, knocking him off his feet. He landed on his back in the brush.

Miri didn't wait to see if she had killed him. She grabbed hold of Gythe and dragged her to her feet.

"We're going to make a run for it!"

She and Gythe ran through the undergrowth, heading in

the direction of the boat with the Bottom Dwellers crashing through the woods behind them. Miri waited tensely for the bat riders to shoot at them, but no green fire flared. They didn't want to risk killing Gythe.

Miri and Gythe knew the woods. They had laid rabbit snares here, and nets to catch birds. Miri followed an animal trail past the field where the dragons were still waiting for stories and a song. Miri barely cast the beasts a glance.

Hearing pursuit behind them, she was shocked to suddenly find her way blocked by one of the Bottom Dwellers. Keeping fast hold of her sister, Miri veered off the path. She was forced to backtrack, heading once more toward the field.

The weeds and bushes clutched at her trousers. She stumbled and almost fell and Gythe pulled her along. Then Gythe tripped over a tree root and Miri caught her, and they kept going. She looked over her shoulder to see the Bottom Dwellers still in pursuit.

Miri tried to circle back around to the *Cloud Hopper,* only to find that way blocked. The bat riders were acting like beaters—boys sent into the woods to beat the bushes to flush out small game and drive it toward the hunters. They were herding Miri and Gythe toward the field. They wanted them out in the open. Miri was too exhausted to try to think why.

Her thigh muscles burned. She was dizzy, gasping for breath. Gythe tugged at her sister, urging her to keep going.

The field opened up before them. The tall grass was sodden from the rain or she might have been able to hide in it. The Bottom Dwellers were behind them and when she and Gythe tried to turn back toward the boat they cut them off.

The dragons were still there, alert and wary. Hearing the sounds of men running through the woods, the dragons reared their heads in alarm. Flames flickered from their mouths. They lifted their wings in warning.

Miri paid no heed to the dragons. She couldn't run much longer and, anyway, there was nowhere to run. She would make her stand on the fringes of the trees where at least they had some cover. She put her arm around Gythe, drew the stowaway gun, and aimed it at four of the Bottom Dwellers, who came running out of the trees behind her. The four saw her and the small pistol and came to an abrupt halt.

"I have only one shot," Miri said, speaking the Trundler language. Gythe had said that when the Bottom Dwellers talked to her, they spoke in the language of the Trundlers. "I can't kill all of you, but I can kill one."

She waited for the Bottom Dwellers to rush her. They stood unmoving. Miri couldn't see their eyes because they were hidden by their helms, but she suddenly realized by the upward tilt of their heads that they weren't watching her.

They were watching the dragons.

"The great beasts are our friends," Miri said boldly.

Grasping her sister's hand, Miri began to back up, moving into the field toward the dragons. Gythe stared at her in astonishment. Miri was lying through her teeth, but she had to risk it.

"If you attack us," she continued, pointing her gun at first one of the Bottom Dwellers then at another, "our friends the dragons will be angry and they will rip you apart."

Gythe understood and she began singing a song, a martial song Stephano had taught her about the Dragon Brigade and the dragons who fought alongside humans. She sang it loudly enough that the dragons could hear.

The Bottom Dwellers didn't move. The dragons thumped their tails on the ground, warning the humans—all the humans—to keep their distance. Miri wondered why, if the dragons were afraid, they hadn't simply flown away.

Whatever the reason, this standoff couldn't continue for long. Miri's arm shook with fatigue, and the hand holding the gun was wet with sweat. She hoped with the last hope left in her heart that Dag and Stephano were still alive and that they had heard the gunshot and were coming to help. If she could just hold out until they arrived . . .

Hearing a shrill whistle, Miri glanced up. Three bat riders circled overhead. As if the whistle was the signal they had been waiting for, the four Bottom Dwellers sprang at her.

Miri fired wildly. She hit one of them, but another grabbed hold of Gythe and tore her from Miri's grasp. Gythe screamed and struck at the bat rider with her fists. Miri rounded on him, punching and kicking, trying to break his hold. In the distance, she heard Dag calling her name.

"Miri! Where are you?"

"In the field!" Miri shouted, using the voice she used when the storms raged and the wind howled in the rigging. "Dag! Help!"

Another bat rider tore her away from Gythe, and threw her to the ground. Miri landed heavily, spraining her wrist and bruising her knees.

"Dag!" Miri yelled, staggering to her feet. "They're taking Gythe!"

The whistle sounded again. A bat rider landed on the ground. The Bottom Dweller carrying Gythe ran to the bat and flung Gythe to the rider, who dragged her onto the back of the bat. Keeping fast hold of her, the rider ordered his bat into the air. Screaming, Gythe frantically reached for her sister as the bat spread its wings.

Miri ran after Gythe, trying to catch hold of her, but the bat flapped off. Miri made a desperate lunge, missed, and fell into the wet grass. She could only watch in grief-stricken horror as the bat rider carried Gythe away.

She heard the bat riders thrashing about in the wet grass, coming for her, but she paid no attention to them. She kept her eyes fixed on the bat rider that had Gythe.

"Miri!" Dag yelled.

Miri looked over her shoulder to see Dag and Stephano running toward her, shouting to draw the attention of the bat riders, who turned to face this new foe.

The bat rider who had abducted Gythe was having a difficult time keeping hold of his prize. Gythe was fighting like a wildcat. Miri heard in quick succession the boom of the blunderbuss, then a pistol shot, and the crackle of green fire.

The dragons were still in the field, wings spread. They appeared to be transfixed by the fight. Eyes wide, they gazed down at the battle raging in front of them. Miri kept her eyes on the bat. Forced to carry the weight of two people, the bat was flying slowly and seemed to be having trouble gaining altitude.

Miri jumped to her feet and ran toward the dragons, shouting and waving her arms.

"Help me!" she pleaded. "I need your help!"

Behind her, she heard more gunfire. Miri kept running toward the dragons.

Verdi reared up and spread his wings, his mane bristling. Viola lowered her head and hissed. Petard, the young male, was wary, but seemed more intrigued than fearful. Miri stopped in front of them. She had to take time to catch her breath. Her words came out in gasps.

"I know you understand me!" she told them. "You saw what happened. They took Gythe. She played her music for you. She sang to you. Help me get her back!"

Miri pointed to the bat carrying Gythe. The bat was dwindling in the distance. Miri spread her hands, entreating the dragons.

"Please! We don't have much time! Help me save her!"

Verdi lowered his wings. Viola quit hissing. Petard looked at the bat, then lowered his belly and chest to the ground. Miri watched, amazed and thankful. The young dragon was inviting her to fly with him.

She ran toward Petard and climbed up onto his foreleg. From there, she took hold of one of the spikes of his mane and pulled herself up onto his back. Petard's bluish-purple scales were rough and dry beneath her hands. She settled herself in the space between the first spine on his broad back and his neck. Gripping with her thighs, Miri rested her back against the spike.

"Grab hold!" Stephano yelled to her.

He was running through the grass toward her, pointing to the spike of the dragon's mane about a foot above her head. Miri clasped hold of the spike with both hands as Petard rose from the ground. The dragon spread his wings, shifting his weight to his hind legs, and propelled himself into the air. His leap slammed Miri back against another spike. Flattened against the spike, Miri stared straight up along the dragon's neck into the clouds.

Viola flew alongside Petard, barking something at him. He looked around at her and roared back, and Viola left, speeding on ahead. Miri clung to the spike with both hands and looked down to see the ground falling away from her. Smoke was rising from the field where the grass had caught fire. She could see Dag clubbing one of the Bottom Dwellers with the butt of the blunderbuss and Stephano standing in the grass watching her.

She looked back into the sky, searching for the bat carrying Gythe. For a terrifying moment she thought she had lost sight of it, then Petard leveled off and Miri saw the bat and Gythe, whose white blouse showed up clearly against the gray clouds. She was sitting in the saddle in front of the

Bottom Dweller, who had his arm clasped around her. Petard flew straight for them.

Viola was closing in on the bat and its rider. Miri kept her eyes fixed on Gythe until the wind in her face made her eyes water, forcing her to blink and look away.

"Gythe, dear, if you can hear Bottom Dwellers in your head, you must be able to hear me!" Miri said. "I'm coming for you!"

Gythe twisted around on the bat, looking behind her, and managed to wave before the Bottom Dweller yanked her back.

Miri was cheered until she realized, now that she was up here, she had no plan, no idea how to save Gythe. The Bottom Dweller had one arm around Gythe, and was holding the reins with the other. Before Miri could decide what she should do, she saw that Viola had her own idea. The dragon swooped down behind the bat and shot a thin jet of flame from her mouth.

The flame struck the Bottom Dweller in the back, blazing through the leather armor. Miri couldn't hear his screams, but they must have been horrible. He slumped in the saddle, either dead or dying.

She had no time to dwell on his fate, because just then she caught a glimpse of movement out of the corner of her eye. One of the other bat riders was flying up to help his injured comrade. Viola must have seen the danger, for she bellowed a warning. Petard snaked his head around, but he was too late; the Bottom Dweller had already aimed his weapon at Petard. Miri flattened herself against the dragon's back and could only watch, horrified, as the fire ball struck Petard on the upper leg.

The ball of green flame was so small compared to the size of the dragon that Miri thought perhaps he would not even feel it. But Petard snarled in pain and Miri was startled to see green lightning arc around the dragon's leg and across his chest.

Wherever the lightning touched his scales, the green fire scorched them, burning the scales black. Petard shuddered and hissed. Viola was flying back to help her brother, but before she could reach him, Verdi soared alongside them. Shielding Petard with his body, Verdi opened his mouth and spewed fire.

Orange flame engulfed the bat and its rider, and they plummeted from the sky, trailing smoke behind them. The three dragons were furious, roaring and howling back and forth.

Miri feared they had forgotten about Gythe. She beat on Petard's neck with her fists and pleaded with him to go after her. Petard calmed down, shook himself, and once more flew toward the bat carrying Gythe, with Viola and Verdi flanking him.

The body of the Bottom Dweller hung from the saddle, arms dangling. Gythe was pulling on the reins, trying vainly to gain some control over the creature. The terrified bat wanted only to flee the dragons. The bat had lost much of its ability to maneuver, however, and before long, Viola and Verdi were able to flank it, keeping the bat penned between them. Whenever the bat tried to escape, one of the dragons was there to stop it.

Gythe reached for Miri, leaning as far out of the saddle as she could without falling.

"Like when we were children!"

"Fly as close as you can!" Miri yelled at Petard.

Petard rose slightly, veering around to come beneath the bat, bringing Miri within arm's length of her sister.

Miri reached her hand out to her sister, and Gythe stretched as far as she could. Finally, Miri's fingers closed over Gythe's wrist, and Gythe clasped her hand around

Miri's wrist, a feat of acrobatics they had performed when they were young, playing in the rigging. Miri pulled with all her might.

As she pulled, Gythe jumped from the saddle into Miri's arms. Miri had to relinquish her hold on the dragon's spike to catch Gythe, and for a heart-stopping moment she thought that she was going to fall and take Gythe down with her.

When Petard saw that his riders were in trouble, he raised his right wing and lowered his left, counterbalancing the weight. Viola gave a satisfied snarl. Grabbing the bat by the wing, she bit it in half, and spit it out.

Miri held Gythe close. The wind blew her tears off her cheeks.

6

Our experiences in life are likened to the hammer and anvil used by God to forge our faith. We are tempered, beaten, made strong yet flexible so we can endure the storms that batter our lives. We bend, but do not break.

—Mother Superior Aylwyn,
Abbess, Saint Erin the Just

Their descent was terrifying. Petard spiraled down rapidly, leaving his passengers to hold on for dear life. The dragon had not been trained to land with humans on his back, a special skill that required the dragon to soar level above the ground, descend slowly, and land gently. Petard was flying too fast. The ground rushed at them. Trees and sky and grass whirled past.

Miri's stomach roiled. She was so frightened she couldn't cry out. She gripped the spike on the dragon's mane with both hands and closed her eyes. Gythe clasped her arms around her sister and braced herself.

The dragon's hind legs hit the ground with a bone-jarring thud. His front legs touched next, slamming Miri and Gythe forward against his neck. Then he settled to the ground and folded his wings. Miri could do nothing for a moment except try to calm her fast-beating heart and catch her breath. She opened her eyes to see Petard's head twisted around. He was staring at her. The muscles on his back rippled, and his eyes narrowed.

"We have to get off, Gythe," Miri said in a strangled gasp, which was all she could manage.

She dismounted hurriedly, sliding down from the dragon's back and landing on his foreleg. Gythe followed and both jumped to the ground. Dag started to run toward them. The female dragon hissed at him and raised her wings. Stephano shouted and Dag stopped.

"Miri, come away," Dag said shakily.

Miri gave him what she hoped was a reassuring smile and then turned back to the dragons.

"Thank you," she said earnestly to Petard. "Thank you for saving my sister."

Gythe made a sign with her hands.

"Gythe says she will sing a song for you tomorrow, a special song to show her gratitude."

The other two dragons gazed at Miri impassively, their eyes hooded, giving no hint of their thoughts. Petard was trying to put up a brave front, but he was obviously in pain. Charred scales ran down the length of his leg and up across his shoulder. Miri was shocked by the extent of the damage.

She and Gythe slowly walked away, conscious that Verdi was keeping an eye on them.

Dag stood waiting for them. Beneath the soot and gunpowder, he was pale.

Stephano was staring at the dragons in awe.

"They have been listening to us!" he murmured. "All this time, they've been listening."

Dag held out his hands to Miri. "I'm sorry. I should have been there to protect you."

"You're here now," said Miri. She clasped hold of his

arm, rested her cheek against his shoulder. "I feel so safe with you. Now we can all go home."

A spasm of pain crossed his face. Miri thought she knew what was wrong.

"My boat!" she gasped. "Something's happened to the *Cloud Hopper*!" Her heart constricted with fear. "It's gone. They burned it. You're afraid to tell me!" She whirled around. "Stephano, tell me!"

"No, no, Miri," Stephano said hurriedly. "The *Cloud Hopper* didn't suffer much damage at all. Gythe's magical spells saved the boat."

"What then?" Miri eyed both men narrowly.

Stephano took a deep breath, let it out in a sigh. "They hit the starboard lift tank. The gas is leaking out. But the boat is fine."

"The boat is fine. We just can't sail it!" Miri drew back to stare at them in dismay. "Is that what you're telling me?"

"Miri, it's not that bad . . . Miri, wait—"

Miri couldn't wait. They had come so close to escaping this prison. Tired as she was, she broke into a frantic run.

She found Rodrigo standing over the smoldering ruins of what had once been their dining table, poking and sifting among the chunks of blackened wood. Rodrigo was a sorry sight. He had a bloody gash on his cheek, and his hair, caked in blood, was straggled about his face. His lavender coat was ruined, his trousers covered in grass stains, dirt, and soot.

He looked up at Miri, who had stopped to catch her breath.

"The lift tank is leaking!" Rodrigo told her. "Is there some way to stop it?"

"I hope to God there is!" said Miri, hurrying to board the *Cloud Hopper*.

Rodrigo followed her onto the ship. "Where's Gythe? And Dag and Stephano?"

"They're safe; they're coming along behind me."

Rodrigo gave her an unexpected kiss on the cheek. "I said a prayer for you both, and you know how I am about praying."

Miri smiled at him wanly. "You don't look so good."

Rodrigo put his hand to his own cheek. "I have a skull-cracking headache and I'm certain this gash will leave a scar." He regarded her anxiously. "Can you fix the leak? You *have* to fix it. You will, won't you?"

Stephano came running up behind them. "Rigo, go look for your tankard."

Rodrigo returned to his search. Miri glanced hurriedly at the sails, the balloon, the hull. A few holes and tears, a couple of charred places on the wood.

"Over here," said Stephano.

He led her to the lift tank, which looked as if it had been bounced down the side of a mountain. Miri could hear the slow hissing of the gas.

"Is there any way we can patch the tank?" Stephano asked.

"What with?" Miri returned bitterly. "Rigo's silk shirt?"

The deck began to heave. The mast wavered in Miri's vision and seemed to be falling down on top of her. She was hot and then she was terribly cold. The next thing she knew Stephano was carrying her over to a chair. He vanished into the hold and returned with a tin cup containing the Trundler liquor known as Calvados. He handed her the cup and hovered over her, regarding her with concern.

"I'm sorry, Miri. I'm a bloody idiot," said Stephano remorsefully. "After everything you've been through . . ."

Miri reached out, squeezed his hand. She was afraid if she said anything she'd end up in tears. She took a drink and the warmth of the liquor drove away the chill. The world wobbled and then slowly settled back into place.

"If it's any comfort, the port-side tank wasn't damaged," Stephano told her, trying to sound cheerful.

Can't we sail with one lift tank? Rodrigo had asked only yesterday.

Could we? Miri wondered.

She was deep in thought when Dag returned with Gythe, carrying the cat in her arms.

"I tried to make her come back to rest, but she wouldn't leave without finding the Doctor," Dag explained. "As it turns out, he found us. I think he was more frightened of the dragons than he was of the bat riders."

Gythe handed the cat to Dag, then ran to her sister. She smoothed back Miri's hair, signing to her repeatedly, asking if she was all right. Miri assured Gythe she was fine, then, with a sigh, she glanced over at the lift tank. Gythe took one look and gave a little gasp. She sank down onto her knees on the deck beside Miri's chair.

"Everything will be fine," Dag said gruffly, resting his hand on Miri's shoulder. "We'll get through this."

Dag's touch warmed and comforted Miri more than the Calvados. She smiled up at him. His hand remained on her shoulder. Miri thought he might actually come out and say the words of love she had sometimes seen in his eyes.

"I'm sorry," Dag said again, giving her a pat. He turned away.

Miri had the impression he wasn't talking about the boat. She gave an inward sigh and forced her thoughts back to their predicament. Ignoring everyone's protests that she needed to rest, she left the chair and walked over to examine the second lift tank, the only tank they had left.

Miri had made a rough guess as to their location when they were first marooned, using the old Trundler maps, the location of the stars, and the sun. She had already calculated the distance back to Rosia and how long it would take them to sail across the vast expanse of the Breath to reach home.

Risky, but we might make it work, she thought. She was about to tell them when Rodrigo gave a glad shout.

"I found it!"

"Found what?" Dag asked.

"The tankard!"

Rodrigo was down on his knees in the charred grass, heedless of the dirt. He picked up the tankard and immediately dropped it with a curse.

"Hot!" he exclaimed, sucking his burned fingers.

He sought out a stick, poked it through the handle, and lifted it. Inspecting the tankard, he gave a low whistle.

"I was right." He hurried to show them, carrying the tankard on the stick back to the *Cloud Hopper.* "Everyone! I was right!"

Stephano started to give him the bad news about the lift tank. "Rigo, the tankard can wait—"

"No it can't!" Rodrigo said excitedly. "Look at this! The tankard was hit by a blast of green fire. Contramagic. The blast destroyed the table, set fire to the grass, and seared the bark and leaves off a nearby tree."

He waved the tankard in the air like a flag. "Observe what the green fire did to that brass lift tank. This tankard should be cracked, dented, maybe even a puddle of pewter. Instead it is untouched, unscathed. A miracle! Or it would be a miracle if it wasn't science. This is astounding. Alcazar's magical constructs protect against the effects of contramagic!"

They stared at him in silence, then looked at each other and looked away.

"My dear friends, you must see how important this is!" Rodrigo faltered.

"It doesn't matter, Rigo," said Stephano, his voice tight.

"What are you saying? Of course it matters—"

"It doesn't because we're stranded here!" Stephano said savagely. "Forever. We're not going home."

Rodrigo paled. "You don't mean that."

Stephano pointed to the wrecked lift tank.

"I can't live like this!" Rodrigo said with a catch in his throat. "There must be a way. There *has* to be a way!"

"There may be . . . ," Miri said slowly. "We use the gas in the remaining tank to fill the balloon. The flight will be dangerous and not very pleasant. There's a possibility we could sink into the Breath and perish."

"I'm dead already," said Rodrigo. "I'll risk it."

"Hear me out," said Miri. "We'll have to lighten the load the boat carries. That means jettisoning everything except what we need to survive the voyage."

She pointed to the cannons.

"They weigh far too much. The cannons and the frog—"

Dag groaned.

"The galley stove, the swivel guns—"

"No," said Dag firmly. "We need the swivel guns—"

"Not if we can't get off the ground, we don't," Miri said flatly. "Rigo's clothes, the trunks, and everything inside—"

"My clothes?" Rodrigo gasped in dismay.

"*And* your shoes," said Miri.

Now it was Rodrigo who groaned. He began to plead, Dag started arguing.

"It's Miri's boat," said Stephano.

The arguing stopped.

"Dag, we'll leave the cannons well oiled and under cover," Stephano continued. "We can always come back for them. Rigo, you were going to need a new wardrobe anyway. Miri, do you really think this will work?"

"I believe it might," Miri said. "We'll be cutting it close, but once we're away from here and out in the shipping lanes, we can hopefully find a vessel that will give us a tow."

"We might find bat riders, too," Dag said grimly. "And we'd have no way to defend ourselves."

"It's up to the rest of you," said Miri. "We either stay here or we sail for home with the knowledge that the voyage will be dangerous. I say we risk it."

"I agree," said Stephano. "But this is life or death. Rigo?"

"I agree, so long as I can keep this," Rodrigo said, holding up the pewter mug.

"I think we could manage that." Miri smiled.

"Gythe?"

She nodded emphatically.

"Dag?"

He heaved a sigh, then said, "It'll be one hell of a job hauling those cannons off, sir."

"We're agreed then," said Stephano. "Let's clean up, patch our wounds, and have something to eat. Tomorrow morning, we start to work."

"I'll mix up the healing potion. Rigo, you're my first patient. I might be able to keep that gash from leaving a scar," Miri added, when he started to protest.

Rodrigo held his tongue and followed her below, still clutching the pewter tankard. Dag remained on deck, bidding a sad farewell to the cannons, especially his favorite, the frog.

In the rebuilt galley, Miri went to work on her potion. She had lost much of her store of herbs in the fire, but she had managed to replace almost all of them and had even found some herbs growing on the island that she hadn't been able to find on Rosia.

She brought out her jars of unguents and potions and began to mix together her famous yellow concoction, singing to herself as she worked. The pungent odor wafted through the galley.

While she mixed up the healing potion known to the others as "yellow goo," Rodrigo stretched out comfortably on Miri's bed to study the remarkable tankard.

"Can I come in?" Stephano asked from the doorway.

"You want to know about the dragons," Miri said, stirring vigorously.

"Did Petard say anything to you? What did you say to him? I know now that they understand us when we speak to them. What happened on the flight?"

Miri thought back to that dreadful experience and shivered.

"I'm sorry, Stephano, I can't talk about it. Not yet. I know it's important to you, but I came so close to losing Gythe—" Miri's voice broke.

"I understand. Maybe later . . ."

Stephano looked so disappointed that Miri relented.

"There was one thing . . ."

"Yes, what?" Stephano asked eagerly.

"Petard was attacked by a bat rider. A blast of green fire hit him. The fireball was small, I didn't think it would do much harm. But the effect on him was horrible. Green lightning sparked over his body. I could feel him shudder in pain. His scales were burned so badly I could see the flesh beneath."

"The same happened to Hroal when he was hit by the fireballs," said Stephano. "Only in his case, I thought he must have sustained multiple hits. Dragons have the ability to heal themselves using their own magic—"

"The contramagic would break down a dragon's magic, just as it breaks down Gythe's protective magic," said Rodrigo from the bed.

"Viola was upset by the attack," Miri added. "I could tell by the way she hovered around him when we landed. The dragons didn't seem surprised to see the bat riders, Stephano. They were alarmed and angry, but not surprised."

Stephano considered this, his brow furrowed.

Miri pointed with her spoon to a stool. "Rigo, put that mug down and sit here."

"You don't seem to realize the importance of my discovery," said Rodrigo. His voice was muffled due to the fact that he was holding his nose. "The tankard took a direct hit from the contramagic and yet there is not a mark on it. Sir Henry must have known the magical steel is resistant to contramagic. *That* is the reason he gave this to me."

He settled himself on the stool.

"Let me see it," said Stephano. Walking over to the galley window, he held the tankard to the fading light. "You're right. Not a mark on it. This is pewter. How do you know the same magic will work on steel?"

"Because Alcazar told me it would," Rigo said with a shrug. "He said he melded the constructs in a pewter tankard to send to Sir Henry because no one would suspect an everyday object of holding the secret to an invention that will revolutionize warfare."

"So a tavern tankard can't be hurt by green fire," said Miri, shrugging. "Rigo, take your hand away from your nose. The smell isn't that bad."

"It is, too," he said under his breath.

Miri ignored him. Washing the blood from his face, she cleansed the wound, then began to spread the yellow goo over Rodrigo's cheek.

He winced and gagged.

"You explain about the steel," he said to Stephano. "I'm busy being nauseous."

"Let me put it this way," said Stephano. "If the HMS *Royal Lion* had been outfitted with protective armament made of this same magically enhanced steel, the ship would *not* have exploded. The green fire would have had no effect on it. What was it Sir Henry said when he gave this to you?"

"Something about others looking at their feet while he looks far ahead to the distant horizon. 'I foresee a time when your country and mine will stand back-to-back battling a foe intent on destroying us both. In that eventuality, I want my ally to be as strong as I am,'" Rodrigo quoted.

He eyed Stephano. "That is conclusive evidence that Sir Henry can't be the one who ordered the Bottom Dwellers to attack us."

"It was someone named Eiddwen. Gythe heard the Bottom Dwellers in her head. Rigo, stop squirming! I'm almost finished. There now. You can go. And don't wash that off! Let it harden."

Stephano had his hand over his nose and mouth. "Go someplace far away."

"I will," said Rodrigo with a plaintive sigh. "I'll go bid farewell to my shoes. I don't suppose I could keep my imported Estaran leather boots?"

Miri shook her head. Rigo heaved a doleful sigh and departed.

"So someone named Eiddwen sent them searching for the boat," said Stephano. "Why?"

"And why come after Gythe?" Miri asked. "Why did they want to take her with them? And who is Eiddwen? Do you know anyone by that name?"

Stephano shook his head. Miri sighed.

"If she did send the Bottom Dwellers after us, they'll come back."

"Most likely," said Stephano. "Though the presence of the dragons on the island might make them think twice." He reached out, stroked her shoulder. "You're worn out. Let's think about this tomorrow."

"There's something I have to do first," said Miri. "I've made up my mind. I've put this off too long. If we don't survive this . . ." She drew in a deep breath. "Would you tell Dag I need to talk to him? In private."

Stephano was silent, regarding her with grave intensity. His hand on her shoulder tightened. Miri felt her cheeks grow warm. She had told Stephano when they first set out on this voyage that she had fallen in love with Dag. Stephano had told her he understood and that he was happy for her, but Miri guessed he didn't and he wasn't.

"Of course, Miri," Stephano said coolly. He paused, then added, using his formal, well-bred tone, "I wish you both joy."

Miri heard him shout for Dag and her courage nearly failed her. She wondered why she was so nervous. She had known Dag for five years now and she admired him. He was strong and courageous, yet he also could be gentle and tender. He had become a father to Gythe. She loved him for the way he loved and protected her sister.

Dag had worked for the gangs of Westfirth after he had left the army. He had done things of which he was ashamed. Dag didn't like himself, and Miri was wise enough to know that if you didn't like yourself, it was hard for you to believe anyone could like you. He would never tell her he loved her. So now was the time for Miri to tell him.

She heard his heavy footfalls tramping down the corridor and her heartbeat quickened.

"Don't be so silly," she scolded herself. "You're thirty-some years old, Miri McPike. Not a giggling girl of sixteen."

Dag entered the galley. He had washed off the worst of the grime and sweat and had removed his armor. He greeted her with the gentle smile he always wore.

"Stephano said you needed me." Dag looked around. "Is it the Doctor? Is he in trouble? Did he eat your potion again?"

"No, it's not the Doctor," said Miri.

She looked down at the hem of her blouse, which she was twisting in her fingers, drew in another deep breath, and let her words tumble out in a rush. "Dag, I know you love me. At least I think you love me. I feel so safe when I'm with you. I want us to be married."

She looked up, smiling, waiting for Dag to say how happy he was and take her in his arms.

Dag didn't say anything. He stared down at his boots.

"Dag, I just said I loved you." Miri drew near him and put her hands on his chest.

Dag wrapped one of his big hands around both of hers and pushed them away. He shook his head. "No, Miri, you didn't. You said you feel safe with me."

He was quiet a moment, then added, "It's not the same."

"Don't tell me how I feel!" Miri said angrily. "Are you . . . refusing to marry me?"

Dag's face contorted in pain. "Let me explain, Miri. Or try to. You know how I am with words."

"I'm waiting," Miri said coldly.

"When the bat riders attacked and you and Gythe were down at the lake, I wanted to rush off to defend you." Dag spoke slowly, thinking about his words before he said them. "Stephano stopped me. He told me that the *Cloud Hopper* was your life. He said you would want me to stay to defend it. He was right."

"Well, of course, he was right," Miri said, "but that doesn't—"

"I'm not finished," Dag said abruptly. "You see me like a father, the man who defends your boat and protects Gythe. You turn to me for help, Miri. You don't turn to me for love."

"You're wrong," Miri protested.

"Am I, Miri?" Dag asked gently.

She wanted to say yes. Her lips moved to form the word,

but there was no sound. He was right. His touch made her feel safe. His touch didn't thrill her. Not like Stephano's touch had once thrilled her. Not like sometimes Stephano's touch still thrilled her.

"You love Gythe and the *Cloud Hopper.* Those are your true loves, Miri. I'm the man who watches over them. And I always will."

Miri couldn't answer him for the burning in her throat. Dag gave a little sigh and turned and walked out of the galley. Miri could have called him back. She could have run after him, told him he was mistaken. Instead she stayed in the galley and let the tears fall down her cheeks.

Night soon put an end to the dreadful day. Stephano paced the deck of the *Cloud Hopper,* gazing up at the stars, watching the fireflies, feeling the sweat dry on his neck. All the while he was picturing Miri and Dag down in the galley, embracing with joy.

He tried practicing his happy smile. He rehearsed words of hearty congratulation. The smile made his face hurt. The words were lies.

He wasn't jealous, he told himself. He and Miri were friends, dear friends. They had decided friendship was the best relationship for both of them. It was just . . . he never thought she'd fall in love with someone else.

At the far end of the boat, Gythe sat on the deck, cradling Doctor Ellington, singing softly to the cat, who dozed on her lap, his eyes half closed. Stephano leaned on the rail and looked at her. She seemed so fragile, her fair hair shining in the lambent light of the moon.

She would have a guardian, Stephano thought. A good man who would give his life for her. And so would Miri.

He was behaving like a spoiled brat, wanting the prize only because someone else had won it.

He heard footsteps coming up the stairs and turned, ready to congratulate the happy couple. The happy couple did not emerge. All he saw was Rodrigo, who grabbed hold of his friend's arm and hustled him down the gangplank.

"We need to talk. Miri asked Dag to marry her," said Rodrigo in a low tone.

"You were eavesdropping?" Stephano asked, frowning.

"My dear fellow, how do you think I have survived at court all these years? Of course, I was eavesdropping."

"I don't want to hear—" Stephano began.

"Dag refused her," said Rodrigo.

Stephano stared, incredulous. "He did what?"

"He said no. He told her she didn't love him. She wanted a father. I was shocked. I hardly expected Dag to be that perspicacious."

"I'll have a talk with both of them—"

"No, you won't." said Rodrigo sternly. "I knew that would be your first impulse and that's why I came to stop you."

"But—"

"My dear friend, I allow myself to be guided by you in matters in which you excel. For example, I do not tell you how to load the swirly gun."

"Swivel gun."

"Precisely. And you do not tell *me* how to handle *affaires de coeur*. You will stay out of this. Dag's refusal was one of the bravest and most selfless acts I have ever witnessed. Don't take that away from him."

"Did he refuse her because of me? Miri and I are just friends—"

"No, not because of you. Haven't you ever listened to Dag talk about his mother? Her religious views?"

"I guess so, but I don't see—"

"She taught him that a man's carnal urges are wicked, sinful. That a woman endures a man's lust because of the need to procreate. There's a reason Dag is friends with that couple in Westfirth who own the whorehouse. He won't inflict his evil urges on any woman he loves."

"Good God!" Stephano was amazed.

"As for Miri, she is looking for the father she lost when she was a child. She thought at first it was you, but you aren't the fatherly type. That failing, she turned to Dag. She mistook her need for a father for the need for a husband."

"How do you know all this?" Stephano felt out of his depth.

"I am a student of human nature, my friend. I find the subject fascinating. Take you, for example."

"Me?" Stephano was alarmed. "What's there to study about me? I'm perfectly normal."

Rodrigo placed his hand on his friend's shoulder and said gently, "Someday we'll talk."

7

The lift tank is starting to supersede the balloon as the primary means of lift on board a ship. Built into the hull at the base of each wing, lift tanks filled with the Breath provide a more stable and better protected means of buoyancy than balloons, of particular importance to the modern warship. Constructs set into the interior of the tank allow for finer control of a ship's trim and pitch. Many ships now combine lift tanks with a single, primary balloon for both lift and ballast.

—*Principles of Modern Ship Design,*
Master Wilhelm Van Vliet

The night passed quietly. Dag handed off the watch to Stephano, who tried to look as if he were completely unaware of what had happened. He apparently failed, because Dag said to him, "You know about me and Miri, sir."

"I know," said Stephano, adding lamely, "I'm sorry."

Dag nodded. "It's all for the best. Good night, sir."

He went off to his bed. Stephano remained on deck, staring out at the stars, thinking about the vagaries of human nature and wondering uneasily what Rodrigo had meant when he'd said *We'll talk.*

Stephano rousted everyone out of bed before the dawn. Afraid the Bottom Dwellers might return to finish the job, he decreed that they should leave the island tomorrow at first light. He and Dag undertook the arduous task of dismantling and removing the cannons and the frog. Miri and Gythe were in charge of inflating the balloon, while Rodrigo carried everything deemed nonessential off the *Cloud Hopper.* He was practically in tears as he bade good-bye to his shoes.

No one spoke of the *affair de coeur,* but everyone could feel the tension in the air. Miri was curt and businesslike, and her eyes were red from crying. Gythe simply looked unhappy, her gaze often going from Dag to Miri. Dag was stoically silent, while Stephano talked too much. Only Rodrigo was himself, deploring the loss of his wardrobe—especially the lavender coat and the Estaran boots—and getting in everyone's way. Doctor Ellington, rousted from his usual place beneath the cannon, departed in high dudgeon, heading into the woods.

No one mentioned the fact that tomorrow morning they would find out if the *Cloud Hopper* was capable of flying or if they would be stranded on this island. At which point, Stephano had decided he would turn to the dragons for help. He didn't mention this to Miri.

Each of the *Cloud Hopper*'s four-pound cannons weighed a shade over a thousand pounds. The short barreled frog weighed about eight hundred pounds. Stephano and Dag suspended the block and tackle from a support spar on the main mast with another set on a nearby tree. The two men hoisted each cannon with the first set of tackle, shifting the weight to the ropes hanging from the tree. Four grueling hours later, the cannons were lying under the tree, covered by spare sail canvas.

Miri and Gythe inflated and secured the balloon. Miri connected a hose from the last remaining tank to the balloon, then carefully opened the valve, allowing just enough precious gas into the balloon so that the amount of lift equaled the weight of the balloon. Once the balloon was inflated, Gythe began connecting the mainstays—the heavy ropes that secured the balloon to the hull of the ship. Miri added more lift gas, to again equalize the balloon's weight.

Gythe climbed up into the rigging to maneuver the balloon into its mooring position between the lower support spar and the top gallant support spar. She connected the top stays to the main mast and the mizzen mast. Finally, she connected ropes known as braces, which controlled the side-to-side movement of the balloon, preventing it from fouling the sails.

Miri attached the braided leather control cables that carried the magical energy from the helm to the balloon, allowing the helmsman to adjust the amount of lift in each of the balloon's chambers. Tomorrow, Miri would finish filling the balloon, using all the gas they had left.

While they worked, they kept watch for bat riders. When Gythe, up in the rigging, put her fingers to her mouth and gave an earsplitting whistle and pointed to the sky, everyone dropped what they were doing. Dag grabbed his blunderbuss. Stephano drew his pistol.

"Not bat riders," Miri reported, relieved. "It's Petard."

"Put the guns down," Stephano ordered.

The wild dragons had occasionally flown over the campsite, appearing more curious than threatening, circling a few times, peering down at the humans and their wrecked boat, then flying off. Generally the three came together. Today there was only Petard.

"He might be here to see if Miri and Gythe are safe," said Stephano. "Wave to him, everyone. Show him we are grateful."

Rodrigo brandished a shirt he happened to be carrying. Miri called out to the dragon to let him know she and Gythe were well and to ask after the dragon's health. Petard circled lower, seemingly interested. Stephano stepped into the center of the clearing.

"We are leaving the island tomorrow morning, Petard," he shouted. "We have enjoyed knowing you and your friends. We will always be grateful to you for saving Gythe's life. We are forever in your debt."

Petard flew over the camp several times, once swooping so low that they could feel the rush of wind from his passing and see the wounds he had sustained in the fight with the demons. The dragon stayed with them only a few moments, then flew off toward the mountain.

"That was odd," Rodrigo remarked.

"He's a dragon," Miri said, as if that explained everything. They went back to work.

By evening, the work was finished, the balloon ready to be completely filled in the morning.

The cannons were hidden away, and the deck cleared of everything except the small table, where they ate their meals, and the stools on which they sat.

Rodrigo had found time to whisper a few words of comfort to Miri. Stephano did not know what his friend said, but Miri let Rodrigo keep his Estaran leather boots. Rodrigo must have spoken to Dag, as well, for Stephano saw Dag shake Rodrigo's hand, something that had never happened in all the years they'd known each other.

Dinner was made up of all the food they couldn't pack. Miri's frugal nature could not bear to see it go to waste. She talked about the morning, speaking cheerfully, assuming they were going to be leaving. No one mentioned the possibility that they might not. Dag was so tired he fell asleep sitting at the table with the cat curled up in his lap. Stephano woke him to send him and the Doctor to bed, saying he would take first watch. Gythe brought out her harp, but no one was in the mood for music, and they made an early night of it.

Stephano was alone on deck, letting himself wallow in homesickness. He missed the noise of carriages rattling past at all hours, the cries of children playing stickball in the street, the shouts of the vendors; all the sights and sounds and smells of humanity. Lost in his memories, he was jolted back to the island when he saw the wings of a dragon blot out the stars.

Stephano thought at first this dragon was Petard. He soon realized he was wrong. This dragon was a stranger, one he had never before seen. The moon shed light enough so that he could see that the dragon's scales glittered green, but not an emerald shade of green like Verdi's scales. This dragon was the dark green of the forest. Larger than the other three, the dragon had an unusually long spike on top of the head.

An elder, he realized, watching with interest.

He had long guessed that a dragon clan or "gathering" was living in the mountain. A gathering was a large group of dragons, perhaps several families, who lived in close proximity to each other. He had kept a watch for other dragons, perhaps out hunting or cooling off in the lake. He had not seen the others in the gathering, and he guessed that after the arrival of the humans, they had confined their hunting to the opposite side of the island.

Stephano was careful not to move, for dragons had excellent eyesight. He kept beneath the balloon, hoping the dragon couldn't see him. He wanted to see what the elder dragon was going to do.

The dragon circled the boat a few times, appearing to study it, though to what end Stephano could not decide. Perhaps nothing more than the chance to view the humans and their contrivance that had so fascinated the dragon young.

The elder dragon made several passes, then winged back toward the mountain.

When the dragon was gone, Stephano shrugged. "As Rigo would say, 'Very odd.'"

He decided not to mention the visit to the others. They had enough to worry about.

At first light, Miri announced she was ready to finish filling the balloon. She slowly added more lift gas, expanding the balloon and allowing Gythe time to make adjustments to the ropes. During the process, Gythe kept an ear cocked, listening for any leaks. Stephano and Dag checked the mooring points where the ropes were tied to the hull. When Miri was satisfied that everything was secure, she completed filling the balloon using the last of the gas.

Rodrigo checked the bridging constructs one last time, and then Miri took her place at the helm and began channeling magical energy through the constructs set in the brass panel. The magic traveled along the cables of braided leather to the constructs inside the balloon. The energy arced through the gas, increasing its natural buoyancy. They all held their breath. The magic flowed unimpeded to the balloon.

Slowly, faltering, with a few wobbles and one heart-stopping dip, the *Cloud Hopper* rose into the air.

No one cheered. They were far too busy. Miri was at the helm, Rodrigo and Gythe were watching the magical constructs, making certain the bridges were working. When Rodrigo rushed over to a cable and began to rapidly draw sigils, Stephano asked tensely what was wrong. Rodrigo only shook his head, too intent upon what he was doing to reply.

As they were drifting up among the trees, the *Cloud Hopper* began to list. Miri sent Dag and Stephano below to shift the water barrels until the boat was once more sailing on an even keel. They came back on deck, just as the *Cloud Hopper* cleared the treetops.

"I think we might make it," said Stephano.

Miri glared at him. "Say your name ten times and then touch wood!"

"Oh, come now—" Stephano began.

"Your full name," said Miri.

Stephano sighed and recited his full name, Stephano Guilluame de Guichen, ten times and then touched his fingers on the railing.

Miri nodded, satisfied, and went back to keeping an eye on the helm.

Stephano gazed down at the island that had been their enforced home for so many long weeks. The green of the forest contrasted with the gray rock of the mountain. The Breath was orangish pink this morning, twining about the island's base so that the island seemed to be floating on a sea of roiling mist.

"A beautiful place," Dag remarked.

"And one I hope I never see again," Stephano said.

"Except to retrieve the cannons," said Dag. He suddenly stiffened. "You see that, sir?"

Stephano grabbed the spyglass from the helm.

"What is it?" Miri called nervously. "What's out there?"

"Dragons," said Stephano. "Three dragons. Looks like *our* three dragons."

"Are they going to attack us?" Dag asked.

"I don't think so," said Stephano. "They appear to be keeping their distance."

"Maybe they're here to make certain we're leaving their island," said Dag.

"Maybe," said Stephano, unconvinced. "Although that must be obvious by now."

As the *Cloud Hopper* sailed deeper into the Breath, the mists swirled and they lost sight of the island and the dragons. The day passed, hot and tense. Miri told them to pray for a favorable breeze, to help push the boat toward Rosia. God must not have been listening, for a breeze did not come. The sails flapped uselessly.

Miri stayed at the helm, nursing the boat along. When she needed to rest, Gythe replaced her. When Rodrigo needed Gythe to help with the magic, which was working in fits and starts, Dag replaced Gythe at the helm. Miri set the boat on a course that would take them in a south-southeasterly direction toward Rosia. She had figured from her calculations that they were about five days away from the continent, taking into account that they were sailing into a headwind. Five long, long days and longer nights for they would be forced to sail after dark.

Night sailing was treacherous. Large chunks of rock that broke off from the islands or the continents drifted about the Breath posing a hazard to ships. Crashing into one of those during the night could end their voyage in a hurry.

The twilight mists were a glorious red color, deepening to purple. The *Cloud Hopper* was sailing over the last of the islands known as the Chain of Pearls. Once they left those behind, they would be entering the vast empty expanse of the Breath.

Gythe took over the helm while Miri prepared the meager meal. Rodrigo sat in a chair, yawning. Dag played with the Doctor to prevent him from going to the galley to pester Miri for food.

Stephano was keeping watch, and just before the sun sank, the mists cleared and again he saw the three dragons.

He blinked, startled, and rubbed his eyes that ached from the long day spent scanning the skies through the spyglass. He thought perhaps he was seeing things, but when he looked back, the dragons were still there. Viola flew in front, taking the lead, the two males flanking her. He watched the dragons for long moments, not saying anything. Then he snapped the spyglass shut, and took his seat at the table.

Miri came on deck carrying a loaf of bread, a round of cheese, and dried rabbit. She set the food on the table. Telling Gythe to eat, Miri took over the helm.

"The dragons are back," Stephano announced, tearing off a hunk of bread.

The others stared at him in astonishment.

"What are they doing?" Miri asked.

Stephano shrugged. "I'm not sure, but I think they may be following us."

"Like a stray dog?" Rodrigo suggested. "Three dragons tied up in the backyard. Going to be hard to explain to the neighbors."

Stephano smiled at the thought. They ate in strained silence. Dag fed the Doctor a portion of his rabbit. Gythe took her sister some food. Miri shook her head.

"I'm not hungry."

The *Cloud Hopper* sailed over the islands, indistinguishable one from another. They flew over thick forests, low hills, open fields, and meadows. As darkness closed in around them, Gythe lit the lantern that hung over the helm. The moon was half full, sailing on a sea of silvery mist. Stephano watched an island slip away beneath the boat and when the island had disappeared, he could see nothing except darkness.

"We are sailing into the Breath," said Miri. "Five days . . ."

Everyone looked up at the balloon tinged with moonlight. God's Breath, carrying them home.

8

Constructs designed to have a healing effect on the human body have always had limited success. Despite years of intense study by devoted church scholars, crafters have been unable to replicate the medicines used by Trundler healers. It is therefore unfortunate, in my opinion, that some of my fellow practitioners continue in the outmoded view that Trundler medicines are heathen witchcraft.

—Dr. Martine Juvalanet,
Physician to the King

A month had passed since the Bottom Dwellers had attacked the Rosian port city of Westfirth. Since the attack, Sir Ander Martel, Knight Protector, had been dividing his time between sitting at the bedside of his charge, Father Jacob Northrop, and crawling through the rubble searching for the body of their companion, Brother Barnaby. Father Jacob had been grievously wounded in the attack, but Brother Barnaby had suffered a worse fate, caught in the explosion that had blown up the Old Fort's gun emplacements.

The weeks since the attack had not brought the knight much comfort.

Father Jacob had suffered a severe blow to the head. The

injury was so serious that for days his life was in peril. The archbishop had sent to the Arcanum for healers, who had treated the priest around the clock, using prayers and healing magicks and even going so far as to perform a procedure known as trepanation, in which a healer skilled in the technique drilled a hole in Father Jacob's skull.

Sir Ander had been appalled by the idea and had argued against it, but the surgeon, Sister Elizabeth, had said that if they did not relieve the pressure on the priest's brain, he would die. Sir Ander had gone to the small chapel in the Old Fort, the residence of the archbishop of Westfirth, where they were staying as his guests. There, he prayed for Father Jacob and for the soul of Brother Barnaby, lighting candles at the altar for them both.

"How could You let this happen to these two good men?" Sir Ander asked God in sorrow and anger.

God answered in a voice that sounded very much like the voice of Father Jacob.

The situation is too complicated. You could never possibly understand, the priest would often say to Sir Ander impatiently. *You simply have to trust me.*

Sir Ander did trust in God. The knight had undergone a crisis of faith many years earlier when his best friend, Julian de Guichen, was executed for treason. Since that time, Sir Ander's faith in God had been steadfast and unwavering, but not blind. He was not above arguing his case with both Father Jacob and God. Sir Ander doubted his arguments altered the opinion of either, but he always felt better afterward.

A week after the surgery, Father Jacob had regained consciousness. Sir Ander was jubilant, at first. His joy did not last, though, for Father Jacob did not recognize his friend and protector. The priest's speech was lucid, but he spoke to only one person—Marie Allemand, the founder of the

Arcanum, known as "Saint Marie." She had been dead for four hundred years.

Sir Ander had fallen into a melancholy routine. He spent the nights on a camp bed in Father Jacob's room, either listening to Father Jacob's snoring or his metaphysical conversations with a dead saint. In the mornings, Sir Ander would rise, eat his own breakfast, and then sit with Father Jacob as his friend ate his own. The priest was in good spirits. He ate well and had put on the weight he'd lost during his coma. But, Sir Ander knew, while his body might be healthy, his mind was not.

Before he was wounded, Father Jacob was considered one of the most brilliant, if difficult, members of the Arcanum. A savant, he was known for his ability to puzzle out solutions to the most baffling mysteries. Now he sat eating rashers of bacon and arguing with Saint Marie over how many angels could dance on the head of a pin.

Finding the sight of the ruin of this great mind terribly depressing, Sir Ander would leave for a breath of fresh air, walking along what was left of the battlements of the Old Fort, observing the rebuilding efforts or searching yet again amidst the rubble for some sign of Brother Barnaby. His fruitless efforts to find the monk were more depressing still.

Sir Ander would return to Father Jacob in the afternoons and talk to the priest, keeping him abreast of events. Sister Elizabeth had said that such conversations might help Father Jacob return to himself, but since Father Jacob was carrying on his own conversation with the saint, Sir Ander had his doubts. He persevered, however.

This morning, over a month since the attack on the city, Sir Ander told Father Jacob the news that had everyone in Westfirth talking.

"King Alaric is going to honor us with his presence," said Sir Ander drily. "His Majesty and his entourage are sailing here on the royal yacht. They will arrive in Westfirth tomorrow. The king is going to tour the site of the battle destruction and to hold a ceremony for those who died aboard the *Royal Lion*."

Father Jacob, his head still swathed in bandages, was sitting up in bed. He wore his nightclothes and a dressing gown over them. The priest was not looking at Sir Ander, nor was he listening to him. He was speaking to an empty chair. As was customary with the secretive Arcanum, one of their healers sat near the priest, listening to his conversation with the dead saint.

The Arcanum healers were always in attendance. At first, when Father Jacob was hovering between life and death, Sir Ander had been grateful for their presence. Now, even though the healers had admitted they were unable to do anything for the priest, they were still here, taking note of everything Father Jacob said. Sir Ander guessed that they were afraid the priest might reveal secrets best left to God and the Arcanum.

"But certainly it may be argued, Sister Marie," Father Jacob was saying, "that, as the great philosopher wrote and I quote, 'Although the senses occasionally mislead us respecting minute objects, and as such are so far removed from us as to be beyond the reach of close observation, there are yet many other of their informations, of the truth of which it is manifestly impossible to doubt.'"

Sir Ander sighed and went back to reading the local gazette's report on the efforts to repair the guard towers. He was interrupted by a knock on the door. Sir Ander rose to answer it, thinking dourly that it must be more healers.

Sir Ander had requested that two guards from the Old Fort's Guard Core stand watch outside the priest's room. Father Jacob had been ambushed in Westfirth only a day before the attack on the city and Sir Ander feared that the person who had missed killing him the first time might try again.

"I have a message for you, Sir Ander," said the guard, saluting. "The archbishop requests your presence. You'll find him in his office."

"When?" Sir Ander asked, frowning. He did not like the archbishop.

"Now, my lord," said the guard. "Sister Elizabeth is here to examine Father Jacob."

Sister Elizabeth was a brisk, no-nonsense woman who had defied convention to become one of the first women to study medicine. She was the surgeon who performed the trepanation on Father Jacob and was credited with saving the priest's life. Short and compact with strong, capable hands, Sister Elizabeth was invariably cheerful, active, and intelligent. The severe folds of the wimple oddly complemented her plump face and her bright, dimpled smile.

"And how are we today?" she asked, whisking past Sir Ander to attend Father Jacob. "Have we been eating?"

"Like a wyvern after a three-day run," said Sir Ander.

He was immediately sorry he had made the reference to wyverns, for it reminded him of Brother Barnaby. The monk had been their pilot for the yacht and he had always harbored a fondness for the recalcitrant and ill-tempered beasts.

"Excellent," said Sister Elizabeth, placing her hand on Father Jacob's neck to take the priest's pulse. She glanced at the other healer, who had risen from his chair. "You are relieved of your duty, Brother Diego. I will stay with Father Jacob for a while. I want to observe him."

Brother Diego nodded and left the room, closing the door behind him.

"It's been almost four weeks now, Sister," said Sir Ander worriedly. "Shouldn't there be some change by now?"

"Of all the miracles of God's creation, the brain is the

most wondrous," said Sister Elizabeth. "One never knows what will happen in such cases, but I remain hopeful."

"I'm glad someone does," Sir Ander muttered. "If you will excuse me, Sister, I have been summoned to meet with the archbishop."

"Before you go, Sir Ander, I need to give you some instructions regarding Father Jacob."

"Yes, Sister," Sir Ander said, somewhat puzzled. "What is it?"

Sister Elizabeth approached him and fixed him with an intense gaze. The dimples that appeared when she smiled had vanished. Her gaze was grave.

"Tread warily, Sir Knight," she said, her voice low.

Startled, Sir Ander was about to ask what she meant, when she cast a warning glance at the door, reminding him that the members of Guard Core were standing outside and although the door might be closed, their ears were not.

"Give a few drops of this concoction twice daily to Father Jacob," Sister Elizabeth added in a more normal tone. "You can mix it in his tea. I will leave it here."

She placed a vial filled with a colorless liquid on the nightstand.

"I will, Sister," said Sir Ander, troubled. "Thank you."

He left Sister Elizabeth seated comfortably in a chair, listening to Father Jacob as he spoke to the invisible Saint Marie, and went to try to find the archbishop's office.

The structure known throughout Westfirth as the Old Fort was both fortress and residence. Since the archbishop had taken up residence there, he had begun referring to the fort as the "archbishop's palace." No one in Westfirth knew it by that name, however, and would snicker at anyone who referred to it by that appellation.

The fortress portion consisted of a stockade, gun emplacements, watchtowers, and docks for naval patrol boats and ships. The gun emplacements had been targeted by the Bottom Dwellers. A single blast from the green beam weapon mounted on the stern of their black ship had sent ten forty-two-pound cannons and four sixty-four-pound cannons sliding down the face of the cliff into the Breath, along with a guard tower and much of the ramparts.

The palace, which was connected to the Old Fort by a series of labyrinthine hallways, had not been attacked and had sustained only minor damage from the shattering explosion—cracks in the plaster, glass windows blown out, a kitchen chimney toppled.

Workmen summoned from all parts of Rosia were busy making repairs on the palace, the fort, the docks, and especially the archbishop's beautiful new cathedral, which lay in ruins. The archbishop, Russell Lovaasen, of Guundaran descent, was a proud and ambitious man. He had promoted the building of a new cathedral in a city that was known for its wicked tendencies and rebellious nature, saying that the cathedral would bring Westfirth back to God and establish the church and her archbishop as a force in Rosia. The destruction of the cathedral had affected Lovaasen far more than the destruction of the fortress. The fact that the enemy had targeted the cathedral, when no other building in Westfirth had been attacked, was not lost on him.

"This is evidence beyond doubt that those who did this were Freyans," the archbishop stated at every opportunity. "All know the Freyans are godless heathens."

Those who held to the belief that the attackers were fiends sent by the Evil One to destroy mankind pointed to the destruction of the cathedral to prove *their* point. Their theory had been extremely popular in the days immediately following the assault, reinforced by wild tales told by survivors of demons who looked as though they had flown out of the cathedral's murals depicting hell.

The churches had been packed with people down on their knees begging God to save them. Everyone expected the Evil One, Aertheum, to come riding in on his black horse to burn the city to the ground. The archbishop had thundered from the pulpit that he was prepared to take on the devil himself.

When days went by and no hellfire erupted from the sewers or rained down from heaven, people grew weary of going to church. A courier arrived from the grand bishop with a letter from His Majesty the king. Suddenly the fiends were not from hell, but a far worse place—Freya, home of Rosia's most bitter enemies.

Sir Ander knew the truth about the foe. They were not fiends, nor were they Freyans. Father Jacob had carefully examined a helmet worn by one of the invaders, and had revealed the results of his examination to Sir Ander and Brother Barnaby moments before the assault on Westfirth. The attackers were men who termed themselves the "Bottom Dwellers" because they lived at the bottom of the world, something that most people would have said was impossible. Sir Ander was not yet certain he quite believed it.

Father Jacob had not told anyone else of his discovery. He had been planning to wait until he could return to the Arcanum to continue his investigations. Sir Ander had considered telling the archbishop what Father Jacob had found, but now that politics were involved, his information, regardless of its truth, would not be welcome.

Sir Ander wondered why he was being summoned, and guessed that the meeting must be connected to the arrival of the king. Sir Ander was not one of the king's favorites. He had been a friend to the rebel cause and although he had not joined the rebellion against the throne, he had been—and still was—in sympathy with the rebels.

Arriving in the antechamber of the archbishop's office, Sir Ander gave his name to the priest who served as the archbishop's secretary. The priest said there might be a short wait. The archbishop had a visitor and there was another person also waiting for an audience. He indicated a monk who was standing by the window, gazing outside.

Sir Ander wandered over to inspect a display of old matchlock pistols that adorned a section of wall. Weapons were not exactly the decoration he would have chosen for the office of a man of the cloth, but he reflected these were probably remnants of a bygone era, when the palace belonged to the marquis who had founded the city. He was examining them with interest when a soft cough caused him to turn. The monk who had been standing by the window was now right behind him.

"Brother Paul," Sir Ander said, astonished.

"Sir Ander," said the monk, bowing. "I hope you are well."

"Fine, thank you," said Sir Ander. "And you? I trust you have recovered from the terrifying experiences at the abbey."

"God be praised, I have. I heard about Father Jacob's injury," Brother Paul added. "I want you to know I have been praying for him."

"Thank you, Brother," said Sir Ander.

"You seem surprised to see me," said Brother Paul with a faint smile.

"I must confess that I am," said Sir Ander. "The last I heard you were residing at the Arcanum under Seal."

"The provost of the Arcanum decided to release me," said Brother Paul. "Given the attack on Westfirth—so similar to the attack on the abbey—he felt there was no need to keep me under Seal. The provost would have consulted Father Jacob before he removed the Seal, but of course, that was not possible given the circumstances. The provost was then good enough to place me in the service of the grand bishop."

"Indeed," said Sir Ander, frowning.

Brother Paul's argument made perfect sense, Sir Ander reflected, and yet he had the feeling Father Jacob would have argued most strongly against releasing the monk. In Sir Ander's mind, there were still a great many unanswered questions regarding Brother Paul.

Brother Paul was as pasty and pale as Sir Ander remembered from the last time they had met at the abbey. Brother Paul had been the nuns' confessor and had escaped the massacre because he had not been at the abbey the night of the murders. He wore tinted spectacles that protected his eyes from the light, even though the office was cool and shadowy, only dimly lit from the sun shining through a stained-glass window. He had told Sir Ander that he was subject to severe headaches and the spectacles helped alleviate them.

"How is Brother Barnaby?" Brother Paul asked. "I assume he is tending Father Jacob."

Sir Ander felt a jab of pain.

"Brother Barnaby was lost during the attack," Sir Ander said, gritting his teeth on the words.

"I am truly sorry to hear this," said Brother Paul sadly. "He saved me from the demons' torment. I will pray for his soul, that he may be fit to enter heaven."

Sir Ander glared at the monk. He wanted to say angrily that if ever a soul was fit to enter heaven without the need for prayer, it was the soul of the gentle Barnaby. Sir Ander swallowed his words. Brother Paul would have been extremely shocked at such blasphemy. Sir Ander changed the subject.

"You are assigned to the grand bishop," said Sir Ander. "Forgive me, Brother, but I thought you had chosen to live a life apart from men, spending your time alone in the wilderness in prayer and meditation."

"That was my intent," Brother Paul conceded. "I was happy in my hermitage and loath to leave it. God made me see that I am needed in the world, to assist others, especially since these terrible events. I offered my services to the grand bishop and he was kind enough to give me the position of courier."

Brother Paul glanced at a leather satchel he had placed on the floor beside him. Sir Ander did not quite see how being the grand bishop's errand boy would help others, but held his tongue. Brother Paul said no more, and Sir Ander was relieved to see the door open and the priest appear, saying the archbishop would see the Knight Protector now and asking Brother Paul if he would be so kind as to continue waiting.

"God bless you, Sir Ander," said the monk. "And may God's blessing be with Father Jacob."

Sir Ander entered the office. The archbishop was standing in the center of the room, still in conference with his visitor. Lovaasen was tall and thin, an energetic and active man in his midthirties. The archbishop was not often found sitting behind a desk. He liked to be out doing God's work, though Sir Ander found it surprising that such work took the archbishop most often to the homes of the elite and powerful, and only rarely to the slums. The archbishop was a friend of the king and had his eye on the grand bishop's miter. Sir Ander was aware, from certain things Father Jacob had said, that the grand bishop, Ferdinand de Montagne, was not overly fond of Lovaasen.

Sir Ander bowed respectfully and waited to be noticed. When he recognized the archbishop's visitor, he understood immediately why Sister Elizabeth had warned him to tread warily. Father Jacob had once named the three most dangerous people in the world: Sir Henry Wallace of Freya, the Countess Cecile de Marjolaine of Rosia, and this man— Dubois, the grand bishop's "creature," his spy, confidant, and agent.

For such a dangerous man, Dubois was not prepossessing in appearance. He was short and pudgy with a round face that bore a mild, pleasant expression. Dressed in nondescript clothes, Dubois was often mistaken for a clerk, a misapprehension he relished, according to Father Jacob. Dubois's clerklike demeanor kept the unwary from noticing the dangerous glitter in the intelligent eyes.

The archbishop was scowling, his cheeks tinged with spots of red, in contrast to Dubois's bland expression. The conversation had apparently been heated, at least on the part of the archbishop.

"Sir Ander, thank you for coming," said the archbishop coldly. "Please be seated."

The archbishop indicated a grouping of chairs placed near his desk. He did not introduce Dubois, nor did he invite the bishop's agent to sit down.

Dubois wandered over to the window, where he affected to be absorbed in watching laborers hard at work outside. He clasped his hands behind his back and rocked a little on the balls of his feet. Every so often, he would cast an oblique glance over his shoulder.

The presence of Dubois made Sir Ander uncomfortable and he had the distinct impression the archbishop felt the same.

"How is Father Jacob this morning, Sir Ander?" the archbishop asked, settling himself in his chair.

"I believe Your Reverence receives the reports of the healers on a daily basis," Sir Ander replied evenly.

"I do, of course," said the archbishop. "But I would like to hear your assessment of Father Jacob's condition."

"Considering the serious nature of the injury he sustained, he has made remarkable progress."

The archbishop drummed his fingers on the arm of the chair and gazed at Sir Ander. Dubois cast a sharp glance at the knight. Sir Ander understood that something was afoot, something he was not going to like. He braced himself as he might have braced himself to endure an enemy bombardment.

"Father Jacob is recovering in body," said Archbishop Lovaasen. "The injury to the brain is quite another matter. Father Jacob is deranged. He talks to a dead saint."

"He does talk to Saint Marie," said Sir Ander. He raised his hand when the archbishop would have spoken. "That does not mean he is mad. May I tell Your Reverence a story?"

The archbishop frowned, but indicated with a gesture that Sir Ander should continue.

"We had in our service a young monk, Brother Barnaby," said Sir Ander, his voice softening. "He was a healer, extraordinarily gifted. He was asked to treat a young woman, who had been on a boat when it came under attack from these same foes who attacked Westfirth. The young woman was so badly frightened that she reverted back to being a child. This woman, Gythe, had no knowledge of what was going on around her. She sang nonsense songs, she played cat's cradle. She was no longer a lovely young woman of twenty. She was a child of six."

The archbishop stirred as though he might ask where this was going. Sir Ander ignored him and continued.

"Brother Barnaby sang with her. He played cat's cradle. He used his healing arts to enter her mind and found Gythe in the darkness where she was hiding. He took her hand and he led her back to us. The last time I saw her, she was once more herself."

"A touching story of the healing power of God," said the archbishop, "but I fail to see—"

"If you will permit me," said Sir Ander. "I believe Saint Marie is doing the same with Father Jacob. I believe that the saint found him in his darkness and she is leading him back to health. After all, the church proclaims that saints can have direct intervention in our lives."

Dubois turned from the window to regard Sir Ander with interest. The archbishop stirred again in his chair, this time with impatience.

"You claim that Father Jacob's madness is a miracle, Sir Ander," said the archbishop, sniffling in disdain. "I was warned you might be difficult."

"I believe my view to be eminently sensible, Your Reverence," said Sir Ander. "We see the healing power of God and His saints, as you yourself just said."

The archbishop picked up a letter. Sir Ander saw Dubois once again rock back on his heels and turn to gaze out the window.

"I have received orders from the grand bishop. His Eminence has made a decision. Father Jacob is to be committed to a lunatic asylum."

Sir Ander was struck dumb. His jaw sagged. He could do nothing for a moment except stare in shock at the archbishop, who affected not to notice.

"You will, of course, be permitted to accompany Father Jacob. His Eminence has sent a carriage to convey the priest to the Asylum of Charenton."

Sir Ander had once visited a lunatic asylum. A brother officer had been confined to one after he'd attacked a group of workmen under the mistaken impression they were Freyan spies. Sir Ander had been appalled at the conditions in the asylum. The inmates were locked up in cells, tied to their beds, babbling and raving. He had left thinking that hell could hardly be any worse and might possibly be better.

And those who were sent to an asylum rarely came out.

"His Eminence is the one who should be locked up," Sir Ander said bitingly. "Father Jacob is *not* insane."

"Given that you are in the grip of strong emotion, Sir Knight, I will overlook such a disrespectful remark," said the archbishop. "His Eminence has read the reports of the healers. Please be ready to depart this afternoon. The healers will prepare Father Jacob for the journey."

"Meaning they will bind him hand and foot, truss him up like a Michaelmas goose, and feed him opium to keep him silent," Sir Ander said angrily. "I won't allow it!"

"You are a Knight Protector, Sir Ander," said the archbishop. "You are sworn to obey orders. You have no say in this matter."

Dubois turned from the window. His expression was mild, as was his tone. "Before we act precipitously, Archbishop, I feel it incumbent upon me to remind Your Reverence of the article in canon law that states that *all* the healers attendant upon the patient must be in agreement before the patient can be committed. I believe one of the healers is opposed."

The archbishop cast Dubois a startled glance, clearly surprised that he had come to Father Jacob's defense.

"And then there is the matter of obtaining the agreement of the members of the family. I believe that Father Jacob has a brother still living—"

"A brother living in *Freya*!" the archbishop snapped, laying heavy emphasis upon the word. "A brother who is a notorious pirate!"

"Nonetheless, I am certain you will not want to do anything that might precipitate possible legal action against the church," Dubois said mildly. "Do nothing in haste, Archbishop. I think you should allow the provost to handle this matter."

"I have orders from His Eminence," said the archbishop, almost shouting. "You yourself brought them!"

"I was not aware what was in the letter. At least let *me* speak to His Eminence before you decide," said Dubois in a soothing tone.

Sir Ander was astonished to receive help from the agent of the grand bishop. Dubois was undoubtedly lying when he said he didn't know about the orders. Dubois knew everything. Sir Ander was quick to accept Dubois's aid, though he couldn't help but wonder why the man had switched sides.

"Monsieur has said all the healers must be in agreement, Reverence," said Sir Ander. "He has indicated that one is opposed. Therefore you must not proceed."

Archbishop Lovaasen shot Dubois a furious glance. The red spots appeared once more on Lovaasen's pale cheeks.

"Four of the healers are," said the archbishop sourly. "Sister Elizabeth is opposed. I plan to speak to her again. I am certain she will soon be convinced that confining Father Jacob until he can recover his senses is in the best interest of her patient."

Sir Ander wondered how long Sister Elizabeth would be able to withstand the pressure the archbishop would apply. Given the fact that this was a woman who could drill a hole into a man's skull with a steady hand, he guessed that she would not yield easily.

"You are dismissed, Sir Knight. I plan to report your uncooperative attitude to the head of your order."

Sir Ander made a stiff bow to the archbishop, cast a grateful if puzzled glance at Dubois, and departed.

Returning to the antechamber, Sir Ander saw Brother Paul was still standing with his satchel, waiting for his audience with the archbishop. Sir Ander walked past the monk without speaking.

He was too upset to return to Father Jacob. The knight

went to the palace garden where he proceded to walk off his anger. He strolled about in the shade of the spreading trees, inhaling the scent of summer roses, and eventually calmed down enough to think rationally.

If not for Dubois, Father Jacob might well have been in a straitjacket by now. Sir Ander wondered again why Dubois had come to Father Jacob's defense. The knight was trying to figure this out when he rounded a corner of the path to find Dubois standing beside an ornamental pond, throwing crumbs to the ducks. Dubois immediately caught sight of Sir Ander. He tossed in the last of the crumbs and beckoned the knight to join him.

"Ah, Sir Ander," said Dubois in his mild voice. "I am pleased to have stumbled upon you. I was hoping we would have a chance for a confidential talk."

Sir Ander guessed that Dubois had not "stumbled" upon him, but had come to this very place hoping to meet him. This notion was borne out by the fact that the pond was in a clearing, surrounded by a brick patio. The trees and clipped hedgerows were some distance away, too far for someone to be able to lurk there, eavesdropping.

"Thank you for your help regarding Father Jacob, monsieur," said Sir Ander. "I must confess I had not expected it, considering that you are the grand bishop's agent."

Dubois gave an enigmatic smile and cast Sir Ander a keen glance.

"We first met at the abbey following that tragic massacre of the nuns. I read Father Jacob's report in which he mentioned green fire, and the destruction of the constructs on the columns and walls of the cathedral. I was reminded of another report Father Jacob had submitted many years ago. It was a report of the destruction of the naval cutter *Defiant*. Green fire was mentioned in that report, as well."

Sir Ander was astonished. "Monsieur has an excellent

memory. Not to mention that the report was placed under Seal, buried. No one was permitted to see it."

Dubois gave a self-deprecating smile. "I am someone who is no one, Sir Knight. One question I need to ask you: You do not believe these attackers are either demons *or* Freyans, do you, Sir Ander?"

Sir Ander frowned and made no reply. The two had been walking slowly around the pond. Dubois came to a stop in front of Sir Ander.

"Father Jacob discovered something about this foe. I knew he could not let the matter of the green fire rest. I also know he was attacked in the streets of Westfirth prior to the attack on the city. Do not look so surprised, Sir Knight. I make it my business to know these things. Now I want to know what he found out about these people. I *need* to know, Sir Ander. Father Jacob would most certainly have confided in you. You may safely confide in me."

"You must be aware, Monsieur Dubois, that I have taken an oath of secrecy regarding Father Jacob and his work."

Dubois made an impatient gesture. "You should consider bending your oath, Sir Ander. The fate of your nation may depend on it."

"I swore my oath before God, monsieur," said Sir Ander.

Dubois lowered his gaze. He was a short man whose head came to Sir Ander's chest. Dubois stared fixedly at a button on the knight's uniform coat for a couple of moments, then shrugged.

"In that case, I bid you good day, Sir Ander."

"Wait, monsieur," said Sir Ander. He owed Dubois something for his intervention with the archbishop. "I promise that when Father Jacob is fully restored to health, I will tell him that you are interested in learning about what he has discovered."

"You are very certain he will recover," said Dubois.

"I am, monsieur," said Sir Ander.

Dubois regarded him thoughtfully. "I warn you, Sir Ander, you do not have much time. The archbishop is undoubtedly writing to the grand bishop and the provost as we speak. I venture to suggest that the surgeon, Sister Elizabeth, will receive a summons to return to the Arcanum. Without her here to intercede for Father Jacob . . ."

Dubois shrugged and left the sentence hanging.

Sir Ander shook his head, frustrated. "I know the grand bishop and Father Jacob have butted heads in the past, but His Eminence chose Father Jacob to investigate the *Defiant*, and the murders at the abbey. Now Montagne is trying to silence Father Jacob by locking him up and telling the world he's insane. Why, Dubois? What's going on?"

"I have rooms at the Ivy. Send for me any time, day or night." Dubois made a bobbing bow. "Your servant, Sir Ander. Oh, by the way, you would not happen to know how to contact Father Jacob's brother in Freya, would you?"

"His brother is Captain Alan Northrop, the Freyan privateer. Captain Northrop tried to kill Father Jacob," said Sir Ander. "Needless to say, the brothers do not communicate."

"I seem to recall hearing as much," said Dubois. "Good day to you, Sir Ander."

Dubois bowed again, sauntered off, and was soon lost amid the shrubbery. Sir Ander gazed after the pudgy little man and thought how much he detested church politics and intrigue. Then he returned to sit with Father Jacob and express his grateful thanks to Sister Elizabeth for her warning.

After leaving the knight, Dubois walked for some time in the garden. He was not enjoying the roses or admiring the hedges that had been fancifully pruned to resemble chess pieces. He was sorting his thoughts and observations, studying them, considering them, classifying them, and—clerklike—tucking them neatly away in the pigeon holes in his mental rolltop desk.

Now in his forties, the only son of a clerk in an accounting firm, Dubois had been sent to a church-run boarding school for boys with the understanding that when he was fourteen, he would obtain a job as a clerk. He was determined not to spend his life as his father had spent it, his back stooped from bending over a desk, spectacles perched on his nose, his index finger permanently stained black with ink.

Even as a boy, Dubois had impressed people with his remarkable mental abilities. His memory was so accurate that he could quote the writings of the saints verbatim. He was observant and inquisitive, a quiet boy who spent his time listening.

The parish priest had considered it a shame that such talents would be wasted toting up numbers all day. He had persuaded an attorney friend to hire the young Dubois as a law clerk. The priest kept an eye on the young man, and when Dubois was in his twenties, brought him to the attention of the grand bishop. Dubois proved himself so useful to His Eminence that before long he had become his most trusted agent.

Dubois kept His Eminence informed about the doings of the king, the intrigues of the Countess de Marjolaine, the plots and schemes of Sir Henry Wallace, and the actions, overt and covert, of other kings and queens, princes, and prelates the world over. Dubois had agents of his own in every royal court. He had agents spying on his agents and spies spying on the spies. Dubois had, in short, become essential to His Eminence, which meant he wielded power over the grand bishop.

Dubois did not abuse his power. A devout man, he was loyal to his master, believing the grand bishop was God's representative here below. Dubois saw himself as God's

agent, protector of the church and protector of the grand
bishop, which meant, as Dubois saw it, that he needed to
know the grand bishop's secrets. Ferdinand de Montagne
trusted Dubois implicitly and, up until now, had been glad to
share his secrets with his confidential agent.

Lately, Dubois had become aware that Montagne had a
secret he was not willing to share; a secret so deep and so
dark that it was literally eating the man up inside. The grand
bishop was dyspeptic; he had visibly lost weight; he was
awake at all hours of the night; and he was in a foul mood.

Granted, the grand bishop was heavily involved in the
worsening situation of the disputed city-state of Braffa, having sided with Estara against King Alaric, for he was allies
with Travia in their claim on the refineries in Braffa that
produced the liquid form of the Breath used to power the
ships of the royal navy. Yet Braffa was not the problem.
Even as Montagne was studying reports on Braffa, he would
toss them aside to read the account of some low-level healer
regarding Father Jacob Northrop.

"Saint Marie," the grand bishop had muttered once in
Dubois's hearing. "What the devil is the man doing talking
to Saint Marie?"

Afterward, the grand bishop had fallen into a dark and
brooding silence and a day later had decided that Father
Jacob was a threat to himself and others and that he should
be sent to a lunatic asylum.

"Is the provost in agreement with this decision?" Dubois
had asked, startled.

"He will be when I have explained the circumstances,"
the grand bishop had said. "Make the arrangements."

"But, Your Eminence—"

"You have your orders, Dubois!" the grand bishop had
said, scowling.

Dubois had read up on canon law and secular law—just

in case—and he had then traveled from the grand bishop's seat at Evreux to Westfirth, ostensibly to carry out his orders, but in reality to assess the situation firsthand. As Dubois had traveled, he had asked himself the same question Sir Ander had asked him.

Montagne is trying to silence Father Jacob by locking him up and telling the world he's insane. Why? What's going on?

Whatever the dread secret was, Dubois thought, not for the first time, it had something to do with those who attacked the abbey and Westfirth.

He glanced at his pocket watch and saw that the afternoon was wearing away. He had an appointment with his physician to examine a gunshot wound Dubois had suffered a month ago at the hands of Lord Captain Stephano de Guichen. The wound was healing nicely, though Dubois found that his shoulder ached when it rained.

On his way out of the palace, he saw Brother Paul leaving the office of the archbishop, undoubtedly the bearer of a furious letter from the archbishop regarding Dubois's meddling.

He was not concerned. He would write his own report to the grand bishop and send it by special griffin-courier. His message would reach Montagne long before the report carried by Brother Paul, who was traveling by wyvern-drawn coach. Dubois would also send a letter to the provost.

Dubois believed that as a duenna protects her young mistress by reading her diary, it was his duty to protect the grand bishop by finding out his secrets. Otherwise, how could Dubois save His Eminence from his enemies?

9

Politics is like the Opera Buffa. Actors in gorgeous costumes glittering with jewels mince about the stage and deliver their lines, eliciting tears and laughter from the enthralled audience. But when the curtain falls, the actors go behind the scenes and take off their masks. And then the true farce begins.

—Alexandro de Villeneuve,
in a letter to his son Rodrigo

King Alaric of Rosia arrived in the city of Westfirth the next day aboard the royal barge, accompanied by a fleet of large warships and a score of yachts belonging to various members of the royal court who were traveling with His Majesty. The king was greeted by the ringing of church bells and the shouts of his subjects who had gathered upon the piers to view the magnificent spectacle.

Shops and businesses had closed for the occasion. People were dressed in their finest. Children clutched small Rosian flags and pickpockets did a brisk business among the crowds jamming the boardwalks. The sailors on the few merchant vessels that had been bold enough or desperate enough to sail into Westfirth paused in their labors to stare at the enormous barge with its glass-enclosed cabin—white trimmed in gold, with matching white and gold silk balloons, one at either end, billowing above the deck. The royal barge was designed for elegant living and slow movement and therefore had no sails. The king stood on deck, waving to the crowds, surrounded by royal bargemen in white-and-gold uniforms.

The merchants and shipowners in Westfirth were glad to see the king, although his arrival meant that the harbor was closed to traffic for the duration of his stay. One reason for His Majesty's visit was to persuade those merchants who had been too fearful to return to Rosia that the Breath was once more safe to travel.

"Of course, King Alaric doesn't dare come himself without bringing half the royal navy along with him," Sir Ander remarked caustically.

He was observing the spectacle from the window in Father Jacob's room. Sister Elizabeth stood by his side, watching with him.

"Most people won't look at it that way," Sister Elizabeth responded cheerfully. She nudged Sir Ander with her elbow. "Only you cynics."

Sir Ander was about to reply when Father Jacob, who had been quiet all morning, suddenly said sharply, "You have nothing to feel guilty about, Sister Marie. You were right to maintain that contramagic is not evil."

"Contramagic?" Sister Elizabeth cast a startled glance at Sir Ander, who turned from the window and hastened to the priest's bedside.

Sitting down beside Father Jacob, Sir Ander said with quiet urgency, "I think it's time you rested, Father . . ."

"Contramagic is a force of nature. One might as well say gravity is evil," Father Jacob continued with spirit. "You and your companions did nothing wrong. You sought knowledge. You sought the truth. Men fear what they do not understand.

You attempted to bring about understanding and thus eradicate the fear."

Sir Ander was sorely tempted to shove a gag in Father Jacob's mouth to shut him up. The mere mention of the word "contramagic" could result in charges of heresy. Even the tolerant Sister Elizabeth was shocked and uneasy.

Fortunately, Father Jacob crossed his arms and sat back in his bed, falling into silent contemplation.

"Let us hope he comes to himself soon," was all Sister Elizabeth had to say.

Sir Ander could tell she was disturbed by what she had heard and he could not blame her. He went back to the window and the two of them watched in silence as the royal barge sailed up to the dock at the Old Fort. The dock had been hastily rebuilt to prepare for this visit and stonemasons and crafters hovered nearby, ready to rush in to make emergency repairs if needed.

The royal bargemen stood at attention. The archbishop, dressed in full regalia, was there to bow and gush as His Majesty walked down the red-carpeted gangplank. He was accompanied by his queen, whose jewels glittered in the sun. The king's gentlemen and the queen's ladies-in-waiting came next. The yachts bearing the other members of the royal court arrived at the dock, disgorging barons and earls, dukes and duchesses. The ladies, assembling on the ramparts, stared and gasped and claimed to feel quite faint at the sight of the wreckage from the attack and the rocks still stained with blood. The men spoke loudly and angrily of the depredations committed by the Freyans and swore revenge.

Sir Ander thought back to those terrifying moments when men lay on the parapet bleeding and dying. He thought of Brother Barnaby falling to his death, and he was sick to his stomach. He was about to turn away in disgust when a small yacht remarkable for its elegance sailed up to the dock. Sir Ander recognized the bumblebee emblem on the balloons. The yacht belonged to the Countess Cecile de Marjolaine.

Sir Ander was pleasantly surprised, though of course she would be traveling with the rest of the royal party. He was a dunce not to have foreseen that she would be in attendance. He watched Cecile step onto the dock, every movement graceful. She made her reverence to the King and Queen and then walked away, refusing to join the crowd of fawning courtiers clustered around their majesties. Sir Ander smiled when he saw that she soon attracted her own crowd of attendant courtiers.

"Will you stay with Father Jacob, Sister?" Sir Ander asked. "I have an errand to which I must attend."

Sister Elizabeth agreed to stay with the priest. She had not yet been sent back to the Arcanum, but it was only a matter of time before she received the summons—unless Dubois could successfully intervene.

Sir Ander hurried to his room and swiftly changed into his dress uniform. He buckled on his sword and sadly eyed the dusty state of his boots. He did not have enough time, however, to polish them.

Long ago Sir Ander had loved Cecile de Marjolaine, when she was sixteen, the most beautiful woman at court. He had lost her to his dear friend, Julian de Guichen. Her rejection had wounded him, but he was not the type of man to let such a loss embitter him. He had remained friends with both Cecile and Julian and was godfather to their son, Stephano.

Sir Ander and Cecile had corresponded over the years. Since he studiously avoided attending court, he had not seen Cecile since the two had risked their lives to meet secretly with Julian in his prison cell the night before his execution. Sir Ander hastened onto the ramparts, searching for Cecile among the throng of voluminous silk dresses, jewels, feathers, fans, and petticoats.

Elegant and aloof, she stood out from the crowd. He had no trouble finding her, and once he did, he slowed his approach, taking pleasure in watching the countess from a distance.

She was still beautiful. Poets sang the praises of her silver hair, gray-blue eyes, and ivory complexion. Tall and slender, she moved with artless grace.

Sir Ander felt a strange sorrow at seeing her after all these years and he could not understand what was wrong. She was still the most beautiful woman he had ever known. Except she wasn't the woman he had known all those years ago. The thought came to him that he might have been looking at a portrait of Cecile de Marjolaine. She was a likeness of herself: cold, remote, detached, revealing no feeling, no emotion. She responded mechanically to the compliments and flatteries, and appeared to be bored with the company and with the proceedings.

And then her gaze fell upon Sir Ander, standing at a respectful distance.

Cecile stepped off the canvas and into life. Her blue eyes shone with pleasure, a faint flush tinged her cheeks, and a smile touched her lips. Sir Ander swept off his hat and made his best military bow. She motioned with her fan for him to advance and graciously smiled at him. Those gathered around her turned to stare at him in whispering wonder.

"Sir Ander Martel," said Cecile, holding out a jeweled hand. "I understand you were present during the attack."

"I was, my lady," said Sir Ander.

The women murmured their sympathies and looked at him with more interest. The men crowded around him, asking him questions about the battle. Cecile stood near him, her dove-colored silk dress rustling. She laid her fingers lightly on his forearm.

"I find this relentless sunshine fatiguing, Sir Ander. That tower over there offers shade. If you would accompany me, I would be interested to hear your account of the battle."

Sir Ander said he would be only too pleased. He and Cecile walked off, leaving her friends and enemies to gossip and stare and speculate.

"We have given them something to talk about," said Sir Ander, glancing over his shoulder.

"Let them," said Cecile.

They stopped in the shadow of the tower, one of the few left standing after the attack. She rested her hand on the stone wall and gazed out into the Breath.

"It is good to see you, my lady," said Sir Ander, regarding her with admiration.

"If you go on to say I am as beautiful now as I was at sixteen I will walk away and not come back," Cecile said with a faint smile. She rested her hand on his. "No gallant speeches between us, dear friend."

"No, my—Cecile," said Sir Ander gently.

"I am so glad you are here!" Cecile clutched him suddenly, with an unusual show of emotion. "You were in Westfirth during the attack. I fear Stephano was also in Westfirth. Is it possible . . . Did you see him? I came here purposefully to find out."

She talked on, not pausing to let Sir Ander answer. "I have heard nothing from my son. Nothing! He was supposed to report back to me. Poor Benoit is frantic and I—"

"Stephano *was* here, Cecile," said Sir Ander, interrupting her. "I wrote to you that I had met him at the Abbey of Saint Agnes. He and his friends and Father Jacob and I traveled to Westfirth together. We were all here during the attack—"

"Oh, God!" Cecile whispered.

"But he escaped," Sir Ander hastened to reassure her. "He and his friends were on a Trundler boat sailing out of the harbor as the attack began. The last I saw, the *Cloud Hopper* was heading into the open expanse of the Breath. I will lay you any odds you like, Cecile, that he and his friends escaped safely. The enemy concentrated their fire on the naval vessels, the fortress, the cathedral, and merchant ships."

"If he is safe, why haven't I heard from him?" Cecile asked. She shook her head, frowning. "I fear he may have fallen victim to the schemes of Sir Henry Wallace. I would have never involved Stephano if I had known Sir Henry was the agent behind the abduction of the journeyman Alcazar. You know Sir Henry, I believe?"

"To my sorrow," said Sir Ander grimly. "He was here at the time, in Westfirth. Stephano mentioned he was on Wallace's trail. Father Jacob warned him to steer clear of the man. Don't borrow trouble, Cecile. There are any number of reasons why Stephano has not contacted you."

"The primary reason being that he hates and despises me," Cecile remarked with a quirk of her eyebrow.

Sir Ander shook her head. "May I ask you a question, Cecile? Why haven't you told Stephano the truth? That you and Julian were reconciled. That the two of you were married. He would not hate you if he understood that you did not abandon his father."

"If people knew the truth, Sir Ander, that Stephano was my legitimate heir, my enemies would become his enemies. Let the world think we are estranged, that I make use of him, that I give him money only to keep him from the disgrace of debtors' prison."

She glanced over her shoulder. "Speaking of my enemies, Her Majesty is causing mischief. I must go."

Sir Ander could see the Queen speaking to her husband,

gesturing at Cecile. King Alaric was observing the Countess and Sir Ander with a frowning glare.

"You are a comfort to me, my friend," said Cecile. "I will let you know if I receive any news of Stephano."

"I will do the same," he said. "God be with you, Cecile."

Cecile shook her head. "I fear God abandoned me long ago, dear friend. Do not walk with me. His Majesty would be displeased."

Sir Ander halted her as she would have walked away. "Cecile, you speak of your enemies. Please promise me one thing: If you are ever in need of help, I have a friend you can trust. Sir Conal O'Hairt. You will find him at the Mother House of the Knight Protectors."

Cecile smiled and left him. She moved languidly, taking her time, refusing to rush. Before joining the King, she stopped to talk to some of the Fort's guards who were on duty. Sir Ander, watching, saw the Queen whisk out her fan with obvious displeasure and say something behind it to a woman standing beside her, a woman with such an exotic appearance, Sir Ander frankly stared. The woman wore a powdered wig trimmed in feathers that contrasted well with her tawny complexion and her large, dark eyes. Her face was lovely, her lips touched with red, her eyes darkened with kohl.

"Striking, isn't she?" said a voice at his elbow.

Sir Ander had not heard anyone approach. He looked around in surprise to find the short, pudgy Dubois standing at his elbow.

Dubois gave a self-deprecating smile. "Her name is Idonia, the Duquesa de Plata Niebla, newly arrived in court and already, as you can see, close friends with Her Majesty. But then you keep charming company yourself, Sir Ander: the Countess de Marjolaine. I congratulate you."

Sir Ander saw no reason to respond. "If you will excuse me, Monsieur, I must return to Father Jacob—"

"How is he this morning?" Dubois asked.

"No change," said Sir Ander shortly.

"That is a great pity, Sir Ander," Dubois said gravely. "A very great pity indeed. You are a devout man, I believe. If I were you, I would speak to the one who might be able to help."

"Who would that be, monsieur?" Sir Ander asked, thinking he perhaps was going to suggest the provost.

Dubois's answer was startling. "Saint Marie."

As Sir Ander returned to the palace he pondered this strange suggestion. Glancing over his shoulder, he saw Dubois lounging in the shadow of the tower, arms folded, his gaze fixed intently upon the striking Duquesa de Plata Niebla.

"God help her," Sir Ander muttered.

He started to return to Father Jacob's room, then stopped. After a moment's hesitation, he changed direction and took a different route. Outside the chapel, he hesitated another moment, then entered.

Every chapel in Rosia had its marble statue of Saint Marie. Her statue in this chapel was located in a small niche in the wall. Lighting a candle, he placed it on her altar. Saint Marie was portrayed wearing armor and carrying a sword, for she was known as a defender of the faith. She had founded the Arcanum and she had died alongside her knights fighting members of a blood magic cult.

Sir Ander had seen portraits of Saint Marie, including the magnificent painting by the famed artist, Lawrence Moreel, which hung in the Arcanum. The statue looked very much like that portrait. The tale was told that Sister Marie passed as a man in order to study in an era when women were not permitted to enter university. Looking at her, Sir Ander could see how she might have been mistaken for a male with her strong, jutting jaw, high cheekbones, fierce eyes, and proud mouth. She had shaved her head in the tonsure and had explained the lack of facial hair on a childhood disease.

A few loyal friends, among them the priest who would eventually be known as Saint Dennis, had known the truth and had helped her keep her secret. Even in later years, when she was honored and admired and everyone knew she was a woman, she had continued to shave her head and wear priest's robes.

Sir Ander placed a candle in the holder on the altar and sat down on a low bench placed there for those who wanted to offer her their prayers. As he gazed up at the statue he wondered how to begin. Now that he was here, he felt a little foolish. Sir Ander believed that saints could and did work miracles, but he couldn't help wonder if Saint Marie was working a miracle by speaking to Father Jacob or if Father Jacob's extraordinary mind had suffered such a terrible injury that he would never recover.

Sir Ander lowered himself to his knees and clasped his hands.

"Blessed Saint Marie, I come to you regarding Father Jacob. I know you are with him. I pray that you are healing him and leading him back to us."

Sir Ander paused, trying to put his feelings into words. "What I fear is that Father Jacob does not *want* to come back. I know him. He is enjoying these metaphysical discussions. He would much rather remain with you than return to harsh reality. We need him, Saint Marie. He is the only one who knows the truth about these fiends. He is the only one who can tell us how to fight them and their terrible weapons."

Sir Ander shook his head. "Father Jacob can be extremely stubborn, Saint Marie. I have heard that you were a match for any man. Send him back. Tell him he has to come home."

Sir Ander took two more candles, placed them on the altar, and said another prayer.

"Be with Cecile de Marjolaine, Saint Marie. Protect and keep her and my godson, Stephano, from harm."

Leaving the chapel, Sir Ander was filled with a sense of peace. He didn't know if that was a sign from the saint or if he was glad to have handed over responsibility for Father Jacob to God.

As he walked back to Father Jacob's room, Sir Ander reflected on his conversation with Cecile. His heart ached for her and her dangerous, difficult, and lonely life. He would have liked to have told the truth to Stephano, to make him understand all that Cecile had done for her son, the sacrifices she had made and would continue to make. The truth was not his to tell, however. Cecile had her reasons and they were damn good ones.

Outside the palace, an orchestra on the royal barge was playing. Sir Ander paused at a window, hoping to see Cecile again, if only from a distance. The royal party had moved on, however, going back to their barges to dress for dinner with the archbishop.

When Sir Ander returned to Father Jacob, Sister Elizabeth greeted him with disturbing news.

"Father Jacob was considerably agitated after you left. I had to summon the guards to help me keep him from leaving the room. Father Diego wanted to bind his wrists—"

"Never!" said Sir Ander angrily.

"We managed to calm him and there was no need," said Sister Elizabeth. She sighed deeply. "God knows I do not want to have to say this, but I really think we may have to consider . . . for his own good . . ."

"Never," Sir Ander repeated, but he uttered the words with less conviction than before.

"The healers are meeting again tomorrow to discuss his case. I will do what I can, but after this incident . . ." Sister

Elizabeth rested her hand on Sir Ander's arm. "God be with you both."

Sir Ander removed his heavy dress uniform coat and flung it over a chair. He went to stand at the foot of Father Jacob's bed. The priest had been quiet. Suddenly he sat straight up and spoke loudly and angrily.

"Again, Sister, I quote the wise philosopher: 'I am assured that there will arise neither peril nor error from this course, and that I cannot for the present yield too much to distrust, since the end I now seek is not action but knowledge!' I seek knowledge! They will not, they cannot stop me!"

Father Jacob sprang out of bed and appeared ready to storm out of the room. As Sir Ander attempted to seize hold of him, Father Jacob struck him a right cross to the jaw.

The priest had been a pugilist in his youth. The blow sent Sir Ander staggering and for a moment he saw stars.

"Ander, what do you mean manhandling me?" Father Jacob said, glaring at him. "I must go to the library—"

Sir Ander stared in glad astonishment. Father Jacob was glaring at *him*. He was speaking to *him*. Not to a dead saint.

"Are you going to the library in your nightdress?" Sir Ander asked, massaging his jaw.

Father Jacob gazed down in perplexity at the long nightgown he was wearing.

"Why am I . . ." He looked about at his surroundings and frowned. "This is not the Arcanum."

He fixed Sir Ander with an accusing glare. "What is going on? Where am I? Why am I dressed like this?" He put his hands to his head, felt the bandages, and started to rip them off.

"Father Jacob, sit down and I will explain everything," said Sir Ander. "And please don't take off the bandages."

"Where is Brother Barnaby?" Father Jacob demanded irately. "Tell him I am perfectly well and he will remove these at once. The bandages itch like the very devil."

"Jacob," said Sir Ander. "Sit down. Please."

"I will not sit down!" said Father Jacob. "Stop treating me like a child and send for Brother Barnaby—"

"Barnaby is dead, Jacob," said Sir Ander quietly. "He was lost in the battle. Do you remember?"

Father Jacob stared at him wordlessly. Pain shadowed his eyes, memories flooding back.

"You and I and Brother Barnaby were at the bastion, talking of what I had discovered about the Bottom—"

Sir Ander put his finger to his lips and cast a warning glance over his shoulder at the door. "Guards outside."

Sir Ander drew closer to Father Jacob and spoke in a whisper.

"We were at the bastion, you and Brother Barnaby and I, when the dragon came to us. Sergeant Hroal warned us that he had seen the Bottom Dwellers coming to attack Westfirth. We ran to one of the guard towers to give the alarm."

"I remember!" Father Jacob said. "One of their ships, a black ship of horror, rose out of the Breath and . . ." He shook his head. "I can't recall anything after that."

"The Bottom Dwellers refitted an old Guundaran warship. It carried a single cannon that fired a beam of green light. The beam destroyed the gun emplacements and blew up the *Royal Lion*. The ship sank into the Breath. All hands were lost."

"I warned the grand bishop . . . ," Father Jacob said softly. "I tried to warn him all those years ago when I saw what happened to the *Defiant*."

He lapsed into silence. Sir Ander waited, knowing and dreading Father Jacob's next question.

"What happened to Brother Barnaby?"

"He stopped to assist a soldier who had been wounded. When the beam hit the gun emplacement, the beam destroyed that side of the cliff on which we were standing. Brother Barnaby lost his footing and fell into the Breath. I was too far away to save him."

Sir Ander sighed deeply.

"I searched the rubble for his body, but there is no trace. I can only assume he is dead."

"He is not dead," said Father Jacob, his voice rasping.

"Jacob, I know this is hard. But I have come to terms—"

"He is not dead, I tell you," Father Jacob said irritably. "How long have I been unconscious?"

"Four weeks. You weren't unconscious, but you weren't with us either."

Father Jacob snorted. "Where was I?"

"You have been discussing theology with Saint Marie," said Sir Ander.

"Oh, come now . . ." Father Jacob stopped. His eyes lost their focus. He gazed inward.

"Saint Marie," he murmured. "Yes, I remember now . . . We must return to the Arcanum at once, Sir Ander. Our yacht was in the shipyard. Was it damaged in the attack?"

"The yacht suffered some minor damage, but our friend, Master Albert, has finished the repairs. We can't leave, however. The harbor has been closed because His Majesty—"

"Of course, we will leave. Tell the person who closed it to open it again."

Father Jacob began rummaging about in his trunk, trying to find his cassock. Sir Ander took the cassock from the wardrobe and handed it to him.

"You must speak to King Alaric, then," said Sir Ander drily. "He was the one who ordered the harbor closed. His Majesty is here to inspect the damage."

"Closing the harbor. I never heard of such nonsense," Father Jacob stated irately. "Send for the archbishop."

Sir Ander smiled inwardly. Father Jacob was definitely back to full health.

"I . . . um . . . don't think that would be wise, Father. The archbishop is a bit preoccupied these days. Quite a lot has happened that you should know about. I can explain what's going on, if you're not too weak—"

"I knocked you on your rump, didn't I," Father Jacob said, smiling.

"You caught me off guard," said Sir Ander, rubbing his jaw and smiling back.

He thought how close he had come to losing this man he honored, loved, admired, and occasionally wanted to throttle. He had to resist the urge to embrace him. Instead, he cleared his throat and returned to business.

"We can't talk here, Father. Too many ears—"

There came a sharp knocking at the door.

"Speak of the devil," Sir Ander muttered, and went to open the door.

Before he could bid them enter, Father Diego swept into the room, accompanied by Sister Elizabeth.

"Sir Ander, I understand that Father Jacob has regained his wits—"

"I never lost my wits," said Father Jacob testily. "Though I have serious doubts about yours, Diego."

Sister Elizabeth laughed, her cheeks dimpling. Father Diego cast her a rebuking glance and turned back to his patient.

"Father Jacob, I strongly insist that you return to your bed. You have been suffering hallucinations—"

"I have been talking to Saint Marie. Do you talk to the saints, Father Diego?"

"I *pray* to the saints," said Father Diego. "I do not hold discourse with them."

"Then maybe you should. Saint Marie performed a miracle," said Father Jacob. "She healed me. Perhaps you question the ability of saints to perform miracles?"

"No, of course I do not . . . ," Father Diego began patiently.

"Good, then get out," said Father Jacob curtly. "I have work to do."

Father Diego gave a deep sigh. "I am here by the authority of the Arcanum and by that authority, Sister Elizabeth and I will examine you."

Father Jacob fumed, but he had to submit to the ministrations of the surgeon. Sister Elizabeth explained the operation she had performed. Father Jacob was quite interested and wanted to see the wound, which meant that Ander had to go in search of a mirror. After asking Father Jacob a few questions to test his memory, Sister Elizabeth pronounced her patient on the road to recovery. She added that Father Jacob must rest—an order she knew he wouldn't obey.

When the examination was finished, Father Diego, who had observed in silence, smiled. "Welcome back, Jacob. Believe it or not, we've missed you."

Father Jacob muttered something that might have been thanks and motioned for them to leave. Father Diego departed, and Sister Elizabeth was about to follow, when Sir Ander stopped her.

"Thank you, Sister," said Sir Ander earnestly. "For saving Father Jacob's life and for not mentioning the conversation you overheard."

"You mean about the contramagic? He was, as Father Diego says, hallucinating." Sister Elizabeth winked. "We'll leave you to your work, Father Jacob," she called as she left.

"About time. And take those confounded guards with you!" Father Jacob ordered.

Sir Ander waited to watch the guards walk off, then he shut the door and locked it. He turned back to find Father Jacob holding up the mirror, trying to see the scar left by trepanation.

"Father, you said Saint Marie healed you because she has a task for you," said Sir Ander. "Is that the truth or did you make that up to annoy Father Diego?"

"Poor Diego. I'm afraid I've been a trying patient." Unable to obtain a good view, Father Jacob put down the mirror. "I told you the truth, my friend. Saint Marie has a task for me."

"What does she want?" Sir Ander asked, uncomfortable with the conversation.

"Saint Marie died unshriven. The evil men who killed her took their time, tortured her. She knew she was dying and she begged them to allow her to make confession. They took cruel pleasure in refusing. They even cut out her tongue so that she could not speak."

Sir Ander had never heard this tale. No one knew the facts of how the saint and her knights had died. They had been ambushed in a wild part of the north country, their bodies left to rot. The search parties found fragments of clothes, armor and weapons, but nothing more. They could only assume the bodies had been dragged off by wild beasts.

"Saint Marie asked me to hear her confession, Sir Ander," said Father Jacob.

Sir Ander was startled. He believed in miracles, but he wasn't certain he believed that for the previous month the blessed saint had been sitting in the chair at Father Jacob's bedside, talking metaphysics and asking him to be her confessor.

"Father, you had a severe head injury. Sister Elizabeth

drilled a hole in your skull, for mercy's sake. Our minds play tricks on us at the best of times . . ."

Father Jacob was shaking his head. "No trick, my friend. Sister Marie wants me to hear her confession."

"But how can she confess to you when she's dead?" Sir Ander asked.

"I don't know. At least not yet." Father Jacob was silent for a few moments, seemingly lost in thought. Then he shook his head. "Nothing comes to mind. Now, tell me what has been going on in my absence."

Sir Ander took the precaution of opening the door and looking up and down the long corridor outside the bed chamber. Satisfied that no one was eavesdropping, he shut the door. Father Jacob sat down and Sir Ander drew a chair close to him and began relating everything that had gone on, from the bishop's decision to commit the priest to a lunatic asylum to Sir Ander's strange encounter with Dubois in the garden.

Father Jacob listened intently in silence. When Sir Ander finished, Father Jacob asked a few questions, desiring clarification on several points. Sir Ander, stiff from sitting so long, rose, stretched, and went to look out the window. The royal barge and the yachts made a colorful show bobbing up and down in the harbor. Members of the crews, with nothing to do, basked in the late afternoon sun. Sir Ander focused on Cecile's yacht, hoping to catch a glimpse of her.

"Do you see her?" Father Jacob asked, coming to stand beside Sir Ander. "Is she there?"

"No," said Sir Ander. He glared at Father Jacob. "Damn it, I am permitted to have secrets of my own! Get out of my head! Stop reading my mind."

Father Jacob chuckled. "I did *not* read your mind. You are wearing your dress uniform. I know how you feel about King Alaric, therefore I know you have no intention of paying your homage to him. However, if Countess Cecile de Marjolaine was part of the royal entourage, you would certainly go to see her. Is she with the king?"

Sir Ander flushed deeply and said nothing.

"I would not ask, my friend," said Father Jacob gently, "if it were not important. Is the Countess de Marjolaine in Westfirth?"

"Yes, Father, she is. She came in her own yacht—"

"Excellent," said Father Jacob. "God works in wondrous ways. I need you to visit the countess and your friend, Monsieur Dubois. You will carry an invitation to them to meet with me here this evening when the clock strikes eight."

"Both of them?" Sir Ander asked, skeptical. "Together? They are bitter enemies."

"They must come together. That way I can explain everything only once. I will not be required to repeat myself as I would if I spoke to them individually."

Sir Ander raised an eyebrow. "This should be interesting. What do you plan to tell them?"

"The truth, Sir Ander," said Father Jacob gravely.

Sir Ander put on his dress uniform coat and began to button it. Father Jacob sat down at the desk to write the invitations. He picked up the pen and then gazed at it in silence. He made no move to start writing. This time, Sir Ander could read Father Jacob's mind.

Brother Barnaby had been Father Jacob's amanuensis, writing all his letters, taking notes of the priest's various investigations.

"I was thinking that we could hold a memorial service for Brother Barnaby," said Sir Ander quietly.

"We will," said Father Jacob, picking up a sheet of foolscap. His pen scratched over the paper. "When Barnaby is dead."

He wrote briefly, shook sand over the paper to dry the

ink, and when it had dried folded it in thirds and sealed it with his own personal seal, not that of the Arcanum. He then jotted a second note and handed them both to Sir Ander.

"Give these to Dubois and the countess in person. Do not entrust the letters to a servant. And do not tell either of them the other is going to be here," Father Jacob added with a chuckle.

"You know, Father, that the countess is supposed to be attending a royal gala this evening and that Dubois might have another engagement. You can't expect them to drop everything to come meet with you."

"I'll wager you a bottle of the finest wine in Westfirth that they come," said Father Jacob, unperturbed.

Sir Ander did not take the bet. Placing the letters into an interior coat pocket, he left upon his errand. He would take a carriage to the Ivy, the inn where Dubois had said the knight could find him, and then he would walk to the countess's yacht.

Before he left the palace, Sir Ander had something important to do. He purchased a bouquet of roses from a flower vendor and brought them to the chapel, where he placed them before the statue of Saint Marie.

"I do believe in miracles. Thank you," he told her.

He had the impression the marble lips smiled.

10

In any royal court, alliances are as fragile as threads of gossamer. Today's bosom friend may thrust his knife into my back tomorrow. I have found it advantageous not to take such betrayal personally. Next week, this same person may hold the key to my political salvation. Of course, keeping a pistol close at hand is never a bad idea.

—Sir Henry Wallace,
Earl of Staffordshire

Sir Ander delivered his messages and returned to the archbishop's palace to find that Father Jacob had been busy in his absence making arrangements for the meeting. He had also entertained the archbishop, who had stopped by to express his joy at the priest's recovery.

"To tell the truth, I believe he only wanted to see if I was in my right mind," said Father Jacob, chuckling. "I was tempted to introduce him to Saint Marie."

"I trust you didn't," said Sir Ander.

"No, no, I was on my best behavior. I asked him for the use of the library for my studies this evening. He graciously gave me permission, telling me the palace will be nearly empty tonight. The archbishop and his staff have been invited to a grand ball to be given on the royal barge."

"The library is a good choice if you want privacy," said Sir Ander. "The room has no windows and only one door, although I suppose there might be secret passages behind the bookshelves. Someone could hide there."

"I checked," said Father Jacob. "No secret passages. The marquis who built this palace was a good, solid, unimaginative old fellow, completely devoid of romance and tight-fisted with his money. He would have never wasted his silver on such frippery. That said, Ander, you must come armed," Father Jacobs added gravely.

"I always do when I am with you, Father," said Sir Ander, smiling. "The list of people wanting to kill you grows longer by the day."

Sir Ander returned to his own room in the palace to bathe, dress, and arm himself. He discarded the dress uniform coat and chose the uniform coat he wore when he and Father Jacob were on a dangerous assignment. The coat had been specially designed for the Knight Protectors and was enhanced with magical constructs meant to protect against various types of attacks, from a dagger in the back to a bullet in the chest. The coat had a special pocket for a stowaway gun and another for a knife. He wore beneath the coat a weskit with similar constructs and his best dress shirt, which was trimmed in lace. He tied his cravat with more than usual care.

Of course, Father Jacob noticed. He was seated in the library, reading a book, when Sir Ander entered. Father Jacob raised an eyebrow.

"Lace cuffs. Attending the ball tonight?"

"We are entertaining nobility," Sir Ander said. "A change from the usual assortment of thieves, warlocks, and murderers you generally invite."

He inspected the room. The library was small and cozy, and smelled pleasantly of leather and vellum. A thick carpet dampened sound. The walls were lined with bookshelves with nooks in between to hang paintings. The furniture consisted of comfortable leather reading chairs, hassocks, and several writing desks. A bottle of very fine sherry stood on the sideboard, along with a plate of small cakes. Father Jacob had lit a single lamp.

"I'll wait at the palace's front entrance to meet them," Sir Ander offered. "I don't trust the servants and I want to see if either of them has been followed."

"Not to mention spending a few moments alone in the company of the beautiful countess," said Father Jacob.

"You are fortunate I took an oath to God to protect you," said Sir Ander. "Otherwise I'd kill you myself."

Father Jacob laughed and continued reading his book.

Sir Ander walked the corridors that led to the palace entrance. As the archbishop had said, the palace was almost empty. The halls were dark, doors closed. He could hear his boots echoing on the marble floor.

Guards stood at the double doors of the entryway, along with a bored footman to deal with any visitors. Sir Ander nodded to the guards, walked out the doors, and stood on the steps to admire the view. From here he could look out over the city of Westfirth and the harbor beyond. The royal barge was aglow with lights, as preparations were being made to receive the guests. The yachts belonging to the members of the nobility were also shining with light, as were the ships of the fleet. In the city, lights gleamed from the windows and on the streets, where the lamplighters were going about their nightly business.

Several ornately designed lamps shed light on the steps leading up to the palace. A few people were in the street— servants hastening upon some errand for their masters or citizens going to view the festivities. Sir Ander observed them keenly, watching to see if any stopped in the shadows. He was checking his pocket watch to ascertain the time when he heard the sound of footsteps and saw a monk mounting the stairs. The monk was carrying a leather satchel and wore dark-tinted spectacles.

Sir Ander recognized Brother Paul.

"Is that you, Sir Ander?" Brother Paul asked as he reached the top of the steps. "Forgive me, but it is difficult for me to see this time of night."

"I am out taking a breath of fresh air," said Sir Ander.

"I heard Father Jacob is fully recovered," said Brother Paul. "God be praised. I was praying for him."

"I'm certain your prayers were helpful, Brother," said Sir Ander politely. He glanced at a nearby clock tower. The time was almost at hand. "Do not let me keep you from your business."

Brother Paul seemed in no hurry to depart. "I was supposed to return to Evreux, as you know. I have just received word that the grand bishop requires me to remain to make certain all goes well with His Majesty's visit. I will be spending the night in the palace. I would like to pay my respects to Father Jacob. Perhaps tomorrow I—"

"We will be leaving for the Arcanum," said Sir Ander curtly. "I will let Father Jacob know he has been in your prayers."

"God's blessing on you, sir," said Brother Paul. He walked off slowly, squinting through his spectacles as he entered the palace.

The guards, recognizing the grand bishop's messenger, waved Brother Paul on past. The footman appeared surprised at the monk's arrival at this time of night and didn't quite know what to do with him, since the archbishop would not be holding audience until the following morning.

Brother Paul said he had been given a room and he knew the way. When the footman let him pass, Sir Ander kept an eye on the monk until he had disappeared in the darkness.

"I don't trust that fellow," Sir Ander muttered to himself. "I can't figure out why. Maybe it's the fact that I can't see his eyes."

The next moment, he forgot all about Brother Paul. The clocks in the churches of Westfirth chimed eight times as a hansom cab rolled up to the entrance. The driver alighted, opened the door, lowered the step, and assisted his passenger to descend.

Sir Ander smiled. In an age where it was fashionable to be late, to make an entrance, the countess had the reputation of being invariably punctual.

She had come alone. Sir Ander hastened down the steps to meet her. She wore a heavy cloak, and her face was veiled. She raised the veil to smile at Sir Ander. Her eyes reflected the lights of the night.

"Thank you for coming," Sir Ander said, taking her hand. "I am sorry to take you away from the royal gala."

"A mysterious summons to meet with the enigmatic Father Jacob. I would not have missed this for all the galas in Rosia," said Cecile.

In that moment, another cab rolled up. A short pudgy man descended. He caught sight of Sir Ander and walked over to greet him. Seeing a lady at Sir Ander's side, Dubois made a bow and took off his hat. Cecile gave a perceptible start.

"Dubois!" she exclaimed.

"Countess de Marjolaine," Dubois returned, startled and sounding not entirely pleased.

"What is the meaning of this, Sir Ander?" Cecile asked in a tone cool with displeasure. "Why is this man here?"

"I should like to know why the countess is here," said Dubois.

"Father Jacob will explain to you both," said Sir Ander.

He offered his arm to Cecile. She hesitated, regarding him intently, then took his arm and permitted him to lead her into the palace. Dubois followed alongside, rubbing his chin and shooting glances into the shadows. They walked in silence through the empty corridors. When they came to the library, the door stood open. Father Jacob, formally attired in his long black cassock, red sash and biretta, was waiting within. He greeted his guests politely and invited them to be seated. He had arranged three chairs in a circle, one for himself and one for each guest.

Sir Ander closed and locked the door. He helped Cecile to remove her cloak and placed it on the back of another chair. Dubois chose to remove his own greatcoat, and kept it with him.

"Countess de Marjolaine." Father Jacob assisted her to a chair. "Many years have passed since I had the pleasure of being in your company."

"The last time we met we had a spirited discussion on the writings of the Chevalier Duvalle," said the countess.

"You espoused his political philosophies, as I recall," said Father Jacob.

"And you opposed them," said the countess with a smile, unable to resist the priest's charm. "We lost track of the hours."

"And angered all your other guests, who could not understand what we found so interesting."

The countess took her seat and drew the veil from her face. Father Jacob turned to greet the grand bishop's agent.

"Monsieur Dubois, I understand I have you to thank for the fact that I am not incarcerated in a lunatic asylum."

"I am glad to see you recovered, Father," said Dubois.

"Though I admit I am greatly puzzled as to why you have summoned me here."

"All will be explained," said Father Jacob. "Countess, may I offer you a glass of sherry? Monsieur Dubois? No? Then I think we may move on to business. Sir Ander, I have laid the magical trap on the door. Anyone who decides to polish the key hole with his ear will receive a most unpleasant shock."

Sir Ander nodded and took up his position by the door.

Father Jacob sat with his elbows on the arms of the chair, pressing the tips of his fingers together. He looked first at the countess and then at Dubois. The lamps were low. Most of the room was in shadow. A single lamp shone on a table near the three who had come together. Father Jacob's eyes, beneath lowered brows, glittered in the light.

He studied his guests for a moment, then said abruptly, "The reason I decided to entrust my discoveries to you both is this: each of you has influence with the two most powerful people in the realm, His Majesty King Alaric and Grand Bishop de Montagne. These powerful men trust you, they will listen to you. I assure you I am not being overly dramatic when I say that this night, I place the fate of millions in your care."

Cecile sat quite still, her hands folded, her beautiful face expressionless. She said nothing.

Dubois sank back in his chair, keeping his face in the shadows. "Why don't you speak to the king and the grand bishop yourself, Father?"

"His Majesty does not trust me because I am a Freyan," said Father Jacob. "I doubt if I could gain access to the royal presence."

Cecile inclined her head to acknowledge that Father Jacob was right.

"As for the grand bishop, just before the attack on West-firth," Father Jacob continued, "I sent His Eminence an urgent message, begging for an audience, telling him I had information regarding the men who had attacked the abbey. The grand bishop refused to see me. In my desperation, I turn to you, Monsieur Dubois. His Eminence must hear the truth."

Cecile stirred slightly. Silk rustled and a hint of perfume scented the air.

"You claim to have discovered information about these 'men,' Father," she said. "I take it they are not demons from hell."

"They are not demons," said Father Jacob. "Although they do have one thing in common with the damned. Both have suffered torments we cannot imagine. Nor are they Freyan, as I suppose you must know from the reports of your agents."

Cecile smiled slightly. "They are not demons and they are not Freyan. Then who are they, Father Jacob?"

"They call themselves Bottom Dwellers."

"How do you know this?" Dubois asked, skeptically. "You sound as if you have spoken to them."

"They did not speak to me, but they did talk to a young monk in my service and also to a Trundler friend of mine. In one instance, the Bottom Dwellers were seeking information. In the other, they were drawn to her by the fact that she is a savant and a Trundler."

"Bottom Dwellers," Dubois repeated, frowning. "The name means, I presume, that they dwell at the bottom. My question is: the bottom of what?"

"The bottom of the world, monsieur," said Father Jacob gravely.

Cecile raised an eyebrow.

Dubois gave a disbelieving cough. "Forgive me, Father, I know you have been ill—"

"And that a surgeon drilled a hole in my head," said Father Jacob with a wry smile. He sighed, and his brow furrowed. "I assure you both that I am well and I am sane. I am also in deadly earnest. I begin by asking what you know of the sinking of the Trundler isle of Glasearrach?"

The countess looked startled. "The island was home to the infamous Pirate King. When his raids on ships disrupted trade and threatened to bring down the world economy, the Council of Bishops and the rulers of all nations came together to attack the island with magicks, casting it down into the Breath."

Father Jacob nodded and continued the tale. "The Pirate King, whose name was Ian Meehan, was holed up in his stronghold on the island, along with many of his followers. In addition, many thousands of innocent Trundlers who made their homes on that island were present when Glasearrach was attacked. History claims that these people perished when the island sank into the bitter cold mists of the Breath. I believe they survived."

Sir Ander saw Cecile unconsciously twisting the ring on her left ring finger—a habit of hers. He was the only person in the world who knew the significance of the plain gold ring, the simple luster of which was lost amidst the brilliance of the diamonds, rubies, and emeralds sparkling on her other fingers. Of all the jewelry she owned, this ring was most precious to her.

Sir Ander's heart ached with the memory. He had been present when Julian had given her that ring, the night before he died. Sir Ander saw that Father Jacob noticed, and the priest's gaze shifted to the ring. When Cecile saw the priest's eyes flicker and realized what she was doing, she covered the ring with her hand.

"You theorize, Father, that these Trundlers survived the poisonous atmosphere and bitter cold and that their progeny have now come back to claim terrible revenge."

"I believe this to be true, Countess," said Father Jacob.

Dubois shook his head. "You have the reputation of being a brilliant man, Father, but that is impossible. Scientific fact—"

"Pardon me, monsieur, but science has no facts when it comes to the Breath," said Father Jacob. "Science has theories that have not been proven."

"Because they cannot be proven," Dubois argued. "Those who have descended that deep into the Breath have never lived to return to tell us."

"Until now," said Father Jacob gravely. "Let me explain. The Bottom Dwellers always destroy the bodies of their dead. Why? To prevent us from discovering the truth about them. When they ambushed me in Westfirth, they burned the bodies of those who were killed. But I managed to rescue a helmet from the flames."

"What could the helmet of a dead man tell you, Father?" Cecile asked.

"A great deal," said Father Jacob. "The helmet was covered in human skin."

Cecile stared at him in appalled silence. Dubois's eyes narrowed.

"I cast a Corpse Spell," Father Jacob continued.

"A spell with which I am not familiar," said Cecile coolly.

"That is because only members of the Arcanum are permitted to cast it, my lady," said Dubois. "Though I believe, Father, you are supposed to have permission from the provost first—"

Father Jacob waved this away as unimportant.

"The energy of a living person remains with the body for a long time after death, Countess," he explained. "The Corpse Spell allows the caster to summon the 'ghost'—"

Sir Ander heard a muffled sound in the hall, as of someone shutting a door somewhere in the distance. He opened the library door a crack and peered out into the darkness.

All was quiet. The doors to the adjacent rooms did not appear to have been disturbed. Sir Ander shut the door and made a sign to Father Jacob, who saw, nodded, and continued talking as though nothing were amiss.

"Contrary to popular opinion, I could not speak to the unfortunate man whose skin had been used to make the helm, but I was able to perceive what he looked like. I saw his face. I felt his pain. His skin had been flayed from his body while he was still alive. He had the extremely pale skin of a person who has never lived in sunshine. Given this and the fact that these people refer to themselves as 'Bottom Dwellers' and that they have a connection to Trundlers, I came to the only logical conclusion: They are the descendants of those who survived the sinking of the doomed isle of Glasearrach."

Sir Ander heard another sound: footfalls. Someone was coming down the hallway, walking with apparent innocence, for the footfalls were not creeping or stealthy. The person walked up to the door and knocked.

Sir Ander glanced at Father Jacob, silently asking if he was expecting anyone. Father Jacob shook his head. The countess and Dubois turned in their chairs; the countess drawing the veil over her face.

"Who is there?" Sir Ander called, opening the door a crack to see.

A man seized the door from Sir Ander, forcing it open. Bright light flared. An object flew past Sir Ander's shoulder, nearly striking him. The person fled, running down the hall.

Sir Ander started to pursue him.

Father Jacob stopped him with a sharp exclamation. "Ander, look at this!"

The object that had been hurled into the room lay on the floor, near the chair in which Dubois was sitting. The object was what was known as a "bulge pot"—a round iron kettle with a bulge in the center used for cooking over an open fire. The pot was fitted with a lid and rolled around a few seconds on the floor, before settling on its side.

Father Jacob and Dubois had both risen from their chairs and were bending to examine the pot. Cecile remained seated. Removing the veil, she gazed at the pot with amused interest.

"Your supper, Father Jacob?" she asked languidly.

Green light suddenly flared, emanating from sigils engraved on the pot. Father Jacob and Sir Ander exchanged glances; both of them thinking the same.

"This is a bomb," said Sir Ander. "Father, take the others and run—"

"No time!" Father Jacob said sharply. He squatted down, placed his hand above the bulge pot, directly over the glowing sigils. Blue light spread from Father Jacob's hand, causing the green glowing sigils to dim slightly.

"Jacob, what the hell are you doing?" Sir Ander demanded.

"The magical sigils on the bomb were activated when the bomb hit the floor. I'm using my magic to disrupt the flow." Father Jacob glanced up at Sir Ander. "My spell won't last long."

Sir Ander nodded. He knew the significance of that terrible green glow. Even as he watched, the blue glow was starting to fade, the green glow strengthening.

"You are a savant, Father!" Dubois was saying urgently. "Use your power to diffuse the bomb's magic!"

"I cannot, monsieur," Father Jacob answered gravely. "These constructs are contramagic."

"Contramagic!" Dubois sucked in a breath.

Cecile leaned forward, regarding the bomb with interest.

"Sir Ander, this bomb is undoubtedly filled with grapeshot," said Father Jacob. "You should escort the countess and Monsieur Dubois from the room—"

"I'm not sure that would be a good idea," said Sir Ander, watching the blue glow diminish as the green glow gained strength. "Any movement near the bomb may very well set it off."

"Sir Ander—" Father Jacob began to argue.

"Father Jacob, shut up," said Sir Ander, "and do exactly as I say. Countess and Monsieur Dubois, I would be obliged if you would both take cover behind that heavy desk. Move carefully. For God's sake, don't bump into anything or knock something over!"

Cecile did as she was told, rising from her chair, gathering up her long skirts, and gliding to the massive oak desk. She took her place behind it, but did not immediately crouch down. Dubois sidled across the floor, keeping a wary eye on the bomb. He reached the desk and stood watching.

"Whatever you are going to do, Ander, you had better hurry!" Father Jacob said tensely. "My magic is failing."

The blue glow was almost gone.

Sir Ander held his hand over the pot's handle.

"When I say the word, Father, let go of the bomb and dive for cover."

Father Jacob nodded.

"Now!" Sir Ander yelled.

Father Jacob let go of the bomb and rolled over backward. Sir Ander seized hold of the pot—now glowing bright green. Whipping around, he flung the bomb out into the hallway, heaving it as far as he could. He slammed the door shut, pressing his body against it as the blast went off.

The floor shook. Books tumbled off the shelves. Paintings fell from the walls. Dust and bits of plaster rained down from the ceiling. The blast blew the door off its hinges, knocking Sir Ander to the floor. Grapeshot struck the one lamp that was lighted, shattering it and plunging the room into darkness.

Sir Ander must have lost consciousness, because the next thing he knew, Father Jacob was bending over him. Dubois was shining a dark lantern directly in his eyes.

"How are you?" Father Jacob asked in concern. "You hit your head on the back of a chair."

"A bump, that's all," said Sir Ander, shielding his eyes and grunting in pain. "Move that damn light! What about you, Father?"

"I am fine," said Father Jacob.

"As am I," said Dubois. He shifted the dark lantern away from Sir Ander.

"Where is Cecile?" Sir Ander asked worriedly, struggling to sit up.

"I am here, covered in dust and plaster, but otherwise unharmed."

Cecile knelt on the floor beside him and placed her hand gently on his shoulder. Her blue eyes were warm and soft with admiration. "What you did was incredibly brave, Sir Ander."

Sir Ander flushed as if he were eighteen and not fifty. He fended off Father Jacob's offer of assistance and rose a little groggily to his feet.

"The blast was loud. Half the palace will be descending on us," Sir Ander warned.

"Countess, you and Monsieur Dubois should not be found here with me," said Father Jacob. "But we have yet a few moments and I must tell you about contramagic."

"Father Jacob, you are speaking heresy—" Dubois began.

"Such 'heresy' almost killed you, monsieur! I will continue to speak heresy until dunderheads such as the grand bishop listen to me!" said Father Jacob angrily. "That bomb was charged with contramagic. The green beam that sank the *Royal Lion* was contramagic. The beam that knocked down a tower in northern Freya was contramagic. The beam that nearly sank the cutter *Defiant* was contramagic. Research those. You will discover the similarities. The Bottom Dwellers are skilled in the use of contramagic, as well as blood magic, as evidenced by the helm made from human skin."

"A blood magic sacrifice," said Dubois.

"Precisely. The Bottom Dwellers attacked us with weapons of contramagic and we had no defense against them, just as I had no way to defuse that bomb. Why? Because the church pronounced this magic evil and forbade anyone to study it!"

Father Jacob slammed his fist down on the desk, sending dust into the air. "That must change!"

Cecile and Dubois stared at him, startled by his passion.

Father Jacob pointed at the destruction in the library. "Do you want proof? The very fact that someone tried to silence me proves that I am right!"

"If you are right, what do these Bottom Dwellers want, Father?" Cecile asked, troubled.

"They want to silence the Voice of God, Countess," Father Jacob replied gravely. "And if we do not find a way to stop them, they will do so."

Sir Ander could hear muffled cries in the corridor, people coming to investigate.

"Father—" he said urgently.

"Yes, Sir Ander. Countess, Monsieur Dubois, the two of you should leave at once," said Father Jacob. "I will return to the Arcanum as soon as the ports open. Contact me there if you have need of me. Please convey all this information to His Majesty and to the grand bishop."

Dubois did not immediately obey. He stood lost in thought. Then he gave a slow nod and murmured, "Well, well, well. This begins to open my eyes. I thank you, Father."

He slid shut the dark lantern, extinguishing the light, and

disappeared into the dusty darkness without another word. Cecile lingered, watching Father Jacob pick up one of the broken lamps. He traced a construct upon it and a soft glow lit the room. Dust continued to drift down from the ceiling.

"You should leave before someone finds you here, Countess," said Sir Ander.

She smiled, unconcerned, refusing to be hurried, and reached out her hand to Father Jacob.

"Once again you have provided me with an entertaining and enlightening evening, Father. You have given me much to consider and reflect upon. I will speak to His Majesty." Cecile gave a little sigh. "Do not depend upon my words changing his mind."

Father Jacob took her hand in his own. "Thank you, my lady."

"Sir Ander . . ." Cecile turned to him and touched his hand.

Sir Ander winced in pain. Cecile was quick to notice and lifted his palm to the light.

"It's nothing," he said, embarrassed. "The handle of the pot was hot to the touch."

"Hot enough to give you a severe burn," said Cecile in rebuking tones. She placed a delicate finger on his palm, traced a construct and spoke a word. The pain in his hand eased. She smiled up at him.

"I am a bit rusty at my magic. I so rarely have a chance to use it. I am glad to see that I have not lost my touch."

Sir Ander helped her climb over the wreckage of the door. Outside in the corridor, the floor was littered with plaster and molding and chunks of stone that had fallen from the walls and ceiling. A large wooden beam had come down, blocking the hall.

"Go in this direction," said Sir Ander, gesturing. "When you reach the end of the hall, follow the corridor to your right. That will lead you to the garden. Once you are there, you will be able to circle around to the front of the palace."

Cecile gave a complacent nod.

"Perhaps I should go with you," he said worriedly. "The halls are pitch dark—"

"We should not be seen together," she admonished him. "Besides, Father Jacob needs you. Do not worry about me. I know how to find my way through the darkness. I have been doing it all my life. Farewell, dear friend. If you should hear from Stephano—"

"I will let you know at once," he assured her.

Drawing the veil over her face, Cecile touched his hand gently and left him.

Sir Ander remained by the ruins of the door, listening to her measured footfalls and the rustle of her skirt until the sounds faded in the distance. Sighing, he turned back to find Father Jacob watching him.

"A singular honor, my friend," Father Jacob said. "To earn the trust and regard of such a remarkable woman."

"We have known each other for many years," said Sir Ander gruffly. He closed his palm over the construct she had traced on his hand and felt the warmth of her friendship. He changed the subject.

"People will be here any moment. What do we tell them, Father?"

"You and I were in the library, peacefully reading, when the door opened and someone threw in a bomb. You picked up the bomb and tossed it out."

Out in the corridor, they could hear men exclaiming over the destruction as they began to clear away the rubble.

"You know you acted like a bloody fool, Ander," Father Jacob added, eyeing the wreckage. "Picking up that bomb. You could have been killed."

Sir Ander touched a hand to his ear. "I'm a bit hard of

hearing from the blast, Father. Did I hear you say, 'Thank you, Ander, for saving my life'?"

Father Jacob smiled. "Perhaps I should say, 'Thank you, Ander, for being a bloody fool.' "

He grew more serious. "I don't suppose you saw the assassin?"

"I caught a glimpse of the person, but the hallway was too dark to see details. A man, I would say, judging by the height and the amount of strength it would take to throw the bomb. Given the use of contramagic, it must have been a Bottom Dweller."

Sir Ander shook his head. "I will be glad to get you back to the safety of the Arcanum. Though I hate leaving Westfirth without some news of Brother Barnaby."

"God has him in His care, my friend," said Father Jacob. He heaved a sigh and ran his hand through his hair, absently knocking off the biretta. "We'll have to find some way to explain this to the archbishop."

"I'm guessing we don't mention the bomb was contramagic," said Sir Ander.

"We do not," said Father Jacob solemnly. "He'd lock us both up in the asylum."

11

*No one trusts Trundlers, which means, in a sense,
that everyone trusts us.*

—Trundler adage

The captain of the palace guard arrived on the scene to investigate the explosion. Father Jacob excused himself, saying he was worn out by all the excitement, and he would return to his room. Sir Ander remained to answer questions. He wasn't much help, for he had not seen the bomber and he could not offer a description of the bomb, explaining everything had happened too fast. The captain said he supposed a great many people must have reason to want Father Jacob dead. Sir Ander agreed and asked if the captain would provide a guard for the remainder of Father Jacob's stay. Father Jacob would protest, he knew, but this time he wasn't going to have his way.

Sir Ander returned to the priest's room to find the door locked. He approved the precaution, though he was astonished that Father Jacob would think of it. He knocked on the door. Father Jacob opened it, and glanced outside.

"Are you alone?"

"Yes," said Sir Ander.

Father Jacob opened the door wide enough for Sir Ander

to enter, then closed it behind him and locked it again. Sir Ander stood staring. The room had been ransacked; clothes strewn about, books pulled from the shelves, and furniture overturned.

"They were looking for the books of the saints," said Father Jacob.

"They didn't find them—" Sir Ander asked, alarmed.

"The books are safe."

Father Jacob led him to one of the trunks. The lock had been forced, the lid opened. Sir Ander looked inside. The trunk appeared to be empty. As Father Jacob drew a construct in the air, sigils flared and the books of the saints shimmered into view, lying at the bottom, no longer hidden from sight by the priest's magic.

"This means the Bottom Dwellers know you have the books," said Sir Ander.

"I fear I am to blame," said Father Jacob. "My conversations with Saint Marie were, as I understand it, the subject of much gossip. The Bottom Dwellers must have found out and assumed I was conversing with the saint because I had read the books she and the others wrote."

Sir Ander was grave. "Worse than that, I'm afraid. You talked of contramagic with Saint Marie."

"Ah, did I?" said Father Jacob. "That was unfortunate."

"Sister Elizabeth was in the room and she heard you. She wouldn't say anything to anyone, though."

"There were guards at the door. Servants in the hall. Sister Elizabeth might have said something to her superior, Father Diego, who could have mentioned it to the archbishop, who could have reported it to the grand bishop. They might have been overheard by secretaries or servants, any one of whom could be an agent for the Bottom Dwellers."

"You believe that there are people here who are actually working to help those fiends?" Sir Ander asked, frowning.

"Of course," said Father Jacob. "Someone knew of Albert's discovery of the prince abbot's journal, remember. That person stole it, read about the writings of the saints, and contacted the Bottom Dwellers, who attacked the abbey to search for the books."

"That's true," said Sir Ander. "I had forgotten about the theft." He glanced around at the mess. "We were going to pack all this up tomorrow anyway. You get some sleep. I'll keep watch."

"You need sleep more than I do. I've been flat on my back for weeks," said Father Jacob with a smile. "Lie down. I have an important letter to write."

Sir Ander didn't argue. He was exhausted and his head hurt. He washed off the dust and blood and then lay down on the camp bed, shading his eyes from the light with his hat. He tried to forget the throbbing of his head by recalling every word Cecile had spoken to him, every graceful gesture. He could still feel the gentle touch of her hand on his. Holding this dear memory close, he fell into an exhausted sleep.

He was wakened by a knocking on the door. The hat had slipped from his face and he blinked at morning light shining through the window. Father Jacob had quit writing and was now reading. He had not noticed the sound of knocking or, if he had, he was ignoring it. Sir Ander left his bed and opened the door a cautious crack. A soldier of the Old Fort stood in the hallway.

"Good morning, Sir Ander," said the soldier, saluting. "I'm sorry for waking you, but there's someone asking to speak to you. A dragon."

"A dragon?" Sir Ander repeated stupidly, still groggy with sleep.

"Yes, sir," said the soldier. "The dragon gave me his name, but the name was longer than he was. Drollgerfig or something like that . . ."

"Droalfrig," said Sir Ander, coming to full wakefulness. "Sergeant Droalfrig."

"Yes, sir, that would be it. The dragon said he and his brother will meet you at the Bastion at midday."

"Sergeant Droalfrig *and* his brother," Sir Ander remarked, shutting the door. "I haven't seen Hroal since the attack on Westfirth when he warned us the Bottom Dwellers were heading this way. I hope the brothers are not bringing more bad news."

"You best speak with them," said Father Jacob. "First, though, I need you to go to the shipyard to make certain the yacht is in readiness. I received a message from the archbishop this morning. He is thankful we were not hurt in the explosion. He knows we would like to leave as soon as possible. He has granted us permission to sail today."

"I'll bet he has," Sir Ander said, grinning.

"I sent a message to Master Albert. He will meet you at the shipyard. We will need to hire wyverns and a driver. Unless you want me to drive?" Father Jacob spoke hopefully.

"I will do the driving," said Sir Ander sternly.

He poured water in the washbowl, borrowed Father Jacob's razor, and began the morning ritual of shaving.

Father Jacob frowned. "I *like* driving—"

"Right into the side of a mountain," said Sir Ander.

"I have told you repeatedly the accident wasn't my fault," Father Jacob said testily. "There was a freak wind gust . . ."

He fell silent. Sir Ander looked in the mirror to see Father Jacob sitting with his finger marking his place in the book, gazing off into the distance. The pain their jests were trying to cover was like a pall in the room.

"I miss Barnaby," said Father Jacob.

"So do I," said Sir Ander.

He washed off the razor and wiped his face with a towel. Going to his room, he swiftly packed his things. He had few personal possessions with him—clean shirts and undergarments, his dress uniform, pistols, sword, and the current book he was reading: an account and analysis of the Blackfire War.

Returning to check on Father Jacob, Sir Ander found the priest had gone back to his reading. "You need to start packing."

Father Jacob paid no attention. Sir Ander buckled on his sword and made certain his pistols were loaded. He was halfway out the door when Father Jacob said suddenly, "The Trundler village is near the shipyard, isn't it?"

"Not far from it," said Sir Ander. "Why?"

"I want you to contact Angus McPike. Tell him I need to speak to him. You might also ask him if he's heard word of his nieces."

Sir Ander was puzzled. "Why would I ask about his nieces?"

"Because Miri and Gythe McPike were with the countess's son, Lord Captain de Guichen, during the attack on Westfirth. Angus might have heard word of them. You could tell the countess, see her again before we leave," said Father Jacob mischievously.

"Start packing," Sir Ander growled.

He was glad to get out in the fresh air, away from bombs and annoying priests. He decided to forgo a hansom cab and walk to the shipyard where the yacht had been towed for repairs.

Only a month had passed since the attack and most of the wreckage left behind had been cleaned up. The exception was a large merchant ship that had crashed onto the roof of a warehouse. Workers were in the process of dismantling the ship. The shipyard was doing a brisk business, repairing damaged ships and boats.

Sir Ander found Master Albert waiting for him to inspect the yacht and make certain it was ready to sail.

Master Albert Savoraun had been friends with Father Jacob and Sir Ander for many years. They had first met him when Father Jacob was investigating the mysterious attack on the naval cutter *Defiant*. That had been the first time they had encountered contramagic. Years later, when Albert had stumbled upon a journal mentioning contramagic in connection with the four saints, he had alerted Father Jacob. Unfortunately the discovery brought the Bottom Dwellers to the abbey, where they had gone on a hate-filled rampage, slaughtering the nuns.

"I was glad to hear that Father Jacob has recovered, Sir Ander," said Albert, shaking hands with the knight. "When weeks passed and there was no change, I feared the worst. I trust he is fully restored to health?"

"He's as cantankerous as ever, if that's what you mean," said Sir Ander, grinning.

They toured the yacht, which had suffered extensive damage from the green fire, requiring the replacement of the port- and starboard-control conduits along with large portions of the hull.

"The crafters tried to place magical constructs over the damaged portions," said Albert. "The attempt failed. No one understands why. The crafters have never seen anything like this."

They both knew the contramagic was responsible. Neither mentioned the word aloud. There were too many people around.

Sir Ander went inside the yacht to find everything much as it had been. The box of dominoes—Father Jacob's favorite game—was on the table. The smell of fresh paint was still strong.

"I didn't know what you wanted me to do with this," said Master Albert in somber tones.

He led Sir Ander to a small trunk tucked into a corner. Sir Ander recognized the trunk and his heart constricted. Inside were Brother Barnaby's few possessions: a clean robe, a leather-bound prayer book that had been a gift from Father Jacob, and a bag of sweetmeats the monk had purchased, probably with the intention of treating the wyverns, who had been his special pets.

"We'll keep this with us," said Sir Ander.

"He had no family, did he?" said Albert.

"We were his family," said Sir Ander.

He gently closed the trunk.

"Everything appears to be in order, Master Albert. Thank you for supervising the work. I hope this didn't interfere with your duties as guild master."

"I was able to manage both," said Albert. "To tell you the truth, I enjoyed the labor. I'll have the lift tanks filled this morning. Should I sail the yacht 'round to the palace?"

"No place to dock it," said Sir Ander. "What with the fleet and the royal barges and yachts clogging the harbor. We'll pick it up here this afternoon. I stored the swivel guns in the fort's armory. I'll have them delivered."

"I purchased two wyverns from a guild brother," said Albert. "They are young, strong, fast beasts. A bit temperamental, but then what wyverns aren't."

They made arrangements to meet later that day. Master Albert left to see to the filling of the lift tanks, and since he still had a few hours until his midday meeting with the dragons, Sir Ander went to the Trundler village to find Angus McPike.

The Trundler village was actually a flotilla made up of Trundler houseboats docked in an area outside the city of Westfirth. The Trundlers and the city officials had reached an agreement that allowed the Trundlers to live in their floating village and sell their wares from their boats, though not in the city.

The Trundlers had fared worse than the city of Westfirth in the attack by the Bottom Dwellers. Their village had been struck with particular ferocity. Sir Ander saw empty docks where Trundler houseboats had once moored; now decorated with flowers or other tokens of grief and remembrance. He worried that Angus McPike might have been one of those killed.

The moment Sir Ander set foot on the pier, he was immediately confronted by several Trundler men carrying clubs. He had come prepared for such a greeting. He was familiar with Trundlers from having visited their village with Father Jacob. He knew they tended to view anyone in a uniform with distrust.

"I'm here to see Angus McPike," said Sir Ander. "Papa Jake sent me. I am Defender."

"I can vouch for this man," said one of the Trundlers. "Come with me, Defender. I'll take you to Angus. How is Papa Jake?" he asked as they walked along. "We heard he was hurt in the attack."

"He's recovered," said Sir Ander. "I was very sorry to hear about the losses your people suffered."

The man's face darkened. "The fiends killed women and children and our old people—all for no reason. We weren't a threat to them. You know our ways. None of our boats carry weapons. We had no way to defend ourselves. It was a slaughter. They told us why," he added grimly.

Sir Ander stared at him, astonished. "They spoke to you? What did they say?"

"We didn't hear them so much with our ears as inside our heads. 'You left our children to die. Now you suffer as we suffered.' I know it sounds strange. You likely don't believe me—"

"On the contrary, I do believe you," said Sir Ander.

The Bottom Dwellers had spoken in the same way to Gythe and to Brother Barnaby, who both said words had formed in their minds. Sir Ander found this information relevant to Father Jacob's theory about the sinking of the Trundler island and made a mental note to relate it to the priest.

They located Angus McPike aboard a houseboat belonging to a fellow Trundler, helping to repair it. Angus was the head of the McPike clan and the chief of the Trundler village. He was in his sixties, still strong and active, still bearing the flame-red hair that was the hallmark of the McPike family. He greeted Sir Ander and left his work to come meet him.

Trundlers paid homage to no king; they followed their own laws. Titles meant nothing to them, and they tended to judge a man on his own merits. Angus McPike liked and trusted Sir Ander and offered his hand in friendship— among Trundlers a mark of high regard.

Angus invited Sir Ander to his own boat, where he insisted they have a "tumble" of Calvados, the potent liquor for which Trundlers were famous. Sir Ander had no desire to drink this early in the day, but to refuse would have been insulting. He agreed to the tumble, short for "tumbler," a glass made of lead crystal, heavy enough to withstand the vicissitudes of life sailing the Breath.

On board, Angus's wife, Anna, was dealing with two wealthy Westfirth matrons who had come to buy Anna's beautiful watered silk. Anna smiled at Sir Ander as she continued her business. Angus escorted the knight down below, where they could sit in comfort and privacy in the galley.

Once the Calvados was poured and Sir Ander had drunk to the health of the family, the health of Papa Jake, and his own health, they settled down to business.

"How is Papa Jake?" Angus asked, his brow creasing in

worry. The priest was popular among the Trundlers. Because they held their own religious beliefs, which were often contrary to church teachings, the Trundlers had long ago been cut off from the church. Father Jacob had, of course, defied the edict. He traveled and worked among the Trundlers at least one month out of every year. "We heard he had been mortally wounded in the attack."

"We nearly lost him," said Sir Ander. His eyes were watering from the burning Calvados. "The healers drilled a hole in his head and he survived."

"A hole in his head!" Angus said slowly, marveling. "Think of that. Our priest is seemingly not an easy man to kill. And so what brings you here, Defender?"

"Father Jac—that is, Papa Jake would like to speak to you in person, Angus. He would come to you, but he is still not fully recovered. He asked if you could meet him at our yacht in the Bollinger shipyard this afternoon."

Angus nodded. "I will be there. Will you have another tumble, Defender?"

"No, thank you, Angus," said Sir Ander, hastily. His head was spinning. "I will not keep you from your work. I do have one question, though," he asked as Angus was escorting him off the boat. "Have you heard from your niece, Miri?"

"Not a word since the attack. No one's seen hide nor hair of her or Gythe or the *Cloud Hopper*. I don't mind telling you I'm worried. Why do you ask? Have you heard something?"

"Miri is friends with my godson, Lord Captain de Guichen," said Sir Ander. "I am friends with his mother and she has not heard from him, either. She is concerned about him."

"Stephano is a right man," said Angus, meaning Stephano was right-minded. He thought like a Trundler. "And my nieces are bonny sailors. If I hear anything, I'll send word."

The two shook hands again. Angus went back to his work

and Sir Ander left to make his unsteady way to the Bastion, to meet with the dragon brothers.

Located at the top of a cliff overlooking the city of Westfirth and its valuable ports, the Bastion had been the base for the famed Dragon Brigade, whose dragons and riders defended those ports that were the lifeblood of Rosino. Home to a score of dragons and their riders for seventy years, the Bastion had been abandoned with the disbanding of the Dragon Brigade.

The fortress had been designed by dragons for their own comfort. Stone walls surrounded a large central courtyard that was open to the sky. Each floor contained workrooms and quarters for the dragons and men who lived here.

The members of the Dragon Brigade would generally arrive at the Bastion on the backs of their dragons. The only other way to reach the fortress was by climbing a series of steps that crisscrossed the side of the cliff. The blast that had destroyed the gun emplacements had also taken out much of this route, as Sir Ander soon discovered.

He had to cut through the archbishop's garden, climb over a wall, then flounder among thick underbrush before he reached the steps. He tore a hole in his trousers, scraped his knee, and cut his hand when he slipped on a loose rock.

By the time he reached the summit he was out of breath, his head throbbed, his muscles burned, and his shirt was soaked with sweat. He had to pause a moment to rest and catch his breath and massage a cramp in his calf, before he walked over to greet Hroal and Droal, who were waiting together in the courtyard.

Both dragons were old soldiers. They stood at attention, their heads up and their necks straight, with wings folded at their sides. Hroal clearly found such exertion an effort. His brother cast worried glances at him. As he drew near, Sir Ander understood why. Hroal had suffered terrible wounds, some of which were still not healed.

These wounds were not typical of any battle injuries Sir Ander had ever witnessed. Dragon scales acted much like armor, though they were far stronger than any armor humans could produce.

Hroal had suffered what appeared to be deep burns on his breast and flanks. Scales were missing in some places, revealing the flesh beneath. The scales that remained had turned black. Hroal appeared to be standing upright by sheer force of will.

"Sergeants Droalfrig and Hroalfrig reporting, sir," said Droal.

Sir Ander recalled that the dragon brothers' speech tended to be short and to the point. He expressed his pleasure in seeing them both again.

"Sergeant Hroalfrig, I am sorry to see you have been wounded. What happened?" Sir Ander asked.

"Hurt in attack, sir. Bat riders. *Roed*. Bad for dragons. Very bad," said Hroalfrig.

"Touch and go, sir," Droalfrig added gruffly. "Pulled through. Couldn't fly for a month. Not up to it."

"I'm not sure he should be flying now," said Sir Ander.

He was intrigued by the statement that *roed* was bad for dragons, and was about to ask what that word meant, when the dragons caused his thoughts to veer off in an entirely different direction.

"Glad to find you, sir," said Hroalfrig. "Came to tell you. Monk. Friend of yours. Information."

"Brother Barnaby!" Sir Ander exclaimed excitedly. "You have information about him?"

"Yes, sir. And no, sir."

Hroalfrig's breathing was labored. He had to pause to catch his breath.

"Blast. Tower fell. Monk fell. Ledge. Monk safe."

Hroalfrig paused again for breath. Sir Ander thought back to the last he had seen of Brother Barnaby. The monk had vanished in a cloud of smoke and crumbling rock when the Bottom Dwellers blew apart the gun emplacement. From what he gathered from Hroalfrig, Barnaby must have fallen onto a ledge. But what had happened to him after that? Sir Ander waited impatiently for the dragon to continue.

"Bat riders," Hroalfrig said at last. "Took monk prisoner. Tried to rescue, sir. Hit by *roed* fire."

"Are you saying that the Bottom Dwellers took Brother Barnaby prisoner?" Sir Ander was astonished. The demons had taken no prisoners at the abbey. They had simply killed. "Are you certain?"

"Prisoners," Hroalfrig confirmed. "Priests. More than one. Black ship."

"Priests . . ." Sir Ander mulled this over.

He recalled hearing reports that several priests who had been in the new cathedral when it came under attack had disappeared. At the time Sir Ander had been preoccupied with concern over Father Jacob, and had paid little attention to the tale beyond thinking sorrowfully that their bodies would probably be found in the rubble. He wondered why the Bottom Dwellers would want to abduct priests.

"What happened to the black ship that was carrying the prisoners?" Sir Ander asked. "Did you see?"

"Sailed away. Into the Breath."

Sir Ander did not know what to make of this news. He didn't know whether to rejoice or to grieve.

"I thank you for coming to me, Sergeant Hroalfrig," Sir

Ander said earnestly. "I know this trip must have been very difficult for you. I feared Brother Barnaby was dead. At least now I have hope that we may yet find him."

The dragons exchanged grim glances. Sir Ander knew what they were thinking, for he was thinking the same. He changed the subject.

"What news of the abbey?"

"Cathedral gone," Droalfrig reported unhappily. "Crashed down. No one there. No one hurt. No one ever comes now. Deserted."

The dragons appeared deeply saddened by this. They had been fond of the nuns, who had been good to them. Sir Ander doubted if the church would rebuild the Abbey of Saint Agnes. The cathedral had been beautiful, with its twin spires in which the nuns hung lanterns to guide sailors benighted in the Breath. Their rest would not be disturbed.

Sir Ander bid the brothers farewell. As he slid and stumbled his way back down the cliff, his thoughts were on Brother Barnaby. The more he considered the probable fate of the young monk the darker and gloomier those thoughts became. He couldn't stop thinking of the helm made of human skin flayed from the body of a blood magic sacrifice.

Sir Ander returned to the palace to find Father Jacob stomping about the room, fuming with impatience.

"Where have you been? What have you been doing?" he demanded, noting with shock the state of Sir Ander's uniform. "Did you get into a brawl?"

"I scaled a cliff," Sir Ander said. He looked around. Books and trunks and clothes were gone. All that remained was a leather satchel. "At least you packed while I was gone."

"Master Albert sent men to take our luggage to the yacht. I had them take everything except the books of the saints. They are here, well protected."

Father Jacob indicated the satchel, which was covered with magical constructs to protect the contents.

"Father, we need to talk—" said Sir Ander, picking up the satchel.

"Not now! We are late as it is. I don't know what took you so long."

Father Jacob stalked out of the room, his impatient strides causing his cassock to flap about his ankles. Sir Ander hurried after him.

"Father, you will want to hear this—"

"I have said our good-byes to the archbishop," Father Jacob continued. "The man could not conceal his joy. He was so glad to be rid of me he loaned me his carriage."

"Jacob," said Sir Ander, seizing hold of Father Jacob's arm. "Stop! I have news of Brother Barnaby."

"Why didn't you say so? What have you found out? No, wait. Not here. Tell me when we are in the carriage."

They left the palace without ceremony. The archbishop's carriage stood waiting. The driver opened the door and placed next to it a box as a step for them to use to climb inside. Once they were settled, the driver closed the door and took his seat in front. He flicked the reins lightly at the horses and the carriage rolled off.

Sir Ander sank back thankfully into one of the luxurious leather seats.

"Tell me about Barnaby," said Father Jacob.

Sir Ander related everything the dragon brothers had told him. Father Jacob's face grew grim.

"This news is not good, my friend."

"I know," said Sir Ander. "The Bottom Dwellers are still trying to find the books of the saints, aren't they? That's the only reason I can think of why they would take priests prisoners."

"There might be other reasons," said Father Jacob. "Some practitioners of blood magic believe that the blood of holy men and women has special power."

He sat in dark thought, his body swaying back and forth as the carriage bumped over the cobblestone streets. Then he sighed. "It does no good to speculate."

"They tortured Brother Barnaby once before. I can't bear to think of the torment he must be enduring down there," said Sir Ander. "I almost wish we had taken him into our confidence, told him we had the books. He could tell them what they want to know and at least then they would stop the torture."

"By killing him," said Father Jacob. "Once they had the information, they would have no more need of him."

He gripped the satchel tightly. "Brother Barnaby needs our prayers. When we reach the Arcanum, I will hold a special mass for him."

Sir Ander sat suddenly forward. "The hell with the Arcanum, Jacob! We should go save Barnaby. We should take the yacht and fly down there and free him from those fiends!"

Father Jacob gave a grave smile. "You are courageous, Sir Ander, and a true friend."

"Then you will do it!" Sir Ander said eagerly. "You will come with me!"

"Of course not," said Father Jacob. "Your suggestion is completely irrational. We have no idea where the island of Glasearrach is located. I doubt if the wyverns would survive the journey. I doubt if *we* would survive. The best way to help Brother Barnaby is to return to the Arcanum where I can continue my studies."

Sir Ander flung himself back angrily in the carriage and sat silent, brooding, then said abruptly, "Very well. I'll go by myself. I'll find a way!"

Father Jacob regarded the knight with affection. "My dear friend, I admire your resolve. I must remind you that you are a Knight Protector. You swore an oath before God . . ."

"The hell with my oath! The hell with God! Where was He when those fiends took Brother Barnaby?" Sir Ander blinked his eyes rapidly and lowered his head into his hands.

He felt the warm and firm pressure of Father Jacob's hand on his arm. "God is with Brother Barnaby, Ander. He has never left him."

Sir Ander wiped his eyes and mouth. Father Jacob offered a handkerchief, which Sir Ander accepted. He blew his nose, then stuffed the handkerchief in the sleeve of his coat.

"You are a good man, Sir Ander," said Father Jacob, sitting back in the carriage. "Just not a very practical one."

Sir Ander made no reply. He grimly stared out the window. He knew Father Jacob was right, but he wanted desperately to be doing something to help Brother Barnaby. Instead he would be languishing at the Arcanum, spending his time sitting in a room watching Father Jacob turn pages.

The carriage continued rolling through the streets. Sir Ander sighed deeply, then said, "I forgot to mention something interesting Sergeant Hroal told me. He was talking about the wounds his brother received in the attack. He was hit by the green fire. The sergeant said something about 'the *roed*.' How the *roed* had a bad effect on dragons. Do you know what he meant?"

"The *roed* . . ." Father Jacob sat, musing. "I know that the word '*raeg*' in the dragon language is equivalent to 'magic.' I would guess that *roed* is the opposite, meaning 'contra-magic.' So that has a debilitating effect on dragons. That is interesting."

He sat mulling this over. Sir Ander sat in silence. When they reached the shipyard he was relieved to find Master Albert and Angus McPike waiting for them. He could stop tormenting himself with thoughts of Brother Barnaby.

The yacht had been hoisted out of the shipyard by cranes and moved to the street. The wyverns, spitting and snarling and snapping at anyone who came near them, were hitched to the yacht, ready to fly. Master Albert reported that the swivel guns had been delivered and were safely stowed, to be taken out and mounted when needed.

Father Jacob said good-bye to Master Albert, shaking his hand warmly, thanking him for all his service and giving him his blessing.

"Albert, I have a question before we part," said Father Jacob. "Those priests who disappeared when the cathedral was attacked. Were the bodies ever found?"

"Not yet, Father," Albert replied. "The searchers assumed they would find the bodies beneath the rubble, but the crafters have shifted most of the rock and they weren't there. Where they went is a mystery. Some are saying God took them straight to heaven."

"I have reason to believe the bat riders took them prisoner, Albert," said Father Jacob. "They are still trying to find the books mentioned in the journal. They know you read the journal. You may be in danger."

"I wish to God I had never seen that journal," said Master Albert bleakly.

"If you had not, we would be facing our doom," said Father Jacob. "Your discovery gives us hope."

Master Albert appeared unconvinced. He shook hands and departed. All this while, Angus McPike had been waiting patiently, leaning against the railing where they had tied up the wyverns.

Father Jacob beckoned to him. "Angus, my friend. I need a word with you in private. We'll go aboard the yacht."

"Let me go first, Father," said Sir Ander.

He opened the door that led from the partially enclosed driver's station, with its black lacquered walls and cushioned leather bench, and entered the yacht. All was as it should be. Their luggage was aboard, the trunks still sealed. A single room occupied most of the interior of the yacht, with small storage compartments in front and a larger one in the rear. The main room served as eating and sleeping quarters, the beautifully carved wooden walls concealing foldout bunks and secret compartments for weapons. Father Jacob came aboard, accompanied by Angus McPike.

"A fine boat, Papa Jake."

"Thank you, Angus. Sir Ander, make certain no one is outside, then shut the door."

Sir Ander returned to report that the only men around were those handling the wyverns. "The beasts are screeching so loudly I doubt if they would hear us even if we shouted."

Father Jacob nodded. He was taking no chances. He spoke in little more than a whisper. "Angus, I need one of your clan to sail to Freya."

"I'm your man, Papa Jake," said Angus.

"I was hoping you would say that. The trip might be dangerous. King Alaric could declare war on Freya any day, which would mean the royal navy will blockade the Freyan ports."

Angus shrugged. "Someone's always declaring war on somebody, Papa. Wars don't affect us Trundlers. What do you want me to do?"

Father Jacob smiled. "I need a letter delivered to a man in Freya. You must give it directly into his hands. No one else must see it. I think it likely you will find him at his house in Haever."

Father Jacob handed Angus a letter sealed with red wax

bearing his initials, *J.N.* Sir Ander saw the name on the letter and felt the hair on the back of his neck prickle. His hands went cold.

Sir Henry Wallace.

Angus took the letter and tucked it into the leather belt he wore around his waist. "I'll hide it away, Papa. They can tear the boat apart plank by plank and they won't find it. Should I wait for a reply?"

Father Jacob shook his head. "That will not be necessary. Thank you, Angus. I am sorry to have to ask you to do this. I have money for your expenses. Sir Ander, you will find a bag of silver rosuns in that trunk—"

"Let it stay in the trunk," said Angus. "For your kindness to my nieces, I owe you more than I can repay. A safe journey to you, Papa, and to you, too, Defender."

Sir Ander waited until Angus had gone and then confronted his friend.

"Why are you writing to Sir Henry Wallace?"

"The less you know, Ander, the better."

"Father Jacob, if they hang you they'll damn sure hang me. I might as well know what for."

"I told Sir Henry what I told the countess and Dubois. I let him know what I had discovered about the Bottom Dwellers and I added that they had tried to kill us with a contramagic bomb."

"You sealed the letter with your signet ring and I suppose you signed it into the bargain."

"I had to sign it," said Father Jacob. "Henry Wallace has to know it came from me."

"Good God, Jacob, if the letter falls into the wrong hands, you will be charged with treason!"

"Most likely," Father Jacob said, his face grave. "I had to warn him, Sir Ander. It is my belief that the Bottom Dwellers have not declared war on Rosia alone. They have declared war on all mankind."

He grew more cheerful, rubbing his hands at the prospect of the journey home.

"And now we should set out for the Arcanum. Do you want me to drive the wyverns?"

12

The *Cloud Hopper* had been sailing for two days, on course
for Evreux. The three wild dragons were still following
them, sometimes flying close enough to be within hailing
range, sometimes flying so far in the distance they were barely
visible through the mists, and sometimes disappearing completely.

The *Cloud Hopper* had left the Chain of Pearls and was
now approaching an area known as the Dustbin, a debris
field created when small chunks of the continental shelf
broke off, were gathered up by the prevailing winds, and

dumped into the Breath. The Dustbin was difficult to navigate even under the best conditions.

Miri intended to sail the *Cloud Hopper* through the Dustbin in order to catch the trade winds. They would lose some time, because they would have to land on an island at night. Flying through the Dustbin was going to be dangerous enough during daylight without attempting the voyage after dark. She hoped to make up the lost time and even gain some when the trade winds blew them swiftly toward Evreux.

Given the tricky maneuvering required to sail the *Hopper* safely among the debris field, Miri stated that she would be at the helm the entire time. She would not allow Gythe or Dag to spell her.

"If anyone sinks this boat, it will be me," she announced grimly.

The voyage was tense. Not only were they going to have to navigate a treacherous debris field, Stephano and the others also had to safely navigate around Miri, who was in a bad mood and wanted everyone to know it. While standing at the helm, watching out for floating chunks of rock, she had time to think and to worry. Her thoughts fluctuated between her disastrous love affair and the potential disaster looming over the *Cloud Hopper*.

As to her love affair, Miri had offered Dag her heart and he had rejected her. Her pride was hurt and she told herself her heart was hurt, as well. Deep inside, she knew her heart was untouched. Dag had been right. She was frightened and bewildered and overwhelmed. She felt responsible for the lives of her friends. She was worried about the dwindling amount of lift gas, about navigating the Dustbin, about running out of food and water. She dared not let them see she was worried. She longed for someone to put his arm around her and let her hide within his protective care. Not wanting to admit such weakness to herself, she blamed Dag for "leading her on," an accusation that was completely ground-less. Dag had behaved like a gentleman. He was, in truth, the personification of the word. The knowledge that she was being unjust to him made Miri even angrier.

She raged at everyone, even the poor Doctor, who fled to the storage closet. The others tiptoed around her: Stephano was insufferably polite; Gythe looked at her with big, sad eyes; Rodrigo oozed charm; and Dag was meek and self-effacing. She detested them all.

On the end of the second day of their journey toward the Dustbin, the sails of the *Cloud Hopper* billowed as the boat felt the first effects of the trade winds. They picked up speed, scudding along through the mists, making good time. About midafternoon Dag sighted the Dustbin ahead of them, the debris dotting the mists, and Miri slowed the boat's speed. Stephano and Dag stood at the bow, keeping a lookout.

"Island to starboard," Stephano called.

Miri adjusted the air screws and steered the *Cloud Hop-per* around it.

"Another to starboard; hold your course."

An island appeared suddenly on the port side, looming out of the mist. Miri barely had enough time to react.

"Sorry, Miri, I didn't see it," said Dag.

"Keep a better lookout next time," Miri snapped.

"I will, Miri," said Dag meekly.

"And stop being nice to me!" Miri snarled.

Dag glanced at Stephano. Miri saw the look and cast an angry glance of her own at Stephano, warning him to keep his mouth shut. She knew she was being unreasonable, but he didn't understand. None of them understood.

The *Hopper* was threading its way through the Dustbin when, late in the afternoon, the air screws stopped turning and the boat began to drift, moving slowly toward a large island, dead ahead.

"What's wrong with the air screws?" Stephano shouted from his post at the bow.

"I don't know!" Miri cried, her hands flashing over the helm without effect.

The air screws wouldn't budge.

"It's the magic!" Rodrigo called out. He pointed to one of the wooden shafts connected to the air screws. "The bridge spells I cast are weakening and—"

"Don't stand there yammering, you fool!" Miri said through gritted teeth. "Fix it!"

Rodrigo opened his mouth, thought better of it, and went to work. He hastily drew a construct. Gythe leaned over his shoulder, guiding the magic through his patch with her hands. Stephano and Dag stood at the bow of the boat, watching the island come closer.

"Got it!" Rodrigo called triumphantly.

The air screws began to turn, and with a relieved sigh Miri regained control of the helm. The *Cloud Hopper* veered away from the island, still coming close enough to it that Stephano and Dag had to shove off the rocks with boat hooks. Once they were safe, Miri rounded on Rodrigo.

"What the hell went wrong, Rigo?" she demanded.

"The magical patch is only a patch, Miri," Rodrigo explained. "Like any patch, it's temporary. I didn't realize *how* temporary."

Miri glared at him. "Make it permanent!"

"I wish I could," said Rodrigo. "Unfortunately, that's not possible. It has to do with the constructs. They're like a layer cake and when one layer falls—"

At the words "layer cake" Miri's brows came together and she reached for the belaying pin she kept under the helm.

"Never mind," said Rodrigo hurriedly. "I'll take care of it."

"*Can* you take care of it?" Stephano asked in a low voice, thinking Miri couldn't hear.

Miri heard. She also heard Rodrigo's answer.

"No," he said bluntly. "The magic will keep breaking down. There's nothing I can do to stop it. I may join Doctor Ellington in the storage closet."

Miri glanced at the balloon that was shrinking in size a little every day and sighed.

Instead of going to the storage closet, Rodrigo went around the boat to check all the patches he'd placed on the *Hopper*. He found a number that were either failing or on the verge of failing. He made repairs and Gythe kept the magic flowing.

Twilight tinged the Breath with pink and purple. Miri had been at the helm all day, refusing to relinquish it. She was bone weary. She hadn't slept in nights. Catching herself dozing off, she told Dag and Stephano to find a suitable place to land.

When they came to one of the larger of the small islands, Miri adjusted the lift and the ballast and lowered the *Cloud Hopper* onto a slab of gray slate dotted here and there with red lichen and green moss. The island was otherwise bare, with not so much as a tree. The *Cloud Hopper* took up most of the space.

Supper was cheerless. They ate their rations in silence. Dag divided his own ration of meat and started to give part of it to the Doctor, who had come out of the storage closet to sit on Dag's knee.

"No need to share your food," said Miri in frozen tones. "You have to keep up your strength. I saved this for the cat."

She brought out a dish of fish heads and other scraps and set it down in front of the Doctor.

"Thanks, Miri," said Dag. Pausing a moment, petting the Doctor, he added in a husky voice, "Miri, I'm sorry. If there's anything—"

"I'm going to bed," Miri said, rising from the table, leaving her food untasted. "The rest of you had better do the same. We sail at first light."

Dag and Gythe and Rodrigo went below. Stephano, standing first watch, remained on the bridge. Miri lay down in the bed, but she couldn't sleep. Wrapping a shawl around her shoulders, she went up on deck. Without speaking to Stephano, she checked the amount of lift gas left in the balloon. She was going to return to her cabin, but found Stephano standing in her way.

He took hold of her hand, twined his fingers through hers.

"You'll always have me, Miri," he said. "I know I'm not much, but I'm better than nothing."

Miri laughed in spite of herself. She squeezed his hand tightly.

"No one else will have either of us, it seems," she said ruefully. "I know I'm being a bitch. It's just . . . Maybe I made the wrong decision, risking sailing through the Dustbin. Maybe we should have gone around—"

"We have the trade winds. We must be close to the shipping lanes. We'll make it to Evreux. We have to. Rodrigo will never forgive us if he misses the summer season at court."

Miri gave a grudging smile. "You always make me feel better. I guess I won't murder you in your bed tonight."

"I'll hide the knives, just in case," Stephano called after her.

Miri went below to her cabin. She moved quietly, feeling her way through the darkness, so as not to wake her sister. She sat down on the edge of the bed. The magic was failing. The balloon was shrinking.

We are near the shipping lanes. We have to be.

———

The night passed quietly. Stephano handed over the watch to Dag. They made their customary exchange.

"Nothing to report," Stephano said.

"That's the way we like it," said Dag.

Stephano went to bed. He was restless and hot and sleep eluded him. When he finally dozed off, he woke to a hand on his shoulder.

"Something you should see, Captain," Dag whispered.

Stephano was awake instantly. He eased himself out of the hammock. Rodrigo was asleep in the other hammock, lying on his stomach, his arms dangling over the edge, breathing softly. He had stumbled out of bed once during the night to check on the magical patches, fixing any that were starting to fail.

Stephano pulled on his boots and met Dag on deck. "What is it?"

"To the north," Dag said, looking through his spyglass.

Stephano put his spyglass to his eye, swept it over the horizon. Darkness filled the sky above and behind, but the sky ahead was lit by the pale, pinkish orange light of approaching dawn. He could see an island silhouetted in the soft light and another island farther beyond. And that was all. Clear skies. They were almost out of the Dustbin. He thought at first this was why Dag had brought him up on deck, then a flash of green light caught his eye.

"There!" said Dag, jabbing his finger.

Stephano shifted the spyglass. He watched for long moments, then lowered it. He could hear the faint boom of cannons.

"Flashes of green," he said, lowering the spyglass. "Cannonfire. Bottom Dwellers attacking a ship?"

"Yes, sir, that's what I thought," Dag agreed. "Merchant ship to judge by the sound of the cannonfire."

Stephano listened and understood what Dag meant. Gun

crews aboard merchantmen were often poorly trained, since they very rarely had to fight. The cannonfire was sporadic, desultory. Once several guns went off almost together, probably an attempt at a broadside.

"Six pounders," said Stephano. He paused, his head cocked. "*That's* not cannonfire."

"Swivel guns," said Dag.

"I never heard of a merchant ship armed with swivel guns," said Stephano.

They both continued to listen and watch. A flare of green fire was followed by an orange fireball and the sound of an explosion.

"Cannon blew up," said Dag, shaking his head. "Poor bastards." He was thinking of the gun crew.

Stephano stirred restlessly. "We should go see if we can help—"

"And do what, sir?" Dag demanded. "Throw rocks at them?"

He glanced at the empty places on the deck where their own guns had been.

"Damn! I forgot." Stephano ran his hand through his hair. "Still, you should wake Miri—"

Dag looked uncomfortable. "Begging your pardon, sir, but could *you* go wake Miri?"

"Sure," said Stephano, smiling in sympathy. He rested his hand on Dag's shoulder. "She'll get over it. Just give her time."

Dag shook his head. Putting the spyglass to his eye again, he went back to watching the battle. Stephano ran below.

"Rigo, rise and shine!" Stephano called out, as he passed their berth.

He heard only a muttered curse in response. Stephano knocked on Miri's door. He still had his hand raised when she flung it open. She was dressed, her hair frowsy. Stephano could see Gythe sitting up in bed, blinking sleepily.

"What's wrong?" Miri demanded.

"Nothing wrong with the *Hopper*. We're almost through the Dustbin. We're near the shipping lanes."

"You've seen a ship!" Miri said excitedly.

Stephano nodded. "Probably a merchant ship. But there's a problem. It's under attack. Bottom Dwellers."

"Son of a bitch," Miri muttered. "Give me a moment to wash and I'll be there."

She shut the door. Stephano returned to the bridge to find Rodrigo standing on the deck in his shirtsleeves glaring at him.

"Why did you wake me? It's still night! I'm going back to bed. Let me know when it's morning . . ."

"We've sighted a ship under attack by Bottom Dwellers. See for yourself." Stephano handed his friend the spyglass.

"I know that look in your eye," Rodrigo said, lowering the glass. "You want to go save them. May I remind you that we don't have any guns."

"I don't want to hear another word about the guns," said Miri, coming up on deck. "Hand me the spyglass."

The sun was starting to rise, providing a better view. A lone island stood out clearly. Beyond that, they could see only the morning mists of the Breath and a long trailing plume of smoke.

"That's a merchant ship, all right," she said.

In the light of day they could see it without need of the spyglass. The merchant ship was a large one. Three masted, though only two now rose from the deck, the other must have been damaged in the assault. Two smaller masts thrust out from the sides of the hull, connecting the upper and lower sails. Long wings ran the full length of the hull. There would be two air screws on each wing with the wheel and the control panels located on the forecastle.

"That's one of the new designs used by the Travian Cartel," said Stephano. "She's a big one."

"And she's on fire," said Dag, watching.

The six gunports on the starboard side were open. Smoke poured out of two of them. There was no sign of the gigantic bats or their riders. That was not necessarily a good sign.

"But she's not sinking. At least not yet. We're going to sail over to see if we can help," said Miri, taking her place at the helm. "Wake Gythe. Throw off the lines."

"Sail over there! You can't be serious!" Rodrigo protested. "For all we know, the Bottom Dwellers have taken control of the ship!"

"He's right, Miri," said Stephano. "We don't know who's on board the ship. And we don't have any—"

"We don't have any bloody guns!" Miri yelled angrily. She glanced up at the balloon and pressed her lips together. She drew in a breath, let it out, forced herself to speak calmly. "We don't have enough lift gas to carry us home. We have barely enough to keep us aloft for the next few hours. So it doesn't matter who is on board that ship."

Miri nodded her head at the burning merchant vessel and added grimly, "If she sinks, so do we."

13

The Travian Trade Cartel is the single most powerful merchant guild in the world of Aeronne. The cartel commands fifty large merchantmen, holds contracts with another thirty, and has seventy smaller ships under its flag. The cartel has exclusive shipping rights with local guilds in Estara, Rosia, Freya, and Travia. Recent mysterious attacks against ships owned or contracted by the cartel have caused them to arm all of their ships, creating what may be termed the third largest navy in the world.

—Countess de Marjolaine,
report to His Majesty's Privy Council

The *Cloud Hopper* sailed past the last island in the Dustbin. The vast expanse of the Breath lay beyond. The smoke from the burning ship could be seen clearly, flowing out in a long billowing plume.

"Ship's name is the *Sommerwind* out of Guundar," Dag reported, keeping watch through the spyglass. "And she's flying a distress flag."

"That's a good sign," said Rodrigo.

The others turned to stare at him.

"I mean, if the Bottom Dwellers *had* taken over the ship,

they wouldn't be likely to send up a distress flag, would they?"

"What he says makes sense," Stephano admitted to Dag.

"That's what worries me, sir," Dag returned. "When Rigo makes sense the world must be about to end."

He continued to watch the ship. "Doesn't appear to be badly damaged. One of the masts came down and took a lot of sail with it. Some of the hull planking is charred. That looks to be the extent of it."

"Is she sinking?" Miri asked tersely.

"Not that I can tell," Dag reported.

"Good thing that captain had sense enough to mount swivel guns," said Stephano. "Probably saved his ship."

Dag nodded in agreement. "Maybe a bat rider patrol like the one that attacked us thought they'd come across easy pickings. They didn't expect swivel guns."

They searched the skies for Bottom Dwellers. The Breath was clear this morning, the trade winds shredding the mists. They saw no bats and their riders.

The wind filled the sail and the *Cloud Hopper* bobbed through the Breath. Miri ordered everyone back to work. Rodrigo and Gythe continued to nurse the magical constructs, while Stephano divided his attention between watching the merchant ship and keeping a nervous eye on the balloon. Dag and the others were doing the same. All except Miri. She kept her eyes fixed on the merchant ship.

Stephano would occasionally glance back at the Dustbin, expecting to see the three dragons. For the first time since they'd left the island, the dragons were not following them. Miri caught him.

"Stop watching for those fool dragons, Stephano!" She snapped. "We have worries enough without them. Rigo, what are you doing sitting about like a lump when the magic is failing? Do you *want* us to sink into the Breath and die?"

Rodrigo had taken a moment to rest. He was back on his feet in an instant.

"There's nothing for me to do," he told Stephano in a whisper that carried clearly to Miri. "The magic doesn't need fixing, at least for the moment. And I can't breathe more Breath into the balloon!"

"Be patient with her," Stephano said.

"I'll try," Rodrigo grumbled. "But she's not making it easy."

The *Cloud Hopper* was now near enough to the merchant ship that they could see activity on board. Some of the sailors were busy fighting the fire, while others were using axes to chop through the tangle of lines to free the fallen mast. They knew when the lookout caught sight of the *Cloud Hopper,* for they could hear him shout. Several of the sailors ran to the railing and began waving their arms.

"Looks like they're motioning us to come within hailing distance," said Stephano.

"That would be a change," said Miri with a grim smile. "Usually they warn us Trundlers to keep away."

Merchant ships generally wanted nothing to do with Trundlers, who were the bane of a ship captain's existence. Trundler boats would sail alongside vessels, offering to sell their wares, which included Calvados. The sailors would manage to smuggle the Calvados on board and end up drunk and unfit for duty.

The *Cloud Hopper* slowly floated nearer to the merchant ship. Miri reversed the air screws, reducing the boat's forward motion so that they would not collide. The *Hopper* was perhaps twenty yards from the ship when Rodrigo pointed to the balloon. Everyone had been so absorbed in watching the *Sommerwind,* they had forgotten about the lift gas.

The balloon had barely enough gas to keep them afloat.

Before Miri could say or do anything, the sailor on board the merchant vessel hailed them.

"Trundler boat. Have you . . . medicine?" The sailor spoke Rosian brokenly and with a thick Guundaran accent. "Our captain is hurt."

Miri turned to Dag. "You speak their language. Tell him we have medicine. But he needs to throw us a line!" she said urgently. "And be quick about it!"

"We have medicine *and* a healer, but we're running out of lift gas!" Dag shouted in Guundaran. "Can you spare some of your reserve gas and give us a tow?"

The sailor nodded and began to yell for his comrades to fetch rope. They tied a weight to the end, then they chose the strongest among them to fling the weight with the rope attached toward the *Cloud Hopper*. The weight arced through the air and missed. The next try failed as well.

"Lubbers," Miri muttered, biting her lip.

On the third try, the weight crashed onto the deck. Dag and Stephano both grabbed hold of the rope, which was attached to a heavy towline. The two men dragged the towline onto the *Cloud Hopper* and secured it to a pair of towing bollards set into the bow.

Once the *Cloud Hopper* was secure and no longer in danger of sinking, everyone on board breathed a heartfelt sigh. Dag bowed his head in prayer. Stephano wiped the sweat from his face. Rodrigo gave a cheer and hugged Gythe. He then went to Miri, laughing, arms outspread.

"Don't touch me," she ordered.

Rodrigo hurriedly backed away.

Miri steered the boat slowly and carefully until the prow was about ten feet above the *Sommerwind*'s stern, taking care to avoid hitting the sails or the *Sommerwind*'s balloons. When the *Hopper* was in position, Miri left the helm to Gythe and ran below to collect her ointments and potions. She came back on deck, carrying a leather bag filled with small jars and bottles.

"Stephano, you're coming with me. Bring your pistols. Rigo, you stay with Gythe and keep the magic working. Gythe, as soon as they swing over a reserve tank, use just enough to fill the main balloon. Dag, I'll need you to translate."

A sailor tossed a tether line for the lift gas tank to Gythe, while Stephano and Dag lowered the rope ladder. Two sailors waited on the deck of the *Sommerwind* to hold the ladder steady. Miri handed the bag to Stephano and nimbly descended, then held up her hands to catch the bag.

"Careful!" Miri called. "I have jars in there!"

"Don't break the yellow goo," said Rodrigo. "We'll all go up in flames."

Stephano tossed the bag down as gently as he could. Miri caught it and waited for Stephano and Dag to join her. Once the two were on board the *Sommerwind,* Miri waved to Gythe, who steered the *Cloud Hopper* away from the merchant ship. Attached by the towline, the *Hopper* floated in the *Sommerwind*'s wake.

"Thank them for the lift gas and tell them I want to keep the *Cloud Hopper* tethered to their ship," said Miri, once they were on board. "Even now that we have lift, I'm still worried about the magic failing."

Stepheno listened as Dag spoke to the sailors in the thick, guttural Guundaran language. He found out that almost everyone on board the *Sommerwind* had suffered some type of injury. Most had burns from fighting the fire, or from being hit by the weapons of the Bottom Dwellers. Some had broken bones or cracked skulls.

Stephano understood a word here and there. When he and Rodrigo were young, their tutor had tried to teach them the language. Guundaran was extremely logical, the tutor maintained; much more so than the fluid, romantic, and illogical Rosian. Stephano admitted the language might be logical, but he never could get past the fact that the verbs apparently all migrated to the end of the sentence. As for Rodrigo, he did not even make the attempt to learn Guundaran, stating he would never have a need for it.

"Have you seen Guundaran women?" he had asked with a shudder.

Stephano heard the word *"kapitan"* several times. The sailors were apparently most concerned about their captain. Once Dag had talked to the sailors and figured out what was going on, he came back to Stephano and Miri to report.

"The *Sommerwind* is a Guundaran ship under contract to a Travian cartel, bound for Evreux. The captain's badly wounded. He's in his cabin below. Their surgeon is either dead or dead drunk; with all sailors talking at once, I couldn't figure out what they were saying. They want Miri to attend to the captain."

"I'll go right now," said Miri.

"Do you need our help?" Stephano asked.

"You'd best stay here, see if you can find out what happened," Miri said "I'll have Dag to translate."

She and Dag accompanied one of the sailors to the captain's cabin. Stephano remained alone on the deck. He looked back at the *Cloud Hopper* to see Gythe at the helm. The balloon was once more fully inflated. She waved at him and he waved back, letting her know everything was all right.

The *Sommerwind*'s able sailors had gone back to their duties. He was wondering if there was anything he could do to help, when an officer approached him. He spoke fluent Rosian and introduced himself as "Leutnant Ben Baumann." Stephano introduced himself as Captain Stephano de Guichen, formerly of the Dragon Brigade. The lieutenant raised his eyebrows at this, but before he could ask questions, Stephano, noticing the lieutenant's uniform was covered in blood, asked if he was hurt.

"Not my own blood," Baumann said, looking down at the dark stains. "The blood of my captain. We were attacked by Freyan pirates riding gigantic bats. Damn and blast them!"

"Our boat was also attacked by these same bat riders," said Stephano. "What makes you think they are Freyan?"

Leutnant Baumann shrugged. "Your king has said so, Captain de Guichen. Freyans wearing these same devil masks attacked the port in Westfirth. Your king has said publicly it will be only a matter of time before Rosia declares war.

"Though I must admit," Baumann added, frowning, "I do not know how Freyans come to be riding gigantic bats or why they use guns that shoot green fire. What are your thoughts? You say you were attacked by them."

Stephano didn't know how to respond. He could have told the lieutenant the bat riders weren't Freyan, that they were a people who called themselves "Bottom Dwellers," that they lived at the bottom of the world, and that he knew this because Gythe had heard their voices in her head. Baumann would think Stephano had been drinking the Calvados.

"I don't believe they are Freyan," he said, adding drily, "despite what my king says."

Leutnant Baumann smiled in understanding. He must have heard that King Alaric disbanded the Dragon Brigade and would guess that Stephano wasn't happy about it.

"If not Freyan, who do you think these people are, Captain? And where do they come from?"

"I don't know, Leutnant," said Stephano. He added gravely, "I'm not sure I want to know."

Leutnant Baumann nodded. He was a typical Guundaran, resembling Dag, only shorter. The lieutenant had the same large-boned frame and strong jawline, with blond hair and a blond beard. He was profuse in his thanks for the medicines and Miri's willingness to help his captain. As it turned out, their own surgeon had been killed in the attack.

"No great loss. The man was useless even when he was sober," said Leutnant Baumann.

He then excused himself, saying he had to determine the extent of the damage the *Sommerwind* had sustained, and see to it that his ship was back on course.

Alone again, Stephano paced the bridge, looking at the ship and thinking that the cartel had spent a lot of money on her. He wondered what cargo she carried.

Stephano was inspecting portions of the hull that had been hit with green fire when Leutnant Baumann returned.

"I have spoken to Fräulein Miri. She says our captain's wounds were not as bad as we first thought. He will soon be well."

"That is excellent news," said Stephano. "I have to say, Leutnant, all things considered, the *Sommerwind* appears to have escaped serious harm. Good thing you had those swivel guns."

"Danken Sie Gott," Leutnant Baumann said. "Our captain is a man of great foresight. Privateers such as the infamous Captain Northrop have been attacking merchantmen, seizing them as prizes. Now these bat riders. We heard rumors that merchant ships sailing in the Breath have vanished without a trace. That is why our captain purchased the swivel guns."

Stephano watched as Baumann and the other officers took readings, consulted charts. He couldn't understand what they were saying, but they were undoubtedly trying to determine how far off course the *Sommerwind* had been driven by the attackers. Sailors climbed the rigging to adjust the sails and the large air screws whirred, bringing the *Sommerwind* about to a new heading.

Leutnant Baumann walked back over to Stephano.

"We are on course again for Evreux, sir. We need to drop off and pick up cargo there, and refill our lift tanks."

"That is good news. We are bound for Evreux ourselves," said Stephano. "That reminds me. We have heard no news for many weeks. Did Evreux come under attack?"

"As far as I know, Captain, the bat riders attacked only Westfirth." Then, with some hesitation, he asked, "I do not like to pry into your affairs, sir, but I am curious as to why a Rosian military officer and a gentlemen such as yourself, sails on a Trundler houseboat? I hope you are not offended."

"Not in the least," said Stephano, laughing. "The story is a long one, Leutnant. To make it brief, when the Dragon Brigade was disbanded I resigned my commission in the navy. Being short of funds, I started my own business. In a small way, my friends are merchants such as yourself."

Leutnant Baumann smiled knowingly. Trundler boats were often used for smuggling.

"I know that Trundlers generally hug the coastline. May I ask what are you doing out here in the shipping lanes, so far off course? Please forgive my questioning, Captain," said Leutnant Baumann, embarrassed. "My ship was attacked by pirates. One cannot be too careful . . ."

Stephano understood. The question was legitimate. And he was going to lie to the man anyway—or at least, not tell him the entire truth. He could afford to be magnanimous.

"Our boat was in Westfirth when that city came under attack. The *Cloud Hopper* was damaged. We were blown off course and crashed on an island in the Chain of Pearls. We were marooned there until we could make repairs. We thought we had enough lift gas to cross the strait, but the tank must have sprung a leak. We had only enough to fill the balloon and we very nearly didn't make it. If it hadn't been for your ship . . ." Stephano shook his head.

Leutnant Baumann listened gravely. "You were in West-firth when the bat riders attacked?"

"Yes, sir," said Stephano.

"The *Sommerwind* was not in Westfirth, thank the good *Gott*. We heard terrible stories from our friends, however. As for our ship, the bat riders attacked us at dawn. There were twenty or more of them, wearing those hideous devil masks and riding monstrous bats. They carried odd-looking weapons, like small cannons, that belched green fire. They hit one of our cannons, which exploded. We feared for a time the fire would spread to the cargo, but we managed to contain it."

"Why do you think they attacked your ship?"

"I believe they were trying to capture it," said Leutnant Baumann. "They attempted to board, but our captain and crew fought them off, and we killed several. We tried to un-mask them, to see who they were, but the bodies burst into flame and we couldn't get near them."

"The same thing happened at Westfirth," said Stephano.

He noticed men hovering in the background, obviously wanting to claim the lieutenant's attention. He thanked Leutnant Baumann for the information and said he would let him get back to work.

"Thank *you,* Captain," said the lieutenant, and with an exchange of bows, he returned to the bridge.

Seeing Dag come up from below, Stephano motioned to him, and the two walked over to the rail.

"Miri doesn't need me," Dag reported. "The captain speaks Rosian. She said we should go back to the boat."

Stephano shouted for Gythe to sail the *Hopper* over to pick them up, and while they waited, Stephano told Dag the news about Westfirth and Evreux and about the attack on the *Sommerwind*.

"Strange, sir," said Dag. "Why do you think these Bottom Dwellers are capturing ships?"

"You saw that black ship of theirs," said Stephano. "It was at least a hundred years old. I'm thinking they're wanting to modernize their navy."

The two crossed the deck, heading for the stern. They had to make their way around the wreckage and the bodies of the dead, wrapped in sailcloth shrouds.

"Do you think it's possible the Bottom Dwellers are working for Freya, sir?" Dag asked.

Stephano shook his head. "We know Bottom Dwellers tried to ambush Sir Henry. And if Freya was planning to go to war with Rosia, Sir Henry would not have given Rigo that pewter tankard. As for Alaric, he has to tell the Rosians something. He can't let the populace think that Aertheum's demonic hordes are going to bring about the end of the world. And, to be fair, Alaric may honestly believe these people *are* Freyans. What I find odd is that the Bottom Dwellers haven't attacked any more cities since Westfirth."

"They're planning something major," Dag predicted.

"That's what I'm thinking," said Stephano.

The *Cloud Hopper* was almost in position, hovering overhead. Rodrigo was about to lower the rope ladder when the lookout on board the *Sommerwind* pointed and shouted.

"Drache!"

14

The death of Empress Elsbeth Octavia without an heir and the subsequent battle for the throne marked the beginning of the end of the Sunlit Empire. The dragons were drawn into the civil war, with some dragons supporting one side and some another. The result was devastating for the dragon duchies, as clan members turned on one another. Grieved to see dragons fighting dragons, some among dragonkind decided they should stop all interaction with humans and withdraw to isolation. The rift was bitter, with those dragons who chose to remain loyal to their human friends accusing their kindred of betrayal.

—Miri McPike,
Mistress of Dragon Lore

Stephano didn't know much Guundaran, but he understood the word for "dragon." He ran to the stern for a better view.

The three dragons were no longer following the *Cloud Hopper* from a distance. They were flying swiftly, heading straight for the *Sommerwind*. Leutnant Baumann was issuing orders.

"What's he saying?" Stephano asked, turning to Dag.

"He is sending men to the swivel guns and the cannons."

"Damn!" Stephano swore. "Keep an eye on our dragon friends. I'll go talk to Baumann."

He turned, only to nearly run into Leutnant Baumann, who had come over to talk to him.

"You are an expert in dealing with dragons, Captain," said Leutnant Baumann. "We have encountered wild dragons before when we fly near the Pearls, and they generally keep their distance. These appear to be coming after us. I don't like this—"

"I can explain, sir," said Stephano, interrupting. "I know these dragons. We met them on the island. They've been following us for days now."

The lieutenant appeared dubious. "Dragons following you, Captain. Why? Did you befriend them?"

"I tried to," said Stephano ruefully. "I didn't think I succeeded, but here they are."

Leutnant Baumann cleared his throat, expressing polite disbelief.

"Fetch Miri!" Stephano told Dag. "If she's not with the captain, she'll be in the sick bay, treating the crew."

While Dag went below to find Miri, Stephano tried to explain.

"Wild dragons are not like those we know as civilized dragons. Those dragons speak our language. They can communicate with us. These wild dragons apparently understand our language, but they either can't speak it or they choose not to do so. When I talked to them, I think they understood me. They never spoke to me, though. I have no idea what they want."

Leutnant Baumann was watching the dragons. "You need to make it clear to the beasts, Captain, that they are to stay away from my ship."

Stephano couldn't blame the man. One swipe of a dragon's tail could knock down a mast or crack open the hull.

Dragons in the Brigade had been trained to maneuver around ships. These wild dragons had probably never been near a ship like the *Sommerwind* before. They might be curious. Or perhaps they were worried about Stephano and his friends.

Miri arrived, returning with Dag. She looked out at the dragons and shook her head.

"Dag told me what was going on. I've been thinking, Stephano. What if these dragons want to go with us to Rosia? Reestablish contact with their kin?"

"I thought of that myself, but if so, why not just fly back on their own? Why follow us?"

"The wild dragons haven't been back to Rosia in hundreds of years. They long ago lost contact with their kin. They know from your stories about the Brigade that you have friends among the noble dragons. They may want you to act as an intermediary. They trust you."

"They have an odd way of showing they trust me. They won't come near me," Stephano said grimly. "Dag and I are planning to return to the *Cloud Hopper*. Unless you need us."

"You can go," said Miri. "I can take care of myself. Think about what I said."

Stephano did think about it. Miri was an expert in dragon lore. She knew dragons as well as any human. He came to the conclusion she might be right. He could devise no other explanation.

He waved his arms at the dragons and both he and Dag shouted at the top of their lungs, telling the dragons to stop, warning them not to come any closer to the ship. Viola was, as usual, in the lead, flanked by Verdi and Petard. The dragons slowed and broke formation. They flew in uneasy circles, keeping near the ship, but not threatening it.

Seeing that the dragons were, for the moment, obeying

his orders, Stephano and Dag arrived back on the *Cloud Hopper* to find Rodrigo had cocooned an irate Doctor Ellington in a dish towel, binding the towel around his legs and body so that only the cat's head and baleful eyes peered out.

"What are you doing with my cat?" Dag demanded.

"You know he doesn't like dragons," said Rodrigo. "He took one look at them and began howling like a banshee and foaming at the mouth. I was afraid he was going to jump off the ship. He scratched me when I tried to pick him up, hence the dish towel. Here, you take him!"

He handed the Doctor to Dag, who unwound the dish towel and hoisted the grateful cat to his shoulder, petting him soothingly all the while. The Doctor dug in his claws, hissed at Rodrigo, and settled down to glare at the dragons.

"Sail the *Hopper* away from the *Sommerwind,* Gythe," Stephano said. "Take the boat out as far as the towline will allow us."

The *Cloud Hopper* slowly drifted off. When the tow line grew taut, Gythe brought the boat to a stop, fearing the towline would snap. Stephano looked over his shoulder, back onto the deck of the merchantman. Gun crews were manning both the swivel guns and the cannons. The lieutenant wasn't taking any chances.

"He's not going to let the dragons keep following us," said Dag. "The crew is nervous enough without dragons trailing along behind the whole voyage."

"I've been thinking," said Stephano. "I have an idea. I believe Miri is right. These dragons want to use us to reestablish communication with their kin. If so, what do we do with them? We can't sail into Evreux with dragons in tow. King Alaric would probably have me arrested."

"What about sending them to the houses of the noble dragons? You still have friends among them."

Stephano shook his head. "These wild dragons were once part of the noble families. There was bad blood, heated arguments. Families split apart. Dragons have long memories and they haven't forgiven their kin for leaving. They would not be pleased to have their wild and uncouth cousins suddenly land on their well-manicured lawns."

"So what are you going to do?" Dag asked.

"I'm going to ask the dragons to take me with them. We'll fly to the Abbey of Saint Agnes and I'll introduce them to the dragon brothers, Hroal and Droal. They can help these three contact their kin."

"You're leaving the *Cloud Hopper*?" Rodrigo asked, startled and dismayed. "Flying off on strange dragons? Leaving us with Miri the Mad Woman?"

Stephano smiled and looked back at the dragons, who were still hovering some distance away. He did not know how long they would remain here, what sort of trouble they might cause.

"Your plan makes sense, sir," Dag said. "The abbey is in a remote location. No one goes there now, not after the Bottom Dwellers destroyed it. The perfect place for these three."

"Well, what do you think?" Stephano asked the others.

Gythe looked out at the wild dragons and gave a tentative nod.

"You want to know what I think?" Rodrigo said. "I think you are using the dragons to avoid having to talk to your mother, admit we failed in our mission. You're going to make me go in your place."

"My mother likes you," said Stephano.

"Everyone at court likes me," said Rodrigo. "That's not the issue. Your mother undoubtedly thinks you are dead. She will be awash in grief—"

"My mother has probably not even noticed I've been gone," said Stephano.

Rodrigo snorted and went on. "The countess will *not* be pleased to have me arrive with news that you are alive and off cavorting with dragons instead of meeting with her to let her know *in person* you are alive. She will want to discuss the very important mission she paid us well to undertake."

"Rigo's right, Stephano," said Dag unexpectedly. "You should go to your mother. I'll fly to the abbey with the dragons."

Gythe and Rodrigo stared at Dag in astonishment. Stephano was surprised, but not as surprised as the other two. Stephano knew something they did not. Gythe was shaking her head violently. Pointing at Dag, she flashed signs with her hands.

"Don't let him! He has never ridden a dragon!"

"Actually, he has," Stephano said. "Though he wasn't supposed to."

Dag grinned at the memory. "I've always wanted to fly again, sir. You know that."

"You haven't been trained as a rider, Dag," Stephano said. "And these dragons haven't been trained to carry riders. The journey is a long one and you'd be riding without a harness or a saddle. The trip will be dangerous and uncomfortable—"

"Not as uncomfortable as it has been for me around here, sir," Dag said quietly.

Stephano knew he was thinking of Miri, and he sympathized with his friend. And he had to admit Rodrigo was right. His mother would be angry and insulted if he did not rush immediately to see her after having been gone for over a month. Not that she cared all that much about him, but she would want to hear what news he could bring her about her enemy, Sir Henry Wallace.

"Let me talk to the dragons," he said at last.

"I can go, sir?" Dag asked eagerly.

"That depends on them," said Stephano.

He waved his arm to draw the dragons' attention, though it was not really necessary, since the three had been staring straight at him. He motioned for them to fly closer. The dragons watched him and stayed where they were. Stephano motioned again, his gesture peremptory, and this time, the three dragons looked at one another. Finally, Viola flew slowly and warily nearer the *Cloud Hopper*.

Down below them, from the deck of the *Sommerwind*, Stephano heard Leutnant Baumann give an order in Guundaran.

"He's telling his gunners to be ready," said Dag.

"Tell them not to shoot! The dragon's coming to talk!" Stephano told Dag, who shouted down in Guundaran.

When Viola was in hailing distance, the dragon slowed, hovering, her wings scarcely moving. She fixed a steadfast gaze on Stephano.

He yelled across the Breath. "I know you can understand us. You proved that when you helped Miri rescue Gythe. I think you and the others are trying to reach Rosia to talk to your kin. If I'm right, give me a sign."

Viola gazed at Stephano and then slightly inclined her head.

Stephano was pleased and relieved. "That's good. That's excellent! I have friends, dragons like yourselves. They live in a remote place. They might know your kin and could help you find them."

Viola raised her head, gazed down her nose. She was interested, and flew a little closer.

"My friend Dag will fly with you, guide you."

Viola was alarmed. Her eyes widened, her foreclaws clenched. She appeared to give the matter thought, however. Her tongue flicked out from between her fangs. Her foreclaws unclenched, then clenched again. She twisted her head around to look at the others, then looked back at Stephano.

"You want to talk this over," said Stephano. "That is fine. Let Verdi and Petard know what I've said."

Viola gazed at Stephano for another few moments, then flew off to consult with the other two dragons. Stephano sighed. He was surprised to find he was shaking, sweating from the strain. He wiped his face and looked around at his friends, especially Gythe.

"Well? What do you think?"

Gythe was smiling. She touched Stephano on the chest. "You are right. They want to find their kin."

"Why now, I wonder?" Stephano asked. "After all this time . . ."

"Maybe the arrival of the Bottom Dwellers," Dag said. "The dragons want to find out who they are and where they come from."

"Viola's coming back," Rodrigo reported. "They're all three coming."

The three dragons flew together, heading toward the *Cloud Hopper.* On the *Sommerwind,* Leutnant Baumann was silent, watching and waiting. Stephano glanced at Dag, who looked nervous, tense. Perhaps he was having second thoughts. Stephano didn't blame him. The prospect of riding an untrained dragon through the Breath without saddle or harness was daunting. The least mistake by either Dag or the dragon could send Dag falling to his death.

The female dragon, Viola, flew closer. She looked pointedly at Dag and then inclined her head in a movement both gracious and graceful.

"They've agreed!" said Stephano.

Dag drew in a deep breath. "Good, sir. Now what?"

"Put on your cuirass and your helmet. You'll need protection from the wind. Take as many loaded pistols as you can carry. Impossible to reload on dragon back if you don't have a saddle or harness. We'll have to plan a route. Gythe, fetch Miri's navigational charts."

As Dag went below to get ready, Gythe reached down for the map that was kept in a chest beneath the helm. She drew it out, then slugged Stephano in the arm with her fist.

"What was that for?" he asked.

"Miri," said Gythe, making the sign for her sister. "She's going to be furious that you didn't consult her."

"I know she will," said Stephano. "And I'm sorry for that. I'm afraid if we delay, the dragons will change their minds or the lieutenant will shoot them. I'm making the best of a bad situation. I hope she'll understand."

Gythe raised her eyebrows.

Stephano gave a wry smile. "All right. I hope she doesn't crack my skull open."

Gythe shook her head and they both bent over the chart to determine the best route.

Dag returned, outfitted in his cuirass and a heavy coat and wearing his helm. He had made up a bedroll and armed himself with four pistols.

He bid farewell to the suspicious Doctor, who sensed something bad was in the offing. The cat dug his claws into Dag's coat and refused to be coaxed off. Rodrigo had to pry loose the angry cat from Dag's shoulder. Holding the spitting and snarling cat by the scruff of his neck, Rodrigo carried the Doctor back belowdecks to the storage closet.

Gythe indicated on the chart the route Dag was to fly, while Stephano explained.

"Look for the floating lighthouses that mark the shipping lanes. Stay between those and they'll guide you to land. You're flying east, so land will appear to your left. We've sailed up and down the coast of Rosia so often you should find a familiar landmark and be able to tell where you are. If you get lost in the shipping lanes, look for the buoy boats. They sail the lanes repairing the magic that keeps the lighthouses afloat and they can help guide you, or you can ask the lighthouse keepers. Now if you fly into fog—"

Dag was watching the dragons, who appeared to be growing impatient. "I'll manage fine, sir. You can't teach me in a few moments what it would take me months to learn. I've flown a dragon before."

"Once," said Stephano. "And you and the dragon were both inebriated."

Dag laughed at the memory. "I don't mind admitting I could use a drink now, sir."

Stephano wasn't smiling. "I shouldn't let you do this."

"I'm carrying four pistols, sir," said Dag with a smile. "I don't see how you can stop me."

Stephano grasped both Dag's big hands, clasping them firmly. "God go with you, my friend."

"Thank you, sir," said Dag. "And with you."

"One more piece of advice," said Stephano. "Hang on for dear life."

"You can be sure of that, sir!" said Dag emphatically.

He turned to Gythe, who flung her arms around him.

"Take care of yourself, dear girl. You're in charge of the Doctor. See that he has a bit of fish at night. Tell Miri . . ." He paused, then said huskily, "Tell her I'm sorry."

Gythe kissed Dag on the cheek. As he turned to leave, he found Rodrigo standing in front of him.

"I don't believe I ever thanked you properly for saving my life. God speed," said Rodrigo.

Dag shook hands with him, then walked over to the rail. Stephano was motioning to the largest of the dragons, the one they had named Verdi for the green color of his scales, indicating he was to fly beneath the *Cloud Hopper*'s keel.

Mounting a dragon from a boat was a tricky maneuver. The dragon had to fly close enough to enable Dag to climb down onto the dragon's back, but not so close that the dragon's mane scraped the keel.

Stephano guided Verdi. The dragon was nervous and his first approach was off by about a half mile. Verdi's next attempt was better, though he was not as close as Stephano would have liked. He did not dare ask the dragon to try again, for fear they would end up with a shattered hull.

Verdi hovered beneath the *Cloud Hopper*. The sun glittered on his green scales. His wings moved gently up and down, holding him in position. His legs dangled, his tail extended out behind. Beneath his wings Stephano could see the deepening orangish pink mists of the Breath and a long, long fall to death.

Verdi twisted his head, glancing up nervously at the *Cloud Hopper*. Dag leaned over the rail, eyeing the distance between him and dragon's back. He gulped.

"Rigo and I could lower you on a rope . . ." said Stephano.

Dag gave a wry smile and shook his head. "I doubt you could support my weight, sir." He drew in a deep breath. "Well. Here goes."

"Dag, wait—" Stephano cried, but he was too late.

Dag climbed over the rail, let go, and plunged down into the Breath.

Gythe was at the helm, keeping the *Cloud Hopper* steady. She was white to the lips. The crew on board the *Sommerwind* was watching, apparently, for Stephano heard some of the sailors cry out in shock. Miri must have been watching, too. Stephano heard a horrified scream. He leaned perilously over the rail, trying to see.

"Rigo, hang on to me!" Stephano ordered.

Rodrigo braced himself and took hold of the waist of Stephano's breeches.

Dag landed half-on and half-off of the dragon's shoulder, just behind the neck. The startled dragon gave a great "whoof!" as Dag came thudding down on him. Dag clutched frantically at the dragon's neck. An experienced dragon would have immediately adjusted his body to assist his rider. Verdi tensed as though afraid to move in case he made matters worse.

Stephano held his breath. After a heart-stopping moment, Dag managed, using all his brute strength, to pull himself onto the dragon's back. He slumped over in relief, closing his eyes and trying to catch his breath. Then he positioned himself on the dragon, resting his back against the spike of the mane. He managed a grin and a wave.

"Ready when you are, Verdi," Dag called.

Verdi did not appear at all sure about carrying a rider, but he flapped his wings and flew out from under the *Cloud Hopper*'s keel. The other two dragons joined their friend. Viola turned her head, looking back at Stephano.

"I will meet up with you at the abbey!" he shouted.

Viola stared at him in silence. Taking the lead, she and Petard and Verdi flew off, heading east, toward the Rosian continent. Stephano was glad to see Dag had taken his final word of advice. He was hanging on to the dragon's neck for dear life.

Rodrigo pulled Stephano back from the rail.

"You might wish I'd let you fall," said Rodrigo in warning tones.

"Stephano de Guichen!" Miri's outraged cry rang across the Breath. "You bring me aboard this instant!"

Stephano winced.

"You could move to Travia," Rodrigo suggested. "Live there under an assumed name. She'd never find you . . ."

Stephano gave a bleak smile. "This was my idea, my decision. I have to face the music."

"Might I suggest a funeral march?" said Rodrigo.

Gythe sailed the *Cloud Hopper* back toward the *Sommer-wind*. Stephano lowered the rope ladder. Two sailors grasped the ladder and held it while Miri nimbly climbed up. Coming on board, she walked straight toward Stephano. Her eyes blazed, her hair flamed red in the sun, her face was pale with fury. She walked up to Stephano and slapped him across the face.

"You bloody idiot!" she cried, her voice shaking with rage. "How could you?"

Stephano put his hand to his stinging cheek. "Miri, I can explain—"

"I don't want to hear," Miri shouted. "You and I are finished, Stephano! Pack your things and get off my boat!"

Gythe had been standing at the helm, watching and listening in unhappy silence. She left the helm. Catching hold of Miri's arm, Gythe forced her sister to turn to face her. Gythe's hands flashed her words. Fire kindled in her usually mild, soft eyes.

"Dag volunteered to go. He said that flying on a dragon would be better than staying around you because you've been making his life miserable!"

Gythe jabbed her sister in the chest. Miri stared at her in shock, taken aback by her sister's sudden and unusual display of anger. Gythe stood with her hands on her hips, glaring at Miri.

"Dag said that?" Miri asked, stricken. "He left . . . because of me?"

Gythe gave an emphatic nod.

Miri was subdued for a moment, then her anger rekindled. "That still doesn't excuse Stephano. He should have never let Dag go. Dag has never ridden a dragon!"

Gythe's hands made emphatic, stabbing gestures. "You had never ridden a dragon, either, and you rode one when you came to save me. You are wrong! You should apologize."

Miri looked at Stephano. "I guess I should have at least given you a chance to explain before I hit you."

"You could have always hit me afterward," said Stephano. His cheek was marked with the red imprint of her hand. "Dag didn't leave because of you. He left because I needed him to take the wild dragons to a place of safety. I couldn't do it because I'll have to go explain matters to my mother. We'll meet up with Dag and the dragons at the Abbey of Saint Agnes."

"Dag will be all right, won't he?" Miri asked pleadingly.

"I won't lie to you, Miri," Stephano said. "Dag's taking a big risk. If it's any consolation, he *has* ridden a dragon before. Do you remember the time the noble dragon, the duke of Ondea, hired us to catch the thieves that had stolen his jewelry collection? The duke had served in the Dragon Brigade, along with his friend, Count Pellerin, who was staying at the duke's castle with us and, well, let's just say the night involved me and Dag, a couple of bottles of brandy for us, and dragon-weed for the dragons. We all decided it was time Dag learned to fly."

"I remember," Miri said slowly, thinking back. "I also remember Dag showing up the next morning, one massive bruise from his head to his toes with a tale about how he fell while trying to scale a cliff to chase the thieves."

"Dag and the duke had problems landing," said Stephano. "We didn't want to worry you . . ."

Miri gazed at him. "I was wrong to slap you, Stephano. But we're still parting company. Leutnant Baumann says we should reach Evreux in a few days. When we do, you will move your things off my boat and pay what you owe us. And now I have to go back to tend to the wounded. I came to fetch more salve."

She went below. Rodrigo walked up behind Stephano, rested his hand on his shoulder.

"She'll get over it. We've been living in each other's pockets for the last month. I know I'm sick to the death of the sight of you myself."

"I may well have sent Dag to his death, Rigo," said Stephano. "I'm not sure Miri will forgive me this time. I'm not sure she should . . ."

The merchant ship was back on course, sailing for Evreux, the *Cloud Hopper* bobbing along behind. Stephano kept watch, trying to see his friend. But Dag and the dragons had disappeared into the mists.

15

Although Rosia controls vast tracts of land, most of the population lives within fifty miles of the edge of the Breath—what is termed "the rim." The majority of the interior is made up of farmland, virgin forest, open prairie, and a few large inland trading towns.

—Lord Jean DuCalie,
famed explorer and cartographer

Dag had deliberately made the leap from the *Cloud Hopper* to the dragon so that he didn't have time to dwell on what would happen if he fell. As it was, he had almost missed landing on his mount. Only a desperate struggle and his own strength had saved him from a horrifying end. Once he was safely settled on Verdi's broad back, he had to take several moments for his pounding heart to slow and the light-headed, sick feeling of terror to pass.

A professional soldier since the age of twelve, Dag had known fear before. Fear was part of a soldier's life and Dag had learned how to cope with it, just as he'd learned how to cope with sleeping in sodden wet clothes, eating tainted meat, drinking stale water, and dodging bullets and cannonballs. He had come to terms with death, at least for himself.

He was still haunted by the deaths of good men he'd ordered to go on the mission that had got them all killed.

Verdi seemed to understand his fear, or perhaps the dragon had been equally terrified. He flew slowly and as steadily as possible, hardly moving his wings, gliding on the same winds that were blowing the *Sommerwind* and the *Cloud Hopper* toward the continent. Verdi's friends flew near. When Dag was able to relax enough to actually look around, he saw Viola on one side and Petard on the other, both watching him and their comrade with what looked to him like anxious attention.

Dag was not particularly comfortable, straddling the dragon's back. The thought of shifting even an inch was frightening. He had a long flight ahead of him, however, and his muscles were already starting to ache. Holding on to the lowest spike on the dragon's mane, Dag slowly repositioned his posterior until he could more firmly rest his back against the first bony protrusion on the dragon's spine.

The only other time Dag had ridden a dragon—the drunken flight with the duke—Dag had ridden in one of the specially designed saddles used by the members of the Dragon Brigade. Dag still counted that evening as one of the high points of his life. He and Stephano had spent most of the afternoon drinking brandy, while the duke and his friend had lit a fire and thrown on a bale of dried burley leaves, what the dragons termed "dragon-weed." The inhaled smoke of the slow-burning leaves affected dragons in much the same way catnip affected cats or brandy affected humans.

They had told stories of the Dragon Brigade and lamented its demise. The brandy had given Dag courage to complain that a common soldier like himself would never have the opportunity to ride a dragon. Only noble dragons could serve in the Brigade and only gentlemen, such as Stephano, could ride them.

Stephano and the dragons had agreed that this was a damn shame and something should be done about it. The result of this was Dag's first dragon flight. He had drunk brandy enough to give himself courage and drown common sense, but not enough to completely cloud the mind. He and the duke had taken off shortly before sunset and, as he still remembered, flew among the orange and purple clouds, soared over the forests and fields, noticing for the first time how many ways God could find to paint green.

No green beneath him now of any shade. Nothing except the mists of the Breath. He didn't let himself think about falling, nor did he look down. He couldn't look down, for the wind rushing in his face made it hard to keep his eyes open. He tried lowering the visor of his helm and that helped some. At least he could see and keep a lookout for the buoy markers.

After flying for what must have been about an hour, Dag relaxed enough to find some pleasure in the solitude and the fact that for a little while, he had no duties, no cares, no responsibilities. He felt a deep and abiding affection for his friends, but for the first time in a long time he could draw a breath that was his own.

He flew past a number of the lighthouses that were more boat than house, each one resembling a Trundler houseboat with a single gigantic balloon and no sails. The lighthouses bobbed up and down in the Breath. The operator kept them in place. The buoy boats visited each lighthouse at intervals to relieve the operator at the tedious work and to strengthen the magical constructs on the boat. An operator on one of the lighthouses was sunning herself on deck when Dag and his dragons flew by. She stared at them in amazement, her mouth agape.

Dragons flew faster than any ship ever built. The *Sommerwind* was still far from Rosia when, shortly before nightfall, the dragons came within sight of land. The three dragons began to search for a suitable place to land, hunt, and sleep. Dag had a vague idea where they were. The ridge of mountains rising up from the coastline was probably the Cassée ridge, which would put him west of Evreux. If that was true, they were not far from the Abbey of Saint Agnes. He and the dragons had only to follow the coastline east tomorrow and they would find it.

The dragons flew inland, leaving the rock-bound coast behind, searching for well-forested areas that would be filled with deer.

When they came to a suitable site—an open field of grass and weeds, Verdi began to spiral down, flying slowly and carefully. Viola and Petard stayed with their friend, with frequent glances at him. When the dragon came close to landing, Dag braced himself. Dragons alighted on their back legs first, settling forward onto the forelegs. Dag and Verdi both came out of the landing safely, though Dag had a lump on his forehead where he'd crashed into the dragon's neck.

The other two dragons landed nearby, one on either side. Dag climbed down slowly and stiffly off the dragon's back, stifling a groan at the soreness in his backside. He kept silent for fear Verdi would think he'd done something wrong. The dragon was gazing back at his rider with a worried look.

Dag patted Verdi on the neck as he would have patted a horse—a gesture that would have deeply offended one of the noble dragons—and said, "Well done, Verdi."

Dag had no idea if Verdi understood him or not. The three dragons stared at Dag a moment as if wondering what to do with him and then, one by one, took to the air. Dag watched them soar away and the alarming thought came to him that they might leave him here, stranded in the middle of nowhere.

There wasn't much he could do about that now, Dag realized, and resigned himself to his situation.

He was wading through tall meadow grass, planning to make camp beneath some nearby trees, when Verdi appeared, flying above him, carrying something in his claws. As Dag tilted his head back to see, the dragon let his burden fall. Dag had to scramble to escape the bombardment. A dead deer landed on the ground, bounced, and came to rest a few feet from where Dag stood. He stared at the bloody carcass in astonishment and then began to chuckle.

Verdi had brought dinner.

The dragons returned shortly after dawn. Dag was waiting for them in the meadow. Verdi landed on the ground. While the others flew overhead, Verdi lay down, his green-scaled body looking like a hillock rising out of the tall grass.

Dag was aware of a keen intelligence behind the glittering eyes, but beyond that, he could glean nothing of what this wild dragon was thinking.

"Verdi—" Dag began and then stopped. "Do you mind if I call you Verdi? I know you dragons have your own names. I don't know what they are and you won't tell us. So we made up our own names for you. I hope that's all right."

Verdi's mouth gaped wide, showing all his fangs. He blinked, his head tilted slightly, and he curled his tail around his hind legs. Stephano could have told Dag that such gestures meant the dragon was in a good mood, pleased with himself and the world this morning, excited to be in this new land, though perhaps a little nervous.

Dag had no idea what the dragon meant, however, and not knowing what else to do, forged ahead.

"Near as I can tell, those"—he pointed to the mountain range—"are the Cassée Mountains."

Verdi turned his head to look.

"Likely that means nothing to you," Dag conceded, "but it means to me that we are west of the Abbey of Saint Agnes, which is where we want to go. The abbey is that way."

He pointed again in a different direction. Verdi turned his head to follow.

"The abbey is near the coast. My idea is that we fly east, hugging the coastline, until we find the abbey. We need to fly low to the ground," he added, "so that I can see the landmarks to guide us."

Verdi looked back at him. Dag could only hope he and the dragon had reached a meeting of the minds. He shouldered his bedroll and approached the dragon, keeping an eye on the massive head. Verdi's eyes followed his movements. Dag remembered that one mounted a dragon by climbing up on the foreleg and from there to the back. He pulled himself up onto the leg, feeling the tough, dry scales beneath his hands, noting with a soldier's interest how the scales were like chain mail, overlapping each other in a way that would distribute an impact across a much larger area than the size of the striking object.

No wonder bullets bounce off, he thought.

Once settled on the dragon's back, Dag grimaced at the pain in his buttocks, then braced himself and indicated with a shout that he was ready.

A dragon trained to fly with a human passenger would leap into the air, then spiral upward to gain altitude, thus sparing the human discomfort. The untrained Verdi sprang straight into the air, using his powerful hind legs to propel his body, and soared upward, his wings sweeping the sky.

The force of the dragon's takeoff flattened Dag back against the spike on the spine. Feeling his stomach drop out of him, Dag held tightly to the front spike and stared straight up past the dragon's head into the clouds. He could see, out of the corner of his eye, the ground rapidly falling away from beneath him. He could do nothing except hang on and pray that he survived and swore that if he did, he would never fly on a dragon again.

Once in the air, Verdi leveled out and Viola and Petard joined him. Verdi spoke to his friends in the dragon's impossible-to-pronounce language. Dag was holding on so tightly his arms began to shake. Chill sweat dried on his neck and chest. When his stomach caught up to the rest of him, he was sorry it did, for he tossed up his breakfast of roast deer meat.

He was heartened to see the dragons heading east, the route he'd told Verdi. Dag felt better as the flight progressed. Verdi and the other three flew low, as Dag had ordered. He recognized several landmarks and was relieved to see that he'd been correct, they were heading in the right direction. But, at that, he almost missed the abbey.

He located the harbor and the dock where the *Cloud Hopper* had docked over a month ago, after surviving an attack by the bat riders—the first time they had ever encountered the Bottom Dwellers. When he didn't see the twin spires of the abbey nearby he concluded, somewhat puzzled, that he must be wrong. Only when they flew into view of the compound and he recognized the stone wall surrounding the cathedral, did he understand why he had not seen the twin spires. He stared in shock at the massive pile of marble, stone, and broken timbers that had once been the ancient, beautiful Abbey of Saint Agnes.

Dag was so appalled by what he saw that he almost forgot to tell the dragons that they had reached their destination. He was about to call out, when he became aware that the three wild dragons had slowed their flight. Even Dag could see they were tense, uneasy.

He discovered the cause. Two larger dragons had taken to the air and were flying toward them, moving slowly, cautiously.

Dag recognized sergeants Hroal and Droal, former members of the Dragon Brigade.

"The dragons are friends of mine!" Dag shouted to Verdi.

The three dragons did not appear impressed. They began circling, drawing closer together.

Greatly daring, Dag gripped with his thighs and raised himself up as far as he could. Holding on with one hand, he waved at the brothers.

The dragon Droal lifted his head in astonishment and called out, "Sergeant!" The dragon barked in his usual laconic form of communication, "Who? What?"

Dag had assumed the meeting between the dragons would be a happy one, a family reunion. But this was a family that had been long divided. Both sides were mistrustful, afraid. He realized in alarm that both were preparing for a fight! God only knew what would happen to him if the dragons decided to do battle in the skies.

Dag had often heard Stephano and Miri talk about the differences between wild dragons and their civilized cousins. He had been skeptical. To him, all dragons looked alike. He now could see the differences for himself.

Droal and Hroal were nearly two times longer than the wild dragons, and their bodies were easily twice as heavy and bulky. Their necks were thicker, their chests broader and more massive. The wild dragons were smaller, sleeker, more graceful and lithe. It was as if Dag were comparing the large, well-fed Doctor Ellington to a lean, scrappy alley cat.

The three wild dragons thrust out their heads and hissed a warning for the strangers to keep their distance.

"These dragons! Friends of mine!" Dag roared again, but this didn't seem to have much effect.

He could feel Verdi's muscles quiver beneath his legs. He had no idea what the three wild dragons intended—flight or fight. Neither boded well for him.

Droal and Hroal took matters in hand. Both slowed, veering off and showing their underbellies to indicate they came with peaceful intent. Droal spoke to the three in the dragon language. The only word Dag understood in the conversation was his own name. Dag didn't know what was being said, but he thought he should respond. When Verdi peered around him, Dag gave an emphatic nod.

After some lengthy discussion, during which the dragons flew in circles, neither side coming too close, Droal spoke.

"All well, sir," said the dragon. "Never met wild cousins. Wild cousins never met us. Suspicious. Finally convinced."

Dag sighed in relief. "Thank you!" He gestured. "You and I—we need to talk."

Droal grunted. "Thought so."

He and his brother flew off, and the wild dragons followed. The sergeants set down in a field near the abbey. After they landed they waited off to one side as the wild dragons, still wary and uncertain, made their own landing. The three wild dragons continued to keep their distance, watching Droal and Hroal with narrowed eyes, wings slightly raised, heads lowered.

Dag slid off Verdi's back and, giving the dragon a pat in thanks for setting him down in one piece, he again had to stifle a groan. Dignity prevented him from rubbing his backside. He walked stiffly over to speak with the dragon brothers.

"Good to see you both again," said Dag. He noticed for the first time the fresh scars from the horrific burns Hroal had suffered. "I notice you've been wounded, Sergeant. Are you all right?"

"Thank you, sir," said Hroal. "Yes, sir. Westfirth. Bat riders."

"We were there," Dag said. "We barely escaped."

"Captain de Guichen. Safe?" Droal asked worriedly.

"All of us safe, thank you. Stephano—that is Captain de Guichen—sent me to speak to you. Our boat was damaged and we had to set down on an island for repairs. We met these wild dragons. Stephano—Captain de Guichen—started telling them tales of the Dragon Brigade and, well, one thing led to another and when we left, these three followed us."

Droal and Hroal listened with grave attention.

"Trouble is," Dag continued, "they understand us well enough, but they can't talk to us. We don't know why they followed us, what they want from us. Captain de Guichen was hoping you might be able to ask them."

"Not easy," Droal said, shaking his head and repeating, "Suspicious."

Hroal said something to his brother in their language. Both dragons looked with interest at Petard. Dag followed their gaze and saw the burns Hroal had sustained were similar to the burns Petard had suffered.

"Roed," said Hroal in grim tones.

At this word, the three wild dragons all looked at Hroal. Dag had no idea what the word meant, but observing the level of interest shown by the wild dragons, he repeated it several times to himself, making a mental note to tell Stephano.

"Bat riders made those wounds," said Hroal.

"We were on the island when we were attacked," Dag said. "That dragon there, the one with the wounds, saved our Gythe from the Bottom Dwellers. Those we used to call demons. They're not. Demons, that is."

"Bottom Dwellers." Droal rolled the words on his tongue. "Why?"

"That is what they call themselves," Dag explained. "Bottom Dwellers. They . . . uh . . . talked to Gythe. We think they call themselves that because they live at the bottom of the world. Deep below the Breath."

The dragon brothers digested this information.

"Is possible," said Droal, after a moment.

"What's possible?" Dag asked.

"The bottom. Dragons went there once," said Droal. "Found land."

"Didn't like it," Hroal added. "Came back. Never went again."

Dag thought this over. "You're saying the dragons flew down below the Breath and survived. They found land. Was anyone living there?"

Droal shook his head. "Long ago. Long, long ago."

Since dragons live to the age of three hundred or more, a long time to a dragon might be a thousand years or more. So if humans were not living on the bottom then, how did they come to be living there now? The answer was beyond Dag's ability to puzzle out.

All this time, the three wild dragons had been conferring. They apparently arrived at a consensus, because the female wild dragon, Viola, raised her head and made a trumpeting call. She walked forward several paces, her wings extended, her belly low to the ground.

Droal raised his head and moved toward her. She halted out of striking range, but close enough to speak. Droal halted when she did.

The two dragons began to converse. Dag walked about; he figured it was less painful than trying to sit down. He listened to the conversation, but it was nothing but roaring, hooting, and bellowing to him. He wandered over to gaze sadly at the ruins of the cathedral and recalled Father Jacob saying how the Bottom Dwellers had left constructs in the stone work designed to weaken and eventually bring down the building. The priest had asked the dragon brothers to keep guard on it, to make sure no one entered.

Not that there was much likelihood of that, Dag thought sadly. The abbey was located in an isolated part of Rosia. No one ever came here anymore except the occasional ship lost in the mists and Trundlers.

Dag's thoughts went to his friends aboard the *Cloud Hopper.* He wondered if Miri had been very angry at Stephano, and how Doctor Ellington was faring without him.

The conversation between the dragons continued. Dag heard a few words he understood, among them "Captain de Guichen" and "Château d'Eau Brisé," the name of Stephano's family estate. Dag couldn't imagine why the dragons would be discussing this.

The midday sun had reached its zenith. He was slowly roasting in his armor. He drank from his canteen; the water was tepid and stale. Sighting some trees in the distance, he decided to walk over, find a seat in the shade, maybe a stream. He hobbled across the field, walking off the stiffness in his muscles. He had nearly reached the trees when Droal called his name.

Dag sighed, turned around, and walked back.

"Clan elders sent dragons," said Droal.

"They did? Why?"

"Bottom Dwellers. *Roed.* Kill dragons. The elders want—"

"Excuse me, Droal," Dag said, interrupting, "what is *roed*?"

"*Roed* is *roed*," Droal said, blinking.

"*Roed,* not *raeg*," Hroal added.

The two seemed to think this explained everything.

Dag gave up on the linguistic lesson. He could see, out of the corner of his eye, the wild dragons listening intently.

"Why didn't the elders talk to *us* about the Bottom Dwellers?" Dag wondered. "I'm assuming the elders speak our language. Someone taught the young ones. If they can't speak it, they understand it."

"*Roed.* Elders don't trust any humans. Sent young to find kin." Droal gave a thump of his tail on the ground.

"Well, now that this is settled, I'm assuming they're going to fly off to look for their cousins."

"Staying," said Droal. "With you."

Dag's jaw dropped. "Me? They're staying with me?"

"You and Captain de Guichen."

"They can't," said Dag flatly. "We live in Evreux. There'd be hell to pay."

"Captain de Guichen's estate. Housing. Saddles. Learn. Dragon Brigade. My idea," Droal said proudly.

"Brother and I," Hroal added. "Teach them to fight."

Stephano's dream of forming his own Dragon Brigade had come true, Dag thought. Just not in the way he'd imagined.

"Good idea, I guess," said Dag, taking off his helm and scratching his head. "Do you know where the estate is located?"

"Been there," said Droal. "Old days."

"Excellent. You take charge of this lot," said Dag, relieved. "I need to get back to Evreux. Do any ships and Trundler boats ever dock here?"

Droal was shaking his head. "Dragons trust you."

"Won't let you go," Hroal added.

"I have to join up with Stephano—"

"Then they will follow. Where you go, they go," said Hroal.

Dag muttered a few swear words in Guundaran and wiped the sweat from his face. He wondered what to do. He looked over at the wild dragons, and the three of them gazed back at him.

Dag gave a philosophical shrug. He'd learned early in his military career to take whatever you were handed and make the best of it. Bellyaching only made matters worse.

"I suppose we'd best get started," he said, and he clapped his helm on his head.

16

Who's watching who, watching who's watching who.
—Rodrigo de Villenueve

The king of Rosia, His Majesty Alaric le Fevre, returned to the royal palace after his trip to Westfirth. Once there, he insisted on ordering eighteen ships from the naval fleet that he had recalled from Braffa to remain to guard the palace. Cecile argued against this. She maintained that the ships were needed to represent Rosian interests in the city-state of Braffa, whose refineries produced the liquefied Breath of God that kept the naval ships afloat.

King Alaric was vengeful, obdurate, with just enough intelligence to be dangerous. He had been a young man when he had ascended to the throne. He believed in his father's delightful secret to ruling: leave all decisions to your ministers and advisers and if anything goes wrong, blame them.

The Countess de Marjolaine was chief among Alaric's advisers. He had wits enough to value her advice and generally abided by it. There were times, however, when he insisted on having his own way. Alaric could be as stubborn as a wyvern, as the saying went, and nothing Cecile said on the subject of the royal navy could deter him from ordering the ships of the line, commanded by his eldest son, Prince Renaud, to remain to defend their king.

To give Alaric credit, he was honestly convinced that the bat riders were Freyans in disguise. Alaric hated the Freyans with a profound and malignant hatred such that if the attackers had been devils sent by Aertheum the Archfiend, Alaric would have been far less concerned. Never mind that Alaric had no explanation for the gigantic bats or the weapons that belched green fire. He had decided they must be secret weapons, developed by the Freyans.

The grand bishop had always fostered Alaric's hatred for the Freyans and now proclaimed loudly that the assault had been a Freyan attack. Cecile was surprised to learn that the stunning and exotic Idonia, Duquesa de Plata Niebla, was adding her voice to those blaming Freya, hinting she had secret information that pointed to the fact.

Cecile had, as was customary, secretly investigated the Duquesa de Plata Niebla. Cecile remembered the woman from the last time she had been at court, years ago. Idonia had remained several months as a guest of the queen. King Alaric, being fond of beautiful young women, had attempted to seduce the duchess. She had fended off his advances, managing to do so in a way that did not offend Alaric, but instead left him intrigued and admiring. She offered as her reason for refusing him the fact that she was dear friends with his wife.

Alaric didn't care two bent rosuns for his wife and continued to try to batter down the duchess's resistance. Just when he thought he had won her, she had announced that she was leaving court to return to her estate because her husband, the duke, was in ill health. She had departed, and Alaric had turned his attentions elsewhere.

Cecile's agents had reported that the duchess appeared to

be exactly who she said she was. Once she was gone, Cecile had forgotten about her.

The duchess had returned older in years, but as beautiful as ever. She wore powdered wigs and powdered her dusky complexion. The white emphasized her black eyes, rose-red cheeks and lips. She was like a red rose among pink and white daisies. She claimed to be a widow now and a wealthy widow at that. Alaric liked his women young and he was no longer interested in bedding the duchess. He enjoyed having her around, however. She flattered him and amused him with her witty *bon mots* and gossip about the latest court scandals.

Cecile had not liked the duchess when she had first come to court. A woman of obvious intelligence, wit, and charm, Idonia fawned over the silly, empty-headed Queen Annemarie. Cecile could think of only one reason for the duchess to spend so much time in the company of a woman who must bore her to tears—the queen could not keep a secret to save her soul. Her Majesty was a flowing font of information.

The night after she returned from Westfirth, Cecile was in her suite of rooms in the palace, working late. She was meeting with her confidential agent, man-of-business, secretary, and trusted confidant, D'argent. The two were going over the countess's dealings related to her large estate in Marjolaine. The wealthiest woman in Rosia, Cecile handled all her business matters herself. She and D'argent were discussing the collection of rents owed by her tenants. The countess's mind was not on her work, however.

She laid down the lorgnette she had been using to read the numbers and sat gazing at a painting on the wall opposite her—a landscape of her country estate done by a famous artist commissioned by her father.

"I am at my wits' end, D'argent," Cecile said abruptly.

D'argent realized she was not talking about the rents. He gave her his full attention.

"How can I help, my lady?"

"In regard to the Duquesa de Plata Niebla."

"Indeed, my lady," said D'argent, sympathetic.

"I thought we had seen the last of her. She was merely an annoyance then. She is now becoming a nuisance."

The two were in Cecile's study, a room decorated with elegance and taste. Fine paintings hung on the walls. The heavy sky-blue velvet curtains had been drawn and the crystal lamps lighted. The salon, a large chamber adjacent to the study, was empty of those who either came to see the countess or to be seen.

Cecile rose from behind her desk, which was hand-carved oak painted white with gold gilt trim, decorated with the countess's insignia, the bumblebee. She opened the door to the salon, making certain she and D'argent were alone. She shut the door and began pacing, her footfalls noiseless on the soft, thick blue carpet. As she walked, she absently twisted the small gold ring.

"I have been seeking to meet with His Majesty on a matter of the greatest importance. I have received information from Father Jacob of the Arcanum that the king needs to hear. Yet the king sends me word that he is not at liberty to see me because he is having a picnic with the duchess or he is playing at quoits with the duchess or going riding with the duchess. If they were having a love affair I could understand it, but Alaric is still sleeping with that blond, bosomy daughter of the Marquis de Cheauvat. Unless something has changed there?"

The countess stopped her pacing to cast an interrogative look at D'argent.

"No, my lady. His Majesty is said to pay nightly visits to the young woman's bedchamber."

"Then he can't be having an affair with the duchess," said Cecile, frowning. "This Idonia is playing a game and it is *not* quoits!"

D'argent said meaningfully, "The queen has been in an excellent humor of late."

Cecile considered this remark. "Now that you mention it, D'argent, I have observed the same. And Her Majesty's good humor is odd, considering the rumors flying about Alaric and the marquis's daughter. Queen Annemarie would ordinarily be shrieking like a fishwife and breaking the royal porcelain."

"The queen and the duchess are always together, my lady. Whenever the duchess is with the king, she makes certain the queen is in attendance. Some say the duchess is conspiring with the king to keep his affair secret from the queen. Whereas I believe . . ." D'argent hesitated.

"Continue, D'argent," said Cecile. "I trust your instincts. What do you believe?"

"I believe the duchess is conspiring with the queen to keep His Majesty from *you,* my lady," D'argent said.

Cecile resumed her seat behind the desk. Picking up the lorgnette, she thoughtfully tapped it on the stack of papers.

"I think you may be right. But why, D'argent? Why is this duchess of nowhere trying to prevent me from talking to the king? It can't be political. The duchy of Plata Niebla is of no value to anyone, not even to the Estarans."

"She is Estaran, my lady," D'argent suggested. "Perhaps she is trying to persuade His Majesty to switch sides."

Estara and Travia were both fighting over Braffa and its refineries. Cecile had convinced King Alaric to side with Travia in the dispute, whereas the grand bishop was siding with Estara. Freya was said to be neutral in the dispute, though Cecile suspected that Sir Henry Wallace was stoking the fire to keep the pot boiling.

Travia and Estara were not at war, probably due more to the shocking attack on Westfirth than the current peace negotiations. Travia and Estara had both been terrified they would be next. After a few weeks had passed with no more attacks, the two countries had gone back to their squabbling.

"If Alaric suddenly decided to favor Estara, it would be disastrous to Rosian interests," said Cecile.

"Not to mention your own, my lady," said D'argent.

"An investment in what may turn out to be nothing," said Cecile with a shrug. "Money I have already counted as lost."

She was still thinking about the duchess. "I believe it is time I took more notice of the Duquesa de Plata Niebla. I have had her investigated before, but this time I want you to conduct discreet inquiries about the woman, D'argent."

Cecile paused, thoughtful, then added with a cool smile, "And if you should happen to run into the clever Monsieur Dubois, you might mention the duchess to him."

"Dubois? The bishop's agent?" D'argent was surprised.

"The little man is like a terrier when it comes to dragging rats out of their holes," said Cecile. "I observed him watching her when we were in Westfirth. We should set him on her trail."

"I will do so, my lady," said D'argent.

Cecile held the lorgnette to her eyes and picked up the document related to the rents. She resumed her examination of the accounts. D'argent took up his pen and the conversation turned once again to more mundane matters of business.

The next day, D'argent attended the king's levee, an informal reception held by His Majesty every morning. During the levee, gentlemen of the court conducted business, exchanged the news of the day, argued over their horses, bragged about their love affairs, and rejoiced in the latest scandals. No gentleman missed a levee if he could help it. It was said that once an ailing count had insisted on being carried to the king's levee on a litter.

D'argent was always present. He greeted friends and was greeted, all the while searching the shadowy corners of the room where Dubois was known to lurk. D'argent eventually found the small, self-effacing man comfortably ensconced behind an enormous porcelain vase, watching, listening.

"Monsieur Dubois," D'argent said.

"Monsieur D'argent," said Dubois.

D'argent bowed gracefully. Dubois gave a little bob. He remained standing in his corner and D'argent joined him. Both gentlemen kept their backs to the wall, looking out over the room filled with men laughing, arguing, whispering, discoursing. His Majesty sat on his throne, discussing with several of his cronies the merits of his new hunting dog.

"The Duquesa de Plata Niebla," said D'argent in a low voice that slid beneath the hubbub.

"Yes, monsieur?" Dubois glanced at his companion and raised an eyebrow.

"A beautiful woman," said D'argent.

"Indeed," Dubois agreed.

"And so fashionable," said D'argent.

"I believe that to be the case," said Dubois cautiously, perhaps not feeling himself capable of judging flounces and petticoats.

"You wouldn't by chance happen to know the duchess's dressmaker?" D'argent asked languidly.

Dubois cast D'argent a sharp glance. "I fear not, monsieur."

"A pity," said D'argent. "The countess admires the duchess's style exceedingly. She was hoping to find out."

D'argent bowed, and Dubois again gave his little bob.

As D'argent moved away, he heard Dubois murmur to himself, "Well, well, well . . ."

D'argent smiled.

Eiddwen had established her identity as Idonia the Duquesa de Plata Niebla years ago, at a time when Xavier, the leader of those known as the Bottom Dwellers, was starting to form his plans for war against those Above. A key part of those plans was to plant a spy in the royal court of Rosia. Eiddwen had been his choice. She had been groomed to play that role, as well as many others, from the time she was a little girl.

The first time Eiddwen had come to court over ten years ago she had stayed only long enough to establish herself as the queen's dearest friend. Eiddwen had attached herself to Queen Annemarie, a vapid, silly woman with no taste, no discretion, and no interest in anything except finding a husband for her daughter and complaining about how badly her own husband treated her.

For the price of some flattery, a few sympathetic tears, and the willingness to listen with a smile to endless hours of mindless blathering, Eiddwen made the queen her boon companion. In return she received important information.

The queen cared nothing for affairs of state, being far more interested in catching the king in affairs of a different sort, and she was continually poking and prying, snooping and spying on him, trying to find which of the noble ladies of the court he was bedding. If along the way she happened to pick up secrets of a sensitive political or military nature she cast them aside or shared them with her friends like bonbons.

As the queen's confidante, Eiddwen could go anywhere, talk to anyone, ask anything. Her own charm, wit, and beauty assisted her. During her current visit she had already gained valuable information about Rosian interests abroad, the king's latest plots to confound Freya, and the movements of the royal navy, all of which she passed on to the Bottom Dwellers through intermediaries.

The same morning of the king's levee, as D'argent was talking to Dubois, Eiddwen was in the chapel of the royal palace, sitting beside the queen, who attended morning prayers regularly. Annemarie was accompanied by her daughter, her ladies-in-waiting, and courtiers who wanted to ingratiate themselves with Her Majesty.

Eiddwen sat on the cold stone pew, absorbed in her own thoughts, paying no heed to the priest's sermon. Despite a few setbacks, such as the failure to assassinate Sir Henry Wallace and Father Jacob Northrop, all was going well in her world. Matters were progressing.

When the time came for prayers, Eiddwen sank onto the kneeling bench. Dutifully bowing her head, she looked down on the marble floor to see if there was a message from her contact this morning. She was not expecting to hear anything because the plans were going well and she was surprised to find, beneath the kneeling bench, a small square of paper. Under cover of dropping her fan, Eiddwen picked up the paper and slid it in her prayer book. Once more seated in the pew, she opened her prayer book to read the note.

Usual place. 2.

Eiddwen shut the prayer book.

"Your Majesty," said Eiddwen, as they were walking from the chapel, "I fear I will not be able to attend your stroll in the garden this afternoon."

"And why not?" Queen Annemarie asked sharply, displeased.

"I have received news regarding my business affairs in Estara, which require that I go into the city to meet with my lawyers," Eiddwen replied humbly.

"Nonsense," said the queen. "Nasty creatures, lawyers. I quite despise them. They must get on without you. I cannot. I will be bored to distraction if you are not with me."

The queen turned to her daughter for confirmation. "Won't I be bored, Sophia?"

"Mama, you are being unreasonable," said the princess with a sweet and understanding smile for the duchess. "Bandit and I will walk with you, won't we, Bandit?"

Sophia asked this question of her spaniel, who was trotting along at his mistress's side.

"Unreasonable! I am certain I am never unreasonable," said Queen Annemarie querulously. "I am the most reasonable person I know. And as for you walking in the garden, you are far too unwell, Sophia. You will bring on one of your headaches."

"I am feeling quite well today, Mama," said Sophia. "The medicine Her Grace was kind enough to prepare to relieve my headaches has helped me."

"Let us hope the medicine cures you," said the queen with a sniff. "No man wants a sickly wife. As for you, Your Grace, if you insist upon soiling your hands with business matters, I suppose I must do without you."

Eiddwen murmured her thanks to the queen and hurried to the guest chambers in the palace where she resided. She removed her silken flounces, feathers, jewels and petticoats, and her white wig. She donned traveling clothes, tied on a broad-brimmed hat with a long veil, slipped on her gloves, and sent word to her coachmen.

The carriage with the coat of arms of the duchy of Plata
Niebla arrived, drawn by two wyverns. Eiddwen entered,
gave the coachman directions, and the carriage began its descent from the palace to the ground.

Eiddwen looked up at the palace through the carriage
window. The Sunset Palace, considered one of the wonders
of the world, floated high above the city of Evreux.

The palace was a breathtaking sight, whether seen by day,
suspended in the air above the lake and mirrored in the waters
below, or by night, when its lighted windows, shining in the
darkness, rivaled the stars. The palace was most beautiful in
the twilight, when magical constructs set in the walls reflected
the colors of the sky, causing them to change color from pink
to orange, purple and blue.

Simple in design, the palace was a square with a tower at
each of the four corners. The entrance consisted of another,
smaller square constructed inside the first, with a smaller
tower at each of those four corners. The palace's beauty lay
in the graceful magnificence of the towers and the fanciful
construction of the one hundred chimneys, each of which
was of a different design, so that the palace, from a distance,
resembled the skyline of a city.

The palace was home to many hundreds of people, including the king and his family, the royal guards, servants,
and retainers, as well as members of the nobility who kept
private residences in the palace, along with their guards,
servants, and retainers. Also living there were the royal
crafters, who maintained the magical constructs that kept
the castle aloft. Multitudes visited the palace on business or
pleasure. The palace teemed with life at almost all hours of
the day and night.

Eiddwen hated the palace and the fools who lived inside
its rotting decadence. She sank back in the comfortable leather

seat to rejoice in the fact that for a few hours she was free of the stupidity of Her Majesty.

The coachman left her outside the gate of the vast enclave of the church of Rosia. Within the walls were the bishop's palace, home of the grand bishop; the university; the grand cathedral; the Mother House of the Knight Protectors; living quarters for the students, the laity, and the nuns and priests. Eiddwen crossed the extensive and beautiful grounds and entered the cathedral through the great bronze doors.

The late morning sun illuminated the stained-glass windows, but did not venture inside, leaving the interior in perpetual cool and shadowy twilight. Few people were in the cathedral, for morning prayers were over and evensong was hours away. Some elderly nuns arranged bouquets of fresh flowers on the altar and trimmed the candles. Two priests walked the aisle, their heads together, talking softly.

The bells of the city were chiming the hour of two of the clock as Eiddwen made her way to one of the small niches in the walls dedicated to the dead; private, ancient chapels meant only for the family. Grilles of wrought iron screened off the chapels, kept out the curious. Only family members had the keys. And, in this instance, Eiddwen.

She removed the key from her glove, glanced around the nave to see that no one was paying attention, and inserted the key into the lock. Then she sat down on a bench that was in deep shadow to wait for her contact.

She did not have to wait long. A monk moved with a slow and solemn step toward the wrought-iron gate. He glanced about, as had Eiddwen, and slipped inside, shutting the gate behind him. The monk wore spectacles of tinted glass and he required a moment to adjust himself to the darkness.

"I am here, Brother Paul," said Eiddwen, raising her veil.

The monk turned his head in her direction and came over to sit beside her. Eiddwen held a lace-edged handkerchief, ready to put it to her eyes. If anyone should happen to pass, they would see only a monk comforting the bereaved.

"How does your work progress?" Brother Paul asked, keeping his voice low.

"Slowly," said Eiddwen. "But well."

"When do you estimate you will be finished?"

"Within the month," said Eiddwen.

Brother Paul frowned. "So long?"

"The work is delicate and exacting and I can move about the palace only after midnight," Eiddwen said irritably. "During the day I am required to dote upon Her Royal Stupidity. I must sleep sometime."

"I was only asking," said Brother Paul meekly. "You needn't bite my head off." He gave a sigh. "You think *your* patience is tried; I spend my days groveling to false priests."

"Speaking of priests," said Eiddwen, "what news of Father Jacob?"

"He recovered his wits, you know," said Brother Paul.

"Yes, I heard that before I left Westfirth. I also heard someone tried to kill him."

"He survived," said Brother Paul bitterly. "That bloody Knight Protector of his saved him!"

Eiddwen's dark eyes glittered in the dim light.

"You!" Eiddwen said. That single word was infused with such venom that Brother Paul rose from the seat and moved nervously away from her, nearer the tomb.

"Yes, me," Brother Paul said defensively. "I had a chance to destroy our enemy and I took it."

"You stupid, stupid man," said Eiddwen, her voice cold with contempt. "You will bring ruin to us all. Did anyone see you?"

"No one saw me near the library," said Brother Paul evasively.

"But someone saw you enter the archbishop's palace. Who?"

Brother Paul shifted his feet. "What does it matter? The priest doesn't suspect me . . ."

"Of course, Father Jacob suspects you!" Eiddwen returned angrily. "He has always suspected you because you were present at the abbey when the attack occurred and foolish enough to remain."

"I had to find the books of the saints. I should think you would want the priest dead. What if he comes to court? He knows you."

"Only by the name of 'the Sorceress.' He has never seen me."

"Sir Henry Wallace has seen you," said Brother Paul accusingly. "He knows you by sight. He knows you are connected with the green beam weapon because you took his money to finance it. You tried to kill him and Father Jacob and you bungled it. I was trying to clean up your mess."

Eiddwen jumped to her feet. Brother Paul flung up his arm and took a step backward, but Eiddwen had no intention of harming him. She flashed him a vicious glance and paced rapidly back and forth a few moments to calm herself.

"What's done is done, I suppose," she said with an irate frown. "If you want my advice, you will stay away from Father Jacob."

"What about that man, Wallace?" Brother Paul insisted. "What if *he* comes to court?"

Eiddwen gave a unpleasant smile. "He would be hanged if he did! Besides, his interests lie elsewhere. He is playing with that magical new steel of his."

The bells chimed the half hour. Eiddwen would have to be returning to the palace or the queen would start to grow suspicious.

"Why did you summon me here, Paul? To display your monumental ignorance?"

Brother Paul chose to ignore her sarcasm. She sat back down and he perched himself uneasily on the bench beside her.

"You have a new assignment. The Princess Sophia. You are to abduct her and bring her Below."

Eiddwen stared at the monk in astonishment. "You can't be serious! The girl is never out of the sight of at least a dozen guardsmen, not to mention her own ladies-in-waiting, any number of servants, and her doting parents. How am I to accomplish this impossible feat?"

"How you handle the matter it is your affair," said Brother Paul. "The order comes directly from Xavier."

Eiddwen gazed, frowning, into the darkness. Her gloved hands knotted the handkerchief.

"Why does Xavier want the princess?" she asked, more subdued.

"Because you told him that she is a savant and that she has some sort of connection to what is happening Below."

"She hears the beating of the drums."

Brother Paul raised an eyebrow, causing his spectacles to slip down his nose.

"I know—it seems improbable," said Eiddwen. "Yet I have seen it for myself. During those times the drums are in use, the princess falls victim to terrible headaches and claims to be tormented by the constant sound of drums beating. It is possible, I suppose, that as the drums break down the magic in this world, they are breaking down the magic within her. Since she is a savant, the magic in her blood is very strong."

"Does she talk openly about hearing drums?" Brother Paul asked, alarmed. "People might begin to suspect."

"I have been dosing the princess with a concoction that sends her into a deep, deep sleep when the headaches start.

Even then she twitches and moans, but at least she isn't babbling. Why does Xavier want her?"

"Orders have been sent out for our people to locate and abduct any savants and bring them Below," said Brother Paul.

"What does Xavier want with savants?"

"That is the business of our blessed saint."

Eiddwen was not pleased. "I could be risking my life in this endeavor. I want to know why."

"Some might start to doubt your loyalty—"

"Doubt my loyalty! I may not have been born Below, but I believe in your cause," Eiddwen said vehemently. "I have worked for that cause all my life, ever since I was a child and Xavier taught me to understand your suffering. He held me in his arms and gave me my name, which means 'holy,' and so I am to him and to our people. Those who dwell Below would not be where they are today, on the verge of victory, were it not for me."

Brother Paul eyed her, irresolute.

"Someone's coming," Eiddwen whispered. Lowering her veil, she put her handkerchief to her eyes.

"Have faith in God, my child," Brother Paul said sonorously.

Eiddwen sobbed and covered her face with the handkerchief. The elderly nuns who had been arranging the altar walked past. Witnessing Eiddwen's violent grief, the nuns stopped.

"Can we be of assistance, Brother?" one asked.

"No, Sister, thank you," said Brother Paul.

Eiddwen shook her head. The nuns gave her their blessing and walked off.

When they were once again alone, Brother Paul said softly, "If I tell you, you must say nothing. I am not supposed to know. I overheard a conversation . . ."

"Why all the mystery?" Eiddwen asked, perplexed.

"You will soon understand. When our island of Glasearrach was attacked, the sinking of the island had the effect of disrupting the Breath. Terrible wizard storms swept over the land Above, plunging the world into chaos for hundreds of years—"

"Yes, yes, I know my history lessons," said Eiddwen impatiently. "Come to the point."

"I will if you will let me," said Brother Paul sullenly. "The Four Saints came together and prayed to God and managed to calm the wizard storms. People in the world Above ascribed the miracle to God. Xavier knows better."

Eiddwen heard the church bell toll the hour.

"What does all this have to do with savants? Be quick."

"We are now experiencing these same storms Below," said Brother Paul.

"There have been storms before—"

"Not like these. These storms are ruinous. Torrential rains, deadly lightning. Rivers flooding, washing away entire villages and destroying crops. And the wizard storms are growing increasingly severe."

"No one knows the cause?"

"Some blame the magic of the drums. Xavier is worried. There are food shortages, rumblings of discontent about the ritual sacrifices. Even rumors of open rebellion. Xavier won't halt the drumming, yet he must find a way to stop the storms. History tells us that Saint Marie was a savant, and we know the other saints were either savants or highly gifted in magic. Xavier theorizes the magical power of savants calmed the storms Above. He hopes it will work Below. He believes the princess to be especially powerful."

"Are you saying Xavier's rule is in peril?" Eiddwen asked, shocked.

"That is why no one is supposed to know," said Brother Paul in a smothered whisper. "The rumors of rebellion are not just rumors."

"And what are these savants to do once they are Below? Pray to a God that doesn't exist?"

"Xavier has a plan," said Brother Paul.

Eiddwen sighed deeply. "I love and respect and honor him. Yet sometimes, I wonder . . ."

"Wonder what?" Brother Paul asked.

Eiddwen glanced at him. Brother Paul seemed a little too eager.

"Nothing." She rose to her feet. "I must be going. I will see what I can do with regard to the princess."

Before they left the chapel, Eiddwen rested her hand on Brother Paul's arm and dug her nails into his flesh.

"Keep away from Father Jacob. You have no need to fear him. No one in the church trusts him. They tried to shut him up in an asylum, for mercy's sake. Let him dig his own grave."

"I have my orders. You have yours," said Brother Paul. He walked away, rubbing his forearm. Pausing, he turned back. "Stay away from the Crystal Market." He walked on before Eiddwen could ask why.

She returned to court and sought out the queen, who decided to punish her by refusing to speak to her. Eiddwen found the change refreshing. Sadly, the punishment lasted only a few moments and soon the queen was going into rhapsodic effusions over the latest wealthy candidate she had chosen to marry her daughter.

Eiddwen was rewarded for her patience with an idea. The queen wanted a husband for Sophia. Why not present her with one? Eiddwen spent the next half hour thinking it all out and decided it might work. Returning to her room to dress for dinner, Eiddwen took a moment to write a letter.

Dearest Lucello,

I hope this letter finds you recovered from the wound you sustained in the failed assassination attempt against Sir Henry Wallace. Forgive me if I did not send you a letter of condolence, but you get no sympathy from me. You botched the job and not only that, allowed him to catch you. You are lucky Wallace only blew off your toe and not your head.

I need your assistance at the royal court. You will travel here immediately to play the part of my nephew, the Conte Osinni. I will explain your duties when you arrive. For the moment all you need to know is that you are from eastern Estara and you are fabulously wealthy. You will need suitable attire. I will see that your expenses are covered.

E.

When the letter was written, Eiddwen set a construct on it that magically rearranged all the letters, so that if it fell into the wrong hands, the missive would be indecipherable. The recipient had to cast the reverse of the magical spell in order to read it. Only her youthful apprentice, Lucello Fabbri, knew the secret.

Eiddwen summoned a footman, gave the letter into his hands with orders to carry it immediately to the post. She then adorned herself with her jewels, her feathers, her silken brocade, and fine lace and went forth to dazzle all who encountered her.

17

It is the responsibility of the church to keep and maintain an accurate account of historical events. The accounting of the world's history is housed in the library in the university, so we may learn from the past. Only the works of Aertheum and his minions are kept hidden, for fear that even the memory of such evil might taint the reader.

—Monsignor Guisepi Nindazi,
Master Historian,
the Church of the Breath

Unlike the countess, who immediately tried to obtain an audience with His Majesty to give him Father Jacob's information regarding the Bottom Dwellers, Dubois did not immediately seek an audience with the grand bishop. This was due to Dubois's personal philosophy regarding life: check and verify.

He did not necessarily believe that every person he encountered was lying to him. Dubois took a less cynical view of humanity. He did believe that it never hurt to make certain.

On his return to his quarters in Evreux, Dubois read through the reports that had arrived from his numerous agents the world over. He met personally with some of them. After that, he paid a visit to the university library.

The building consisted of two floors. The lower floor was one large open room filled with desks and chairs all neatly arranged. Books stood in high wooden shelves that ran the length of the walls. The shelves were of such height, the librarians had to climb ladders to reach the books. The library's high ceiling was adorned with paintings depicting the sky at various times of the day and night, replete with pink and purple and golden clouds for sunrise and sunset, a dazzling sun at noontime, and darkness and stars and the moon at night.

The second floor was a balcony that overlooked the floor below. Those perusing the books on the balcony level could gaze down onto the first floor or look up at the ceiling. The library was deathly quiet, the silence broken only by the rustling of a page, the occasional cough or whispered word.

The head librarian, an elderly monk, sat at his desk on the first floor, ready to assist. Dubois inquired where he might find books written on the sinking of the island of Glasearrach. The priest directed him to a section on the second floor, saying he would find two shelves of books dealing with that subject.

Dubois discovered that most of the books were about the Pirate King, Ian Meehan, and the events that led up to the sinking of the island. He read several accounts of how the nations of the world put aside their differences to bring down the nefarious Meehan by sinking the island but he could not find anything with regard to the event itself.

Very odd, Dubois thought. Since that event changed the course of history.

Dubois went back to ask the librarian if he might find books or manuscripts regarding this time period in another location in this library or perhaps in another library.

The librarian happened to be perusing a book containing engravings of dragons chasing some savage-looking humans carrying spears. He raised his head to peer at Dubois over a pair of spectacles perched precariously on the end of his nose.

"Our collection of books on the Pirate King and Glasearrach is the most extensive in the world," the librarian replied in rebuking tones.

"But the authors of the books are modern," Dubois murmured. "I was hoping to find information written by those who must have witnessed the event."

"Hardly to be expected, monsieur, given the terrible aftermath," said the librarian.

"Might books on this subject be found in the Library of the Forbidden?"

"It is called 'Forbidden' for a reason, monsieur. Only the provost of the Arcanum has access to those books. I doubt if you would find anything about the sinking of the island. Only books deemed dangerous to the faith are stored there."

"Still, given the calamitous nature of the event, someone must have written about it," Dubois argued mildly. "For example, the church must have kept records. The church keeps records about everything."

The priest considered his argument and found it lacking. "The church was fighting for the lives and souls of their flock. The priests of the time must be excused for not taking time to put pen to paper—if there were such things as pen and paper to be found in those dark days."

Dubois politely thanked the librarian for his help and left him to his reading.

And so, Dubois pondered, he found himself in a cul-de-sac. He had no way to verify Father Jacob's claims except to wonder if the very absence of evidence that people were still alive on the island as it sank was, in itself, evidence.

Dubois briefly considered attempting to gain access to the Library of the Forbidden. He immediately discarded the idea.

The library was located in the Arcanum, under the auspices of the provost. The Grand Bishop de Montagne himself would find gaining access to the library difficult, if not impossible. Those who wondered why such books were not destroyed had only to reflect upon the inscription that was set in stone above the vault's iron doors: KNOW THY ENEMY.

Dubois decided not to delay his report to the grand bishop any longer. On the day of Midsummer Revels, when people filled the marketplaces and thronged the shops, preparing for the evening's feasting and dancing, Dubois obtained an audience with Ferdinand de Montagne, grand bishop of the Church of the Breath.

Dubois entered through a secret passage that led to a small closet attached to the grand bishop's office—a closet hidden behind a tapestry. Listening at the door of his closet, Dubois could hear someone moving about the room—Montagne, by his heavy footfalls and long strides. The grand bishop was an extraordinarily tall man, well over six feet, and large of girth. Ascertaining that the grand bishop was alone, Dubois made himself known by softly rapping on the door.

"Enter, Dubois," Montagne called.

Dubois opened the door, then drew aside the tapestry that concealed the door's presence. He found Montagne seating himself at his desk.

"Ah, Dubois," said the grand bishop, motioning for his agent to be seated. "You have excellent timing. I was just about to send for you. I need you to deliver this letter. Help yourself to food and wine while you wait."

The grand bishop's wine was excellent. Dubois poured himself a glass and then waited in silence while the grand bishop wrote his letter, signed it, and sealed it with a signet set in a silver seal.

"Take this to the Estaran ambassador. Confidential, of course," said the grand bishop, handing the letter to Dubois.

"The departure of the royal navy from Braffa means that Estara can move her own ships into position. I have pledged my support."

Money would be flowing from the Rosian church coffers into the coffers of the Estarans. The Church of the Breath was very powerful in Estara. If Estara—and by extension the church—gained control of the flow of the liquid form of the Breath known as the "Blood of God," the church would become considerably more wealthy and very powerful.

Dubois tucked the letter into a secret inner pocket of his coat.

"This brings me most providentially to my first report, Eminence," said Dubois. "I have received information from one of my agents that the Freyans are sending their fleet to Braffa."

"You misspoke, Dubois," said Montage, frowning. "You meant to say that Freya is sending a fleet to Rosia. This, of course, means war—"

"I beg your pardon, Eminence," Dubois interjected. "I did not misspeak. At the instigation of Sir Henry Wallace, Freya is going to be dispatching ships to Braffa. King Alaric left them an opening when he ordered the fleet away—at your urging, I believe . . ."

Montagne was silent, glaring at Dubois.

"I will alert the Estarans," Montagne said at last. "What else do you have for me?"

"I have a message to you from Father Jacob."

Montagne grimaced. His stomach made a rumbling sound.

"The mere mention of that man's name brings on my dyspepsia. I confess, Dubois, that on hearing Father Jacob had lost his wits I was tempted to thank God for His mercies. I did not, but the thought crossed my mind."

"You are only human, Eminence," Dubois murmured.

The grand bishop sighed in acknowledgment. He looked

at Dubois sharply. "Why did Father Jacob send *you* to report? That is not like him. Why did he not come to annoy me himself?"

"You have not heard the news, Eminence?" Dubois asked. "I would have thought the archbishop would have informed you immediately."

The grand bishop rubbed his forehead. "The archbishop is forever sending me reports. He writes three or four reports a day. I am at least a week behind. What happened?"

"An attempt was made on Father Jacob's life. Someone tossed a bomb into the room where we were meeting. I myself very nearly fell victim."

"Good God, Dubois!" the grand bishop exclaimed, shocked. "I have heard nothing of this. Are you all right?"

"I am fine, Eminence," said Dubois. "No one was injured, thanks to the quick thinking and courage of the Knight Protector, Sir Ander Martel. He picked up the bomb before it could go off and threw it out into the hall. The blast took out a portion of the wall and knocked down several ceiling beams."

The grand bishop was clearly shaken. "I have never been fond of Sir Ander Martel, as you know. But the knight has done me a great service and I will see to it that he receives a commendation. Dubois, I say this from my heart. I do not know what I would do without you."

Dubois was pleased and touched. He gave a self-deprecating smile and went back to business.

"You may thank the knight for saving the life of the Countess de Marjolaine, as well. She was also in the room when the attack was perpetrated."

"The countess! You and the countess! Both meeting with Father Jacob." The grand bishop glowered and put his hand on his stomach. "What was the meeting about?"

Dubois did not immediately answer. He turned around in

his chair to look toward the large antechamber where the monsignor and members of his staff worked and greeted those seeking an audience with the grand bishop.

"They are in the cathedral," said the grand bishop, understanding Dubois's silent question. "Monsignor is directing the preparations for this evening's Midsummer service."

"If Your Eminence does not mind, I will check to see that no one is in the antechamber." Dubois went to the door, opened it, peered out, closed it, turned the key in the lock, and resumed his seat.

"I am not going to like this, am I?" Montagne asked with a heavy sigh.

"I fear not, Eminence," said Dubois.

He went on to make his report on Father Jacob's theory of the Bottom Dwellers, quoting the conversation verbatim, including everything said by Father Jacob, himself, and the countess.

As he talked of the priest's theory that the attackers were not Freyan, but people who lived at the bottom of the world, the grand bishop interrupted with a snort.

"Ineffable twaddle," he stated. "You say the surgeon drilled a hole in the man's head. His brains must have leaked out. People who live at the bottom of the world indeed!"

"People skilled in the use of contramagic," said Dubois.

The grand bishop had been twiddling the silver seal, switching it back and forth from one hand to the other, tapping it on the desk. At Dubois's words, Montagne froze. He stared at the silver seal as though wondering what it was, then deliberately laid it down on the desk.

"I am going to pretend I did not hear you speak heresy, Dubois," Montagne said sternly. He rose to his feet. "I think you should leave now."

Dubois stood up. "The bomb that came so near to killing us was set with contramagic constructs."

The grand bishop stiffened. His countenance altered. He unsteadily sank down in his chair, as if his legs would no longer support him. He motioned for Dubois to be seated.

"Tell me," was all Montagne said.

"The bomb was a crude device, Eminence. A kettle packed with gunpowder such as any anarchist might make. Yet, in one aspect, it was quite remarkable. The device designed to cause the bomb to explode was powered by constructs of contramagic."

Montagne fixed Dubois with a cold stare.

"You are my most trusted agent, Dubois, but even you can go too far."

"It is because I am your trusted agent that I must tell you what I saw, Eminence," Dubois returned. "Otherwise your trust would be misplaced. I saw the constructs on the bomb myself. They glowed green and were like none I have ever seen before."

"Are you a crafter, Dubois?"

"God did not so bless me, Eminence. I am a humble channeler."

"Then you could not possibly know if you were looking at contramagic or pea soup!" said the grand bishop angrily.

Dubois was not a crafter, but channelers worked with magical constructs and Dubois, with his amazing memory, was familiar with many thousands of these constructs. He knew their derivation, understood how and why they worked. He had been aware the moment he saw those on the bomb that the green glowing constructs were like no other constructs. They were familiar, used the same basis six sigils: earth, air, fire, water, life, death, but they were put together wrong. Something made them alien, strange.

Dubois inclined his head in acknowledgment and did not argue. He would not win the argument and he would succeed only in further angering the grand bishop. Dubois had done his job, made his report. Let the grand bishop do with it what he would.

"The countess saw this green glowing bomb, too, I suppose," said the grand bishop. "What did she make of it?"

"She did not say, but she listened to Father Jacob with great attention."

"The countess is an intelligent woman. She would not believe this lunacy," said Montagne with a smile.

The smile was ghastly, so obviously false that Dubois winced. He pitied the man. Montagne was sincerely devoted to the church and to his God. He might have his faults, ambition among them. But he was at heart an honest man, a devout man, a man with no skill at deception or deceit.

"I think it possible the countess finds Father Jacob's theory plausible," said Dubois.

The grand bishop heaved a deep sigh and then belched. "My poor stomach! I won't be able to eat for a week! The countess has undoubtedly taken this wild tale to the king. I must go to the palace immediately, attempt to undo whatever damage she has done."

"I doubt very much if His Majesty will believe her," said Dubois. "It is in King Alaric's interests to believe these attackers are Freyan."

"They *are* Freyan, Dubois," said Montagne angrily. "Not so-called Bottom Dwellers! I am surprised that you, a rational man, could believe it. Do you have anything else to report?"

Dubois understood that he was being asked to leave and he dutifully rose to his feet.

"Only a question, Eminence. If I might change the subject—"

"Please do!" the grand bishop said through gritted teeth.

Dubois inclined his head. "What does Your Eminence know of the Duquesa de Plata Niebla?"

The grand bishop was confounded. The subject was so far afield he had to pause a moment to try to put a face to the name.

"The duchess of where? Oh, yes, I remember. All I know is that she is said to be wealthy and she is a fine-looking woman. Why?"

"In other words, you know very little," said Dubois, frowning. "Everyone seems to know very little. We cannot be too careful about those who are close to the person of His Majesty, especially in these troubled times. You will not mind, Eminence, if I pursue a line of inquiry regarding the duchess?"

"An excellent notion, Dubois," said Montagne heartily. "His Majesty's safety is of paramount importance."

He walked over to Dubois and placed a large and heavy hand on his shoulder.

"Pursue this mad Bottom Dwellers notion no farther, Dubois. Let this go. For your sake. For the sake of us all . . ."

The grand bishop gave Dubois's shoulder a squeeze that was meant to be affectionate, but which ended up being painful, for the shoulder he squeezed was the one in which Dubois had been shot. Dubois winced, murmured he would consider the grand bishop's advice, and left through the tapestry.

As he traversed the secret passageway, he reflected on the grand bishop's enigmatic warning. *For your sake*, Dubois could understand. He was in danger of being declared a heretic. What intrigued him was the last line.

For the sake of us all . . .

He wished His Eminence would tell him the truth. He would guard the grand bishop's secrets with his life, but he could not guard them if he did not know the secrets his master was so desperate to conceal.

The Countess de Marjolaine had finally been granted an audience with His Majesty. She had sent him a message telling him she had received important information regarding Sir Henry Wallace. The king had sent back an immediate reply, ordering her to attend him at once. Alaric hated Freya with a profound and abiding passion, and his antipathy for Henry Wallace ran deeper than that. Alaric blamed Wallace for a failed attempt on his life.

The king was in his private chambers. The countess met him in the room Alaric liked to call his "study." Shelves were lined with leather-bound, gold leaf–embossed volumes that he had never read. The walls were adorned with a portrait of his father, hunting scenes, and a very fine painting of the floating palace at sunset.

A large window looked down upon the city of Evreux, many hundred feet below. The most notable feature in the landscape was the grand bishop's palace. Alaric liked to stand here and reflect upon the fact that he floated in the clouds while his former friend and bitter political rival, Ferdinand de Montagne, was stuck down on the ground.

The king's secretary admitted Cecile. She found Alaric standing at the window, as was his wont, admiring the ships of the royal navy patrolling the skies around the palace.

"The Countess de Marjolaine, Your Majesty," said the secretary.

The king turned. Cecile made a deep curtsy. Alaric responded with a frown and a peremptory gesture for her to come join him.

Alaric Le Fevre was fifty-four years old. He was a tall man, slender, with a long narrow face, a long aquiline nose, a wide mouth with thin lips. He sported a narrow brown mustache and a beard that was trimmed to come to a point in front. His brown hair was starting to go gray and he often wore wigs to conceal it. His brown eyes were unreadable, and his expression generally guarded and wary. His followers said he was a master at concealing his thoughts. His detractors said that he had no thoughts to conceal.

He and Cecile had been lovers many years ago. She had slept with him for one reason—to gain influence over him. She knew his many weaknesses and his few strengths. She despised him, but she was loyal to him and worked hard to further his interests, because his interests were the interests of her country. She was loyal to him for another reason: King Alaric alone stood between Cecile de Marjolaine and the many political enemies she had made over the years.

"What has that fiend, Wallace, done now?" Alaric demanded, scowling.

"Freya is preparing to send their fleet to Braffa, Your Majesty," said Cecile.

"Are they, by God?" Alaric said, his face lighting with pleasure. "Going to Braffa! We scared them off."

He chuckled and looked out proudly at the *Spirit of Rosia,* which had just sailed into view.

Cecile bit her lip and gave an inward sigh.

"Your Majesty, I fear this news is not cause for celebrating—"

Alaric swung round on her. "What do you mean, Countess? Of course, the news is good. If the bloody Freyan navy is heading to Braffa, they won't attack us."

"If the Freyan fleet succeeds in reaching Braffa, Freyan ships could blockade Braffa *and* the refineries that produce the Blood of God, cutting off our supply."

The countess gestured toward the *Spirit of Rosia.* "Our new ships rely on the liquid form of the Breath to stay afloat. Without the lift gas, our fleet will be languishing on the ground."

Alaric scowled at this news, which did not suit him. He had to admit she was right, but still it did not suit him.

"What do we do?" he demanded.

"You must order the fleet back to Braffa immediately," said Cecile.

Alaric's scowl deepened. "That will leave us unprotected. This may all be a Freyan trick. They needed only one ship to destroy the *Royal Lion* at Westfirth, using that infernal secret weapon of theirs."

"I have news with regard to that attack, Your Majesty," said Cecile. "I met with Father Jacob Northrop of the Arcanum. He made a study of the attackers. They were the same as those who murdered the nuns at the Abbey of Saint Agnes. They are *not* Freyan."

She went on to relate to the king, as Dubois had related to the grand bishop, how the attackers were known as Bottom Dwellers, descendants of the survivors of the sinking of Glasearrach. She did not tell him about the bomb, for she would have to bring up Sir Ander Martel. Alaric's memory was long, especially for those he hated. He would ignore the assassination attempt completely to focus upon the fact that Martel had been a friend of Julian's.

As Cecile spoke, she saw Alaric's thin lip begin to curl in scornful disbelief before she was halfway through her account. When she went on to mention contramagic, she saw she had lost him completely.

"Magic that isn't magic." Alaric gave a contemptuous laugh. "We have never heard of anything so stupid. Not to mention the church considers it heresy. You should not be talking about such evil."

He eyed Cecile coldly. "This Father Jacob Northrop is Freyan."

"True, Your Majesty."

"That explains everything," said Alaric with a shrug.

He stood very tall, put his hands behind him, and turned his back on her.

"We will speak to the grand bishop about this Father Jacob. We will see what Montagne has to say."

Alaric expected to frighten her by naming the grand bishop. The king assumed Montagne would refute her claims and side with him on the question of Freya. Alaric and Montagne might be foes at the moment, but the king was always one to hedge his bets.

Cecile had foreseen his use of this tactic and she was prepared.

"Indeed, I was about to urge Your Majesty to speak to His Eminence," said Cecile.

"You were?" Alaric slightly turned his head. His eyes narrowed. "Why?"

"Ask the grand bishop about the collapse of the watchtower in northern Freya and the attack on the cutter *Defiant*. Ask him if those were the result of contramagic. He will find it difficult to deny the charge. If he does, say you have proof."

"*Do* we have proof, Countess?"

Cecile raised an eyebrow. "Does that matter, Your Majesty?"

She had placed Alaric in a quandary. She was well aware he didn't believe a word she had said about contramagic or about the Bottom Dwellers, having convinced himself the attackers were Freyan. Yet she knew Alaric would dearly love the idea of accusing the grand bishop of lying, putting Montagne on the defensive.

"I do so love watching Montagne squirm."

The king chuckled, and was about to give her what she knew would be a favorable reply, when their conversation was interrupted by a commotion outside the door.

A shrill voice cried out, "I am your queen. I go where I will! I don't care what your orders are, you stupid man. Open this door immediately, sirrah, or I shall have you flogged!"

The door opened. The secretary cast an apologetic glance at the king, who rolled his eyes and muttered something beneath his breath as his wife swept into the room.

Queen Annemarie was tearful, distraught. She pressed her handkerchief to her nose and sniffed loudly. Behind the handkerchief and the tears, her eyes were shrewd, suspicious. Despite the fact that Cecile and Alaric had not slept together for over twenty years and that Alaric was currently conducting an affair with the sixteen-year-old daughter of a marquis, the queen was as jealous of Cecile now as she had been twenty years ago.

Alaric let the world know that he admired and respected Cecile, and valued her advice. He trusted Cecile, shared confidences with her, while he would not tell his despised wife what he had eaten for breakfast. Annemarie watched for every opportunity to try to catch the two in some compromising situation, hoping to force Alaric to cast off Cecile, banish her from court.

As Cecile curtsied to the queen, she caught a glimpse of the Duquesa de Plata Niebla hovering in the doorway, not daring to enter the king's private chambers. The duchess was accompanied by a handsome young man. Cecile had heard about the duchess's nephew, whose romantically dark good looks were being discussed behind all the fluttering fans in court.

The king glowered. He knew his wife was putting on a show and he knew the reason why. He did not bother to hide his contempt.

"You know we dislike these interruptions. We were in the middle of business. Disturbing reports have reached us out of Freya."

"I am sure this news from Freya could not be nearly so distressing to you as the fact that your daughter is near death!" Annemarie cried, her bosom heaving. "I have sent for the physicians!"

The one soft spot in this hard man was his daughter, Sophia. He changed in an instant from despot to doting father.

"Sophia? Is she ill again?" the king asked anxiously. "What is the matter?"

The queen made the most of her victory. "Her headache was so terrible, she fainted from the pain. I fear if we cannot find her darling, she may die!"

" 'Darling'? What darling?" The king was confused.

"Bandit is missing!" the queen wailed dramatically. "We have searched and searched, but he is nowhere to be found! The duchess believes the loss of her pet brought on this latest attack. When Sophia came to, all she could talk about were drums. Of course, she meant her dog."

"Her dog!" The king stared at his wife in amazement. The look on his face was so comical that Cecile had to turn her head to hide her smile. "This is about a dog?"

Bandit was the princess's spaniel and he was aptly named, for he was a little thief with a fondness for iced cakes and shoe leather. The dog disappeared about once a week. He was generally discovered in the larder begging for treats from the cook or hiding beneath someone's bed, chewing on a slipper.

Sophia was a sensible young woman. Though she doted on Bandit, she would not fall ill just because her dog was missing yet again, Cecile reflected, concerned. Sophia had spoken of drums before, hearing the sound of drumming when her headaches were very bad. If she said *drums,* she meant drums. Not dogs . . .

The queen gave way to hysterics. The duchess, with a curtsy and an apologetic glance at the king for her intrusion, hurried in to comfort the queen. The young man remained in the doorway. He looked embarrassed, not knowing what to do with himself.

The secretary returned.

"Monsieur D'argent," he announced, and D'argent entered the room in haste.

Cecile forgot about the princess and her dog. D'argent's expression was grave. He would never have presumed to enter the king's chambers except for some urgent reason.

"Your Majesties, forgive the sudden intrusion. I am the bearer of terrible news—" D'argent paused, looking from the sobbing queen to the king. "But then, you have heard—"

"If you are here about that blasted dog—" the king began.

"Dog?" D'argent shook his head. "I am not here about a dog, Your Majesty. The glass walls of the Crystal Market have shattered. The market was filled with hundreds of people shopping for the Midsummer's Eve feast. They cannot begin to count the number of dead."

18

The architectural world has recently benefited from the development of new strengthening and connecting magical constructs. Such constructs allow for a stronger and more secure base, giving an architect the option to use different materials in ways that were not available to them before. The Crystal Market's glass "bricks" are possible only because of these new constructs.

—Antoine Capet,
master crafter and architect

The Crafters' Guild Crystal Market was a marvel—an enormous structure built out of thousands of bricks made of glass, not clay. The glass bricks were infused with, strengthened, and held together by magical constructs. The architects and crafters declared the glass bricks to be harder and more durable than granite.

The Crystal Market was one of the most popular places in Evreux. Vendors from all over the world came here to sell their wares beneath the glittering glass dome. One could buy everything: exquisite lace shawls from Bheldem, sherry from Estara, or spice cakes from the Aligoes Islands. Since this was a holiday, the hall would have been filled with people.

Those in the room were too horrified to speak. Alaric had to put his hand on the back of his chair for support. He looked immediately to Cecile.

When the queen saw the look, her face flushed in anger. She broke the silence by saying, "I am sure this is very shocking, but have we all forgotten poor Bandit?"

Alaric cast his wife a disgusted glance and said coldly, "Get her out of here."

"You should return to the princess, Your Majesty," said the duchess, trying to lure the queen away. "She should not hear this terrible news from someone else. You should be the one to tell her."

The queen refused to leave. "I will not be sent off like a servant!"

Alaric ignored her and turned to D'argent.

"How did such a disaster happen?"

"No one seems to know, Your Majesty," D'argent replied. "Survivors say they heard the sound of the glass cracking. Someone shouted that the ceiling was going to fall. There was pandemonium. People were trampled trying to flee. Those inside were cut to ribbons. The carnage is reported to be awful. The gutters of Market Square are said to be ankle deep in blood."

"Thank you," said Alaric. He had turned quite gray. "You may go."

D'argent shot a look at the countess, indicating he had something of importance to relate to her in private. She gave an oblique nod and promised to join him when she could. D'argent departed.

News of the tragedy was spreading through the palace. Cecile could hear cries and screams and calls for His Majesty. Alaric walked over to the window and stood gazing out at the mists of the Breath slowly twining about the palace. Far below, hundreds of his people lay dead, dying.

The queen burst out suddenly, "If you will do nothing to find our darling's little dog, I shall think you are a cruel and heartless father!"

Alaric's expression hardened. He was being made to look foolish and that angered him. The duchess was quick to see his anger and she did her best to once more try to urge the queen away.

Queen Annemarie pushed her aside. "He has no care for the sufferings of his dear child—"

"Enough!" Alaric thundered, enraged. "Call out the palace guard. Send them to search for the princess's damn dog. Now leave me, all of you!"

"Thank you, my dear," the queen said, sniffing.

She swept from the room with a glance of triumph at Cecile, who coolly took no notice. The duchess, looking extremely uncomfortable, dropped a curtsy and left rapidly, taking her nephew with her.

"Your Majesty, you should summon your ministers—" Cecile began.

"Leave me," he ordered.

"I do not like to bring this up at the time of such a terrible disaster, but what should we do about Freya—"

"Do what you like," he said coldly.

He was going to leave the Braffan turmoil to her to solve. If she made the right decision, he would take the credit. If she made the wrong move, he would disavow her. Precisely what she had expected, which made her wonder why she should suddenly be so angry. She gave a deep curtsy and departed.

The halls outside the royal chambers were crowded with the inhabitants of the palace exclaiming over the disaster in loud, high-pitched panic. When Cecile emerged from the royal presence, they clustered around her, clamoring for information.

She said curtly she knew nothing more about this than they did, and pushed through the press of terrified people. To add a touch of the macabre to the tragedy, servants and guardsmen were crawling about on the floor, peering under tables and calling Bandit's name in wheedling tones.

Cecile arrived at her chambers to find that the astute D'argent had cleared the salon of courtiers and had dismissed the viscount, her secretary. D'argent was waiting for her in her office.

"Someone you should meet, my lady," said D'argent. "Give me one moment."

D'argent vanished. The countess sat at her desk, reflecting wearily that after more than twenty years of service to this weak king, propping him up, making him look effective and intelligent, she should not be angry with him. She might as well be angry with a wolf for slaughtering rabbits. Such was the nature of the beast.

D'argent returned, accompanied by a well-dressed gentleman who was deathly pale, with blood on his face and clothing. He was holding a cloth pressed to a large gash on his head. He bowed to the countess and demurred when D'argent brought forth a chair.

"I fear I will get blood on it . . ."

"Nonsense, monsieur, you are injured," said Cecile. "Be seated. D'argent, summon one of the healers—"

"Nobody, please, my lady," the gentleman gasped.

He sank into the chair, and D'argent poured a glass of brandy, which the man thankfully accepted. He gulped it down, shuddered.

Cecile looked to D'argent for an explanation.

"My lady, this gentleman is Monsieur Reynard Moreau. He is one of the architects who designed the Crystal Market. Reynard and I were friends at university. He brought me word of the disaster."

"I came as soon as it happened," said Moreau.

He was shaking, and not from his wounds, which were minor. He was shaking from fear.

"Monsieur Moreau has come to you for help, my lady," said D'argent. "He is afraid that he will be blamed for the tragedy."

He has good reason to be afraid, Cecile reflected. Someone has to be held to account. The wretched man could face execution if evidence came out that the architectural design was flawed. And he might well deserve it.

"What have you to say, monsieur?" said the countess in cool tones.

"I didn't know where else to turn," said Moreau. "I fear I will be arrested at any moment—"

"Then you should be quick about it," Cecile said.

"I brought this, my lady." Moreau removed a piece of paper from an inner pocket of his coat. The paper was frayed and worn. "I ask you to read it. The report is not long."

The report was stained with blood from the man's hand. Cecile picked up her lorgnette and rapidly scanned the report.

"Dear God," she murmured.

She read again more slowly, then laid the paper down on the desk. She lowered the lorgnette to gaze at Monsieur Moreau.

"You wrote this report?"

"Yes, my lady."

"The report is addressed to the grand bishop. You gave it to him and kept a copy."

"Yes, my lady."

"The report is dated six months ago. Is that correct?"

"Six months, yes, my lady."

Cecile handed the report to D'argent. He read through it, shook his head, and handed it back to the countess. She started to return it to the architect, then changed her mind.

"If you have no objection, monsieur, I should like to keep this. If you are arrested, it would be better if this were not found upon your person. Evidence such as this has a way of vanishing," she added drily.

Moreau shuddered again at the mention of arrest and gulped down another proffered glass of brandy. Some color began returning to the man's face, and his hands stopped trembling.

"How did you come to write such a report?" Cecile asked.

"When the Crafters' Guild members first began to notice the cracks and the strange behavior of the glass bricks they brought the matter to my attention. I investigated and I was concerned enough by what I found to write this report to the grand bishop. I took it to him in person."

Cecile tapped the report with the lorgnette. "You state that the magical constructs set in the glass bricks were starting to fail, the failure was occurring at an alarming rate, and it appeared to be growing worse. Is this what you told him?"

"Yes, my lady."

Cecile referred again to the report. "You said that the magical contructs were, and I quote, 'behaving strangely.' You could feel the glass bricks 'vibrate,' the magical constructs 'break apart' beneath your fingers." She frowned. "I am a crafter myself, monsieur. I know magical constructs can weaken over time, but magic cannot be destroyed. The constructs cannot 'break apart.'"

"I myself would have said such an occurrence was not possible, my lady. And yet, I saw it. I felt the glass vibrate. I saw the constructs fracture. I was reminded—you will think this odd—I was reminded of the musical instrument known as the glass harp."

The glass harp was more a drawing room curiosity than a true musical instrument. The performer ran chalked fingers around the rims of crystal glasses filled with water, each glass with water at a different level. The vibration of the glass by means of the friction of the fingers created different notes. The performer caused the glass to "sing."

"I heard the same sort of eerie singing sound, my lady."

Cecile was perplexed. She had no reason to doubt this man. She could not imagine him creating a lie so elaborate. "What is causing the magic to act in this strange manner?"

"That is what I asked myself, my lady. And what I asked the grand bishop."

"What was the grand bishop's reply?"

"He assured me that the magic was undergoing a natural cycle. He explained that magic waxes and wanes like the phases of the moon. Indeed, my lady, the fractures in the constructs *do* appear to occur more frequently at some times than at others. And it is true that the Crystal Market was the only building so severely affected, though that might be because the crystal bricks rely far more heavily on magic than other ordinary brick or stone. A building made of real brick, for example, does not require magical constructs for strengthening to the same extent as a building made of glass."

Cecile was silent as she turned this over in her mind. Her gaze went back to the report, still on her desk.

"I don't suppose there were witnesses to the conversation between you and the grand bishop?"

"No, my lady," said Moreau. "I wanted to bring my associates, but the grand bishop said he would meet with me only in private."

"I gather you did *not* believe what the grand bishop told you about the magic."

Moreau gave a faint smile. "I studied the science of magic in university, my lady. I know for a fact that magic does not 'wax and wane.' When I tried to present this view to the grand bishop he interrupted me, asking if I believed what the writings of the saints tell us—that magic is the Voice of God and that God can speak or be silent as He wills."

"What did you say, monsieur?"

"What could I say?" Moreau made a helpless gesture. "How could I tell the grand bishop I believed the writings of the saints to be lovely poetry, but certainly not science. I assured him I was a faithful son of the church. Then he asked me if there was a possibility my findings might be flawed. Perhaps I had 'imagined' the whole thing. I was terrified and I stammered that there was always that possibility. What else could I have said?"

"Nothing," Cecile murmured.

"And all the while I knew we were just moments away from disaster. I have gone to the Crystal Market daily to conduct research on how and why the magic is fracturing. I was there today when . . . when . . . the vibrations became alarming. There was that strange singing sound and then . . . Oh, God!"

Drops of sweat broke out on Moreau's forehead. He tried to swallow and gagged. D'argent silently poured more brandy and handed the goblet to him. The countess waited for him to recover himself, while Moreau mopped his forehead and continued to relate what had happened.

"I was standing just inside the main entrance, talking to one of the crafters employed to maintain the magic. I heard a splintering crack like a gunshot. A brick from the ceiling fell and then . . . there was a cascade . . . The screams . . . I hear them now. I will hear them forever."

Moreau put his hand to his face. His shoulders shook, and he sobbed aloud. D'argent rested his hand on his shoulder in sympathy and looked at the countess.

"What do we do, my lady?" he asked.

Cecile thought of Father Jacob, what he had told her about

the green beam and contramagic. "Monsieur Moreau, did you see flashes of green light prior to the disaster?"

"No, my lady," said Moreau, puzzled. "Why?"

"Nothing. Just a fancy of mine," said Cecile. "I fear, monsieur, that you are right. You are in danger. You will most assuredly be arrested and silenced. We must take steps to prevent such an occurrence."

Cecile rang a silver bell that stood on her desk. The countess's lady's maid, a middle-aged woman who had been with the countess since she had first come to court, responded to the summons with alacrity.

"Marie, take this gentleman with you. Disguise him as a palace servant and guide him to the kitchen by the back stairs. D'argent, fetch the carriage, then meet Monsieur Moreau in the kitchen and escort him to the safe house on the Rue Laplace. After that, go to his office and remove all reports pertaining to the Crystal Market. Monsieur Moreau can tell you where to find them. Do you have a wife, monsieur? Family?"

Moreau shook his head.

"Good. That makes matters easier. D'argent will arrange to smuggle you out of the country. I am afraid you must become an exile, Monsieur Moreau. At least for a time."

A relieved Moreau expressed his gratitude, as Marie led him from the room. D'argent remained to receive further instructions.

"You might well fall under suspicion yourself, D'argent," she said.

"I fear that may happen, my lady. Moreau said he asked one of the palace footmen where he could find me."

"When the guards question you, tell them your friend was wounded and in shock. He was talking gibberish. You put him in a hackney cab and that was the last you saw of him."

"Yes, my lady. What do I do with the reports?"

"Send them by our most trusted messenger to Father Jacob Northrop at the Arcanum."

D'argent nodded.

"Send funds to the Sisters of Mercy to provide help for the victims and to say a mass for the dead."

"Yes, my lady."

"That will be all, D'argent. Thank you."

As he was about to leave, Cecile stopped him at the door.

"Oh, and one more thing," she said. "Arrange for the crafters to make a dog collar for Bandit. A jeweled collar set with a magical construct that will permit his mistress to find him should he become lost. Hopefully that will spare us more of the queen's histrionics."

"An excellent idea, my lady."

Cecile read Moreau's report once again, then carried it to the music room. Rarely used, the tower room was kept locked except for those rare occasions when Cecile held a musical evening or went there to play. She unlocked the door, entered, and lit a lamp. A pianoforte and a standing harp stood in the center, surrounded by chairs for musicians and rows of chairs for a small audience. Heavy velvet curtains covered a bay window. The walls were decorated with paintings of a variety of shapes and sizes, from small oval portraits in gilt frames to large paintings portraying two ships in full sail, a dragon count in his court finery, and others of a more musical nature.

Cecile shut and locked the door behind her, then carried the lamp to one of the small portraits at the far end of the room. She touched the face of the woman in the portrait, and a magical construct flared briefly. She removed the portrait, exposing the wall behind, blank except for the outline created by the rubbing of the frame. Cecile drew a magical construct on the wall and watched the edges of a secret cabinet appear. She drew another magical construct, unlocking the cabinet, and removed an iron box that she opened with yet a third magical construct. She kept various important papers inside the box, including her marriage certificate and her will. She started to add the report to these, then paused.

A miniature lay at the bottom of the box, nestled in a corner. The small painting was an oval watercolor done on porcelain and framed in gold: a man's face, a beloved face, the face of Julian de Guichen, her husband, and the father of her son. Another miniature lay beside it, a portrait of Stephano in his Dragon Brigade uniform. She had commissioned the portrait without his knowledge, hiring the same artist who had painted his formal portrait when he received his knighthood.

Cecile lifted the two miniatures and thought how alike the two men were. She touched them both to her lips, then replaced them inside the box. She added the report to the other contents, shut the box, and returned it to the cabinet. She replaced the magical constructs and the painting, then doused the light. Sitting down in the chair behind the harp, she ran her fingers over the strings in the darkness, feeling the strings vibrate beneath her fingers, listening to the music they produced.

She remained there alone and thoughtful far into the night.

The grand bishop was at work in his study, putting the final touches on the Midsummer's Eve sermon, which was always one of his most popular. He was reading certain passages aloud, admiring how they sounded, when the door burst open and the monsignor rushed into the room.

The grand bishop looked up in astonishment at such rude and untoward behavior. The monsignor was in his forties, quiet, circumspect, and discreet. His robes disheveled, his hat missing, he stood in the middle of the room panting for breath, for he had come to the grand bishop on the run.

"Monsignor," the grand bishop said sternly. "Get hold of yourself. What do you mean by this intrusion?"

"Eminence!" the monsignor gasped. "The Crystal Market has collapsed!"

Montagne could not believe he had heard right. "What did you say?"

"The Crystal Market has collapsed. The glass ceiling apparently just . . . shattered. The dead . . . the wounded . . . I have ordered my staff . . . all the priests to go . . ."

Montagne felt the blood drain from his face. He was deathly cold. The monsignor stood waiting for orders and trying to catch his breath. He regarded the grand bishop with concern.

"Are you well, Eminence?" asked the monsignor, now growing alarmed. "Forgive me! I should not have sprung news of this terrible tragedy on you so suddenly. I will fetch a healer—"

"No, no. I am . . . fine," Montagne managed, though with a great effort. His jaw was tight, hard to move. His lips were numb.

By God's miracle, a part of his brain continued to function. He would never afterward know how. He heard himself issuing orders. All priests and nuns were to go to the site, do what they could to help. He told the monsignor what he should do with the bodies of the dead, where they were to house the casualities.

He even had the presence of mind to realize that the surviving crafters would be making wild speculations. That must not be allowed. Montagne was about to order that the crafters who had worked on the Crystal Market should be sent to the Arcanum, placed under Seal. He remembered at the last moment that Father Jacob was at the Arcanum.

"The Asylum of Charenton," said the grand bishop. "Send them there, where we can minister to them in their grief."

Montagne sat for a long time without moving. When he finally came to himself, the monsignor had gone. The grand bishop had no recollection of the man leaving and very little of what he had said to him. He remembered only consigning the crafters to an insane asylum. He gave a shivering sigh.

Church bells all over the city were ringing wildly. Evreux would be in chaos. People would expect their grand bishop to take charge, share in the grief, the agony.

Montagne sat writhing in guilt like a bug on a pin. He tried to stand, but his limbs failed him. He slid from his chair onto the floor and crouched down on his knees. Bowing his head, he clasped his trembling hands. Tears filled his eyes.

"Oh, God! It is true, then!" Montagne whispered. " 'The sins of the fathers *are* passed on to the childen.' "

He shuddered. "Our children are coming to slay us!"

Dubois was visiting a lady friend of his—a widow of ample proportions who resided in a small, well-kept house on a quiet street in an unprepossessing neighborhood. The widow was in her forties, pleasant, cheerful, discreet, and an excellent cook. All in all, she was well worth the money Dubois paid to keep her. The widow's house was located not far from the Crystal Market, and they both heard the crash and the screams. Dubois left immediately to find out what had occurred.

He viewed the ghastly sight with shock and disbelief. Dubois was not a soldier. He had never been on a field of battle, but he had heard the stories of those who had and he imagined this was what a battlefield must look like, only far more horrible. They were hauling out the bloody, mangled remains of little children.

The Crystal Market had broken apart in the center. The enormous glass rotunda, so tall that huge trees flourished beneath it, had come crashing down. Inside the market people had been shopping, clapping at the feats of the jongleurs and tightrope walkers, listening to strolling musicians, eating, drinking, laughing with family and friends. And they died in a cascade of splintered glass.

Death was a great equalizer. The poor man died alongside the rich. Lords and ladies from the royal palace died next to pickpockets from the alleyways. Entire families were wiped out in a single moment. People were cut up like meat in a butcher's stall. Arms and limbs sliced off. Skulls cleaved in two. Bodies impaled, shards of glass pinning them to the floor. Rivers of blood streamed from the market and flowed out into the streets. The first some in Evreux knew of the tragedy was to see the water in the gutters run red.

Glass bricks falling from the building had exploded on impact, sending sharp pieces of glass flying into the crowds who had been walking the boulevard on this festival day. People cut by the glass were dazed and bleeding. Some wandered about in shock, others knelt on the ground, holding dying loved ones in their arms.

The din was horrible: screams and shrieks from those still trapped inside, the cries of those outside, the shrill whinnies of carriage horses hit by the glass, the howls of wyverns smelling the blood, the whistles of constables, the frantic clanging of church bells.

And still there was the terrible sound of breaking glass, for bricks continued falling, causing more walls to collapse.

Dubois's gorge rose. The smell of blood made him nauseous. He staggered over to a tree, threw up, and felt better. Then he ventured as close as he could to the site without risking being hit by falling glass.

The structure had been designed with the great rotunda in

the center and two long wings of glass extending on either side. The fall of the rotunda had brought down a portion of both wings. Some parts of the market hall remained standing, though the bricks in those parts were starting to crack. The constables were doing what they could to keep people from going near the disaster. In some cases, they had to physically restrain desperate people from rushing inside to find their loved ones.

To add to the confusion, crowds of gawkers were converging on the area, getting in the way and hampering the efforts of healers and physicians and priests trying to tend to the wounded and give final rites to the dying.

The constables and city guardsmen were outnumbered and in need of help. King Alaric's decision to recall the royal navy from Braffa proved to be beneficial. His eldest son, Prince Renaud, was admiral of the fleet. His flagship was sailing above the city at the time of the disaster and he happened to be on the bridge at the time. He saw the building collapse.

The prince was a hard man, known to be a strict disciplinarian, not loved by either his officers or his crew. He was a man of action, however, blessed with more intelligence than his parents. The prince immediately dispatched marines and sailors to the market to assist, and soon the ship's boats set out from the larger naval vessels loaded with men. The marines cordoned off the area, pushed back the crowds, and told people to go home.

Dubois was neither a healer nor a physician, so there was little he could do to help. He walked gingerly on the broken glass that covered the street, avoiding stepping in pools of blood, watching, listening, observing. He was twice stopped and ordered to leave. He drew out his credentials from his coat pocket and showed them. The marines bowed and let him alone. Dubois was present when the monsignor and his staff arrived.

The monsignor gathered his staff around him and spoke to them in low tones. Dubois sidled over unobtrusively to eavesdrop.

"—looking for guild members who were present when the hall collapsed," the monsignor was saying. "We need to record their accounts of what they saw before they talk to anyone. Their testimony might become muddled or confused. We have conveyances waiting to take them to the Asylum of Charenton, where they will be treated and questioned in quiet surroundings. Remove them from the scene swiftly, quietly, circumspectly."

Dubois was intrigued. He had assumed the collapse to be a tragic accident. Now he wondered.

Watching the priests of the monsignor's staff fan out, Dubois thought it might be instructive to hear for himself what these crafters had to say. He searched about until he saw a young woman wearing the emblem of the Crafters' Guild on her gown. She was standing in front of the hall. Tears streamed unchecked down her cheeks. She was staring at the wreckage and talking to herself.

Dubois walked over to her. "Mademoiselle, is there something I can do to help you?"

She turned to him. "Did you hear it? The singing?"

"Who was singing, mademoiselle?" Dubois asked.

"The glass . . . ," she said. "The glass was singing. And then . . . gone . . ."

Dubois was about to ask more. He was bumped from behind.

"Pardon me, monsieur," said a priest, firmly elbowing Dubois aside. "I will assist the young lady."

Dubois could have produced his credentials, showing him

to be an agent of the grand bishop. But he had the feeling that in this instance, the priest would have referred him to the monsignor, who would have referred him to the grand bishop. Dubois murmured something to the effect that he hoped the young woman would soon recover, and backed away. The priest blessed him for his concern, put his arm around the crafter, and led her to a waiting carriage.

Glass singing. Crafters present when the hall collapsed transported to an insane asylum.

Dubois continued roaming about the vicinity of the market until long after nightfall, picking up shards of glass, studying them, letting them fall. Darkness came as a blessing, covering the scene of the destruction as the shrouds covered the bodies of the dead. The gawkers went back to their homes or gathered in the taverns.

The only people who remained were the marines and those searching for survivors or trying to do what they could to help. The wounded had been carried to the houses of healing. Some of the bodies of the dead that could be identified had been claimed by their families. Others would have to wait until morning. And there were those who would never be identified . . .

The monsignor had decreed that the grisly remains be placed in coffins to be buried in sacred ground. Coffin makers throughout the city would work well into the night.

Dubois was feeling weary and he was turning his steps toward his lodgings when a wyvern-drawn carriage descended from the sky to land on the large, tree-lined boulevard that ran in front of the Crystal Market.

The carriage was private, belonging to the nobility, and must have come from the palace. Carriages had been coming and going from the palace all day, bringing those who feared friends or loved ones might have been caught in the collapse, as well as those overcome by morbid curiosity.

The carriage stopped at the corner underneath a streetlamp. Dubois cast the carriage a cursory glance. At the sight of the coat of arms emblazed on the side, Dubois paused. He did not recognize it, a red two-headed eagle on a gold field, quartered with a silver chalice on a black field. Since he was familiar with the armorial devices of all the members of the royal court, he was naturally curious and he watched to see who the occupant of this carriage could be.

He had to endure a slight delay. The driver was having difficulty controlling the wyvern because of the scent of blood in the air. The driver shouted that he could barely hold the beast, and bid the occupant to be swift.

The carriage door opened. A woman descended. She wore a long cloak and a hat with a veil over her face. She stepped lightly and nimbly onto the pavement and glanced around. Dubois drew back farther into the shadows.

Thinking she was alone, the woman lifted her veil. She stood gazing at the wreckage of the Crystal Market. The broken, shattered glass sparkled and glistened. The blood was black in the moonlight.

The woman's lips parted in a smile.

The driver warned that he could not control the wyvern much longer. The woman returned to the carriage. She shut the door and the driver plied his whip. The wyvern snapped at him, then plunged forward. The carriage rolled down the street, the wheels crunching over broken glass.

Dubois stared after the carriage until the wyvern took to the air.

"Well, well, well," he murmured.

He had recognized the lovely face of the Duquesa de Plata Niebla.

Dubois had two mysteries to unravel: one of crafters, singing glass, and the grand bishop's order that they be whisked away to an asylum; and one of a beautiful noble woman who smiled at the sight of mangled corpses. Which should he pursue?

Dubois had no difficulty making the decision. God had caused the duchess to fall from heaven right in front of Dubois for a reason. God wanted him to pursue the investigation of the duchess, and leave the grand bishop and his secrets to Him.

19

With your funding, we will develop a new weapon that will bring Rosia to its knees. Be aware that development of this weapon will not come cheaply. I will require you to provide the means to cover all costs. Once completed, the weapon will have a multitude of applications. Help me revolutionize warfare as we know it.

—Eiddwen, in a letter
to Sir Henry Wallace, ten years ago

The nation of Rosia was in mourning. The corridors of the palace that were usually busy and bustling, filled with laughter, perfume, flirtations, and arguments, talk of music and art, business and hounds, politics and horses, were almost empty. Those who walked there did so with heavy tread. When people met, they talked in hushed voices.

The grand bishop had issued a statement that the disaster was due to a flaw in the architectural design, and a warrant had been put out for the arrest of the architect. The statement also read that a memorial service honoring the dead was to be held in the cathedral on the morrow.

The day of the service, the king and queen were in attendance, accompanied by their oldest son, Prince Renaud, and

members of the royal court. The queen was dressed all in
black, wearing a hat with a traditional mourning veil over
her face. She wept loudly and copiously throughout the service. The king was attired in a calf-length black coat trimmed
in silver, with black stockings and weskit. He was silent,
reserved. He had issued a proclamation, expressing the nation's sorrow.

The service was led by the archbishop of Evreux, Father
Guiar. Grand Bishop Ferdinand de Montagne was in attendance, but he did not speak. He was haggard, ashen, and said
to be in ill health. The choir sang of redemption and hope.
The organ music swelled, the trumpets soared. People of all
rank and station filled the cathedral. Those who could not
find a seat stood on the grounds outside in a gently falling
rain. The air inside was redolent with the suffocating smell
of wet black crepe.

Cecile did not attend the service. She remained in the
palace to keep the princess company. Sophia had wanted to
attend the memorial service, but the king forbade it. Generally the doting Alaric gave his daughter anything her heart
desired. This time, he refused to listen to her pleas. He said
that she had recently been very ill, the weather was inclement, and she would find the service too upsetting. He would
invite the Countess de Marjolaine to stay with her.

The queen had protested shrilly within the hearing of the
servants that the countess was a bad influence on her daughter, filling her head with music and literature, talking to her
of history and politics. Sophia was in danger of becoming
clever. How was the queen to acquire a husband for a girl
with the reputation of being clever?

Alaric was in no mood to listen to his wife's rantings and
he had walked out on her, saying curtly that Sophia would
stay and the countess would stay with her.

Cecile went to the princess's chamber prior to the service to find the king alone with his daughter listening to her play the pianoforte. Alaric had no ear or taste for music. He was listening only because Sophia was playing. His gaze was fixed on his daughter, his expression unusually somber, contemplative. Catching sight of the countess, he rose abruptly. He bent over his daughter, smoothed her hair, and kissed her gently on the crown of her head.

Sophia stopped playing to look up at her father in surprise. Alaric was rarely given to displays of affection, even to his most beloved child.

"Play something more cheerful, Sophia," he said. "I do not like to see you so sad."

"I keep thinking of those poor people who died," Sophia replied. Her eyes were red rimmed. "I wish you would let me go to the cathedral."

"I do not want you falling ill again," said Alaric gently. He was always gentle when he spoke to her, using "I," never the cold and formal "we."

"Look, my poppet, here is the Countess de Marjolaine coming specially to cheer you up. She is your guest. You must entertain her properly."

Cecile curtsied to the king and the princess.

"I must speak to the countess before I leave for the cathedral," Alaric continued. "Play that piece I like. The one you played the other night. The . . . uh . . ."

"Sonata, Papa?" Sophia asked. "This one?"

She played several bars.

"Yes, yes, that's the one," said Alaric.

Sophia found the music among the sheets of music on top of the pianoforte and arranged it on the stand. She began to play. Alaric took one more moment to regard her fondly, then walked over to the window on the side of the long room opposite from the princess. He motioned Cecile to join him. The view was dismal. The clouds closed thickly around the palace. Raindrops splashed against the glass.

"The Duke of Piette lost his daughter in the Crystal Market," said Alaric in a low voice under the cover of the tinkling music. "She was Sophia's age, almost to the day."

"I heard, Your Majesty," said Cecile. "A terrible tragedy."

She was dressed somberly in a gown of deep maroon trimmed with black velvet ribbons and black lace falling from the sleeves. She wore a black feather in her hair and jewels of onyx. She knew Alaric had something else on his mind. The real reason he had invited her to stay with Sophia was to have a private talk with her. She waited patiently for him to reveal what he was thinking.

"We met with the grand bishop yesterday," said Alaric abruptly. "Montagne looks terrible. He says his stomach troubles him."

"That might not be all that is troubling His Eminence," said Cecile coolly.

Alaric waited for her to elaborate, but she waited to hear what Montagne had said. After several moments of uncomfortable silence, the king proceeded.

"We told him what you told us about this priest of yours and his strange theories."

"What did Montagne say?"

"That Father Jacob was a lunatic," Alaric said angrily. "The grand bishop was furious. He knew all about your meeting with Father Jacob. He said he was dismayed to hear that you had not only listened to such heretical talk, but that you were spreading it. He said I was to warn you to look to your soul. You know I cannot protect you from the wrath of the church!"

What Cecile knew was that if she were accused of heresy, the king would be the first to throw a blazing torch onto the oil-soaked wood. She watched the water running in rivulets down the windowpane and thought about leaving the palace, returning to her estate. Leave behind the intrigue, the spying, the lying and pandering, the flattery, the false smiles and polite mouthings. She would retire with her books, her music, her memories . . .

But that would mean leaving her beloved country in the hands of fools.

Cecile gave considered approval. "You played the matter most cleverly, Your Majesty. I congratulate you on your triumph."

Alaric eyed her narrowly. He quite obviously had no idea what she meant, but he didn't want to say so. He waited for her to tell him what triumph he had gained and how he had gained it.

"Montagne is angry because he is afraid, Your Majesty," said Cecile. "He is afraid because the arrow you loosed struck too near the mark."

The sonata ended. They both fell silent until Sophia began playing a waltz.

"Hmmmm," Alaric muttered, frowning, noncommittal, but glad to hear more.

"You know Montagne. He is generally cool and reserved. The very fact that he forgot himself and began hurling threats means you touched a raw nerve. Your Majesty realizes that if it could be proven the grand bishop has completely mishandled the church's governance of magic, the crown would be justified in taking control."

Alaric drew in a deep breath, let it out slowly through his nose. He was the absolute monarch of Rosia. His navy ruled the world. He held the power of life and death over his subjects. He controlled everything except the one thing he wanted, the single most powerful force in the kingdom—magic. Centuries ago, during the Sunlit Empire, magic had belonged to Rosia's kings. Then came the Dark Ages. In a desperate effort to save his kingdom from chaos and civil unrest, King Armond Tiernay gave the church control over magic. King Alaric daily cursed this weak ancestor of his. He had always longed to take the magic back.

"We would need proof of the church's mismanagement," said Alaric. "Something other than a lunatic Freyan priest with a hole in his skull."

"What if the grand bishop had been warned months ago that the Crystal Market was in danger of collapse and he chose to conceal the warning rather than admit the church had made mistakes?"

Alaric's eyes glittered. "Is that true? Can that be proven?"

"I will need time. We must move slowly and deliberately, build an ironclad case. Above all, we must move in secret. I need not tell Your Majesty that what we are doing is very dangerous. If any hint should reach His Eminence—"

"You may rely upon us," said Alaric, and in this if in nothing else, Cecile knew she could trust him.

Alaric would never jeopardize his chance of achieving his dearest wish, his heart's desire. He departed for the memorial service in such a good mood he was forced to temper his joy to suit the sadness of the occasion.

Cecile was alone with the princess, a rare occasion they both enjoyed. Sophia was fifteen, with a slender build, chestnut hair, and a soft, winsome face. She was generally surrounded by her ladies-in-waiting, whose companionship she might have enjoyed had these ladies been close to her own age or of her own choosing. They had all been selected by her mother, however, and although they flattered and petted her, Sophia was smart enough to know they were spying on her for her mother. Consequently, she viewed them more as prison guards than companions. This day, the ladies-in-waiting had all been given leave to be with their families.

"You played the waltz well, Your Highness," said the Countess, coming over to sit beside the princess. "I would say you must have practiced it a great deal lately."

Sophia blushed and lowered her eyes.

"The waltz has become my favorite," she said shyly.

"Ah, and is there a reason for this?" asked the countess.

"I have been longing to tell you!" Sophia said, her eyes lighting. They dimmed a moment later, filling with tears. "I feel so guilty, though. I should not be playing waltzes or thinking of . . . of dances when so many have died."

"Come, my dear, we will speak of this matter of the waltz quietly together in your room," said the countess.

The two left the grand salon and walked to the princess's chambers. They were greeted by a flop-eared, brown-eyed spaniel that tumbled about at the feet of the princess, tangling himself in the hem of her skirts and begging to be picked up. Sophia lifted the dog and kissed him on the nose. He licked her face and snuggled in her arms.

"Ah, I heard someone found Bandit," said Cecile. "He seems quite recovered from his ordeal."

"It started when he chased the Duchess of Waverly's cat. You know the one she named Alfonso, that horrid white fluffy beast she makes her servant carry around on a silk pillow. The duchess was extremely upset. I can't think why. She should be glad Bandit gave that fat, lazy cat some exercise. Anyway, Alfonso ran down I don't know how many flights of stairs to the bottom of the palace. Bandit never gave up the pursuit," Sophia added proudly. "Spaniels are hunting dogs, you know. I wish I'd seen the chase.

"One of the servants caught Alfonso, but Bandit got away. Where do you think they found him? He was in the kitchen pantry!" Sophia laughed and nuzzled the dog with her chin. "Such a smart dog! Cook discovered him on top of a table in the larder. He'd eaten an orange pudding and some of a roast goose when she caught him. Of course, he was hungry after all that running, poor dear."

Cecile began to laugh. Sophia was delighted.

"See, Bandit, you have made the countess laugh. She is so solemn and serious all the time. We almost never see her happy. And now, with your new collar, you will never be lost again!" Sophia cuddled the dog.

"I would keep him away from Alfonso," said Cecile.

"Indeed I will. Dreadful beast. Look where he scratched Bandit on his poor nose!" Sophia exhibited the dog. "I cannot thank you enough for the magical collar, Countess. You must tell me how it works."

Sophia held up Bandit to show off the collar. The countess duly admired the new dog collar, which was made of leather set with a diamond, one of a pair cut from a single stone.

A crafter had placed constructs in the two diamonds, connecting the jewels. The crafter set one diamond in the collar and mounted the other onto a silver compass. The next time Bandit got lost, the servant who took care of him would channel magical energy into the compass and the unique connection between the two halves of the diamonds and constructs would point the compass toward the collar.

Cecile explained how the collar worked. Sophia tested it by making Bandit "hide" in the wardrobe, where he began to chew on one of her shoes. She scolded him by giving him sweetmeats and then she and Cecile sat down to an elegant luncheon, which included neither orange pudding nor roast goose.

The princess's chambers were decorated in shades of rose and mauve, with white moldings trimmed by gold gilt. The rooms were filled with every luxury. Fine paintings hung on the walls, including one done of Bandit in a white neck ruff that the spaniel had eaten while sitting for his portrait. Crystal lamps gave off a rosy glow. A fire burning in the grate took the edge off the rainy damp.

After they had finished dining, Sophia sat down on the floor to play with Bandit. The countess took a turn about the room. As Cecile drew near the fire, she noticed a new miniature placed in a prominent position on the mantelpiece.

"What is this?" she asked, lifting it.

Sophia glanced up. She made a face. "Prince Dieder Oertker of Travia. He wants to marry me. Mama says he's very rich, but I think he's very fat. Here, Bandit. We will show the countess your new trick. Fetch your ball and you shall have a sugarplum."

Sophia rolled the ball. Bandit watched the ball roll past him, yawned, and scratched at the new collar. Sophia laughingly crawled after the ball herself to show him what he was supposed to do.

"We will try this again," said Sophia, feeding the dog a sugarplum as a reward for not behaving.

Cecile watched the princess romping with the little dog and looked from the girl to the miniature. The artist had painted an extremely flattering portrait, but he could do little to alter the round, corpulent face and full, flabby lips. Cecile knew Prince Dieder, a scrofulous reprobate, whose vices were the sort people spoke of in whispers. He was old enough to be Sophia's grandfather.

Prince Dieder was said to be desperate for an heir, his only son having died of smallpox. The prince had married two young wives in recent years trying to produce a new heir and buried both women; rumor had it they had died of his brutal treatment.

Royal marriages were not meant to be love matches. This marriage was attractive from both a monetary standpoint—the prince was fabulously wealthy—as well as a political one. The wedding would more firmly establish ties between the royal families of Rosia and Travia.

Cecile resolved to mention what she knew of the prince to King Alaric. He had thus far refused to arrange a marriage for his daughter, seemingly unwilling to give her up, despite the queen badgering him about it. Sophia was certainly old enough to wed, and relations with Travia had been strained since he had pulled the royal navy from Braffa, leaving Travia in a weakened position. Add to this the fact that the royal coffers were almost empty after the huge expenditures made to refit the naval ships to use the liquid form of the Breath and she feared Alaric might be persuaded to make the deal.

"Impossible," Cecile murmured. "She is still a child."

She placed the miniature on the mantelpiece facedown and asked the princess to tell her the story of the waltz. Sophia curled up on a divan, her dress gathered around her ankles. Bandit slept in her lap.

"A fortnight ago, before I was so ill, I was with my ladies-in-waiting in the salon. Lady Angelina and I were playing duets when Lucello . . . I mean the conte"—Sophia blushingly corrected herself—"came into the room."

"The conte?" Cecile asked.

"The Conte Osinni," said Sophia. "The nephew of the Duquesa de Plata Niebla. You must have seen him at court. He is so handsome and elegant, with beautiful manners. He does have a slight limp. He was wounded in some battle or other. He was an officer and says the wound was minor, but I know he must have done something very heroic. What was I saying?"

"This handsome Conte Osinni came into the room."

"Oh, yes, Lucello . . . I mean the Conte Osinni stopped and stared about in confusion. He is new to the palace, you see, and he'd gotten hopelessly lost. He apologized and started to leave, but Lady Angelina whispered to me that she heard he played the pianoforte beautifully. I could not find the courage to invite him to play for us, but he overheard and he offered. My ladies longed to hear him and so I permitted it.

"He looked through my music and found the waltz and said he knew this must be one of my favorites. He sat down on the bench beside me. I was going to move, but he asked me to stay and turn the pages for him. I was still going to move, but Lady Angelina pushed me down and my other ladies were all laughing. I was so embarrassed I couldn't move a muscle.

"He played and looked at me the entire time. His eyes are deep brown and he has black eyelashes and his hair is chestnut and smooth. He has elegant hands with long, tapered fingers. His smile is lovely, warm and yet melancholy. I see the shadow of some secret sorrow in his eyes."

Sophia went on to talk about the Conte Osinni and the impromptu concert and how he had played not only the waltz, but more pieces as well. Sophia had at last found courage to turn the pages and once his hand had brushed hers, quite by accident. He had made a lovely apology, so her ladies told her.

Cecile listened and thought to herself that she had been wrong. Sophia was not a child. She had emerged from the silken cocoon of childhood, but her wings were still delicate, too fragile to fly. She was basking in the sunshine of a young man's smile, warming herself in a glorious state of infatuation.

Cecile made a mental note to find out what she could about this handsome count. Thus far, her agents could tell her nothing about the Duquesa de Plata Niebla except that she appeared to be what she claimed to be.

Sophia continued talking about the count: what he said, how he said it, what he was wearing, how he wore it. Cecile was only half-listening. She let Sophia chatter happily. Her thoughts turned to other, more serious matters.

D'argent had managed to smuggle Monsieur Moreau onto a ship bound for the Aligoes Islands. D'argent had located the architect's reports and removed them from the office only moments before the church officials arrived with an order from the grand bishop to seize all documents, arrest everyone, and close down the business. D'argent was currently engaged in copying the reports. He would provide her with a set and send one to Father Jacob.

Cecile's spies had been at work in Freya, reporting that Sir Henry was spending an inordinate amount of time at a naval shipyard. They could not find out what he was doing, for the shipyard was heavily guarded. Cecile had no doubt that he was using the formula for the magically enhanced steel to armor a sailing vessel. If that proved successful, he would armor the entire Freyan fleet. For the moment, she could do nothing to stop him.

Thinking of Sir Henry turned her thoughts to Stephano. She had still not heard from him. She reminded herself time and again of Sir Ander's encouraging words. She would not let herself think that Stephano might be dead and yet she couldn't help herself. When Sophia jumped up and began to waltz with Bandit for a partner, Cecile was thankful for the distraction.

She watched the princess whirl about the room, holding Bandit around the middle. His ears flying, he barked wildly. Cecile was glad to see Sophia well and happy. King Alaric had told her that this last illness had been extremely bad. She had been in terrible pain, half out of her mind. She kept pleading with her healers to "make the drumming stop." The Duquesa de Plata Niebla had given her a dose of some herbal concoction, which had caused Sophia to fall into an exhausted sleep.

Cecile supposed she should say a word of caution to Sophia for dreaming too much of this handsome count, whom no one seemed to know. Cecile's gaze went to the mantelpiece, to the miniature of the corpulent old prince. Hopefully Sophia would not be forced to marry him, but she would be bartered off to some man someday.

When she was married her days of waltzing, of turning pages for handsome young men, and even of romping with her little dog would be over. Such days, bright with sunshine, were fleeting and, once gone, would never come again.

Let her at least have these moments of innocence and joy to look back upon, Cecile thought. She kept silent on the subject of the count and enjoyed watching Sophia waltz.

The Duquesa de Plata Niebla accompanied the royal party to the cathedral. She was heavily veiled, so that no one would notice that while everyone else was weeping, her eyes were quite dry. She sat through the service and tried to keep from dozing off. When the service finally ended, the people filed out of the church to discover the rain had ceased. The sun came out, which the archbishop termed God's blessing. The king and queen entered the royal carriage to return to the palace. Members of the court followed in their own carriages. The mourning period would last thirty days. During that time parties, balls, galas, celebrations of any kind were prohibited out of respect. The theaters were closed, as were the opera houses.

The halls of the palace were empty as the noble lords and ladies went immediately to their rooms and shut their doors. The queen had wanted Eiddwen to remain with her, to discuss the service and gossip about what everyone had been wearing. Eiddwen had work to do and she managed to escape the queen, saying that she was so overcome with grief she needed to be by herself.

Once locked safely in her own chambers, Eiddwen poured herself a glass of champagne and raised the glass in a silent toast.

"To Xavier and the success of your grand experiment."

Xavier Meehan XIV, the ruler of the Bottom Dwellers, had proven that the plan to slowly choke off the Voice of God in the world Above would work. The plan had been the dream of his grandfather; his father had developed the means to make the dream a reality; and the son had turned the dream into a nightmare for those in the world Above.

On the sunken island of Glasearrach, at the bottom of the world, men and women sat in a sacred circle, beating their drums and chanting the sacred chants that were slowly breaking down every magical construct in every church, ship, dwelling, and palace in the world.

Eiddwen had never seen the drums. She had heard them described by Xavier during one of the few brief times he had spent Above, and by Brother Paul and others. She longed to see them. She could imagine them—a hundred drummers seated in a circle in the sacred temple.

The drummers beat drums inscribed with ancient constructs designed to channel contramagic. They chanted the words to blood magic rituals, the only magic known to be able to control the contramagic. The drumming created a resonance in the Breath that spread the effect of the contramagic to the world Above. This effect was slower, more gradual than the green fire weapons, for it was spread over a large area. The shattering of the Crystal Market was proof that the voices of those Below could silence the Voice of God Above.

The large drums were made of wood covered in human skin taken from sacrifices in blood magic rituals. Priests skilled in the heinous art burned contramagic constructs onto the skin and then flayed it off the bones while the victims screamed in agony. Blood magic gained its strength through pain and terror.

Eiddwen had been a student of blood magic, raised in a cult of blood magic followers. She and her young protégé, Lucello, known as "the Warlock," had used blood magic to terrorize various locales in Rosia in order to stir up civil unrest and draw the attention of the authorities, keep them occupied investigating grisly murders instead of reports of ships disappearing in the Breath and of towers collapsing.

Her plan had worked well, almost too well. The seduction of a nobleman's daughter had attracted the attention of Father Jacob Northrop and he had nearly caught Lucello. The young man had managed to escape only by persuading the nobleman's daughter to sacrifice herself, giving him time to flee. Eiddwen had shut down the operation.

Her thoughts went to what Brother Paul had been saying about unrest among Xavier's subjects. Eiddwen was concerned. She had warned Xavier to keep his sacrifices to a minimum, otherwise he would start to frighten people and they would turn against him. As it was, Xavier was beginning to frighten her. A person could become addicted to the killing, just as one could become addicted to opium.

Eiddwen took off the mourning clothes she had worn to the service and hung them in the wardrobe. Although she was playing the part of a wealthy noblewoman, she employed no lady's maid, much to the shock of every noblewoman in the palace. The notion that Eiddwen dressed and undressed herself was, to the pampered and powdered ladies of the court, quite appalling. The queen had almost fainted when she heard.

Eiddwen had concocted a story that her last lady's maid had been an assassin employed by her political rivals in Estara. Given the volatility of Estaran politics, no one doubted this tale. She claimed the maid had tried to smother her with a pillow while she slept, and she said she had never been able to trust another maid since.

The idea of not trusting a servant was true, so far as it went. Servants were often employed as spies, and Eiddwen was in the palace on a dangerous mission. She could not risk being discovered. The deeper truth was that she could not stand having another person around her. She liked being alone. She had never had friends as a child in the orphanage where Xavier's followers had discovered the exotically beautiful and highly intelligent little girl. A child with no parents to cause problems. They deemed her to be suitable for their purposes and had spirited her away, taken her to meet Xavier.

He had given the orphan child a name and had handed her over to his followers to raise. She had been unusual in that she had never wanted friends. She trusted no one, cared for no one. If she took a lover, she did so for reasons that had nothing to do with love.

Eiddwen arrayed herself in a beautiful silk chemise adorned with lace and a black silk dressing gown embroidered with flowers. She shook out her black curls and let her hair fall about her shoulders. Attired for her night's work, she went to the bed, reached into a slit she had made in the mattress, and withdrew a large roll of paper. She spread this out on the bedroom floor, got down on her knees, and began studying the diagrams. A soft knock on the wall made her frown.

Rising to her feet with an exasperated sigh, she went over to the panel and passed her hand over a magical construct set in the wall. The secret door slid open and a young man entered. He was wearing a poet shirt, trousers that buckled just beneath the knee, shoes, and stockings. He was handsome with large brown eyes, a fine nose, and a strong jawline. His eyes and smile were both touched with a hint of melancholy. He seemed to be saying to every woman he met, "I have some secret sorrow that only you can understand."

Eiddwen was proof against those sensuous eyes. She regarded him with annoyance.

"What are you doing here? I did not send for you."

"No, you did not," said the young man. He tried to take hold of her. "I'm lonely and you look ravishing."

Eiddwen shoved him away. "Go back to your room, Lucello. You take far too great a risk coming here. Someone might have seen you."

Lucello pouted. "Do not be so cruel to me, Eiddwen. It has been so long . . ." He tried to kiss her.

Eiddwen gave him a cold and glittering look. Lucello backed away. He walked over to the bed, sat down, and scowled.

"Why won't you make love to me anymore?"

"Because you are here to make love to the princess," said Eiddwen.

Kneeling again on the floor, she smoothed out a corner of the paper and bent down to study it more closely.

He shrugged. "I can do that in my sleep. She already adores me."

"And she must go on adoring you," said Eiddwen.

"Until when?" Lucello asked impatiently. "Living here is like living in a mausoleum! I shall go out of my head with boredom. Other women in this palace will be glad to have me in their beds if you won't. I might go pay a visit to one right now."

Eiddwen shifted her head slightly to look at him. "You will obey me, Lucello. You know what will happen if you don't."

"You may threaten me all you like, Eiddwen, but you need me to seduce the princess," Lucello said with a shrug.

"You can't make this plot of yours work without me. I'll do as I please."

Eiddwen smiled at him. "Dear Lucello, if you were discovered in your bed with your throat slit from ear to ear, I would be very sorry. Mainly because I would have to make other arrangements with regard to the princess."

Lucello tried to meet her eyes and failed.

"I wasn't serious. You know that."

Eiddwen resumed her perusal of the paper.

"What are you looking at that you find so damn fascinating?" Lucello asked in sulky tones.

"An architectural rendering of the ground floor of the palace," she replied. Rolling up the paper briskly, she rose to her feet. "Or rather it would be the ground floor, if the palace were actually resting on the ground."

"What are you plotting now?" He left the bed and came to stand close to her.

"I have work to do, Lucello," she said.

"You know you want me," he said.

His voice was soft, his eyes filled with longing, yearning. His voice, his eyes had seduced many young girls, luring them to his bed, to enslavement, to death.

He put his arms around her and tried to kiss her neck.

"I love you, Eiddwen."

She turned away. "Be a good boy, Lucello. Go to your room and stay there."

The young man flushed with rage and shame. His body trembled. He caught hold of her arm. "I know how to kill, Eiddwen! You taught me!"

"Don't be a bore, Lucello," she said.

He glared at her, his hands twitching as if he longed to put them around her throat. After a brief struggle with himself, he muttered a curse and left by way of the secret panel.

Eiddwen sat down at her dressing table in front of the mirror.

"He is starting to think too well of himself," she said to her reflection. "He is becoming a nuisance."

Yet, there wasn't much she could do. Despite what she had said to the contrary, she needed him. She had to carry out this latest strange scheme of Xavier's to abduct savants.

She could send Lucello away, leave without the princess, tell Xavier . . . Tell him what? That she refused to obey him?

Eiddwen shivered. She feared no one in this world and she didn't believe in the next. But she went in awe of Xavier. He had guided her life from the time she was a child and although he had never harmed her, never spoken harshly to her, he had a way of shriveling her soul, making her feel small and helpless.

Once she had dealt with her original assignment, she would deal with the princess.

The clock chimed one. Eiddwen touched her lips with carnelian and her cheeks with rouge, smearing the rouge as though she had spent the night in pleasurable pursuits. To add to the fiction, she mussed her curls and unfastened some of the ribbon ties on her dressing gown. She pulled a silk mask—that staple of clandestine lovers—over her face.

The palace was dark, quiet. Eiddwen began the long trek down to the palace's lowest level. What would be the ground floor—if the palace was on the ground.

20

The difficulty has not been in creating the magical metal, but in creating a viable way to use the metal on a gunboat. We have determined that a refitted merchantman will be better suited than a naval gunboat, providing the structure needed to support the weight of the steel plating. Having reached this conclusion, I am pleased to report that the work proceeds well. The gunboat will be ready as scheduled and on budget.

—Sir Henry Wallace,
report to Queen Mary of Freya

The rain had stopped in Rosia. The gray clouds had moved on to drench Rosia's enemy, the nation of Freya. The downpour had ceased for the moment, allowing Sir Henry and his friend of twenty years, Admiral Randolph Baker, to venture out to inspect Sir Henry's invention.

Admiral Baker stared at it, walked around it, then said with a powerful snort, "I think the bloody boat looks god-awful."

"I find her beautiful," said Sir Henry.

Both men laughed. The admiral was a stout man of medium height, deeply tanned from his years of sailing. He wore a white periwig to conceal his baldness. Admiral Baker was a "thoroughgoing sailor" as the saying went, and despite his stern, dour demeanor, his men respected him. His nickname belowdecks was "Old Doom and Gloom" because he was a pessimist who anticipated the worst possible outcome. When something went right, the admiral would shake his head and mutter, "It is only temporary."

The two men were in a salvage yard located on the outskirts of Haever. Sir Henry had purchased the yard because it was littered with the wooden hulks of wrecked ships, rusting lift tanks, wooden masts stacked like cordwood, piles of rope rigging, limp balloons, and rolls of canvas sails—the perfect cover for Sir Henry's clandestine operations.

Salvage ships came and went, towing their prizes behind them. Men crawled over the ships, taking them apart. At the rear of the salvage yard in a fenced-off, restricted area, men worked on the construction of an experimental gunboat armored with the new magically enhanced steel invented by the genius, Pietro Alcazar.

The gunboat was surrounded by a fence reinforced with unseen, magical traps meant to deter invaders. One entered through a gate that was locked by ordinary locks requiring a key to open, as well as by magical locks requiring a magical key. Alcazar's workshop was inside the fenced-off area. He labored here six days a week, assisted by a journeyman and his apprentice, as well as a blacksmith and his apprentice, assigned to build the steel panels for the gunboat currently being inspected by Sir Henry and Admiral Baker.

Despite Sir Henry's praise, the gunboat was anything but beautiful, looking like no other gunboat that had ever set sail. Long sheets of the new steel angled down along the hull from the main deck. Lighter sheets of steel extended out from the keel along the underside of the hull. The prow, covered in the lighter weight steel, extended out from under the heavy armor.

A pair of steel-covered wings, each mounted with a large air screw, helped maneuver the heavy ship. Sir Henry had added bracings and lift tanks beneath the heavy upper armor. A pair of masts supported sails and ballast tanks.

"How have the tests gone?" Admiral Baker asked in a glum tone that implied he expected the worst.

"Exceedingly well," said Sir Henry. "Bullets fired at point-blank range left a few marks on the steel, but that is all. We sailed the gunboat around the point and fired a twelve-pound cannonball at it. You can see here where it hit."

Sir Henry indicated a small dent in one of the steel panels. Admiral Baker leaned close to inspect it. He stood up, gave a noncommittal grunt.

Sir Henry was annoyed. "By God, you are a hard man to impress, Randolph."

"The way you carried on about this miraculous steel, Henry, I expected you to say the damn cannonball went up in a puff of smoke. Still, I suppose one could term it satisfactory," Admiral Baker conceded grudgingly.

Sir Henry grinned. He was in a good mood, pleased with the experiments on the steel. Not even his friend's gloomy aspect could ruin it.

Of the four friends at Grafton University, Henry had been the brainy schemer, Alan Northrop the smooth-talking cavalier, Simon Yates the analytical thinker, and Randolph Baker the dour pessimist. Though vastly different in personality, the four were inseparable. They had two things in common: They were all ambitious for power and wealth and they were all second sons, which meant they would have to find that power and wealth on their own. The four termed themselves "The Seconds."

Simon Yates, now confined to a wheelchair by a bullet in his spine, worked in government intelligence. Randolph Baker had chosen a naval career after he graduated, as did

Alan Northrop. The two had tried to persuade their friend Henry Wallace, whose father was a "red judge" on the high court, to join them in the navy. Sir Henry decided his path to glory lay in serving his country in a different way. A chance encounter with Crown Prince Godfrey landed Henry a job in the Office of Foreign Affairs. He had gone on to become one of the most powerful men in Freya.

Randolph Baker had risen to the rank of lord admiral in Her Majesty's navy. Captain Alan Northrop would have undoubtedly attained high rank, but for a scandal involving his older brother, Jacob.

The truth of what happened between the brothers was known to only a few, Sir Henry among them. All the public knew was that Jacob had fled to Rosia and Alan had inherited the family fortune. Quitting the navy that would have left him a lieutenant all his life, he had purchased his own ship. Captain Alan Northrop was now an extremely successful privateer, so successful that his queen had thought fit to honor him with a knighthood. The rakish rogue was now *Sir* Alan Northrop, much to the amusement of his friends.

"I am convinced this magical steel will withstand a hit from the green fire those demons used to sink the *Royal Lion,*" Sir Henry continued. "Unfortunately we have no way of testing that. Too bad we don't have that green beam weapon Eiddwen invented, the weapon that almost sank the *Defiant.* The weapon *I* paid for."

"Damn female made a fool of you, Henry," said Admiral Baker. "You aren't the first man to fall for a pretty face. You won't be the last."

"It wasn't Eiddwen's pretty face I was after," said Sir Henry drily. "I wanted that weapon. We saw what it did to the cutter. They've made improvements since. You should have seen King Alaric's pride, the *Royal Lion,* go down. They sank her with one shot."

"Wish I had seen it!" said Admiral Baker. "When is Alan coming to captain this marvel of yours?"

"His ship has only just docked," said Sir Henry. "He has to remain with his ship to supervise some repairs and wait for some prize he captured to arrive. Speaking of prizes, when does the rest of the fleet sail for Braffa?"

"Day after tomorrow if the winds hold," said Admiral Baker. "We're almost finished provisioning. It's a beautiful sight, the fleet. A dozen two-deck ships of the line, eight frigates, and ten sloops. The heavy frigates *Griffon, Intruder,* and *Duke Edmond* and the sloops *Halian, Wartin*, and *Packford* are already on the way east to meet with four ships of the line, then on to the Straits de Domcáido.

"I hope your bloody plan works, Henry," the admiral added. "You've got me taking the main fleet south around the Star's Feet and that will add at least seven days to the voyage. Damn war might be over by the time I get there."

"Sending part of the fleet through the straits will keep the Estarans busy, make them think that the rest of the fleet is on the way. The rest of the fleet *will* be on the way, just not the way the Estarans, the Travians, and the Rosians expect. As for the extra time . . ." Sir Henry shrugged. "There won't be a war. No one wants to offend Braffa by attacking it. The Braffans would shut down the refineries that make the Blood, which keeps the ships afloat. The standoff over Braffa will continue, while I conduct secret negotiations with the Braffan government. When those are concluded, the arrival of the Freyan fleet will assure the Braffans that we mean to support their determination for independence."

"That assumes your negotiations go well," said Admiral Baker, gloomily shaking his head.

"I have no reason to think they won't," said Sir Henry, smiling.

Their conversation was interrupted by a man carrying a

leather satchel, walking into the shipyard with a hurried stride.

"Ah, the inimitable Mr. Sloan," said Sir Henry. "You appear to be bursting with news, Mr. Sloan. I can practically see it oozing out of your boots."

"Indeed, my lord," Mr. Sloan replied gravely. "A terrible tragedy has occurred in Rosia. Two days ago, the Crystal Market hall collapsed. The number of dead may never be known, but it must be well into the hundreds."

"What was the cause?" Sir Henry asked sharply.

"Smitten by the hand of God," suggested Admiral Baker.

"The cause is unknown, my lord," said Mr. Sloan. "Our agents are trying to find out, but information is difficult to obtain. All the guild crafters who worked on the market have mysteriously disappeared. They were spirited away on orders of the grand bishop."

"We know this for a fact?" Sir Henry asked.

"Yes, sir. I received this report from one of our agents in Evreux. She hastened to the scene the moment she heard about the disaster. She was wearing the guild emblem in order to obtain access to the site and was examining some of the glass bricks when she was seized by one of the church guards, who insisted that she accompany him. He put her in a carriage with other crafters and gave the driver orders to take them to the Asylum at Charenton. She jumped from the moving carriage and managed to escape. I have here her full report, my lord."

Mr. Sloan indicated the leather satchel.

"How very strange," said Sir Henry, thoughtful. "I wonder why the hall collapsed."

"God's balls, Henry, it's a thousand dead Rosians!" said Admiral Baker explosively. "We should be celebrating. Who gives a damn how the bloody hall fell down."

Sir Henry saw Mr. Sloan about to make some remark. He

apparently changed his mind, however, for he remained silent.

"You have something more to say on the subject, Mr. Sloan," said Sir Henry. "Speak freely. Admiral Baker is in our confidence, as always."

"Yes, my lord. Our agent has been a crafter for twenty years. She states in her report that she never saw anything like this. According to the crafters who were with her in the carriage, the glass bricks had been covered in magical constructs. They claimed the magical constructs on the bricks had been erased."

Sir Henry's good mood evaporated.

"Bosh!" Admiral Baker snorted. "Impossible."

"Not so impossible. The constructs on the watchtower at Upper Alten were erased," said Sir Henry. "The constructs on my mansion were erased. But in those cases, the fiends attacked them with green fire."

"No one reported seeing flashes of green fire at the Crystal Market," said Mr. Sloan. "Yet something caused the magic to fail."

Sir Henry thought of the astounding letter he had recently received from Father Jacob relating all he knew about the Bottom Dwellers, about contramagic, about the attack on the abbey, the destruction of the *Royal Lion,* the collapse of the watchtower. Slowly the pieces of the puzzle were coming together to form an extremely ugly and horrifying picture.

Father Jacob had risked his life writing this letter, for if it became known he was corresponding with Rosia's enemy, he would be executed for treason. Sir Henry appreciated this fact and had not mentioned the letter to Admiral Baker. There was really no need. Baker considered Father Jacob a traitor to his church and country and would thus refuse to believe anything the man said. Mr. Sloan knew, of course. Franklin Sloan knew everything.

Sir Henry was roused from his musings by a polite cough from his secretary.

"I'm sorry, Mr. Sloan, you have more news to report?"

"Yes, my lord. When I came through the gate in the fence just now, I checked the magical traps. One was tripped."

"Only one?" Admiral Baker gave a dismissive sniff. "Must've been rats."

"I do *not* believe it was rats, my lord," said Mr. Sloan stiffly. "I myself hired the crafter to place the magical traps according to my own specifications."

"The admiral was jesting, Mr. Sloan," said Sir Henry, hastening to soothe his secretary's ruffled feelings. He cast a glance at the admiral, whose suggestion that Mr. Sloan's traps were of such a simplistic design that rats could set them off was offensive in the extreme.

"Yes, damn it, man, don't be so blasted serious," said Admiral Baker, taking the hint.

Mollified, Mr. Sloan proceeded with his report. "The crafter surrounded the gunboat with a clay slurry set with magical constructs. I activate the magic nightly. If anyone larger than a small child sets foot on the slurry, the magic retains evidence of an intruder."

Mr. Sloan led them to the starboard side of the gunboat and pointed to the ground. He passed his hand over the magical slurry. A part of the slurry began to glow red, revealing a partial footprint. Mr. Sloan pointed out several other areas where the intruder had stepped in the slurry.

"How could someone break into the yard?" Admiral Baker asked.

"He wouldn't have to if he were an employee, sir," said Mr. Sloan. "He had only to conceal himself until after closing hours."

"Astute reasoning, Mr. Sloan," said Sir Henry. "What did our intruder want?"

"Sabotage," suggested Admiral Baker.

The three men boarded the boat. They examined the helm, the steering, the rigging, the lift tanks, the balloons, the hull, the twelve-pound cannons, and the sixteen swivel guns. They found no signs that anyone had tampered with anything.

"Maybe our intruder just wanted to get a look at it," said Sir Henry, puzzled.

"My lord," Mr. Sloan called from a different part of the gunboat, where he had been examining the steel plates, "you need to see this."

He pointed to a spot on one of the plates. Sir Henry peered at it closely and muttered, "Damn and blast it!"

"What is it?" Admiral Baker thrust his face near the panel. "I don't see a goddamn thing."

"The damage here, sir," said Mr. Sloan, touching the panel with his finger.

The admiral peered at it, practically pressing his nose to the steel. He frowned, straightened. "Looks like someone threw acid on it. Why the devil would anyone do that?"

"Admiral Baker's description is most apt, my lord," said Mr. Sloan. "I recall observing something similar when the demons attacked your house with their green fire weapons. Wherever the green fire struck them, the metal pots and kettles, pipes, and the downspouts looked as if they had been hit by acid. In those instances, the metal had almost completely dissolved."

"You're saying a demon sneaked in here, blasted this panel with green fire, and left." Admiral Baker shook his head. "Makes no bloody sense. Why wouldn't he just blow up the goddamn boat?"

"Because he was here to discover something far more important," said Sir Henry. "He wanted to find out if this steel can withstand contramagic. We will inspect the other panels. Mr. Sloan, go fetch Alcazar."

Mr. Sloan left upon his errand. Sir Henry and Admiral Baker inspected every panel. They found no signs that any of the rest had been damaged.

Mr. Sloan returned, accompanied by Pietro Alcazar, inventor of the magically enhanced steel. Formerly a journeyman at the Rosian Royal Armory, Alcazar had sought to sell his invention to Sir Henry, hoping to pay off gambling debts. He had sent Sir Henry a pewter tankard inscribed with magical constructs that strengthened the metal. Realizing the worth of this invention, Sir Henry had gone to Rosia personally to bring Alcazar to Freya.

"Mr. Sloan says you wanted to show me something, my lord," said Alcazar, wiping his grimy hands on a rag.

A small, slender man of a nervous temperament, Alcazar was fond of his work, devoted to his family, and addicted to baccarat. Sir Henry had made Alcazar a wealthy man and also a virtual prisoner. Guards escorted Alcazar from his home in Haever to his workshop every morning and took him back to his home every night. Alcazar was not permitted to go near gambling dens, much to the relief of his family.

"Look at this." Sir Henry pointed to the melted spot.

As Alcazar examined it his eyes widened. He stepped back, staring at the spot with evident dismay and confusion.

"Did the steel melt?" Sir Henry asked acerbically.

"It would appear so, my lord," said Alcazar, flustered. "But that's not possible."

"Yet it happened," said Sir Henry grimly. "So apparently it *is* possible."

"I . . . I know, but . . ." Alcazar gazed at the panel in bewilderment. "It isn't poss—"

"Don't say it's not possible when it clearly is possible!" Sir Henry snapped. "Check the magical constructs present in that spot."

"My lord, the magical constructs are a part of the steel itself. The constructs would not show up as constructs *per se*—"

Sir Henry glared, frustrated. "There must be some way to tell if the magical constructs in the steel have been broken or destroyed."

"Magic cannot be destroyed, my lord," said Alcazar. "That is the first law—" Seeing the expression on Sir Henry's face, Alcazar gulped and began again. "There . . . uh . . . might be a way. I can cast a spell that causes the constructs to glow faintly—"

"Just do it!" Sir Henry said through gritted teeth.

"Yes, my lord."

Sir Henry was not a crafter. He gestured to Mr. Sloan, who was a channeler, to keep a close eye on Alcazar, observe the experiment. Channelers could not build magical constructs themselves, but since they could channel the magic through the constructs, they had the ability to see them. Alcazar began swiftly tracing magical constructs over the steel. Mr. Sloan leaned close to follow the progress.

Sir Henry and Admiral Baker stood nearby, waiting in silence. When the spell was complete, Alcazar and Mr. Sloan peered intently at the panel. Alcazar gave a little gasp. Mr. Sloan raised his eyebrows.

"Well?" said Sir Henry.

"The magic in that one spot is gone," said Alcazar. "I don't understand . . ."

"Mr. Sloan," said Sir Henry. "Can you confirm?"

"Master Alcazar is right, my lord. When he cast the spell, the entire panel begin to glow, as one would expect. Except that one spot. It remained dark."

"There is the possibility . . . ," Alcazar said timidly.

"What, damn it?" Sir Henry said.

"You remember Monsieur Rodrigo, my lord. I was talking with him on board the ship about the magical steel. As you recall, it was his theory that inspired me—"

"Yes, yes, get on with it!"

"We got to talking about the theory of magic and Monsieur Rodrigo mentioned contramagic, how its constructs could erase magic. He said that's what happened when the green beam of light hit the *Royal Lion*."

"And you never thought to tell me this?" Sir Henry demanded. He was pretending to be angry, since he had been eavesdropping on the two himself. As had Eiddwen . . .

"The study of contramagic is evil, my lord," said Alcazar, looking shocked. "I did not want to imperil my immortal soul. I told Monsieur Rodrigo I wouldn't listen to such talk. He laughed. I didn't think he was serious . . ."

"Oh, he was serious, our Monsieur Rodrigo," Sir Henry said grimly.

He began to pace about the yard. Admiral Baker squinted at the panel. The rain had started again, but no one seemed to notice. Alcazar wiped his face with his sleeve and started to speak. Mr. Sloan, seeing Sir Henry absorbed in thought, shook his head.

Sir Henry stopped his pacing, turned. "Tell me, Master Alcazar, did anyone hear you and Monsieur Rodrigo talking about contramagic?"

"That's what frightened me, my lord," said Alcazar. "Monsieur Rodrigo wouldn't keep his voice down. I was afraid someone would overhear and report us. A lot of people were on deck. My brother and his family and, of course, the sailors."

Mr. Sloan cast a sharp glance at Sir Henry.

"You said Eiddwen was disguised as a sailor, my lord."

"True, Mr. Sloan," said Sir Henry, his expression dark. "True. I fear this confirms my earlier suspicions."

"It's not my fault, my lord!" Alcazar babbled. "I didn't tell anyone! I kept quiet—"

"No one's blaming you. Get back to work!" Sir Henry snapped.

Alcazar returned to his workshop, casting uncertain glances all the way, as though expecting to be struck from behind.

"Eiddwen," Admiral Baker said, astonished. "That thrice-cursed female?"

"I told you she smuggled herself on board that blasted ship," said Sir Henry. "I feared she might have eavesdropped on their conversation and now it seems I was right. She needs to know if she has reason to be worried about this magical steel shielding a ship against her demonic green fire. She wouldn't dare risk coming back to Freya," Sir Henry continued, thinking out loud. "She would assign the job to one of her confederates."

"The question is, how did they find out where we are producing the steel?" Mr. Sloan asked.

"An excellent question," said Sir Henry. "I will have a talk with Master Alcazar."

"Must have been a bloody great disappointment to the demon," said Admiral Baker. "All that work for a smudge."

"He's right, my lord," said Mr. Sloan, struck by the admiral's remark. "He fired at only one small portion on one panel. That wouldn't prove much. He should have tested the other panels and yet he didn't. Perhaps something happened to alarm him—"

"Rats," said the admiral, winking at Sir Henry.

Mr. Sloan pointedly ignored the admiral's jab. "There are tenement houses nearby, my lord, as well as two taverns.

People are on the streets at all hours. The intruder could have seen or heard something that alarmed him and he fled."

"Either that or his weapon malfunctioned," said Sir Henry.

"An excellent suggestion, my lord," said Mr. Sloan. "We must consider the possibility that the intruder left before he had concluded his experiment."

"And in that case, he will be back," said Sir Henry exultantly. "Mr. Sloan, did you have the magical trap replaced? Or add any constructs to the fence?"

"No, my lord. I thought perhaps you might wish to examine it before I summoned the crafters."

"Excellent," said Sir Henry, rubbing his hands. "Don't touch it. Leave everything as he left it."

"Are you daft, Henry?" Admiral Baker stared at him. "You sound as if you *want* the demon to finish what he started."

"That is precisely what I do want, Randolph," said Sir Henry. "If he does, Mr. Sloan and I will be waiting for him."

Sir Henry gave Mr. Sloan his instructions for the evening's "entertainment," as Admiral Baker termed it. The secretary departed. Sir Henry and Admiral Baker walked over to the workshop to have their talk with Alcazar.

"Damn sorry I can't stay here to help catch your demon, Henry," said Admiral Baker. "I have to return to the flagship to see that all is ready for the voyage to Braffa. You must promise to write with all the gory details."

"Let us hope there will be no gore," said Sir Henry.

"Damn it, man, have a little fun," said Admiral Baker, slapping his friend on the back.

The interior walls of the workshop were black with soot from the melting crucibles and the forge fire, where the smith was hard at work preparing the pig iron, limestone, canisters of purified gases drawn from the Breath, and a tank of the Blood of God. A young apprentice was cleaning the infusing chamber where the liquid metal would be carefully mixed with the gases. Alcazar sat on a tall stool at a large stone table, scrawling magical constructs on the stone. He would stare at them, shake his head, and rub them out in frustration.

"What are you working on, my friend?" Sir Henry asked, sending his sharp glance into every corner.

"A way to improve the steel," said Alcazar eagerly. He was never happier than when talking about his inventions. "I was thinking—"

Sir Henry interrupted. "Where is your other workman? The journeyman. I forget his name—"

Alcazar glanced around vaguely and blinked. "You mean Brice? Isn't he here? He must be around somewhere."

Sir Henry noticed the smith's young apprentice avert his face and become immediately absorbed in his work. The apprentice was sixteen with a mop of red hair and freckles. He quaked at the sight of the famous spymaster bearing down on him.

"Now, lad, don't be frightened," said Sir Henry in kindly tones. "Do you know where we might find Master Brice?"

"N-n-no, m-m-my lord," the young man replied, going white beneath his freckles.

The blacksmith ceased his work and looked up. "Brice hasn't been to work in two days, my lord."

Alcazar was amazed. "He hasn't? Why didn't you say something, Ronson?"

"I did, sir," said the blacksmith in long-suffering tones.

"What do you know about this, my lad?" Sir Henry asked the apprentice.

His tone was kind. The expression in his eyes was not. The young man quailed.

"Master Brice said he had come into a . . . bit of money and . . . and if anyone asked . . . I was to say he was took sick . . ."

He cast Sir Henry a pleading glance. "I didn't think nothing of it, my lord! Brice was always goin' to the prizefights. I thought he'd got lucky on a bet!"

The young man was shivering with fear.

Sir Henry sighed. "Calm down, lad. I am not going to skin you alive. Any time you hear of someone who works here coming into 'a bit of money,' inform me."

He and Admiral Baker exchanged glances. "Now we know how the secret got out."

Alcazar was bewildered. "What secret? I don't understand."

"Your bloody journeyman is a bloody traitor!" Admiral Baker shouted.

"Oh, my God!" Alcazar almost fell off his stool. "I didn't know, Sir Henry. You must believe me!"

Sir Henry didn't answer. He and the admiral walked out of the workshop. They didn't speak until they had left the salvage yard and were waiting for the admiral's coach.

"That Alcazar's a dunderhead," said Admiral Baker at last.

"He's a genius," said Sir Henry drily.

"Same thing." The admiral grunted. "How the devil did Eiddwen find out this Brice chap was working for Alcazar?"

Sir Henry shrugged. "Easy enough. If I were Eiddwen I would have planted agents in all the shipyard taverns and guild halls with orders to keep their ears and eyes open. Sooner or later they're bound to hear someone talk about strange steel or merchant ships being turned into gunboats. I hope Brice enjoyed his earnings as soon as he was paid. Eiddwen never leaves loose ends."

The admiral chuckled. Sir Henry reported the matter to

the Haever constabulary, not going into detail, of course, but saying he had an interest in a man who had disappeared. Two days later, the constables informed Sir Henry that the body of a man answering Brice's description had been found floating in the river, a knife in his back and a wad of banknotes in his pocket.

21

I am intrigued with the new constructs your man Alcazar has submitted for patent. In my experience, innovation more often comes from the independent crafter looking at a problem through a new lens, as my old mentor used to say, than from the constricted methodology of the guild hall. That said, you may be interested in seeing these latest submissions regarding improvements in firearms. As I did with the new guns with the rifled bore, I will pass this on to your man, Mr. Sloan.

—Simon Yates,
in a letter to Sir Henry Wallace

While the admiral and Sir Henry were enjoying a meal of beefsteak and roasted potatoes at Sir Henry's club, Mr. Sloan was inside a rag and bottle shop, purchasing two shabby peacoats such as were worn by sailors. He took the peacoats to what was known as a "sigil shop" located on a side street.

A sign hanging outside the sigil shop featured six magical sigils connected in a circle. The six were the original six sigils first used by ancient man to create magic: air, earth, fire, water, life, death. The sign signified that the shop dealt in the business of making and selling magical constructs.

Mr. Sloan entered, carrying his peacoats underneath his arm. The proprietor, Mistress Brown, a crafter who had taken over the business after her husband had run off with a wine merchant's daughter, was exceptionally skilled at her work. She could have found employment in any of the larger magical houses had she not been left to care for two little boys.

Mistress Brown had been struggling to make ends meet before being discovered by Mr. Sloan, who always kept an eye out for talent. He had given her one or two jobs and had found her to be efficient and very discreet. After that, he had placed her on retainer, making life much easier for her and her children.

Mistress Brown was with a customer when Mr. Sloan entered. She smiled at him and hastened to get rid of the customer, who wanted magical constructs placed on a set of crockery to stop the clumsy kitchen girl from breaking them.

After the customer left, Mr. Sloan greeted Mistress Brown, then added, "It might be well if you were to close for the day, ma'am."

Mistress Brown obeyed immediately. She lowered the shutters, shut the curtains, and locked the door. She and Mr. Sloan repaired to a back room where she did her work. The walls were lined with bookcases containing books on constructs. A large table took up most of the area. She lived above the shop. Mr. Sloan could hear the sound of small boots thudding on the floor over their heads.

"It sounds as if your boys are thriving, ma'am," said Mr. Sloan politely.

"They are indeed, sir, thank you. And thank Sir Henry for placing them in such an excellent school. I could have never afforded such a luxury myself. Now what can I do for you, Mr. Sloan?"

"I need magical constructs on these two jackets, ma'am," said Mr. Sloan. He laid the peacoats down on the table. "Protective constructs, guarding against the usual—bullets, knife blades."

"Of course, Mr. Sloan. I can place those on the fabric in either ink or embroidery. The embroidery will take longer, of course, but will be more lasting."

"Ink if you please, ma'am. I need these immediately. I will wait for them, if that is convenient."

"Quite convenient, Mr. Sloan," said Mistress Brown. "I'll just get started—"

"One more thing, ma'am," said Mr. Sloan. "I need you to add constructs to protect against contramagic."

Mistress Brown stared at him. The color drained from her face. She forced a smile.

"You will have your little jest with me, Mr. Sloan . . ."

"I never jest, ma'am," said Mr. Sloan. "I am very much in earnest."

"Mr. Sloan, what you ask is impossible," said Mistress Brown in hushed tones. She cast a fearful glance at the room above and added, "Not only that, sir, we could both be arrested for talking about such evil!"

Mr. Sloan gazed at her intently. "You are a gifted crafter, ma'am."

"The most gifted crafter in the world could not do what you ask, Mr. Sloan. In order to build a construct that would protect against . . . what you ask, I would first have to have studied . . . that sort of magic. That is forbidden."

Mr. Sloan had expected the answer. Still, he and Sir Henry had thought it worthwhile to try.

"Very well, mistress. I understand. I assume I can trust to your discretion?"

"You may, Mr. Sloan," said Mistress Brown. She started to say something, then checked herself.

"Yes, Mistress Brown? Speak freely."

"I fear you are in some sort of terrible danger, Mr. Sloan. Perhaps I could add something more to the coat—"

Mr. Sloan recalled the green fire weapons. "A good idea, ma'am. Constructs that guard against flame would be a welcome addition."

"That I can easily do, Mr. Sloan," said Mistress Brown with a relieved smile. "If you would take a seat in the waiting room, I will set to work."

Mistress Brown spread one of the peacoats out on the table. Dipping a steel pen in ink, she began to painstakingly draw the complex magical constructs on the coarse fabric. Mr. Sloan watched a moment, then went to the waiting room and sat down in a stiff-backed chair. He took out a well-worn book containing the writings of the saints and began to read it, as was his daily habit.

Sir Henry parted cordially with Admiral Baker, wishing him a prosperous and safe voyage. Admiral Baker wished Sir Henry good luck with the demon hunting and ordered his carriage to take him to the wharf. Sir Henry returned to his home in Haever.

He indulged himself by going to the nursery to play with the baby. The nursemaid stood looking on in stern disapproval. A father was meant to see his child only at teatime, when Baby had been washed and dressed and was deemed suitable for presentation. The father might perhaps chuck the baby beneath the chin or pat its little head. The idea that a father should actually set foot in the nursery, pick up Baby, and play with him was shocking.

"I almost gave notice," the nursemaid confided to the cook. "Such goings-on in a respectable household. It's not natural."

Sir Henry left the nursery to seek out his wife. He found her arranging a bouquet of flowers in the drawing room.

"I will be working late at the palace tonight, little Mouse," he told her. "Do not wait up for me."

Lady Anne made a face. "We are to dine with the Winterhavens, my dear. Had you forgotten?"

"You must make my excuses," said Sir Henry. "Affairs of state."

"Poor Henry," said Anne, gently touching his face as he bent to kiss her. "You do not take a moment's ease. My aunt works you too hard. I will complain to her that I never see my husband."

She said this with a mischievous smile. Lady Anne's aunt was the queen.

Sir Henry gave her a kiss. "Enjoy yourself tonight, my dear, but you must not stay out late. Are you certain you should go? You look tired."

He spoke in anxious tones as he regarded his wife worriedly. Lady Anne was small boned, with delicate features and large eyes, resembling the "Mouse," which was Henry's pet name for her.

"I am fine, my love," said Lady Anne, smiling up at him. "Lady Winterhaven needs me to make a fourth at whist. I will be home before midnight, I promise." She gave a charming little pout. "I don't suppose you could make me the same promise? That you will be home before midnight?"

"I fear not, my Mouse," said Sir Henry. "This Braffa mess . . . I have reams of paperwork . . ."

He kissed her, marveling as always how she could possibly have come to love him. Equally marvelous was the idea that he had fallen in love with her.

Sir Henry did not travel to the palace, as he had told his wife. He ordered the coachman to take him to a small apothecary shop. Sir Henry entered and nodded to the proprietor, who was busy grinding up something with a mortar and pestle while a customer waited. The proprietor gave a slight jerk of his head toward the back. Sir Henry continued on through a door into a large office, where he found Mr. Sloan waiting for him.

"I see you have the coats, Mr. Sloan."

"Yes, my lord. I asked Mistress Brown about the contramagic. She refused to accede to the request. I am afraid I distressed her with the question, my lord."

"It was worth a try, Mr. Sloan. Oddly enough, I find myself in agreement with my old foe, Father Jacob. We will rue the day we banned the study of contramagic."

Sir Henry and Mr. Sloan changed clothes, putting on slouch hats and the shabby-looking peacoats now embellished with protective magical constructs. Both men armed themselves with several loaded pistols, which they dropped into capacious pockets. Sir Henry added a stowaway pistol, and Mr. Sloan thrust a large knife into his boot. Both carried small bull's-eye lanterns, which they wore on lanyards around their necks. These small lanterns contained glowing magical constructs behind shutters that concealed the light.

"As I did not think it would be wise for us to be seen carrying your newly acquired rifles, my lord, I concealed two of them at the salvage yard. They are loaded and ready for use."

"We are facing one man, Mr. Sloan, not an army," said Sir Henry with some amusement. He grew more serious. "And the goal is to take this man alive for interrogation. We know he is using a contramagic weapon. That means he is likely one of the Bottom Dwellers *and* he is in contact with Eiddwen. The information he could provide us will be invaluable."

Mr. Sloan nodded to indicate he understood. "Still, one should always be prepared, my lord."

"True, Mr. Sloan. I have not had a chance to practice with the new rifles," Sir Henry added, adjusting the bull's-eye lantern around his neck.

"I believe you will be impressed with the accuracy and ease of firing, my lord," said Mr. Sloan.

They waited until the customer was gone and the shop empty before they left. One reason Sir Henry had selected an apothecary shop as cover for his operations was that all manner of people, from fine gentlemen to humble street sweepers, could be seen coming and going and not raise suspicion.

Mr. Sloan had a carriage waiting. He mounted the driver's box, while Sir Henry took his seat in the back. They set out through the streets of Haever just as night was falling and the lamplighters were plying their trade. The rain clouds had moved off.

Henry gazed out the window. Men were leaving work, entering the taverns for a nightly "wet." Women were sitting on the doorsteps, gossiping with their neighbors and shouting at children to come home for supper. In the well-to-do parts of the city, men and women were dressing in their finest, putting on their jewels, preparing to go to dinner or to the theater or the opera. Nursemaids were putting the children to bed.

Henry felt a sudden surge of love for these people, *his* people, from the whore plying her trade on the corner to Her Majesty the queen, from the ragged street urchin to his own dearly beloved baby son. His people; his responsibility. He was tasked with guarding them, keeping them safe.

He touched the pistols in his pockets and reflected that these people would never know what he had done for them, how many had died by his command because he deemed them a danger to his plans. Her Majesty knew some of what he did, but certainly not all. Ignorance is truly bliss.

He thrust out his long legs, folded his arms, leaned back comfortably in the leather seat, and pulled his hat over his face to take a brief nap. He woke as the carriage pulled up to an inn located near the salvage yard.

Mr. Sloan entered the inn and returned with one of Sir Henry's trusted operatives. The man unhitched the horses and led them into the stables behind the inn.

"Fields will have the carriage waiting for us upon our return, my lord," said Mr. Sloan, referring to the operative.

"Very good, Mr. Sloan," said Sir Henry.

Mr. Sloan and Sir Henry proceeded to the shipyard on foot. The neighborhood was a rough one and both men kept their hands on their pistols. They stayed in the shadows, walking around the pools of radiance cast by the streetlamps. Sir Henry considered it highly unlikely anyone was watching them, but he had lived as long as he had by never taking chances.

Keeping in mind that Eiddwen's agent had probably secured a job in the salvage yard, the agent would have to find a place to hide himself when the yard closed and the workers departed. Even then, Alcazar often worked far into the night, which meant that his guards and apprentices would also be present. With tenement housing only a block away, and two taverns that did not close until midnight, the intruder would be forced to remain until the early hours of the morning to experiment with the panels. He would not want anyone to see flashes of green fire or hear the muffled sound of the weapon going off.

Sir Henry fit the key to the gate in the fence surrounding

the salvage yard and he and Mr. Sloan entered silently. Sir Henry had ordered Alcazar to leave his workshop on time tonight. Alcazar had not asked questions. Knowing Sir Henry was angry over the journeyman, he'd been only too happy to obey.

Mr. Sloan and Sir Henry dared not risk using the bull's-eye lanterns in case the intruder should see them. The glow from streetlamps provided light enough for them to find their way through the salvage yard. They concealed their movements by ducking behind stacks of wood from ships in various stages of dismemberment.

Mr. Sloan had selected as a vantage point the hulk of a ferry that had caught fire on one of the inland seas. The fire had broken out while the ferry was docked and she had gone down in shallow water, which made for an easy salvage. The two men settled themselves inside the hulk on planks of wood stretched between sawhorses. They were about ten yards from Alcazar's workshop and the gunboat. They settled down for a long and tedious wait that might come to nothing.

A distant church bell tolled the hours. The time between strikes seemed so long that Sir Henry was starting to wonder if the blasted clock was broken. He had nearly reached the conclusion that their intruder was not coming when Mr. Sloan touched his arm and indicated a shadowy figure approaching the gunboat. Sir Henry's heart quickened with excitement.

The intruder was about six feet from the gunboat when he stepped into the light. Sir Henry caught a glimpse of a face out of hell. He and Mr. Sloan exchanged rueful glances. They had neither of them considered that the Bottom Dweller might have changed from his work clothes to his demonic armor.

The fact that he had done so made perfect sense, Sir

Henry thought. He would not only have excellent protection, but if anyone happened to report seeing a demon in a salvage yard, the person would probably be locked away in an asylum.

Mr. Sloan had lifted his bull's-eye and was about to raise the shutter to shed light on the intruder when Sir Henry nudged him. The Bottom Dweller had no idea he was under surveillance. Sir Henry wanted to see what the man did.

The intruder lifted a device that resembled a small cannon and rested it against his shoulder. Sir Henry recognized the weapon. He'd had an extremely close and unpleasant look at such a gun when Bottom Dwellers had ambushed him and Father Jacob in Westfirth. The intruder aimed the weapon at a panel on the gunboat—a different panel from the one he had previously chosen—and fired. A ball of green flame struck the panel. The green fire hit the steel panel and fizzled out.

Sir Henry could barely keep himself from raising a cheer. Ironically, he was grateful to the Bottom Dweller, for this test could not have been conducted without him. The intruder made some adjustment to the weapon, and then fired again at the same panel, though in a different part of the panel, with the same result. Sir Henry had seen enough.

He raised his pistol and nudged Mr. Sloan, who uncovered the bull's-eye, sending a beam of bright light stabbing through the darkness. The intruder whipped around. He was wearing the hideous demon-faced helm and leather armor, the same one Sir Henry remembered from the Bottom Dwellers in Westfirth.

"You have two pistols aimed at your heart," Sir Henry said coolly, cocking one of his pistols as Mr. Sloan cocked his. "Drop your weapon and surrender."

Instead of obeying, the intruder raised the gun.

"Damn!" Sir Henry swore. "Try to only wound him, Mr. Sloan. I want him alive."

Two pistol shots rang out almost simultaneously. The Bottom Dweller staggered as the bullets struck him. He did not fall, nor did he drop his weapon.

Green light flared. Mr. Sloan bellowed a warning and threw himself in front of Sir Henry. The ball of green fire caught Mr. Sloan in the shoulder, spinning him around and sending him flying. His bull's-eye lantern shattered, the light went out. Sir Henry was half blinded. He could see nothing for a moment except a dazzling blur of green.

"Mr. Sloan!" Sir Henry called, drawing a second pistol and ducking down behind a crate.

No answer.

Sir Henry rubbed his eyes until the blur went away. He could not find the Bottom Dweller in the darkness, but he could hear harsh breathing, shuffling feet, muffled swearing, and then the sound of a metal object hitting the ground. A noxious odor filled the air. Sir Henry choked, coughed, and hurriedly covered his mouth and nose. He kept his pistol raised, still searching for the Bottom Dweller, even as he tried to find out what had become of Mr. Sloan.

"Franklin! Where are you?" Sir Henry yelled, risking inhaling the fumes. He coughed again.

Hearing a groan and seeing a sudden flicker of green flame out of the corner of his eye, he rose from behind the crate to see Mr. Sloan on the ground. His coat had caught fire, but the flames were dying out. Sir Henry coughed again. The smoke must be poisonous, for he was starting to feel light-headed.

He started to go to Mr. Sloan. He heard pounding foot-falls and the demonic face was suddenly right in front of him, so close Henry could see the glittering eyes behind the helm. The intruder grabbed Sir Henry by the throat. Desperate to fend off the attack, feeling himself losing consciousness, Sir Henry pressed his pistol against the man's ribcage and fired. The man grunted, stumbled, and sagged to the ground.

Sir Henry knelt beside the Bottom Dweller, seized hold of the helm and tore it off. The man's skin was chalk white, his huge eyes black and glittering with hatred.

"Who sent you?" Sir Henry gasped, grasping the man by the leather breastplate and shaking him. "Did Eiddwen send you?"

The man's lips twisted in fury and he said something Sir Henry couldn't understand.

"Was it Eiddwen?" he asked again.

The life drained from the eyes, and before Sir Henry knew what was happening, the corpse burst into flames, burning Sir Henry's hand. He cursed and scrambled backward to escape the searing heat. He could hear the burning flesh pop and sizzle. The stench made him gag.

"Are you all right, sir?" Mr. Sloan called weakly.

"Rest easy, Mr. Sloan. I am fine. The intruder is dead, more's the pity. Let me see what happened to you."

Sir Henry hurried over to where Mr. Sloan was trying to struggle to his feet. Sir Henry pushed Mr. Sloan gently back to the ground, lit his bull's-eye to examine him.

Mr. Sloan's coat was charred and blackened and partially burned away in the vicinity of the shoulder, which had taken a direct hit. Sir Henry silently thanked Mistress Brown for the magic constructs inked onto the fabric, which had saved Mr. Sloan from more serious harm.

The smoke of the burning corpse drifted in their direction. Mr. Sloan retched. "What is that horrible smell, my lord?"

"Hellfire and damnation, Mr. Sloan," said Sir Henry. "Our Bottom Dweller intruder burst into flames. Can you stand up?"

Mr. Sloan nodded. Sir Henry assisted his secretary to his feet and together they stumbled away from the smoke into the fresh air.

"Once again, I owe you my life, Mr. Sloan," said Sir Henry. "I would say 'thank you,' but I fear my thanks on these occasions is becoming monotonous."

"I was only doing my duty, my lord," said Mr. Sloan.

Sir Henry smiled. "Throwing yourself in front of demonic fire is not generally considered to be among the duties of a secretary."

He paused a moment, then added, "You know that I am grateful, Franklin."

"Yes, my lord," said Mr. Sloan. Embarrassed by the praise, he changed the subject. "What is that you are holding, my lord?"

"The man's helmet. I ripped it off his head." Sir Henry felt squeamish touching it, remembering how Father Jacob had said the helmets were made of human skin. "You would not describe me as 'sensitive,' or delicate in my feelings, Mr. Sloan?"

"Certainly not, my lord."

"Nor am I given to the 'creeps' or the 'horrors.' Yet, I swear to you, Mr. Sloan, the sight of that man's face made my skin crawl. The eyes were huge, like the eyes of rats that spend their miserable lives in the darkness of tunnels and sewers belowground." He paused again. "Or the eyes of one who has lived on an island at the bottom of the world."

"You are thinking of Father Jacob's theory, my lord," said Mr. Sloan.

"The man's strange appearance doesn't prove the priest's theory, but it does appear to corroberate it. We will send the helm to Simon for analysis, find out if it is made of skin. Too bad we couldn't take the man alive. I did ask him who had sent him, if it was Eiddwen. He made some reply, but I couldn't understand the language. Something to do with storms and witches."

"Indeed, my lord," said Mr. Sloan. "Could you remember exactly?"

Sir Henry thought back. " 'Stormy dead' and 'all witches reddening.' "

Mr. Sloan looked grave. "Was it this, my lord? *'Storm yn dod. Ni allwich redeg.'* "

"That or something very close, Mr. Sloan. Do you understand it?"

"I do, my lord. The language is that of the Trundlers. As your lordship knows, I spent many years in the royal marines where I had the honor of meeting your lordship—"

"And saving my life," Sir Henry inserted.

Mr. Sloan acknowledged that with a nod and continued. "Several sailors aboard the ship on which I was serving were Trundlers, and I learned the language from them. The dying man said: 'The storm is coming. You cannot run.' "

"Trundler language," said Sir Henry thoughtfully. He sighed. "Once again bearing out Father Jacob's theory."

He noticed Mr. Sloan wincing. "How are you feeling, Mr. Sloan? You have a nasty burn on your shoulder."

"The wound does sting a bit, my lord, but I am fit for duty."

"Excellent. Then if you feel up to it, let us see what clues our demon friend left behind."

By the light of the bull's-eye lanterns, they searched the grounds. When Sir Henry came to the remains of the intruder's body, he was stunned to see that it had been reduced to ashes. He stirred the pile with the toe of his boot, but found nothing, not so much as a fragment of bone. A few feet away Mr. Sloan located the weapon, which the Bottom Dweller had flung down after he had shot Mr. Sloan. The two men examined it with interest.

The cannonlike weapon measured three inches in diameter and four feet long. The barrel was made of brass banded with iron and was outfitted with a handgrip and a shoulder rest. Odd-looking magical constructs had been engraved in the brass and iron.

"Do you recognize these constructs, Mr. Sloan?"

"I do not, my lord," said Mr. Sloan, shaking his head.

"Could they be contramagic?"

"Since I have no knowledge of the subject, I would not venture to make a guess, my lord."

"And there is no one we can ask," said Sir Henry, frustrated. "Not without being accused of heresy!"

"There is *one* person, my lord," said Mr. Sloan. "Father Jacob Northrop."

The two exchanged glances.

"Yes, well, I must think about that," said Sir Henry.

They walked over to inspect the steel panels.

"Here's where he fired. Again, nothing but that strange acidlike burn," said Sir Henry with satisfaction. "Poor Eiddwen. She will be sadly disappointed. I am almost sorry he did not live to report this news to her."

"He could have sent a report after his first visit, my lord. That is what I would have done."

"We cannot assume the demon was as competent as you are, Mr. Sloan, but you do have a point. If Eiddwen does hear it, I hope she chokes on it," Sir Henry added grimly.

He glanced over his shoulder at the pile of ashes, then looked around the yard. "There is nothing more we can do here. We will clean up, then go home to our beds. We have earned our rest this night."

They picked up the strange weapon and the helm, wrapped them in a tarpaulin that had been covering part of the damaged ferry. Mr. Sloan obtained a broom from the workshop and swept away the ashes. They drenched the greasy burned spot on the ground with buckets of water, but were not able to remove all traces.

"Instead of a greasy patch, we now have a greasy wet patch," said Sir Henry ruefully. "The workers are sure to take notice."

"Alcazar could tell them he was doing some experimenting, my lord," Mr. Sloan suggested. "The workmen are accustomed to his oddities."

"An excellent idea, Mr. Sloan."

They left the salvage yard, walking the deserted streets to the inn where Field was waiting for them. Mr. Sloan would have driven the carriage, but because of his injury, Sir Henry would not permit it. Instead, Sir Henry made Mr. Sloan sit in the carriage and took the reins himself, much to Mr. Sloan's chagrin.

When they returned to Sir Henry's house, it was silent. Sir Henry's hours were so erratic that he had ordered the servants never to wait up for him. He and Mr. Sloan conferred quietly in the entryway. Mr. Sloan asked for his instructions before retiring to his own chambers—a set of rooms above the carriage house. Sir Henry had been turning things over in his mind. He had reached a decision.

"I fear I must ask you to forgo sleep this night, Mr. Sloan."

"I am at your lordship's service, as always."

"First, take yourself to Dr. Fosgate and have that burn treated."

Mr. Sloan smiled faintly. "Yes, my lord."

"Next, shut down the salvage yard for the next few days. You will have to find a way to explain to Alcazar the absence of the gunboat."

"Indeed, my lord." Mr. Sloan raised an eyebrow.

"Tell Alcazar I am running the boat through additional tests or some such thing. He is to continue producing the steel to make more panels. Bring in an additional smith and more workers. I want enough panels to outfit every ship in the fleet defending the homeland."

"That will take some time, but I will arrange it. Should I dispatch a messenger to Captain Northrop, asking him to meet you at the salvage yard in the morning?"

Sir Henry smiled. "You know my mind, Mr. Sloan. No, I will speak with Northrop myself. He is my friend, but he has his faults—the chief being he cannot keep his damn mouth shut. No hint of my plans must become known to anyone."

"I understand, my lord. Are you still sailing to Braffa, or should I send a message to the admiral?"

"I am still traveling to Braffa, Mr. Sloan," said Sir Henry. "After a small detour to Rosia."

"You will be putting yourself in grave danger traveling to Rosia, my lord," said Mr. Sloan.

Sir Henry shrugged. "I spent the ride here considering my options, Mr. Sloan. Bottom Dwellers caused the collapse of the Crystal Market. I do not know how they did it, but I am as certain as death that they did. I am convinced they will attack Freya next and when they do, we must be prepared. 'The storm is coming. You cannot run.' I need to speak to Father Jacob."

"Is a reunion between the priest and the captain wise, my lord? After all, Captain Northrop *did* try to kill his brother."

"I will deal with Alan," Sir Henry said.

"Yes, my lord. Is there anything else?"

Sir Henry did not immediately respond. The only sound to be heard in the slumbering house was the ticking of a clock in the front parlor. The muffled tick, tick, tick put Henry in a somber mood. Life's moments slipping away, never to be recovered.

He placed his hand on Mr. Sloan's arm. "I leave the care of my wife and child to you, Mr. Sloan."

"A sacred trust, my lord," said Mr. Sloan.

The two said good night. As Mr. Sloan left on his errands, Sir Henry walked upstairs. He went first to his room, where his beloved Mouse was sleeping soundly. He kissed her forehead. She smiled in her sleep.

He then crept into the nursery, padding softly, careful not to wake the nursemaid. He leaned over the cradle, looking at his son. He was such a tiny mite of a thing, his head covered with brown fuzz. Sir Henry touched his fingertips to his lips, then placed his fingers on the child's head, giving him a silent blessing.

After that, he changed his clothes, picked up a portmanteau that was always packed, and scribbled a hurried note to his wife saying that he had been called away to deal with the situation in Braffa. He ended with his expression of enduring love, left the note on her dressing table, and departed.

22

Everything in nature serves a purpose—or so science teaches us. (Even bloodsucking ticks, though I can't fathom how they are useful!) If we accept that magic is a force of nature inherent in all things then we must also accept that contramagic is a force of nature. Then what purpose does it serve other than to erase constructs we create? We know that over time, all magical constructs fail and must be renewed. We have always believed that this was the result of magic simply fading away. What if this is not the case? What if contramagic acts to weaken the constructs in a natural cycle that balances the magic? If so, the Bottom Dwellers might have developed the means to create an imbalance that will disrupt the cycle and end up destroying all magic everywhere.

—Thoughts on Contramagic,
Rodrigo de Villeneuve

Rodrigo de Villeneuve's perspective on life might have been summed up as: Why bother? He was often in lust, but had never bothered to fall in love. He was a skilled crafter, but had never bothered to excel at his craft. He was a talented musician and composer, but had never bothered to take lessons or write down any of his compositions. He had developed the theory of how to produce magically infused steel, but had never bothered to try to put his theory into practice.

This didn't mean Rodrigo couldn't bother when he chose to. During the ill-fated revolution, he had risked his life searching the battlefield to find Stephano, carry his wounded friend to a secret location, and nurse him back to health. He had used his skill as a crafter to deal with the Bottom Dweller who had sneaked aboard the *Cloud Hopper* to attack Gythe and he had fixed the broken magic aboard the ship. Such times of "botheration" were rare, however.

He was going to some bother now, experimenting with a few of the rudimentary constructs of contramagic he'd managed to puzzle out while trying to find a way to repair the damage the contramagic was causing. He likened the slow, painstaking process to that of a person trying to teach himself to read. He theorized that if he understood contramagic, he could devise magical constructs to neutralize the destructive effects. He kept his work secret.

Contramagic. The study or even the mention of the word was forbidden by the church. Such magic was deemed "evil." When Rodrigo was young, he'd tried to learn more about it, mainly because he'd been ordered not to study it. He remembered holding forth on the subject at a tavern, after having imbibed several glasses of cheap sherry.

"Contramagic uses the same six basic sigils, just turned upside down, as it were, and bound together by some sort of mysterious something," Rodrigo had argued.

He had always enjoyed tossing such conversational bombshells, and he had chuckled over the shocked looks on the faces of his friends as he unsteadily made his way back to his room that evening. His laughter had ceased abruptly when a large chunk of stone had crashed to the sidewalk at his feet. Rodrigo had looked up to see a tonsured head looking down at him. A suddenly sober Rodrigo had realized that this was no accident. Either he had been extremely lucky or the attack was a warning. He had never told anyone, not even Stephano, about that night. Rodrigo had taken the hint and abandoned his study of contramagic. And there was another reason. Miri would be outraged and even Stephano would be uneasy.

Rodrigo was also working to heal the rupture between Miri and Stephano. At the moment Rodrigo was having more success with the contramagic.

The *Sommerwind* and the *Cloud Hopper* were sailing side by side, battling unfavorable winds that were blowing them steadily westward. The *Sommerwind*'s smith and crafters had repaired the *Hopper*'s damaged lift tank and filled it with lift gas, so that the houseboat was now sailing under her own power. Miri remained aboard the *Sommerwind,* to tend to the captain and injured crewmembers. Gythe was at the helm of the *Cloud Hopper.* The captain of the merchant vessel was improving under Miri's care.

"The miracle of yellow goo," Rodrigo remarked.

Miri reported that although weak from loss of blood, the captain was able to come on deck, inspect the repairs, and tell the crew he was pleased with the progress.

That day the wind changed, blowing the ship and the houseboat in a westerly direction. They lost several days fighting the headwinds. Leutnant Baumann told Stephano that this was normal this time of year. They would soon make up the lost time and arrive in Evreux only a few days behind schedule. The crew of the *Sommerwind* was in a good mood.

The same could not be said of those on board the *Cloud Hopper*. Miri spoke with Gythe daily, standing at the ship's rail and shouting instructions for Gythe and Rodrigo, who had been drafted into helping concoct more of Miri's herbal remedies. They sent the bottles and jars from the *Cloud Hopper* to the *Sommerwind* in a basket tied to a pulley.

During these times, Miri did not speak to or even look at Stephano, and when Rodrigo tried to talk to her on Stephano's behalf, Miri silenced him with a glare.

"The words froze on my lips," Rodrigo told Stephano. "I swear I had icicles hanging from my teeth."

The cat, Doctor Ellington, was the most miserable of all. He missed Dag and refused to be comforted. He would not eat. He crouched in a ball beneath Dag's chair, giving out an occasional sorrowful yowl.

The days passed with no change in the routine or in anyone's spirits. No one was happy. Rodrigo, lying in his hammock at night, would hear Stephano pacing the deck for hours on end.

"I'm facing the truth about myself," Stephano had told his friend. "When we first encountered the dragons, I dared to dream as I haven't dared to dream in years, ever since I resigned my commission. I dreamed of riding dragons. And now I have sacrificed Dag to that dream. He's probably dead, and God knows what has become of the three dragons."

Rodrigo was at his wits' end. He conceded that Stephano had a right to wallow in self-pity, but it was becoming quite boring. He conceded, too, that Miri had a right to be angry at Stephano, but she had signed on to this ill-fated job to find the journeyman, Alcazar, with just as much eagerness as had the rest of the Cadre. She would have been happily sharing in the money they would have received from the countess if the gamble had paid off. Miri had no reason to chuck everything out the window just because the job had gone up in a ball of green fire, so to speak. Rodrigo had felt compelled to point these facts out to both Miri and Stephano, with the result that now they were both angry at *him*.

At night, Gythe would tether the *Cloud Hopper* to the *Sommerwind.* The smaller boat bobbed along behind, floating slightly above the larger vessel. They had been sailing the Breath for five days and nights. Gythe thought they must be near the Rosian coastline. The morning of the sixth day dawned in lovely colors of red and purple. Gythe must not have been awake yet because Rodrigo could hear Stephano tromping about on the bridge. Rodrigo would have liked to have gone back to sleep, but he had to check the magical constructs.

He yawned, went to the galley, put the kettle on, and dozed off until the whistling woke him. He dumped the hot water into the teapot and waited for the tea to steep. Pouring the tea into the cup, he thought it looked rather weak, then realized he'd forgotten to add the tea. Sighing deeply, Rodrigo remedied the situation and carried two cups up onto the deck.

He found Stephano looking down at the deck of the *Sommerwind,* watching Leutnant Baumann and his midshipmen cast the ship's position with their sextants.

"Breakfast?" Rodrigo asked, offering the tea.

Stephano took a swallow and promptly burned his tongue.

"You're up early," said Stephano. "Gythe isn't even awake yet."

"I couldn't sleep," said Rodrigo. "Not with you stomping up and down on my head for hours."

"I was thinking about Miri," said Stephano. "She's right. It *is* time that we parted company. Forming the Cadre of the Lost was meant to be a glorious adventure. We'd take a few risks, make lots of money, and have a good time doing it. Nothing has turned out as I planned. We've earned a pittance, barely enough to keep us afloat, and I've nearly gotten us all killed."

"What is wrong with you?" Rodrigo demanded. "You never used to take such a gloomy view of things. As for the Cadre, we may not have made much money, but at least we made *some*. If you disband the Cadre, what will we live on? I have my allowance, but that will only cover my half of the rent, not the necessities of life, such as fine wine and velvet waistcoats."

Rodrigo had been living off an allowance given to him by his father. After his father's death, Rodrigo's older brother became responsible for maintaining the allowance. Fortunately for Rodrigo, his older brother was a good-hearted man who had always been fond of the scapegrace and would, Rodrigo hoped, continue to support him.

"I'll take a job as a clerk," Stephano said.

"My dear fellow, I hate to say this, but you wouldn't last two minutes as a clerk. You are hopeless at bookkeeping and your handwriting is atrocious."

"Fencing master, then," said Stephano.

Rodrigo envisioned their home being invaded by small boys with swords.

"God help us!" he exclaimed, shuddering. He laid his hand on Stephano's shoulder. "Don't make any rash decisions. Be patient with Miri. She'll forgive you. She always does."

"Not this time, Rigo," said Stephano, sighing. "Not this time."

He threw himself down in a chair, narrowly avoiding sitting on the cat, who fled with an irate howl. Rodrigo went about the boat making adjustments to the bridging constructs. The sky was lead-crystal blue with wisps of the

Breath trailing past like silken scarves. He wondered what sort of money fencing masters earned these days.

Miri appeared on the deck of the *Sommerwind*. She looked at the *Cloud Hopper* and called up to Stephano. She had not spoken to him in days. Rodrigo left his work to hurry over to assist in what might turn out to be truce talks.

"Where's Gythe?" Miri shouted. "She should be at the helm now! Is something wrong?"

"I don't think so," Stephano yelled back.

"Go check on her."

Stephano headed down below. Miri stood waiting, her arms crossed over her chest.

Stephano returned, his expression grave. "Miri, come here at once!"

"What's the matter?" Miri asked, alarmed.

"Just come!"

Stephano lowered the rope ladder. Miri told Leutnant Baumann she was leaving the ship, then kilted up her skirts and climbed the ladder.

"What is it? What's wrong?" she asked anxiously. "Is Gythe ill?"

"I don't know," said Stephano. "I've never seen her like this."

Miri hurried off, going down below to the quarters the sisters shared.

"What is the matter with her?" Rodrigo asked.

"The door was shut. I could hear Gythe inside. It sounded like she was singing—not those childhood songs she sang when she went away from us that time. I couldn't understand the words, but her song sounded . . . angry."

"An angry song?" repeated Rodrigo skeptically.

"Remember that opera we attended where the baritone tries to seduce the soprano with threats to kill her lover, the tenor, unless she sleeps with him? The soprano agrees, but when he tries to kiss her, she stabs him. She sings a song telling him how much she loathes him, how she enjoys watching him die. That's the sort of song Gythe was singing."

"My dear fellow, the end of the second act! You were awake! I'm so proud of you!" said Rodrigo in a voice full of emotion.

The door leading below flew open with a bang, startling Doctor Ellington, who dove for his hiding place beneath the cannon, only to again discover that the cannon was no longer there. The Doctor retreated underneath the table.

Gythe ran onto the deck. Her face was pale, her cheeks crimson. Her blue eyes had darkened to gray. She stood on deck, wildly staring around, then hurried to the rail. Miri came on deck, trying to catch up to her sister. Gythe clutched the rail and stared into the Breath. She then turned back toward Miri and began to make frantic signs with her hands.

"She says they're coming to kill us!" Miri reported.

"Who's coming to kill us?" Stephano asked, searching the skies. "There's not an enemy in sight."

Miri shook her head helplessly. "She won't tell me. She's not rational. I've never seen her like this. Stephano, I'll take the helm. You and Rigo talk to her."

Gythe shrieked, drawing their attention. She was leaning over the rail, pointing toward the sky below the keel. Rodrigo peered down.

"Is the Breath supposed to be doing that?" he asked uneasily.

Miri looked over the side.

"No," she said. "It isn't."

The lookout on board the *Sommerwind* must have seen the strange phenomenon, too, because he shouted out a warning. Leutnant Baumann took one look and they could hear him telling a midshipman to go below to summon the captain.

On a normal day, Rodrigo would look down into the

Breath and see, far below, a mass of pinkish orange clouds that seemed so thick he always fancied he could lie down on them, as on a feather bed. The sight was deceptive, of course. The Breath at that depth was made up of nearly impenetrable fog. Rodrigo remembered the time the *Cloud Hopper* had been hit by gunfire and drifted down into the cold, gray mist.

At that depth, the Breath was rarely disturbed; the wind, if it blew at all, was light. Slight swirls sometimes ruffled the top. Today the Breath was an ugly mass of churning, boiling black clouds. Strange green lightning glowed among the dark clouds or streaked from one to another.

"Is that a wizard storm?" Stephano asked, referring to the magical disruptions in the Breath that sometimes seemed to come out of nowhere.

"A terrible one! The green lightning is contramagic," Rodrigo said, unable to control the tremor of fear in his voice. "The clash of the magic in the Breath and the contramagic is creating a wizard storm worse than any normal wizard storm, and a normal wizard storm almost sank us!"

Gythe stood transfixed, staring into the boiling clouds, her body rigid, her face white.

"Rigo, take her below!" Miri ordered. "Stephano, slip the towline. We don't want to be tethered to the *Sommerwind* in gale-force winds."

Rodrigo tried to persuade Gythe to come below. She pointed to the storm and then made a slashing motion across her throat.

"She says again they're coming to kill us," said Miri. "I'm afraid she's right. If we're caught in the storm, the winds will tear the boat apart."

The clouds were rising, bubbling upward, congealing in a gloppy mass like some hideous pudding about to boil over. The wind was strengthening, blowing east toward Rosia.

"We can't escape it," said Miri, her voice straining to be heard above the shrieking wind. "We'll have to ride it."

Houseboats such as the *Cloud Hopper* were not meant to withstand the force of hurricane winds or wizard storms, one reason Trundlers usually sailed close to the shoreline, where they could shelter when necessary. If the boats were caught in the Breath during a storm, they would attempt to "ride the storm," outrunning it by riding the leading edge of the wind.

Rodrigo looked over at the *Sommerwind*. Captain Leydecker was on deck, shouting commands while hobbling about with a crutch, his leg in a splint. The sailors were running to put on more sail. The maneuver was tricky; the amount of sail had to be calculated just right. If they set too much sail the wind might carry away spars or blow down a mast; too little, and they'd risk the storm overtaking them.

"Rigo," Miri said, casting him a pleading glance, "you *have* to keep the magic working!"

Rodrigo shook his head. "Those clouds are crackling with contramagic, Miri. A single strike could destroy every magical construct on this boat. If that happens . . ." He didn't finish the sentence.

Gythe was still staring, mesmerized, into the roiling clouds. The *Cloud Hopper* soared through the air, riding the storm winds. The *Sommerwind* was doing the same, keeping abreast of the *Cloud Hopper*. The storm moved rapidly, surging up from below, as lightning flared and thunder boomed.

Stephano tried to drag the Doctor out from under the table, intending to take him to the storage closet for safety. The terrified cat clawed him, leaving a bloody streak on his wrist, then dashed off, with a swearing Stephano in pursuit.

"Never mind the cat," Rodrigo told Stephano, stopping

him as he was going below. Rodrigo felt a strange, unnerving calm. "We're not going to be able to outrun it."

The heavy greenish black clouds bubbled like viscous soup, bubbled upward, spreading out, filling in the sky below, turning everything black beneath the *Cloud Hopper*'s keel. The sun, shining above them, was untouched by the storm spiraling up from Below and made the clouds that much darker by contrast.

The wind that had been blowing the *Cloud Hopper* and the *Sommerwind* toward the safety of the shore suddenly shifted direction. The sails emptied, and flapped helplessly. The wind veered again, the boat heeled and rocked. Rodrigo lost his footing, and Miri was thrown sideways, and had to fight to maintain control of the helm. Aboard the *Sommerwind,* every hand was on deck, even the cook, battling to save the ship.

Gythe had stopped singing. Her lips were parted. Her breath hissed between her teeth. Her face was livid, and her blue eyes seemed almost as bright as the lightning. Her hands gripped the rail tightly, the knuckles white.

Jagged green bolts flashed, perilously close. Thunder boomed.

"There is evil in that storm," said Rodrigo.

"Contramagic isn't evil!" Stephano yelled over the gusting wind. "It's a force of nature! Remember?"

"Contramagic *isn't* evil," Rodrigo agreed. His lips were stiff. He could scarcely move them to speak. "Yet there is evil magic creating this storm. I feel it. And so does Gythe."

As the clouds closed in around them, stinging rain blasted them and lightning crackled, coming ever nearer. The thunder was only three or four heartbeats behind the bolts. They lost sight of the *Sommerwind* in the gray sheets of rain, though they could hear the creak of the timbers and sometimes shouted commands.

"Rigo, take Gythe and go below!" Stephano ordered. "I'll stay with Miri!"

Rodrigo lurched across the deck. He was soaked to the skin, with water dripping into his eyes. Gythe was standing in the rain and wind and sizzling lightning, her eyes raised to heaven. Her lips were moving: she was singing.

Rodrigo thought she must be in some kind of shock, that perhaps she had retreated to her childhood again as she had done the last time they faced danger. Perhaps it was for the best, he thought. When the end came, she wouldn't know it . . .

"Gythe, dear," he began.

Gythe shook her head vehemently. Her hair was plastered to her face. Her lips were still moving, and her voice grew louder. Rodrigo tried to take hold of her, to force her to come with him out of the storm.

Gythe rounded on him, her eyes blazing, and she struck him in the chest with both hands. Astonished, he stumbled backward, lost his footing on the slippery, rain-swept deck and went sprawling. When he tried to get back to his feet, the wind knocked him down.

He managed to pull himself up by grabbing on to a rope. Through the lashing rain, he could barely see Stephano helping Miri at the helm, both of them struggling to remain upright in the whipping wind. A green lightning bolt streaked past, so close to the *Cloud Hopper* that Rodrigo could hear it sizzle. The thunderclap was almost simultaneous, and half deafened him.

Gythe was not holding on to anything. She stood tall and surefooted on the canting deck, her hands raised, her voice audible clear and pure above the howling of the wind. Rodrigo recognized the song.

She wasn't singing Trundler songs at all. She was singing prayer chants, such as he'd hear the priests sing on those days when his mother had forced him to attend holy services. But how did Gythe know such chants? Trundlers didn't go to church. Trundlers didn't believe in saints, or in God for that matter. How did Gythe come to know a prayer to Saint Castigan?

Gythe was sopping wet. The wind swirled around her, yet seemed not to touch her. It was as if she were standing in the eye of the storm. Her hands were still raised to the heavens, and as she continued singing, the wind began to die down. Lightning flickered angrily among the gray clouds, and thunder rumbled, but from a distance.

"I think the storm's moving off," said Stephano in disbelief.

"We've had a lucky escape," said Miri.

Rodrigo opened his mouth. He was going to say something to them, to tell the truth of what had happened, when Gythe turned to face him. Her eyes were as clear as the blue sky that was clearing above them.

"You did that," Rodrigo said, awed.

She placed two fingers on his lips.

"Say nothing!" she was telling him.

Gythe's eyes darkened. She touched his forehead, and drew back her fingers, stained with blood. She pointed to the blood and then to the receding storm clouds.

"Blood magic," Rodrigo said, suddenly understanding.

Gythe gave an emphatic nod.

"Gythe—" Rodrigo hesitated. "You weren't singing Trundler songs. You were chanting a prayer. A prayer to Saint Castigan!"

Gythe blinked at him in bewilderment. She pointed to herself, as if to say, "I was?"

"Didn't you understand what you were saying?" Rodrigo asked.

Gythe shook her head.

"Then where did you learn the prayer? From that priest, Father Jacob?"

Gythe shook her head, and a dreamy, faraway look came into her eyes. She made a circle with both her hands around her head, as of hair cut into a tonsure. Her eyes smiled.

"Brother Barnaby," said Rodrigo, bewildered. "But how . . ."

Gythe touched her heart, then her ears, as if to say "He talks to me. I talk to him."

She put her hand on Rodrigo's lips again. She glanced over at Miri and looked back at him sternly and lifted her finger in warning.

"You're right," said Rodrigo. "Best Miri doesn't know that you are communing with Brother Barnaby. I'll keep your secret."

Gythe kissed him lightly on the cheek, then ran off to find Doctor Ellington. Miri called after her, but she pretended not to hear, as she disappeared down below.

Rodrigo saw Stephano talking earnestly to Miri. His voice was too low, Rodrigo couldn't understand what he was saying, but he hoped his friend was trying once more to ask Miri to forgive him.

He was doomed to disappointment. Miri turned her back on Stephano, spoke to him over her shoulder. "Go check for damage. And tell Rigo to make certain the magic is holding."

She brushed her wet, straggling red hair out of her eyes and went back to her duties at the helm.

Stephano looked at her a moment, then walked despondently over to inspect the hull near where Rodrigo was standing.

"We were damn lucky," Stephano told his friend.

"You don't look as though you consider yourself lucky," Rodrigo said.

Stephano shrugged. He glanced at Rodrigo. "You're bleeding."

Rodrigo dismissed this as unimportant. "Listen to this passage from the books of the saints, my friend: 'And it is written that the four saints came together and stood in the full fury of the storm and raised their arms to heaven and cried to God for mercy. And the storm ceased to rage . . .'"

Stephano stared at him. "Good God, Rigo! Don't tell me you've found religion!"

"I am not sure what I've found," said Rodrigo.

In the days to come, with steady winds and fair weather, the *Sommerwind* sailed safely to Evreux, arriving at the docks about midday. The *Cloud Hopper* had detached itself from the merchant ship and was now preparing to travel to the place where Miri and Gythe usually docked. The time for parting had come. Stephano and Rodrigo were going to their house in the city. Miri and Gythe were staying on the boat.

The four stood on the deck of the *Cloud Hopper,* all of them uncomfortable. Stephano's trunk, with his few belongings, stood on the deck.

Gythe gave Stephano a kiss on the cheek and a sad and wistful smile. Miri stood with her arms crossed, her expression cold and forbidding.

"I'll let you know when I hear from Dag," said Stephano.

Miri flashed him a look that made him feel as if he'd been turned to stone. She walked off, stepping on Doctor Ellington's tail, who screeched in pain and protest.

"Welcome home," said Rodrigo.

23

With the king's declaration of the disbanding of the Dragon Brigade, our service to our country comes to an end. The deeds of glory and valor of both men and dragons now belong to the past. I am honored to have served with you. I am honored to have been your commander. Though we are disbanded, I will keep my oath to defend our country and I know each of you will do the same, for we are the courage of a nation. We are and forever will be the Dragon Brigade.

—Sir Stephano de Guichen,
lord captain of the Dragon Brigade

Stephano had always liked his modest dwelling, located in a comfortable, merchant-class neighborhood of Evreux. The three-story house, with six windows on both the second and third floors facing into the street, and one window and an arched door on the ground floor, was not particularly beautiful. It looked very much like every other house on the block. But on the morning of their return to Evreux, when he saw his house, tears filled his eyes. He would not have traded his house for the Sunset Palace.

He and Rodrigo had come home straight from the *Cloud Hopper*. When Stephano asked Miri what her plans were,

Miri said shortly she didn't know, and she would have to think about it. She told him she would drop by his house later to discuss the matter and visit Benoit to make certain he was all right.

Stephano had thanked Captain Leydecker and Leutnant Baumann for their assistance. Captain Leydecker was profuse in his praise of Mistress Miri, saying he would be forever in her debt, firmly believing she had saved his life. Stephano and Rodrigo had shaken hands and taken their leave.

They had ridden in a hansom cab, Rodrigo declaring he could not be seen walking the streets of Evreux in what was left of his fine clothing.

"I would be ruined," said Rodrigo. "Simply ruined."

The cabdriver had taken one look at the two shabby customers carrying a trunk between them, and insisted on payment in advance. Fortunately, they still had money, due, as Rodrigo pointed out, to the simple fact that there had not been anyplace on the island to spend it.

When he and Rodrigo arrived at their house, they were comforted to see a thin trail of smoke rising from one of the two chimneys.

"Wonderful!" Rodrigo exclaimed ecstatically, dropping the trunk. "Benoit is here and he has a fire going. I will have a bath. A bath that lasts for hours. Sorry, but you will have to wait your turn."

The door was locked and Stephano had no idea what he'd done with the key. He took hold of the door knocker—a dragon done in brass—and rapped loudly. They waited a considerable time. Stephano could picture Benoit, swearing to himself in annoyance, hobbling to answer.

The door opened a crack. An eye peered out. "Get along with you! No beggars." Benoit started to slam the door.

Stephano inserted his foot. "Benoit! It's me!"

Benoit stared at him a moment and then fell over backward, landing on the floor with a thud.

Rodrigo gasped. "Good God, Stephano, you've killed him!"

The two hurried inside. Stephano went down on his knees beside Benoit and propped him up.

"Benoit, I'm sorry. Are you all right?"

Benoit's eyelids fluttered.

"Rigo, go fetch some water—"

"Brandy . . . ," Benoit murmured faintly.

Rodrigo ran to the kitchen.

"We don't have brandy," said Stephano.

"We do now," said Rodrigo, returning with a crystal snifter. "Very fine brandy, too. Vieille Reserve if I'm not mistaken."

"What did you pawn to buy brandy? The furniture?" asked Stephano, trying to sound severe.

"A gift from your lady mother, sir," said Benoit.

He sipped the brandy and looked at Stephano with watery eyes.

"I am glad to see you, sir. You, too, Master Rodrigo. So very glad!"

Benoit embraced them both, then held out the snifter, indicating the need for more brandy. Stephano and Rodrigo between them assisted the old retainer to his comfortable chair by the kitchen fire.

"We're starving," said Stephano. "Is there anything to eat?"

"I would be glad to cook for you, sir," said Benoit. "But I'm feeling a little dizzy. The joyous shock of seeing you come back from the dead, sir—"

"We'll fend for ourselves," said Stephano, grinning.

"Indeed we will," Rodrigo called, reporting from the larder. "I've found a beefsteak pie, cold chicken, a round of cheese, sausages, fresh baked bread, a full barrel of beer, and several bottles of wine. From your mother's cellar, if I'm not mistaken."

Stephano fixed his eye on Benoit.

"The countess thought I was looking unwell, sir," said Benoit defensively. "I told her I had lost my appetite—"

"You seem to have found it," said Stephano. "Bring some of everything, Rigo."

While they ate, they assured Benoit that Miri and Gythe were well and that they would soon be coming to see him. Stephano made no mention of the trouble between them.

"As for Dag—" Stephano began.

Benoit slapped himself on the forehead. "That reminds me, sir. A letter came for you from Dag only an hour ago. He's visiting your estate. One of the tenants delivered it."

"Dag at my estate!" Stephano was confounded. "What in the name of all that is holy is he doing there?"

"He's alive, at least," Rodrigo stated.

"That is true, thank God," Stephano said, relieved. "How is he? Are the dragons with him? What did he say?"

Benoit drew himself up. "I have no way of knowing, sir," he said stiffly. "The letter was addressed to you. I would never open your private correspondence."

"Never?" Stephano asked with a wink at Rodrigo.

Benoit stole a sly glance at his master. "Well, perhaps in this one instance I might have taken a peek, sir. I deemed this might be an emergency. Your honored mother was so extremely worried, I took the liberty."

Stephano gave a solemn nod. "I'm certain you had good reason. What does Dag write?"

"He is well. He is visiting your estate with five dragons, two of whom apparently you know from the Brigade days, sir. He adds in a postscript that you should come as soon as possible. The letter was quite brief, sir."

"Dag isn't much of a correspondent, I should guess," said Rodrigo.

"More likely he doesn't want to set down what he knows in writing," said Stephano. He sighed and pushed himself to his feet. "We might as well throw on some clean clothes and go see my mother now. Get the worst over."

Rodrigo stared at him, horrified. "First we will bathe and then change into our *court* clothes. Then, when we are suitably attired, we will go to see your mother. You owe me, for getting us off that island."

Stephano smiled. Just as he had predicted.

"How would you like to see the old estate again, Benoit?" Stephano asked as he was going up the stairs to his room.

"Very much, sir," said Benoit. "I will heat water for baths. Oh, there is something you gentlemen should know before you leave. There's been a terrible tragedy in Evreux."

He told of the collapse of the Crystal Market. Stephano and Rodrigo listened in shock.

"Do they know what caused it?" Stephano asked.

"All manner of rumors are floating about, sir," said Benoit.

"When did this happen, Benoit?" Rodrigo asked.

"Let me see . . . three days ago, sir. Midsummer's Eve."

"The day of the storm . . ." Rodrigo observed.

"What does that have to do with it?"

"I think it a strange coincidence," said Rodrigo in somber tones. "You say some friends of mine from court were among the dead."

"Yes, sir," said Benoit. "I'm sorry, sir."

Rodrigo sighed deeply. "I will be in my room. Let me know when the bath is ready."

"I am going to add lavender and rose oil, sir," said Benoit, rising to put on the kettle. He wrinkled his nose. "You will forgive my saying this, but there is a strong odor of smoked fish about you both."

Before he took his bath, Stephano wrote a note for Benoit to deliver to his mother, apprising her of his return and saying that he would be pleased to wait upon her in the early evening if she would deign to receive him and Monsieur de Villeneuve.

Benoit traveled by hackney cab to the palace. He gave the message to D'argent, who read the few words, and, smiling broadly, carried the note to the countess. She was in the middle of a meeting with the Estaran ambassador, endeavoring to convince him that Freya was deliberately provoking the Estarans into going to war and that the Estarans should not rise to the bait by attacking Travia.

She motioned for D'argent to enter. He whispered to her as he handed her the note. She read it without expression, handed it back to him without comment, then continued with her meeting. By the time the Estaran ambassador left, he promised to at least consider her advice.

When he was out the door, Cecile closed it and then, feeling faint, leaned against the wall and, putting her hands to her face, she whispered over and over, "Thank God! Oh, thank God!"

Rinsing her eyes with cold water, the countess told D'argent to invite Stephano and Rodrigo to a private supper at the hour of eight.

At the appointed hour, Stephano and Rodrigo, dressed in somber-colored mourning, arrived at the palace. Rodrigo carried the pewter tankard in a velvet sack tied with a ribbon.

D'argent himself was waiting at the palace entrance to receive them. He expressed his pleasure at seeing them alive and well. Stephano answered curtly. As always, when facing a meeting with his mother, he was in a bad mood. Rodrigo was more gracious. He thanked D'argent, who cast a curious glance at the velvet sack.

"A memento of our travels we have brought for the countess," said Rodrigo.

"From an old friend," Stephano added drily.

D'argent raised an eyebrow, but made no comment. He conducted them through the palace corridors to the countess's private chambers.

Several people walking the halls recognized Stephano and Rodrigo, especially Rodrigo. The ladies in particular were delighted to see him. They gave him their rouged cheeks to kiss and demanded to know how he could have deserted them all this time. He said he had been home on family business. None of the women paid any attention to Stephano, who had put on his court face, which Rodrigo had likened to the face of one of the palace's gargoyles.

As the three were walking through the hall, Rodrigo talked with D'argent about those who had died. Stephano was ahead of them, not paying attention, trying to imagine the Crystal Market in ruins. He had the sudden strange sensation that someone was watching him. Stephano turned his head to see an exotic-looking woman had stopped in the hall to stare at him. Stephano was so struck by her beauty that he stopped to stare back. Rodrigo stopped because he bumped into Stephano.

"My dear fellow, do watch where you are going—"

"Who is that?" Stephano asked in a low voice.

Rodrigo looked at the woman. She was dressed in muted elegance in a midnight-blue gown of velvet and silk. She wore an elaborately coiffed white wig. Her complexion was dusky, her cheeks rose red.

"I have no idea," said Rodrigo. "Do you want to be introduced to her?"

"No," said Stephano. "I was just wondering—"

"You *are* interested. I will find out—"

"That's not what I—"

"D'argent," said Rodrigo, ignoring Stephano's protests, "who is that amazingly beautiful female?"

"The Duquesa de Plata Niebla, sir," D'argent replied. "The young gentleman is her nephew, the Conte Osinni."

"Where the hell is Plata Niebla?" Rodrigo asked.

"Estara, I believe, sir," said D'argent.

"Ah, of course. No country breeds such beautiful woman as Estara," said Rodrigo.

The duchess resumed walking, glancing at them over the rim of her fan from beneath thick black eyelashes. She was accompanied by a handsome young man in his midtwenties who walked with a slight limp and a silver cane. He paid scant attention to them.

Rodrigo and Stephano both bowed. The duchess paused. She seemed to be trying to make up her mind whether to speak or simply accept their admiration and pass by. At last she lowered her fan and walked over.

"Monsieur de Villeneuve," she said, her voice a rich contralto. "A pleasure to see you again."

"I never forget a face, Your Grace," Rodrigo said. "Especially one as lovely as yours. I am devastated to admit, therefore, that I cannot remember where exactly we have met."

"I am Idonia, the Duchess of Plata Neibla. Have you ever been to Plata Niebla?" the duchess asked.

"I have not had that pleasure," said Rodrigo, adding gallantly, "but if all the women are as lovely as you, Your Grace, I will make plans to travel there at once."

"Do not leave us too quickly, monsieur," said the duchess, smiling.

Stephano found her fascinating. He liked the fact that she

did not simper and blush and giggle behind her fan. Unlike most women at court, she was forthright and outgoing. He tried to think of something witty to say and failed utterly.

She introduced her nephew, who placed his hand on his heart and bowed. He resembled the duchess only in that he had dark hair swept back from his forehead. He had large brown eyes of astonishing clarity and a sulky mouth.

"I know you will be heartbroken, gentlemen," the duchess said with a laugh, "but I must leave you. My nephew and I have been summoned to attend the queen and we are already late. I hope now that we are reacquainted, Monsieur Rodrigo, I will not lose you again."

Rodrigo reached into an inner pocket and produced a silver case inlaid with gold. He opened it, withdrew a card, and handed it to the duchess.

"My card," he said. "A simple note will bring me to languish at your feet in admiration."

The duchess laughed again, a delightful, rippling sound. Accepting the card, she slipped it into an embroidered reticule she wore on her wrist. She thanked him and dropped a curtsy. Her nephew bowed gracefully, stifled a yawn, and the two departed.

"My dear fellow, congratulations," said Rodrigo in a low voice, as they went on their way. "You have made a conquest!"

"What are you talking about?" Stephano asked irritably. "She never looked at me."

"That means she was quite taken with you," Rodrigo assured him. "She was being coy."

Stephano shook his head. "A woman like that has never been coy in her life. Do you remember where you met her?"

"No, and that is puzzling. How could I forget such a face?" Rodrigo gave this a few moments thought, then dismissed the matter with a shrug. He gave the duchess no more thought.

The duchess was, however, thinking a great deal about Rodrigo. Eiddwen and Lucello continued down the hallway on their way to the royal quarters. Eiddwen's brow was furrowed. She flicked her fan open and closed, open and closed, paying no heed to Lucello, who was brooding over something and wanted her to know he was unhappy.

As the two were walking past the music room, which was closed due to the period of mourning, Eiddwen suddenly veered off. She opened the door, grabbed hold of Lucello, and dragged him into the dark and empty room.

"What the devil are we doing in here?" Lucello asked petulantly. "Bad enough I have to watch you flirt with that fop—"

"That 'fop' as you term him, was the man I told you about on board the *Silver Raven*. I am certain he recognized me from the ship. He covered it well, with all that talk about not forgetting my beautiful face. But I am sure he knows me."

"What if he did? He's a buffoon," said Lucello dismissively. "And what would he say? That he thinks the last time he saw you, you were a sailor? That's ludicrous."

"Don't let him fool you," said Eiddwen. "Villeneuve only plays at being a buffoon. I overheard him talking to the journeyman, Alcazar. The two were discussing contramagic. He was coming too close to the mark. I sent our troops to the island where they were marooned to find and kill the clever Monsieur de Villeneuve. They reported they had done so. Why the devil is the bastard still alive?"

"Because your Bottom Dwellers bungled it," said Lucello contemptuously. "I don't know why you are surprised. Those uncouth savages bungle everything."

"May I remind you, Lucello, that *you* are a guttersnipe

I saved from prison. *You* would still be an uncouth 'savage' were it not for me."

"Then let me take care of the fop," said Lucello eagerly. "I'll see to it that he doesn't remember anything ever again."

"Don't be absurd."

Eiddwen opened the reticule and took out Rodrigo's card. She gazed at it a moment, turning her plans over in her mind. She handed him the card.

"You will not be able to attend the princess tonight. I will make your excuses. Disguise yourself as one of the servants and leave by the servants' exit. Go to La Farge . . ."

"I'll do it myself. No need to waste good money on La Farge."

"I have said before: You must curb your appetites while we are in Evreux, Lucello," said Eiddwen bitingly. "I mean it. Do not make me tell you again."

Lucello's eyes flared, then smoldered. "I am not a child, damn it! You treat me like a child!"

He crushed the card in his fist and angrily walked toward the door. Eiddwen gave an inward, irritated sigh. She had only herself to blame. She had taught this boy to kill. He was like a bear she'd raised from a cub. He danced to her tune and ate from her hand, but bears were wild beasts and someday he might slip his chain and turn on her. She had to keep tossing him honeycombs.

"You may come to me tonight," said Eiddwen.

Lucello stopped and looked warily around. "Truly? You're not toying with me?"

Eiddwen bit back a sharp response. "I will be in my chambers after midnight. Come to me then. And now you must leave. La Farge will need time to make arrangements. You have the card?"

Lucello waved the card with Rodrigo's address. It was crumpled, but readable. Lucello went on his way, walking rapidly, swinging his silver cane and humming the waltz tune the princess Sophia had played for him.

Eiddwen watched him go. One day he was going to choke on that honeycomb.

D'argent escorted Stephano and Rodrigo to the countess's chambers. They entered through the salon, passed through her office, and into her private room, where servants appeared to take their capes and hats. D'argent then escorted them down a hallway decorated with paintings and works of sculpture. Flowers in porcelain vases perfumed the air with the fragrances of roses and lilies. Soft light illuminated the paintings, shone on the sculptures and the flowers.

"I assume you sent your own mother a letter letting her know you are safe and well?" Stephano asked Rodrigo as they were walking down the hall.

"I wrote her the moment we arrived," said Rodrigo. "I would like to take a few weeks to visit her. I haven't seen her since my father's death . . ." Growing misty-eyed at the thought, he took out a handkerchief to wipe his nose.

Stephano smiled sympathetically. "I'll be going to my estate to meet with Dag. Yours is nearby. We can travel together."

D'argent opened the door to the drawing room, ushered Stephano and Rodrigo inside and, closing the door after them, departed. The Countess de Marjolaine was arrayed in her evening splendor, wearing a night-blue silk moiré gown decked with lace, and with a train in the back that fell from the shoulders. Her hair was beautifully arranged, trimmed with feathers and roses. She wore a necklace of sapphires and diamonds with matching sapphire-and-diamond bracelets and rings.

She stood by the fire, reading a book through her lorgnette.

At Stephano's entrance, she looked up, lowered her lorgnette, closed the book, placed it on the mantelpiece, and extended her hand to be kissed.

"I am glad to see you well, Stephano," she said languidly.

Stephano bowed over his mother's hand. She touched his palm with her fingertips as cold as the diamonds that adorned them. She then gave her hand and a smile to Rodrigo.

"Monsieur de Villeneuve. Permit me to offer my personal condolences on the death of your father."

"Thank you, Your Grace," said Rodrigo, bowing.

"We will dine in an hour. Please be seated," said Cecile.

She sat with her back straight, no slouching. Stephano perched on the edge of an uncomfortable chair and thought longingly of his own warm kitchen and his friends gathered around the table. That made him think of Miri; he banished the thought hurriedly.

"No other guests tonight?" he asked, glancing about the drawing room.

He had been in this room only once before, on the occasion of his commission in the Dragon Brigade. Then the room had been filled with light and people, drinking and talking and laughing. He had not observed many details then for he had been floating on a cloud of happiness and pride. The room was dark now, lighted by only a few elegant lamps set here and there on small tables.

"We are in the period of mourning over the collapse of the Crystal Market," said Cecile. "During this time, gatherings are considered *de trop* . . ."

"Ah, yes, I was shocked to hear about the collapse," said Stephano. "A terrible tragedy. Is the cause known?"

"It is under investigation, I believe," Cecile replied.

"Benoit said he heard that crafters who had been in the vicinity when the market hall collapsed were rounded up and whisked away," said Rodrigo.

Cecile gave a cool smile. "Dear Benoit. He does enjoy listening to drivel. Will you take some wine?" She motioned to a servant, who came forward to pour a ruby-colored liquid into crystal goblets.

Rodrigo held the goblet to the light, admiring the color. He put the glass to his lips, rolled the wine on his tongue, swallowed, and closed his eyes in bliss.

"To think I went for weeks without such sustenance." Rodrigo gave a delicate shudder. "I have no idea how I survived."

"Not to mention, Mother, that Rigo here had to bathe in a creek and eat fish soup on a daily basis."

"And leave my shoes behind," Rodrigo said mournfully. "You cannot imagine, Your Grace, the deprivations we endured."

Stephano happened to glance at his mother as they were jesting. She had turned exceedingly pale, and tears glimmered in her eyes. He was so astonished at the sight of his mother exhibiting emotion that he looked at Rodrigo to see if he had noticed.

Rodrigo was motioning to the servant to pour him another glass of wine, however, and when Stephano turned back, his mother's face was cold, without expression. No trace of tears. They must have frozen.

"I know it's not fashionable, Mother, but let's have dinner now," said Stephano abruptly, breaking in on Rodrigo's tale of how the cat, Doctor Ellington, had one day climbed a tree and refused to come down. "All that talk of fish soup has made me hungry."

Rodrigo coughed and cast Stephano a rebuking glance. Stephano knew he was being rude, but he didn't care. He wanted away from this place, away from his mother, away from the fine crystal and the smell of perfume and roses and noiseless servants gliding about on thick carpeting.

His mother smiled. "One can tell you were marooned on an island, Stephano. You have forgotten your manners. Dinner will be served in an hour and not before. *You* might enjoy dining on underdone beef, but I do not."

Stephano, ignoring the servant, poured himself another glass of wine. For lack of anything else to do, he walked over to the fireplace and stared unseeing at a figurine of a shepherdess. Cecile turned to Rodrigo.

"I am most intrigued by whatever it is you are keeping in the velvet sack, monsieur."

"A trifle, Your Grace, which I thought you would find amusing," said Rodrigo lightly.

Lowering his eyelids, he cast a glance at the servant.

Cecile saw the glance and understood. Telling the servant they would wait upon themselves, she dismissed the man. Rodrigo was about to open the velvet sack. Cecile shook her head.

"Stephano, I feel a draft. Please ascertain if that door is shut."

Stephano walked over to the door. He yanked it open, to find the servant standing outside.

"What are you doing?" Stephano demanded.

"I thought I would wait here in case madame wanted anything," said the servant in some confusion.

"She won't," said Stephano.

"Very good, my lord," said the servant and bowed himself away.

Stephano looked up and down the hallway and saw no one else. He shut the door and turned back.

"Who is he spying for?"

"The grand bishop," said Cecile in bored tones.

"Then get rid of him!" said Stephano, adding sarcastically, "Oh, no, I forgot. That's not how the game is played, is it, Mother? You keep him around because you know he's the grand bishop's agent and therefore you can feed him the information you'd like the grand bishop to know. But since the grand bishop undoubtedly knows that you know, what the devil is the point?"

"Forgive him, Your Grace," said Rodrigo. "I've tried my best to educate him, but one can only do so much."

"I understand, monsieur," said Cecile. "I appreciate your efforts."

Rodrigo drew the pewter tankard from the velvet sack and handed it to the countess. She saw an ordinary-looking vessel, as could be found in any number of taverns, and looked back at Rodrigo, mystified.

"A fine specimen of its kind, no doubt," she began, "but I fail to see . . ."

"The gift is not from me," said Rodrigo. He drew his chair closer. "I am but the messenger. The gift is from Sir Henry Wallace."

Cecile said nothing. Her eyes flickered. She bid Rodrigo to continue with a look.

"The tankard was crafted using the magical enhancements developed by Pietro Alcazar that strengthen steel," said Rodrigo in hushed tones. "The journeyman sent this tankard to Wallace, who tested it and recognized the value of this innovation. This tankard brought Sir Henry to Rosia at peril to his life. He apprehended Alcazar with the intent of taking both the journeyman and the tankard back to Freya."

"He succeeded," said Cecile.

"The man is deucedly clever, Your Grace. We failed to stop him from abducting Alcazar and nearly got ourselves killed in the process. Still, we did come away with this. Sir Henry gave this to me, before he left us on that island. He said to present this to you, with his compliments."

"But . . . Why would he do such a thing?" Cecile stared at

the tankard in perplexity. "Such magically enhanced steel will give Freya an immense advantage over us. It might even give them victory! Why share this knowledge?"

"The fact is that we would have developed these constructs anyway," said Rodrigo, adding with becoming modesty, "Truth be told, I advanced the theory of the magically enhanced steel myself. I wrote a small treatise on it. Alcazar read my treatise and went on to prove my theory was correct."

"You knew this invention was possible?" Cecile asked, amazed. "And you did nothing?"

"It was a theory, Your Grace," said Rodrigo with a charming smile. "A theory concocted after a night of drinking what I recall was extraordinarily bad brandy. Oh, the sad life of a student.

"But never mind all that," he continued. "What's important is that Wallace knew I had developed the theory. He knew I knew and so he gave me the tankard. But there is another reason, a more important reason, Your Grace."

"And what might that be?" Cecile asked, eyeing him coldly.

Rodrigo left his chair. He walked over to her and said softly, "Contramagic."

Cecile's eyes widened. She rose to her feet with a silken rustle.

"Congratulations, Rodrigo," said Stephano. "You've shocked my mother."

"What do you know of contramagic, monsieur?" asked the countess. "Did you write a treatise on that, too?"

"I could have, Your Grace," said Rodrigo. "But we all know what would have happened to me. While we were on the island, the tankard withstood a direct hit from the green fire from the Bottom Dwellers—"

"You know the truth about them?" the countess asked,

astonished. She answered her own question. "But, of course. You met with Father Jacob. Sir Ander told me as much. Pray go on."

"The tankard was not damaged," said Rodrigo.

"Whereas when the contramagic fire hit the cannons on the *Royal Lion,* it erased all the strengthening constructs. When those cannons fired, they exploded, taking out the entire gun deck and igniting the ship's powder magazine. The *Royal Lion* blew apart, killing everyone on board," said Stephano, adding in grating tones, "Are you spying on me now, Mother? Talking to Sir Ander?"

"Sir Ander is my friend," said the countess, her eyes flashing. "He wrote to me of his great pleasure in meeting you. Though I must say the way you are behaving I can't think why."

Stephano remembered Sir Ander had been gracious and kind to him, how warmly he had spoken to Stephano of his father.

"Forgive me, Mother," said Stephano. He reflected with a sigh that he rarely endured an audience with his mother during which he didn't end up apologizing for something. "I did enjoy meeting Sir Ander. He is an excellent man. Please overlook my words. Too much wine on an empty stomach."

He meant the last remark to be funny, but he couldn't help thinking of the lean meals, the fear they would be stranded on that accursed island, and he put more feeling into his words than he had intended. His mother regarded him a moment.

"I am the one who is thoughtless. Of course you would be hungry. I will order dinner to be served immediately."

Cecile turned her lustrous eyes upon Rodrigo. "I know why Sir Henry sent the tankard to me. These Bottom Dwellers are a threat to us all. He foresees a time when our two countries will be fighting as allies, fighting for our very

existence, perhaps. Therefore, Monsieur de Villeneuve, I ask
you to report to the royal armory tomorrow morning. Bring
with you a copy of your treatise. I will meet you there. I
will explain to Monsieur Douver, the master armorer, that
you will be in charge of supervising the production of the
steel—"

Rodrigo's jaw dropped; his eyes widened. He was—for
the first time Stephano had known him—struck dumb.

"Congratulations, Mother," said Stephano, amused.
"You've shocked Rodrigo."

"My dear lady," said Rodrigo, finding his voice. "You are
not in earnest—"

"I am always in earnest," said Cecile, a frown line mar-
ring her forehead. "Is there a problem?"

"A problem!" Rodrigo gasped. "Me! In an armory! With . . .
with dirt and . . . and . . . smelting!" He appealed to Stephano.
"They smelt there, don't they? I believe I heard that they
smelt in armories. I can't be anyplace where men smelt!"

The countess's frown deepened.

"Consider making this 'sacrifice' for your country, monsieur," she said caustically.

Rodrigo recovered himself. "If I can find it, I will send
your master armorer a copy of the treatise, Your Grace. That
is the best I can do. I am leaving tomorrow to travel to Argonne to visit my mother."

"Are you?" Cecile asked in a dangerous tone that made
Stephano shiver.

Rodrigo blanched a little, but kept smiling. "I am, Countess."

Cecile put her hand on the door handle and looked at
Stephano. "I must speak to the servants. Talk to him."

She left the room. Stephano could tell his mother was angry by the way she held her head, the tap of her heels, even

by the irate swishing of her gown. He realized, after a moment, that the pewter tankard was gone. He had never seen his mother remove it.

Rodrigo was pouring himself another glass of wine. "I don't believe I have ever suffered such a severe shock. Not even when the Bottom Dwellers shot me."

"Stop clowning, Rigo," Stephano said. "I hate to say it, but in this instance my mother is right. Rosia needs that magically enhanced steel. You can't make a joke of this."

"Stephano, I understand. I do," Rodrigo said earnestly. "I love my country as much as the next man and if I thought I could help, I would. But I would be completely useless, I assure you. Smelting." He shuddered.

"It might be an adventure," Stephano suggested.

"I've had adventure enough for a lifetime, my friend," said Rodrigo. "Plead to your mother on my behalf. She'll listen to you."

"Since when," Stephano muttered.

When the countess returned, she asked Rodrigo for his arm and he complied, escorting her down the hall. Stephano moodily followed. They entered a room that was ablaze with candlelight gleaming in the crystal wineglasses and shining off the polished silver. Servants stood behind each chair, while other servants hovered nearby, waiting to bring in the silver tureens with the soup course and pour the wine.

The countess indicated that Rodrigo should sit at her right hand. He was in his element, talking of music and the opera, asking the countess what he had missed in his absence and when that topic languished, shifting the conversation effortlessly to the political situation in Braffa.

The countess listened with her customary calm demeanor and kept the talk flowing smoothly. Stephano spoke when required and then only in monosyllables. His appetite was ruined. He ate the marvelous food without tasting it and drank sparingly of the wine. Every so often, his mother would turn her gaze on him.

She said nothing. She didn't have to. Stephano understood her silent communication. He knew the importance of this invention. He knew that lives were at stake. He knew, better than most, the dreadful nature of the enemy. And all the while, Stephano tried to picture Rodrigo in the royal armory, sweating in the heat of the forge fires, shouting to make himself heard over the din of hammering, covered in the soot that turned the skin permanently black.

At the end of the meal, the servants placed the port on the table, along with cheese and walnuts and grapes. The countess rose, pleading fatigue.

"I will leave you gentlemen to your wine. Ring the bell when you wish to leave. The servants will see you out."

Stephano and Rodrigo rose to their feet. The countess swept out, casting Stephano a final piercing look, silently ordering him to deal with Rodrigo. Stephano dismissed the servant, and began to pace restlessly.

Rodrigo forked a bit of cheese, savoring it. He reached for the decanter. "Will you have some?"

Stephano shook his head. "You've drunk enough for both of us."

"I am making up for lost time, my friend," said Rodrigo, who was in an excellent mood. He burst out rapturously, "Your mother is a wonderful woman! You malign her. She was charming to me at dinner. She said nothing, of course, but I believe she has given this matter of the magical steel considered thought and concluded I was right. I shall not smelt."

Stephano remembered the look his mother had flashed at him as she went out the door. The look had not been charming.

"I'm not so sure of that, Rigo," said Stephano, sighing. "I'm sick of this place. Let's go home."

"Agreed," said Rodrigo. "I'll just take the port with us. It looks lonely."

Picking up the crystal decanter, he tucked it lovingly under his arm.

24

*I would far rather be on the field of battle than in my
mother's drawing room. On the battlefield, you know
your enemy. You are surrounded by friends and comrades to whom you entrust your life. At court, the enemy is all around you, yet you have no idea who they
are. You must live your life as if you were behind enemy lines, waiting to be discovered. Soldiers share a
camaraderie born in conflict. Courtiers share para-
noia, born in mistrust. And yet my mother seems to
revel in it.*

—Stephano de Guichen,
in a letter to Sir Ander Martel

During the carriage ride home Rodrigo drank port and sang
arias, even attempting to sing all four parts of a quartet and
coming closer to succeeding than Stephano would have
thought possible. He was achingly sober and spent the ride
staring through the windows at the streetlamps: landbound
stars that followed the streets in sparkling lines, straight or
curved, crossed and crisscrossed.

He looked back at the Sunset Palace. The magical stone
that had been radiant with the hues of the sunset now glim-

mered softly with moon glow. Here and there a light shone
in one of the mullioned windows.

The ships of the royal navy floated above the palace. They
were rigged with their running lights—brass lamps—shining
red and green. Men would be awake on board the ships: the
officer of the watch making his rounds; the lookouts keeping watch . . . for Freyans.

Beyond the lights of Evreux was the Breath, a ridge of
solid darkness dividing the glittering darkness of the city
from the glittering darkness of the starlit heavens. A few
lights shone in the Breath: a merchant ship sailing into port;
a patrol boat guarding the shoreline.

He looked out into the night and thought how much he
loved his country, his people. His father had loved his country. Julian de Guichen had died for his country, though since
he had been executed as a traitor, there were few who would
ever know that or believe it. Stephano listened to Rodrigo
singing and wondered how he was going to manage to persuade his friend to work in the royal armory.

Every man had his price, so they said. Stephano reflected
gloomily that there was not enough velvet, satin, silk, and
lace in the world to convince Rodrigo to enter a foundry.

No use talking to him tonight, he thought, listening to yet
another aria. Stephano resolved to speak seriously to his
friend in the morning.

They arrived home as the clocks were chiming one. The
neighborhood was quiet. It was a respectable neighborhood;
everyone went to bed at a decent hour. The only light was a
streetlamp about half a block down. Benoit would be sitting
up waiting for them, cozily tucked in his chair by the kitchen
fire. Stephano opened the front door, calling for Benoit as he
entered so that he didn't alarm him.

No answer.

Stephano assumed that Benoit had fallen asleep after the rigors of the day. The trunk was empty. Benoit must have unpacked their things. He hoped Benoit had brushed and cleaned his Dragon Brigade coat. Stephano turned to see if Rodrigo needed assistance walking.

Rodrigo was steady on his feet despite the amount of wine and port he'd consumed. He was an effervescent drunk, not mean or surly, not sloppy or sentimental. He was not staggering, though Stephano noted that his friend did take extra care when crossing the hall. Witty and charming, he would tumble into his bed with a smile and wake refreshed. Stephano, who drank half as much as his friend and generally ended up feeling twice as bad, looked upon Rodrigo as a marvel.

"You go upstairs," said Stephano. "I'll check on Benoit."

Rodrigo gaily assented. He was still carrying the decanter of port, though there was considerably less now than when they had left the countess. The decanter was cut crystal, decorated with the bee insignia of the de Marjolaines. Stephano would have to remember to return it to his mother.

"Can you make it?" he asked Rodrigo dubiously, seeing his friend pause to scrutinize the first step.

"My dear fellow, I could dance the fandango if I wanted," said Rodrigo, referring to the lively Estaran dance then currently in vogue. "Would you like to see me?"

"No, no, I believe you," said Stephano hastily. "I'll meet you upstairs."

"Will you take a final glass of your mother's excellent port before you go to bed?" Rodrigo asked.

"No, I've had enough of my mother for one night," said Stephano grimly.

Rodrigo smiled. "Tell Benoit to wake me early so that I can pack."

"How early is early?" Stephano asked.

"Noon would be about right," said Rodrigo. "Good night, my friend."

Gripping the decanter in one hand and the stair railing in the other, he began to negotiate the stairs with as much care as if he were scaling a mountain.

Stephano watched to make certain his friend didn't fall and when Rodrigo had safely reached the summit, went to the kitchen. A lamp was burning. A glass of wine—partially drunk—was on the table. Benoit was not in his chair.

"That's odd," Stephano remarked.

Nothing irritated Benoit more than to see guests walk away from the table leaving behind wine or beer or whatever they were drinking. He considered this an insult to the host. This had actually become a joke among the Cadre. Rodrigo would sometimes leave a bit of wine in his glass just to hear Benoit berate him. The idea that Benoit would not finish his wine was unthinkable.

Stephano was concerned enough that he picked up the lamp and walked across the hall to Benoit's bedroom. Opening the door softly, he looked inside. The old man was in his bed, lying on his back, his nightcap on his head, the blanket pulled up to his chin. Benoit's mouth was open. He was breathing loudly.

Stephano stood a moment, looking fondly at Benoit. The family retainer had known Stephano before Stephano had known himself. Benoit had ridden with his father to bring home his infant son from the nunnery where his mother had sought refuge to give birth to her bastard child. If the mother superior of the nunnery had not contacted Julian, he would have never known he was a father. Stephano might have been raised an orphan for all his mother cared. She had wanted only to go back to court and to her lover, the king.

That was the story he'd heard from his embittered grandfather. Stephano thought back to tonight, that shadowed look of dread in his mother's eyes. He had not imagined it or at least he didn't think so. He wondered, for the first time, what the true story might be. His father had never talked about Cecile, had never spoken her name. Perhaps Julian had not known the truth, either. If there was a truth to know.

He thought of his cutting remark about Sir Ander and remembered his mother's swift defense. The knight had remained Cecile de Marjolaine's loyal friend after all these years. Sir Ander was a good man, honest and God-fearing. Was it likely he would be steadfastly loyal to a woman who was little better than a common whore?

Stephano asked himself this question and it occurred to him that he could ask Sir Ander. The knight had wanted to talk to Stephano about his mother when they had met at the Abbey of Saint Agnes. Stephano had coldly refused.

"Next time we meet," he said to himself.

He closed the door to Benoit's room and ascended the stairs. The second floor of the house consisted of a parlor that doubled as library and office; Rodrigo's bedroom and dressing room; and Stephano's bedroom and dressing room. The third floor was a formal dining area, a large room that Rodrigo termed grandiloquently "the ballroom." The third floor was kept closed, the few pieces of furniture covered with cloth. Stephano had never held a ball in the ballroom, nor was he ever likely to. He detested such events and while Rodrigo adored them, giving fancy dress balls and elegant dinner parties cost money. Rodrigo never gave up hope that someday they would be able to afford it.

Certainly not now, Stephano thought. Not with the Cadre disbanded and me with no way to earn a living.

He used the lamp to light his way up the stairs. He paused on the landing on the second floor and glanced around. He still had the feeling something wasn't right. Benoit and the unfinished wine and the fact that the old man always waited up for them—if for nothing else than to hear Rodrigo relate the latest court gossip.

Stephano couldn't see anything out of the ordinary. Telling himself he was jumping at shadows, he looked in on Rodrigo, who was in the parlor, sprawled in a chair in front of a barely glowing fire. Another oddity—Benoit had not been up to tend to it. Rodrigo was drinking the last of the port and yawning at the embers.

"There were times I thought I would never see this room again," said Stephano.

Rodrigo smiled. "Good night, my friend. And thank you."

"For what?"

"For bringing us home," said Rodrigo.

"We stayed true to each other. The Cadre. That's why we survived." Stephano sighed. "And now that's gone."

"When Miri hears Dag is alive and well, she'll be in a better frame of mind. Leave the door open. I'll finish the port and then I'm off to bed."

Stephano bid his friend a good night and went to his bedroom, which was the last room at the end of the hall. He opened the door and heard behind him, over his right shoulder, someone draw in a soft breath.

Stephano's gut clenched. Every nerve in his body tingled. He didn't stop to ask questions. A person hiding behind a door was not here for a chat. Stephano swung his body toward the sound, taking the lamp with him as he pivoted.

The light reflected off the blade of a knife. Stephano flung the lamp in the assassin's general direction. The lamp struck the man in the face. Glass shattered. The man gave a grunt of pain and dropped the knife.

From down the hall, Rodrigo called out sternly, "Stephano? What did you break now? That had better not be the hand-painted porcelain water pitcher—"

The light was gone. Before it went out, Stephano had

caught a glimpse of his attacker: a man wearing a cloak and tricornered hat, his face covered by a black silk scarf, with eyeholes and slits for the nose and mouth.

Stephano yelled, "Assassin!" and ran for his sword, which he kept in the baldric, hanging from the bedpost. He had the advantage in the semidarkness, because he knew where he was and what furniture was around him, whereas his attacker would be left to fumble about.

"Assassin?" Rodrigo was bewildered. "Stephano, are you . . . Ulp!"

Stephano heard his friend cry out, then the sound of a door banging and feet pounding. His heart sank. There was more than one killer in the house.

Pale light from the streetlamp shining through the windows cast two long silvery rectangles of light on the floor. Stephano was three jumps away from the bedpost when strong arms wrapped around his legs, taking him down.

Stephano landed flat on his stomach. His assailant twisted to his feet. Stephano, glancing back, saw the barrel of a pistol aimed at his head. He rolled under the bed.

The gun went off, the bullet striking the floor where his head had been. Stephano crawled out from under the bed just as the assassin was drawing another pistol. Reaching up, Stephano snagged a pillow and tossed it at the window.

The assassin turned and fired. The bullet blew a hole in the pillow and smashed through the glass. Stephano clambered to his feet, grabbing the sword from the baldric. He lunged at the attacker, only to see the blade enveloped in a swirl of black cloak, fouling the weapon.

Stephano swore and tried to free his blade from the tangled cloak. The assassin gave the cloak a snap, yanking the sword from Stephano's hand, and flung the weapon, still wrapped in the cloak, across the room. He drew another pistol. Stephano's own dragon pistol was inside a box in the closet, so that wasn't any help. He seized hold of the hand-painted porcelain water pitcher and flung it at the pistol, striking as the man fired, spoiling his aim.

The bullet hit the wall behind Stephano, who was ready with his fists. The assassin was fumbling in his pocket for either a knife or yet another pistol. The shrill, piercing sound of police whistles brought both Stephano and his attacker to a halt.

In what Stephano would later recall as one of the more ludicrous moments of his life, he and the man trying to kill him stared at each other in mutual astonishment.

True, there had been the sound of gunshots, but when people in Evreux heard gunshots, they tended to shutter the windows, bolt the doors, and go back to bed. Few went to the trouble of summoning the constables and even if his neighbors had done so, the nearest constabulary was half a mile away.

"La Farge! Coppers!" yelled the lookout who had been posted on the sidewalk below.

The assassin raised his hand to his forehead in salute, then he ran across the room and coolly dove through the broken window, taking out the frame and the rest of the glass. Stephano ran to the window and stared down to see the assassin make a hard landing on the sidewalk among shards of broken glass and smashed wood. One of the man's accomplices helped the assassin to his feet. The last Stephano saw of him, he was hobbling off down the block in company with two others. The police whistles were growing louder.

"Damnation!" Stephano swore.

Sounds of swearing and thumping came from the hallway. Stephano found his sword, freed it from the cloak, and ran into the hall.

Seeing him, Rodrigo yelled excitedly.

"I've got him! I've got him!"

Stephano stopped to stare.

Rodrigo, with a courage born of port, had jumped onto his assailant's back, wrapped his legs around the man's waist, and covered his eyes with his hands. The man was flailing with his fists and staggering blindly about the hallway, deliberately bumping into walls in an effort to knock Rodrigo off him.

"Let him go, Rigo!" Stephano shouted, choking back an inclination to laugh. "The constables are coming!"

"But I've got him!" Rodrigo protested. "They can arrest him!"

"Let him go!" Stephano said grimly. "The police aren't coming for him. They're coming for you!"

Rodrigo lost his grip and slid off the man's back. The assassin fled into the darkness. Stephano could hear him thundering down the stairs. Rodrigo was standing in the hall, gaping at him.

"Me? What—"

"Grab money from the strongbox!" Stephano ordered.

"Why—"

"Just do it!"

Stephano heard shouting from the street; someone had caught sight of the assassins. Several of the constables broke off from the main group to give chase, probably thinking they were the men they had come to arrest.

Stephano ran into his room, flung open the closet door, and grabbed the two most valuable objects he owned: his Dragon Brigade uniform coat and a box made of oak, bound in iron. He noted Benoit had, indeed, cleaned his coat. He thrust his sword into his baldric, slung it over his shoulder, and ran back into the hallway. Rodrigo was stuffing two bags of silver in his pockets.

"Would you please tell me what's going on?" Rodrigo pleaded.

"My mother is what's going on," said Stephano angrily, grabbing hold of Rodrigo's arm and propelling him down the stairs.

Reaching the ground floor, they headed for the kitchen and the back door. Stephano blessed the assassins. If they had not attacked, he and Rodrigo would have been sound asleep when the constables invaded their home.

So much for thinking his mother cared about him.

As he and Rodrigo rushed out through the back door, they heard the shattering sound of the constables breaking down the front. Stephano and Rodrigo ran through the backyard, trampling Benoit's garden, and out the back gate. One of the constables, coming around a corner, saw them and let out a yell.

Stephano darted into an alley. "This way!"

"Why would your mother hire assassins to kill us?" Rodrigo asked, hurrying to keep up.

"My mother didn't send the assassins," said Stephano. "She sent the police to arrest you."

"Then who sent the assassins?"

"I have no idea," said Stephano. "No more questions! Save your breath for running!"

Shouts and whistles indicated pursuit was right behind them. They had a good head start and they knew the neighborhood. They ran down alleys, crashed through hedgerows, and scaled walls. When they could no longer hear whistles, Stephano called a halt. He had a stitch in his side that was painful, but at least it was not a knife. Rodrigo bent double, his hands on his knees, gasping for breath.

In the light of a streetlamp, Stephano placed the box he was carrying on the sidewalk, opened the box, and drew out his dragon pistol, the small bag of shot stored alongside the weapon, and the tin of powder. He began loading the pistol.

"I don't suppose I can go back for a change of clothes?" Rodrigo asked plaintively. He was wearing his count finery—silk coat, lace, velvet pantaloons, silk stockings.

Stephano looked up. "Rigo, someone wants us dead. Not to mention the fact that my mother has a warrant out for your arrest. She sent the police to haul you off to a foundry."

"I'll hide at my mother's—"

"You told *my* mother you were going to visit your mother. The police will be there, as well."

Rodrigo gave a bleak sigh. "So where are we going?"

"The Cloud Hopper," said Stephano, rising to his feet. "I hope you're right about Miri forgiving me. Otherwise . . ."

"I'll be smelting," said Rodrigo gloomily. "Or dead. I'm not sure which would be worse."

Stephano tucked the loaded pistol into his coat, leaving the box behind. The two headed for the harbor.

Miri and Gythe always docked the *Cloud Hopper* at a public wharf near Dag's boardinghouse. When in Evreux, the two women did not join their fellow Trundlers in the Trundler village of houseboats. The village was located about ten miles from the city, which had meant the sisters would have a long way to travel to reach Stephano's house, where the Cadre met. They liked to be close to Dag and they knew he liked having them nearby.

This area of the harbor was home to warehouses and businesses dependent on the canal traffic. Long barges loaded with goods were tied up for the night. Empty barges were waiting to be filled in the morning. The streets were deserted but Stephano and Rodrigo kept to the shadows, not taking chances. Arriving at Canal Street, Stephano stopped behind the corner of a building. He took hold of Rodrigo, dragging him back when he would have walked on.

"The *Cloud Hopper* is just down the road—" Rodrigo protested.

"I know," said Stephano.

Flattening himself against the wall, he peered down the street. He drew back with a curse.

Rodrigo groaned. "What now?"

Stephano gripped Rodrigo by the arm and pulled him into the shadows. "Down the boardwalk. The *Cloud Hopper*."

Rodrigo looked and let out his breath in a low whistle. "D'argent!"

"And he's brought friends," said Stephano bitterly.

The *Cloud Hopper* was lit up like the royal barge on His Majesty's birthday. Constables swarmed over it, flashing their bull's-eye lanterns into the water barrels and peering beneath rolls of sailcloth. D'argent held a handkerchief to his cheek with one hand. A constable had hold of Miri, who was swearing at him. Gythe stood blocking the door to the hold, threatening anyone who came near her with the belaying pin.

"I'm an idiot!" Stephano muttered. "Of course, my mother would realize the *Cloud Hopper* is the first place we would go."

"Will they take Miri and Gythe to prison?" Rodrigo asked worriedly.

"Not if I can help it," said Stephano grimly, drawing his pistol.

Miri kicked the constable in his privates. He doubled over and she broke free. Gythe snatched up Doctor Ellington, made a rude gesture at D'argent, and hurried to join her sister. The two women ran down Canal Street. The constables started to go after them.

"Leave them," D'argent ordered, loud enough for Miri

and Gythe to hear. "We have the boat. That is what we came for." He dabbed at his face with the handkerchief.

"The boat," said Stephano. "So we can't get away."

"We have money," said Rodrigo. "We could hire a coach or horses or—" He saw the expression on Stephano's face. "Your mother will have all those places watched, too."

"My mother is nothing if not thorough," said Stephano.

The two waited in the shadows for Miri and Gythe, who were walking down Canal Street in their direction. As if God himself were taunting them, the skies clouded over, and rain began to fall.

"Me without a cloak. Another silk coat ruined," Rodrigo said with a sigh.

Neither of them had brought a hat either. The rain drummed on their heads and ran into their eyes. Stephano and Rodrigo moved to the shelter of an overhang.

The constables on board the *Cloud Hopper* loosened the tie ropes. One took his place at the helm. They steered the houseboat away from the dock and out into the canal. Gythe and Miri stopped to watch until the houseboat disappeared into the darkness.

Rodrigo gave a mirthless laugh. "Good luck trying to figure out how to keep the magic working."

"They only have to go as far as the impound lot," said Stephano.

Miri and Gythe resumed walking. When they came level with Stephano, he softly called their names. Miri started, looked around, and saw him. She stared at him from beneath the hood of her cloak, her arms folded across her chest. Then she slowly walked over to them. Gythe trudged alongside her sister, sheltering the Doctor from the rain with her cloak.

"They've impounded my boat," Miri said.

"Miri, I'm so sorry—" Stephano began.

"This is your doing, then."

"Mine, actually," said Rodrigo meekly.

"You'd better tell me," said Miri with a sigh.

Rodrigo explained the situation.

"I'll get your boat back, Miri," he added, remorseful. "I'll go to the master smelterer and offer myself—"

"No, you won't," said Stephano wearily. "You can't go back. Someone hired assassins to kill us, remember?"

Miri shifted her gaze to him. "Assassins."

Now it was Stephano's turn to explain.

"There were four of them," he said in conclusion. "Professionals. They fled when they heard the constables' whistles. Aside from trying to kill us, they actually did us a favor. Warned us the police were coming."

Miri regarded Stephano in silence. Gythe stood behind her sister, her face a pale glimmer beneath her hood, her eyes large and unhappy.

Miri's lips twitched. She put her hand to her mouth to try to stop the laughter, but that didn't help. The laughter rolled out of her. She laughed loud and long, laughed until she had to wipe the tears from her eyes and leaned weakly against a wall.

"Oh, Stephano, Stephano," Miri said when she could talk. "Only you would be saved from a man trying to kill you by a man coming to arrest you. That's why I love you. When I don't hate you."

Stephano's answer was to take Miri in his arms. He held her tightly, his own eyes wet, and not from rain.

Miri smiled up at him and freed herself from his embrace. She put her hands on her hips. "So they've impounded my boat and driven you and Rigo into hiding. The question is, what do we do now?"

"You and Gythe have relatives in the Trundler village," said Stephano. "You could go stay with them. Rigo and I will—"

Gythe shook her head emphatically and clasped her hands together.

"Gythe is right. We're not splitting up," said Miri.

"But back on board the *Cloud Hopper* you said—"

"I know what I said." Miri cut Stephano short. "Gythe and I talked it over. She made me see I was wrong. She is wise, my little sister. We've enjoyed the good times with you. We'll stick with you in the bad."

"What good times is she talking about?" Rodrigo asked in a low voice.

Stephano glared at him and changed the subject. "What happened to D'argent? I saw him with a handkerchief plastered to his face. I hope you punched him."

Miri glanced at Gythe, who grinned and held up the Doctor. Only his head was visible, peering out of the cloak. He looked wrathful. Gythe shaped her fingers like claws.

"He scratched D'argent!" Stephano said, grinning. "Good for the Doctor. I owe him some sardines. And speaking of the Doctor, I heard from Dag. He's safe at my estate outside Argonne with the three dragons and the two dragon brothers. He writes that he is fine and he has news to tell us."

"Of course, he's fine," said Miri. "I knew he would be. And even if he wasn't, he made the decision to go. I was wrong about him, too. I've been wrong about a lot of things lately."

She took hold of Stephano's hand and squeezed it. "I'm sorry."

"I am the one who is sorry," said Stephano. "And I will get the *Cloud Hopper* back, Miri. I promise."

He pushed his wet hair out of his eyes. "But, in the meantime, we'll have to leave Rosia, lay low for a while until I can find a way to persuade my mother *not* to have Rigo arrested—"

"*And* find out who is trying to kill us," said Rodrigo.

"That, too," said Stephano.

The four were silent, thinking.

"I have an idea," said Miri. "Come with me."

"Where?" Stephano asked.

"Never mind. I'm in charge now," said Miri.

"I don't suppose this involves bed and a hot bath," said Rodrigo hopefully. When no one answered him, he answered himself. "I didn't think so."

They left the sheltering overhang and plunged into the rain, which was now falling in torrents.

The storm had let up a little and the clocks in the church steeples were chiming four times when Miri announced that they had arrived at their destination. She pointed to a large ship tied up at the dock. The ship was dark save for the running lights. Even without the lights Stephano would have recognized the checkered balloons of the *Sommerwind*.

He looked at Miri in perplexity.

"The *Sommerwind* is bound for Braffa," said Miri. "They're stopping at Argonne to take on water and supplies and make some additional repairs before the long voyage."

Stephano stared at her. "Argonne! That's where Dag is and my estate— Which, of course, you already knew. Miri, you are a genius! Will Captain Leydecker take us on, do you think?"

"The captain owes me for saving his life." Miri cast a sly glance at Rodrigo. "As for you two, I hear he's looking for deckhands—"

"Deckhands!" Rodrigo gasped and shuddered. "Swabbing decks and keel-hauling and dancing hornpipes . . ."

He stopped. The other three were grinning at him.

"Oh, I see. Very funny." Rodrigo sneezed. "May I point out that while we're standing in the rain having fun at my expense, I'm catching my death of cold."

"Going to my estate will be risky, Miri," Stephano said. "We'll have to dodge the constables—"

"And assassins," said Rodrigo with another sneeze.

"All in a day's work," said Miri, shrugging.

"Speaking of work," said Rodrigo. "Do you think this little misunderstanding we're having with your mother means she is going to stop paying us?"

"Let's tally up the score," said Stephano. "We bungled the job she gave us, refused to sacrifice ourselves for our country, and now we're on the run. What do you think?"

Rodrigo sighed and sneezed again.

25

And God's voice led blessed Saint Marie across Rosia to a mountain rising from an inland sea, its steep slopes covered in aspen and fir. Saint Marie looked on the mountain island and knew that God had led her to the site of the bastion that would forever guard God's Word.

—The Life of Saint Marie,
Father Ralph Hayden

The branch of the church known as the Arcanum was founded by Saint Marie about five hundred years ago during the Dark Ages, to defend and protect an embattled faith. The church in those times was beset by enemies from without and within. Terrible storms raging in the Breath had disrupted trade and communication between nations, plunging wealthy nations into poverty and poor nations into chaos. Rivers and inland seas rose, flooding farmlands and washing out entire cities.

Famine and disease killed many who survived those disasters. Neighbor fought neighbor over scraps. The church tried to help, but the nuns and priests were overwhelmed, as they, too, were forced to struggle to survive.

Those who practiced the evil form of ancient magic known as "blood magic" thrived during this time as the desperate

turned to warlocks and witches for help. Many would come
to discover that the price they paid for wealth and power was
too terrible, but by the time they did, they were sunk so deeply
in depravity they could not claw their way out.

The headquarters of the Arcanum was located in the
Citadel of the Voice, an impregnable bastion whose walls,
towers, dwellings, and the original church had been magically carved out of the mountain. Hundreds of years later,
the Citadel had grown and expanded. Many structures dotted the mountain's rugged slopes in clusters. Each cluster of
buildings was built around a central courtyard beautifully
landscaped with flowers, hedges, and fountains.

The oldest structures had all been built at sea level. The
Citadel had grown upward, climbing the mountainside. There
was now the library, the hospital, the prison, the dortoir for
the priests and one for the nuns, the provost's mansion, and
the dortoir for the guardians of the Citadel, the monks of
Saint Klee. The various clusters were connected by covered
walkways and staircases leading up the side of the mountain, from one level to another. They were further protected
by curtain walls, set with watchtowers. The cathedral stood
at the very top, its delicate spires rising high above the fortress walls, as though disdaining their protection, seeming
to reach up to touch heaven.

Built for a more brutal time, the fortifications now served
to protect the inhabitants from the elements, rather than
from an enemy. Gun emplacements set into the sides of the
mountain had long since been turned into gardens and court-
yards, as the Citadel came to rely on magic instead of cannonballs.

The Citadel of the Voice was rumored to be an awful
place, a towering fortress on a hidden island that lay beneath
perpetual brooding clouds beset by fierce, cold winds whip-

ping the waves of the inland sea and sending them crashing upon the shore. The Citadel was the Voice of God in His wrath—a bastion of dark dungeons, dismal cells, and forsaken oubliettes.

Sir Ander chuckled at the notion, which never failed to amuse him. He had friends who ascribed to this belief, and he wished they could see him this fine morning, standing on the ramparts, basking in the bright sunshine that sparkled off the crystalline blue waters of the inland sea. The citadel was in truth one of the most beautiful places on Rosia.

The island was surrounded by the sea, and the sea was surrounded by the Kartaign Mountains. These were not young, fang-edged mountains. They were old, their sharp peaks worn by time, rounded and softened and thickly forested. There were no passes through the mountains. The Citadel was not marked on any map. The only way to reach it was by sailing through the air over the mountains, then traveling across the inland sea. Lookouts on the walls could observe approaching ships long before the ships could observe the lookouts.

Those traveling to the Arcanum on church business were welcomed at the Carriage House. Yachts and coaches landed in the carriage yard—a large, flat strip of land running alongside the sea. Stables housed wyverns and griffins.

Sir Ander admired the view and listened with pleasure to the voices of the choir practicing a new hymn. The hymn praising God was well suited to the beauty of the day. For a moment, he let the music and the sun and the rolling swell of the sea wash over and submerge his sorrow, worry, and regret.

Sir Ander was not alone on the ramparts. The nuns, priests, and monks of the Arcanum who inhabited the Citadel often walked here. Many were out this morning, enjoying the beauty of the day before the heat drove everyone into the cool shadows of the scriptorium, the library, the chapel, or the cathedral; into the privacy of their own cells or the comradeship of common rooms.

Sir Ander was the subject of stares and whispered talk. He wasn't supposed to be here. The Citadel kept no standing army. In all the years of its existence, it had only rarely been attacked. And in the extremely unlikely event that the Citadel did come under assault, secret, powerful magicks, put in place and operated by the warrior monks of Saint Klee defended it. The monks also guarded those "guests" who had been sent to the Arcanum under Seal.

As a Knight Protector, Sir Ander guarded Father Jacob when the priest was away from the Citadel. His duties as guardian were not required inside its protective walls. Sir Ander and Father Jacob had returned to the Citadel over a fortnight ago and Sir Ander should now be back in the Mother House in Evreux. He had instead taken lodgings in the Citadel's guesthouse, which usually was reserved for visiting bishops and other dignitaries.

The provost was not pleased, but he had no jurisdiction over the Knight Protectors and he could not order Sir Ander to leave. Only a ranking officer of the Knight Protectors could issue such an order and since the commandant respected Sir Ander and knew the knight must have good reason for his decision, the order for his removal would not come very swiftly.

Sir Ander was not here of his own voilition. He was here because Father Jacob had asked him to remain. Sir Ander was not certain why. Perhaps, he mused, it was to protect the priest from starvation. Sir Ander saw to it that Father Jacob stopped his work long enough to eat and occasionally poke his nose out for a breath of fresh air.

Father Jacob had his own quarters, but he was rarely in them. He was more often to be found in the library, working alone in a small reading room, translating the works of the saints they had unearthed in the Abbey of Saint Agnes. Sir Ander was the only person permitted to enter the reading cell, which resembled the "guest" cells far below in the prison, except that it was furnished with a desk and a comfortable chair in addition to a cot and chamber pot. The library had several such secure reading cells, since the priests and nuns of the Arcanum often worked on sensitive projects.

When the clock in the bell tower struck eleven, Sir Ander turned to leave the ramparts to fix a tray of food to take to Father Jacob. He halted at the sight of a large yacht sailing over the sea, bound for the Citadel. The yacht was instantly recognizable as belonging to the grand bishop. The others on the ramparts stopped to stare and speculate.

Sir Ander took one look and hurriedly left. He had a grim foreboding this visit had something to do with Father Jacob.

Sir Ander returned to his room in the guesthouse to put on his formal uniform coat, shirt, breeches, and boots. He tucked his hat under his arm and ascended the steps to the library. Crossing the courtyard, he approached the library, a large stone structure, rectangular in shape with three stories and two towers. He entered through the bronze double doors, which had been designed to look like the two pages of an open book.

Inside was a large room filled with myriad bookshelves, desks, and chairs. Large windows admitted the sunlight by day; lamps lit the library by night. Sir Ander whispered a greeting to the head librarian, who worked behind a large desk and inquired of each visitor what business he had in the library. Accustomed to the knight by now, the head librarian returned his greeting pleasantly and waved him on.

Sir Ander walked past the rows of shelves and desks. Reaching the north tower, he greeted the warrior monk who was posted at the bottom of the stairs that led to the reading rooms and the Library of the Forbidden at the very top level. The monk regarded the knight with cool appraisal, then stood aside to allow him to pass through the arched doorway. Narrow spiral stairs led to the upper three levels and the reading rooms. At the top, on the fourth level, locked and magic-locked, and locked again was the Library of the Forbidden, where works of a dangerous or heretical nature were housed. A private staircase, guarded day and night by warrior monks, led to that library. As he passed he gave a cheery good morning to the monks, who did not respond. The warrior monks of Saint Klee never spoke unless forced to do so by dire necessity.

Sir Ander proceeded down the hall to Father Jacob's reading room on the third level. Dusty sunlight slid through slit windows. This level was deathly quiet; not even the songs of the choir rose this far. Sir Ander's boots, ringing on the stone floor, made an ungodly racket.

He found Father Jacob absorbed in his work, reading with one finger to mark his place in the text, while he made notes on a sheet of paper in a bound book. Sir Ander took out his key to unlock the iron gate.

"Did you remove the warding spell?" he thought to ask before inserting the iron key.

Father Jacob gave an annoyed mumble that might have been a yes.

"Are you certain, Father?" Sir Ander persisted. "I still have burns on my hand from the last time you said you had removed the spell."

Father Jacob looked up from his reading.

"Ander, what do you think I've found?"

Sir Ander sighed and gingerly touched the key to the lock. No sparks flew, so he deemed it safe to open.

"Tell me later. The grand bishop's yacht—"

Father Jacob wasn't listening. "You remember when we

were in the underground room in the Abbey of Saint Agnes, the room where the saints had conducted their secret work on contramagic. We found the desks with their initials carved into them: *M, D, C, M,* and *X.* Marie, Dennis, Charles and Michael. We could not figure out what the *X* meant. You theorized that *X* marks the spot, as I recall. Perhaps a treasure map."

Sir Ander tried again. "Father Jacob, the grand bishop—"

"Bother the grand bishop!" Father Jacob exclaimed. He laid his hand on the book. "I know what the *X* stands for. The *X* is the initial of a fifth person—Xavier."

"A fifth person?" Sir Ander repeated, intrigued.

"There were *five* friends, Ander!" said Father Jacob. "Five priests, presumably close friends, all of them studying contramagic."

"Who was this Xavier?"

"Ah, that's the question. Who was he? Why have we never heard of him? Why isn't his name inscribed on the book with the other four? I wonder . . ."

Father Jacob fell silent, gazing thoughtfully into the shadows.

"Father Jacob, I know this is fascinating, but it must wait. The grand bishop—"

He was interrupted by the sound of slippered feet shuffling down the hall. The head librarian peered at them through the iron grille.

"Father Jacob, you are summoned to the provost's office."

"Ah, I knew it," said Sir Ander grimly.

Father Jacob was leaning back in his chair gazing up at the ceiling. Sir Ander knew that look: the unfocused eyes, the movement of the lips in and out, in and out. The priest wasn't in the Citadel. He was somewhere off in the distant past, trying to part the curtains of time.

"Father Jacob—"

"He can't hear you, Brother," said Sir Ander.

"But he's sitting right there." The head librarian raised his voice. "Father Jacob!"

Father Jacob sat up and frowned. "I'm not deaf. Well, Brother, what do you want?"

"You are summoned to the office of the provost," the head librarian repeated patiently. "The grand bishop has arrived and he requests that you attend him immediately."

"Tell the grand bishop I'm busy," said Father Jacob.

He returned to his reading and note taking.

The head librarian was a middle-aged monk devoted to the Order of Saint Thomas, patron saint of knowledge. He and the other monks spent their days in the peaceful, quiet confines of the library, their only upset the mishelving of a book. And now here was Father Jacob refusing a summons to attend the grand bishop. The poor librarian staggered from the shock and stammered incoherently. "Father Jacob . . . The grand bishop . . . no one . . . I couldn't possibly . . ."

Sir Ander rescued him. "Tell the provost Father Jacob will be there presently."

The head librarian cast the knight a look of intense gratitude, then hurried away.

"You have been summoned, Father," said Sir Ander. "You know you have to go, so don't make me carry you."

Father Jacob looked obdurate for a moment, then muttered irritably, "I'd like to see you try! Oh, very well. Let us get this over with so that I can return to work."

He pushed himself up out of the chair, grimacing at the stiffness in his legs and back, and started out the door.

"You can't appear before the grand bishop looking like you've been sleeping in your cassock," said Sir Ander.

"What's wrong with the way I look?" Father Jacob demanded indignantly. "And for your information, I *have* been sleeping in my cassock."

"There's a large gravy stain on your sleeve and what appears to be dried soup that dribbled down the front. You haven't shaved in days. Your hands are black with ink and there's ink on your chin and the side of your face." Sir Ander wrinkled his nose. "And when was the last time you bathed?"

Sir Ander herded Father Jacob out the door of the cell and clanked it shut behind. He persuaded the priest to bathe, shave, put on a clean cassock, and rid himself as much as possible of the ink on his hands and face. When Sir Ander deemed his charge presentable, they climbed the stairs that led to the provost's dwelling, located near the summit.

"I don't know why you're insisting that I accompany you," Sir Ander stated. "The grand bishop sent for you, not me. His Eminence and I don't get along, as you well know."

"I need you as a corroborating witness in my defense."

"You haven't been accused of anything. At least not yet."

"I'm always being accused of something," said Father Jacob mildly. "You can take notes like Brother Barnaby."

"I am *not* Brother Barnaby," said Sir Ander sternly.

"I know that, my friend," said Father Jacob in gentle tones.

"I had a dream about Barnaby the other night," said Sir Ander in subdued tones. "Do you remember the time when we were investigating the massacre of those young people in Capione, when he told me he could not understand how I could justify killing another human being, even one as evil as the Warlock?"

"I remember," said Father Jacob.

"Brother Barnaby told me in my dream that he understood now. He asked me to pray for him."

"What do you think the dream means?" Father Jacob asked.

"That I've been thinking a lot about Brother Barnaby," said Sir Ander with a faint smile.

"And he's thinking of you," said Father Jacob earnestly. "He is not dead, Ander. He's reaching out to you. You must let him know you support him with your prayers."

Sir Ander only shook his head.

They arrived at a quaint, old-fashioned building that had once been a chapter house, but which now housed the provost's office, as well as rooms for those who served the provost. Sir Ander and Father Jacob were shown into the office by the provost's secretary. He had been reluctant to admit Sir Ander, since only Father Jacob's presence was requested, but when Father Jacob insisted he required the knight's attendance the secretary decided that he would let the provost decide and announced both of them.

The provost was seated at his desk. The grand bishop, Ferdinand de Montagne, was standing at the window, staring out at the magnificent view of the mountains reflected in the water. He had his back to the door and did not turn around as Father Jacob and Sir Ander entered.

Provost Phillipe rose to greet his guests with a warm handshake and a cordial smile. Those who met Provost Phillipe were often astonished that this mild-spoken, scholarly looking man was the head of the Arcanum, one of the most feared institutions in the world.

Some said Phillipe had been placed in this position by the Council of Bishops on order of Montagne, who wanted a provost he could control. If Montagne thought that, he soon found out he had been mistaken. Phillipe of Allamaine possessed a rare quality: He had the scholar's ability to assess a situation and make an unbiased judgment. He expected good of men and yet was not shocked when they fell short. He seemed never to be angry or upset. Nothing ever disturbed his equanimity. Yet when he made a decision, it was said that the mountain on which the Citadel was built was more likely to shift its position than Provost Phillipe.

The provost was short and stocky with a round face, made rounder by the tonsure and a pair of round spectacles. He was dwarfed by the towering Montagne. If the provost was the mountain, Montagne was the storm wind that occasionally blew in to rage and cast his thunderbolts. When the storm was gone, the mountain remained unmoved.

The provost bade his guests be seated and took a seat himself. He did not sit behind his desk, which might have been intimidating to his guests, but joined them in a cozy circle. His office was dark and cool in the heat of the day. The room was small and well furnished with comfortable leather chairs. Curtains were closed on all the windows except the one where Montagne stood.

The grand bishop turned around to greet his guests. Sir Ander was shocked at the man's appearance. Montagne was gray with fatigue, and the flesh around his eyes was puffy. He had visibly lost weight. He frowned at the sight of Sir Ander, who remained standing, proud, upright. Montagne had never forgiven Sir Ander for his loyalty to Julian de Guichen during the Lost Rebellion. Sir Ander, for his part, had never forgiven Montagne for his betrayal of his friend.

"I understand, Sir Ander, that you have refused to obey orders to return to the Mother House," said the grand bishop.

"Your Eminence is mistaken," said Sir Ander. "I have not yet received my orders."

"I have sent word to the commander of the Knight Protectors that I require Sir Ander to remain with me," Father Jacob said, annoyed. "He is instrumental in my investigations of the books we discovered at the Abbey of Saint Agnes."

"I don't see how a Knight Protector can possibly be instrumental in your studies," said the grand bishop caustically. "Does he read to you aloud?"

Father Jacob rose to his feet.

"I am glad we had this chance to talk, Eminence. If you will excuse me, I have work to do—"

"For God's sake, Jacob, don't be such a pain in the ass!" The grand bishop was practically shouting. "Sit down!"

The provost raised an eyebrow, lowered his head, and rubbed the side of his nose. Sir Ander exchanged glances with Father Jacob, who resumed his seat.

"You heard, of course, about the collapse of the Crystal Market hall," said the grand bishop abruptly.

"A terrible tragedy. We held a mass for the dead," said Provost Phillipe.

"We held a great many masses for the dead," said the grand bishop in heavy tones. "The funerals were too numerous to count. Our priests were overwhelmed. Coffin makers worked day and night, and the cemeteries are now filled with fresh graves. So many little graves . . . small children. So many flowers. And all of them wilting . . ."

He sighed deeply and shook his head. The provost motioned discreetly for Sir Ander to be seated; apparently he was going to be permitted to stay. Sir Ander moved quietly to a chair beside Father Jacob, who was regarding the grand bishop with grave intensity.

"You put out a report, Eminence, that the failure of the crystal bricks was due to the architect's design, that the building was structurally unsound," said Father Jacob. "I happen to know for a fact that is not the truth."

The grand bishop frowned. "How do you know this for a *fact,* Father Jacob?"

"Because I received a report from the architect himself stating that the magic in the crystal bricks was failing. A report he gave to you months before the collapse."

The grand bishop was livid. He struggled to speak, choked on his anger, and finally managed to squeeze out words. "Who told you that?"

"A friend, Eminence," said Father Jacob gently. "A friend to the church."

The grand bishop bowed his head. His anger drained out of him, and he seemed to collapse, shrivel up.

"God help me," he said in a low voice.

He tried to walk toward a chair, staggered, and nearly fell. Sir Ander and the provost both sprang to their feet, fearing the man might collapse. He waved them away.

"I am fine," he said, leaning against the back of the chair, gripping it with both hands. "I have not been sleeping well."

He sank unsteadily into the chair. The provost summoned one of the brothers who served him and ordered brandy for the grand bishop and a pot of tea. When the tea and the brandy arrived, the provost dismissed the servant and handed around the steaming cups himself. They drank their tea in silence. The brandy restored Montagne. Some color returned to his face.

"You have not told anyone about this report, Father Jacob."

"No, Eminence. Not even the provost." Father Jacob gave a small nod of apology to the provost, who gave a mild smile. "And I feel confident in saying that the person who sent the report to me will remain silent, as well."

The grand bishop nodded. He drew in a deep breath and passed his hand over his face.

"I read that report months before the collapse." The grand bishop spread his hands helplessly. "What was I supposed to do? Close down the Crystal Market? And if so, what was I to tell the people of the world? Was I to say to them that the Crystal Market, the pride of the Crafters' Guild, the symbol of God's gift to us, is cracking like an eggshell?"

"No, Eminence," said the provost. "You could not say that."

"I thought we had time," the grand bishop continued. "I

set the most skilled crafters to work to try to fix the magic, find out the cause . . . God forgive me. I thought we had time."

Father Jacob shook his head and looked very grave. "Tell me what happened."

"A number of crafters were present when the collapse occurred, working to repair the magical constructs set in the glass bricks. They had been able to stay abreast of the repair work. They had seen no drastic disruptions in the magic, nothing to alarm them. And then something changed."

Father Jacob sat forward eagerly, nearly upsetting his tea that stood forgotten and untasted on a small table at his side. Sir Ander rose and quietly removed the cup so as not to spill tea on the provost's fine rug.

"Almost immediately following the collapse, we took the crafters who had been present to a quiet place to hear their reports. They talked of the glass 'singing' and 'quivering' right before the glass bricks shattered. They said, one and all, that the magic failed utterly, catastrophically. They could do nothing to stop it."

"Did you speak to your agent Dubois?" Father Jacob asked. "Did he tell you about the helm I recovered, about the Bottom Dwellers?"

"He told me. I told the provost."

"Then you both must be aware that this failure was caused by contramagic."

"You don't know that!" said the grand bishop angrily. "Demons did not attack the Crystal Market—"

"Nor Freyans either, I suppose," Father Jacob remarked.

The grand bishop sucked in an angry breath.

"The Bottom Dwellers caused this catastrophic failure, Eminence," Father Jacob continued. "Just as they have been causing magic to fail throughout the world. What else did the crafters tell you?"

The grand bishop was seething. He was being interrogated by one of his own priests and he could do nothing except submit to the questioning. His hands curled around the arms of the chair. Sir Ander had the impression Montagne would have been happy to curl them around Father Jacob's throat.

"Some reported hearing sounds other than the singing. Several said they had heard a drumming sound, very faint. One young woman described it as the sound of 'a hundred beating hearts.'"

"'A hundred beating hearts,'" Father Jacob repeated thoughtfully. He jumped from his chair and began to pace about the room. "The Bottom Dwellers have contramagic weapons, but neither the bat riders nor their black ships were anywhere in sight when the market collapsed. Yet I am convinced they are responsible. The question is how? How did they knock down a structure when they live at the bottom of the world? A hundred beating hearts . . ."

The provost placed his fingertips together and looked at the grand bishop.

"Father Jacob," said Montagne impatiently, "I came for answers, not to listen to wild theories—"

"That is my answer, whether you want to hear it or not," said Father Jacob, rounding on them. His eyes glittered. "I do not know how they are attacking us, though I have an idea. Blood magic. The helm I recovered was made of human skin. The Bottom Dwellers have found a way to use blood magic to fuel contramagic."

He resumed his pacing and thus he did not see the alarmed look the provost cast at the grand bishop, nor did he see the darkening of Montagne's brow, the tightening of his lips. Sir Ander saw both and shifted uneasily in his chair. He sensed approaching danger and wished he could whisk Father Jacob out of the room.

Father Jacob saw nothing. He was muttering to himself.

"I once saw a soprano shatter a glass with a single note. Perhaps the same theory applies to the Crystal Market, though at the moment I cannot explain how they managed it . . ."

"Perhaps you can find the answers at the scene of the disaster, Father," said the grand bishop. "I came here to take you back with me to Evreux to investigate this tragedy."

Father Jacob was tempted. He stood with his head down, his hands behind his back. Then he shook his head.

"No, I cannot leave my work here."

"I could make this an order," said the grand bishop, frowning.

"You could, Eminence," Father Jacob conceded. "And I might learn much in my investigation that was useful. However, I believe I will learn more if I remain here. You term my theory about the Bottom Dwellers 'wild ravings.' I believe I am close to discovering the truth."

Sir Ander observed another exchange of meaningful glances between the grand bishop and the provost.

"I recommend a substitute, Provost. You know Father Antonius," Father Jacob continued. "He is knowledgeable about engineering magic. He was once responsible for maintaining magical constructs in a floating fortress."

"I do not want anyone else to know about this," the grand bishop said.

"Soon everyone will know, Eminence," said Father Jacob gravely. "Magical constructs are failing the world over. They will continue to fail, and unless we find a way stop these attacks, more buildings will fall. Ships will sink. People will die, not only in Rosia, but in every nation."

He fixed both men with a piercing gaze. "We face a foe who is using contramagic to try to silence the Voice of God. If this foe succeeds, the world will be plunged into another Dark Age far worse than the first. It is my fear that if God's voice is silenced, we will never hear Him speak again."

Montagne's jaw tightened; a muscle in his neck twitched. The provost sat quite still, giving no hint of his thoughts. His mild expression was perhaps a little more solemn, but that was all.

"Very well, Father Jacob," the grand bishop said tightly, biting the words. "Stay here. Continue your work."

"Thank you, Your Eminence," said Father Jacob.

The grand bishop gave him a bitter glance. What else could he do after Father Jacob's dire warning? Sir Ander almost pitied the man.

The provost rose to his feet. "Thank you for coming, gentlemen. We will not keep you longer."

Sir Ander stood up, glad to leave and take Father Jacob with him. All in all, the meeting had turned out far better than he had anticipated. No blood had been shed. Father Jacob had other ideas, however.

"With regard to my work, Provost," said Father Jacob, "in order to continue my research, I need to have access to the Library of the Forbidden."

The grand bishop stiffened. The provost was shocked. He raised his eyebrows. His spectacles slid down his nose. Yet he managed to retain his customary mild tones.

"The Library of the Forbidden exists for a reason, Father Jacob. Works of evil, exposing the darkest parts of men's souls, are contained within."

"I am not seeking to study blood magic spells, if that is what you fear, Provost," Father Jacob said irritably.

"What do you seek?" the grand bishop demanded. "The provost is familiar with the catalog of books in the library. What is the book for which you are searching?"

"I will know when I find it," said Father Jacob.

The grand bishop gave a sour smile. "As the provost says, we are allowing you great liberty already, Father. Do not try our patience."

" 'Ignorance is the foe,' writes Saint Dennis!" Father Jacob declared angrily. " 'Knowledge is salvation.' When will you learn the truth of this? If it were up to me, no book would be forbidden! Come along, Sir Ander."

Father Jacob turned on his heel and walked across the floor, his cassock snapping around his ankles.

"Father Jacob!" The provost called after him in mollifying tones. "As I said, I am familiar with the catalog of the Library of the Forbidden. There are no books on contramagic, if that is what you seek. You would be wasting valuable time."

Father Jacob did not look back; he did not reply. Flinging open the door, he stalked out, with Sir Ander following. As he left, he glanced over his shoulder. Montagne and the provost were conferring, their heads together, their voices low. He could not hear what they were saying. The secretary glided past the knight and closed the door.

Sir Ander caught up with Father Jacob. Neither spoke until they had returned to the reading room in the tower. Father Jacob slammed his hands on the desk.

"Montagne is an ass, a nincompoop!"

"He is also a man with something to hide," said Sir Ander.

"What do you mean?" Father Jacob asked sharply.

Sir Ander told him about the exchange of alarmed looks he had seen between Montagne and the provost. "They know much more than they are telling you, and they are afraid you're going to find out."

"You are right, my friend. They prevent me from entering the library," said Father Jacob in thoughtful tones. "And yet they allow me to study these books which they know contain the saints' work on contramagic."

"Montagne is terrified. He sees the future you foretold coming to pass," said Sir Ander. "He hopes you can find a way to stop the destruction of magic."

"He hopes I can do that without discovering the truth. He is willing to risk disaster to keep this truth secret. This truth, whatever it is, must be terrible."

He was silent, speculatively eyeing Sir Ander, who knew exactly what the priest was going to say before he said it.

"I must enter that library, Ander! These books I am reading now are preliminary works. Descriptions of experiments in contramagic, jottings, notes taken of conversations, a few equations and diagrams, the philosophic ramblings of Saint Charles on the subject. This was the beginning, the steps of a baby learning to walk. That is probably why the saints left these books behind. Their work in contramagic was far more advanced than what I have here."

"How can you possibly know that?"

"Because the Pirate King used contramagic weapons," said Father Jacob. "History doesn't tell us so, of course, since we're not permitted to talk about it. But think back to the old Trundler legends and songs about the Pirate King. One goes this way: 'The green fire of his baleful glare shot the ships out of the air.' And another: 'Green were his eyes and green his fiery gaze and green the grass that covered their graves . . .'"

"Maybe the man just had green eyes, Father," said Sir Ander wryly.

Father Jacob cast him a baleful look.

"Let us say you are right—" Sir Ander began.

"I *am* right," said Father Jacob.

"I'm not sure where Trundler songs lead us, Father. Provost Phillipe claims there are no books on contramagic. Do you think he would lie to you?"

Father Jacob did not answer immediately. "I respect and admire the provost," he said at last. "But he, like the grand bishop, would do anything to defend the church."

"And what about you, Jacob?" Sir Ander asked, regarding

his friend earnestly. "You gave up your family, your inheritance, your country. You almost gave up your life for your faith. This truth might well bring about the church's destruction."

"If the church is built upon a mountain of sand, it will fall anyway. My care must be for the innocent. I need to enter the library."

"Very well, Father. But to do so, you will have to fight your way past the warrior monks, undo complex magical warding spells, crack open specially made locks, all without setting off every alarm in the Citadel."

"You have a succinct way of summing up the problem, Sir Ander," said Father Jacob, nodding. "I will give the matter thought."

"Jacob, I wasn't 'summing up the problem,'" Sir Ander said, exasperated. "I was telling you breaking into the Library of the Forbidden is impossible."

"'With God, all things are possible,'" said Father Jacob.

Sir Ander gave up. "I'm going to dinner. Are you coming with me or should I bring a tray?"

Father Jacob stood with his hands clasped behind his back, staring intently at the books on the table.

Sir Ander sighed. "I'll bring you a tray."

26

Saint Marie envisioned the Citadel of the Voice as a bastion of learning and light in a world of ignorance and darkness. The Citadel was designed to be a place of beauty, soothing for the mind and the spirit, where God's defenders would come to learn and arm themselves against the followers of Aertheum and those who would harm the innocent. Since her death, I have made it my goal to complete her mission. It is my hope that she would be pleased with what we have built.

—Saint Dennis,
second provost of the Arcanum

Sir Ander tried to ease his worries by taking an evening stroll on the ramparts. Generally he found pleasure in admiring the stars above and the ripples gliding over the calm surface of the water below. This night he barely glanced at the stars. Father Jacob had taken his dinner on a tray and gone back to work. He had not said anything more about trying to break into the Library of the Forbidden, but Sir Ander knew with certainty that the priest would not give up the dangerous idea.

The risk was very great and the chance of reward seemed

slim, since Father Jacob would be searching for a book with no idea what book he was searching for. Sir Ander did not know how many books were in the library, but given the amount of evil in the world he judged the number must be significant. Father Jacob might need days for his search and he would have minutes, at most, before the monks of Saint Klee used their powerful magicks to subdue and capture him.

The risk to Sir Ander was also very great and one that could be easily avoided. He could return to the Mother House.

He smiled to himself. He knew perfectly well he would never leave his friend to undertake this mission on his own. Father Jacob was a genius, a savant, but he was not skilled at burglary. Sir Ander remembered with a shake of his head the night they had removed books from the secret chamber in the abbey. Eager to study his find, Father Jacob would have left a gaping hole in the floor of the catacombs visible to all the world if Sir Ander hadn't insisted they take time to conceal it.

He happened to walk beneath one of the many magical lights—a pair of bronze arms with bronze hands cupping a glowing ball of light in their upturned palms—and saw with a start that he wasn't alone. A monk was coming from the opposite direction.

"God's peace be with you, Sir Knight," said the monk as he walked past.

"Brother Paul?" Sir Ander exclaimed, stopping him.

"Sir Ander Martel. Forgive me for not recognizing you, my lord. I am pleased to see you."

"What brings you here, Brother?" Sir Ander asked. Unlike the monk, Sir Ander could not say he was pleased to see Brother Paul.

"As you know, I spent time in the Arcanum after the tragedy at the abbey," Brother Paul replied. "I have been visiting friends I made among the monks."

He blinked his watery eyes, barely visible behind the dark spectacles. The light shining down on him emphasized the pallor of his skin, like the underbelly of a fish. A sudden thought flashed into Sir Ander's mind, a thought so shocking he lost track of what Brother Paul was saying. Sir Ander ended the conversation abruptly and hurried off, leaving the monk to stare after him.

Sir Ander hurried to the library, ascending the stairs that led up to the tower two at a time. He was startled to find the door to the reading room unlocked, standing wide open. Father Jacob was pacing up and down in the hallway. The disciplined warrior monks mounting guard over the stairs that led to the Library of the Forbidden were silently keeping him under observation.

Sir Ander spoke to him several times and finally had to stand directly in the priest's path to force him to take notice. Father Jacob could see by Sir Ander's expression that he had news. He returned to the cell, followed by Sir Ander, who shut the wrought-iron door with a clang.

"What is it?" asked Father Jacob.

"I ran into our friend, Brother Paul, just a few moments ago. Do you know, Father, that he looks exactly like your description of a Bottom Dweller."

"Probably because he is one," said Father Jacob dryly.

Sir Ander gaped at the priest. "How do you know? And when were you going to tell me?"

"I thought you knew," said Father Jacob, raising his eyebrows. "Isn't it obvious?"

"Not to me it wasn't," said Sir Ander, exasperated. "When did you figure this out?"

"Oh, almost immediately. I suspected him at once of being complicit in the attack on the abbey. Brother Paul knew

Albert had found the journal of the prince abbot. The mother superior and the nuns knew that, as well, but the women had work enough to do to keep body and soul together. The idea that one of them would want to steal a journal did not make sense. The thief was skilled in the art, leaving no trace behind. Again, to my mind this ruled out the nuns. We are left, therefore, with only Brother Paul.

"Next, it was Brother Paul who wrote the account of the 'eyewitness' to the grand bishop. I asked myself, why would the monk who had discovered the horror in the abbey take time to write such a long and lurid account? Because Brother Paul wanted to convince us that demons sent by the Evil One had been responsible. He overplayed his hand and made a glaring error when he quoted the poor woman who survived, by writing, 'The demon yelped.' That gave me the first indication that the attackers were men, not demons."

"I follow you so far," said Sir Ander.

"Then I made a mistake," said Father Jacob, sighing and lowering himself into his chair. "I should have immediately gone to interview that sole witness. Instead I decided to investigate the scene. That left the poor woman to the mercy of Brother Paul."

"He killed her."

"Of course he did. He killed her and threw her body into the Breath, then told us that she had taken her own life. There were many other clues: someone familiar with the library had searched it; Brother Paul's determination to make us believe that the attackers were demonic; his eagerness to help—"

"Wait a moment, Father. The Bottom Dwellers took Brother Paul prisoner when they captured Brother Barnaby. They tortured him!"

"To further convince us of his innocence. And that also gave him the opportunity to question Brother Barnaby. The

Bottom Dwellers were growing frustrated by now. Brother Paul knew the books were in the abbey, but he had no idea where. He hoped Brother Barnaby knew, but we didn't tell Barnaby we had found the books, so that proved to be of no help to him."

"You sent Brother Paul to the Arcanum under Seal. After he was questioned, the provost released him. Why didn't you ask that they keep him here?"

"I believed him to be involved in the attack, but I couldn't prove it," said Father Jacob. "And you must remember, I had no knowledge of the Bottom Dwellers at the time. I didn't know anything about them until I recovered that helm in Westfirth and cast the Corpse Spell on it. After that came the attack and my head injury. I had no idea he'd been assigned to the staff of the grand bishop. Someone in high office recommended him for that position. Which shows us there is more than one Brother Paul in the church."

"That's not a pleasant thought," said Sir Ander.

"A thought to keep one awake at night," said Father Jacob. "I believe it likely that the Bottom Dwellers have spies and operatives not only in the Church of the Breath in Rosia, but also the church in Freya, and in the halls of power of every nation in the world."

Sir Ander was quiet a moment, thinking over all the priest had said. A thought occurred to him. "It was Brother Paul who tried to kill us with the contramagic bomb in the archbishop's palace."

"A mistake on his part. He acted alone, on impulse. He knows that I suspect him. I would guess his superiors were not pleased when they found out he had betrayed himself by such a rash act."

"Brother Paul's here now, Father," said Sir Ander, chilled. "He's in the Citadel. I just saw him."

"He's come for the books of the saints," said Father Jacob.

"Or to kill you."

"Probably both," said Father Jacob with a shrug. "He's very energetic, our Brother Paul."

"I don't know how you can be so damn calm about this," said Sir Ander. "We could go to the Mother House. You would he safe, there."

"That is not possible. My work is here."

"All right, at the least, I'm going to ask the warrior monks to stand guard over you—" Father Jacob was shaking his head. "Why not?"

"Any one of them could be a Bottom Dweller."

Sir Ander muttered words not generally heard in the walls of the Citadel and flung himself into a chair.

"So what do we do?"

"We remain vigilant," said Father Jacob.

The night passed peacefully. Sir Ander stayed with the priest in the reading room. He tried to read one of the books of the saints, but he was not a crafter and he couldn't make heads or tails of the theoretical and philosophical discussions. The book did have the effect of putting him to sleep, slumped back in the chair. At the sound of a voice calling Father Jacob's name, Sir Ander woke from a bad dream with a start.

Sunlight filled the room. A nun responsible for the daily delivery of mail stood outside the reading room.

"Father Jacob," she said again. "I have a letter for you."

Father Jacob was on his cot, his hands clasped over his breast, deep in slumber. He didn't stir.

"I'll take it, Sister," said Sir Ander.

"Good morning, Sir Ander. This came for Father Jacob and this came for you," said the sister, delivering two letters.

Sir Ander recognized the handwriting on his letter and the bee insignia on the wax seal. He slid his letter into an inner pocket and examined the letter for Father Jacob. The envelope was plain, with no return address. Sir Ander didn't recognize the handwriting, but that wasn't unusual. Father Jacob had a wide and varied correspondence. Sir Ander tossed the letter on the desk and went out to use the lavatorium.

He returned to find Father Jacob awake, tousling his hair and gazing at the envelope. The expression on his face brought Sir Ander up short.

"What's wrong now?"

"I know the handwriting," said Father Jacob in an altered voice.

He was holding the letter in his hand, his fingers trembling. He took hold of the letter opener, slit the envelope, and drew out the contents. He glanced at it, then let the paper fall to the desk.

"May I see it?" Sir Ander asked.

Father Jacob pushed the missive across to him. Sir Ander picked up the letter, which was written on foolscap, folded into quarters. In the center of the sheet was a drawing, crudely and hastily done, of a dog, a retriever, with a pair of crossed arrows above him and a hunting horn below. Beneath that was scrawled:

> *Denidus, Soles the 14, noon, Peu de Sable, Capione, Public docks. Someone will come.*

"Denidus, Soles the 14. That's tomorrow's date," said Sir Ander, returning the letter to Father Jacob, who made no move to pick it up. "The writer wants to arrange a meeting. Do you recognize this drawing?"

"Yes," said Father Jacob.

Sir Ander waited expectantly.

"The drawing is my family crest. This letter is from my brother."

Sir Ander stared. "The brother who tried to kill you?"

"I have only one brother," said Father Jacob. "Why, after all these years, would Alan want to meet with me . . ."

He began to gather up his notes. "Ready the yacht, Sir Ander. We leave for Capione within the hour."

"Absolutely not," said Sir Ander. "Alan Northrop is a pirate, a criminal—"

"Which is why you are coming with me," said Father Jacob, placing his notes inside one of the books of the saints. He then stuffed the books, one by one, into a leather satchel that fairly bristled with protective magical constructs. "If this were just another boring family reunion, I would go on my own."

Sir Ander raised his eyes to heaven. "God, make this stubborn priest listen to me!"

Father Jacob chuckled. "Last night you wanted to leave the Citadel because staying here wasn't safe. Now you want to stay here because leaving isn't safe."

"You know what I mean." Sir Ander was in no mood for levity.

Father Jacob gave his friend a rare warm smile. "I do, Ander, and I am grateful for your care. If you will go ready the yacht, I will let the provost know we will be away from the Citadel for a short time."

"He'll breathe a sigh of relief," Sir Ander muttered.

He descended to the Carriage House and ordered the yacht to be made ready to sail. While he was waiting for the wyverns to be harnessed, he took time to read Cecile's letter. It was very short and appeared to have been written in haste.

You will be glad to know your godson has returned safely.

"Thank God for some good news," said Sir Ander.

Capione was a port city like Westfirth, although both cities would have taken insult at even that general comparison. The harbor at Capione was located some distance (about five miles) from the city and although the harbor and warehouses and shipyards attendant to it supported the city, Capione preferred to view itself as a resort destination, catering to the upper classes. Noble lords and ladies had been coming to the city since the days of the ancient Sunlit Empire to indulge in the famous mineral baths and view the magnificent Étapes du Père waterfalls and caverns.

As for the docks and the warehouses, Capione saw itself as a duchess forced to maintain ties with the younger sister who had run off to marry a merchant. The wealthy merchant—commerce—paid the duchess's upkeep, but no one in Capione mentioned that. She continued to look down her nose at him.

Capione was nestled in the foothills of the mountains. Fine old mansions surrounded by green forests could be seen scattered among the hillsides. The city itself was small and elegant, taking pride in its ancient buildings and carefully preserving them. The city of Capione was staid and quiet at night, while the harbor was boisterous and raucous. Visitors had their choice of entertainment.

Father Jacob's yacht, *Retribution,* arrived in Capione early in the morning. Sir Ander piloted the yacht toward the harbor. He drove the yacht himself because he could not yet bear to find a replacement for Brother Barnaby, and Father Jacob was not permitted anywhere near wyverns. When he moored the yacht at the public docks, the sight of the black yacht with the gilt trim and the symbol of the Arcanum painted on the sides created some consternation among the inhabitants. The arrival of the Arcanum generally meant that someone was in serious trouble.

Sir Ander's first act upon arrival was to visit a tavern and assure everyone that the church was not going to outlaw strong drink or force the taverns to close on the sabbath. He bought a round for the patrons, telling them that he and Father Jacob were here to take the waters. He gained much goodwill, drank a tankard of an excellent brown ale, and gleaned information, which he reported on his return to the yacht.

"No Freyan vessels, either merchants or naval, have been sighted in the Breath in recent days. Although, as the sailors pointed out to me, there are so many inlets and channels and coves along the coastline that a fleet of ships might escape observation."

"As a privateer with a considerable bounty on his head, my brother would take care to stay well hidden," said Father Jacob. "We will see what the morrow brings. My meeting with him is to be in the afternoon. Since we are supposed to be here to take the waters, shall we go to the springs?"

Sir Ander made a face. "You know I hate that stuff. It tastes like rotten eggs."

"We can wash it down with ale."

"You have a bargain."

The next morning, they made their visit to the famous fountain in the center of Capione, drank the mineral water, and went to the tavern at the dockyard for a lunch of roast beef and the brown ale. After lunch, they returned to the yacht to wait.

The clocks were striking the hour when there came a

knock on the door. Sir Ander answered, pistol in hand. He was startled to find a Trundler lad of about twelve.

"Where's Papa Jake?" the lad inquired.

"I am here," said Father Jacob, coming to the door.

"I am to say that you are to come with me," said the lad. "And if you are Defender, I'm to say that you may come, too."

"That's good, because I was coming anyway," said Sir Ander.

He was outfitted for the occasion with his broadsword, long knife, several throwing knives tucked in his boots, the dragon pistol, and a pocket pistol in his waistcoat.

"You are a walking armory," Father Jacob observed.

"Because you are a walking target," said Sir Ander.

He and Father Jacob accompanied the Trundler boy to a wherry tied up nearby. This wherry was operated by a man introduced by the boy as his da. Neither Da nor the wherry were in the cleanest condition. The boat had a broad beam and low gunwales, rather like a long raft. A single thin support mast and four mooring lines secured the balloon, and a small pivoting air screw propelled the boat.

Sir Ander gave the boy a coin, which the lad took, and then departed. They were left with Da, who said nothing for the entirety of the trip. In response to Sir Ander's question about where they were bound, Da grunted once and spit over the side twice.

Da ferried them along the shoreline until he reached one of many coastal inlets that all looked alike: rocky crags and trees. Da steered the wherry into the inlet, taking several twists and turns. Trees lined the shore on either side. Sir Ander noted places where the branches had been recently snapped off or left dangling.

"Looks like a ship sailed through here," Sir Ander pointed

out. "Your brother is undoubtedly waiting for us in this god-forsaken wilderness where no one will ever find our bodies."

Father Jacob smiled. "A ship did pass through here, but it wasn't a large ship. A heavy frigate such as privateers sail wouldn't fit into this small inlet."

"You've never told me much about your brother," said Sir Ander. "Is he older, younger?"

"Alan is younger, two years my junior. He was sixteen when I left Freya. The last I saw him was twenty years ago, when he and his friend, Sir Henry Wallace, tried to kill me."

"You never said why."

"That is a long story. And unless I am mistaken, we have arrived at our destination."

Da had steered the wherry around yet another bend in the inlet and they came within sight of a monstrosity of a gun-boat. The name painted on a hull covered with metal plating was HMS *Terrapin*. The gunboat took up almost the entire inlet, its steel sides rubbing against the trees along the shore-line. Patches of sunlight dappled the steel panels that armored almost every inch of the boat. A few crewmen were visible on deck, sweating in the heat as they worked.

Sir Ander gave a low whistle. "Damn thing's aptly named. It looks like a floating turtle!"

"Monsieur de Villeneuve told me when we were together at the abbey about a journeyman who had invented steel infused with magic that would withstand bullets. I believe we are looking at the result."

"Stephano never mentioned that to me," said Sir Ander.

"The mission was secret. Monsieur de Villeneuve was not supposed to have told me, but he was under the impression at the time that I was going to throw him into an oubliette. He was eager to confess his sins."

Da maneuvered the wherry alongside the *Terrapin*. Sail-ors lowered a covered gangplank, one with side railings so that those boarding did not fall into the Breath. Sir Ander boarded first, followed by Father Jacob. They were met by a man wearing the uniform of a Freyan naval captain.

Alan Northrop was of medium height with wavy black hair, light brown eyes that were almost amber, dark eyelashes, and heavy brows. He had a strong jaw, prominent cheekbones, and a deeply tanned complexion. He stood with his hat beneath his arm.

"Welcome aboard. I am Sir Alan Northrop, Captain of His Majesty's ship *Terrapin*," he said with a bow.

"Sir Ander Martel of the Knight Protectors," said Sir Ander, bowing stiffly in turn.

Captain Northrop noted the knight's armaments. "You will not need your weapons, sir. Allow me to relieve you of them."

"I'll be damned if I will—" Sir Ander began heatedly.

"We are guests aboard this ship, Sir Ander," said Father Jacob. "You will have no need for your weapons."

Sir Ander eyed the captain. "Do you give me your word, sir, that Father Jacob will be allowed to depart freely and safely?"

"You have my word, sir," said Captain Northrop. "Please give me your word that you will relinquish all your weapons, including the pocket gun in your waistcoat and the knives in your boots."

Sir Ander handed over his weapons to a lieutenant as Captain Northrop watched closely. He took time to admire the dragon pistol.

"A fine-looking weapon, sir. I don't suppose I could induce you to sell it to me?"

"Not for all the gold in the world, sir," said Sir Ander.

Captain Northrop shrugged and turned to Father Jacob. "Do I call you 'Brother,' brother? That would be ironic, not to mention redundant."

"You look well, Alan," said Father Jacob.

"You look well yourself, Jacob," said Alan, adding coolly, "More's the pity."

He smiled at Sir Ander, who was eyeing him grimly.

"Relax, Sir Knight. I am teasing. The quarrel between my brother and I is long past. But we can catch up on family gossip later. My friend has risked a great deal to speak with you, Jacob. He is in the cabin below. If you will come with me, I will take you to him. Don't trip over that cable, brother. It would be a shame if you broke your neck."

Captain Northrop laughed. Sir Ander wasn't amused. He stayed close to Father Jacob as they descended the stairs into a cramped, dark corridor barely big enough for the three of them. Captain Northrop knocked on a door.

"He's here," he called.

"Send him in," said a voice.

"The meeting is private, Sir Ander," Captain Northrop said, barring the knight's way. "Not even I am invited." He opened the door.

"Father Jacob," said the man inside.

"Sir Henry," said Father Jacob.

He entered and shut the door behind him.

27

Angered by what was seen as the increasing wealth and ambition of power-hungry priests, and suspecting them of secret allegiance to Rosia, our good king brought about the Reformation, establishing a church based on a true devotion to God. Most Freyans stood strong with their king and the new church. A few stubbornly clung to the old faith, most notably the Earl of Chester, who launched a bloody civil war. With his capture and execution, the rebellion fell apart and eventually ended.

—The Rise of the Church of Freya,
Father Edmund Brannigan

Captain Northrop smiled at Sir Ander, who was squashed up against a bulkhead.

"If you will accept my hospitality, sir, I have a comfortable chair in my cabin and an excellent bottle of Estaran wine I will be glad to share."

Sir Ander could hear muffled voices from inside the cabin where Father Jacob and the other man who had tried to kill him sat together.

"Or you can remain stubbornly hanging about in the corridor, Sir Ander," Captain Northrop continued. "I warn you, their conversation might be a long one. I have given you my word as a gentleman that your charge will be safe. If you refuse, I will think you question my honor."

He grinned when he said this, causing Sir Ander to very much question Captain Northrop's honor. The knight reflected, however, that he might learn something from the captain that Father Jacob would find useful and he grudgingly agreed to accompany Captain Northrop.

Ducking his head as he walked to avoid bumping it on the low ceiling, Sir Ander picked his way through an assortment of tools, ropes, and cables that littered the deck. When they came to another small cabin at the end of the corridor, Captain Northrop stood aside to allow his guest to enter first.

"Leave the door open," said Sir Ander, taking a seat.

Captain Northrop gave a good-natured, charming smile and offered Sir Ander a glass of wine. Sir Ander declined, preferring to have his wits about him. Captain Northrop poured a glass for himself. The constant sounds of banging and hammering came from various parts of the ship. Apparently the *Terrapin* was a work in progress.

"A very fine Estaran blend," Captain Northrop said, holding the wine to the light. "I labor under the impression you don't like me very much, Sir Ander."

"I find it hard to like a man who tries to kill his own brother," said Sir Ander.

"You have heard Jacob's side of the story, no doubt."

"Father Jacob has not told me anything beyond the fact that he fled Freya to avoid being persecuted for his faith," said Sir Ander. "I had no idea he had a brother until we were investigating the attack on the destroyer *Defiant* and we discovered that you and your friend, Wallace, were behind it."

"You bring up a painful memory, Sir Ander," Captain Northrop said, wincing.

Sir Ander thought this an odd statement, considering that

the captain and Wallace had succeeded in almost sinking the destroyer. He let it pass.

"Would you like to hear the family history?" Captain Northrop asked. "Come now, Sir Ander, admit it. You are curious."

"I would prefer to hear more about this remarkable-looking gunboat," said Sir Ander.

Captain Northrop laughed. "I'll wager you would. The *Terrapin* belongs to Sir Henry. I am merely her captain, and so it would be ungentlemanly of me to gossip about her. To return to my brother, I will begin by saying our family was highly respected, well-to-do."

Sir Ander had to admit he was curious to hear the story of how Father Jacob had come to flee his homeland, so he settled himself to listen.

"Our father owned a fleet of merchant vessels. My mother came from a family who owned a shipbuilding operation. The alliance was mutually beneficial to both families, though I believe my father married my mother for love. She was very beautiful. I take after her. Jacob favors our father."

Captain Northrop drank his wine. Sir Ander's attention was divided between listening to the captain's story and trying to hear what was being said down the corridor. The two men were keeping their voices low, for he could hear nothing.

"My mother was an intensely devout follower of the Church of the Breath," Captain Northrop continued. "This was during the time of the Reformation in Freya when there was tenuous peace between the Church of the Breath and the Freyan church. My mother was wont to attend mass on a daily basis. My father was not a religious man and saw no harm in his wife practicing the old faith. He would not have felt the same about his children, but he was gone from home a good deal of the time, for he captained one of his own ships, and so he did not know that Jacob was indoctrinated.

"He accompanied my mother to mass morning, noon, and night, and he sang in the choir. When the priests found out that he was gifted in magic, a savant, they were thrilled. They sank their claws into him—"

"You will please speak more respectfully of the clergy, sir," Sir Ander interrupted.

Captain Northrop shrugged. "As you will, sir. The priests ran a school for young crafters and they invited Jacob to attend, even offering to pay his tuition. Jacob excelled, of course. He loved the study of magic, and admired the priests, to the point where he talked of becoming a priest. If my father had been home more, he would have put a stop to such nonsense. My mother hid it from him, however, and by the time he found out, it was too late."

Captain Northrop poured himself another glass of wine.

"As for me, I was never in any danger of becoming a priest. I was a born sailor. My father took me on my first voyage when I was six, and I loved it. The mists of the Breath in the early morning, the exhilarating feel of riding the wind. I knew then where my heart lay."

"As did your brother," said Sir Ander.

Captain Northrop contemplated the wine, turning the glass in his hand, staring into the red depths. "Jacob was father's favorite. Odd, isn't it? I was the son who took after him, yet father was always talking of Jacob—the son who was a savant, who would do great things when he joined the business. And so when Jacob announced that he was going to Rosia to become a priest, our father was appalled. He refused to believe it, at first.

"When Jacob assured him he was serious, Father flew into a rage. He threatened; my mother wept; the servants gave notice. The row lasted for weeks. My father couldn't stand to look at Jacob, and left on another voyage. While he was gone, my mother fell ill, diagnosed with a cancerous tumor in her belly. The healers could do nothing for her, and after a long, painful illness, she died a horrible death."

Captain Northrop lifted the wineglass to his lips. "So much for God's mercy, eh, Sir Ander? After all the time and prayer our mother had devoted to Him, He made her suffer like that. Doesn't seem fair, does it?"

Sir Ander thought of how he had wrestled with his own faith after Julian's terrible death. He thought, too, of the loss of Brother Barnaby. "We are not meant to understand. We are meant to have faith."

"That's what Jacob said. I told him faith was just an excuse, God taking the easy way out."

"If you're expecting to shock me, sir, you will be disappointed," Sir Ander said with a slight smile. "I said the same to myself at one time in my life. I found my faith again."

"I never had any faith to lose," said Captain Northrop wryly. "During this period, our good king Osward issued the order that shut down the monasteries. The crown seized their holdings. An edict proclaimed that anyone who followed the teachings of the Church of the Breath was a traitor to Freya and subject to death.

"Many of Jacob's priest friends fled to Rosia. They pleaded with Jacob to come with them, saying he wouldn't be safe in Freya, but he refused. This was during the time our mother was ill, and he would not leave her. I suppose I have to give him credit for that. When mother was on her deathbed, Jacob wrote to father, telling him to come home. Our father didn't return in time, which left Jacob to handle the funeral. He followed Mother's wishes, which she whispered to him as she lay dying. The funeral was conducted in secret, at midnight, by a Rosian priest. Servants talked. The neighbors discovered we were hiding this priest in the house. Our father arrived at our home the same time as the soldiers.

"Jacob helped the priest escape, but he did not have time to flee himself. The soldiers arrested Jacob and our father. Jacob had concealed me in one of the priest-holes or they would have arrested me, as well. I was sixteen and alone in the house. The servants had all fled. I was trying to think of something to do, when Jacob appeared. He'd used his wonderful savant magic to escape. He said he'd tried to convince our father to come with him, but our father refused, saying he would rather face death than be deemed a traitor to his country. Jacob had come home to bid me good-bye. He was going to Rosia.

"I flew at him in a rage. Jacob was always good with his fists, and I ended up on my ass before I knew what hit me. I told him he couldn't leave our father to face this alone. Jacob said he was the criminal. Our father would be safe once he was gone. I didn't believe him. I vowed to Jacob that I would hunt him down like the traitor he was and kill him. Five years later, when my friend, Sir Henry, heard that Jacob had sneaked back into the country on some secret mission for the church, we found him. I kept my vow then—or tried to. I was not a particularly good shot at the time."

Captain Northrop saw the expression on Sir Ander's face and laughed. "Are you sure you won't have some of this excellent wine?"

Sir Ander shook his head. "What happened to your father?"

"As it turned out, Jacob was right. Friends in court intervened on our father's behalf. Certain people were paid off and he was set free. The business suffered for a long time after that, however. Clients didn't trust a family of traitors. My father worked hard to prove himself a loyal subject of the crown and eventually the business revived. We never truly lived down the scandal, though." Captain Northrop gave a bitter smile. "There is a reason my friend Randolph is an honored and respected admiral and I am a glorified pirate."

"Yet you seem to have done well for yourself," Sir Ander

observed, indicating the Estaran wine. "A case of that would cost me a month's pay."

Captain Northrop poured another glass, finishing off the bottle. "Some people consider me lucky. I was a second son with no prospects and suddenly I was the first son with the world before me. I attended university and purchased a commission in the navy, then left that when I was passed over time and again for promotion. I bought my own ship. A cousin now manages the business for me. I'm a successful privateer, a wealthy man. Yes, I have done well for myself. And I owe it all to Jacob."

Sir Ander heard the ironic tone in the captain's voice. "You should know, Captain Northrop, that your brother has done an incredible amount of good as a priest. Countless times, he has risked his life to save innocents. When you tried to kill him, you say you missed. I say God's hand intervened."

Captain Northrop smiled faintly. "You mean God nudged my elbow so that my shot went wide and then He tampered with Henry's pistol so that it misfired. All this so my brother could live to pray another day."

Sir Ander decided he didn't much like Captain Northrop. The knight was thinking he'd rather wait in the corridor, when he heard the sound of a door opening and Father Jacob's voice calling for him.

"The meeting has ended," said Captain Northrop, rising. "Thank you for letting me ramble on, sir."

Sir Ander was already on his feet and out the door. He found Father Jacob in the corridor, looking for him, with Sir Henry nowhere in sight. The door to the cabin where the two had been meeting was closed.

"Ah, there you are, Sir Ander," said Father Jacob, catching sight of him. "Ready to leave?"

"*More* than ready," said Sir Ander emphatically. "How did your meeting go? What did that man want with you?"

"We cannot talk here. Suffice it to say, my friend, I did not see how matters could possibly grow worse." Father Jacob sighed. "But they are now worse."

They moved to one side of the corridor to allow Captain Northrop to squeeze past them.

"The wherry is waiting to take you to Capione," said Captain Northrop. "If you will follow me . . ."

He led the way back up the stairs and onto the top deck. The wherry had traveled some distance down the inlet, and at a signal from Captain Northrop, Da released the lines that were holding the wherry to a tree and sailed back. Father Jacob, Sir Ander, and Captain Northrop stood waiting in silence.

Captain Northrop said abruptly, "You never asked about our father."

"How is he?" Father Jacob asked.

"Dead," said Captain Northrop. "He died of a fever he contracted in the Aligoes."

"I didn't know, Alan. I will keep him in my prayers."

"He does not need your prayers!" Captain Northrop had dropped the bantering façade. He was angry, his eyes dark and brooding. "He needed you, Jacob! Father was never the same after you left. You broke his heart. He never understood how you could betray your country. How you could betray *him*!"

"God called me to His service, Alan," said Father Jacob simply.

"God!" Captain Northrop gave a mirthless laugh. "Where was your God when our father was dying? Where were you? He called for you. Where was his Jacob? I held him in my arms. I had to tell him you weren't coming."

Father Jacob was quiet, sorrowful, grieving. Sir Ander stood by, helpless to intervene. He would fight Father Jacob's foes, would place himself between Father Jacob and knives, bullets. But he could not protect his friend from such pain as this.

"I do not know what to say, Alan."

What could the man of faith say to the man of the world? Father Jacob reached out toward his brother.

"I am sorry—"

Captain Northrop struck his brother's hand away.

"I am sorry, too, Jacob," Alan said harshly. "Sorry my shot missed!"

The wherry nudged up against the *Terrapin,* and the crew again lowered the covered gangplank. Sir Ander and Father Jacob crossed it and took seats in the wherry. The crew of the *Terrapin* raised the gangplank, and Da steered the wherry among the trees.

As they slowly pulled away from the gunboat, Father Jacob sat in silence. Sir Ander looked back to see Captain Northrop standing on the deck, his hands clasped behind him, staring at them.

Then they rounded a bend in the inlet and the *Terrapin* was lost to sight.

"That was unpleasant," said Father Jacob.

"Family," said Sir Ander.

He had family of his own.

The two left Capione that afternoon. Sir Ander again drove the yacht, holding the wyvern's reins and keeping an eye on the brass panel that regulated the flow of magic into the lift tank. The journey was peaceful. The wyverns were well fed and as docile as could be expected for the recalcitrant beasts. He'd had to put a stop to them snapping at each other only once, sending a small electrical jolt that traveled through the harness to remind them to tend to their business.

The jolt was painless, but Sir Ander always felt guilty whenever he was forced to resort to such tactics. In his mind's eye he could see Brother Barnaby gazing at him in sorrowful dismay. The notoriously bad-tempered wyverns loved Barnaby, as did all creatures. The monk would have said a gentle word or two to calm them. Sir Ander had tried a gentle word, only to have one of the wyverns spit at him.

Father Jacob opened the door that led from the cabin to the driver's compartment in the front of the yacht.

"May I join you?"

"Of course. Just don't annoy the wyverns."

"Stupid beasts," said Father Jacob, settling himself.

The wyverns, hearing his voice, whipped their heads around to glare at him. Sir Ander shouted at them and they sullenly returned to the business of flying.

"What did you and Sir Henry discuss?" Sir Ander asked. "Must have been important for him to risk his life traveling to Rosia."

"It was important," said Father Jacob somberly. "He told me the true identity of the woman we call 'the Sorceress.'"

"Henry knows her? That doesn't surprise me," Sir Ander said.

"Her name is Eiddwen. She is associated with the Bottom Dwellers. That came as no surprise, since she sent them to kill us in Westfirth. What I didn't know was that *she* was the one who provided Sir Henry with the design to build the green fireball weapon that nearly sank the *Defiant*. After learning that her weapon worked, Eiddwen vanished, taking the weapon with her, leaving Sir Henry in a very embarrassing position with his queen."

"My heart bleeds for the man." Sir Ander grunted. He glanced at Father Jacob. "Do you trust him? If this Eiddwen is really in league with these Bottom Dwellers and has been all this time, why would she get involved with the Warlock and all those gruesome murders and blood magic rituals in Capione?"

"I have been thinking about that. Sir Henry describes Eiddwen as extremely intelligent, calculating, fearless, and amoral. Everything she does has one focus: to advance her goals, which means these murders were committed for a reason, not for some sort of perverted pleasure, which is what I first thought. As I told the grand bishop, I believe the Bottom Dwellers are using blood magic to enhance and stabilize the effects of the contramagic. Eiddwen was conducting experiments with the blood magic and contramagic."

"Where is this woman now?"

"Henry doesn't know. She stowed away on board his ship when he was escaping from Westfirth with the journeyman, Alcazar. He dropped her off at some remote location. He has agents searching for her, to no avail. All he knows is that she is still working with the Bottom Dwellers. She told him as much.

"Sir Henry also told me that this journeyman, Alcazar, did in fact invent magically infused steel, which he sold to the Freyans. Henry has the man a virtual prisoner, manufacturing the steel for him. That strange-looking ship was outfitted with the magic steel. Apparently cannonballs have almost no effect on it. And according to Sir Henry, the steel can defend against contramagic."

Sir Ander stared at him. "You mean the green beam weapons? How can Henry possibly know that?"

"Eiddwen sent one of her agents to test the steel. Henry and his man, Mr. Sloan, caught the Bottom Dweller in the shipyard firing a green fireball weapon at the steel panels. They killed him, but apparently not before the man was able to report back to Eiddwen. They found evidence that the intruder had been there once before."

"Why would Henry tell you all this?" Sir Ander asked suspiciously. "He's betraying Freyan interests and that is not like him."

"He is a patriot, that is true. He is also a visionary. He has told me this for the same reason I wrote him all the information I obtained regarding the Bottom Dwellers. Both of us foresee a time when Freya and Rosia will be fighting back-to-back for our very survival."

"You know that if either his queen or our king find out the two of you are sharing information—"

"We would be drawn and quartered, our heads stuck on pikes," said Father Jacob calmly. "We both know the risks."

He added, after a moment's pause, "But I am very sorry you are involved, Ander. I should not have permitted you to come with me to this meeting. You should return immediately to the Mother House to request reassignment. Tell them you find working with me to be impossible."

"They already know that, Father," said Sir Ander, grinning. "I was assigned to you as a punishment, remember?"

Father Jacob frowned. "I could force you to go—"

"How?" Sir Ander asked, amused. "I can be just as stubborn as you, Father, and almost as good with my fists."

Father Jacob was silent a moment, then he said quietly, "I value your friendship, Ander. I don't tell you that often enough."

"You've *never* told me," said Sir Ander. He glanced at Father Jacob. "But I know it, just the same."

Embarrassed by his own emotions, Sir Ander steered the conversation back to the original topic.

"So what will the Bottom Dwellers do now?"

"Sir Henry believes—and I agree with him—that when Eiddwen discovers that his magical steel can repel contramagic, she will urge the Bottom Dwellers to act swiftly, accelerate their plans."

Sir Ander was grim. "What plans? They don't appear to have any plans, other than butchery. First they attack the abbey and murder nuns, then they blow up ships in Westfirth, then massacre innocents in the Crystal Market. Who knows where they will strike next or what devilry they will perpetrate?"

"I think it's safe to say that wherever they strike, we *won't* be ready for them, since we stuipdly refuse to learn anything about contramagic! I *must* find a way to the Library of the Forbidden!"

"Provost Phillipe said there are no books on contramagic in the library."

"Then where are they? Because I know from the books of the saints that they must be somewhere!"

Father Jacob sat hunched over, his brow furrowed, his expression grim. Suddenly he lurched bolt upright and seized hold of Sir Ander's arm with such force he nearly knocked him off the bench.

"Good God, Sir Ander, I've been blind as a beetle!" Father Jacob tried to grab the reins. "We have to get back to the Arcanum, to stop Brother Paul! Tell these beasts to fly faster!"

The startled wyverns began flailing wildly, clawing and biting each other, threatening to snap the cables and tangle the lines. The yacht rocked back and forth perilously.

"Jacob, what the— Let go, damn it, Father! It won't help if we crash!"

Sir Ander elbowed the priest aside and at last managed to bring the wyverns under control.

"What's this about stopping Brother Paul? Stopping him from doing what?"

"He didn't come to the Citadel to kill me," said Father Jacob. "I'm not the only one who wants to know what is in the Library of the Forbidden."

"Do you really think he can find a way to break into the Library when you can't?" Sir Ander asked skeptically.

"He won't act alone," said Father Jacob. "I know where the Bottom Dwellers will launch their next attack."

28

The joy and terror of experimentation is the possibility of attaining the unexpected. Joy in that you have discovered something new. Terror in that you may have unleashed effects over which you have no control.

—Sister Marie Allemand,
first provost of the Arcanum

Sir Ander landed the yacht in the carriage yard at the lowest level of the Citadel. He had been worried that they might find the Citadel already under assault, but the early morning was peaceful, the sun shining in a cloudless sky. A cool breeze blowing from the mountains had brought a drop in temperature. Once the yacht was safely moored, he handed care of the wyverns over to the lay brothers who worked in the stables, and went to confer with Father Jacob.

"I will go warn the provost, Sir Ander. You go to the master of the warrior monks. Tell them to find Brother Paul and bring him to the provost for questioning. And they should ready the Citadel's defenses. Tell them to prepare to defend against contramagic."

"How do the monks know about contramagic?"

"They are warriors," said Father Jacob shortly. "They

studied the attack on Westfirth as they study every attack, in order to learn about the attackers. The master knew I had been there and he came to me with questions. I told him what I had discovered about the Bottom Dwellers, their weapons, their armor. I told him what little I know about contramagic. He listened in silence and left in silence. I have no idea if I was any help."

Sir Ander walked swiftly across the stable yard, heading for the stairs that led to the guardian compound of the monks of Saint Klee. Their compound was built out on a jutting promontory, at a far distance from all other buildings in the Citadel. Although the monks lived and worked here, they kept to themselves. They did not worship in the cathedral, instead praying in their own private chapel. They trained in their own training ground in their compound, surrounded by walls of stone and walls of faith and discipline. The monks did not speak unless someone spoke to them and then their responses were limited to gestures or, if absolutely necessary, a few brief words.

The monks had been responsible for the Citadel's defenses since the Citadel's founding by Saint Marie. Their order dated back to the time immediately following the collapse of the Sunlit Empire. According to legend, Klee had been a Freyan soldier in the wars that eventually brought down the empire.

A giant of a man, with long blond hair typical of the northern region of Freya, Klee (pronounced in Freyan as "clay") was renowned for his courage and ferocity in battle until God reproached him. The ghosts of all the men he had slain appeared before him. With them, they brought all the children and grandchildren who would never be born.

Horrified, Klee began to develop methods of fighting without the use of weapons. Magic would be his weapon and he would kill only as a final resort.

The monks of Saint Klee remained true to their saint's teachings. Over the centuries the monks had developed specialized magicks, which they kept secret. They would do everything in their power to subdue a foe, not kill him, although they were permitted to kill if innocent life was threatened.

Shortly after the Citadel's founding, the monks were tested when the Citadel was attacked by an army of blood wizards and their knights. The wizards, having just killed Saint Marie, thought that without her the Citadel would be vulnerable. They miscalculated and they paid dearly for the mistake. So many were lost during the battle that the cult was broken, and had never fully recovered.

The path that led to the monks' compound was steep, and difficult and arduous to navigate. Sir Ander was winded by the time he arrived at the gate. He spoke to the gatekeeper, saying that he needed to see the master on an urgent matter.

The gatekeeper did not move or make a sound that Sir Ander could detect and yet within moments the gate opened and the master walked out. Like the rest of the monks, he wore his hair long in honor of their saint, abjuring the tonsure. He dressed in crimson robes worn by both the men and women of the order who, nameless, considered themselves as one. The bright robes stood out in contrast to the black robes of the priests and nuns of the Arcanum.

The master was a tall, spare man, seemingly made of gristle, bone, and muscle, with shoulder-length steel-gray hair. He stood waiting to hear why he had been summoned.

"Master, I come from Father Jacob," said Sir Ander. "We have reason to believe—very strong reason to believe—that the Citadel is likely to come under attack from the same foe that struck Westfirth. We do not know when, but we believe the attack to be imminent."

The master's expression did not change, and he said nothing, only stood, waiting expectantly.

Sir Ander lowered his voice. "Father Jacob asked me to tell you he believes it probable the enemy will be using weapons of contramagic."

The master accepted this information with equanimity, gazing steadily at the knight. Sir Ander found his silence and lack of emotion disconcerting. Had the master heard him? Did he understand the dire nature of the situation? Was he going to do something, sound the alarm, mobilize his monks? If Sir Ander had given this news to the commander of the Knight Protectors, there would have been shouted orders, drums beating, trumpets blaring the call to arms.

Sir Ander was seriously tempted to pinch the man, just to get a reaction, when he realized suddenly that the gatekeeper was gone. Sir Ander had not seen the monk leave. The master remained alone, waiting patiently.

"We . . . uh . . . have evidence, Master," Sir Ander continued, floundering, "that the monk known as Brother Paul is one of these Bottom Dwellers. We believe he has been acting as a spy for them. Father Jacob believes it is imperative that you find Brother Paul, place him under arrest, and bring him to the office of the provost . . ."

Sir Ander's words died away. No alarm had been raised, no command given, yet the monks of Saint Klee were now filing out of their compound, moving to their assigned posts throughout the Citadel. The master was still silent, still waiting.

Sir Ander tried to remember where he'd left off. "As to this Brother Paul, I have a description of him—"

"We know," said the master, finally breaking his maddening silence.

"Ah, yes, good. I should tell you one more thing. Father Jacob says the target may be the Library of the Forbidden."

The master's eyelids flickered. He was no longer looking at Sir Ander. A shadow flowed over the ground. The sun, which had been shining only moments ago, had disappeared behind a large brownish gray storm cloud that was moving rapidly, inexorably nearer. As Sir Ander watched, the shadow overtook the mountains and flowed down the sides.

Sir Ander felt the hair on his neck prickle.

"Master, that's no storm. That's—"

He turned to the master, but he was no longer there.

A bell in the monks' compound began to clang. The bell was inscribed with magical constructs that triggered magical constructs in other bells, causing them to ring. Soon every bell in the Citadel was clanging.

Once yearly, Father Jacob had told Sir Ander, the alarm bells rang in the Citadel. Everyone in the fortress took part in the drill, going to his or her assigned place in case of attack. The Citadel's inhabitants had come to view the annual drill as a kind of holiday, a break from the routine. They even held a feast afterward to mark the occasion.

This day was not a drill.

People were caught by surprise and instead of immediately going to their places, they wasted time by rushing out into the quadrangles, the streets, and the gardens to demand to know what was going on. The sight of the crimson-robed monks moving swiftly to their posts answered their questions.

The Citadel was under attack.

The word spread as the bells rang. No one panicked, though there were tight lips and pale faces as people finally hurried to where they were supposed to go.

Sir Ander had no assigned place. His assignment was Father Jacob, who was probably on his way to meet with the provost. Sir Ander ran for the stairs that led to the provost's dwelling, all the while searching for Father Jacob along the way. He feared he would never find the priest in his black cassock in this throng of black-robed priests and nuns, all racing to be somewhere else.

Fortunately, Father Jacob found him. He was waiting at the bottom of the stairs.

"Sir Ander! I've been looking for you. Thank God you're tall and *not* dressed in black!"

Father Jacob seized hold of the knight, separating him from the crowd and hustling him into a garden where they could speak in relative quiet.

"Did you ever see such chaos? These men and women are supposedly rational human beings." Father Jacob shook his head in disgust. "Listen. We don't have much time."

He cast a glance skyward at the cloud that was already down the mountain and moving toward the inland sea. The reddish brown fog was starting to dissipate, and they could see the outlines of a large and ungainly black ship.

"That ship is like the one that sank the *Royal Lion*," said Sir Ander. "And took out the side of a mountain. Can the Citadel's defenses hold?"

"Against contramagic? We are about to find out. If I am right, the Bottom Dwellers won't dare risk bringing down the mountain because they might do damage to the library."

"Where is your assigned post? I'll come with you."

Father Jacob gave an impatient wave. "I don't know, and I don't care. That doesn't matter now."

"Then where are we going?"

"To the library, of course," said Father Jacob.

Sir Ander was appalled. "You're going to break into the library? You can't be serious!"

"What better time than during all this confusion? Besides, if the defenses fail, you and I will be needed to stop the Bottom Dwellers from entering it."

Sir Ander thought quickly. He was armed only with the

weapons he'd brought aboard the yacht: his broadsword, his dragon pistol, and the pocket pistol.

"I'll need the pistols that the countess gave me," he said. "The ones that have no magic. They are in my quarters."

"A good thought," said Father Jacob. "I'll meet you there. Don't dawdle."

Father Jacob hurried off, pushing his way through the crowd toward the path that led to the library. Sir Ander paused to glance again at the enemy ship. The fog had cleared, and he could see, flanking the black ship, a horde of bat riders. He broke into a run.

Father Jacob arrived to find the main library in a state of confusion. Those inside whose assigned posts were elsewhere were trying to leave, while those outside tasked with taking up the defense of the library were trying to get inside.

Father Jacob took one look at the knot of people tangling in the main entrance and left, circling around to the back of the building. He had observed some time ago that the latch of one of the lead-paned windows on the ground floor did not close properly. He had reported the broken latch to the crafters in charge of maintaining the buildings. But because in the Citadel, as with every other structure in the world, the magic was failing at an increasing rate, the crafters had all they could do to maintain the magical constructs that kept the buildings standing. He doubted they had taken time to repair a broken latch. He was right. He managed to pry open the window from the outside.

Father Jacob took one last look at the enemy ship bearing down on the Citadel and silently commended himself and his friends into the hands of God, then hiked up his cassock and crawled through the window.

The room was empty. Those who had been studying had

left to go to their posts. He ran down a corridor, turned into another corridor, and came to the main part of the library. The warrior monks were already in position, guarding the tower stairs and the main entrance. Priests and nuns were busy with their various assigned tasks: carrying valuable books and sacred objects to places of safety, hauling buckets of water and bales of straw, rolling up carpets that could catch fire.

As Father Jacob approached the stair that led to the tower, he saw that two monks now stood guard now, instead of one.

"I have valuable books in the reading room on the third level," said Father Jacob.

The monks indicated with a nod that he could proceed.

Father Jacob dashed up the stairs. Circumventing those two monks had been the easy part. The warrior monks guarding the Library of the Forbidden would be a different matter. He could not very well say he had left books in there.

He passed his own little reading cell and slowed his pace, thinking about how to deal with the warrior monks. He was skilled in martial spell-casting as well as with his fists, having studied the gentlemanly art of pugilism in his youth. He was forced to concede that while he might put up a good fight, the monks of Saint Klee would likely make short work of him.

His wits were his best weapon.

He came to a narrow arched entrance. In the shadows beyond was a spiral staircase that led to the top of the tower. A monk stood beneath the arch, the crimson of his robe a smear of color in the shadows. One of the warrior monks was always posted at the bottom of this staircase.

Father Jacob hid behind a wall, observed the monk, and formulated his plan of attack. The monk would have heard the alarm, but he would have no way of seeing what was going on, for there were no windows at the top of the tower.

Father Jacob said a prayer, thinking this was likely the first time anyone had ever asked God's help in breaking and entering a library. Leaving his hiding place, Father Jacob burst into the corridor.

"Did you hear the alarm, Brother?" he called. His voice boomed in the silence, echoing off the walls. "The Citadel is under attack!"

The monk emerged from the shadows. He cast an inquisitive glance at the priest.

"The same foe that attacked the harbor at Westfirth. I provided information about them to the master. He has no doubt communicated this to you and your fellows. The foe will be using contramagic."

The monk indicated with the slightest of nods that he was aware of the nature of the enemy.

"I believe their objective is the Library of the Forbidden," Father Jacob continued. "They have come to find books on contramagic. I need to enter the library and secure these books. I ask that you let me pass."

The monk fixed his intense gaze on Father Jacob. A shadow darkened the monk's eyes. The monks respected and trusted Father Jacob. But just how far did that trust go?

"Wait," said the monk.

He turned and began to climb the spiral stairs that led to the tower room above. Father Jacob followed along behind. Hearing his footsteps, the monk stopped on the stair and looked back.

"Oh, you meant me to wait below," said Father Jacob. "I'm sorry. I misunderstood. Still, since I've come this far . . ."

The monk gave a slight shake of his head and continued. Arriving at the top level, the monk ducked beneath a low archway. Father Jacob stopped to study his surroundings.

The archway led to a narrow corridor about twenty paces long, bare and cold and dark, with stone walls and a cobblestone floor. Lanterns hanging from hooks on the walls gave off dim light. The corridor ended at a gate made of steel bars arranged in a strange, complex pattern. The gate guarded a door of solid oak with intricately carved magical constructs surrounding the seal of the Arcanum: a sword and a staff crossed beneath a flame set on a quartered shield. The door had no visible sign of a lock, latch, or handle.

Two monks guarded this door. They had also heard the alarm and were wondering what was going on. While the monk who had spoken to Father Jacob went to confer with his fellows, Father Jacob remained in the shadows, observing the gate and trying to figure out how to open it. The design of the steel bars reminded the priest of a crosshatched pen and ink drawing with bars running vertically and others horizontally, crossing and crisscrossing, seemingly at random.

The gate had been designed five hundred years ago by Saint Marie. The provost was the only one who knew the key to the operation of the gate. When forbidden texts had been confiscated, they were listed in the catalog, which was itself kept secret, then placed in a depository in the wall on a revolving tray. After the door closed, the tray swiveled, dropping the book into the darkness. Once a year, the provost entered the Library of the Forbidden to sort the books and shelve them.

The monks spoke together for only a moment before reaching consensus. Father Jacob saw at once that the decision was not going to go his way and he walked down the shadowy corridor to confront them. One of the monks moved to stop him, pointing emphatically toward the stairs leading away from the library, indicating he was to leave.

"Answer me this, Brothers," said Father Jacob. "Has a monk wearing dark spectacles recently come around here, asking questions about the Library of the Forbidden?"

The monks exchanged glances and Father Jacob knew he

was right. Before he could explain, an explosion shook the walls and the floor, sending dirt and dust cascading down from the ceiling.

"The Bottom Dwellers have launched the assault," said Father Jacob, wiping dust from his face.

The monk again pointed emphatically toward the stairs and actually broke his silence.

"Go somewhere safe, Father."

Father Jacob knew in his soul, by everything he held sacred, that he was meant to enter the library. If Brother Paul and the Bottom Dwellers managed to break through the Citadel's defenses, they would come here, and he doubted very much if three warrior monks could stop them.

"Let me at least remain to help you. I have fought this foe before," said Father Jacob earnestly.

Another booming explosion shook the tower. From below came cries and shouts and more blasts, followed by screams.

"The enemy is in the library," said Father Jacob.

Again the monks conferred by a silent exchange of glances.

"Our post in the event of an attack is at the bottom of the stairs," said one of the monks. "You will accompany us, Father."

"Go to your post! Leave me here to guard the gates," said Father Jacob. "If the enemy gets past you, I may not be able to do much, but I will do what I can to stop them."

With the sounds of the battle raging below growing louder, the monks must have decided they had no time to argue with Father Jacob. Or perhaps they simply realized that his offer to guard the library made sense. In either event, the monks departed in haste.

Alone in the darkened corridor, Father Jacob breathed a pleased sigh and went back to studying the gate. He was gazing at it intently when he felt the air stirring, as though someone had brushed the sleeve of his cassock.

Thinking it was one of the monks coming back to order him away, he turned, ready to argue.

He was astonished to find Saint Marie standing beside him.

"You have come to hear my confession," she said.

Father Jacob was startled. He had forgotten that she had asked him.

"I would be glad to do so," said Father Jacob. Another explosion rocked the tower. "I fear this is not a good time—"

Saint Marie laughed. Her laughter was robust, boisterous, infectious. She was wearing the robes of a provost, white trimmed with black and edged in gold. Her silver hair was cut in the tonsure as she had worn it in her youth when she had disguised herself as a priest. Her face was aged, care-worn, soft with sorrow, yet serene. She had never lost her faith in God, and had always believed in the goodness of men, even as she had fought against the darkness that often possessed them.

Her laughter died, but her smile remained. She shifted her gaze from him to the steel gate.

"Beautiful, isn't it? The gate is a puzzle, you know."

"That is obvious to the trained observer," said Father Jacob.

"Can you solve it?" Saint Marie asked. "Can you find the key that will allow you to enter the library?"

Father Jacob had come here for that purpose, but now doubt assailed him.

"I am forbidden to enter," he said.

Again, he felt her touch, as cold and light and sharp as a snowflake.

"God has given you great gifts, Father Jacob. You risked

all you had for the sake of Him. If you believe that God gave you His gifts so that you might take up His sword and fight His foes, defend His people, then no risk is too great. Believe in Him."

Father Jacob stared intently at the steel gate, searching for the glowing lines and sigils of the magical constructs in order to understand how the magic worked. Try as he might, he couldn't see them. He frowned in frustration, and spoke a phrase of command that should have caused the constructs to illuminate. Still the gate remained dark. Father Jacob drew in a slow breath.

"There *is* no magic," he said softly. "The gate is only a gate, a puzzle made of steel bars."

He was dimly aware of the din of battle in the distance. The noise distracted him, and he resolved to shut it out. Moving nearer to the gate, he examined the bars closely. Some of the bars had holes drilled in them, seemingly at random.

Jacob scanned one of the bars, followed it to another and from there to another. He envisioned one bar sliding over and dropping into a hole that caused another to move and that triggered another . . .

"I know!" he breathed.

But where to start? Which bar was the first? If he moved the wrong bar, the steel gate would seal shut and only the provost could reset it.

Father Jacob was now intensely intrigued by the puzzle, by the challenge. His gaze went swiftly from one bar to another, mentally calculating where each would fall, thinking how the next bars would react, rejecting, starting over. And then in an instant, the puzzle fell into place, one bar after the other after the other.

Father Jacob set his hand on a single bar about a finger's breadth from the floor.

"God forgive me," Father Jacob said softly.

"Believe in Him," said Saint Marie again.

Father Jacob leaned near and shifted the bar, causing it to slide across and clank into a hole. He watched in awe as one by one, the bars shifted and moved and fell into place. The gate had been made with such skill and precision that even after all these years every bar moved smoothly, sliding either up and down or across. His eyes followed the swift progress until the last bar dropped into a hole that had been drilled into the floor. Pivoting on this last bar, the gate slowly swung aside.

Behind it stood a wooden door covered in ancient, outmoded warding constructs. Jacob had little difficulty in their deconstruction. He spoke the arcane words, his hands running swiftly from one construct to the other, and as he touched the last of the sigils their light shimmered and faded. He gave the door a gentle shove and it creaked open.

He had, after all, missed something—removing the right construct, saying the right word. Alarm bells began ringing throughout the library, probably throughout the Citadel. Between the other alarms, the gunshots and shouts and cries and crackling and sparking of magicks, he knew only one person would hear and understand: the provost. He shrugged, took down a lantern from its hook on the wall. By its light, he and Saint Marie entered the Library of the Forbidden.

The first thing he did was stumble over a pile of dusty books that had been dumped in the depository. They lay in disarray on the dust-covered floor. Father Jacob held the lantern above them, curious to see what they were.

"Look at this!" he exclaimed, bending over them.

"No time, Father," said Saint Marie.

Father Jacob straightened. He held the lantern high and gazed around. The chamber's wall followed the curve of the tower. Shelves had been built into the walls, each shelf neatly labeled so that the provost would know at a glance where to store the books. A very old desk had been shoved against a wall. Other than the desk, there was no furniture. No chairs, no tables. Browsing was not encouraged. The floor was bare except for a few books that had fallen off the shelves, looking very much as if they had tried unsuccessfully to escape. One might have expected the room to smell of brimstone and decay. Instead, the fragrance of old leather and vellum was rather pleasant.

"Such a waste," muttered Father Jacob, walking past the shelves lined with knowledge languishing in the darkness.

Looking at the titles, he had to concede that many of these books were undoubtedly evil and might lead the ignorant astray. Books containing blood magic spells and rites and rituals, for example. Not far from those, however, he came across sections dedicated to books of a scientific nature. Some questioned the existence of God, others advanced theories that the magic in the Breath was merely a phenomenon of nature.

"Do we have such little faith in God and in ourselves that we are threatened by ideas?" he asked. "A treasure trove of wisdom from all ages is shut up here—lost to us!"

"The creation of the Library of the Forbidden was not my doing, though I suppose I provided the impetus," said Saint Marie with a sigh. "This tower room was once my office. That was my desk. After my death at the hands of the blood wizards, Father Dennis began to see enemies lurking in every shadow. He confiscated books he feared were dangerous. He was afraid of the knowledge. As was I."

"We are always afraid," said Father Jacob. "We should face what we fear, not hide from it."

"I learned that lesson," said Saint Marie. "But I learned it too late."

Father Jacob came to the last of the shelves and looked around, puzzled.

"Where are the books on contramagic?"

"The provost told you. There are none here."

"I don't understand," said Father Jacob. "The books you and the others wrote, the ones you refer to in the books I found at the abbey. They must be somewhere. Where are they if they are not here?"

Saint Marie smiled at him. "It is time you hear my confession, Father Jacob."

She turned and walked away and faded into the darkness.

"Sister Marie!" Father Jacob called after her.

There was no answer.

He stared about the library in frustration and disappointment, wondering about the books, wondering what she meant by *hear my confession*?

"How I can hear her, if she won't talk to me?" he muttered. He paused and said thoughtfully, "Or maybe she did."

He considered her words, *He was afraid of the knowledge. As was I.* And the sorrow in her voice as she said, *I learned that lesson. But I learned it too late.* She had brought him to the library to hear her confession. . . . *This was my office . . .*

Father Jacob hurried past the bookshelves and went over to the old desk that had been pushed to one side, out of the way, forgotten. The desk was of oak and extremely heavy, probably the reason it had been moved aside, and not taken from the room. He opened drawers, holding the lantern over them, searching inside. They were all empty. He spoke a word and passed his hand over the desk, hunting for magical constructs, but found none.

He looked at the desk again. It was plain, not a construct in sight. He decided to search the drawers one last time before giving up. He repeated the spell . . . and this time he was rewarded! The remains of an old, old magical construct gleamed feebly from the bottom of the lowest drawer.

The construct had probably once been a powerful illusion spell. Only a few lines and a squiggle remained, the illusion having long since disappeared. Father Jacob could see what had long ago been hidden—a drawer within a drawer. He tried to open it, only to find that it was stuck. He could feel something inside. He painfully squeezed his hand into the drawer and after an effort eventually managed to free the object. He drew out a book. The volume was slim, bound in black leather with faded gold lettering on the front.

My Confession

Inside was her name: Sister Marie Allemand.

Father Jacob placed the lantern on the floor, sat down on the cold stone, and leaned his back against the wall. Oblivious to the sounds of battle, he settled himself to read.

29

For centuries, we have been charged with defending the Citadel of the Voice. We vow to defend the Arcanum. We vow to defend those who live and work within the Citadel. And because we vow to defend the grace of God, we try to fulfill the first two vows without the taking of human life.

—Master of the monks of Saint Klee

A vast courtyard paved with flagstone ran between the two guesthouses used by dignitaries visiting the Citadel. Sir Ander crossed the courtyard on the run, keeping a watch on the black ship as he headed for his quarters. A warrior monk in crimson robes was moving people along, urging them to take cover.

The hospital was also on this level, though some distance away from the guesthouses. Healers, physicians, and surgeons hastened to take up their duties. Sir Ander caught a glimpse of Sister Elizabeth, who looked grim and did not see him.

Across the courtyard from the guesthouses were the communal dining hall and large kitchen with adjacent outbuildings, gardens and vineyards, barns and staff quarters. A curtain wall connected by guard towers encircled this entire side of the mountain.

Sir Ander was ten steps away from his guesthouse when the monk shouted to him to take cover. He bolted for a nearby doorway just in time to escape being knocked down by a blast of wind that took off his hat and sent it flying.

The wind caught up dead leaves and flowers, snapped small trees, flung dust into his eyes, and flattened him back against the wall. The monk sought shelter alongside Sir Ander.

"What is going on, Sister?" he yelled over the blasting wind.

"My brethren are casting, 'Air as Wall,'" she replied.

Two other monks had taken positions on his side of the curtain wall between two guard towers. Each monk twirled a staff in his hands. They chanted words and the whirling staves became a blur of blue magic.

"I need to reach my quarters!" Sir Ander shouted, pointing to the other guesthouse. "My pistols!"

The monk cast him a sympathetic glance, but shook her head. "Wait. It is not safe."

Sir Ander fumed as gale-force winds howled through the courtyard.

"At least tell me what they are doing!" he said.

"Magical constructs etched into the stone run along the top of the wall and extend up the sides of the towers," she told him. "The magic of the staves transmits magic to the constructs on the wall. The wall and the towers form a channel through which the magical wind will flow with ever increasing ferocity."

The two warrior monks stood in place whirling their staves, their feet firmly planted and their robes whipping about them, the constructs on the wall glowed brighter and brighter.

The bat riders flanking the black ship had spread out, flying to attack different parts of the Citadel. Sir Ander saw a large number of them heading in the direction of the library.

He cursed the loss of precious time, but there was nothing he could do. Gale force winds roared around him.

Several bat riders had caught sight of the apparently un-defended opening between the guard towers and were flying toward it. The lead bat riders hit the wall of air at full speed and split apart, disintegrating in horrible masses of blood and fur, flesh and bone.

The bodies of these bats and their riders rebounded off the air wall and struck their comrades flying close behind. Bats screeched and flapped, and their riders plummeted to a bone-crushing death on the rocks below. The first wave of the en-emy had utterly collapsed. The survivors—those that had been in the rear—broke off the attack and flew away to regroup.

The commander of the black ship must have witnessed the destruction, for the ship changed course and began sail-ing in their direction. The gun mounted on the prow of the black ship, slightly larger than a swivel gun, but a hundred times more lethal, took aim at the wall.

Sir Ander remembered the *Royal Lion*. He remembered what had happened to Dag's magical pistol when the contra-magic hit it. His nonmagical pistols had been designed for this very reason.

"Take cover!" Sir Ander roared at the monks. "Throw down the staves!"

He turned to the warrior monk, who was regarding him with cold disapproval.

"You don't understand!" he told her. "If the staves are hit by the contramagic—"

He was too late. The green beam struck the "Air as Wall." Constructs blazed fiercely blue and then faded as the green contramagic broke the constructs apart. The wind began to die. The bat riders flew to attack, approaching the wall more cautiously, firing their shoulder-mounted green fire guns as they came.

The two other monks were trying to renew their spell. The staves flared with blue flame. A green ball of fire hit the staff of one of the monks. The magicks collided, blue and green crackling fiercely. The staff blew apart. Sharp wooden shards pierced the monk's body, and he fell to the ground, clutching at one of the shards that had gone through him like a spear. His comrade flung his staff at one of the diving bats, then ran to check on his companion. One of the riderless bats swooped down on him, striking him with its clawed feet and biting at his head.

The warrior monk and Sir Ander ran to help. Noxious red fumes spread from the bat riders' armor and rolled down over the courtyard. Sir Ander began to cough and choke. The monk managed to grab a handful of the bat's fur. Blue lightning crackled, and the bat fell to the pavement, writhing and twitching. Sir Ander examined the injured monk, who was bleeding from numerous bat bites. None looked to be serious.

The warrior monk waved at him. "Go on, sir!" she shouted, coughing in the smoke.

"Heaven forfend!" a woman cried, coming up behind Sir Ander.

He turned to see Sister Matilda, a nun visiting from his homeland of Travia to lecture about an ancient scroll she had discovered. Sir Ander and the sister had spent an enjoyable evening discussing the homeland Sir Ander had not visited in many years.

Sister Matilda was now standing behind him, her face pale with horror. Sir Ander rose hurriedly and pushed her toward the guesthouse.

"Go to your room, Sister. Lock the door and stay there until this is over!"

"But . . . that young monk—"

"He is with Saint Klee, Sister. He died to protect us."

Sir Ander escorted the nun back to the guest hall, shoved her inside, and shut the door. He hoped to God she would heed his advice. Using the curtain wall as cover, he ran for the guesthouse where he was staying in a ground-floor room.

He went straight to a large wooden chest at the foot of his bed and began pulling out its contents. He was already wearing his belt with his broadsword. He added a long dagger to that, then grabbed up the baldric that had loops for his pistols. He thrust powder flasks and extra bullets into his pockets and tucked his dragon pistol into his belt. He took out the construct-free pistols from the chest, loaded them, and slid them into the heavy leather loops on his baldric. Thrusting a pair of throwing knives into sheathes stitched into each boot, he remembered the poisonous red smoke, grabbed a handkerchief, and tied it around his neck.

At the bottom of the trunk lay several glass vials that had belonged to Brother Barnaby. The monk had made a vow to his own patron saint to never take a human life. Yet because he traveled with Father Jacob and was often placed in dangerous situations, Barnaby had devised a variety of ways to defend himself. He had concocted a liquid made of distilled Estaran hot peppers and finely ground black peppercorns and poured it into vials. Tossed into the face of an attacker, the liquid caused excruciating pain, but did no long-term damage. Father Jacob had playfully dubbed the mixture "Barnaby's Revenge."

After stuffing the vials into his pockets, Sir Ander ran to the window to assess the situation. Several small boats, each drawn by three gigantic bats and carrying a contingent of troops, were pulling away from the black ship.

"Ground forces," Sir Ander muttered.

Once the Citadel's air defenses had been disabled, the ground troops would land. The black ship had again changed course, seeking a new target—a guard tower on the opposite side of the mountain from the library. Father Jacob had been right. Brother Paul would have warned his comrades to leave the library tower untouched.

Black smoke billowed into the sky, mingling with the noxious reddish smoke that still roiled off the attackers. Buildings were on fire. He couldn't see what had been hit.

Sir Ander ran out the door and entered the courtyard to find that Sister Maltida had ignored his warning. She was out in the courtyard trying to assist the monks, overcome by the smoke. One was on her hands and knees, retching; the other had passed out. She was ministering to them and did not see the bat rider jump off his bat and come running toward her.

He did not intend to kill this victim, Sir Ander saw at once. He was going to take her prisoner.

"Run, Sister!" Sir Ander yelled.

Sister Matilda looked up and saw her danger, but instead of running, she flung herself protectively on top of the injured monk.

Sir Ander wished that just once in his life, one of these stubborn faithful would listen to him. He drew the dragon pistol, took careful aim, and fired. The bat rider staggered as the bullet tore through his chest. The bullet slowed him, but he kept running.

"Sons of bitches just won't die!" Sir Ander swore in frustration.

Running toward the sister, Sir Ander drew his second pistol and shot the bat rider again. The Bottom Dweller fell to his knees, blood pouring from another hole in his chest, and finally crumpled.

"Are you all right, Sister?"

The nun was staring transfixed at the dead man. She was deathly pale and Sir Ander feared she was going into shock. She needed something to take her mind off the terror.

"Sister!" Sir Ander shook her. "Stay strong! These monks need your help."

Sister Maltilda swallowed hard, licked her lips, and managed to nod her head. Sir Ander lifted the unconscious monk and carried him inside. The other monk was able to stagger to her feet and follow them.

"Now do as you're told, Sister," Sir Ander said. "Stay here with them and shut the door. If you know any locking constructs, this would be a good time to use them."

He reached into his pocket, brought out Barnaby's vials. "Take these. The fiends wear helms that cover their eyes, but not their mouths. If one of them gets near you, throw this directly into the mouth. It won't kill, but it will give you time to escape."

Sister Maltilda managed a wan smile as she took the vials, clutching them tightly. "Thank you, Sir Ander. God be with you."

"God better be with us all," Sir Ander muttered as he left.

He reloaded each of his pistols on the run. A group of monks dashed past him, carrying what appeared to be barrels filled with fireworks, such as were fired on His Majesty's birthday to the delight of the crowds. Sir Ander trusted these fireworks would do more than produce oohs and aahs. He had almost reached the stairs that led to the library level when he was half blinded by a blaze of dazzling green light. An explosion rocked the ground.

One of the guard towers crumbled and collapsed. Stone blocks rumbled down the side of the mountain, destroying the stairs that led to the hospital.

One of the small boats drawn by the giant bats landed in front of the hospital. Bat riders climbed over the sides and were met by monks wielding their magic. Sir Ander shook his head and kept going. He had to reach Father Jacob.

Sir Ander took the shortest route to the library, climbing

the main stair up the side of the cliff to the library's front entrance, a beautiful plaza encompassed by a colonnade with fluted stone columns.

He climbed the stairs as fast as he could. The black ship was almost lost to sight in a haze of reddish, noxious smoke and the black smoke, which he could see now was coming from the docks at the base of the mountain. He could barely make out the green beam gun swiveling around and then smoke swirled and he lost sight of it.

Reaching the top of the stairs, he stopped to catch his breath and reconnoiter. The poisonous smoke was making him feel light-headed so he used the handkerchief to cover his nose and mouth. Green light flared and he saw the black ship's weapon fire. Smoke rose, this time from the cathedral.

Not far from where he stood, two warrior monks manned a large metal tube aimed at the black ship. One of the monks touched his hand to the tube, and constructs flared blue. A dozen rockets burst from the tube and soared through the air. These rockets were joined by dozens more, launched from the tops of other buildings. The rockets rained down on the black ship and wherever they hit, they burst into white-hot flame that quickly spread.

Soon one of the sails was burning, along with the rigging. Fires sprang up on the deck. The ship's crew was forced to abandon their duties to fight the flames.

Sir Ander cheered. The sight renewed his energy. He headed for the library, only to find that, as he had feared, it was under assault.

Two bat riders flying ahead of a small boat intended to dart between the columns of the encircling colonnade to reach the library entrance. Chains of magical arcing constructs wound round the columns. One of the bats soared over the chain, slamming his rider into the stone ceiling, probably breaking the rider's neck, for he went limp. The magical chain caught the second rider in the throat, garroting him, taking off his head.

The Bottom Dweller who was captaining the boat saw what happened to his escort and brought the boat in for a hard landing. The troops climbed over the sides, some firing their contramagic weapons at the monks manning the chains, others running in the same direction as Sir Ander— the entrance to the library.

"Cover me!" Sir Ander bellowed.

Five warrior monks stepped out in the open, exposing themselves to contramagic fire. They carried no weapons, only small bags. The bat riders raised their guns. Sir Ander dashed across the open space behind the monks. As the bat riders fired, the monks tossed their bags into the air. The bags exploded, filling the air with glittering blue dust. The green contramagic fire hit the dust and rebounded, engulfing the Bottom Dwellers in their own green flame.

Sir Ander made it safely to the library entrance. He had been praying that he would arrive ahead of the enemy. His prayers ceased when he almost fell over the bodies of two monks lying on the floor at the foot of the staircase.

Several charred, greasy spots and a trail of blood on the stairs indicated that the monks had managed to kill or wound several of the enemy before they were taken down.

Sir Ander could hear explosions coming from the levels above. The bat riders who had survived the attack must have gone up the stairs. He climbed the stairs, taking them two at a time. When he reached the landing on the second floor he heard foosteps behind him and saw a warrior monk coming up the stairs.

"Brother, I need your help!" Sir Ander shouted. "The enemy is headed for the Library of the Forbidden!"

The monk asked no questions. He joined Sir Ander and the two ascended the next flight of spiral stairs. Sir Ander drew his pistol, holding it in front of him as he climbed. They met no resistance at first. As they neared the Library of the Forbidden they could hear sounds of movement coming from above. Both slowed, moving cautiously.

The monk was as silent as the smoke drifting in the air. Sir Ander tried to emulate him, but his leather boots creaked and his sword clanked. The monk took the lead, leaving Sir Ander to guard the rear.

The monk came to a sudden halt, flattening against the wall and motioning Sir Ander to do the same. Using the curve of the wall as cover, the monk peered up the stairs and indicated that Sir Ander was to look. Moving as quietly as he could, Sir Ander took a quick peek. Two Bottom Dwellers were guarding the landing and two more were in the hall beyond.

Sir Ander swore under his breath. The door to the Library of the Forbidden stood wide open. The attention of the Bottom Dwellers was focused on the library.

Sir Ander moved back and drew both pistols.

The monk exhibited the glittering blue grenades he carried. Leaning near, he whispered, "Draw their fire."

Having seen the grenade in action, Sir Ander understood the plan.

He shouted out Father Jacob's name, letting the priest know he was coming, and ran up the stairs. He cocked the first pistol, aimed, and fired. The bullet struck the Bottom Dweller in the back of his head, penetrating the helm. The man dropped down dead.

At the sound of the gunshot, the other three Bottom Dwellers turned around and raised their weapons. Sir Ander lunged sideways, as the monk leaped in front of him and tossed two grenades into the air. One of the bat riders fired. Green light flared, followed by a blazing flash of blue when the contra-magic hit the wall of glittering powder and bounced off, catching the Bottom Dweller in his own deadly blast.

The two in front of the library door fired. The monk ran back down the stairs, joining Sir Ander, who was reloading his pistols. The monk tossed another grenade. Green light flared and blue magic crackled, half blinding Sir Ander. When the light faded, he was glad to find that both he and the monk were still standing.

Pistols again in hand, Sir Ander took another look into the hall. The two Bottom Dwellers were reloading their strange weapons. Sir Ander raised his pistol, fired, and missed, the bullet hitting the wall behind one of the Bottom Dwellers. At least the shot had been close enough that the man had been forced to duck. Sir Ander was about to fire again, when he heard Father Jacob's voice cry out in alarm and then a gunshot.

"Jacob!" Sir Ander cried fearfully.

No answer. Sir Ander had one bullet left and no time to reload. The monk tossed another blue powder grenade, filling the air with sparkling dust, just as one of the Bottom Dwellers fired. The resultant blast caught the Bottom Dweller, sending him reeling back against the wall.

"Go to him!" the monk yelled at Sir Ander.

Sir Ander slid the pistol into the loop in the baldric, drew his sword, and ran through what was left of the sparkling powder. The last Bottom Dweller dropped his weapon to grab hold of a sword with a curved blade from a harness on his back.

Sir Ander attacked the man with several fast, straight thrusts to the chest that forced him to fall backward as he parried. The Bottom Dweller sidestepped a vicious slash at his arm and slid in close, his blade aiming at Sir Ander's throat. Sir Ander blocked the attack.

Swords locked together, and sparks flew. The two struggled, then Sir Ander managed to drive one of his sword's quillons into the man's throat. The Bottom Dweller staggered backward and Sir Ander slammed his fist into the enemy's jaw.

His broadsword followed, and blood sprayed from a gaping wound in the man's neck. Sir Ander kicked the body out of the way and drew his pistol.

"Go for reinforcements!" he yelled to the monk.

The sound of rasping, heavy breathing disturbed Father Jacob's reading. He glanced up to see Brother Paul standing warily inside the open door. He was on guard, knowing from the alarms that someone had opened the gate, wondering if the person was still inside.

"Come in, Brother," said Father Jacob, rising and closing the book. "I have been expecting you."

He slid the volume of the confession underneath the desk, picked up the lantern, and walked toward Brother Paul, who had to shield his sensitive eyes from the bright light.

"I know the voice . . ."

"Father Jacob, Brother."

"Father! Thank God! I heard the alarm and I feared the demons had broken into the library," said Brother Paul, squinting, still trying to see. "Could you douse the light, Father? It is making my head ache."

Father Jacob tapped the glass and the light went out. The library was dark, the only light now emanating from a lantern hanging on a hook outside the door. The light gleamed on the crown of Brother Paul's head, faintly illuminating his pallid face.

"I would imagine the light does cause you pain," said Father Jacob in sympathetic tones. "Since you lived most of your life Below with only glimpses of the sun. You must have found the pain of the bright sunlight excruciating when you first arrived here from your homeland."

"I don't know what you are talking about, Father," said Brother Paul. "I was born in Rosia."

He took off the dark spectacles and looked searchingly about the room. His eyes were unusually large and liquid. His gaze was drawn to the bookshelves. His hands twitched. He was nervous, edgy.

"You should go for help, Father. I will stay to guard the library."

"The books you seek are not here," said Father Jacob.

"What books?" said Brother Paul. "I came because I heard the alarm—"

"You came for the books on contramagic," said Father Jacob. "They're not in the library. I was surprised myself. My research into the books of the saints I discovered in the abbey led me to believe they were here."

"You should not speak of such evil," said Brother Paul in a low voice. He stared, unblinking, at Father Jacob, who was slowly and steadily moving nearer.

"You were commanded to break into the Library of the Forbidden in search of the books on contramagic. This entire assault was a diversion, giving you the chance. All a wasted effort," said Father Jacob. "As I said, the books you seek are not here."

The sounds of the battle raging below echoed up the tower stairs. From where Father Jacob was standing, he had a clear view of the corridor. He could see flashes of green and blue fire. Brother Paul's hand slipped up the sleeve of his robe and returned carrying a pistol.

He pointed the gun at Father Jacob.

"Where are the books, Father? What have you done with them?"

"Why do you want them?" Father Jacob asked curiously. He was still holding the lantern, hiding it behind the folds of the skirts of his cassock. He continued to talk, keeping Brother Paul's attention fixed on his face.

"Your people know far more about contramagic than did

the saints, Brother Paul. These weapons you have invented are quite marvelous."

"Tell me where you have hidden the books!" Brother Paul said angrily.

"I don't have them."

Brother Paul aimed the pistol at Father Jacob's head. "You're lying!"

"You can search through all the shelves, Brother. I won't try to stop you. You will not find them," said Father Jacob gently. "They are not here."

Brother Paul looked rattled. He waved the gun with an unsteady hand. "Then you're coming with me."

He motioned with the pistol. "Walk in front. Behave as if nothing is the matter. I'll take you over to the ship. You will visit my world. Who knows," he added with a twitching smile, "you might even be reunited with your friend, Brother Barnaby."

"Barnaby!" Father Jacob repeated sharply. "What do you know about Brother Barnaby?"

"Walk!" said Brother Paul, waving the pistol about recklessly.

Father Jacob started to walk slowly past Brother Paul. A loud explosion sounded nearby, rattling the shelves, followed by smaller blasts and a pistol shot and Sir Ander's bellowing voice calling out for Father Jacob. Brother Paul blanched and glanced over his shoulder uncertainly.

"The battle is lost," said Father Jacob. "Your comrades are not coming. No one has to know about this, Brother. Give me the gun and we will talk . . ."

Brother Paul brought up the pistol swiftly and aimed it at Father Jacob's head. A spasm of hatred contorted his face. He cocked the hammer.

Father Jacob whipped the lantern out from behind his skirt and activated the construct. The lantern blazed into a dazzling white light. Father Jacob aimed the beam directly into Brother Paul's eyes.

He cried out in pain, and flung up his arm to cover his face. Father Jacob dropped the lantern and seized hold of Brother Paul's wrist to try to wrest the pistol from his grasp.

The two men reeled back and forth. The pistol discharged, the bullet whizzing past Father Jacob's ear. Brother Paul flung the empty pistol to the floor and reached into his robes. The light flashed off the barrel of a small pocket gun.

"Drop the gun, Brother!" Sir Ander yelled.

He ran into the room. He was bloody and disheveled, covered in grime. He held his pistol in his hand, aimed it at Brother Paul.

"Don't kill him, Ander!" Father Jacob cried. "He knows something about Brother Barnaby!"

"Drop the gun, Brother Paul," Sir Ander ordered again. "Give up. The fight is over."

"Tell us about Barnaby," Father Jacob said urgently. "Is he alive?"

"He is alive," said Brother Paul with a ghastly grin. "I am sure he wishes he wasn't."

He thrust the barrel of the gun into his mouth.

Father Jacob made a desperate lunge and managed to seize hold of the monk's arm, jostling his aim just as Brother Paul pulled the trigger.

The bullet tore through his cheekbone, shattering his jaw, transforming his face into a grisly mess of blood and brains and slivers of bone. He slid down the wall to the floor.

"Damnation!" exclaimed Sir Ander in pity and sorrow. "What the devil did he do that for?"

Father Jacob was on his knees beside the dying man. He placed his hand on Brother Paul's chest in blessing.

"God's peace be with you," said Father Jacob.

The blood gurgled in Brother Paul's throat. His blood-stained hand seized hold of Father Jacob's cassock, dragged him close to hear. Brother Paul said two foul words and fell back, dead.

Sir Ander was grim-faced. "I'm sorry you had to hear such filth, Father."

"I've heard worse," said Father Jacob, sighing. He gently closed the one remaining eye. "Poor man. To be consumed with so much hatred. May God have mercy on his soul."

"The nuns in the abbey were good to him," said Sir Ander wrathfully. "I saw how he and his friends repaid them. I hope he burns in hell's fire for eternity."

He reached down to help Father Jacob to his feet. "Are you all right?"

"I'm as fine as can be expected, considering I'm likely to be arrested any moment. Are the warrior monks outside?"

"Not now, but they will be here soon. I sent the one who was with me for reinforcements."

"How goes the battle?" Father Jacob asked.

"I lost track of what was happening when I ran in here. Last I saw, we were holding our own. A good thing you told the monks what you knew about contramagic."

"Is it safe to leave?" Father Jacob asked.

"Leave the library? Yes, we cleared the enemy from the stairs—"

"No, I mean leave the Citadel."

"You mean *now*?"

"I dare not wait."

Returning to the desk, Father Jacob bent down, reached underneath, picked up the book off the floor. He thrust the slim volume into his cassock before Sir Ander could catch a good look at it.

"You heard the alarm. We should escape during the confusion, before anyone can stop us."

He walked rapidly out of the library and into the hall. He glanced at the bodies of the Bottom Dwellers lying on the floor, shook his head in frustration and sorrow, and ran down the stairs. Sir Ander had to work to keep up. He heard another explosion. The black ship must still be firing.

When they reached the landing, Sir Ander stopped. "Get behind me, Father. There might be more Bottom Dwellers on the ground floor. I am still required by my vow to protect you."

Father Jacob flattened himself against the wall to allow Sir Ander to squeeze past.

"Even though I've broken the church's law?" Father Jacob asked, half in jest, half in earnest.

"I took an oath to God, Father, not the grand bishop," said Sir Ander drily. "One question," he asked, as they ran down the last flight. "Why did Brother Paul kill himself?"

"He feared the fate that awaited him," said Father Jacob.

"He could have told the provost that he was there to protect the books," said Sir Ander. "You couldn't have proved otherwise."

"He did not fear us," said Father Jacob gravely. "Brother Paul had assured his superiors the books on contramagic were in the Library of the Forbidden. The Bottom Dwellers launched this attack to obtain the books. He would have had to explain to his superiors that they had gone to all this trouble for nothing. I would guess his people do not view failure kindly."

"So the provost was right about the books," said Sir Ander. "I'm sorry, Father."

"Brother Paul failed," said Father Jacob. "I did not."

He added with a sigh, "I almost wish I had."

30

For the Arcanum to function, it must remain an autonomous order within the structure of the Church of the Breath. The provost reports to the Council of Bishops, and cannot be beholden to any single member, including the grand bishop. Only by maintaining this separation can the Arcanum remain an effective means for fighting corruption of the soul and not become a weapon in the internal politics of the church.

—Father Raynard du Galinea,
seventh provost of the Arcanum

Father Jacob and Sir Ander reached the ground floor of the library to find that the invading Bottom Dwellers had either been killed or driven off. Priests and nuns were helping the healers tend to the wounded, covering the faces of the dead, granting God's blessing to the dying. Warrior monks remained at the entrance, for the sounds of battle could still be heard raging in other parts of the Citadel.

Books were strewn all over the floor. In some instances, the shelves had fallen down or had been overturned to form crude barricades. Charred and greasy spots on the floor marked the final resting place of the Bottom Dwellers, whose magical armor immolated the bodies after death.

Despite their haste, Father Jacob and Sir Ander slowed their pace, not wanting to call attention to themselves by running. Father Jacob kept his head bowed, his face averted; Sir Ander walked at his side. No one paid any attention to them except a nun who was hurrying past with a handful of blood-soaked rags. Seeing blood on Sir Ander, she stopped to ask if he required assistance. He told her no, he was not seriously hurt. She thanked God and hastened on. The smell of blood mingled with the smoke of burning.

"So many dead and wounded," said Father Jacob.

"It was a hard-fought battle, but the monks did their job," said Sir Ander. "They fought off the invaders and set fire to their black ship."

"How did they manage that?"

"Incendiaries," said Sir Ander. "The monks launched rockets that ignited on impact and burned like a son of a bitch. Pardon the language, Father. The last I saw, the Bottom Dwellers were running around the blazing deck in confusion, trying to put out the fires."

"Will they launch another assault?"

"I doubt it. The Bottom Dwellers hit us with everything they had at the outset. Where are we going?" Sir Ander asked in a low voice.

"We're leaving the library the same way I came in," said Father Jacob. "I don't want to encounter the monks if I can avoid it."

"They have no way of knowing it was you who broke into the library," said Sir Ander.

"Don't bet on that," said Father Jacob grimly.

They climbed over the upended shelves and piles of books, treading on broken glass and staying out of the way of any monks. The room with the casement window through which Father Jacob had entered was in the rear of the library, far from the main entrance.

Sir Ander crawled through the window first and stopped on the lawn outside to assess the situation.

A smokey haze made it difficult to see. The last time he'd caught a glimpse of the enemy ship, it was on the opposite side of the mountain. He couldn't see any of the bat riders, but he could still hear in the distance the crackles and booms of magical discharges, shouts and screams and sporadic pistol fire. He guessed this meant that some of the Bottom Dwellers were still fighting.

At least there were no bat riders here and no warrior monks.

"You can come out now, Father," said Sir Ander.

Father Jacob climbed through the window. He took care to shut it before joining Sir Ander.

"I still hear fighting," said Father Jacob.

"Covering their retreat, most likely. Which way are we going now? The monks will be guarding all the stairways that lead to the carriage yard."

"Not the old stumble steps," said Father Jacob.

Sir Ander stared at him. "The stumble steps? You can't be serious! We'll break our necks! We might as well throw ourselves off the side of the mountain now."

The "stumble steps"—so named because they would cause an enemy to stumble—dated back to the time of the Citadel's construction. Built as a defensive measure, the steep, narrow stairway with its uneven steps had been designed to discourage an attack by sea. With the development of magical defenses, the stumble stairs were no longer needed and had been allowed to fall into disrepair.

Consisting of nine hundred steps carved out of the bedrock, the stairway plunged straight down the side of the mountain. Navigating the stairs was not pleasant. A misstep could send one tumbling off the rocky cliff. The magical constructs that had been placed to maintain them had failed long ago. In addition to being uneven, the stairs were broken and crumbling.

"No one will be expecting us to take that route," said Father Jacob.

"Because we're supposedly rational human beings," Sir Ander grumbled. "Where's the entrance?"

He had seen the stairs every time he brought the yacht into the Citadel, a thin line of gray going straight up the side of the mountain. He had never used them and he had no idea how to reach them. All he knew was that a guard tower stood at the top. The Citadel had a great many guard towers.

"The entrance is not far from here." Father Jacob started off at a brisk pace.

"I was thinking about what that wretched Brother Paul said about Barnaby. That he was still alive. I wish there was some way we could rescue him," said Sir Ander, walking alongside the priest. "I've said this before, but I keep thinking we should be trying to save him, not running around looking for moldy, old books. I'm sorry if I offend you, Father, but that's how I feel."

"You do know that we would never survive the voyage below the Breath," said Father Jacob.

"The Bottom Dwellers sailed here from Below and they survived," Sir Ander argued.

"With specially designed ships and powerful magicks," said Father Jacob.

Sir Ander grunted and walked on very fast, his head down. He could feel Father Jacob's worried, sympathetic gaze.

"I know I'm being irrational, Father," Sir Ander said after a moment. "It's just . . . it's Barnaby . . ."

"I believe with all my heart that finding those books will help us find him," said Father Jacob earnestly.

"I pray you are right," said Sir Ander, sighing. He peered through the smoke. "I hope you know where you're going. I can't see a damn thing."

Father Jacob opened his mouth to reply and began to cough in the smoke. He had no handkerchief, for he was constantly using them to clean his ink pens. He put his hand over his nose and mouth and kept going.

No one ever came to this part of the Citadel anymore except the occasional shepherd and his dog tending the flocks of grazing sheep that kept the grass trimmed. The steeply sloping ground made walking difficult. Father Jacob and Sir Ander slid or skidded much of the way down, fetching up at last against the inside of the curtain wall.

The walking was easier here, as was the breathing, for the smoke had not settled this low. They made their way along the wall until they came to a small, squat, and extremely old guard tower dotted with arrow slits, through which guards defending the stumble steps in ancient days would have a clear shot at any enemy bold enough to try to climb them.

A wooden door banded with iron set into the wall at the bottom of the tower permitted access.

"This tower is never used anymore," said Father Jacob. He tried the door, which opened easily. "The lock is broken. No one bothers to refresh the spells."

Inside, the tower was dark and cool. The only sounds were angry squeals of the rats, the tower's current residents, disturbed by their coming. The two men waited until their eyes could adjust to the dimness, then searched for the door to the stairs.

It was easy to locate. The door was blocked by a trestle on which was a sign that read in large, bold letters: DANGER.

"A sign. That's all?" said Sir Ander. "No magical warding spells?"

"They assume no one in his right mind would go down those stairs," said Father Jacob.

"Which shows they never met you," Sir Ander stated.

He removed the sign and shifted the trestle. This door was locked, but the lock was rusty and gave way when Sir Ander kicked it. He opened the door, stepped out onto the first step, looked down and closed his eyes. He did not suffer from a fear of heights, yet the sight of the stumble steps plunging straight down the side of the mountain made him queasy.

"Too bad we didn't bring any rope," said Father Jacob.

"Too bad you had to break into the damn library," said Sir Ander with a grunt.

"You speak a true word there, my friend," said Father Jacob somberly.

Sir Ander saw the priest slip his hand into the pocket of his cassock where he had secreted the slim volume he had taken from the library, checking to make certain the book was safe.

Father Jacob had been unusually quiet since they had left the library. Sir Ander had attributed this to seeing a man blow half his head off or that he was thinking of Brother Barnaby. Now Sir Ander wondered if the priest was thinking of that small book.

"God be with us," said Father Jacob, and he began to descend the stairs.

The trip down the stumble steps turned out to be one of the most terrifying events in Sir Ander's life. The stairs were uneven and irregular, cracked and crumbling, and in some places were completely missing. He was at times forced to resort to simply letting go and sliding on his rump, fetching up against a scrub tree or boulder. Once his heart stuck in his throat when a step cracked under Father Jacob's foot, causing the priest to fall. He tumbled into Sir Ander, nearly sending them both down onto the foam-covered rocks below. By the grace of God, Sir Ander was able to hang on and save them.

He was never so glad to see anything in his life as the eight hundredth and ninety-ninth step. By the time he reached it, his hands were bruised and bloodied, his breeches were torn and his knees skinned. Father Jacob's cassock had a large rent in the back, and he was limping.

"Given a choice between fighting an army of demons or going down those damn stairs again, I'd choose the demons," said Sir Ander fervently. "Can you walk?"

"Bruised my ankle," said Father Jacob. "There's the Carriage House. We don't have far to go."

They made their way to the stable yard. At first they saw no one. The stables had not come under attack, probably because they contained nothing of value to the Bottom Dwellers. Sir Ander wondered what had happened to the lay brothers who worked here. He gave a shout.

"Sir Ander!" a voice called out in response. "Is that you?"

The lay brothers had been hiding in the barn. They emerged, filled with questions, for they had not been able to see what was going on. Sir Ander answered their questions briefly, then said he and Father Jacob needed to leave immediately on urgent business.

The lay brothers were dubious as to whether that would be possible. The wyverns had been thrown into a panic by the sounds of the explosions. Sir Ander was insistent and he and the lay brothers searched the stables until they found two wyverns who appeared calmer than the rest. With the help of Sir Ander, the lay brothers managed to harness the beasts to the yacht.

"Looks like we made it safely so far," remarked Sir Ander in an undertone.

He climbed up to the driver's compartment and assisted

Father Jacob. Reaching out to unlock the door, Sir Ander stopped in alarm and grabbed hold of Father Jacob, preventing him from entering.

"What is it?" Father Jacob whispered.

"The door was unlocked," said Sir Ander in smothered tones. "Someone is inside. Wait here."

"I'm coming, too," said Father Jacob. "If the monks are waiting for us, you'll need my magic."

Sir Ander conceded the point. He had his sword, but if the magic-wielding monks of Saint Klee were waiting to ambush them, his sword would be useless. He thrust the door open with a bang. He and Father Jacob barged inside. Both came to a startled, dumbfounded halt.

Ferdinand de Montagne, grand bishop of the Church of the Breath, was standing at the window, gazing outside. Hearing the two men enter, Montagne turned to face them.

"Eminence!" Father Jacob exclaimed, amazed. "What are you doing here?"

"You defied us and broke into the Library of the Forbidden. I guessed you would be intent on leaving to pursue your ill-fated obsession."

Montagne was a tall man; his head almost brushed the cabin's ceiling. His voice was ragged, weary, his face gray with fatigue and illness. He did not appear to be injured, though his fine robes were stained with soot and blood and smelled strongly of smoke.

"I seek the truth, Eminence," said Father Jacob gravely. "Please do not try to stop me."

"You know damn well I cannot stop you," said the grand bishop, adding caustically, "You must think yourself very clever, Jacob, to have taken advantage of this tragic situation to enter where you were forbidden."

"If you intend to try to shame me, Eminence, I will say in my defense that you left me no choice," said Father Jacob.

His face darkened. He was growing angry. "I asked permission and was denied."

"Where are you going?" Montagne asked abruptly.

"Since you will exert all your efforts in attempting to thwart me, I prefer not to say."

"Did you find the books on contramagic?"

"I did not, as Your Eminence knows."

"You plan to go in search of them."

Father Jacob stirred restlessly, his anger mounting. "You have looked the enemy in the face, Eminence. You have witnessed for yourself the terrible threat the Bottom Dwellers pose to the world. They have already murdered countless hundreds: the nuns at the abbey, the crew of the *Royal Lion,* the innocents in the Crystal Market. Their deaths might have been prevented, as well as the deaths of the enemy, for they are also God's children. The church knew the truth . . . and did nothing. You knew the truth . . . and did nothing."

The blood had risen to Montagne's face. He made no answer, and the blood slowly drained, leaving his skin sallow.

"All these years," Father Jacob continued, "you have known far more about contramagic then you would admit. You recognized from Brother Paul's letter that the so-called demons who attacked the abbey were using weapons of contramagic. You knew the collapse of the Crystal Market was caused by contramagic. You have done everything in your power to try to prevent me from discovering the truth. As a result, thousands are dead! Needlessly!"

Montagne's jaw worked, a vein in his neck twitched. He swallowed and remained silent.

"I don't understand, Father," said Sir Ander.

"Grand bishops down through the centuries have known far more about contramagic than they have ever admitted."

Father Jacob drew the book from his pocket and held it up in front of Montagne's face.

"Saint Marie knew the truth. She blamed herself. She made her confession in this book."

The sunlight glimmered off the title, *My Confession,* stamped in gold. Sir Ander thought back to the time when Father Jacob had first told him Saint Marie had come to him to ask him to hear her confession.

"The truth about what, Father?" Sir Ander asked.

"The church took the innocent work Saint Marie and the others had done on contramagic and used it to develop powerful weapons that sank the island of Glasearrach and plunged the world into centuries of darkness and despair. Worse than that, Eminence, you have known that magic throughout the world is failing and that the Bottom Dwellers are the cause! Instead of revealing the truth, so that the nations of the world could work to stop them, you persist in lies, denials, fabrications!"

"There is more to it than that!" Montagne said heavily.

"More to what?" Father Jacob asked, frowning, startled by the man's intensity.

The grand bishop closed his eyes, his mouth worked in some private agony. He swallowed, as though tasting bitter medicine, and shook his head, refusing to answer.

"What do you intend to do, Jacob? Denounce me?"

"I do not know yet," Father Jacob said shortly.

Outside the yacht, the wyverns were screeching and squabbling. One of the lay brothers holding the reins shouted that he could not control them much longer. Montagne rubbed his eyes.

"Do not pursue this course of action, Father. You will end up destroying that which you are trying to save."

"We can no longer live in ignorance and fear, Eminence."

"God help you, Jacob," said Montagne.

He left the yacht. Moving shakily, he almost fell as he tried to climb down off the driver's seat. Sir Ander went to assist him, clasping him by the upper arm and helping him descend. The grand bishop walked with slow and faltering steps past the astonished lay brothers, never seeming to see them. Sir Ander waited to make certain Montagne was safely on his way, then he returned to the yacht.

"I wonder what he meant—'there is more to it,'" Father Jacob said, musing.

"Whatever it was, that 'God help you' wasn't a blessing. It was a threat, Father."

"You shouldn't come with me, Ander," said Father Jacob. "Once I leave these walls, I will be a fugitive. The full force and might of the Arcanum will be exerted against me."

"God didn't add conditions to my service," said Sir Ander. "God didn't say that I was to guard you only during calm days. He meant stormy nights, as well."

"We are facing a hurricane, my friend," said Father Jacob, sighing.

Sir Ander took his place in the driver's box. "Do we travel to the palace? Speak to the king? Tell him about the Bottom Dwellers?"

Father Jacob gave a rueful smile. "How close do you think we would get before we were arrested? If by some miracle we did manage to talk to His Majesty, he would not believe me. He did not believe the countess. I have no proof."

"So where are we going?"

"The dragon realms," said Father Jacob.

"Dragon realms!" Sir Ander repeated, amazed.

"The duchy of Talwin to be exact."

Father Jacob placed his hand on Sir Ander's shoulder. "I am being very selfish in allowing you to come, my friend, but I honestly do not think I could make this journey without you."

He went inside the yacht and shut the door.

Sir Ander's mind was in turmoil. Dragon realms! What

did dragons have to do with any of this? He forced himself to concentrate on flying the yacht, finding something calming in the familiar task of preparing to set sail. He touched constructs set into the brass control panel, channeling the magical energy into the lift tanks and the ballast tank.

He could feel the yacht respond as he increased the buoyancy and it slowly rose from the ground. He touched a second set of constructs that guided magical energy along the braided leather control lines connected to the wyverns' harnesses, allowing him to direct the beasts. His first task was to locate the black ship. He did not want to end their journey by flying the yacht into the enemy's gun sights.

As the yacht drifted upward, he could see the fires on the docks below blazing out of control. No one was fighting them. They were letting them burn out. The smoke that had been a curse was now a blessing, concealing the *Retribution*'s departure. Sailing above one of the guard towers, he sighted the black ship. It was limping away. He brought out the spyglass from underneath the helm and put it to his eye.

The Bottom Dwellers had managed to bring the fires on board under control, but their ship had sustained considerable damage. One mast was broken and several sails had been destroyed, as had much of the rigging. He could see sailors and even soldiers in demonic armor working on the deck. Bat riders accompanied the ship, but their numbers had been considerably reduced.

He scanned the deck and saw a group of prisoners huddled near the stern. As he watched, two Bottom Dwellers grabbed one of the nuns and dragged her across the deck to where the green beam-firing cannon was mounted. The nun fought, struggling against her captors.

Bottom Dwellers hauled the woman to the gun and forced her to bend over it. One drew a knife and slit her throat, almost severing the head from the body. Blood gushed, spilling onto the gun. The Bottom Dweller who had murdered the nun rubbed her blood into the weapon.

A blood magic ritual. Sick to his stomach, Sir Ander lowered the glass.

The yacht sailed over the walls of the Citadel. The magical defenses that might have stopped Father Jacob had been knocked out by the enemy.

A sign from God? Sir Ander wondered.

The moment he left those walls behind, he became an outlaw.

He smiled, shook his head, and turned, opening the door a crack. "Father, could you bring me a cup of tea?"

Sir Ander settled back comfortably, touched the controls, and gave the wyverns a little tingle on their backsides. The beasts flapped their wings and the yacht sailed north to the dragon realms.

When evening fell on the first day of their journey, Sir Ander was concerned about where to land for the night. Ordinarily he would have chosen a town or city with stables for the wyverns and an inn with good food and drink. He did not think it likely that the word would have already been sent to search for them, but he wasn't taking chances. Sir Ander landed the yacht far from civilization, setting down in a large, grassy sward.

He fed what meat they had in storage to the wyverns, enough for a meal tonight. The next night when they landed, he would have to hunt. He released the wyverns from their harness and hobbled them so that they would not fly away. Once they were fed, he walked about a bit to stretch his legs and then went back inside the yacht. He found Father Jacob where he had left him that morning, seated in his reading chair. The slim volume lay closed in his lap, his hand resting on it.

"I hope you're not picky about dinner," said Sir Ander. "I didn't have time to stock up on fresh food and I fed the dried beef to the wyverns. That leaves us smoked cheese, hardtack, and the last of the apples. I'll go hunting tomorrow when we stop for the night."

"I'm not hungry," said Father Jacob.

"You should eat something."

Father Jacob stood up wearily. "I moved heaven and hell to find this book and now I wish I hadn't. The grand bishop was right, my friend. I could end up destroying the faith I have dedicated my life to defending."

"I don't believe that, Father," said Sir Ander.

"I may not have a choice."

"There's always a choice," said Sir Ander, sitting down to eat. "Explain what happened to the island of Glasearrach."

"Saint Marie does not go into detail, but this is how she describes it."

Father Jacob flipped through the pages of the book until he found the passage. He read aloud: " 'Imagine you want to take down a gigantic fortress. You bring in sappers to plant huge kegs of gunpowder beneath the walls and legions of crafters to ignite the gunpowder. The resulting explosion blasts apart the very bedrock on which the fortress stands and sends shockwaves rumbling through the ground. The fortress splits asunder. Now imagine this same scenario using contramagic to sink an island. The powerful opposing forces of magic and contramagic collide, sending shockwaves through the Breath . . .' "

Father Jacob closed the book.

"She blamed herself and her friends. If they had not discovered contramagic and learned how to use it, the tragedy of Glasearrach would not have happened."

"You say her friends. Did you find out anything about the fifth friend, Xavier? Why no one ever heard of him?"

"His tragedy was perhaps the greatest. If Marie and the others were responsible for the sinking of the island, Xavier was responsible for the depredations of the Pirate King. His name was Xavier Meehan. He was the brother of Ian Meehan, the Pirate King.

"Shortly after their discovery of contramagic, Xavier made a visit to his homeland. No one knows what truly happened, but Marie speculates that while he was there, he told his brother—in all innocence—about the wonderful work he had been doing. His brother saw at once how he could use this new magic to his advantage. He forced his brother to design contramagic weapons that he used with devastating effect against his foes. I would imagine they were much like the green beam weapons his descendants are using against us now."

"What happened to Xavier?"

"We have no way of knowing. Marie writes that they never saw him again. Hearing of the weapons of the Pirate King, Marie and the others recognized that he was using contramagic. Appalled by what they had created, they took their work to the Council of Bishops and confessed that they were the ones responsible. They were imprisoned. The church declared contramagic evil and forbade anyone to use it. Then the church went against its own precepts and used contramagic to sink Glasearrach. They almost destroyed the world."

Sir Ander chewed hardtack. "So what does any of this have to do with the dragons? How are they involved?"

"I know where to find their research on contramagic. Saint Marie writes that she and her Knight Protectors took the books to the palace of the Duke of Talwin for safekeeping. Why she took them to the dragons is a mystery, however."

"What I don't understand is this," said Sir Ander. "If Saint

Marie and the others were responsible for creating this great evil, as the church viewed it, how did they come to be canonized?"

"Because they quelled the storms. We have always been taught that the calming of the storms was a miracle. It may have been in part, but there is a basis in science. Marie and the others knew magic and they knew contramagic. They knew the wizard storms were caused by the clashing of the two forces and they theorized that although they could not end the magical storms, they could diminish their severity. By this time, the situation was so dire that the church had no choice but to release them from prison and let them try. When they succeeded, the church declared them miracle workers, blessed of God."

"A very clever move," said Sir Ander wryly.

"Indeed it was. The church put the four into an untenable position. If the four told what they knew about the sinking of Glasearrach, they would destroy the church. People needed God; they needed faith and the four agreed to keep silent. But Saint Marie was plagued by guilt. She could not die without confessing the truth."

Father Jacob shoved away his plate, his food untouched.

"Now I understand," said Sir Ander quietly. "As you said, you are faced with the very same choice. You know the truth about the Bottom Dwellers and the failing magic. What are you going to do?"

"Turn the matter over to God," said Father Jacob.

31

*Since the time of the Sunlit Empire, the fair city of
Capione has been the playing field for the games of
the rich and powerful.*

—Anonymous

Dubois was in Capione, continuing his investigation of the
Duquesa de Plata Niebla, when he heard the news about the
attack on the Citadel. Dubois's agents had learned little of
any use about the duchess in the region of Plata Niebla. He
had concluded that the investigation was going to come to
nothing, when he discovered she had purchased a château in
the picturesque town of Capione. He had decided to travel
there himself, to conduct his investigation in person. He
was in the inn, partaking of hot chocolate and croissants for
breakfast, when a special courier arrived with a pouch
marked "Private."

Dubois opened the pouch, drew out the contents, and began to sort through them. One letter caught his attention. He
stared at it a moment, prey to a deep foreboding. The envelope was sealed with red wax imprinted with the official
seal of the church.

Dubois had received only a few "red seal" letters during
his career. A red seal meant dire news. He slit open one end

of the envelope with a small knife, taking care not to tamper with the seal, which was magical. If he broke it, the letter would go up in flames. He was startled to recognize the handwriting of Montagne. The grand bishop had not wanted to trust even the monsignor, his secretary, to write it.

The letter began: "The Citadel has come under attack!"

Dubois was so astonished he had to read the sentence twice to make certain he understood it correctly. Rising hurriedly from the table, he went to the door of his room, checked to make certain he had locked it, then returned to finish the letter.

Montagne described the attack of the black ship and the bat riders. He wrote that the occupants of the Citadel, led by the monks of Saint Klee, had managed to drive off the attackers. Many had been wounded, some had died, and it was feared some had been taken prisoner.

Dubois noted as a point of interest that the grand bishop no longer referred to the attackers as "demons" or "Freyans." He did not term them "Bottom Dwellers," either. He merely called them "the enemy."

Dubois's chocolate grew cold while he pondered this astonishing news. The Citadel had not come under attack for hundreds of years. Why was it attacked now? What was the objective? If the Bottom Dwellers wanted to kill people and cause fear, they would have chosen another target, such as Evreux. Few would ever hear about the attack on the Citadel. The Arcanum would keep that a closely guarded secret.

He continued reading and found the answer.

Montagne wrote that during the attack, Father Jacob Northrop had broken into the Library of the Forbidden, searching for books on contramagic, despite the fact that the provost had told the priest he would not find any such books.

"This did not deter Father Jacob," Montagne added.

Father Jacob and Sir Ander had fled and were now

considered fugitives. The grand bishop believed the priest was still searching for the forbidden books. Montagne ordered Dubois to drop whatever he was doing and pursue them. When he located them, he was to inform the monks of Saint Klee, who were also searching for them. The monks would see to it that the two were returned to the Citadel.

Montagne ended by warning Dubois that he was to say nothing of the attack or the escape of Father Jacob to anyone.

"Well, well, well," Dubois murmured.

He sat down in an easy chair, crossed his legs, put his fingertips together, pressed his two index fingers against his lips and pondered what to do. Dubois knew that finding Father Jacob when he didn't want to be found would be difficult. Montagne must know that, too, but he was desperate. This led Dubois to wonder: *Why* was the grand bishop desperate? Given the terrible nature of this enemy, wouldn't the logical course of action be to support Father Jacob in his search to find a way to stop them? Not send Dubois and warrior monks to arrest him?

"What do you fear the priest will discover, Eminence?" Dubois asked the letter.

The letter providing no answer, Dubois finished eating the croissants, placed the letter on the plate, and tapped the seal with the knife. The letter went up in flames. Dubois stirred the ashes with the knife and then dumped them into what remained of the chocolate. He threw the chocolate into the slops jar.

Dubois wondered how the grand bishop expected him to find Father Jacob when he was forbidden to mention his crime to anyone. Usually when conducting a manhunt, Dubois would have sent word to his agents worldwide. He would give descriptions of the priest and Sir Ander, providing names, known aliases. He could not ask them to find Father Jacob if he could not name or describe Father Jacob.

His Eminence is not thinking logically, Dubois reflected. So what was he to do?

He had only just arrived in Capione to start his discreet inquiries into the duchess. Given her nearness to the royal family, Dubois considered this investigation of extreme importantance. He rubbed his forehead.

He would truly like to find Father Jacob, if for no other reason than to learn why the priest was driving the grand bishop to desperation. But Dubois couldn't very well jump into a carriage and rush off to find him, because he had nowhere to rush to. Father Jacob could be anywhere in the world by now.

Dubois decided to spread the word that he was interested in information regarding a priest of the Arcanum who might be in company with a Knight Protector. Since there were any number of priests of the Arcanum, most of them accompanied by a Knight Protector, Dubois would be deluged with leads. But he couldn't think of anything else to do.

Sending this order out to his agents and receiving information back would take time. In the interval, he would continue with his investigation of the duquesa. He dashed off a note to the grand bishop, which read: "Message received. Starting now." Dubois wrote letters to his agents and dispatched them. This done, he mounted his horse and, following directions given to him by the innkeeper, rode to the Château de Sauleschant.

Dubois did not go immediately to the château, but stopped first in a nearby village to gather information. The village was small, poor, and shabby. The only establishments in town were a tavern that also served as a post office and an apothecary.

Dubois went first to the tavern. Owners of taverns were

generally pleased to have customers. Dubois was therefore taken aback when the owner glowered at him and demanded to know what the devil he wanted.

Dubois meekly told the proprietor that he was writing a book on the noble families of Rosia and was interested in the history of the current owner of the château, the Duquesa de Plata Niebla.

The tavern owner eyed Dubois, decided he looked harmless, and gave him a grudging welcome.

"Beg pardon, monsieur. I thought you was one of them ghouls who came to gawk at where the murders were done."

"Murders?" said Dubois. "Ah, yes. I remember."

The Murders of Capione. Gazettes throughout Rosia had been filled with the gruesome details of the tragic story. People had talked of nothing else for months. He ordered a beer for himself and one for the tavern keeper.

"I recall I did hear something about those," he said offhandedly. "A nobleman's daughter was one of the victims. Opium and blood magic."

He started to switch the subject to the duquesa, but the tavern owner, seeing that Dubois was not the least bit interested in the murders, immediately told him all about them.

The murders had occurred only a short time ago, most of them in Capione, but some in the surrounding region. A young man known as the Warlock had gained a following among the disaffected youth of the community, luring them into his evil clutches and then killing them in horrible ways too gruesome to describe. The daughter of Viscount Devroux had been a victim, along with a local lad, whose body had been found in a nearby field. Or rather, parts of his body had been found.

"The Arcanum even sent a priest," said the tavern owner with relish. "Name of Father Jacob Northrop. He and the viscount's soldiers attacked the coven where this Warlock was said to be holed up. The priest couldn't capture the fiend, but he did drive him away. Though it will be a long while before any of us feel safe in our beds."

"Father Jacob," said Dubois to himself. "He was in Capione when the grand bishop sent for him to investigate the murders of the nuns at the abbey. An odd coincidence."

Dubois was always suspicious of coincidences.

He expressed proper horror and said again he was here to research the château.

"Was the duquesa in residence at the time?" Dubois asked. "What a shock she must have suffered."

"She was here," said the tavern keeper. "The soldiers paid her a visit, asked if she wanted them to provide a guard, seeing that she was a woman and alone. She was very polite, thanked them for their concern and said from what she had heard, she was far too old to be of interest to the young Warlock."

"How did the château come to be for sale?" Dubois asked. He purchased two more drinks and settled back to listen.

The original owners, the Desmarals, dated their heritage to the Sunlit Empire, when a knight had distinguished himself in service to his king and had been given the land as a gift. The extensive Desmaral family had flourished for a number of centuries, even managing to survive the Dark Ages. The unfortunate tendency of cousins to marry cousins had produced a strain of madness in the family, however, which had resulted in the last heir killing his wife and children and then hanging himself in the wine cellar.

He had died in debt. The executor put the estate up for sale. The mansion had been purchased by the wealthy, mysterious duquesa, who said she came to Capione to take the waters. Dubois gave the tavern owner a description of the duchess. The tavern owner had seen her only once, on the day she had taken possession. The entire village had turned out to welcome her. He said the description fit her.

Knowing perfectly well that the duchess was in Evreux, Dubois asked innocently if she was then currently in the château. The tavern owner said he didn't think so. He could provide directions, if Dubois wanted to view the château, which was a fine example of architecture of that period.

The château was about five miles from the village, situated on a hill that overlooked a picturesque valley. The tavern owner warned Dubois that the château was haunted by the ghost of the last of the Desmarals, who was said to roam about the building with a noose hanging around his neck.

As Dubois rode to the château, he wondered if the duchess had made peace with the ghost or if she had ordered him out of her house. From what Dubois had seen, the Duquesa de Plata Niebla was a woman of strong will, not someone to put up with a ghost.

He arrived at twilight and stopped at the end of the drive to reconnoiter. The château must once have been magnificent. The structure was massive, solid, with a columned portico and a turnabout drive. A great many chimneys attested to the vast number of rooms. The duquesa appeared to care little about her investment, however. The masonry needed repair. The garden was overgrown with weeds.

Dubois rode his horse along the tree-lined drive. He was halfway to the château when his horse began acting strangely. The beast shook his head and looked nervously about, snuffling and blowing. Dubois's natural caution had prompted him to ride on the side of the road, keeping in the dark shadows of the tree line. He couldn't see anything to cause alarm, but he approached the château even more warily.

He knew the duchess was not at home. He had made certain of that before he left. He could see no signs that the mansion was inhabited. Yet his horse was growing more and more agitated.

Dubois discovered the reason when he reached the end of the drive. He found two griffins, tethered to tree limbs. The griffins were saddled and harnessed and showed signs of having recently been ridden. They were aware of his approach. Their large, lion bodies rose to a crouch at the sight of him, their bright glittering eyes keeping careful watch. One gnashed his beak and began cleaning it with a paw.

Dubois dismounted and led his unnerved horse to the woods on the other side of the road, downwind of the griffins and out of sight of the château. He tethered the horse to a tree limb and went back to have a closer look at the griffins.

Smarter, faster, and far more reliable mounts than wyverns, griffins were used by the military, royal messengers, diplomatic couriers, and private citizens wealthy enough to own them. The expense of keeping and maintaining griffins was great and one had to be specially trained to ride them. No one ever "hired" griffins.

Dubois advanced as close as he considered safe. Griffins were not bad tempered like wyverns, but the dignified beasts were generally cool to strangers. A snap from their powerful beaks could take off a man's head. The griffins kept watch on Dubois as he drew near, but were otherwise not disturbed by his presence.

Dubois stopped just short of head-snapping range. He looked at the harness and the saddles and noted that the leatherwork was quite fine, expensive, with no sign of military markings. Footprints in the dirt beneath the trees led to the gravel turnabout drive. The prints were of two sets of feet—two men wearing riding boots.

Dubois was intrigued. Two men had flown here on griffin back when they could have just as easily and far more cheaply hired horses or carriages. He could think of two reasons. The first, the men were in a hurry. Griffins flew extremely fast, almost as fast as dragons. The second, the men wanted to remain unobserved.

They might be thieves. He discounted that. Men who rode griffins were not here to steal the silver wine decanters.

Dubois would not have described himself as a man of courage. He often said he had too much sense to be courageous. He was not a gentleman, like Lord Captain de Guichen, and thus was not required to fight duels or stand his ground when someone was shooting at him. That said, Dubois was not a coward, either. He could be brave when bravery was required.

These gentlemen, whoever they were, had something to do with the duquesa. He needed to know what. Dubois reached into his coat, to the specially designed pistol sheath, and drew out the double-barreled pistol set with magical targeting constructs. He loaded the pistol and grabbed his dark lantern. Keeping to the deepening shadows, he made his way to the château.

The front entrance consisted of a set of double doors that must once have been very fine, but which exhibited the same lack of care as the rest of the structure. One of the doors stood ajar.

"You gentlemen entered with impunity," Dubois murmured. "You have no fear of being discovered, for you didn't bother to close the door."

He *did* fear discovery, so he crept around the side of the château to the rear. Here he found the servants' entrance. This door, far less magnificent than the front door, was locked. Dubois numbered lock picking among his many talents and he soon let himself in. He carefully and softly shut the door behind him.

A narrow entryway led to an enormous kitchen on his

right, the pantry on his left, and another locked door farther down the hall. He wondered if that was the infamous wine cellar where the unfortunate man had hanged himself. The entryway was dark. The only light came from windows in the kitchen, and night was falling fast. Dubois stood quite still, held his breath, and listened.

He could hear at least one man tromping about on the upper level. A booming voice, the type that belongs to sailors or military men, said loudly and irritably, "We've searched every room of this bloody house. She's not here. We should return to the *Terrapin* before someone sees the boat and reports us to the authorities."

Dubois was startled. The man was speaking Freyan. Having spent considerable time in the Freyan court, Dubois was fluent in the language. He could not place the voice. The second man answered in a much quieter manner. Dubois could not make out what was said.

The first voice boomed out irascibly, "What the devil are we looking for now? I doubt if you'll find the money you paid her." He gave a rakish laugh.

The other man was silent. Perhaps he was not amused.

The two men started clumping down the stairs. Dubois realized they were descending to the ground floor. He ducked into the pantry. He opened the shutter of his dark lantern, flashed the light about, then slid the panel shut. The pantry was merely a pantry. The shelves were empty, nothing of interest. Dubois left the door open a crack and peered out into the hall.

The footsteps came closer and closer. Dubois saw lights flashing; both men were carrying dark lanterns. He heard them walking through the kitchen and then they appeared in the hallway directly opposite him. Dubois was so astonished he had to choke back an audible gasp.

He was looking right into the face of his old foe, Sir

Henry Wallace. The man with Sir Henry was the pirate, Captain Alan Northrop, one of the most sought-after criminals in Rosia. Both had come expecting trouble. Sir Henry carried a pistol in one hand and the dark lantern in the other. Captain Northrop was holding a pistol and Dubois could see the butt of another pistol tucked into his belt.

Dubois gave an inward sigh of regret. He had spent much of his life pursuing Sir Henry Wallace, hoping to catch the Freyan spymaster on Rosian soil so that he could bring him to justice. Now he had him but he could do nothing. Dubois was far too sensible to think he could try to arrest Wallace and Northrop and survive the encounter. He might, however, learn something of value. He composed himself to listen.

"Here it is," said Sir Henry, walking down the hall, out of Dubois's line of sight. "Behind this door. It was once a wine cellar or so she told me."

"That's where the bastard hanged himself," said Captain Northrop.

He remained standing in the entryway.

Sir Henry chuckled as he fiddled with the lock. "Afraid of ghosts, Alan?"

"It's bad luck to go into a room where a man's killed himself," Alan said. "What did this Eiddwen of yours do in there, anyway?"

Dubois's ears pricked. Eiddwen? Who was Eiddwen? Some relation to the duchess?

"She had turned the cellar into a laboratory. This is where she and her people constructed the green beam weapon. I came here to finalize the plans on the sinking of that cutter. She had demanded more money and after all the money I had already paid her, I wasn't about to give her more without some idea of what she was doing with it. She brought me to this room to show me the green beam cannon, which was almost assembled. It was impressive, as you know. On the basis of that, I gave her the money."

"Do you think she has more weapons like that stashed away down here?"

"Weapons, plans, who knows," said Sir Henry. "We know she's lived here recently. Maybe she left some clue as to where I can find her now."

There was a clicking sound. The door opened with a creaking of rusted hinges. After a moment's silence, Sir Henry said, with a catch in his throat, "God almighty . . ."

"What?" Captain Northrop demanded, raising his pistol. "What is it? A ghost?"

"Not a ghost," Sir Henry replied. "Though I could almost wish it was. Come see for yourself."

Captain Northrop walked with obvious reluctance toward the door to the wine cellar. Dubois lost sight of the two men and he risked opening the door a little wider until he had them in view.

"Good God!" Captain Northrop exclaimed. "Is all that . . ."

"Blood," said Sir Henry. His expression was grim. "The stains are old, but there's no doubt."

"This is a far cry from gun schematics, Henry," said Captain Northrop in a tone of revulsion. "I take it this gore wasn't here when you were here."

"No," said Sir Henry.

"So what happened?"

"Blood magic rites," Sir Henry said. "See the manacles on the walls? That's where she kept her victims chained. In this isolated mansion, down here in the cellar, no one would hear the screams."

"You're certain it was Eiddwen who did this? They said the mansion was owned by some Estaran duchess. Maybe she did it."

"More likely Eiddwen murdered her and stole her identity," said Sir Henry. "Father Jacob told me Eiddwen was involved in blood magic. She worked with that apprentice of hers, the Warlock. Those murders in Capione were his doing and now we know she was involved. Some of those young people probably died right here."

"I've seen men with their heads smashed to a pulp, their guts hanging out, the scuppers running with blood. And I never felt like puking until now," said Captain Northrop. "Let's get out of here."

"This woman has made threats against my family. And I have no idea where she is!" said Sir Henry. "For all I know, she might be sneaking up on my wife right now . . ."

Dubois crept silently into the hallway. Both men had their backs to him. Northrop still held his pistol, but it wasn't cocked. Sir Henry had lowered his gun.

Dubois cocked his own pistol.

At the sound, Captain Northrop swore and raised his gun.

"Don't move!" Dubois ordered. "Drop your weapons. What is the colorful Freyan expression, Sir Henry? 'I have the drop on you.' I could kill you both right now, but I won't. I need information."

Sir Henry and Captain Northrop exchanged glances. There wasn't much they could do. One of them might fire a shot, but Dubois would most certainly kill the other. The two men gently laid their pistols on the floor.

"Now remove the pistol you have in your belt, Captain. And you, Sir Henry, the pocket pistol you carry beneath your coat. Place them on the floor as well."

"Who is this bastard?" Captain Northrop demanded, doing as he was told. "He looks like a bloody clerk."

"His name is Dubois," said Sir Henry. "He works for the grand bishop of Rosia. His looks are deceiving. I consider Dubois my equal."

"You honor me, Sir Henry," said Dubois earnestly, with a little bow. "Keep your hands in the air, please."

"Why are you here, Dubois?" Sir Henry asked.

"The rule is: The person with the gun asks the questions," said Dubois. "This Eiddwen you talked about. What does she look like? Describe her."

Sir Henry shrugged. "She's about thirty-five years of age. Her appearance is quite striking. She has a mane of black hair and dark eyes and a dusky complexion."

"All of which could be disguised with wigs and powder," said Dubois. "Does she have a distinctive physical trait or characteristic?"

"It would help me, Dubois, to know why you want to know," said Sir Henry, starting to grow annoyed. "You heard me say she has made threats against my family—"

Dubois pondered a moment, then said, "The Duquesa de Plata Niebla, the owner of this château, is at this moment in the royal court of Rosia."

Sir Henry cast Dubois a sharp glance.

"The devil she is," he said harshly.

"I don't understand—" Captain Northrop began.

"You will, soon enough," Sir Henry told him. "Is she alone or with someone?"

"She is with her nephew. A young man in his midtwenties, perhaps. He is handsome with a pouting mouth. He walks with a limp."

Sir Henry's brow darkened. "The bastard walks with a limp because I shot off his toe. What does this duquesa look like?"

Dubois described the duchess, adding, "She wears powdered wigs and her face is heavily rouged and powdered. She might as well be wearing a mask. That is why I asked about the physical trait."

Sir Henry thought. "Eiddwen has a chipped tooth."

Dubois sorted through his mental files and brought up several images of the duquesa. "Right incisor. The chip is small, noticeable only when she smiles."

"You see, Alan, I told you Dubois was my equal," said Sir Henry. "Yes, that is Eiddwen. Dubois, you and I need to have a serious talk and I find that difficult to do when the blood is draining from my arms. If you will allow us to lower our hands . . ."

"Kick your pistols toward me," said Dubois.

Both men did as they were told. One after another, the pistols slid across the floor toward Dubois. He gathered them up and placed them in the pantry behind him, all the while keeping his own pistol trained on the two men.

"Very well, Sir Henry, I am all attention," said Dubois.

"You are aware that I have no love for King Alaric. If I thought Eiddwen was in the royal palace merely to kill Alaric, I wouldn't lift a finger to stop her. But I believe she is plotting something far more terrible, something that will have dire consequences not only for Rosia, but for Freya and the rest of the world, as well. You are familiar with Father Jacob Northrop?"

"I am," said Dubois. He glanced at the captain. "I believe he is your brother, monsieur?"

Captain Northrop made no response.

"Father Jacob knew Eiddwen as 'the Sorceress,'" said Sir Henry. "*I* knew her as the woman who tricked me into helping her build a contramagic gun. She took the weapon and my money and disappeared. I gave no more thought to her until I discovered she had sent her Bottom Dwellers to kill my wife. Then her Bottom Dwellers ambushed me in West-firth, along with Father Jacob."

"I know this to be the truth," Dubois conceded. "I was in Westfirth at the time of the ambush. I was on your trail at the time. I very nearly caught you."

"You gave me some extremely bad moments, Dubois," Sir Henry admitted. "To continue, a short time ago, I received a note from Father Jacob. He told me everything he had discovered about the Bottom Dwellers, about contramagic, about the weapons they used. I connected this with what I knew about Eiddwen. I will not bore you with details, but we both have come to the same conclusion: Eiddwen is an agent of these Bottom Dwellers. She is skilled in magic, contramagic, and blood magic. She is intelligent, fearless, clever, cunning, cruel, and sadistic. And you say she is in the royal palace."

"If you don't believe Henry, take a look inside that wine cellar," Captain Nothrop added grimly.

Dubois was deeply troubled. He knew Sir Henry Wallace, knew he could lie and lie well when it suited his purpose. Dubois did not think the man was lying now, though.

"And now, what do you intend to do with us, monsieur?" Sir Henry asked. "Since, as you say, you have the drop on us."

"I will let you go," said Dubois.

Captain Northrop started moving in the direction of the pantry to retrieve his guns. Dubois blocked his way.

"I will keep your pistols. A small memento of our meeting."

"The devil take you, monsieur! I'll be damned if I let some weasely clerk—"

Dubois pointed his pistol at the captain's head. "I assure you, Captain, the weasely clerk will shoot you without hesitation."

"Meet me at the griffins, Alan," said Sir Henry. He gripped Captain Northrop by the shoulder and shoved him toward the back door. "I'll buy you more pistols."

"We will meet again, monsieur," Captain Northrop vowed angrily.

He shook off Sir Henry's grip and stalked out the door,

slamming it with such violence that the wood cracked. Sir Henry smiled and shook his head.

"Alan always was a hothead. I have a piece of advice. Return to the palace. Find Eiddwen. And put a bullet in her brain."

Dubois did not relax his guard. He held the pistol on the Freyan spymaster as he walked toward the door.

"A pleasure talking with you, Dubois. Give my regards to the grand bishop."

Sir Henry Wallace walked out. Dubois stepped to the door and watched the two as they made their way by the light of their dark lanterns to where they had left their griffins. He wondered if they might wait to ambush him and decided in the negative. Sir Henry Wallace had been in earnest when he talked about this Eiddwen and the suspicion that she was plotting something world shattering.

The question was: What to do about her? All very well for Henry to talk about assassinating her, but then Dubois would never find out what she was doing in the palace. Were there more like her? Other agents? What was this Warlock doing with her? How was he involved?

"I could take her into custody under the authority of the grand bishop, but Her Majesty the queen would be furious over the arrest of her favorite, as would the king," Dubois said to himself, frowning.

Relations between the king and the grand bishop had been strained of late. With rumors of the Freyan navy heading to Braffa and His Majesty and the grand bishop on opposing sides of the conflict, a quarrel between the two men over this duchess could very well land Rosia in the center of an armed conflict.

He knew that whatever he did, he would have to do it circumspectly. The thought came to him that he could take the Countess de Marjolaine into his confidence. She, too, had suspected there was something not quite right about the Duquesa de Plata Niebla.

Dubois took a fancy to Sir Henry's pocket pistol and tucked it into his coat. He dropped the other weapons into an empty barrel and then, curious, he went to look inside the wine cellar.

He knew what to expect and yet he wasn't prepared for the gruesome sight. Blood had stained the stone floor red. Blood covered the walls, especially in the vicinity of the manacles. The blood had even splashed on the ceiling.

Dubois took one long look, then said a murmured prayer for the souls of the victims and closed the door.

He walked back across the gravel drive to where he had left his horse. He did not use the dark lantern. He relied on the moon to light his way. Although he was fairly certain Sir Henry would not kill him, Dubois thought it best not to offer the Freyan too much in the way of temptation.

Reaching the tree line, Dubois was relieved to find the griffins were gone. He was glad to know he had judged Sir Henry rightly.

Dubois mounted his horse. He took one last look at the château. The building was gray and cold in the moonlight. Dubois rode away, thinking to himself that after all the dreadful deeds that had taken place inside that place, God would be more than justified in burning it to the ground.

Dubois was not an assassin. Unlike Sir Henry, Dubois had never killed anyone. Yet after viewing the wine cellar, he thought that if he should come upon Eiddwen, he might act upon Sir Henry's advice and put a bullet in her brain.

32

Matters have gone from bad to worse in Argonne. The Duke de Bourlet has openly defied the king and gathers an army to defend the duchy. Julian de Guichen has proclaimed his loyalty to the duke. He marches with the armies, as does his young son, Stephano. All know the king has goaded the duke into this fight. He will attack them with the full might of the kingdom and the church. This rebellion is lost before it can ever begin. Perhaps you might still save your friend. Destroy this letter after you read it.

—Grégoire de Villeneuve,
in a letter to his younger brother, Rodrigo,
written at the time of the Lost Rebellion

The Travian merchant ship, the *Sommerwind,* sailed from Evreux, having taken on cargo, passengers, and one new member of the crew. Miri was the new crewmember, replacing the inebriated surgeon. Stephano and Rodrigo paid for their passage and were given the small cabin merchant ships often reserved for passengers. Gythe offered to help with repairing the magical constructs damaged by the contramagic fire and Rodrigo startled everyone by offering to assist her.

"My dear fellow, otherwise I would go out of my head with boredom," said Rodrigo.

Stephano was skeptical. "You are giving up tranquil days spent lounging on deck and basking in the sun. You embrace boredom! Why the change?"

He eyed Rodrigo, who was looking particularly innocent, and lowered his voice to say grimly, "I know the real reason. You're studying contramagic."

"Me? Study?" Rodrigo gave a light, airy laugh and walked off.

The weather was fine when they left Evreux bound for Argonne and remained pleasant throughout the voyage. They saw few other ships sailing the Breath and no sign of the enemy, perhaps due to the increased presence of the Rosian navy patrolling the coastline.

Four days sailing brought them to the port city of Argonne in the duchy of Bourlet. Here the *Sommerwind* was planning to take on additional cargo and supplies for the long journey to Braffa.

The port of Argonne was the last stop for all ships traveling to the eastern nations of Estara and Braffa and the first stop for those ships making the return journey. The docks were usually crowded with ships that sometimes had to wait in line for space, hovering in the Breath until they could enter. The *Sommerwind* arrived to find the wharves almost empty.

The harbormaster, who had sailed out to guide the *Sommerwind* to its berth, explained the situation to the captain in gloomy tones.

"What with the rumors of war with Freya, the Travians threatening to blockade Braffa, and pirate attacks, it is a brave ship's captain that takes to the air these days, Captain Leydecker."

"I've heard the rumors about the blockade. Is the situation

in Braffa really this bad, sir?" Captain Leydecker asked. "Braffa is my next port of call."

"That's the problem, sir, we don't know," said the harbormaster. "Rumors. All we hear are rumors! There was a significant decrease in shipping after the attack on Westfirth, and this business with Braffa is making the situation worse. No captain wants to sail that far only to find he can't deliver his goods.

"Now, mind you, Captain Leydecker," the harbormaster added with a wink, "I do not advocate breaking the law, but a captain who *did* manage to run the blockade would find it well worth his while."

Stephano, loitering on deck, happened to overhear the conversation and smiled. The harbormaster was drumming up business for the Travian cartel. A ship's captain who risked running the blockade and managed to sneak past the warships could name his price when it came to delivering goods.

Stephano leaned on the rail and gazed at the mountains in the distance. His family estate was located in the foothills of those mountains. The Château d'Eau Brisé was named for a series of rapids formed by the confluence of two rivers flowing down out of those mountains. The château was located near the rapids, which were known by the locals as "*d'Eau Brisé*" or Shattered Water.

Stephano had not been to his home in many years, ever since he could no longer afford to live there. The income he received from the tenants who still farmed the land barely paid the taxes. About once a year, Rodrigo would delicately suggest that Stephano sell the estate and Stephano would delicately tell Rodrigo what he could do with that suggestion.

Stephano's plan was to someday restore the family estate to its former glory. He saw himself riding across the fields, meeting with his tenants, greeting guests in his own house, inviting his friends to sit down with him at a great feast. He dreamed of seeing Benoit take his usual place of pride, standing behind the master's chair, pouring the wine, lording it over the other servants. He dreamed of asking the noble dragons and the men who had served with him in the Dragon Brigade to return for a reunion.

His dreams were only dreams, and he had to admit there was not much chance they would ever come true. On this visit, he would have to meet with Dag and the dragons at the château in secret during the night. His mother would have agents watching the house, ready to alert constables armed with warrants to arrest him and Rodrigo. And being arrested was the least of their worries. Someone had hired assassins to kill them and he had no idea who that person was. He trusted he had thrown the assassins off the trail, but he could not risk lowering his guard.

As he stood staring at the mountains, Miri came up to him and slipped her hands around his arm. "Are you happy to be home?"

"Not this way," said Stephano. "Having to sneak into my own house like a thief."

"So what's the plan?" Miri asked.

"I can't make any plans until I find out what Dag has learned about the wild dragons. Captain Leydecker says we're going to be stopping here for a few days. He's waiting for the delivery of some sort of special cargo. You and Gythe and Rigo should go into Argonne, rent rooms—"

"Don't be silly, Stephano," said Miri crisply. "We're coming with you."

"It's not safe—"

"Stephano de Guichen, I've heard you and Benoit talk all these years about your château and I'm not going to miss the chance to finally see it."

Stephano turned his back on the mountains to remonstrate with her.

"Miri, I can't allow you to come. This time I mean it, so don't even bother to argue."

"I don't need to argue," said Miri. "I'm in charge, remember? You will need Gythe's help with the wild dragons. And I need to talk to Dag," she added more somberly. "Make things right between us."

"Miri, listen—"

She raised her hand to cut him off. "Who found the means to escape from Evreux?"

"You did," said Stephano with a smile that ended in a sigh. He turned back to the mountains. "But this isn't the way I wanted to welcome my friends to my house."

"I know," said Miri gently. "I know."

The *Sommerwind* sailed into port. Captain Leydecker and Leutnant Baumann shouted orders. The sailors ran to their tasks with unusual eagerness, looking forward to shore leave. Lines snaked down from the ship to dockworkers who caught them and tied the *Sommerwind* to her moorings. The captain was supervising the helmsman, who had the tricky job of reducing the amount of magical energy arcing through the lift gas, providing just enough to allow the ship to nestle into the berth.

Stephano and Miri went below to tell the others. They entered Stephano's cabin to find Rodrigo tying his cravat in front of a piece of tin he had transformed into a mirror. Gythe sat cross-legged on the bed, teasing Doctor Ellington with a feather.

"What's the plan?" Rodrigo asked.

"Miri and Gythe are coming with us to d'Eau Brisé," said Stephano. "That wasn't my original plan, but Miri has modified it."

"You're still going to find a way for me to see my mother," said Rodrigo.

"I'm sure your house is being watched. We'll have to find a way to smuggle you inside. I hate all this sneaking about!" Stephano said, scowling.

"I'm sorry," said Rodrigo remorsefully. "It's my fault. I should have agreed to smelt."

Stephano shook his head. "Someone tried to kill both of us, remember? After we've dealt with the wild dragons, we'll have to find somewhere to hide, while I try to placate my mother and discover who wants us dead."

"I have a better idea," said Miri. "We have a job offer. Captain Leydecker wants to hire us to sail with him to Braffa. He's been hearing rumors that Travian ships are blockading the refinery ports in order to pressure Estara into giving up her claim to Braffa. He has to deliver this cargo to the refineries, which means he's considering running the blockade."

"I'm confused," said Rodrigo. "The *Sommerwind* is under contract to a Travian cartel. Why would the Travians stop one of their own ships?"

"Captain Leydecker would have make a detour to Travia to obtain permission to deliver his cargo. That would mean bribing the right government officials, obtaining the proper paperwork, all of which could take weeks. Not to mention disclosing the nature of his cargo."

"Do we have any idea what this mysterious cargo is?" Stephano asked.

"None," said Miri. "All I know is that it is to be delivered to one of the Braffan refineries, and he is to pick up an extremely important shipment while he's there."

"This ship isn't a tanker. It's not outfitted to haul the liquid Breath that the Braffans refine. I wonder what's going on."

"Don't you be too inquisitive, Stephano. It's none of our business."

"I know. I'm just curious, that's all."

Stephano came to easy terms with Captain Leydecker. The captain needed Stephano's military expertise in evading the Travian warships and he would be in command of the landing party that delivered the cargo. When Stephano asked offhandedly about the nature of the cargo, the captain shook his head and changed the subject.

That night, as Stephano and Rodrigo were preparing to go ashore, Miri appeared at their door. She came bearing two navy-blue coats with matching trousers.

"Officers' uniforms. From the captain. He said you might find them useful."

"For what?" Rodrigo asked with a glance and a shudder. "A bonfire to keep us warm during the long winter nights?"

"For disguise, fool," Miri told him.

Captain Leydecker had learned something of their situation from Miri, who had explained that the Countess de Marjolaine, Stephano's mother, was angry with her son and seeking to have him arrested. Familiar with the countess's reputation, the captain understood.

"I wouldn't be caught dead—" Rodrigo stopped. "Oh no, Stephano, you will not make me dress up in that ridiculous outfit—"

"The uniforms are perfect," Stephano exclaimed. "The police have descriptions of two Rosian gentlemen. They won't be looking for two Guundaran ship's officers."

Rodrigo eyed the uniform, which consisted of a long coat of royal blue, trimmed in lighter blue with brass buttons. Along with the coat was a white shirt with a white weskit, royal-blue breeches, and a blue tricorn hat.

"The sleeves need to shortened and a nip taken in here at

the waist. I know a tailor who could transform this into something wearable."

"I hear smelters wear leather aprons," said Miri.

Rodrigo sighed deeply and put on the uniform.

They stayed the night in an inn and the next day, using some of the money Rodrigo had rescued when they fled the house, Stephano purchased new dresses for Miri and Gythe that would befit passengers on board a merchantman. In their finery, the four walked right past a constable, who tipped his hat to the ship's officers and their ladies.

Stephano hired a closed, wyvern-drawn carriage to take them to his château. He chose to drive the carriage himself, sitting on the box in the front.

"Want one of us to keep you company?" Rodrigo asked.

Stephano shook his head. He would have to survive the flood of memories. He needed to be alone.

He could not count the number of times he had flown this route on dragonback with his father. When he was little, his father would set him in front on the dragon saddle. As he grew older, Stephano had ridden his own dragon. The two had flown side by side, laughing, talking, jesting with other dragon comrades, who often accompanied them, flying down from their fortress located in the mountains near the château.

Those dragons had departed when the duke and his followers had rebelled against the king. Many of the dragons had gone reluctantly. They had believed in the duke's cause and had wanted to stay and fight. The Supreme Gathering of Dragons, made up of the heads of the noble dragon families, had decreed that the dragons would not take sides in the conflict. They ordered the dragons who served with Julian in the Dragon Brigade to return to their homes in the dragon duchies.

Years later Stephano had encountered some of those dragons when he had joined the Brigade. They had been embarrassed to face him, but Stephano had earnestly assured them that he understood, and bore them no ill will. He had served with them in the Brigade, he had been their commander. He had chosen never to ride any of them, however.

As it turned out, the memories were not as painful as he had expected. Only one battle had been fought in this part of Bourlet. He flew over the site and saw cows grazing on the battlefield. The scars of war were no longer visible, covered now by grass and clover.

As the carriage sailed over the confluence of the two rivers, he smiled to hear the exclamations of awe and wonder from Miri, who had never seen such a magnificent sight. Leaving the river behind, he flew low over Rodrigo's family estate. Rodrigo leaned out the window, looking down yearningly at the house and grounds.

Stephano hailed his friend and pointed. Two constables could be seen strolling openly along the long driveway. The constables craned their necks to peer up at the carriage.

Rodrigo hurriedly ducked back inside and shut the window.

Stephano guessed that constables would be waiting at his house as well. He had written Dag a note before they left Evreux, apprising him of the situation, and another brief note when they arrived in Argonne, telling him they would meet after dark. He landed the carriage a couple of miles from the house in an open field that had been a dragon training ground.

They arrived in the late afternoon. Stephano stabled the wyvern and the carriage inside a building used by his father to store dragon saddles and harnesses. The carriage came with a hobble for the wyvern—a heavy weight that Stephano chained to the wyvern's hind leg. He had bought a haunch of deer meat before they left. Gythe, who was fond of animals, even the bad-tempered wyverns, fed the wyvern and saw to it that the beast was comfortably settled.

Stephano took a moment to look out over the training field, nothing more than a vast expanse of dirt. The grass had been worn away years ago by dragons and their riders practicing their takeoffs and landings. Stephano could see his father in his shirt and breeches and boots walking with his wide stride over the field, waving off a dragon who was coming in too fast or working with exemplary patience to make a new recruit understand what was expected of him.

The sight of three hayricks, spaced far apart, stacked up in the center of the field, brought Stephano up short. He was wondering who had built them and why when Rodrigo called his attention to five dragons, flying from the direction of the mountains.

Stephano recognized sergeants Hroal and Droal and the three wild dragons, Verdi, Petard, and Viola. The five were flying in formation, with Sergeant Droal in the lead.

Stephano took off his hat and waved as the dragons circled overhead. Sergeant Droal dipped his wings and bellowed a greeting.

"Welcome home, sir! Watch this."

The other brother, Hroal, landed on the ground at the end of the training field and gave an order.

"Ground attack!"

Petard circled the field, then dove down on the first hayrick, setting it ablaze with his fiery breath. Viola came next. She skimmed the ground, set her hayrick on fire, and flew off. The third dragon, Verdi, flew too low and crashed into his target, demolishing the hayrick and nearly demolishing himself. He managed to pull out of the dive at the last

moment, flying upward with bits of straw and wood clinging
to him, much to the merriment of his companions who hooted
and jeered. Sergeant Droal was on the three in an instant,
roaring at them to maintain order.

"Well done!" Stephano called out. He was close to tears.
He thought of the constables who might be watching.

"You best leave now," Stephano shouted. "There's been
some trouble—"

"Heard, sir," said Droal. "They wanted to show you."

He indicated the three young dragons.

"Wanted to make you proud."

Sergeant Droal saluted with another dip of his wings. The
dragons flew back toward the mountains.

Stephano turned to Gythe, who was laughing and clapping her hands.

"Our work paid off," he said to her.

She grinned and threw her arms around him.

Miri only shook her head.

"So what are you going to do with three young dragons?"
she asked.

"I have no idea," said Stephano.

"You never plan ahead," Miri said with a sigh, falling into
step beside him.

"Maybe that's because whenever I do make a plan, we
end up marooned on an island or someone tries to kill us or
my mother wants to throw Rigo in prison," Stephano returned
with a smile. "So I say, what's the use?"

The weather was fine for a walk, cooler in the countryside than in the city, with a breeze blowing down from the
mountains. They could not see the château, for it was hidden by trees. A lane lined with the famous pines of Bourlet
led from the training ground to the main dwelling. The air
sparkled with the pleasantly sharp scent of pine needles.

Assailed by memories at every turn, Stephano was glad

to have the chance to work off his emotion with physical activity. He kept a worried eye on Rodrigo, who was unusually quiet. The sight of his home had affected him deeply. Gythe's face was soft with sympathy. Miri would glance at both Stephano and Rodrigo every so often and give them a warm smile. Doctor Ellington enlivened the walk by attempting several times to escape from his basket.

They arrived at the château just as the light was starting to fail, as Stephano had planned. The lane split, one road going to the back of the property, the other to the front drive.

"I told Dag we'd meet him in the back," said Stephano.

The lane wound around a small, stream-fed lake where Stephano had often gone swimming and fishing as a boy, and ended in the stable yard. Stephano stopped on the shore of the lake. From here, he could see his house.

The château was modest, constructed of gray stone with two towers, one at each end, connected by the main part of the dwelling. The house had three levels and contained eight bedrooms and servants' quarters. Outbuildings consisted of a small guesthouse, a long house, a chapel, and a barn.

He could see the outbuildings from the lane and he could tell even at this distance that they were in a state of disrepair. The barn bore a gaping hole in the roof, and one of the windows in the chapel was broken, which meant there would be water damage inside. The roof of the long house—a structure used for storing dragon-riding equipment—was starting to sag in the middle. The gardens that had been Benoit's pride were overgrown with weeds and grass. The hedges that Benoit had kept clipped were now ragged.

"Your home is beautiful," said Miri.

"It used to be," said Stephano in husky tones.

"It's beautiful," Miri repeated, clasping his hand.

He smiled, not trusting himself to speak.

Night had fallen so gently none of them had really noticed

it. A light shone in one window on the ground level of the château.

"That's the kitchen," said Stephano. "You and Gythe go around to the back of the house, Dag will be waiting for you. He'll let you know what's going on. Rigo and I will wait here. If the coast is clear, put a candle in the window. You have your story in case the constables are there?"

"We were traveling to Argonne on the main road. We stopped for a picnic luncheon and we didn't tie the horse up properly," Miri recited. "The horse ran away and took the carriage with him. We'll be fine, Stephano. Stop fretting."

She and Gythe adjusted their bonnets and set out, taking Doctor Ellington, who was still confined to the basket and letting them know he wasn't happy. Stephano went to sit on a low retaining wall. Rodrigo joined him, first brushing off the wall with his hand, then spreading out a handkerchief so as not to dirty his trousers.

The two sat in silence. Stephano kicked his boots against the wall until he remembered how Benoit had always scolded him for scuffing the heels. He got down off the wall and began to pace restlessly.

"This brings back a lot of memories," said Rodrigo.

"Too many," said Stephano harshly. "I'm sorry I came."

The night deepened. A nightingale whistled cheerfully from a tree, starting his song when the other birds had ended theirs for the day.

"Miri and Gythe have been gone a long time, don't you think," Stephano said. "Something's wrong . . ."

A light flared in the window. Miri moved the candle back and forth.

"That's our signal," Stephano said.

"Should I light the lantern?" Rodrigo asked.

"Don't risk it," said Stephano. "Stay close to me."

He knew every bit of this land, every rock, every hedge,

every ditch. Reaching the back of the house, they went around to a door set below ground level. A small flight of stairs led down to it.

"This door leads to the kitchen," said Rodrigo. "Do you remember the time we stole the mincemeat pie? We were escaping out this very door when Cook caught us and chased us with a ladle, thumping any part of us she could reach. My ears rang for days. I haven't eaten a mincemeat pie since."

Stephano cautiously opened the door and looked inside.

Dag sat at the table petting Doctor Ellington, who was once more at home on his shoulder. The cat's purrs resounded through the room. Miri was lighting a fire in the enormous kitchen fireplace. Gythe was chopping up carrots and throwing them into an iron pot. No one else was in sight.

Stephano gave a relieved sigh, opened the door wide, and walked inside.

Dag rose immediately to his feet, disturbing Doctor Ellington, who jumped onto the counter and went to see what Gythe was doing.

"Good to see you, sir!" Dag said heartily.

He and Stephano shook hands. Dag laughed at Rodrigo in his uniform.

"What's the matter?" Rodrigo demanded, offended. "I think I look quite nautical."

"That's one word for it," said Dag, winking at Stephano.

"Have the constables been here?" Stephano asked.

"As a matter of fact, they're here now," said Dag. "I told them to wait in the dining hall."

"Dag, what the hell—"

"If you'll come with me, sir," said Dag coolly. "You, too, Rigo. You don't have much choice. They know you're here."

Stephano put his hand on his pistol.

"They only want to talk, sir," said Dag. "No need for your gun."

Miri rose from lighting the fire, wiping her hands on her apron. Gythe put down the knife. She picked up the Doctor and held him close. Both women were grave, solemn.

They walked down the familiar corridor that led to the dining hall. Stephano had no idea what was going on. Despite Dag's reassurances, he kept his hand on the pistol in his pocket. Rodrigo followed slowly and reluctantly. The door at the end was closed. Dag opened the door and then stood aside.

"You go first, sir."

Stephano halted. "Tell me what's going on."

"You'll find out, sir," said Dag.

Stephano glanced back at Rodrigo, who gave an unhappy shrug. Drawing in a breath, Stephano walked through the door and into the vast hall with the high-beamed ceiling. He stopped, stared.

The hall was filled with men, some of them standing, some seated around the enormous oaken table that dated back to the time of his great-great-grandfather. The men were grinning, nudging each other with their elbows. A man wearing a constable's uniform left the group and came striding toward them. The constable stopped, clicked his heels, and saluted.

"Captain de Guichen," he said formally.

"Lucielle, isn't it?" Stephano said, recognizing the man. "Francois Lucielle?"

"*Chief Constable* Francois Lucielle," the man said proudly. "I have a warrant for your arrest, Captain. Signed and sealed by His Majesty."

Constable Lucielle grinned. "And I'd like to see the man in Bourlet who would serve it on you, Captain!"

The men at the table laughed and cheered.

"I don't understand," said Stephano, bewildered.

"We stood with you against the king then, Captain, and

we stand with you now!" said the constable. "Welcome home, sir. Welcome home to you, Master Rodrigo!"

The men in the room raised their voices in welcome, then quieted as an elderly man with gray, grizzled hair and beard stepped forward. Stephano recognized one of his tenants, a farmer named Lebrett. Lebrett had always been a leader in the neighborhood and now he had been elected spokesman, apparently. He doffed his hat and cleared his throat.

"We are glad to have you back among us, Captain. Home where you belong."

Someone raised his voice in a huzzah and the rest joined in. Farmer Lebrett insisted on shaking Stephano's hand and the rest of the men crowded around him and the amazed Rodrigo. Stephano recognized tenants, neighbors, local shopkeepers, the blacksmith, a former stable hand, and the gardener. The women came into the room bringing their children, who gazed in awe at this man who rode on the backs of dragons. The elderly cook who had chased them with the ladle now threw her arms around them both and burst into tears.

Farmer Lebrett called for a speech. Everyone fell silent, looking expectantly at Stephano. He gazed around at them, his heart full.

"Life has been hard for you," he said. "The king punished you for siding with my family and the duke. He ordered his troops to burn homes and crops, steal your horses and slaughter your cattle. Many of the men in this room were arrested on suspicion of aiding the duke's cause."

His neighbors nodded, remembering. Stephano remembered, too. After his father's death, Stephano had struggled to maintain the land and buildings himself, with only Benoit to help. Stephano was seventeen, too proud to ask for assistance. Debts piled up. He was forced to sell everything of value and even that was not enough.

"All these years, I thought you blamed my family for your hardship," he continued after a pause to clear his throat.

"Not so, Captain!" someone called out.

"Say the word," said another, "and I'll go to war with you again!"

"You will not, you daft old man," said his wife, and the speech ended in laughter.

"I wish I could invite you to feast with me as my father used to do," Stephano said. "We have no provisions—"

"Never mind that, Captain," said Farmer Lebrett. "We brought the feast to you."

The women carried in baskets of bread and fruit and trays laden with roast beef. Two men wheeled in a huge round of cheese and hefted it on the table. Two other men rolled in a barrel of beer. Stephano turned to Dag, who had been watching this and grinning hugely. Miri and Gythe were by his side, wiping away tears.

"Dag," said Stephano, "I can't thank you enough—"

"Wasn't any of my doing, sir," Dag said. "Your neighbors planned all of this. You're a hero, sir, as well you should be."

Rodrigo was talking to the chief constable. He came back, his face glowing with excitement. "That excellent, wonderful man tells me it is safe to go home. Those constables we saw are there to *keep* me from being arrested."

Stephano smiled. "That's good news. Bear in mind that someone sent assassins after us."

"I'll ride with him, sir," Dag offered. "See to it he gets home safely."

"Give your mother my love," said Stephano, embracing his friend. "And do *not* visit your tailor! That's the first place anyone who knows you would come looking for you. Dag, keep an eye out."

With Dag as escort, Rodrigo departed, too happy to even mind—much—about the tailor.

When the feast was ended and the last neighbor took his leave, somewhat the worse for beer, Miri and Gythe retired to the guesthouse, saying they would clean up in the morning. Dag had not yet returned. Stephano was alone in the château. Taking the lantern, he went from room to room, opening them up, walking through them.

Most rooms were empty. He'd been forced to sell much of the furniture to pay the bills. All that was left were the articles that had been too heavy to move, such as the oaken table downstairs. The walls were bare. Benoit had removed the family paintings, wrapped them in cloth, and stored them away for safekeeping.

He wandered into the library, his father's favorite room. Julian had not owned many books. Those he did own he had loved. Stephano had taken some of his favorites with him when he moved. All that remained were a few books on dragon lore. Brushing off the dust, he set them on the desk. Miri would be interested in those.

He roamed about the room and almost fell over a painting shrouded in cloth that had been placed up against a wall. He wondered why Benoit had left this here instead of storing it with the others.

Curious, Stephano uncovered it. The painting was the portrait of his father that had always occupied a place of honor in the library. The portrait, a gift from the duke, had been painted by a famous artist. Stephano held the lantern close so that the light shone on his father's face.

Julian de Guichen was wearing the uniform of a knight of the Dragon Brigade. He had been twenty-five at the time, looking forward to a future filled with hope and promise. The portrait was an excellent likeness.

Stephano knew why Benoit had not taken it to storage. His father belonged here, in the room he had loved. Stephano covered the painting and walked through the rest of the house. The memory of his father walked with him and, thanks to his friends and his neighbors, the memory was no longer fraught with pain. His father's voice and his laughter filled every room.

Stephano went last to his bedroom. His bed was still there. The old, carved oak frame with its bedpost and canopy was so heavy that only a dragon could have shifted it. He remembered as a little child his father coming to check on him every night, standing by the side of his bed and gently stroking his hair. Stephano remembered lying in this bed the night after his father's execution, giving in to the grief he had proudly kept hidden, sobbing until he had no tears left and his sobs were dry and burning.

Stephano touched the pillow, where he fancied he could still see the indent of his head. He smoothed the pillow and said a silent prayer for that boy and for his father, then left and closed the door. Stephano made himself a bed in the kitchen in front of the fire. Wrapping himself in his cloak, he gazed into the flames a long time. When he finally fell asleep, he had the dreamlike impression that he felt his father's hand stroking his hair.

33

*For many years, we dragons have met our human
bretheren at the location in the human duchy of
Bourlet known as Shattered Water to train in the art
of war. There dragons and riders practice together
until we become a single well-honed weapon. We
once served our king and country with honor and
pride. Today, though the training fields lie fallow, we
dragons remember and honor the name de Guichen.*

—Count Orgbrindle,
clan Greashear

Stephano was rudely wakened in the morning by a heavy cat
landing squarely on his chest. He opened his eyes to find
Gythe and Miri standing over him, smiling.

"Good morning, Doctor," Stephano said, yawning. "Oh,
no, you don't!"

Doctor Ellington had curled up on Stephano's chest,
ready to settle down for the remainder of the day. Stephano
removed the Doctor, who considered being offended, then
saw a hole in the wall surrounded by mouse droppings. The
cat went to investigate.

"Dag is back from Rodrigo's," Miri reported. She walked
to the counter and started unloading eggs from a basket—a

gift from a neighbor. "He says everything is fine. No one followed them. Gythe is wild to go visit the dragons. She wanted to wake you up before dawn, but I made her let you sleep."

"Thanks." Stephano yawned again and stretched.

"I talked to Dag," said Miri.

"I'm glad," said Stephano lamely.

He picked up his blanket, started to toss it over the back of a chair, caught Miri's eye, and folded it neatly.

"I said I was sorry. Dag said he was sorry. Not much more to say after that." Miri began cracking eggs into a bowl.

"I guess there wouldn't be," said Stephano.

He was uncomfortable with this conversation. Rodrigo was so much better at these things. He pulled on his shirt and began to put on his boots.

"You're the only man I ever truly loved, Stephano," Miri said in matter-of-fact tones.

Stephano stopped with his boot in his hand to stare at her in consternation.

Glancing at him over her shoulder, Miri began to laugh. "You look as though I just threw a bomb at you. Don't worry, It won't go off. It was something I realized last night, that's all. You're safe."

Stephano pulled his boot on. He could feel his face burn. "I . . . I think I'll go for a swim."

"Breakfast will be ready when you get back," Miri told him cheerfully.

After breakfast, Dag, Gythe, and Stephano decided to visit the dragons. Miri stayed behind, planning to spend the day in the library, studying the books on dragon lore.

Dag and Stephano walked across the lawn to the old training grounds with Gythe, skipping and dancing ahead of them. She had no harp, for she had left the instrument on the *Cloud Hopper,* but she sang the songs she had sung for the dragons and twirled among the grass and the weeds and the wildflowers.

Stephano was tempted to join her. His dark mood had lifted. He was glad he had come home. He had vowed in the night he would find a way to restore his family's honor, repair and rebuild his lands, and work with his tenants. He would become a good and true lord. He didn't know how, yet, but he would find a way.

He listened with interest to Dag's enthusiastic account of riding a dragon. Stephano had heard it all before—every time a dragon rider came back from his first flight. He never tired of listening, experiencing his own thrill again and again.

"The wonderful quiet!" Dag said, awed. "As though you've left the world of the living far below. I swear to you, sir, I came closer to God in those moments than ever in my life. It was as though He held me in His hand and carried me above the fields and over the valleys. I saw the sun shining like molten gold on a lake; puffy clouds that seemed as though I could sleep on them; a storm in the distance, the lightning forking across the sky."

"You've seen all that from the *Cloud Hopper*," said Stephano, amused.

"It's not the same, sir," Dag said earnestly. "Not the same at all. When I'm on the boat, I'm standing on the deck. When I'm with Verdi, I'm flying! I'm flying like the dragon is flying. We're a team. Verdi knows what I'm thinking and I know what he's thinking. I hope they'll stay, sir," he added wistfully.

"Do you have any idea why they followed us?" Stephano asked. "I assume Hroal and Droal have talked to them."

"They did, sir. They wouldn't tell me. They said they wanted to talk to you first."

The three young dragons were waiting for them in the

field, as were Hroal and Droal, former sergeants in the Dragon Brigade, now retired. Gythe would have run to greet the young dragons. Stephano restrained her. He could see they were ill-at-ease, nervous. Viola fluttered her wings. Petard churned up the ground with his claws. Verdi, his eyes on Dag, was switching his tail slowly back and forth.

"They're upset about something," Stephano told Gythe. "We should find out what's going on first."

Gythe didn't answer. She was helping Dag deal with the irate cat, who had been riding on Dag's shoulder. At the sight of the dragons, the Doctor ruffled his fur, dug in his claws, and flattened his ears. Gythe tried to pry the cat loose, a task she finally accomplished after a good deal of hissing and spitting. The Doctor gave the dragons a final snarl, just to let them know he wasn't afraid, then stalked off with dignity.

Gythe sucked at the scratches on her hand, while Stephano walked forward to meet with the sergeants. The two dipped their heads in respect, flicked salutes with their wings and thumped their tails on the ground to express pleasure.

"Good to see you, sir," said Droal, "back in the old place."

"Good, sir, very good," said Hroal. "Belong here."

"Thank you both," said Stephano. "And thank you for your care of the wild dragons. I am glad to find out you have been training them."

"Asked us to train them, sir," said Droal.

"The wild dragons asked you?" Stephano was astonished.

"Want to fly with you," said Hroal.

Stephano was pleased, but perplexed.

"I was hoping when we first encountered these dragons that they might want to learn to carry human riders. I told them stories about the Brigade, but I wasn't sure they understood."

"They did, sir. Elders still remember humans. Told stories to the young. Not good, some of the stories." Droal shook his head.

"Bitter," Hroal added sadly. "Don't trust humans."

"I guessed as much," said Stephano. "That's why they were afraid of us. But if that is true, why did the elders teach their young the human language? And why did the elders permit the young dragons to come after us?"

Hroal and Droal glanced at each other. Hroal nodded to his brother, indicating Droal was to speak. Stephano noticed with concern that Hroal still appeared to be recovering from his wounds. He settled comfortably on the ground, leaving his brother to explain.

"Elders don't know the young ones left," said Droal.

"Good God, sir!" Dag exclaimed. "They ran away from home!"

"Dragon Brigade," said Droal by way of explanation. "Heard the stories. Adventure. Glory."

Dag was grinning at Stephano. "Here's your chance, sir! Our own Dragon Brigade."

"What should I tell them?" Droal asked.

Stephano had secretly nursed a hope that this was the reason the wild dragons had followed him. He hadn't let himself believe it, hadn't wanted to be disappointed. He had imagined himself flying again so many times. The ground below, the dragon's wings shredding the mists of the Breath . . . He could offer to escort the *Sommerwind* . . .

Gythe punched him in the arm. "Miri," she signed. "She needs to know. Now."

Stephano came back out of the clouds.

"You're right. I have to talk to Miri before I decide. I'll go alone. You and Gythe wait here."

"Good luck," Gythe signed.

"Thanks," Stephano said, sighing. "I'll need it."

He walked back to the château and sought out Miri in the library, where she was happily engrossed in reading one of his father's books. She was so deep in her studies that she didn't hear him enter.

He stood looking at her for long moments. He had been thinking about the wild dragons, making plans. He had to try to make her understand.

He braced himself. "Miri, we need to talk. I know about the wild dragons, why they're here, what they want."

"Good! Tell me," said Miri.

She closed the book, sat back in the chair, and smiled at him.

Stephano removed a sheet from one of the other chairs, raising a cloud of dust. He paused a moment to sneeze, then sat down. The beginning was the easy part. The hard part would come at the end.

Stephano ran his hand through his hair, embarrassed. "The young dragons have been training with Droal and Hroal. They claim they left without permission from the elders."

"You don't believe that?"

"I don't know what to believe." Stephano remembered the elder dragon, circling their boat the night they left.

"Then send them back," said Miri.

"I don't think they'll go. They want to stay with us," he said, avoiding her gaze.

"You have your heart set on flying again." Miri sighed. "I knew the moment I set eyes on those dragons that you would be back up in the clouds."

Stephano stood up, took hold of her hands, and held her fast when she tried to pull away. "I need you to understand. The joy you feel at the helm of the *Cloud Hopper,* riding the storm wind, that's the joy I feel when I'm flying. I've ridden dragons since before I could walk. They are my life, Miri, as sailing your boat is yours."

She looked up at him, then gave a grudging smile. Slowly she drew her hands away. He let her go.

"What are you going to do about Captain Leydecker?" she asked briskly. "You promised you would sail with him."

"I was thinking he might like having dragon riders protect his ship," said Stephano.

"Dragon *riders,*" said Miri, emphasizing the plural. "You mean you and Dag and Gythe. She'll want to fly. She's talked of nothing else . . ."

"Come see the dragons for yourself," Stephano urged. "How much they've learned. Gythe asked me to bring you."

"You trust these beasts, even though you don't know why they're here."

"We all have secrets," said Stephano, his eyes fixed on her.

Miri blushed deeply and said nothing.

She and Stephano reached the practice field to find only Hroal and Droal. Stephano glanced around.

"Where are the wild dragons?"

"Up there, sir," said Droal.

Dag and Verdi were flying far above them. Dag had rummaged about the estate during his time here and found the dragon-riding equipment in the storehouse. Verdi was now outfitted with a saddle, Droal having explained to both Dag and Verdi how to strap it onto the dragon. Catching sight of Miri below, Dag and Verdi did a rolling maneuver in midair; the straps in the saddle holding Dag secure as the dragon flipped upside down.

Stephano was proud of his pupil, though he did wish Dag had chosen a more propitious time to show off his skills. Miri was clutching his arm so tightly she seemed likely to cut off the circulation.

Gythe was riding Petard. Stephano had hoped Gythe would choose the steadier, more stable dragon, Viola, but Petard was obviously enamored of Gythe, and she clearly loved the young dragon. In the end, the two had chosen each other. Stephano was actually glad he was left with Viola, the natural leader. The two of them would make a good team.

The dragons had now begun to practice landings. Dag and Verdi were the worst at landing that Stephano had ever seen and he had small hope they would improve. To see Verdi hit with such force Stephano figured Dag would be lucky if he had a tooth left in his head.

Gythe and Petard landed next. Petard flew in at exactly the right speed, dropping down as lightly as an autumn leaf spiraling to the ground. Gythe unhooked the straps that held her in the saddle, took off the helm, and climbed down from the dragon. She gave Petard a pat on the neck, which obviously pleased the dragon, then ran to her sister.

Gythe's pale hair streamed behind her and her blue eyes shone. She was laughing and breathless. Her body quivered with excitement.

Miri watched her and couldn't help but smile, even as she sighed. "What have you done, Stephano?"

"Gythe has always lived in the shadow of your protection, Miri. Let her feel the sunshine."

Miri held her arms wide. Gythe ran to her sister's embrace and the two hugged and wept. Dag joined them, covered in dirt and bleeding from where he'd bitten his tongue.

"Did you see that barrel roll, sir?" he asked proudly.

"I did," said Stephano. "I saw the landing, too."

"We were a little rough," Dag conceded, spitting blood. "Can't quite seem to get the hang of that. We'll keep working on it, though."

Gythe kissed Miri and then ran back to Petard to remove the heavy saddle. She refused to allow anyone to help her, insisting that she must learn to do this herself.

"Stop it, Stephano," Miri said.

"Stop what?" he asked.

"Grinning like you've caught a glimpse of heaven."

Her voice trembled as she spoke. Stephano put his arm around her.

"Don't be mad if I say I did, Miri. To see dragons flying above my house again; to fly with my friends . . ."

"You're going to get yourelves killed," Miri said.

"Miri . . ."

"I know, I know." She turned to him, clasped both his hands in hers. "Promise me you will look after them, Stephano. The three people I love best in the world are in your care."

"I do promise, Miri, with all my heart."

Stephano drew her close. She gazed up at him and seemed to relax in his arms. He was overcome with love and tenderness and he bent to kiss her.

Miri hurriedly averted her face and pulled away.

"Don't, Stephano, please," she said in a low voice.

Stephano saw Dag watching and thought he understood.

"And take comfort from this, Miri," Stephano said teasingly, "if anything happens to us, you'll always have Rodrigo."

He fled before Miri could hit him.

The training continued for several more days as they waited to hear word from the captain of the *Sommerwind* that they were ready to sail. Rummaging about in the cellar, Stephano discovered some old Dragon Brigade flight coats. He couldn't find one large enough to fit Dag, so Miri managed to cobble one together, cutting a coat apart and sewing in gussets to expand it. A training coat that had belonged to Stephano as a boy fitted Gythe. She was so charmed with it, she insisted on wearing it all day and would have slept in it if Miri had permitted.

Stephano worked his pupils—all of them, dragons and

humans alike—hard. He taught the riders how to rappel from a hovering dragon, and instructed dragons and riders in the use of the bosun's pipe, teaching them to communicate by means of various calls. The dragons, with their excellent hearing, could detect the high-pitched whistles over long distances. The use of the bosun's pipe, which could be worn around the rider's neck, was far quicker and more effective in battle than shouted voice commands.

Stephano demonstrated to Dag how to load and fire weapons when riding on the back of a dragon. He did not teach Gythe to use weapons because he knew Miri would be opposed; this was a line he could not cross.

Stephano would not have taught Gythe to use weapons anyway. For Gythe, riding the dragon was like singing her songs, playing her harp, working her magic. She found wondrous pleasure in flying, and he was not about to sully her joy by teaching her how to kill.

Stephano and Sergeant Droal took Petard aside one day to counsel the young dragon on taking extra care to protect his rider. Stephano was glad to see the dragon, who tended to be a little feckless, settle down and appear to take their concerns seriously.

"Above all, Petard," said Stephano earnestly, "if there's any fighting, you need to fly Gythe to safety. Never mind what she says. Those are *my* orders."

Stephano practiced flying with Viola and found that, just as he had hoped, the dragon was quick and eager to learn. With some jealousy she had been watching her two comrades work with their riders, and she was glad to show off her own skills. Stephano was pleased and told her they would make a good team.

Viola said something to Sergeant Droal, who translated. "Call her 'Lady Viola.'"

"What?" Stephano was startled. "Why?"

"Your stories. Lady Cam. Partner. Friend. Same." Droal shook his head sadly. "Wild dragons. Know nothing. Noble. Common. All the same to them. Savages."

He went on to explain that wild dragons had their own hierarchy, which was very simple. The elder dragons wielded the authority in the clans. Other than that, all the dragons held equal status. This was quite different from the class-conscious civilized dragons, who lived and died by titles and rank. Sergeant Droal had tried to explain the concept of dukes and duchesses, counts and princes of dragonkind and why noble dragons considered themselves better than the common dragons such as himself and his brother. The wild dragons had been extremely confused.

Stephano decided that if Viola wanted to be called lady, he would do so, and gladly. He had a feeling that he and Viola were going to form a bond almost as close as the one that had existed between himself and Lady Cam.

He was coming off the field after practice, hot and sweaty, dirty and happy, when Sergeant Droal called out that he and his brother would like to speak to him. He saw at once that something was wrong. The two brothers had always treated the lord captain with the utmost respect and deference. Now they both appeared very uncomfortable as they approached him. Hroal looked at Droal and jerked his head, urging his brother to speak.

"Come out with it, Sergeant," Stephano said at last, addressing Droal. "What's on your mind?"

"Practice gone well, sir," said Sergeant Droal.

"Yes, I think it has," said Stephano. "I'd like another six months or so, but that's not going to happen."

"No, sir," said Droal. He and Hroal looked at each other again.

"If that's all, sergeants—"

"Secrets, sir," said Droal abruptly.

"You need to be more specific," said Stephano.

"Young ones," said Hroal. "Secrets."

"Saw them. Heads together," said Droal. "Talking. I come up. Quit talking. Look furtive."

Stephano frowned. "Did you manage to overhear anything they were saying?"

"Heard them say '*raeg* men.'"

"'*Raeg* men,'" Stephano repeated, puzzled. "What does '*raeg*' mean?"

"Opposite of *roed*," said Hroal.

"And what does that mean?"

"Us. Our being. *Roed* and *raeg*."

"I'm sorry, but I don't understand," said Stephano.

"Those you call 'bat riders,' *raeg* men," said Droal.

"They were talking about the bat riders? Why would they be secretive about that?"

The dragons had no answer.

"Just thought you should know, sir," said Droal.

He saluted and the two dragons took to the air, leaving Stephano to ponder what they'd told him. He had already guessed the young dragons were keeping secrets from him. He wasn't surprised, nor was he particularly worried. Dragons tended to be private regarding their own affairs. Lady Cam and Stephano had been together a long time before she shared personal thoughts and fears. It was natural the young dragons should have secrets.

Yet, he was trusting his life to them, trusting the lives of his friends . . .

A shadow washed over him. He looked up to see Viola flying above. The dragon circled him several times. Her purple scales shimmered in the sunlight, some taking on a blue tint, others flaring red. He admired her, thought how beautiful she was; how beautiful and how wild. She was different from the noble dragons he had known. Smaller, sleeker, faster, she was quicker to think and react. She dipped her wings and flew off.

Stephano returned to the château to talk to Dag, found him taking a swim in the lake. Stephano stripped off his clothes and joined him. When the two were toweling themselves dry, Stephano related the conversation between himself, Droal, and Hroal.

"I trust Verdi, sir," said Dag stoutly. "I've served with a lot of men and I'm a fair judge of character. I trust that dragon with my life."

"Even though they're keeping secrets from us," said Stephano, running his fingers through his wet hair by way of a comb.

"You and I have secrets, sir," said Dag, shrugging. "We trust each other."

Stephano sought out Gythe and found her in the music room. She'd discovered the clavichord that had belonged to Stephano's grandmother. The instrument had been badly out of tune. Gythe had tuned it herself, saying it was much like tuning her harp, and was picking out one of the Trundler songs.

"I need to talk to you, Gythe, about the wild dragons. I need your opinion."

He told her about his conversation with the sergeants, his own misgivings. Gythe listened attentively.

"What do you think we should do?"

Gythe smiled and then simply lifted her arms as if she were flying. Considering the matter settled, she went back to her music.

Last, Stephano talked to Miri. She was in the kitchen, kneading bread. She had flour up to her elbows, flour on her face and in her hair. She slapped the dough, picked it up, threw it onto the flour-covered board, and listened to Stephano.

"They're young, about sixteen in our years," said Stephano in conclusion. "Maybe I *should* send them home."

Miri dug the heels of her hands into the dough, flipped it over. "Remember when you were sixteen? You fought alongside your father in the rebellion. What would you have done if he had tried to send you home?"

Stephano was silent, thoughtful. His father *had* tried to send him home. Miri left her bread dough to put a floury hand over his.

"Petard saved Gythe's life on the island because of her music and your stories. You have to let the dragons fly with you. Otherwise they might go roaming about the countryside and get into all manner of trouble."

"Then just Dag and I will take the risk. I won't let Gythe fly . . ."

"I'd like to see you try to stop her," Miri said briskly. "You've made a change in Gythe. For the first time since our parents died, she's happy. Truly happy."

Stephano watched her knead the dough, wondering how to say what was in his heart. "Thank you, Miri."

"For what?" she asked, thumping the dough.

"For your support. And your friendship."

They were alone in the kitchen. He started to put his arm around her.

"Don't you come near me, Stephano!" Miri scolded, fending off his advances with a dough-covered wooden spoon. "I just cleaned those breeches you're wearing and I don't want flour all over them Now go make yourself decent for supper."

But she smiled at him as he left.

The next afternoon, a sailor brought word from the captain that the *Sommerwind* would sail in two days' time. Stephano still had to negotiate with the captain about hiring on dragon riders and he decided they should leave the next morning. He sent word to Rodrigo, who sent back word he would be ready, adding in a postscript that they were going to be astounded when they saw what he had done to spruce up his uniform.

"That gives me cold chills, sir," said Dag.

"You're not alone," said Stephano.

Rodrigo joined them the following morning, arriving with a large, heavy crate and wearing a uniform resplendent with gold braid, gold buttons, gold frogs, and epaulettes.

"How do I look?" he asked Stephano.

"The admiral of the fleet pales by comparison," Stephano replied. He looked at the crate and asked curiously, "What's in there?"

"Books. From my days at university," Rodrigo replied. "Books on magic theory and philosophy. A little light reading for the voyage."

Stephano eyed his friend. "You're up to something."

"Reading a book!" Rodrigo smiled. "How dangerous can that be? Now if I were writing one, that would be a different story. The scandalous tales I could tell . . ."

They traveled to Argonne, where Stephano met with Captain Leydecker and Leutnant Baumann on board the *Sommerwind* to explain his plan that three dragons and their riders would escort the ship to Braffa. Once Captain Leydecker recovered from his astonishment, he had a great many questions: Where would the dragons sleep since the ship would not be stopping on the way, how would the dragons get along with his crew? Stephano explained that the dragons would take turns sleeping on the deck near the stern. As for the crew, they need have no fear. The days when dragons ate humans were long past.

Captain Leydecker appeared dubious. He and Baumann walked to the bridge to hold a private conference. Stephano could not hear what they were saying, but Baumann appeared to be urging the captain to accept the dragons. Captain Leydecker was by nature a cautious man and he seemed to be having reservations. The lieutenant cast a glance toward the cargo hold and said something in low tones. The captain looked that direction, as well. Then he nodded and both men returned to Stephano.

"We are agreed, sir," said Captain Leydecker.

They came to terms on payment, which was lower than what Stephano had hoped, but far more than he would have made otherwise. His only problem now was persuading Rodrigo to relinquish the gold epaulettes.

"I will," said Rodrigo, taking off the gold-trimmed coat with regret. "But please don't tell my mother. She was so impressed when she saw me in my uniform. The dear woman thinks I'm finally going to amount to something. I would hate to disillusion her."

The next morning, the *Sommerwind* sailed with a fair wind, heading east for Braffa. Three dragons, with their riders, flew alongside.

34

To a dragon, a human guest is considered to be "a jewel upon the pillow of hospitality." For those fortunate enough to be invited to spend time in a dragon's household, they can look forward to days filled with splendor, music, art, and excellent conversation. I never spend my holidays anywhere else.

—Contessa Christina Mandalay

Sir Ander looked down with interest as he flew the yacht over the city of Ciel-et-terre, which could be roughly translated as meaning "Sky and Land," so named because the city was built in the mountains and thus close to the sky. Ciel-et-terre was one of three cities in the dragon duchies where humans resided.

Long ago, when the noble dragons first began to interact with humans, the dragons found much in the human culture they admired, particularly the arts. After visiting the grand palaces of their human counterparts, the noble dragons built palaces of their own, hiring human architects, crafters, and masons, and bringing them and their families to the dragons' province of Ondea. The humans built their own town there, and as more and more humans came to offer their services to the dragons in return for dragon gold, the town grew to become one of the largest cities in Rosia.

But that was in the past. Ciel-et-terre's prosperity was now sadly at an end. The city was now practically deserted. Sir Ander looked down from the yacht on empty streets. No carts, no wagons, no people hurrying about their business. A single person walked across a plaza in front of a church.

The yacht's door opened behind him. Father Jacob looked out. "May I join you?"

Sir Ander was pleased and relieved to see the priest. Father Jacob had spent much of their journey absorbed either in his thoughts or rereading Saint Marie's book. He ate barely enough to keep body and soul together, and endlessly paced the deck of the yacht, back and forth, back and forth, his hands behind his back. Sir Ander calculated that Father Jacob was likely walking the same distance they were flying.

"We are over the city of Ciel-et-terre," observed Father Jacob, taking a seat beside Sir Ander.

"It appears to be deserted," Sir Ander commented. "What happened?"

"King Alaric happened," said Father Jacob drily. "His decision to disband the Dragon Brigade. Your godson, Stephano, was not the only human to be adversely affected by the king's foolish act. The dragons as a nation were offended and angered. The noble dragons withdrew from court and went back to their own lands. In retaliation, they ordered humans to leave the dragon duchies.

"Construction halted on the dragon palaces, workers and artisans were dismissed. Rumors began to circulate among the human population that the dragons were going to attack them. People fled and, with tensions still running high, they have not returned."

Sir Ander shook his head at the folly of both species.

"Sounds like the situation was bungled from top to bottom. Who are these noble dragon friends of yours we're going to visit?"

"The duke and duchess of the Talwin clan, the largest and oldest of the dragon gatherings, named for the Tall Winds, the thermals that rise from the mountains. I was a guest in their palace many years ago, shortly after my arrival in Rosia. You know that I have always been interested in dragons and their history and religious beliefs. I spent several months with the duke and his mate pursuing my work in that field."

Sir Ander had never heard this. "So you fled your home to follow your faith, but you didn't go to a monastery. You went to visit dragons."

"I was young. I had watched my mother die a horrible death. I had seen my faith maligned, my brethren persecuted. I was angry, unhappy, grieving. I had thought I would find peace in the church here. Instead, I found only more questions. I left to pursue my studies among the dragons."

"Did the dragons help you find your faith?" Sir Ander asked.

"Heavens, no!" Father Jacob chuckled at the thought. "Dragons have their own religious beliefs that are quite different from ours. Dragons have no concept of God or the Evil One. They do not believe in an afterlife, no heaven or hell. Dragons believe in living life in the moment. Contentment is found in being at peace with oneself, accepting what life brings. The duke and duchess were very kind to me, very patient. For though dragons do not think as we do about religion, they have a deep fondness for theological discussions. They encouraged me to talk with them. I learned about myself from dragons."

They left the city far behind, flying over thick forests broken occasionally by large swathes of fields where the land had been cleared for farming. Father Jacob suddenly leaned forward and pointed. "The duke's palace. Up ahead. You can see the walls."

Sir Ander landed the yacht in a field near the palace. Once the yacht was landed and secured and the wyverns fed and settled, Sir Ander and Father Jacob changed into their finest clothes. Father Jacob wore his black cassock and biretta, with a red sash around his waist. He rarely wore the sash, which he claimed restricted his breathing. He said the dragons would appreciate the formality, and so Sir Ander struggled into his dress uniform and polished his ceremonial sword for the occasion.

The palace was the largest structure of any kind Sir Ander had ever seen, as well as the strangest. It was eight stories high, perhaps a mile or more in length, and looked as if it had been designed by an architect having an opium dream.

The palace of the Duke and Duchess of Talwin was built to resemble the palaces of humans, though on a much larger and far grander scale. Unlike human palaces, dragon palaces did not act as fortresses. If the dragons ever felt threatened, they simply retreated to their ancient caves in the mountains. Dragons were fond of towers, crenelations, ramparts. They liked chimneys and gabled roofs, mullioned windows, stained-glass windows, arrow slits in the walls, columns, porticos, and gargoyles. Double doors, single doors, iron-banded doors, so many doors Sir Ander had no idea which was the main door. Small doors for humans and doors for dragons that were forty feet tall.

Father Jacob led his friend to the correct door, which was a door within a door. They rang a bellpull and it was as if all the church bells in Evreux began ringing at once. Every tower had its bell and every bell rang with a different timbre. The sound was wondrous, and Sir Ander listened, enchanted.

They had no idea what sort of reception they would receive. Father Jacob had not sent word of his coming to the duke and duchess, fearing that a letter he wrote might be intercepted by the Arcanum.

A young man answered the door. He was dressed in the bright colored tunic, garishly colored tights, and soft leather slippers of a jongleur. Father Jacob stared, startled. The jongleur invited them inside with a warm and engaging smile.

"I just happened to be passing when I heard the welcoming bells. Come inside." The young man waved his hand. "The duchess is in the main chamber. Go ahead and announce yourselves. I would do so, but I'm late for rehearsal."

The sounds of the bells faded away as the jongleur lightly ran off. Father Jacob and Sir Ander stood in the entryway, listening to the last echoes. Then the house was silent.

"Things have changed since I was here," said Father Jacob in regretful tones. "The duke and duchess had a staff of hundreds: footman, pages, cooks, servants, as well as artists, entertainers, musicians. Their home was filled with music and talking and laughter."

He sighed deeply, as Sir Ander stared at the large cavernous chamber, the vastness of which overwhelmed his senses.

Enormous granite columns supported a cathedral-like ceiling beautifully painted with the cycle of a day, beginning with the portrayal of the sunrise in the eastern part of the castle, proceeding through to sunset and the night sky with the moon and stars. The real sun stone though hundreds of windows, casting hundreds of shafts of sunlight, all slanting down to illuminate the marble floors.

Paintings decorated the walls. Sir Ander did not know much about art, but even he could recognize works by the masters. The dragons never used furniture, but they had thoughtfully provided furniture for their human guests. The tables, chairs, and sofas were all placed against the walls, to be out of the way of the dragons, along with pianofortes, clavichords, and harps. Trumpets and hunting horns hung on hooks on the walls. Hearing the sound of violins, he looked across the chamber to see four musicians playing their music for the entertainment of a large dragon, who had turned her head to observe her new guests.

The dragon was about forty feet in height, and her scales were green, as were her wings and tail. She was an imposing sight.

"Stop gaping," said Father Jacob, latching on to Sir Ander's elbow. "That is the duchess. I'll introduce you."

"Father Jacob Northrop," called the duchess, as they approached. "How good to see you again."

She dismissed the musicians, who departed with bobbing bows of respect.

"I am pleased that Your Grace remembers me," said Father Jacob. "Sir Ander Martel, I have the pleasure of introducing you to Her Grace, Drohmir, Duchess of Talwin."

"Sir Ander, you are most welcome," said Drohmir in rich, melodious tones.

Sir Ander made a deep bow, said he was pleased to make her acquaintance, and after that he was silent. Overawed by his surroundings and the regal dragon, he decided to leave the conversation to Father Jacob.

"I regret that I could not send you advance notice of our coming, Your Grace."

"You are an old and cherished friend. Please do not concern yourself with such formalities, Father," said Drohmir. "I am glad you came. Will you and your Knight Protector be staying with us? As you recall, we have rooms in the towers we make available to human guests."

"We do not want to inconvenience you, Your Grace. We will stay on our yacht, which is nearby."

Sir Ander was relieved. He could not imagine living in this lofty, drafty, cavernous palace.

Drohmir lowered her head politely to be able to speak more comfortably to her human visitors, and turned her shining eyes to Sir Ander.

"I am sorry you could not have visited us in better days, Sir Knight. We hosted a great many human guests. We had servants to wait upon them, cooks to prepare food for them. All that has changed. We have only a few guests these days, a group of traveling musicians and jongleurs. I have a fondness for music, as you may have gathered. Our guests wait upon themselves now, Father," Drohmir added with a sigh.

"We don't mind, do we, Sir Ander?"

"Not at all, Your Grace. If you would·like, I could bring some chairs."

The dragon gave a graceful nod. Sir Ander carried over chairs for himself and Father Jacob and placed these in front of the dragon. The two men sat down. The dragon lowered herself to the floor and wrapped her tail around her feet. The floor shook as the dragon moved.

"I hope that you plan to remain with us for some time, Father," Drohmir said. "I do enjoy human conversation. The duke and I are very fond of each other, but after living together for two hundred years, we run out of things to talk about."

"I would like nothing more than to stay for an extended length of time, Your Grace, but we are here to meet with you and the duke on a matter of some urgency."

"The duke has gone to a gathering of the clans in the Oscadia Mountains, a supreme council. He does not plan to return for a week at least."

"I am sorry to hear this, Your Grace," said Father Jacob, clearly dismayed. "My need to see the duke is very great. Can you send a message to him?"

"Even if I could send a messenger, he could not leave a meeting of the supreme council, Father." The duchess saw the priest's unhappiness and she was distressed. "Is there anything I can do to assist you?"

Father Jacob considered. "I hope you can, Your Grace. Shortly after the Dark Ages, a nun named Sister Marie

Allemand came to visit here. Her arrival would have been before the duke was born. She would have been a friend of the duke's esteemed parents."

"I do not recognize the name of this nun," said Drohmir regretfully. "If the duke's parents knew of her, they never spoke of her to me, nor did the duke. You could wait for his return . . ."

Father Jacob shook his head. "There is not time, Your Grace. Lives are at stake."

"I am truly sorry, Father," said Drohmir regretfully.

Father Jacob's brow furrowed. He rose to his feet, clasped his hands behind his back, and began to pace about the room.

So we came all this way only to crash headlong into a mountain, Sir Ander reflected gloomily.

The duchess observed Father Jacob with concern. The dragon was obviously distraught over having to disappoint her guest. Dragons pride themselves on their hospitality, considering nothing too good for those who visit them.

"Father Jacob," Drohmir said suddenly, "I've had a thought. The duke's family retainer is still alive. He might remember this nun. His name is Vroathagn. He was retainer when you were here."

"I remember him," said Father Jacob, pleased and relieved. "Vroathagn was an excellent manager. He had quite a gift for dealing with humans."

"He was a marvel. We have never found another dragon to replace him," said Drohmir.

"Vroathagn was quite old when I knew him," said Father Jacob. "I am surprised he is still alive."

"He is a tough one," said Drohmir. "He is crippled, however, and no longer able to fly. But his wits are sharp as a fang, as the saying goes. I will take you to him, if you would find that agreeable."

"I would like that immensely, Your Grace," said Father Jacob.

The duchess rose ponderously, carefully uncurling her tail, lest she accidentally knock over her guests. The sounds of violins started up again, this time from a different part of the palace.

"What does a dragon retainer do?" Sir Ander asked Father Jacob in a low voice as they moved their chairs back against the wall.

"Much the same as their human counterparts," Father Jacob answered. "They run the household, manage the business affairs of the estate. The retainer also acts as a diplomatic liaison between the human guests and their dragon hosts, settling misunderstandings, explaining the ways of dragons to humans and the ways of humans to dragons. That was quite important in the days when dragons would entertain human ambassadors, royalty, nobility, and high-ranking members of the church."

"You seemed surprised to find the duke absent. Do dragons often hold these supreme councils?"

"No, they do not," Father Jacob replied, casting Sir Ander a sharp glance. "A supreme council brings together the heads of all the clans. They hold such large gatherings only in times of crisis."

"Do you think this meeting has to do with the Bottom Dwellers?"

"I would stake my hope of heaven on it," said Father Jacob.

Sir Ander and Father Jacob accompanied the duchess across the enormous chamber. On their way, they passed two of the musicians, young women, carrying what looked like their laundry. The women were in good spirits, singing songs as they went about their work. They paused to curtsy respectfully to the duchess and merrily greeted Sir Ander and Father Jacob. Obviously life among the dragons was still pleasant for these humans, despite having no servants to wait upon them.

"The dragon clans meet so rarely, Your Grace," said Father Jacob, advancing the length of her body to walk alongside her. "The duke and the other dragon clan leaders must have important matters to discuss."

Drohmir inclined her head in polite agreement. "These are troubled times, Father."

He waited for her to elaborate, but she said nothing more. She was uneasy, Sir Ander noted. He had to quicken his pace to avoid being swept away by her twitching tail.

"You do not attend the council, Your Grace?" Father Jacob asked.

"I invited the musicians to spend the summer," Drohmir replied. "It would be impolite of me to leave my guests. The duke knows my views and he will express them for me. I do not enjoy supreme council meetings. I much prefer my music."

The duchess led them toward the rear of the palace. They left the grand chamber by way of a tunnel, entering a part of the palace that had been designed to more nearly resemble the caves that had once been the dragons' homes. The chambers were much smaller than the grand chamber, with no windows and no furniture. The floor was dirt, packed as hard as stone.

"Dragons sleep here," said Father Jacob to Sir Ander. "Despite building these grand palaces, dragons are only comfortable sleeping in small, enclosed chambers. The nursery would be here, as well. I'm surprised we don't see any young dragons. The duke and duchess are of breeding age."

The chambers were cool and airless, with a very strong odor of dragon. Sir Ander was once more extremely thankful he was sleeping in his own comfortable bed in the yacht.

Drohmir led them to a chamber in the very back of the palace. The chamber had no doors; apparently dragons had no need for privacy. She asked that Father Jacob and Sir Ander wait in the hall until she checked on the elderly dragon.

"He may be asleep," she said. "If so, you will need to wait until he wakes. Rousing Vroathagn from a deep slumber is quite impossible."

Drohmir advanced and peered into the darkness. "Ah, good. He is awake. Vroathagn, you have visitors. An old friend of yours, Father Jacob Northrop, would like to speak with you. He is accompanied by his Knight Protector, Sir Ander Martel."

She moved aside to allow Father Jacob and Sir Ander to pass. They entered the chamber, which was snug and warm. Fine paintings hung on the walls: landscapes portraying the mountains that had once been the ancient homeland. A thick bed of fresh straw cushioned the old dragon's gnarled limbs and aching joints. The duke and duchess were making certain their faithful servant's final days were filled with comfort.

Vroathagn raised his head. His body was failing him, his wings useless, his limbs shriveled. His scales were quite gray and falling off, leaving bare patches of flesh. His eyes were clear and bright, however, and very shrewd.

"Father Jacob, how pleasant to see you again," said Vroathagn in a dry, rattling voice. "You were one of the good sort of humans. Always so polite and good natured. Easy to serve. Never one to complain."

Sir Ander raised an eyebrow, wondering if the dragon had the priest confused with someone else.

"Vroathagn, Sir Ander and I have traveled a long way on a matter of great importance. I came to see the duke, only to find he is gone. The duchess thought you might be able to help."

"I will be of service if I can, Father," said Vroathagn.

"A nun named Sister Marie Allemand came to visit the duke's father. She would have been accompanied by several

Knight Protectors. Do you recall meeting her or hearing stories of her?"

Vroathagn listened intently, his eyes fixed on the priest. He nodded slowly. "I remember her. She was here before the Time of Storm and Sorrow and she came again several years later, after the storms had abated."

Sir Ander wondered what the Time of Storm and Sorrow was, then realized the dragon must mean what humans know as the Dark Ages.

"She was here *prior* to the Time of Storm and Sorrow?" Father Jacob asked, startled.

"Sister Marie and her friends—a group of priests. Their names were . . . let me see . . . Father Dennis, Father Michael, Father Charles, and Father Xavier. They came here to study."

"Father Xavier," Father Jacob repeated with a glance at Sir Ander. "You have an excellent memory. What were the five studying?"

"The *roed* and the *raeg*," Vroathagn said.

"What is that?" Father Jacob asked.

Before the old dragon could answer, the duchess made a rumbling sound in her chest. Her claws scraped the stone floor, her tail thumped against one of the walls.

"We were discussing a nun, I think," said the duchess. Her tone was cool, no longer quite as hospitable.

Father Jacob took the hint. "Please continue, Vroathagn."

"There is not much more to tell, Father. Sister Marie and her companions spent many months here. They wrote down what they learned and took the books with them when they left."

Sir Ander was about to ask what was in the books. Father Jacob stopped him with a look.

"Sister Marie returned some years later, you said," said Father Jacob.

Vroathagn gave a soft, sad sigh.

"Sister Marie had changed a great deal. I remember the

duke saying he would not have known her. When she was here the first time, she was always talking, always laughing. She and her friends were excited by what they were learning. Good friends, they were. Very close. When she came here again, after the Great Rending sank the island, Sister Marie was old beyond her years and seemed weighted down by grief. She had lost the gift of laughter."

"What happened to the books?" asked Father Jacob. "She left them here with you. What became of them?"

Vroathagn's eyes narrowed. "How do you know about the books, Father? Sister Marie said they were secret."

"Saint Marie told me about the books, Vroathagn," Father Jacob said. "The books on contramagic."

"Take care, Vroathagn," the duchess warned.

Father Jacob understood her perturbation. "I know this subject is a sensitive one, Your Grace. A subject you dragons do not like to discuss openly—"

"The subject is not sensitive to *us,* Father," said Drohmir sharply. "You humans are the ones who have forbidden us to speak of it."

"A terrible mistake with tragic consequences," said Father Jacob. "A mistake I am trying to correct, if I am not too late. Saint Marie wrote about the books in her *Confession.*"

He drew out the small book from his pocket to show the dragon. He quoted the words from memory. "'I saw the terrible evil we had caused and I was going to destroy the books that contained our research. Then I realized that the knowledge was not evil. The evil lay in men and what we did with that knowledge. I have decided to take the books on contramagic to my friend, the Duke of Talwin, for safekeeping until the day when humanity gains wisdom.'"

Vroathagn closed his eyes and Sir Ander feared the old dragon might have fallen asleep.

"Her very words. I can almost hear her voice." The dragon's

eyes flared open. "No one knew about the books, not even Sister Marie's Knight Protectors. She told the Knights the strongbox they carried contained sacred relics. She gave the books to the old duke for safekeeping."

"I would like very much to have them," said Father Jacob. "I believe Saint Marie led me here for that purpose."

Vroathagn eyed him shrewdly. "Have you gained in wisdom as she says, Father?"

"I hope I have, Vroathagn," Father Jacob replied in grave tones. "I need to understand contramagic."

He turned to the duchess. "You have agents in the human kingdoms, Your Grace. You know we are under attack from a foe that is skilled in the use of contramagic. They have created contramagic weapons that have proven devastating to us and to dragons, as well."

"We were speaking of books, Father," said the duchess coldly. "Tell him where to find them, Vroathagn."

"I will be glad to tell you, Father," said Vroathagn. "If you give me the key."

"Key? What key?" Father Jacob demanded.

"Sister Marie told the duke that the one who came for the books would have the key."

"Key! I have no key!" Father Jacob said in frustration. "What key could she mean? Unless there was a key with her when she was killed. If so, it has long since been lost."

He ran his hand through his hair, knocking off the biretta. Sir Ander retrieved it. Father Jacob paid no heed. He stood frowning at the floor.

"Key . . . What could that be . . . Ah-ha!" he shouted in triumph.

He opened the book to the first page and showed it to Sir Ander. Beneath the words, "My Confessions," Saint Marie had written the phrase, "The key to my soul."

Father Jacob showed the book to Vroathagn.

"That is the key," said the old dragon. "Sister Marie told the duke the key would lead a wise man to the books. They are in a strongbox banded with iron and locked with magical constructs. The old duke hid the box in the vault beneath the pigsty."

"I can show you how to find it, Father," said Drohmir. Having at first been so welcoming, she now appeared eager to be rid of them and willing to do anything to hasten their departure.

"Thank you, Your Grace," said Father Jacob.

He thanked Vroathagn, who said he was glad to have been of service.

"A pigsty," Sir Ander said. "I have to dig a box out of a pigsty."

"I'll help," said Father Jacob.

"Damn right you will," said Sir Ander.

Sir Ander did not want to go rooting around a pigsty in his best dress uniform. He was going to return to the yacht to change, but the duchess offered him clothes that had been left behind by some human laborers. Once he had changed, he asked where he could find shovels. The duchess led them first to a toolshed and then to the pigsty, which was located behind the palace. He was relieved to discover there were no pigs.

"We have no one to take care of them anymore," Drohmir explained. "And I know nothing about pigs."

Apparently she didn't know how to clean up the muck either. Sir Ander had to concede that the duke had found an excellent place to conceal a vault.

The duchess said coldly she would leave them to their work. She returned to the palace and soon they heard the sounds of violins. Drohmir was seeking solace in the music.

"I fear I have upset her," said Father Jacob.

"She certainly didn't like the talk about contramagic," said Sir Ander, handing the priest a shovel. "What I still don't understand is why Saint Marie left the books here. And why did the five priests come to the dragons to study? What were they studying? Dragons?"

"Contramagic," said Father Jacob. "One of the priests, Saint Michael, came from Ciel-et-terre. He would have been raised around dragons."

"But what do dragons know about contramagic?"

"Ah, to that I have no answer," said Father Jacob. He had kilted up the skirts of his cassock. "Help me over the fence."

Sir Ander and Father Jacob both began to dig where the duchess had indicated. Father Jacob proved to be inept with the shovel and when he accidentally tossed a load of filth onto Sir Ander's boots, Sir Ander ordered him out of the pigsty.

He had dug down about four feet when the shovel scraped against something hard. Sir Ander cleared away the remaining muck and dirt with his hands and uncovered a stone slab set into the ground. He and Father Jacob squatted down to examine the slab that was locked with magical constructs.

"I hope they used human magic," said Father Jacob. "If these constructs are dragon magic, I'll have to ask the duchess to remove them."

"I think she's more likely to remove us," Sir Ander grunted.

Feeling the ground shake, Sir Ander stood up and looked around to see Drohmir coming toward them.

"Have you found anything yet?" she asked.

"We have located the vault, Your Grace," said Sir Ander.

Father Jacob was on his hands and knees, casting a magical spell on the stone slab. He passed his hand three times over the stone surface and the constructs appeared.

Father Jacob sat back on his heels. He stared at the constructs blankly. Sir Ander gave a low gasp of shock.

Blue sigils gleamed. Green sigils shone. Both together. Green lines of magic intertwined with the blue.

"The *roed* and the *raeg*," said Father Jacob softly, awed. "Magic and contramagic intertwined."

"That's impossible," said Sir Ander.

The shadow of the dragon's head fell over them.

"Not for us," said Drohmir. "You were not meant to see this. If I had known the vault was bound by dragon magic, I would not have allowed you to find it."

Father Jacob rose to his feet, wiping his hands. He faced the dragon. "See what? Contramagic and magic working in union? Why should I not see that?"

"Your concern is these human books. Take them away and ask no more questions. I will remove the constructs, Father," said Drohmir. She sounded more sorrowful than angry. "Stand aside."

Moving ponderously, the dragon stared intently at the box. She did not move a claw that Sir Ander could see, yet the glow of constructs, green and blue, began to slowly diminish, and finally faded away altogether. When the dragon had deconstructed the magic, she thrust one claw beneath the heavy stone slab and pried it open.

The vault was about six feet deep. The walls were lined with stone protected by the same magic. The only object in the vault was the strongbox. A crude ladder consisting of a series of iron rungs had been built into one wall.

Father Jacob climbed down the ladder to examine the strongbox, which was locked by magic. He passed his hand over the box. The warding constructs were made by a human, for they gleamed blue and appeared to Sir Ander to be extremely complex. Father Jacob pondered them, trying to figure out how to unlock the magical spells. At last he smiled.

"Three keys," he informed Sir Ander. "Saint Marie was thorough. The strongbox is extremely heavy . . ."

"I will lift it for you," said Drohmir.

"That would be kind of you, Your Grace," said Father Jacob. He looked up at her from the bottom of the vault. "I am truly sorry to have upset you. That was not my intent."

The duchess picked up the heavy strongbox with her claws and lifted it out of the vault. Father Jacob climbed the ladder and the duchess replaced the stone slab. Father Jacob shook down his robes.

"Your Grace, we need to talk," he said to the dragon.

"It would be best if you left now, Father."

"I cannot leave without the answers, Your Grace. Saint Marie and her friends were studying contramagic and how it *works with* magic, as opposed to destroying magic. They came to the dragons because they knew you have the ability to control both magic and contramagic. The *roed* and the *raeg*. An ability you have kept hidden from us."

Drohmir gazed at him steadily. She said nothing, but she did not turn away. In the distance, the violins had stopped, replaced by harp music.

"You must have heard of the collapse of the Crystal Market," Father Jacob continued. "Your agents would have told you. Perhaps they also told you that before the crystal blocks shattered, crafters reported feeling the crystal shiver beneath their hands. They watched in horror to see the magical constructs vanish. Some said they heard a sound as of a heart throbbing or drumming. Very faint and distant."

"A drumbeat . . . ," Drohmir said. "No, Father, I had not heard about humans hearing a beating drum."

"You understand what they mean, don't you, Your Grace," said Father Jacob. "You hear it, as well."

A shudder rippled through Drohmir's body, her mane crackled. Her claws dug into the ground.

"That is why you keep the musicians," said Father Jacob gently. "They drown out the sound."

"We hear the drumming," said Drohmir harshly. "A throbbing, like the beating of a heart. The sound comes from the depths of the Breath. We don't understand how, but when the drumming starts, magic fails. And worse.

"The drum beat is killing us."

Sir Ander changed back into his uniform, then loaded the heavy box into a wagon loaned to them by the musicians. While Father Jacob conversed with Drohmir, Sir Ander drove the strongbox to the yacht. He stowed the box away safely in the secret compartment underneath the yacht, which Father Jacob had termed "the coffin," then drove the wagon back to the palace.

He found Father Jacob still in conversation with Drohmir. The musicians were playing softly at the far end of the chamber. Every so often, Drohmir would stop talking and tilt her head to listen.

"Drohmir has been telling me what has been happening to the dragons," said Father Jacob, motioning Sir Ander to join them. "Dragon scholars have long known that dragon magic is in the blood, not the brain, like human magic. A dragon's magic is a part of her, like her scales or her bones or her wings. As you saw, Her Grace was able to remove those constructs by turning her thoughts to them. What we did not know because we were too ignorant to know, is that dragons have both magic and contramagic in their blood. The one complements and reinforces the other."

"Why doesn't one destroy the other, as we've seen for ourselves happen with contramagic?" Sir Ander asked.

"The dragon's body maintains the two in a delicate balance. Now that contramagic has begun radiating up from

Below, the balance has been disturbed. Our own magic is failing, crumbling beneath the onslaught. The same is happening with the dragons, only worse. Because the magic and the contramagic are inside them, the effect on them is lethal."

"Wounds heal far more slowly, if they heal at all," Drohmir explained. "We are easily fatigued. We are aging much more rapidly. But the toll on our eggs is far worse."

"I wondered why I did not see any young dragons about the palace," said Father Jacob quietly. "Drohmir told me why."

"Some of our children died before they hatched," said Drohmir, her voice soft and grieving. "Those few that survived were weak and sickly and did not live long. If this attack continues, dragons will soon be extinct."

"The dragons are meeting in supreme council to discuss the crisis," said Father Jacob.

"We are desperate to find a way to stop this. We did not know the source, but you say, Father, that the drumming comes from people at the bottom of the world. How is that possible?"

Drohmir's mane rippled along her back. "According to the old stories, dragons flew down there centuries ago. The journey through the Breath was perilous. Many turned back, unable to endure the cold. Those who fought their way through reported that they found a vast body of water, cold and murky, and swampland. They deemed the place uninhabitable. We saw no humans. I did not think humans could have survived."

"I believe those on the doomed island of Glasearrach were forced to find a way to do so, Your Grace. We are a tough species. I would be glad to tell everything I know about the Bottom Dwellers to the supreme council."

"I will take you there on the morrow, Father," said Drohmir. She cast an apologetic glance at Sir Ander. "Your Protector must stay behind. The duke knows you, Father. He does not know this knight."

Sir Ander did not like leaving his charge to the care of the dragons. He could tell by the expression on Father Jacob's face, however, that no amount of arguing would convince the priest to forgo making this journey.

Drohmir rose to her feet. "And now, I am certain you will want to return to your yacht before darkness falls. I will see you in the morning."

Drohmir inclined her head, then moved through the empty palace, going back to listen to the music that drowned out the sounds of death.

Sir Ander and Father Jacob walked in silence back to the yacht. Father Jacob was undoubtedly thinking about all the information he'd gleaned. Sir Ander was trying to figure out how to convince the duchess to take both of them to this supreme council. The sun had set behind the mountains, filling the sky with bright shafts of gold and orange. They entered a thick stand of trees that surrounded the palace, following a faded old trail. A rustic bridge spanned a rushing stream.

"So you plan to attend the supreme council alone," Sir Ander said.

"Don't be upset my friend. So far as I know, a human has never before been invited to speak to the supreme council. The duke knows me. He can vouch for me. What will you do?"

"I am probably safest here," said Sir Ander.

"The days will be long for you, I fear," said Father Jacob.

Sir Ander laughed. "Days of peace and quiet with absolutely nothing to do. No one trying to kill me. No one talking to dead saints. Did you see that stream back there? Probably teeming with trout. I haven't been fishing since—"

Sir Ander stopped dead and thrust out his arm, halting Father Jacob. They were still in the tree line, still in the shadows.

"What's wrong?" Father Jacob asked.

The afterglow lit the sky. Evening mists lay in the field in which they had landed. Ahead of them was the yacht, parked in the open field. A faint glimmer of light shone from a back window, shining through a chink in the curtain.

As they watched, two men wearing the crimson robes of the monks of Saint Klee emerged from beneath the yacht, carrying the strongbox between them.

"Curse my arrogance!" Father Jacob said grimly. "I am not the only one who knew where to find the books on contramagic—"

"No time for that now, Father!" Sir Ander grabbed hold of the priest's arm. "More monks will be watching the yacht. We have to run—"

"Too late," said Father Jacob.

Magical light began to glow, shining around him. Sir Ander turned to see the monks of Saint Klee approaching, light shining from the monks' hands. Father Jacob's eyes rolled back in his head. He staggered and them slumped to the ground and lay there, unconscious.

Sir Ander reached for his pistol. A hand caught hold of his from behind. A strong, sinewy arm circled his neck. Sir Ander struggled to free himself. The hold on him tightened.

"Relax, Sir Knight," said the monk. "I am not going to harm you. You will go to sleep. When you wake, you will be in the Citadel."

The darkness came very fast.

35

For now, the Braffan High Council believes they have Rosia competely at their mercy and will force us to dance to their tune. If they ally with Sir Henry Wallace, they will find themselves dancing with the devil.

—Countess Cecile de Marjolaine

The Countess de Marjolaine sent a message to His Majesty requesting that she be permitted to see him on a matter of the most alarming nature. His Majesty had canceled his levee that day due to an attack of lumbago, which was keeping him bedridden. He had given orders that no one was to disturb him. The countess was certain that he would not refuse to see her, and she was right. The page returned with the message that the king would allot her a few moments of his time, but only if she came immediately.

The countess looked at herself in the mirror. She was no longer Alaric's mistress, but he was flattered to think that she took care to dress to please him. She was wearing a new gown of black silk trimmed with rose-colored ribbons. The sleeves ended at the elbow in a cascade of lace. The hem of the skirt was gathered and held in place by silk rosebuds in a style that permitted the wearer to reveal her ankles. The very next morning, every lady in the court (except those with thick ankles) would be summoning her dressmaker to the palace.

Cecile added a lace cap with rose ribbons, and a necklace of rubies that had been a present from His Majesty. Upon arrival, while waiting to be admitted into His Majesty's presence, Cecile asked a servant if Her Majesty was with the king. The servant reported that the queen was supervising the Princess Sophia's deportment lessons. Cecile received this news with pleasure. Sophia's deportment or lack thereof would occupy the queen for hours.

Cecile entered the royal bedchamber to find Alaric, clad in breeches and a shirt, lying facedown in bed with a cloth spread with powdered mustard, flour, and egg whites across his back. The heat from the mustard relieved the pain of the lumbago. The king's physician and assistants hovered near.

"I am sorry to hear you are not well, Your Majesty," said Cecile, with a deep curtsy.

"Damn lumbago. It is all the fault of that wretched stag we hunted yesterday," Alaric complained. "We rode after the beast for an hour at least and lost it in the brambles. We woke this morning and could not move. Well, Countess, what is so important that you have to disturb us when we are in agony?"

"The matter is confidential, Your Majesty," Cecile replied with a glance at the physician.

"Get out of here," Alaric ordered, waving at the physician. "And take this stinking concoction off our back. It's done nothing except burn off a layer of skin."

The physician removed the pungent cloth. He and his assistants gathered up their ingredients and departed.

Alaric rolled over with a groan.

"Help me to a chair," he said to Cecile, dropping the

royal "we" as he generally did when the two of them were alone.

She assisted him to rise. Grimacing in pain, he hobbled to a chair and sank into it with a groan.

"I do not like growing old, Cecile," Alaric said after he was settled. "We rode for hours when we were young and then made love all night. Do you remember?"

Cecile poured him a glass of wine and brought it to him. He eyed her approvingly.

"You're still a damn fine-looking woman, Cecile. I wouldn't mind taking you to my bed again."

"Those days are past us, Your Majesty," said Cecile.

"So they are," he said, sighing. "So they are. Now what is so important that you drag me from my mustard plaster?"

"Several ships from the Freyan fleet are in Estara, Your Majesty."

Alaric frowned. "Estara? What the devil are the bloody Freyans doing there?"

"They were attempting to sail through the Straits de Domcáido. The Estaran navy caught them and refused to allow them to pass. Neither side has fired at the other, at least not at last report. There can be no doubt, Your Majesty. The Freyans are going to try to take Braffa." She would have liked to have added, "I told you so."

Alaric was so incensed he forgot his pain and started to stand up. He fell back with a grimace and a muttered curse. "Are the Freyans going to invade?"

"They have no need to invade," said Cecile bitterly. "With Travia threatening to blockade Braffa and Estara threatening to take Braffa by force, the Freyans can claim they are there to protect the Braffans from their enemies. The Braffans will hail Freya as a protector and invite them to stay."

"Might as well ask the wolf to protect a lamb! That bastard

Wallace is behind this. How long can the Estarans keep the Freyans bottled up in the Straits?"

"Until the first foggy morning in the Breath, Your Majesty. The ships might have already slipped through."

"What are the Travians doing?"

"The Travians have asked *us* for help. Since they have no navy, they are hiring ships from the Guundaran."

"How did we get into this mess? How did this happen?" Alaric demanded angrily.

Cecile would have liked to tell the king that it happened because he had panicked and ordered the Rosian fleet out of the region. If the Rosian navy had remained there in strength, the Freyans would not have dared send their ships. Cecile had to swallow the words, which would have only infuriated him.

"Your Majesty, what is done is done. You must consider what to do now."

"What do you advise?"

"You should immediately order Prince Renaud to send the Braffan expeditionary force north to Caltreau, take half the northern fleet and set sail for Braffa. They should travel the northern route and show our Travian allies we are acting to counteract Freya's aggression. The longer we can hide our movements from the Freyans and the Estarans, the better. You can't conceal the fleet's sailing from the grand bishop, but if we move quickly we can catch him off guard, before he has time to warn his Estaran friends."

The king shifted in his chair, trying in vain to find relief from his back pain. He considered what she said, then made his decision.

"His Highness will sail with his flagship and two frigates. That is all. The remainder of the fleet stays to guard the palace."

"But, Your Majesty, that is hardly enough—"

"I will not compromise my safety and the safety of the capital. I am going back to bed. Summon the physician on the way."

Cecile left the audience mentally and physically drained. Returning to her chambers, she found the salon filled with people. Upon her entrance, everyone immediately jumped up and pushed their way forward, calling out her name, hoping to attract her notice. She swept past them, telling the viscount in a loud voice that she was not holding audience that day. She entered her office, shut the door, sat down at her desk, and rubbed her temples.

Her maid, Marie, appeared with hot tea. Marie had been with Cecile since she had first come to court at the age of sixteen and knew that after meeting with His Majesty, the countess would be in need of restorative refreshment.

"Thank you, Marie," said Cecile gratefully.

Marie poured the tea and set out a dish of pound cake. She then stood waiting quietly, her hands clasped before her. The countess knew immediately something was wrong. Generally Marie glided silently in and silently out.

"What is it, Marie?" Cecile asked, drinking her tea.

"There is talk in the servants' hall, my lady," said Marie. "I thought you should know what was being said."

"Please sit down," said Cecile.

Marie hesitated, then sat on the edge of a chair.

"The talk is about the Princess Sophia, my lady, and Conte Lucello, the handsome young man with the limp. I wasn't going to say anything to you, because I have no evidence, but I fear Her Highness may have been indiscreet. I say 'may' because this talk could be nothing but malicious gossip."

"What have you heard?" Cecile asked, troubled.

"One of the gardeners claims he saw the two in the garden late at night. They were locked in an amorous embrace."

Cecile was alarmed. "Do you place credence in this report?"

Marie considered. "The man is well known to exaggerate. But I have no doubt, my lady, that he did see something, though perhaps nothing more than the conte kissing the hand of the princess. Still . . ."

"You are right. This rumor could do serious harm. Has it reached Her Majesty, do you think?"

"Her Majesty is trying to arrange a marriage for the princess with some wealthy Travian prince. She would be furious if she heard this rumor. It is well known that the conte's aunt, the Duquesa de Plata Niebla, is promoting the match between the conte and the princess, and she is working to keep the queen in ignorance."

"Keeping Her Majesty in ignorance is not terribly difficult," said Cecile drily. "Ignorance is her normal state of being. What do you hear about the Duchess of Plata Niebla?"

"She is very private, my lady. She keeps no servants. No one knows anything about her or her nephew. I did hear something very curious about her, however. She is rumored to walk about the palace late at night."

Cecile shrugged. "She has a lover."

"So one would presume, my lady. Yet the circumstances were odd. I heard this from one of the footman of Lord Amalfi. His lordship being unable to sleep, he roused his footman in the middle of the night and sent him to the kitchen to fetch hot milk. Being half asleep, the young man took a wrong turn and ended up in the lower regions of the palace. He came upon the duchess, wearing only a negligee. He was shocked, as you can imagine. He thought at first she might be sleepwalking and didn't know whether to speak to her or not, for fear that her spirit might not find its way back to her body. He is a very superstitious young man, my lady."

"I assume the duchess *wasn't* sleepwalking," said Cecile.

"No, my lady. She told him she had lost her way in the palace and asked him to show her how to return to her rooms. He did so, my lady, and that was an end to it."

"She hasn't been seen wandering about since?"

"Not that I know of, my lady."

"How very odd," said Cecile, frowning. "She wouldn't be meeting a lover in the pantry. Thank you, Marie, for bringing this to my attention."

Marie rose, curtsied, and departed. Cecile sat at the desk, twisting the small golden ring, and thinking about how best to handle this delicate situation.

It was not surprising to her that the duchess was promoting the match. Marrying her nephew to the princess would ensure her place at court for the rest of her life. Cecile knew better than to try to warn the queen to guard her daughter from the count. The queen would immediately tell the duchess and Cecile did not want to give the duchess reason to be aware that she knew what was afoot.

Unfortunately, she thought, telling Alaric was likewise useless. If he knew this young man was toying with his daughter, he would overreact, exile both the young man and the duchess, create a scandal where there was none. *At least not yet.* She felt this was her fault; that she should have been paying more attention to Sophia. If she had, the girl might have confided in her, and she could have interceded, counseled her.

Cecile sat down and wrote a charming note to the princess, inviting her to the music room at four of the clock. The noise of the pianoforte would effectively drown out a confidential discussion. She then summoned D'argent.

After that, she started to drink her tea, only to discover it had grown cold.

D'argent arrived within moments. Grave and composed, he bowed to her, took his seat, and drew out his notebook.

Cecile regarded him with profound gratitude. No wild, erratic winds ever disturbed the man's calm. She could trust him with her reputation, her life. More important, she could entrust to his care the lives of those she held dear.

"What word of Stephano?" she asked.

"I was about to come to your ladyship when I received your summons," said D'argent. "Your son is in Bourlet at the family estate. I considered it useless to try to have him and Monsieur Rodrigo arrested there. The locals are extremely loyal to the memory of his father."

"As they should be. Perhaps someday Stephano . . ." Cecile sighed and left the sentence unfinished. "He has no idea I am paying the taxes on the estate, does he?"

"No, my lady. I have arranged it so that the money appears to be coming out of his pension. Fortunately your son has no interest in accounting. He allows Monsieur Rodrigo to handle the finances. I suspect Monsieur Rodrigo is aware of the truth, but he knows better than to reveal it."

"Monsieur Rodrigo! I should like to wring that man's neck!" Cecile said. "Yet, even without him, the master of the armory reports that work on duplicating the magically enhanced steel is progressing well. Keep the warrant active, however. Being arrested might teach my son and that clever friend of his a lesson. What is Stephano doing at the estate?"

"Training dragons, my lady."

"What else?" Cecile murmured. "He is his father's son."

She sat for a moment in silence. Her memories were like the miniature she kept of Julian, hidden away in a dark recess to be taken out every so often and brought into the light.

D'argent, sensitive to his mistress's moods, waited patiently. Rousing herself, Cecile made a small gesture with her hand as if waving away the past, and returned to the present.

"Have you heard anything from the inimitable Monsieur Dubois regarding the Duquesa de Plata Niebla?"

"I know only that Dubois made a journey to Capione," D'argent replied. "He has not yet returned. I have left word at his lodgings that I am to be informed the moment he arrives."

"Very good. Something strange regarding the duchess has come to light." Cecile related the tale of the duchess's midnight peregrinations.

D'argent listened with his customary attention. "That is, as you say, most unusual. I happen to know the young footman in question and he is a steady lad, though, as Mistress Marie says, given to an unfortunate belief in country superstitions."

"I would like you to investigate this further, D'argent," said Cecile. "My thought is that if the duchess made one foray to the lower parts of the castle, she will make others. She is a cold and calculating woman who does nothing without a reason."

"My view of her exactly, my lady."

"D'argent," Cecile said, stopping him as he was going out the door. "Be careful."

D'argent raised an eyebrow.

"There is something sinister about this woman," Cecile continued. "When her lips smile, her eyes remain empty and dark."

"Like the eyes of a snake," D'argent suggested.

"I think I would see more life in the snake," said Cecile. "She is dangerous, D'argent. I worry about what she may be plotting."

"You may rest assured that I will take every precaution in my dealings with her, my lady."

D'argent departed, leaving Cecile to prepare for her meeting with the princess.

Cecile was seated at the pianoforte when the Princess Sophia arrived with Bandit trotting along behind. As Cecile rose and curtsied, she saw at a glance that the young woman was in love. Sophia was always beautifully dressed—her mother saw to that—but she herself had never taken much interest in her appearance. Today she had endeavored to hide a few pimples with powder. Her gown was new, and she was wearing a pair of new shoes.

"Those shoes look small for you," said Cecile.

"They do hurt my feet," Sophia admitted. "But *he* says my feet are so dainty . . ."

She blushed prettily as she spoke and, turning to hide her blushes, ordered Bandit to go sit in a chair. The dog, as usual, pretended not to understand. He sat at her feet, wagging his tail.

"You are a very bad dog," Sophia scolded and to punish him for his refusal to obey, picked him up and kissed him.

"What piece shall we play?" asked Cecile.

Sophia chose a duet from a popular opera about star-crossed lovers.

"Tell me about this 'he' who thinks you have dainty feet," said Cecile with a smile.

Sophia missed her fingering and this mistake ended the duet. Cecile continued to play the music as they talked.

"I told you about him, Countess," said Sophia, her flush deepening. "The Conte Osinni, although he says I am to call him by his given name, Lucello. He is the most handsome, the most charming, the most wonderful man I have ever met. He dances so well. He says such lovely things to me."

Sophia talked of the type of wine Lucello liked, his favorite foods, the books he read because she recommended them, the poetry she read because he loved it. He was well educated, it seemed, and well traveled. He did not like to hunt. He abhorred bloodshed, he told her. He sang, he danced, but only waltzes, due to his limp. He was a crafter, but had never studied the art of magic. He adored Bandit. Sadly, the dog did not like the conte.

"Bandit bit him," Sophia said. "I was mortified. I made him go without cake for two whole days."

"Has this Lucello made advances, Sophia?" Cecile asked quietly.

Blood rushed to Sophia's face, and she hung her head, glancing at Cecile from out of the corner of her eye.

"He kissed my hand, my lady," Sophia said in guilt-ridden tones. "And I am ashamed to say that I did nothing to stop him."

Cecile breathed an inward sigh of relief, even as she tried her best to look stern.

"You know that was most improper, Your Highness."

"I know," said Sophia. "I scolded him severely and he asked my pardon a dozen times. He said his feelings over-came him."

"Sophia, it would be better if you did not spend so much time in the company of the young conte. If he loves you—"

"Oh, we have never spoken of love, my lady!" Sophia pro-tested.

"Haven't you?" Cecile asked.

Sophia could not look at her. "He said . . . He did say . . . he loved me."

"And what did you say?"

"I ran away without saying anything."

The conte was certainly doing everything in his power to seduce the princess. Perhaps the young man did truly love her. Cecile had her doubts.

"You did well, Sophia. You will be careful?"

"Yes, my lady."

"And feel free to confide in me, my dear. You may tell me anything. I will understand."

"I know you will, my lady," said Sophia, warmly. "Thank you."

Cecile began to say more, when there was a knock on the door.

"The Travian ambassador, my lady. He says the matter is urgent."

"I will be there in a moment."

"I should go," said Sophia. "It is almost time to dress for dinner. Thank you." She impulsively threw her arms around Cecile, gave her a kiss, and said softly, "You were right. These terrible shoes are too small! I'm going to take them off at once."

Sophia gathered up Bandit, who had fallen asleep, and carried him away. Cecile left her music and went to meet with the Travian ambassador.

36

*A spy has many tools at his command. The ability to
disguise oneself is perhaps the most valuble. Someone taking on the persona of another person must
become the person, live and breathe that person. If
you are disguised as a starving beggar, you must
starve.*

—Sir Henry Wallace

The next day, the Braffan pot boiled over. His Majesty was
feeling better and decided to hold his levee. It turned into a
fiasco. The grand bishop arrived to demand publicly that the
king send the entire naval fleet to deal with the Freyans.
Furious, Alaric declared he would add two frigates and a
couple of patrol boats that were guarding the coast of Bourlet, a duchy he didn't much like anyway, but that was all.

Montagne maintained that this wasn't good enough, and
the two got into a violent argument, in the midst of which
ambassadors from Travia and Estara, along with a representative of the Braffan High Council, joined the fray, to the
delight of those who had thought this was going to be just
another gossip-filled levee. Travia stated they were prepared
to send their fleet to protect Braffa from Freya. Braffa said
they didn't need Travian protection and demanded that

Estara immediately withdraw her ships and allow the Freyan ships safe passage. This set off howls of rage and protest from the grand bishop, and from both Travia and Estara. His Majesty ended the levee, stalked out in a royal huff, and sent immediately for Cecile.

"Fix it," he told her when she arrived.

"Somewhere—probably in Braffa—Sir Henry Wallace is laughing," Cecile muttered beneath her breath.

She could not find a way to "fix it." The best she could do was to cool tempers, stop the hotheaded Estaran ambassador from challenging the Travian ambassador to a duel, placate the grand bishop, and attempt to prevent Alaric, who was in a towering rage, from committing political suicide. She went from one meeting to the next until late in the afternoon, when she finally returned to her chambers, drained and worn out.

She entered through a private door to avoid facing the crowd in her salon, sank down at her desk, and then sent for D'argent, who had impatiently been awaiting her return.

"I am sorry I could not see you sooner," she said. "This Braffan situation is a disaster. Sir Henry has beaten us this time, I fear."

"No need to apologize, my lady."

"You have news about the duchess?"

"I do, my lady. I found her last night on the lower floors of the palace—"

He was interrupted. The countess's secretary knocked, then opened the door.

"I told you I was not to be disturbed, Viscount—" Cecile said, annoyed.

"A Monsieur Dubois has arrived, demanding to see you, my lady. I said you were not receiving, but he is very insistent—"

Indeed, Cecile could see Dubois hovering in the doorway.

"My lady!" Dubois called urgently. "I *must* speak to you!"

The generally unemotional and self-effacing man attempted to shoulder the viscount out of the way.

"Please enter, Monsieur Dubois," said Cecile, to the disappointment of the viscount, who had been hoping to be able to toss this fellow out on his ear. "That will be all, Viscount."

The viscount withdrew with a haughty air as though to say the countess could not blame him if she chose to entertain clerks.

Dubois was still wearing his cloak, and carried his hat in his hand. His clothes were wrinkled and mud-stained, and he was puffing, out of breath.

"I beg your pardon for my disheveled appearance, my lady," said Dubois. "But I deemed not a moment must be lost."

Cecile had known Dubois for many years and had never seen him so disturbed.

"Please be seated. Have you eaten?"

Dubois shook his head. He bowed to D'argent, apologizing for the interruption. Cecile rang for Marie and ordered sandwiches and coffee.

"A drop of brandy," she suggested.

Dubois took a seat, drank the brandy, and then fanned himself with his hat.

"I have been to Capione," he said. "I visited the Château de Sauleschant, the estate of this so-called duchess."

" 'So-called,' " Cecile repeated, the words chilling.

"I will explain," said Dubois. "But, first, I must tell you who was also there: Sir Henry Wallace."

"So the duchess is in league with Wallace," said Cecile, drumming her fingers on the desk.

"No, my lady. I could almost wish that were true," said Dubois.

He related his tale, telling what he had learned about the duchess at the inn and how he had discovered Wallace and Captain Alan Northrop searching the house. Dubois gave her a word-for-word account of what he overheard them say and finished by describing the gruesome scene in the wine cellar.

Cecile listened in growing horror, so appalled she felt incapable of asking a coherent question. All she could think of was this murderer, Lucello, laying his bloodstained hands upon the princess.

When his tale was concluded, Dubois devoured the sandwiches and drank the coffee.

"We must expose this woman and her accomplice. I must immediately inform His Majesty."

Cecile was on her feet, ready to go to the king. Dubois rose to prevent, giving a polite cough of apology as he stepped to place himself in her way.

"Exposure will not be easy, my lady," he cautioned. "I have no evidence. The duchess will simply deny everything. And I cannot call Sir Henry as a witness," he added drily.

"You are right, monsieur," said Cecile, growing calm in an instant. She resumed her chair. "We must find another way. D'argent was just telling me about the duchess's strange behavior here in the palace. She has been seen making midnight rambles."

"I found the duchess on the lowest level of the palace last night," said D'argent. "The scene was exactly as we heard the footman describe. She was in dishabille and claimed to have been there to meet a lover."

"The bottom of the palace?" Dubois asked, frowning. "She was down there last night and you say she has been down there before?"

"According to the report of a servant," D'argent replied.

The three sat in silence: Dubois pondering, D'argent wondering, and Cecile trying to decide what to do. Her main concern was for Sophia.

"Whatever else, the princess must be removed from danger. I will take her to my estate— Yes, monsieur?"

She said this to Dubois, who had bounced to his feet with such suddenness he upset the coffee cup he had been balancing on his knee.

"We must go to the ground floor of the palace," he said. "At once! Not a moment is to be lost!"

"I will be glad to, monsieur," said Cecile. "I must first send word to the princess—"

"Now!" Dubois shouted. He forgot himself so far as to stamp his foot. "Immediately!"

"Considering what we now know of this woman, I think it would be best if we do as he says, my lady," said D'argent, troubled. "The lower chamber of the palace is dark and drafty. You should bring a cloak."

"And lanterns," said Dubois.

D'argent left to fetch dark lanterns. Cecile rang for her cloak and wrote a note to the Princess Sophia, saying she wished to see her. The three set out, taking the back passages to avoid having to answer questions. Cecile covered her head, concealing her face with the hood of her cloak.

The palace proper had four levels. Each of the towers had an additional two levels. The upper two levels housed the private chambers of the king and queen, and the residences of members of the nobility. Here were the audience rooms, guest rooms, music rooms, ballrooms, galleries, libraries, morning rooms, evening rooms, and so forth. The third level contained the kitchens, pantries, wine cellars, granary, common docks, servants' quarters, carriage houses, stalls for the royal wyverns and griffins, and the guardsmen's barracks.

The very bottom level was a large warehouselike chamber that had been specially constructed to house sixteen enormous lift tanks, filled with the liquid form of the Breath known as the Blood of God. The lift tanks were inscribed with magical constructs and operated much like the lift tanks on the royal navy's new warships to keep the palace floating in the air.

They arrived at the bottom level to find it empty. The crafters had left for the day. There were no windows, and the darkness of the immense room seemed to swallow up the beams of their lights.

"What are we looking for, Dubois?" asked Cecile, gazing around. "What do you suspect that woman was doing down here?"

"I do not know, my lady," said Dubois grimly. "All I know is that she is a sorceress who is skilled in contramagic and I very much doubt if she was entertaining a lover among the lift tanks."

As Dubois and D'argent flashed their lights about the chamber, Cecile saw a large rat skitter out of hiding. She grimaced in disgust and gathered her cloak more closely about her legs.

"What is wrong, my lady?" D'argent asked, noticing her shudder.

"A rat," Cecile replied. "The thing crawled out from under the tank."

"You should go back to your chambers, my lady," said D'argent, glancing down at her low-cut shoes. "You are not dressed for this."

She gave a dismissive shrug. "I fear we are out of our element here. Perhaps we should summon the royal engineers. They can tell us if something is amiss."

The royal engineers were crafters expert in the field of engineering magic. They worked down here during the day, checking the levels of the liquid in the tanks, assisting with filling the tanks when necessary, making certain the tanks were functioning properly, and repairing any magical constructs that were starting to break down.

"We will need to provide them with some explanation for why we summoned them, my lady," Dubois replied. "Otherwise they will think we are lunatics."

"You are right, of course, monsieur," said Cecile with a slight smile.

Dubois sent his light stabbing into the darkness, searching the area around the tanks from ceiling to floor and scanning the tanks themselves.

"A fool's errand, my lady," D'argent said softly. "We have no idea—"

"What is that?" Cecile cried suddenly, pointing.

Truth to tell, she was more concerned about rats than anything else. She had been nervously watching for rodents when she noticed a faint green glow coming from beneath one of the lift tanks.

Dubois and D'argent hurried to investigate.

"Please stay back, my lady."

The two men squatted down on the floor, peering underneath the tank, which was mounted on stone supports. Cecile, paying no heed to Dubois's urging, drew near to see. Dubois went down flat on his stomach, crawled partway under the tank, and carefully and gingerly retrieved something.

He stood up, holding the object in his hand. D'argent shone the lantern on a broken shard of lead crystal about the size of Dubois's palm. The crystal glowed a faint green. A faint shimmer of green glowed from the constructs that covered the surface of the lift tank.

"You are a crafter, my lady," said Dubois. "Do you recognize those constructs?"

"You and I have seen them and this green glow before." She recalled her brush with death with vivid clarity. "They are contramagic. Did they do any damage?"

"I wonder . . ." Dubois stood in thought a moment, then said, "I believe it is time to summon the chief engineer."

"The engineers live with their families in quarters in the level above. I will go," D'argent offered.

He left. The countess waited in the darkness, trying to think about contramagic and not rats. Dubois fidgeted beside her, flashing his light around.

"If you do not mind being left alone for a moment, my lady, I would like to check something," he said at last.

"I will be fine," said Cecile. She held out her hand. "Before you go, let me see that object."

"I don't know, my lady—" Dubois was reluctant. "We have no idea what it does . . ."

"That was not a request, monsieur," said Cecile.

Dubois handed over the piece of lead crystal, then left upon his errand. Cecile examined the crystal closely. It appeared to be part of a broken bottle, perhaps a perfume bottle or a bottle containing smelling salts. The constructs etched upon the glass were no thicker than a strand of hair. The workmanship was exquisite, the worker skilled. If Eiddwen had crafted this magic, she had taken a great deal of time and trouble. To what end?

Dubois returned. His expression was grim. "I found the same glow beneath another tank, my lady. I pulled out another piece of crystal. I didn't check them all, but I'm guessing we'll find the same beneath each of them."

D'argent returned with one of the engineers. They had disturbed the man at his supper, apparently, for he was trying to swallow something and wiping his mouth as he came. He was a large man with a full, black beard and a cheerful countenance. He was astonished beyond measure to come upon Cecile down in the depths of the palace. He stared at her, incredulous, then made a flustered bow.

"This is Master Henri," said D'argent. "Chief engineer. He disparages our discovery."

Master Henri flushed, embarrassed. "It's just that some of the lads in the palace sneak down here and get into all manner of mischief, my lady. What you've found is likely a broken wine bottle—"

"This is no wine bottle, Master Henri," said Cecile, and she held out the lead crystal. The green glow was starting to fade. The constructs were barely visible.

Master Henri took the crystal and held it to the light. His thick brows creased.

"I must admit, these constructs are singular, my lady. Still, I wouldn't put it past those lads—"

" 'Those lads' had nothing to do with this," Dubois interrupted testily. "The constructs are contramagic, Master Engineer."

Master Henri drew back to regard the three with dark suspicion. "Whatever you gentlemen and lady are plotting, I will not be involved. I bid you good night—"

"We are not plotting anything, Master Henri!" said Cecile sharply. "We are trying to foil a plot. Monsieur Dubois— who is, by the way, an agent of the grand bishop—found this crystal shard underneath the lift tank. Inspect the tank to make certain everything is as it should be."

Master Henri was clearly loath to have anything to do with them or their green glowing crystal. The Countess de Marjolaine was a powerful force in the kingdom, however, and he could not very well refuse to obey her command. Master Henri activated the lights that hung from the ceiling, filling the chamber with a bright glow, and began to inspect the lift tank. The constructs he cast caused the magical constructs on the tank to glow with blue light.

"All appears to be in order, my lady," he said coldly.

"Check the bottom of the tank," said Dubois.

Master Henri cast him a glance of deep suspicion, but he did as he was told. Flattening himself on his back on the floor, he edged his way beneath the tank. There was silence, then they heard him gasp. Cecile and Dubois and D'argent exchanged glances. Master Henri wriggled his way from underneath the tank. His face behind the black beard was pale.

"Some of the constructs on the bottom of the tank are gone, my lady," he said, sounding dazed. "Others are eroding. Even as I watched, I saw a construct vanish before my eyes!"

"Can you stop the destruction?" Cecile asked urgently.

"I can't stop it, my lady, because I don't know the cause," said Master Henri in helpless tones.

"Check the other tanks," said Dubois.

Master Henri dashed off. Cecile looked down at the crystal in her hand. She looked at Dubois and D'argent.

"This was a bomb," she said quietly.

Master Henri returned. He was haggard and distraught. "I checked three tanks. The magic is failing on each of them. I have to assume the same is happening with the rest of the lift tanks."

"You and your engineers can replace the magic that is being destroyed," Cecile said. "How long will that take?"

Master Henri regarded her steadily.

"My lady, you don't understand. The magical constructs were put in place when the lift tanks were built. We would have to remove every tank and start over from the beginning. The work would take months. Maybe a year."

Cecile's throat constricted. D'argent was pale and grave. Dubois shook his head and asked the question they were all thinking.

"And what happens, Monsieur Henri, when the magic on

the tanks fails? Is the palace in imminent danger of falling out of the sky?"

Master Henri swallowed and glanced about in confusion.

"I . . . I don't know, Monsieur," he said. "Such a catastrophe has never been contemplated—"

"Contemplate it," said Cecile.

"My lady, I must evaluate the situation . . ."

"Master Henri, six hundred people live and work in the palace!"

"I know, my lady," he said unhappily. "This has all been so sudden. The liquid Breath in the lift tanks will continue to work until the constructs are gone and perhaps a short time after that. Many of the constructs are still in place. I have no way of knowing how fast that green magic will do its devil work. All I know is that I can't stop it."

"We are talking about evacuating six hundred people!" Cecile said, shaken. "All of them panic-stricken."

"Worse than that, my lady," D'argent added in grim tones. "The palace floats above Mirror Lake. If the palace were to fall out of the sky, it would crash into the lake. The water would overflow the banks and flood the city. We will have to evacuate all of Evreux."

"If there was time . . . ," Cecile murmured.

"As I said, my lady, the liquid in the tanks will remain viable, though unstable." Master Henri was thoughtful. "It might be possible to lower the palace slowly. I will know more after we have investigated."

"Report to me the moment you know anything," said Cecile.

"Report to you, my lady?" Master Henri was uneasy. "His Majesty—"

"Should not be troubled with this business until we have more information. When I know what our options are, I will inform His Majesty. The decision, of course, will be his. Master Henri"—Cecile fixed him with a look—"you will tell only your engineers about this. *No one else*. And you will swear them to secrecy. On pain of death."

"Yes, my lady," said Master Henri.

"If anyone else discovers this, I vow to God I will have every single one of you hanged."

Master Henri swallowed. "I understand, my lady." He bowed and hurried away to alert his engineers.

"We know now what Eiddwen has been doing down here at night. Sabotaging the lift tanks," said D'argent. "The question is: What do we do with her?"

"She has no way of knowing we have discovered her plot," said Cecile.

"But she must be planning to leave the palace soon," D'argent pointed out. "Before it crashes to the ground."

"Leave Mistress Eiddwen to me," said Dubois, opening his coat to reveal the concealed pistol. "I have full authority to arrest her. The question is: What do I do with her?"

"Before we do anything with her, there is something important we must consider," Cecile said. "The Sunset Palace is the most visible symbol of the strength of the monarchy. If we evacuate the palace and lower it to the ground, the people of Rosia will want to know why. And we have no answers. His Majesty will be made to look weak, vulnerable."

"And think of the ensuing chaos," said D'argent. "Even if it is lowered slowly, the palace will fall into the lake. Thousands of people will be forced to flee their homes. Where will they go? Who will care for them? The evacuation alone could plunge the country into turmoil."

"After the disaster with the Crystal Market, rumors are already spreading that magic is failing. Those will grow stronger," said Dubois. "You are right, Countess. This would create a crisis of faith that could destroy our church and our country. We cannot evacuate the palace. And yet we can't wait for the palace to plummet from the heavens. Our only option is to find a way to counter the contramagic. And only the duchess can do that."

"Bring Eiddwen to my chamber," said Cecile. "Be discreet, Monsieur Dubois. No one must see you. There is a back entrance to my rooms that leads to a closet. My maid will meet you in the passageway."

Dubois nodded and hastened off.

"My lady, from what we hear, this woman is a murderess many times over," said D'argent. "She is extremely dangerous. We can't keep her locked in your bedroom."

"An excellent point, D'argent, and one I had considered. Go to the Mother House of the Knight Protectors. Ask for a knight called Sir Conal O'Hairt. Tell him I am in urgent need of his assistance. Say that Sir Ander recommended him. Make haste. We have not a moment to spare."

"I leave now, my lady," said D'argent.

"And yet we may already be too late," Cecile said softly.

37

*We do everything in our power to keep our children
from harm, yet we let them fall in love with impunity.*

—Anonymous

Cecile made her way up the stairs and through the servants'
passages to her chambers. She did not want to meet anyone
on the way. The time was now evening. In the palace, the
noble lords and ladies would be dressing in their finery,
looking forward to dining with friends or His Majesty, who
was fond of entertaining. Later there would be dancing, and
flirting, for the young. Their elders would sit down to cards
and gossip; governesses would be supervising their young
charges, feeding and sending them to bed. Nursemaids would
be rocking cradles and singing lullabies.

Cecile tried not to imagine what would happen if the
Sunset Palace, this enormous structure of marble and granite, glass and wood and magic, were to suddenly plunge to
the ground. No one could survive. In one horrific moment,
the country of Rosia would be left without a king, without
ministers. Foreign nations would lose their ambassadors.
Entire noble families would be wiped out. The disaster was
too terrible even to contemplate.

Cecile would have to tell the king tonight, but she needed as much information as she could gather in order to advise him. Alaric was never at his best during a crisis. He tended to dither, decide one way and then another. This would be worse. He would most likely refuse to believe this tale of contramagic bombs and, to be honest, who could blame him? She would need to provide proof. He would need to hear the report of the master engineer, which meant Master Henri had better have answers. And Eiddwen had to be removed, handed over to the Knight Protectors who could keep her safe while they sent for the Arcanum inquisitors to force her to talk.

Cecile slipped into her chambers. She summoned Marie, telling her to keep watch in the passageway for Monsieur Dubois.

Marie knew better than to ask questions. "A note arrived for you, my lady. I believe it is from the Princess Sophia. You will find it on your desk."

Marie left to take up watch in the passageway. Cecile went through to her office. The viscount was gone, thank God. She vaguely recalled giving him permission to leave early to attend a musical evening. Cecile picked up the note and was about to set it aside, thinking it was only a response to the note she had sent earlier, when something about the handwriting caused her to examine the note with more attention.

Sophia's handwriting was as neat as that of a clerk. She wrote slowly, forming every letter perfectly. The princess had not learned to read or write until only a few years ago. The queen herself was illiterate, believing that a girl needed to know only one thing and that was how to catch a husband. Cecile had taught Sophia, much to her mother's ire. The king sided with Cecile, saying his daughter would grow up to be an educated woman. The princess was quite proud of her accomplishment and she took great care when she wrote anything.

The letter should have been addressed formally, "Countess Cecile de Marjolaine," but the envelope had only one word and that was illegible. It might have been "Countess" or "Cecile" or a confused combination of both. Cecile turned over the envelope. The back was smeared with sealing wax that had dripped all over the envelope. The hand holding the wax had been trembling.

Filled with foreboding, Cecile seized the letter opener, sliced through the envelope, and tore out the letter. She scanned it swiftly, then sank back in her chair. The letter fell from her hand. Cecile felt suffocated, unable to catch her breath. The room seemed to be tilting. She closed her eyes, forced herself to breathe. Once the room settled back into place, Cecile picked up the letter and read it again.

My dearest friend,

I am not supposed to be telling you this, for Lucello warned me to keep our secret, but I am so filled with joy that I had to tell someone. Lucello has asked me to be his wife. I know that Papa would forbid our marriage, but I cannot live without Lucello. I adore him with all my heart and therefore I have agreed to elope with him. We are going to the dragon duchies. I know nothing about this, but Lucello says we can be married there, since the law is different or something.

I fear you will be angry with me, Countess, but please don't be. There is a good reason I am running away. Lucello told me that his aunt, the duchess, found out that Papa has agreed to my marriage with that horrid Travian prince. Lucello told me stories about the prince, how he has the pox and he beats his wives. I would sooner die.

You must tell Papa, Countess. You will know what to say. He will be furious, but I hope in time he will forgive me and welcome Lucello as his son.

Countess, you understand what it is to be in love. Wish me joy!

The letter was signed simply, "Sophia." There were two postscripts:

1. *The duchess goes with us as chaperone. We are to hire a post chaise so that no one will know us. I am to disguise myself with a veil! So romantic!*
2. *I am taking Bandit. He cried when he thought I was going somewhere without him and I can't bear to leave him behind.*

Cecile sat with the letter in her hands. Her fingers were so cold she could no longer feel them. Her own youthful folly and indiscretion came back to her. So many lives forever shattered, destroyed. Her husband's cruel death at the hands of a jealous king. A bastard son who had always hated and despised her.

"If only, if only, if only I had paid more attention! If only I had talked to Sophia, warned her. My fault," Cecile said in a choked voice. "This is my fault. And now, what is to be done?"

She dropped the letter and sprang to her feet, running to the door with the idea that there might yet be time to stop them. She flung the door open, only to find Dubois standing on the other side. One look at his expression and she knew all was lost.

"The duchess is gone and her nephew with her," Dubois reported, entering and shutting the door behind him. "She has escaped us!"

"That is not the worst of it." Cecile picked up the letter and showed it to him.

Dubois read it. He looked at her, aghast.

"This is terrible!"

"Beyond terrible," said Cecile. "Think of the scandal. Sophia's reputation—"

"'Scandal'!" Dubois repeated. "'Reputation'! Consider what this means, Countess! Eiddwen and Lucello are cold-blooded, ruthless, sadistic killers who deal in blood magic. God knows what they mean to do with the princess! If we are lucky, Eiddwen plans to merely use her as a hostage, for the duchess must know that we would eventually find out what she had done and come after her. If not, and they contemplate some unholy rite—"

Dubois shuddered. He laid the letter down on the desk. "You must tell the king to call out the guard—"

"No!" Cecile said firmly. "You discount the scandal, but I cannot. Sophia's life will not be ruined as was mine. We cannot tell the king. He will need all his wits about him to deal with the contramagic crisis. This terrible news would destroy him. He would be able to think of nothing else."

Dubois was grave. He knew the king by reputation, knew that she was right in what she said.

"There is only one thing to be done. I will go in pursuit of the princess," said Cecile.

"You, my lady!" Dubois gasped. "You can't be serious! The danger, the risk is too great!"

"Sophia trusts me. She will listen to me."

"My lady, no, you must think this through—"

"I have, monsieur. As you say, Eiddwen may be using the princess as a hostage. If you send an army, Eiddwen might harm her."

Cecile sat down at her desk and began to write. At last she could think calmly, make plans with a clear mind. The room was silent except for the ticking of a small clock on the mantelpiece. Dubois roamed about, fiddling with his hat, twirling it in his hand, dropping it twice. Cecile paid him no heed. She wrote two letters, both of them short, and enclosed both in envelopes, sealing and stamping them with the sealing ring that bore her insignia, the bee. One letter she handed to Dubois, the other she tucked into the bosom of her gown.

"Once you have Master Henri's report, take this letter to His Majesty," she said.

Dubois gave a dry cough. "His Majesty would not admit me to the royal presence . . ."

Cecile smiled. "Grand Bishop de Montagne is in the palace. He was at the levee and he remained to meet with the king's ministers. Once you know the extent of the peril, go to Montagne, tell him everything. He will accompany you to the king. The grand bishop and I have been on opposite sides of a good many conflicts, but I respect his intelligence, as I respect yours, Monsieur Dubois. With God's help, you both will be able to advise His Majesty in this crisis."

Dubois made a little bobbing bow to acknowledge the compliment.

"I have written to His Majesty that due to the danger, I have taken Sophia with me to my country estate. We have left quietly, so as not to start a panic."

Dubois considered this, and nodded to indicate his approval. "Though I still do not like the idea of you pursuing these murderers alone, my lady."

"I will not be alone. Ah, here is D'argent and Sir Conal. Welcome, Sir Knight. Thank you for coming so swiftly."

"Countess de Marjolaine," said Sir Conal with a deep bow. "I am honored to be of service."

Cecile had never met Sir Conal O'Hairt, but she had heard her friend Sir Ander speak highly of him, once telling her that if she ever required help she could turn to Sir Conal.

He was a short man with curly hair and the sunburned, leathery skin of one who spends a great deal of time outdoors. He had broad shoulders, muscular arms and a thick neck, with the look of a Trundler about him, which would explain his name. Cecile was surprised and concerned to observe that he walked with the aid of a cane.

Sir Conal saw the direction of her glance. "Knee goes out on me sometimes, milady. Nothing I can't handle."

He was not apologetic, merely explanatory. His light blue eyes met her gaze without flinching. He stood calmly under her scrutiny: respectful, but not intimidated; a man who knew his own worth; an honest man, loyal and courageous, or he would not have been chosen to be a Knight Protector. Sir Ander had said she could trust him. Cecile felt she would have trusted Sir Conal even without her friend's recommendation.

"What has gone wrong, my lady?" D'argent asked, alarmed. "Where is the prisoner?"

"Monsieur Dubois will explain while I change my clothes. I won't be long. Are you armed, Sir Conal?"

"I am, milady." Sir Conal pulled aside his cloak to indicate the baldric he wore, with its loops for pistols. He was also carrying his sword at his side.

"Excellent. You and I will be making a journey. We will need to travel fast and light. A young woman has been persuaded to make an elopement. I have reason to believe her seducer and his accomplice are bound for the dragon duchies. I must stop them for the sake of this young woman's reputation. I would like you to accompany me. They are traveling by post chaise. What is the fastest way we can catch up with them?"

D'argent looked astonished and troubled at this news. He glanced at Dubois, who only shook his head sadly and twirled his hat.

Sir Conal was giving the countess's request careful consideration. "Flying in the dark is much too dangerous. I would suggest we, too, travel by post chaise, milady. We can follow them, perhaps catch up to them."

"Please make the arrangements, Sir Conal. We will leave the palace using the common docks, not the front entrance."

Sir Conal wasted no time asking questions, nor did he try to talk Cecile out of going, as she had half expected. He simply bowed and left. As Cecile went to her dressing room, she heard Dubois hurriedly telling D'argent what details they knew about Eiddwen's escape and the abduction of the princess.

Cecile returned dressed for travel in a plain woolen gown, dun colored with long sleeves and linen petticoats. The days were warm in Evreux, but she and Sir Conal were traveling north into the mountains, where the weather would be cooler. She wore lace-up boots and thick stockings. An unhappy looking Marie hovered behind Cecile, carrying a hooded cloak and gloves and a purse heavy with silver.

Cecile handed to D'argent the second letter she had written.

"This is for Stephano."

D'argent was extremely grave. "My lady, I beg you to reconsider. Send me with Sir Conal."

"Thank you, D'argent. I need you to remain here. Accompany Dubois to His Majesty."

"My lady—"

She held out her hand to him. "Take care of Stephano, my friend. He won't admit it, but he will need your help and guidance."

D'argent could not speak for his emotion. He kissed her hand, then slipped the letter into an inner pocket.

"Godspeed you on your mission, Monsieur Dubois," said Cecile, drawing on her gloves. "I am glad to have been working *with* you, for once."

Dubois placed his hand over his heart and made a deep bow. "God go with you, Countess."

"Marie, I will take the back way out," said Cecile.

Sir Conal was waiting for her at the common docks. Knight Protectors were often seen at the palace, especially today, with the grand bishop and his staff present. The common docks were busy. Supply wagons were making evening deliveries, servants were coming and going on errands for their masters, and military conveyances carried officers from the ships. No one paid much heed to the pair.

Cecile kept her hood drawn low over her face. She said nothing as she climbed into the griffin-drawn chariot in which Sir Conal had arrived. He had changed his clothes, no longer wearing the uniform that would connect him to the Knight Protectors. He was dressed as a military officer, which would account for the sword he wore at his side.

"Who is the young woman, milady?" he asked, assisting her into the chariot.

Cecile explained their mission. Sir Conal listened without comment, though his expression darkened and he shook his head when he heard the identity of the person who had been abducted.

"I do not like to say this, milady, but you know it is possible these two are *not* taking the princess to the dragon duchies. They could be taking her anywhere."

"I thought of this, Sir Conal," Cecile replied. "They are hiring a post chaise. Only a select few inns in Evreux offer post chaises for hire. We will stop first at the inn that is located on the King's Highway leading north. Hopefully we will hear news of them."

The clock struck ten times as they arrived at the inn. Lights shone from the windows. Other carriages stood in the

yard. The inn was busy this time of night. Sir Conal alighted
from the coach and gave Cecile his hand to assist her. As she
stepped down, Sir Conal said quietly, "While I secure the
post chaise, you find out if the three have been here, milady.
You can ask without arousing suspicion."

Sir Conal demanded a post chaise and the fastest horses,
saying he was on an errand of the utmost urgency. Sir Conal's
air of authority sent men scurrying to carry out his orders
and brought the innkeeper himself to supervise. He cast a
wondering glance at Cecile, who stood in the yard, her hood
still drawn low over her head. The innkeeper noticed the
fine quality of her clothing. He ventured to suggest she might
find the waiting more comfortable inside.

"Thank you, sir," said Cecile. "We will not trouble you
long, I hope. This road leads to Ellif and from there to the
dragon duchies."

"Yes, that is true, madam."

"I am seeking news of three people who may have passed
this way earlier in the day. A young man with a limp and a
young woman with a small dog. They would be accompanied by an older woman, a duenna."

"They were here this afternoon, madam," said the innkeeper. "I remember them because of the little dog, who got
loose and ran off. The young woman was going to chase
after it. The older woman stopped her, saying they were in a
hurry and to leave the dog behind. The young woman was
most distraught. The young man caught the dog, and they
proceeded."

"Did they say where they were bound?"

The innkeeper chuckled. "They had no need, my lady.
We see many such young couples. A young man and a young
woman traveling in haste on the main road that leads to the
dragon duchies. A wedding is in the offing, I would say."

Cecile thanked the innkeeper for the information. Within

moments, a small, fast chaise drawn by two horses rolled into the yard.

"What did you find out?" Sir Conal asked in a low voice.

"They were here this afternoon," Cecile reported. "They hired a post chaise, making no secret of the fact they were going to the dragon duchies. I fear they have several hours' start."

"We can follow their progress on the road, milady," said Sir Conal. "They will have to change horses at the rest stops, as will we, and we will hear news of them. And if they leave the road, we will find that out, as well."

"We have lost a great deal of time," said Cecile.

"We are on their trail, milady," Sir Conal said with a reassuring smile. "We will catch them. You should try to sleep. Rest easy. We are all in God's care."

He lit the carriage lamps, mounted the driver's box, and snapped the whip. The horses plunged ahead and soon hit their stride, galloping over the road. The chaise shook and rattled and swayed perilously from side to side. Cecile held on tightly to the strap to avoid being tossed around.

She made herself as comfortable as was uncomfortably possible. Wrapping up in a blanket, she wedged herself in a corner and closed her eyes, trying to take Sir Conal's advice. She remained awake, however, aware of every jounce and jolt in the road. Eventually she gave up and, as the night deepened, she leaned out of the chaise window to look back at Evreux, now behind them. In the distance, the Sunset Palace, illuminated by night, glittered among the clouds like a star come down from heaven.

We are all in God's care.

Cecile had once placed Julian in God's care. She had prayed to God on her knees, begging Him to save her husband from a cruel death. God had not cared then. She did not see why He should start caring now.

Drawing off her glove, she clasped the plain golden ring and turned it around and around.

Dubois and D'argent waited together in the countess's office for Master Henri. D'argent had ordered a light supper. Neither man was particularly hungry and they only picked at the food. When the door opened without ceremony and Master Henri entered, both Dubois and D'argent jumped to their feet.

"What have you found out?" Dubois demanded.

Master Henri looked about. "Where is the countess?"

"She is indisposed," said D'argent. "Make your report to us. We are commissioned to carry it to the king."

"All sixteen tanks are affected," said Master Henri. He was pale and haggard and filthy from crawling around under the tanks. "Some worse than others. We can keep the magic functioning for a time. I don't know how long."

He paused and wiped a hand over his face.

"Yes, go on," said Dubois.

Master Henri was clearly reluctant. "I need to say something first, gentlemen. My engineers and I have noticed in the past few months that the magic has been failing. Nothing serious. We've had to replace constructs more often, that is all. We didn't report it. We don't want to be blamed—"

"Master Henri, we found the bomb fragments. We know the person responsible. This is not your fault," said D'argent, exasperated.

"You will tell that to His Majesty, monsieur," Master Henri pressed anxiously. "We don't want to be arrested."

"Yes, of course, we will!" Dubois shouted. "Stop wasting time! What should we tell the king?"

"Tell His Majesty," said Master Henri slowly, "the palace is already starting to sink."

38

A plump little doe wanders into the forest and is threatened by a wolf. A bear sees the doe and attacks the wolf. A griffin sees the doe and attacks the other two. The intelligent doe would take this opportunity to run. The ignorant Braffan doe stays to glory in the fight, ignoring the fact that the victor will surely devour her.

—Lutr Ulfskjald,
former Braffan council member

The *Sommerwind*'s journey to Braffa had thus far been uneventful. Fair winds carried the *Sommerwind* along at a rapid clip. The wild dragons with their riders flew escort, two dragons on duty while one slept in the open area on the stern castle that had been cleared for them. The crew had been nervous around the dragons at first; no one wanting to venture near the slumbering dragon. But when several days and nights had passed peacefully with the dragons showing no signs of intending to devour anyone, the crew relaxed.

This day, Petard was sleeping, his large body impossibly curled up into a tight ball, his nose tucked beneath his wing, his tail wrapped around him. His eyes were slits of gleaming red. Miri wondered if dragons kept watch even as they slept, or if the partially open eyes were meant to deter predators. She wished now as she had wished in the past, that there was some way to talk with these dragons.

She and Rodrigo were together on the deck of the *Sommerwind,* both of them taking a break from work. Gythe was sleeping in the small cabin. Miri had never seen her sister so relaxed, so filled with joy, and she was glad she had relented and permitted her sister to ride. Gythe had even stopped talking about Brother Barnaby, although sometimes, when a shadow passed over her face, Miri knew Gythe was thinking of the young monk.

Dag was flying Verdi in the lead. Stephano and Viola flew near the ship; a more difficult task, for they had to make certain they kept a safe distance from the rigging and the balloon, not wanting to tangle a wing in the ropes or rip the balloon with the dragon's tail.

Catching sight of his two friends standing on the deck, Stephano waved to them from the back of the dragon. He was laughing for no apparent reason with his head thrown back, his arms spread as though he would embrace the sky.

"Look at him," said Miri with a touch of sadness in her voice. "He's with the one female who can ever make him truly happy."

"A dragon," Rodrigo agreed glumly. "I wash my hands of him."

Stephano was happy, unconditionally happy. He had no self-doubt, no worries, no concerns—other than trying to train Gythe to behave more like a dragon rider; and he feared he was going to have to give up on that.

He looked down on the mists of the Breath beneath him in the shipping lanes, tasted the sharp, pure air in his mouth, and reveled in the stillness. People spoke of the Voice of God. Stephano felt closer to God in His silence.

He gave Miri and Rodrigo a salute, then he and Viola flew ahead of the ship to join Dag, who was practicing loading his pistols while on dragon back, a feat that could be tricky due to the motion of the dragon. Dag had learned how to aim and fire from the back of the dragon, shooting at small balloons Miri launched from the deck. Dag had always been an excellent shot and he soon surpassed Stephano in skill in hitting the target.

Dag took his escort duties seriously. Gythe and her dragon, Petard, by contrast, were completely undisciplined. The two flew all over the sky, sailing far above the merchant ship, diving down beneath the keel, hiding in the clouds, and then bursting out to startle the others. Stephano had tried several times to explain to Gythe the duties of an escort. Gythe had listened, her eyes dancing with merriment, and after the lecture she and Petard flew off to do exactly as they pleased.

"You should talk to her, Miri," Stephano had said, frustrated. "Explain to her that she needs to take her dragon riding seriously."

"As you told me in Bourlet, Stephano, Gythe is a grown woman," Miri had replied tersely. "If she doesn't have to listen to me, I guess she doesn't have to listen to you either."

Miri worked in the small surgery belowdecks, nursing the crew's various ailments from broken bones to chilblains. Rodrigo had proven his worth by using his skills as a crafter to make the same magical repairs to the *Sommerwind* as he had made for the *Cloud Hopper*. When Rodrigo wasn't working on that, he was down in his cabin doing something mysterious that he wouldn't discuss.

"My dear friend," he said to Stephano when he had questioned him about his belowdecks activity, "I suppose I am permitted to have secrets."

"If the beautiful wife of some count was on board, I wouldn't have to ask what you were doing," said Stephano drily. "That not being the case, I was just wondering. You spend so much time alone in there . . ."

"I could be composing an opera," said Rodrigo.

"Are you?" Stephano asked, surprised.

"No," said Rodrigo. "But I could be."

He walked off and that was the end of that.

As for the last member of the Cadre, Doctor Ellington earned his keep by killing rats, which he presented as gifts to various people, leaving the prizes in unoccupied shoes.

That afternoon the *Sommerwind* sailed into the contested Straits de Domcáido. They sighted the ships of the Freyan fleet skirting the Estaran coast, coming as close as they could without actually venturing into Estaran territory. Estaran ships dogged them, letting the Freyans know they were under surveillance.

Nervous about calling attention to his vessel, Captain Leydecker ordered Stephano and his dragon riders to keep clear of the stand-off. The *Sommerwind* was nearing Braffa and what was potentially a volatile situation. Every time they had encountered another merchant ship, Captain Leydecker had slowed to ask for news about the situation in Braffa, while Miri questioned any Trundlers they happened to run across.

They heard rumors, received conflicting information. The Travians were blockading the refinery ports; the Travians weren't blockading them; the Rosian fleet was on its way; the Rosians had said they would not get involved; and so on and so forth.

"I have no idea what to believe," said Captain Leydecker.

"What do you hear from the cartel?" Stephano asked.

"The last I heard, the Travians were hiring Guundaran mercenaries to man ships that are older than I am and in worse condition," Captain Leydecker replied.

"One thing I know for certain, Captain," Miri said. "The Trundlers are fleeing this part of the world. Every Trundler boat we've met is leaving and not planning to come back. My people have a nose for trouble."

"The question is, Sir, what do you plan to do if we find the refineries are blockaded?" Stephano asked.

"People are counting on me to make my delivery," said Captain Leydecker grimly. "I don't see that we have a choice."

"True, sir, but we don't want to sail blindly into a blockade," said Leutnant Baumann. "The Travians would like nothing better than to get their hands on our cargo."

"Pardon me," said Rodrigo, "I am a bit confused. If a Travian cartel is your sponsor, why would Travian ships confiscate your cargo? Wouldn't you all just have a hearty laugh, shake hands, and be on your way?"

Captain Leydecker snorted. "The blockade ships' officers and crew receive a percentage of the prize money. Once a Travian captain got his hands on our cargo, *he* would give a hearty laugh, all right. He'd say, 'Bad luck, gentlemen, this is now mine.'"

Stephano was longing to ask about this mysterious cargo. The words were on the tip of his tongue. He saw Miri fix her eyes on him, warning him to keep silent. The cargo was none of their business. He was being paid to protect it and that was all he needed to know.

For the time being . . .

"From what we hear, the city of Braffa is still open to shipping," said Leutnant Baumann. "It might be wise, sir, to put in overnight at Port Vrijheid instead of sailing to the refinery; ask around, see if we can obtain reliable information."

Captain Leydecker frowned at this suggestion. He was a hardheaded businessman. He owned his ship and would share in the profits once he paid off the Travian cartel who sponsored him. Stephano knew what the captain was thinking.

Leydecker was nervous about the talk of war. He wanted to make his delivery and return to Rosia as quickly as possible.

"I agree with the lieutenant, sir," said Stephano. "A day's delay would be better than losing your cargo. We'll have some idea what we might be facing."

Captain Leydecker eventually, though reluctantly, agreed.

The next day, the *Sommerwind* arrived at Port Vrijheid. Stephano and the Cadre had visited the city before, but only briefly.

Very briefly. They had arrived in the *Cloud Hopper* to do a job, putting up as usual in the Trundler enclave not far from the port. Unfortunately, they had found themselves in the middle of a Trundler blood feud between the McPike clan and the Stewart clan. Miri had upheld the honor of the McPikes, with the result that the Cadre was forced to leave Port Vrijheid in something of a hurry.

Stephano's first consideration was the dragons and what to do with them. He did not want to create an uproar by taking the dragons anywhere near the city. Dragons had never lived on Braffa and there was no telling how a populace unfamiliar with dragons would react to the sight of them. He and Dag and Gythe flew inland, heading for the cedar forests that blanketed the western hills. Here the dragons could hunt and find a comfortable, secure place to sleep.

They landed in an open field. Their riders dismounted and took off the heavy saddles and harnesses. Dag stowed these in a ravine and covered them with tree branches, while Stephano explained to Viola that he and his friends would be gone for the night, but that they would be back the next morning.

"Listen for the whistle," he said, indicating the bosun's pipe.

Viola gazed at him steadily. Even though she never spoke to him, Stephano was now confident she understood him. She had a way of tilting her head and fixing him with her glittering eyes. He felt that he often knew what she was thinking. Not even Lady Cam had responded so swiftly to his commands, acting on his thoughts before he'd spoken the words aloud.

The dragons did not appear worried or anxious about being left alone. They shook out their manes and arched their backs, glad to be free of the saddles. They listened politely to Stephano and the moment he had finished, took to the air.

"I think they're hungry for fresh meat, sir," said Dag.

"I know the feeling," said Stephano. "Salt pork is starting to stick in my throat."

He and Dag and Gythe rejoined the *Sommerwind* and the ship continued to Port Vrijheid. Captain Leydecker recommended an inn, the Misty Sunrise, and paid them for the first part of the voyage. Rodrigo jingled the fat purse.

"We have rosuns for a change, friends! Let us enjoy ourselves. There will be no talk of business at the table. We will be dining on real food tonight and no one will be trying to poison me."

Stephano shook his head. "I'm going to be sorry I asked, but who is trying to poison you?"

"The ship's cook."

"That's because you're stealing his glass jars. He knows it's you. You're a very inept thief," said Miri, laughing.

"Why are you stealing glass jars?" Stephano asked, amazed.

"The thought has occurred to me that I need to defend myself in case I'm attacked," said Rodrigo.

"You're going to pelt your attacker with glass jars," said Dag, grinning.

"Would you rather I used a pistol?" Rodrigo asked.

"God forfend!" Dag said fervently.

"Cook will never miss the jars, and that's no excuse to try and poison a man. I take back any small criticism I may have made of your cooking, Miri," Rodrigo added magnanimously.

"Small criticism!"

Miri's eyes flared. Gythe grabbed hold of her sister before she could inflict bodily harm on Rodrigo, and dragged her off to visit the shops. Stephano, Rodrigo, and Dag, accompanied by the Doctor, took rooms at the inn. The place was small by Rosian standards, but clean and comfortable.

The Misty Sunrise was run by a ship's captain who had retired due to poor health. He had named the inn after his ship, and pieces of the vessel were on display throughout. Rodrigo stumbled over a spar on his way to his room.

When the inn's owner found out that they had sailed on the *Sommerwind* with his friend Captain Leydecker, he thought nothing too good for them. There being no other guests at the inn, he asked them to join him for dinner.

"Damn rumors about war," the owner grumbled. "Driven away all my customers."

The captain served them a Braffan specialty—a spicy stew from the Aligoes of beans, sausage, beef, and pork known as *feijoda* accompanied by fresh-baked bread and cold ale. Miri asked how to make the dish. Rodrigo ate three helpings, complaining only that there was no wine. When Stephano started to ask the captain about the blockade, Rodrigo kicked him under the table.

"No business while dining," he said.

After dinner, they gathered in the parlor beneath a painting of the *Misty Sunrise*—the ship, not the inn—which hung above the mantel. Gythe and Miri showed off new hats.

Dag played with the Doctor. Stephano relaxed. His belly was full, and a pleasant weariness was setting in. He and the others were talking of going to bed early, when the parlor door opened and Captain Leydecker appeared, accompanied by the owner and a woman of middle years, a Trundler by her looks, for she was dressed in traditional Trundler garb, wearing a short skirt and trousers.

Remembering the Trundler blood feud, Stephano cast an alarmed glance at Miri. She smiled reassuringly.

"Different clan," she whispered.

"I am sorry to barge in upon you," said Captain Leydecker. "But there's news you should hear. This is Annie Glennane. She runs a ferry that takes refinery workers back and forth to their jobs on the islands. Annie, tell them your story."

Stephano asked Annie if she would like something to drink and ordered a round of ale for everyone. Annie sat down in a chair, smacked her lips over the ale, and was going to launch into her tale when Doctor Ellington jumped into her lap. Dag apologized and started to retrieve his cat.

"I'm fond of cats. The beast can stay," said Annie, petting the Doctor, who arched his back and rubbed his head on her chin. "As for my tale, here it is. My man and I operated our refinery ferry for twenty years. Since he died, I've kept it going. Mayhap you gentlemen don't know much about these refineries."

Stephano admitted that they didn't. None of them had ever visited one.

"Right, then." Annie finished her ale and asked for another, while Doctor Ellington made himself at home in her lap. "The refineries are located on small islands situated above the pockets where they mine the pure Breath. In these pockets the Breath is so thick that it's nigh near liquid. The workers drop down great hoses and suck up the Breath. They remove any impurities and refine it into the liquid form of the Breath you know as the Blood of God. Tankers come once a week to pick up the liquid and carry it to the mainland.

"The refinery workers and crafters and the mercenaries who guard them live on the island. They work in shifts. Seven days on, seven days off with their families. The shifts overlap, so that every three days, we ferrymen carry workers to the islands and bring workers back."

She cocked an eye at them to see if they understood. Stephano nodded and nudged Rodrigo, who had drifted off to sleep.

"Sorry. Fascinating." Rodrigo sat bolt upright and stifled a yawn.

Annie eyed him with disfavor and continued. "I was supposed to make my usual run a few days ago, but couldn't. Damn sail ripped and I had to patch it and reset some constructs. As it turns out, my Mickey—him that was my husband—must have been watching out for me. Those ferrymen who went to the refinery on Bloeddruppel Een island never came back. No sign of them."

"So the Travians *are* blockading the refineries," said Stephano.

"Damn Travians!" Annie made a rude gesture. "That's what they can do with themselves."

"The people I've talked to say the Travians have seized the refineries," Captain Leydecker told them. "The Freyan fleet slipped past the Estarans and is on the way to Braffa. The Travians decided to steal a march on the Freyans and took over the refineries before the Freyans could get their hands on them."

"The Freyans have a treaty with Braffa," said Stephano, considering the ramifications of this news. "Rosia has a treaty with Travia, which means that if Freya attacks Travia, Rosian ships would have to come to Travia's defense. We could be teetering on the brink of all-out war."

He turned to Annie. "Did anyone actually see Travian ships blockading the port? Has anyone seen Freyan warships in the area?"

"No, sir," said Annie shortly, scowling as if she didn't enjoy being questioned. "Just because no one saw them doesn't mean they're not there."

"True," said Stephano thoughtfully. "It seems odd, that's all. I don't see Travia risking a war."

Annie gave a flick of her hand. "Never mind your war, sir. My friends have families on that island and they haven't heard from them. They are worried sick. The skipper of the *Elspeth*—her being a tanker—sailed to the refinery for their weekly pickup. He was due back yesterday. We haven't seen hide nor hair of him. Something's wrong!"

Annie picked up the cat and rose to her feet. "There, that's my tale. If there's nothing more you fine folk want to know, I have to be up early. I have six young ones to feed. I'll be taking my leave."

She handed Doctor Ellington to Dag, said a few words to Miri and Gythe in the Trundler language, thanked Stephano for the ale, and departed.

"Are things as bad as she says, Captain?" Miri asked worriedly.

"There's not a man on Braffa willing to venture out of Port Vrijheid now," Captain Leydecker answered. He paused and Stephano knew what was coming next.

"But you are still planning to make your delivery."

Captain Leydecker nodded. "As I told you, sir, people are depending on me. I was thinking that you and your dragons could fly with us when we go. You could reconnoiter, find out what's going on. I'd be glad to pay extra."

"Of course, Captain," said Stephano. "Are you certain you want to risk your ship?"

Captain Leydecker hesitated, then said, "I don't want to, Captain. But I'm not only delivering cargo. I'm picking up cargo for a very important person. I was paid well not to ask questions. We'll meet up with you in the morning."

After the captain had gone Dag asked, "What do you think is going on, sir? Would the Travians really go this far?"

Stephano turned to Rodrigo. "Your father was ambassador to Estara. He spent time in the Travian court on diplomatic missions. What do you think?"

"My father always spoke of King Rupert of Travia as a levelheaded man, cautious, slow to act. Rupert doesn't want a war with Freya. I could envision him ordering a blockade, but he wouldn't dash in to seize the refineries."

"What about Freya?" asked Stephano. "Our old foe, Sir Henry, is probably mixed up in this somehow."

"Freya is putting herself forward as Braffa's friend. They are going to save her from the evil men who want to ravish her," said Rodrigo. "Freya is undoubtedly hoping the Braffans will give the refineries to her as a reward from a grateful nation."

"And if the Travians *did* take over the refineries, they wouldn't keep quiet," said Stephano. "They'd want the world to know they gave Freya a black eye. We've heard nothing from them."

"And there would be no reason to keep the ferrymen and tanker crews prisoner," Miri pointed out.

They were silent, even the Doctor, who'd gone to sleep on Dag's shoulder. The silence grew so profound Stephano could hear the creak of the timbers, the wind rattling in the eaves and the whispering of mice running across the floor. Doctor Ellington woke, growled, and jumped off Dag's knee.

"There is another possibility, sir," said Dag slowly.

"I thought of that," said Stephano. His tone was grim. "The Bottom Dwellers need lift gas for their black ships."

"Gythe, you've sensed the Bottom Dwellers before when they're near. You've heard their voices. Can you hear anything now?" Miri asked.

Gythe touched her ears and shook her head. "Silence."

Rodrigo yawned, nearly dislocating his jaw. "My friends, we could stay up all night speculating. We'll find out for ourselves soon enough."

"Rigo's right," said Stephano. "We need to be up before dawn. The *Sommerwind* will take us to the dragons. Gythe, Dag—"

"Not Gythe," said Miri flatly.

"Why not me?" Gythe demanded, her hands flashing.

"We agreed, Gythe," said Miri firmly. "You made a promise to me. I would let you ride the dragon, but not into danger."

Gythe stamped her foot. Her face flushed, her eyes flared. "I am old enough to decide this for myself! I don't need you to protect me. Petard and I are going whether you like it or not."

Miri said nothing. Her face paled. She pressed her lips together, cast a sharp glance at Stephano. This was his decision, after all.

"Gythe, you're not going," he told her.

Gythe rounded on him. Her flush deepened. She pointed at her sister. "You always take her side!"

"This has nothing to do with Miri," said Stephano. His voice was stern. "You may know how to ride a dragon, Gythe, but you're not a dragon rider. You are undisciplined and reckless. You don't listen to me, and you don't obey orders. And neither does Petard."

Gythe stared at him in disbelief, stung by his words. Her lower lip quivered, and tears shimmered in her eyes.

Miri saw her sister's distress and relented. "Stephano, don't be so hard on her—"

"This needs to be said, Miri." Stephano turned back to Gythe. "I was wrong to let you ride. When you tell me that you and Petard are ready to stop gallivanting and obey my orders and you want to learn to become a dragon rider, I will teach you. But until then, you will not ride."

Gythe blinked rapidly and wiped her nose. She seemed to still want to be angry, for the flush burned on her cheeks.

After thinking a moment, however, the flush faded. She walked over to Stephano, placed her hand over his heart.

"You are right. I have been thoughtless. I am sorry. It won't happen again." She cast him a pleading glance, hoping he'd reconsider. "Please let me ride!"

"You will remain on board on the *Sommerwind* with Miri and Rodrigo," said Stephano.

Gythe lowered her eyes, then gave a tremulous smile.

"Take Petard with you," she said with her hands. "The fault is mine, not his."

"I'm not so sure about that," said Stephano. "The dragon seems to be as heedless as you are. I will have a talk with him before I decide."

Gythe picked up Doctor Ellington and buried her face in his fur, finding comfort in the cat. Dag awkwardly patted her on the shoulder.

"Thank you, Stephano," Miri said softly, drawing close to him.

"I didn't ground Gythe for you, Miri," said Stephano. "I was the one at fault. I didn't want to say no to her. None of us ever say no to Gythe."

"So now you're blaming me," Miri flared.

"I blame myself," said Stephano. "If Gythe had died, her blood would have been on my hands."

He walked to the window, where he stared out into the night. He could feel Miri's eyes on him, but he didn't turn around.

Miri left him and went to her sister. She put her arm around Gythe and they retreated to their room. Dag sighed heavily, put Doctor Ellington on his shoulder, and headed for the door.

"You know I'm right, Dag," Stephano said abruptly.

"You didn't need to make her cry," Dag said.

Stephano didn't answer.

"But yes, you were right, sir," Dag added.

He shut the door and Stephano heard Dag's heavy footfalls tromping slowly up the stairs.

"Maybe I shouldn't have been so hard on her, Rigo," said Stephano.

"Hard on her?" Rodrigo walked over to stand beside his friend. "Remember what your father did to you when *you* went for a joy ride?"

Stephano gave a faint smile. "The time when Lieutenant Stanchi, Lord Skaerangir and Lady Kinetrille and I decided to practice our newly aquired martial skills by raiding a fortress—"

"Except the 'fortress' was a local farmhouse," said Rodrigo, grinning. "You set fire to a barn and stampeded a herd of cattle. The farmer's wife had hysterics. The farmer came after you with a pitchfork."

"We didn't mean to set the barn on fire," said Stephano ruefully. "I can laugh about it now, but it wasn't funny then. When we landed, my father hauled me off the dragon bodily, dumped me on my ass in the muck, and told me I was grounded for a month. I had to reimburse the farmer out of my Brigade pay. When my father upbraided me, he said, 'Our work is serious. We defend a nation.'"

He turned from the window, the memory warm and faintly sad inside him. He and Rodrigo went up the stairs to their rooms.

"You did what you had to do about Gythe, Stephano," said Rodrigo. "That is why you are the commander of the Dragon Brigade and I am but a humble sailor. By the way, I learned how to dance the hornpipe. Shall I show you?"

"For God's sake, no!" said Stephano, shuddering.

39

The Blood of God is so valuable, so sought after, that humans will likely end up spilling their own blood over it. If I were God, I would not want my name attached.

—Monsieur Dubois

The three Braffan refineries that processed the Breath of God, turning it into the liquid known as the Blood of God, were located on three small islands floating in the Breath. Although the location of the refineries was supposed to be secret, anyone who wanted to find them could simply, as Stephano pointed out to Captain Leydecker, follow the tankers and ferryboats that made regular runs to the refineries. Stephano did not tell the captain their fears that the refineries might have been attacked by Bottom Dwellers. The captain had worries enough as it was.

So what was this mysterious cargo? The *Sommerwind* had no tanks. The captain wasn't picking up the liquid. Yet he said the cargo was valuable, and the only valuable cargo at the refineries was the Blood. Stephano spent the time while flying toward their destination in useless speculation.

The three dragons and their two riders stayed near to the *Sommerwind*. Stephano allowed Petard to fly with them because, he reasoned, the dragon would simply follow them anyway. Stephano lectured Petard as he'd lectured Gythe and when he had finished, Viola took over, hooting and roaring in anger. She didn't say much, but before she was finished, Petard had his head down around his knees. Scoldings and reprimands could not subdue the young dragon for long, however. When Petard took to the air, his eyes gleamed with excitement, though he took care to keep Verdi between him and his sister.

This morning, Gythe was contrite and subdued. Dag had placed Doctor Ellington in her care, and she and the cat boarded the *Sommerwind* without a single murmur of protest.

Before Miri and Stephano parted, she took him aside.

"Gythe and I spent the night talking," she said. "I've promised to quit being so protective. She's a 'woman growed' as my uncle would say. It won't be easy for me. She still seems so fragile."

"She *was* fragile, Miri. She's not anymore. She's changed."

"Has she?" Miri was grim. "Gythe told me Brother Barnaby counseled her last night. He helped her find her courage."

"Brother Barnaby! I hoped she had stopped thinking of him."

"She still claims she hears his voice. She won't tell me much. She says the monk is suffering and that makes her sad. And she says she talks to Petard."

"Like she sings to the cat. At least *you* are talking to me," said Stephano.

"You did what I should have done a long time ago," said Miri, sighing. "But I'm afraid someday she will fly away on that dragon and I'll never see her again."

"Gythe will never fly far from you. And neither will I," said Stephano, smiling. "Take care of Rigo. See to it he's not poisoned."

"If he is," Miri said with a glint in her eye, "I'll be the one to do it."

This region of the Breath was far outside the shipping lanes. The Breath itself was different in this part of the world. As they sailed farther, the lovely reds, oranges, and pinks of the mists gradually gave way to a thick layer of greenish gray mist that into swirled and eddied beneath them. The temperature rose and the air was humid. Stephano was sweating in his Dragon Brigade uniform coat.

Above the mist, the morning sky was a clear, deep blue. He could see the faint imprint of a half moon and a single, sparkling star. The *Sommerwind* began to slow her forward progress and raised a triangular red flag, the signal that they were close.

Leutnant Baumann shouted from the deck of the *Sommerwind*, "Refinery dead ahead, Captain."

All Stephano could see was a gray and green mass that appeared to be floating on a misty pond. The ship came to a halt. Stephano had arranged with Captain Leydecker that he and Dag would fly to the refinery to investigate. Stephano motioned to Petard, and the young dragon joined them. The *Sommerwind* floated in the Breath, keeping her distance.

The gray-green mass turned into hundreds of islands floating in the Breath. Some of the smaller islands were nothing but gray rock. The larger islands were covered in thick vegetation, which accounted for the humidity. Huge trees rose from the surface or clung to the sides of the islands, jutting out at odd angles, their roots dangling in the mist. The islands were separated by channels through which ships could sail. Wisps of fog drifted among the trees, obscuring the view ahead.

No wonder the refineries are difficult to find, Stephano

thought. He didn't see the island they were searching for until they were almost on top of it.

The island was not so much an island as a large chunk of floating rock shaped like a kidney bean. Perhaps two hundred yards across, the island had been stripped of vegetation, and most of its area was occupied by a stone building in the form of a *U*.

Captain Leydecker had provided Stephano and Dag with a description of the refinery so they would know what to expect. This building, the largest on the island, was the living quarters for the workers, crafters, and soldiers.

In the central part of the building were sleeping areas for the men and women, a common room, laboratories, and a kitchen. Wings on either end were used for storage and warehousing. A smaller, detached stone building to the north of the central building was the armory where they stored ammunition for the six thirty-two-pound cannons that were located at strategic points around the island.

Supplies for the refinery, including spare parts and tools, were stored in small wooden outbuildings. The laboratory was in another stone building across from the living quarters. Two enormous round tanks, located at either end of the kidney bean, held the liquid distilled from the Breath. Near the tanks stood two enormous glass vats, surrounded by coiled tubing, copper tubs, and wooden tubs, encased in scaffolding. This was where the refining process took place.

Tubes attached to large pumps mounted on two large floating rafts snaked down into the Breath to reach the pocket of pure Breath far below.

At the south end of the island, Stephano saw a contraption that looked like an arm bent at the elbow—the docking arm. Due to the small size of the island and the fact that there was very little space on which to land, tankers and ferries had to tie up there. When a tanker or a ferry arrived, workers extended the docking arm outward using a series of cranks and pulleys. The arm provided a secure place for ships to dock, safe from the jagged margins of the island.

"Security measure," Captain Leydecker had told them. "If the workers don't recognize the ship and the ship doesn't respond to a hail with the correct code, the workers won't extend the docking arm."

Tankers docked at the north end of the island. The huge tanks took days to fill, so the crew would land the tanker and then depart, traveling back to the mainland on a ferry. When the tanker was full, the crew would return to sail it to its destination.

As they approached the island, Stephano could see nothing out of the ordinary: no signs of Travian ships sailing a blockade; no bats or their riders. All seemed quiet and peaceful until they flew close enough to the island to have a clear view. Then the hair on the back of Stephano's neck prickled.

The time was now midmorning. He should be seeing workers climbing on the scaffolding, crafters walking from one building to another, crews filling the docked tanker.

But the refinery was deserted, with not a single person in sight.

Stephano signaled to Dag that he was going to fly in low. Dag signaled back, warning him to be careful. He, too, had noticed the unusual inactivity. Stephano motioned for Petard to keep watch above, and he was glad to see the young dragon obey his orders, flying in large circles over the island.

Stephano and Viola swooped down as close as they could come without smashing into the scaffolding that surrounded the large vats. He scanned the island. A thin trail of smoke rose from a burning building. He now could see the people— or what was left of them.

Bodies littered the ground. Not all of them were human. Some were the carcasses of dead bats.

Viola made a sound, a kind of rumble meant to draw his attention. Stephano looked up to see Dag gesturing to a large crater surrounded by rubble and more bodies.

Dag raised the visor of his helm to yell, "They blew up the powder magazine, sir."

The tanker had also been attacked. One of the masts was splintered, and part of the deck and hull were still burning. The punctured balloons dangled like silk scarves from the rigging, and more bodies lay on the deck. At the south end, the docking arm had been broken at the elbow.

"Son of a bitch," Stephano swore.

He motioned for Dag and Verdi to fly closer. The *Sommerwind* waited, floating in the Breath about a mile distant. Captain Leydecker and Leutnant Bauman would have their spyglasses trained on them, and would be impatient to hear what they had found.

"Bottom Dwellers were here. Don't see much we can do, sir," said Dag heavily. "Looks like they butchered everyone, set fire to the place, then left."

Stephano was gazing, frowning, at the refinery. Something wasn't right. "They didn't do that much damage. The main buildings are still standing. I think we should investigate. First we need to tell Captain Leydecker he's not going to be making his delivery."

They turned, intending to fly back to the *Sommerwind*. Both were startled by the unmistakable sound of a gunshot. They looked back to see a man standing outside the southern end of the dormitory, frantically waving his hat in the air. As he did so, a streak of green fire forced the man to duck for cover back inside the building.

"Apparently the Bottom Dwellers didn't leave. Not all of them," Stephano shouted at Dag. "At least one survivor! A bat rider has him pinned down inside that building! There might be more. Tell Leydecker we're going to rescue them."

Dag hesitated. "What do we do once we have them, sir? We can't take them out on the *Sommerwind*. The docking arm's wrecked. The ship can't dock."

"We can't leave them here. The Bottom Dwellers might come back," Stephano said, frustrated. "Ask Leydecker. Maybe he can think of something."

Dag nodded, wheeled Verdi around, and flew back to the *Sommerwind*. Stephano studied the island, trying to figure out how to proceed. Viola could not possibly land, not without risking serious injury. The flaming green streak had come from a wooden building located at the foot of the scaffolding, across from the southern end of the living quarters. A Bottom Dweller with some type of weapon must be holed up there. The weapon wasn't firing the usual ball of fire, but it appeared to be just as deadly. Stephano considered having Viola destroy the building with her flaming breath, but he decided he couldn't risk it.

A dragon such as Lady Cam, who had been trained in warfare, knew how to control her breath so that she could shoot a thin stream of flame onto a building, setting it on fire, while not harming surrounding structures. If he asked Viola to breathe on it, she might blast it with a fireball that would set the entire island ablaze.

Stephano checked to make certain his pistols were loaded, and his knife in his boot. He added a powder horn and a pouch of bullets and waited impatiently for Dag to return. When Dag and Verdi flew back, Stephano pointed to the ground, indicating he was going to descend. Dag showed he understood by flourishing a pistol.

Stephano uncoiled the rope ladder that was standard equipment for a dragon rider.

"Take me over to that scaffold," he told Viola.

Viola flew in low to hover just above the scaffolding. Stephano could feel the dragon's body quivering. Her mane rippled, a shiver contracted her scales. They had practiced this maneuver several times, but always under safe conditions. Stephano assumed she was worried about him and he patted her on the neck to show he was pleased with her.

He took off his helm and stowed it, attached the rope ladder to the saddle, unbuckled his harness, and climbed out of the saddle. He descended the rope ladder, moving slowly and carefully to prevent the ladder from swinging. Out of the corner of his eye, he saw another green flash. He heard the buzz of a bullet as a thin line of green fire streaked past him. The Bottom Dweller hadn't fired at him. He was aiming at Viola.

The dragon hissed in alarm. Her body jerked and her wings flapped wildly, making the ladder swing precariously. Stephano was forced to let go, and he fell the rest of the way, landing heavily on the platform. He crouched down, looking to see the location of the sharpshooter. Now he knew there were at least two, for this shot had been fired from a different building, somewhere off to his left. The thought registered that this wasn't the bat riders' usual mode of attack. They'd invented some sort of new devilish weapon that apparently fired bullets.

"Probably laced with contramagic," he muttered to himself.

He looked up to see if Viola was all right and was startled to see that the dragon had fled, flying away from the refinery, hooting at Petard.

Stephano was worried. He told himself that she was only leaving to give Verdi room to fly in with Dag. He didn't like the way she was behaving, her terrified reactions.

Verdi and Dag flew down, the dragon coming in extremely low. Stephano held his breath, hoping the clumsy dragon wouldn't accidentally take out the scaffolding and him along with it. Verdi hovered ponderously overhead. Dag climbed awkwardly down the rope ladder and landed on the platform with a thud that shook the frame. Stephano had his pistol drawn, covering Dag while watching for the sharpshooter.

No one fired.

Viola roared and Verdi, after circling a few times, flew away to join the other two dragons. Stephano watched them. The dragons were flying in agitated circles, talking between themselves.

Dag crouched behind him. "I spoke to Leydecker and explained the problem. Miri says—"

"Not now," Stephano ordered.

Motion caught his eye. A hand holding a weapon appeared in the window of the laboratory. Stephano nudged Dag.

"Look at that pistol! That's not their standard-issue weapon, not like those long guns they used against us. And I'll swear something that sounded like a bullet hit the scaffolding right below me."

"You're right, sir." Dag examined the weapon with a critical eye. "Looks similar to a horse pistol."

Stephano rose slightly, to see if he could get a better view. A green flash, a green streak, the same strange wail, and a bullet hit the beam near Stephano's head, ricocheted off. A burning pain tore through his cheek. Dag fired at the sharpshooter and the hand holding the pistol disappeared.

"Missed the bastard!" Dag grumbled. He eyed Stephano with concern. "You all right, sir?"

"Spent bullet grazed my cheek. Hurts like a son of a bitch, though," said Stephano. He drew back his hand to see it was covered in blood.

Dag examined the wound. "Damn! That's nasty looking sir! Your skin is . . . scorched!"

"Feels like I was hit with a red-hot poker!" Stephano said, wincing at the pain.

A second bullet slammed into the scaffold near Dag, this shot from the first sharpshooter, the one who had fired at the man with the hat. The bullet embedded itself in a wooden post. A thin curl of smoke rose from the wood.

"Pretty damn clever, sir," said Dag grimly. "The long guns the Bottom Dwellers used against us were intended to take out large targets. These pistols are meant to kill people."

"They don't dare use the long guns that shoot the fireballs. They could blow up the island and they want the refineries intact for the lift gas," Stephano realized. "That's something to remember. We might be able to use that against them."

"How many out there, sir?"

"I've seen two. No telling how many more."

"Sir, about Miri—"

"Miri will have to wait. Let's get safely down on the ground, then we can talk."

Stephano counted three levels with a platform on each level. Flights of stairs connected the platform with another flight leading to the ground. He and Dag would be relatively safe on the scaffolding. The wooden frame would continue to provide cover. Once on the ground, they would have to cross an open area to reach the entrance to the living quarters. They could see the man who had waved the hat standing in the doorway, holding the door partly open. Every so often Stephano caught a glimpse of the man's tricorn.

"The hell of it is those two sharpshooters are in different buildings, one in the laboratory in front of the living quarters and one in that building below us to our right." Stephano pointed them out. "The moment we step into the open, they'll have us in a dandy crossfire."

"I brought something we might be able to use to clear out at least one of them, sir," said Dag.

Reaching into his coat, he produced a bag containing

three glass jars, each with a cork stopper, each filled with some sort of black gunk.

"What's that?" Stephano asked. "Lunch?"

"Rigo says they're homemade grenades, sir," said Dag in dubious tones. "He handed the bag to me while I was back at the *Sommerwind* talking to Captain Leydecker. Rigo concocted the mixture, apparently. Said we might find it useful."

"So that's why he's been stealing glass jars," said Stephano. "How does it work?"

"He says I touch the squiggle and it blows up on impact."

Stephano considered. "The closest sharpshooter is in that building right below us. He fired from a front window at the fellow with the hat and he shot at us from a back window. Assuming he's watching us from the back, my hope is that he will move to the front to shoot at me when I make a run for the door. My next hope is that the man in the door is armed and can cover me. That's when you throw that thing in the back window. Hopefully it will take out at least one sharpshooter."

Dag shook his head. "There's a lot of 'hope' in that plan, sir. Too much, if you ask me."

Two flashes of green fire and two bullets slammed into the wooden beam near them, one over their heads and one at their feet. Where the bullets hit, the wooden frame started to smolder, the contramagic eating into the protective constructs. Stephano didn't like to think what it might be doing to his flesh that stung and burned.

"Their aim is improving," said Stephano. "You keep one grenade. Give me the bag with the other two."

Dag handed over the bag and Stephano tucked it into an inner pocket. He checked to make certain his dragon pistol was loaded.

"Remember the fight in Westfirth, what that damn magic did to my pistol, sir," Dag reminded him. "Almost took my hand off."

"Thank you so much for reminding me," Stephano muttered. "I was wondering what else to worry about. Ready? Here we go."

He leaped to his feet and ran down the stairs, keeping low as he ran. He could hear Dag thudding along behind him. Stephano waited tensely for the sharpshooters to fire again. He reached the lower platform and still nothing.

Those guns act like any other pistols, he thought. They must have to take time to reload.

He saw a flash of green from the laboratory and dropped to his belly. The bullet hit the frame right where he had been standing, showering him with wood splinters and cinders. Jumping to his feet, he dashed down the last flight of stairs and kept running, heading for the living quarters.

The man in the doorway opened the door and stepped out. Raising his pistol, he fired in the direction of the second sharpshooter.

"Go on! I'm right behind you, sir!" Dag yelled.

Stephano had to cover only about ten yards, but it looked to him to be a hundred. He put his head down and ran, expecting every moment to feel a bullet slam into his back. He was almost to the doorway when a blast behind him knocked him flat.

A wave of heat washed over him. He staggered to his feet and lunged for the door, where the man with the hat caught and steadied him. Stephano turned to see the building housing the Bottom Dweller engulfed in flame. Dag was sitting on his butt on the ground, bleeding from a cut on his head.

"Cover me!" Stephano told the man.

He ran back to Dag, who was groggily trying to stand up, but not having much luck. Stephano grabbed his arm.

"Good Lord! I never expected *that,* sir," Dag said, dazed.

"Are you all right?"

"I can't hear you, sir. If you're asking if I'm all right, I will be once my ears stop ringing."

The man in the hat fired again and yelled for them to hurry. Stephano dragged Dag to his feet and the two made a mad scramble for the door. They ducked inside, and the stranger slammed the door shut just before two bullets slammed into it.

Once his eyes adjusted to the dimness, Stephano saw brooms and mops leaning up against the wall, a couple of buckets, several barrels stacked near the door, a chest, and some tools. He was in a store room. A door on an interior wall must lead to the main living quarters.

"Thank you, sir," he was about to say to the man with the hat when the man took a good look at Stephano and burst into laughter.

"God bless my soul! If it isn't Captain de Guichen. Of course! It *would* be you flying around on a dragon! I am glad to see you managed to escape that island," the man added, still chuckling.

Stephano blinked and peered into the shadows, waiting for his eyes to adjust. The voice sounded familiar.

"I'll be damned!" Stephano gasped, amazed. "Sir Henry Wallace!"

The man bowed. "Your servant, sir."

Stephano could only stare. "What the devil are *you* doing here?"

"I could ask the same of you, Captain," said Sir Henry.

Before he could reply, Dag raised his pistol and aimed at Sir Henry's head.

"Give me one good reason why I shouldn't shoot this bastard, Captain! We could have died on that blasted rock!"

"Come now, Sergeant, I had more faith in you and your

friends than that. I knew you'd survive," Sir Henry said, adding with a smile, "Put the gun down. I'm not your enemy—at least not at the moment. I'm here on a diplomatic mission."

Dag snorted and Stephano eyed Sir Henry skeptically.

"I can prove it to you, Captain. This way."

Sir Henry opened the door and waited politely for them to precede him. Dag eyed him and didn't move.

"I don't trust him, sir. Maybe he's behind this attack."

"I don't trust him for an instant," said Stephano. "But in this case I think he's telling the truth about being here as a diplomat. Look at his clothes."

Sir Henry was wearing a white shirt with lace cuffs, a white cravat trimmed in lace, a blue brocade weskit, a dove-gray dress coat trimmed with silver buttons, and fine leather boots.

Dag's brow furrowed. "You've been around Rigo too long, sir. What do his clothes have to do with it?"

"He looks as if he's been dining with the queen. Not the way *I* would dress if I were planning to attack a refinery," Stephano pointed out. "His coat is torn and stained with blood—"

"And I have gunpowder residue on my cuff," Sir Henry added, exhibiting his sleeve.

"I guess you're right, sir," said Dag reluctantly.

Sir Henry motioned for Stephano to move closer.

"I am here with two officials of the Braffan council," Sir Henry said in a low voice. "I regret to say the third died in the assault. I was thinking it might be best if we kept our somewhat complicated relationship to ourselves."

"Why?" Stephano snorted. "Don't your friends know they're dealing with a spy, a thief, and an assassin?"

"I am loyal to my country as you are to yours, Captain," Sir Henry replied coolly. "We have a common goal—to escape from this island alive. Nineteen men and women are dependent on us. We drove off the fiends once, but they'll be back. Shall we come to terms, Captain? Friends for the duration of the crisis?"

Nineteen people, not counting Sir Henry. Stephano was dismayed. What was he going to do with them? He realized Sir Henry was still waiting for an answer.

"Let's just say we won't be enemies."

Stephano entered the common room where the workers relaxed during their downtime. The long dining tables had been pushed aside to make space for the wounded, who lay on mattresses that had been dragged from the beds and spread out on the floor.

Stephano counted fourteen men and five women. Most of the walking wounded were helping to treat their comrades whose wounds were more serious. Six of these lay on the mattresses. One man's head was swathed in bloody bandages, leaving only his nose and mouth exposed. One of the women had a broken leg. Almost all the workers had burns that must have been caused by the fiery green bullets. Two bodies were covered with sheets.

The room smelled of blood, gunpowder, and death. These people had only to look out one of the slit windows to see the bodies of their friends lying on the ground, yet the survivors were composed and calm; those not ministering to their wounded fellows keeping watch at the windows for the enemy to return to finish them off.

The building had been constructed with an eye to security. Each side had five windows, narrow, long, and rectangular. The windows were open, not covered with glass. Presumably the climate on these islands was always warm, though heavy with humidity from the junglelike vegetation on the surrounding islands.

Those windows on the refinery side had a view of the *Sommerwind*. The other windows faced out into the Breath.

If the Bottom Dwellers returned to finish what they'd started, they'd fly in from that direction.

The workers must know they could not survive a second major attack, yet they were going about their duties calmly, even the wounded enduring their pain in stoic silence. Stephano was impressed. The life of a refinery worker must not be an easy one, isolated on this barren rock, laboring day and night to produce the Blood that brought wealth to their small nation. These people were tough, resilient. They had endured what must have been a horrific attack, watched friends die, all the while knowing the enemy would return.

Sir Henry introduced Stephano to the workers, speaking in Travian, which was the official language of Braffa.

"My friends, this is Captain de Guichen, formerly of the famed Rosian Dragon Brigade."

Before Stephano could say a word, a man dressed in fine clothes like Sir Henry lunged forward to seize Stephano by the hand.

"This is Lord Bjorn Westhoven of the Braffan High Council," said Sir Henry.

Lord Bjorn was about Stephano's age, in his thirties, with a smile that was charming, ingratiating, and pitifully hopeful. He had a handsome, fleshy face with the sallow complexion of a man who liked his port wine and perhaps other stimulants. He spoke Rosian with such a thick accent Stephano could barely understand him.

"You come in answer to our prayers to rescue us, sir!"

"I fancy rescuing us will prove difficult, Lord Bjorn," a woman said.

"Frau Madeleine Aalder, also with the Braffan High Council," said Sir Henry.

Stephano had first seen her down on her knees, tending to

the wounded. Now she rose to her feet and walked over to join the conversation.

"What? Why?" Lord Bjorn asked anxiously. "I see a ship out there. The *Sommerwind,* if I'm not mistaken. We can sail away in that."

"The docking arm is broken, Lord Bjorn," said Frau Aalder. "The ship cannot dock. Unless we can fly out on those dragons, we're still trapped here."

Frau Aalder was a tall, spare, lanky woman with gray hair tied back in a severe knot, and a frank, direct gaze. Stephano was startled by her brutal candor, though he had to admit she had made an accurate assessment of the situation.

Frau Aalder did not curtsy, but further confounded Stephano by reaching out to shake hands with him like a man. She had an astonishingly powerful grip.

"You are wounded, Captain."

"A graze," said Stephano.

"Sit down and let me tend to it," she said.

"Oh my God, this is not happening!" Lord Bjorn groaned. He sagged into a chair and put his head in his hands.

Frau Aalder gave him a pat on the shoulder and told him to "Buck up."

Stephano said the graze was nothing, but Frau Aadler insisted, shooing Lord Bjorn out of the chair and telling Stephano to shut up and sit down.

As she washed the wound and smeared some sort of salve on it that eased the burning, Stephano asked what had happened. Sir Henry gestured to a man in a torn uniform, wearing a bloodstained bandage tied around his head. His right arm was in a sling.

"Sergeant Cuyper," said Sir Henry. "The sole survivor of the refinery's mercenary unit."

The sergeant was Guundaran, built much like Dag, with

the same military bearing and stoic demeanor. Like most mercenaries, he spoke excellent Rosian.

"Broken wrist and a bump on the head, sir," said the sergeant, noticing Stephano regard him with concern. "I was near the powder magazine when it blew. Knocked me senseless for a time. The gentleman"—the sergeant indicated Sir Henry—"saved my life by dragging me inside this building before the fiends could kill me."

Sir Henry shrugged this off. "Tell Captain de Guichen what happened, Sergeant."

"We were attacked by fiends from hell, sir. That's what they looked like, though this gentleman calls them 'Bottom Dwellers' and says they are humans like ourselves."

Stephano regarded Sir Henry with interest. "You know about these Bottom Dwellers? How?"

"As you recall, Captain, they tried to kill me in Westfirth. I don't much like people who try to kill me and I decided to find out what I could about them."

"And what did you find out?"

"That their hatred transcends borders, Captain," said Sir Henry coolly. "We must put aside our differences—for a time."

"For a time . . . Ouch!" Stephano winced under Frau Aadler's ministrations.

"The Bottom Dwellers have captured the other two refineries. They caught the people off guard, took them by surprise. They fell without a fight," the sergeant continued. "The fiends would have seized this one, too, but we were ready for them. That wrecked tanker you see on the dock managed to escape the assault on the second refinery and sailed here to warn us that we were the next target."

"How did you and the council members come to be here?" Stephano asked Sir Henry.

"As bad luck would have it, the members of the Braffan

council and I happened to be touring the refinery when the captain told us that this place was about to come under attack. There was no time to escape." Sir Henry smiled and gave a fatalistic shrug. "You can see what's left of the boat that brought us amidst the ruins of the docking arm."

Stephano grunted. He didn't believe for one moment that Sir Henry Wallace had come to the refinery to gape at the vats and admire the scaffolding. But there was no point in confronting him. He would only lie, and at this point his reason for being here probably didn't matter. Stephano turned back to the sergeant.

"You had time to prepare a defense."

"Yes, sir. We caught them in an ambush and managed to drive them off, but not before they'd done considerable damage. Most of my unit died when they blew up the powder magazine, including my captain and lieutenant."

Sergeant Cuyper spoke matter-of-factly about the deaths of his comrades. But when Dag said something sympathetic in Guundaran, the sergeant cast him a grateful glance.

"The Bottom Dwellers didn't expect a fight, Captain. There were only a few of them. They will be back in greater numbers," said Sir Henry. "We have no powder, no ammunition. We won't survive the next assault. As you saw, they're armed with different weapons than they used in Westfirth."

"I noticed," said Stephano drily. He gingerly touched his cheek, now slathered in ointment. "They left sharpshooters behind. How many?"

"Your sergeant blew up one. That leaves one in the laboratory and another one in the building adjacent to the lab." Sir Henry pointed out the window. "There might be more hiding in those other buildings. We have no way of knowing until they fire on us."

"Stick your head out the door," Dag growled. "Let's see who blows it off."

"An amusing fellow, your sergeant," remarked Sir Henry.

Stephano would have grinned, but Frau Aadler had stuck a plaster on the wound, and moving his facial muscles hurt.

"Frau Aalder is right. The *Sommerwind* can't land with the docking arm destroyed, so I'm not sure—"

"Begging your pardon, sir," said Dag, interrupting, "I've been trying to tell you. Miri says she can fly here in the pinnace. Captain Leydecker wasn't going to let her. He told her it was too risky. But you know Miri." Dag shook his head in admiration. "She was ordering the crewmen to start filling the balloon as I was leaving."

"Excellent idea!" Fran Aalder exclaimed.

She had been listening to their conversaion and now she took charge, bustling about with energy, issuing orders to the other survivors.

"The pinnace will be on its way soon to pick us up. We'll need to have the wounded ready to transport. I want some of you men to haul in some mattresses—"

She was interrupted by loud roarings and hootings from the dragons.

The next moment one of the lookouts called, "The fiends are out there, Sir Henry! They're heading this way."

Another lookout, keeping watch on the opposite side of the building, turned to Stephano.

"Looks like your dragons are leaving, Captain."

Stephano and Dag exchanged startled glances and hurried to the window.

"Maybe they decided to fly off to guard the *Sommerwind*," Dag said hopefully.

Unfortunately, the dragons were heading in the opposite direction, away from the *Sommerwind,* away from the refinery, away from the enemy. The dragons were fleeing toward a small tree-covered island.

Stephano felt as though he'd taken a punch to the gut.

"Sir, we can't let them go!" Dag said urgently.

"I'll call them." Stephano walked over to the open slit window. He drew out the bosun's pipe.

"Don't get yourself shot, sir," Dag warned.

Stephano had to risk it. He leaned out the window, put to the pipe to his lips and gave the summons call, making it as loud and shrill as he could. Seeing a flash of green fire, he hurriedly ducked back inside. A bullet smashed into the wall.

"I wouldn't do that again, sir," said Dag. "Any response?"

Stephano looked out the window. He shook his head. The dragons had landed. He could barely see them, the color of their scales blending with the foliage.

"Maybe they didn't hear," said Dag.

"They heard," said Stephano.

"Captain," Sir Henry called, "you better come see this."

He had been looking out his window through a spyglass. He lowered the glass and handed it to Stephano, who looked out and swore beneath his breath. The enemy was approaching and he couldn't begin to count the swarm of bats and riders. Worse, they had brought with them one of their infernal black ships.

"The same type of ship as the one that sank the *Royal Lion*," said Stephano. He handed the spyglass to Dag. "Check on the progress of the pinnace."

"They're almost finished filling the balloon on the pinnace, sir. She'll be ready to launch soon," Dag reported. "Miri's on board. I can see her red hair!"

He added in an undertone, "What do you think's wrong with the dragons, sir?"

"I have no idea," said Stephano. "And we don't have time to worry about them. We'll need to get rid of those sharp-shooters before Miri lands. How many pistols do you have, Sir Henry?"

"Two. I managed to retrieve three more from the dead."

"I have two and Dag has two . . ."

"Here, sir," said Sergeant Cuyper, "I won't be needing this. Not with my busted arm."

The sergeant held out his weapon.

"By God, sir!" Dag exclaimed, regarding the weapon in admiration. "This is one of those long guns with the rifled bore!"

"Like the one carried by that assassin you sent to kill us," Stephano muttered in the direction of Sir Henry.

"Harrington acted without orders, Captain," Sir Henry returned. "Besides, you had your revenge on the wretch. I'm a fair shot, Captain," he added coolly. "I need powder and ammunition. If you have some to spare . . ."

Dag cast Stephano a glance, pleading with him not to trust this man. Stephano didn't have much choice. They would need all the guns they could get.

"I didn't bring much," said Stephano, handing over his powder horn and ammunition. "Just what I could carry."

Sir Henry began loading his pistols. Lord Bjorn, who had been silent until now, touched the rapier he wore at his side. He gave a wan smile.

"I'm rather a good swordsman," he said.

"Let's hope we don't need you, my lord," said Stephano cheerfully. He went to join Sir Henry and the sergeant at the window.

"God help us if we're left to depend on Lord Bjorn," Sir Henry said, loading his pistols.

Stephano smiled and immediately regretted it. He scratched at the stiffening plaster. Frau Aadler shot him a disapproving look and he quickly lowered his hand.

"Where are the sharpshooters again?"

"One is in that building across from us, Captain," said the lookout, pointing. "That's the laboratory. The other is in the adjacent building to the north. The fiends haven't shifted position, at least not that I've seen."

"What goes on in the laboratory?"

"I've asked. The workers won't tell us," said Sir Henry. "The process for refining the Blood is secret."

"Secret!" Stephano gave an incredulous laugh. He glanced around at the workers. "You people realize that in a matter of hours, the Bottom Dwellers are going to be running this refinery! Your secret isn't going to be secret much longer!"

The workers' expressions darkened. They were clearly unhappy, but they remained stubbornly silent.

"I'm sorry," Stephano said with a sigh. "I realize you people are only doing your jobs. I don't suppose it matters what's in there."

"Unless there's something that's likely to blow up the entire island," said Sir Henry, who must have been thinking along the same lines as Stephano.

"No, sir," the worker said with a faint smile. "Nothing like that."

"Pinnace has set sail," Dag reported from the window.

He picked up the rifle and began loading it as the sergeant pointed out the weapon's features.

"I've always wanted to fire one of these," said Dag. "Just get me a clear shot at those fiends, sir. That's all I need."

Stephano drew his pistols and turned to Sir Henry. "Ready, sir?"

"Do you have a plan, Captain?"

"Not getting killed?" Stephano suggested.

"As good a plan as any," said Sir Henry gravely. "Then, yes, sir, I am ready."

40

My research has led me to develop an application of constructs that could prove useful in defending against contramagic. I need a way to test my hypothesis. If I am wrong, my experiment—and myself—may be short-lived.

—Journal of Rodrigo de Villeneuve

On the *Sommerwind*, Captain Leydecker was on deck trying to reason with Miri.

"I'll be fine, Captain. The pinnace seems to handle just like the *Cloud Hopper*." Miri gave him a reassuring smile. She inspected the balloon, looked around the small boat, and found all to her liking. "I've been sailing boats like this since I was tall enough to reach the helm."

"I do not doubt your skills as a sailor, Mistress Miri, but it is much too dangererous—" the captain began.

Both of them heard the loud hoots and roars coming from the dragons and they turned to look in their direction. The three dragons were flying away from the refinery. Looking past them, into the Breath, Miri saw the Bottom Dwellers, the bat riders, and their black ship.

She looked back to the dragons, sucked in a breath, and bellowed her sister's name. "Gythe! I need you!"

Miri returned to the argument with Captain Leydecker. "Landing on that island is going to be tricky and you can't spare any of your officers or crew. Not with *that* coming."

She jerked her thumb at the black ship and the attendant bat riders. Looking around the deck of the *Sommerwind*, seeing no sign of her sister, Miri shouted Gythe's name again.

"Take two of my best marksmen, then—"

"Thank you, sir, but there isn't room in the pinnace," said Miri earnestly. "We don't know how many survivors we may have to transport. And, let's be honest, two marksmen aren't going to be much help against that lot. I have to leave now. Where is my sister?"

Gythe came running up from below.

"Where have you been?" Miri demanded.

"I was putting the Doctor in the pantry," Gythe signed.

"Never mind the damn cat!" Miri said angrily. She glanced at the captain, and shifted to speaking in the Trundler language. "What's wrong with the fool dragons? Right when they might be useful, they've flown off! They've abandoned Stephano and Dag!"

Gythe was startled. The dragons were now several miles away.

"They're afraid . . ."

"*They're* afraid! We're all afraid!" Miri snapped. She looked at Gythe worriedly. "Are the Bottom Dwellers talking to you?"

Gythe shook her head. "They don't know I'm here."

"I wish you would go below—"

Gythe tossed her head. Her hands flashed. "We've discussed this, sister! I'm not going to hide. If the *Sommerwind* is attacked, I can help fight them."

"Pinnace is ready to set sail, Mistress Miri," Leutnant Baumann reported.

"Be careful!"

"You, too!"

Miri kissed Gythe and embraced her, then climbed the ladder that led into the pinnace.

The balloon was now completely filled. The crew was holding onto the ropes, ready to let go when Miri gave the order. She took her place at the helm and studied the brass plate with the magical constructs engraved on it. The ship was Guundaran and despite what she had told the captain, Miri had been worried that the constructs might be difficult to understand. She saw with relief that they were similar to those on the helm of the *Cloud Hopper*. If anything, they were even less complicated.

Designed to serve as a lifeboat or to carry crewmembers and supplies between ship and shore, the pinnace was outfitted with a small lift tank built into the gunwale, a single balloon, and a small sail on a lone mast. Long rows of bench-like seats in the center could be removed if necessary. The boat was not armed. The helm was situated at the rear of the boat, so the helmsmen could see where to steer.

Pinnaces were meant to be used only for short distances. They did not provide the most comfortable ride. Being small and light, pinnaces were affected by every ripple, eddy, and current in the Breath. No sailor wanted to be caught in a pinnace during a storm.

"Or in a demon attack," Miri muttered.

She put that worry out of her mind.

Running her hands over the helm, she was getting the feel of the boat and making certain everything was working. She was about ready to shove off, when she was startled by a "Whoops!" followed by a thud. She turned to see Rodrigo sprawled on the deck underneath the ladder.

"Missed the last rung," he explained, rising to his feet and brushing off his clothes.

"What are *you* doing here?" Miri demanded.

"Coming with you," Rodrigo replied.

"Rigo, I don't have time for your foolery—"

"I'm not fooling, Miri. I'm coming with you. I can help," Rodrigo said. "I've been working on something. I can't explain it, but I think it could be useful against the bat riders."

Miri was surprised. For once in his life, Rodrigo seemed to be serious. She didn't have time to argue.

"Sit down on that bench and don't move."

"Yes, ma'am." Rodrigo meekly did as he was told.

Miri ordered the sailors to cast off. The pinnace drifted away from the *Sommerwind*. When they were clear, Miri sent the magical impulse to the air screws, and they began to whir. She adjusted the sail and headed the small boat in the direction of the refinery.

"What happened to the dragons?" Rodrigo asked, taking sudden notice of the fact that they weren't around. "What are they doing way out there? Did Stephano send them away?"

"They fled. Gythe says the beasts are afraid of the Bottom Dwellers," said Miri grimly. "I'm not surprised. I've been expecting some kind of trouble from them."

"You never said anything," said Rodrigo.

"Who would listen to me? Certainly not Stephano. I haven't been around dragons as much as he has, but I've studied their lore for many years. I guess I understand them as well as any human can. And that's the point."

"I don't follow you," said Rodrigo.

"Take Doctor Ellington. To Dag and Gythe, the cat is a loved friend, a trusted companion. To me, the Doctor is a cat who hangs around because he wants smoked fish. To Stephano, the dragons are comrades-in-arms, friends, companions. Viola and Petard and Verdi are not comrades, they're not friends. Those names are not even their names. They're here for their own reason."

"What do you think that reason is?"

The dragons had landed on the distant island, close enough to see what was happening, but not close enough to be in danger.

"These dragons may be a hundred years old, but in dragon terms that means they're adolescents," she said. "They've been playing make-believe, pretending to be warriors. Now the make-believe has turned real and they're afraid."

"Stephano's been playing make-believe, too," said Rodrigo quietly.

"I know," said Miri with a sigh. "I fear this is going to end badly all around."

She eyed Rodrigo, who was removing a large wad of silk from beneath his coat. "If that's a new shirt, it's one of the ugliest I've ever seen."

"It *is* a rather gruesome shade of red," Rodrigo admitted. "I didn't have much choice. I had to use what silk I could find."

"What do you mean? Where did you find it?"

"Down near that bad-smelling place I believe is known as the bilge, where they store the rope and sailcloth and nets and such like."

"And the spare balloons!" Miri was shocked. "Did you cut up one of the spare balloons?"

Rodrigo was down on his hands and knees on the deck, heedless of the dirt, smoothing the silk with his hands. Now that it was spread out, she could see he had made his own crude balloon, formed of two pieces of silk sewn together. He sat back on his heels and looked up proudly at Miri.

"I even did the sewing myself. Comes from years of observing my tailor. What do you think?"

She was busy trying to keep an eye on their destination and on the black ship that was crawling steadily closer.

"I think Captain Leydecker will toss you overboard if he

finds out you cut up a spare sail," said Miri severely. "Why did you bring a limp balloon on board anyway?"

"You will see," said Rodrigo.

Rising to his feet and hauling the silk with him, he lurched across the rocking deck, heading for the small lift tank. "Once I fill my balloon with some gas from the lift tank the balloon will take flight. How does this valve work?"

"Rigo, don't you dare touch that!" Miri cried.

"I won't syphon off much gas," said Rodrigo. "Just enough to fill the balloon. Do I turn this crank thing—"

"No!" Miri howled. "You don't know how to work it! If the valve sticks, the lift gas will all leak out and we'll sink! Rigo, I'm warning you—"

Miri stopped, stared, then gasped. "Oh, God!"

Rodrigo heard her and turned, alarmed. "What?"

Miri pointed.

The island on which the refinery had been built was little more than a large chunk of rock, a part of a continent that had broken off and gone drifting out into the Breath. She could see the underside of the island and three bat riders who had apparently been clinging, hiding there since their failed attack, waiting for their comrades to return. They now had swooped out of hiding and were flying toward the pinnace.

Miri glanced over her shoulder. They were too far from the *Sommerwind*. They would never reach the ship before the demons were upon them.

"Miri," said Rodrigo tensely, "tell me how to work the valve. I need to fill the balloon!"

"One more word about your stupid balloon—"

"I swear, Miri, this will help us! That's why I made it! The balloon is covered with magical constructs. I don't have time to explain. Miri, please—"

"I'll fill it!" Miri snapped, watching the bat riders flying nearer. "You come here and watch the helm. Put your hands here and here and don't move. Don't so much as twitch!"

Rodrigo gingerly placed his hands on the symbols where Miri had shown him and froze. Miri ran over to the lift tank.

"Fill the balloon all the way," Rodrigo told her.

"I'm an idiot," Miri muttered. "A bloody idiot. And I'm going to die an idiot."

She cranked open the valve until she heard the gas start to escape, then swiftly clamped the opening of the silk balloon over the valve. The balloon filled rapidly. Miri shut the valve, then deftly tied the balloon with the bit of string Rodrigo had borrowed from the cat.

"Don't let go of it!" Rodrigo warned.

Shaking her head at her own folly, Miri carried the balloon back to Rodrigo. He took it from her and gazed up at it lovingly. She saw a green flash and cringed. One of the bat riders had fired his fireball long gun at them. The Bottom Dwellers were only finding their range, however. The fireball trailed off harmlessly into the Breath.

"Whatever you're going to do with that thing you'd better do it quickly," Miri told Rodrigo.

He held the balloon by the string and began running his hand over the silk, drawing lines, connecting lines, forming magical constructs. Being a channeler, Miri could see the constructs start to glow with a faint blue radiance.

"You have a balloon that glows in the dark," she said caustically. "How is that going to help us?"

"I am going to use it to create a magical shield around the pinnace," Rodrigo explained.

Miri shook her head and drew her pistol. Cocking it, she laid it on the helm. The three bat riders were separating, planning to come at them from different directions. They raised the long guns. They were in range.

"Rigo, get down!"

Rodrigo paid no attention to her. He was still drawing magic constructs on the balloon.

Green fire flared. Two fireballs slammed into the pinnace; one hitting the hull, the other tearing a hole in the sail. She couldn't see what happened to the third. The pinnace reeled. Miri gripped the helm with both hands. Rodrigo fell backward into a bench, ending up in a seated position, still managing to keep firm hold of the balloon.

Miri cast an embittered and angry glance at the dragons, who were watching from the safety of their little island. The young one, Petard, appeared to be arguing with the others, hooting and lashing his tail. His sister Viola roared at him, ducked her head, and flared her wings. Petard backed down. Verdi was off to one side, staying out of the quarrel.

"Ready!" Rodrigo announced.

He held the glowing balloon in both hands, cupping it by the bottom. Moving to the center of the pinnace, swaying with the motion of the boat, Rodrigo raised the balloon into the air, holding it as high as he could reach.

The three bat riders were again taking aim.

"Rigo, get down!" Miri pleaded.

"In a minute," he said, gazing up at the balloon, oblivious to anything else.

Miri grit her teeth and aimed her pistol at the Bottom Dwellers. She wouldn't hit anything. They were too far away, out of range. She felt the need to do something.

"Ah . . . there . . ." Rodrigo breathed gently. "You see? Look at that!"

Miri stared in wonder at the magical blue glow starting to radiate from the balloon, lighting up the pinnace, glittering in the air.

Green balls of flame sizzled through the Breath. Miri

ducked behind the helm. The green fireballs struck the blue glow . . . and the contramagic disintegrated. The flames fell harmlessly around the pinnace in sparkling green drops.

"It works!" Rodrigo cried. "Did you see that, Miri? It works!"

He sounded completely amazed.

"You mean you didn't know if it would?" Miri gasped.

"My reasoning was quite sound," said Rodrigo. "I needed to put it to the test. I've been thinking about magic and how it reacts with contramagic and it occurred to me that if there is indeed a connection between the two, then that connection should work both ways. Contramagic erases constructs and neutralizes magic, like an alkali does to an acid. The problem is, I kept focusing on the effect that contramagic has on constructs when I should have been concentrating on how the two coexist . . ."

Miri had no idea what he was talking about. She muttered, "Yes, yes" every so often and went on with her work. The pinnace was drawing closer to the island. The bat riders were still out there, reloading, probably puzzled as to why their attack had failed.

Rodrigo paused to make some adjustments to the balloon, then prattled on.

"Granted, it takes a lot more magic to neutralize contramagic, but it can be done. Since magic is inherent in the lift gas in the balloon I drew a construct that would project that magic into a shield—"

Miri interrupted. "Fascinating. How long will the shield last?"

"Ah, that's a good question," said Rodrigo, gazing up at the balloon. "Since I have never created such a complex construct before, I can't say. Those hits weakened it. I can try to shore it up, but I'm not sure how long that will last. How far are we from the refinery?"

"Not far," said Miri.

The bat riders had flown out of range to reload their weapons. Now the three were coming back to the attack, swooping around the pinnace. Miri crouched down behind the helm. The blue shield held; the green flames struck it and scattered like starbursts. Miri was elated. Rodrigo shook his head dejectedly and began hurriedly tracing lines on the balloon.

"My constructs are breaking down and the lift gas is leaking out. I can't do much more to repair them."

"If you can hold the bat riders off for just a little longer, we should reach the island," said Miri, eyeing the distance to the refinery, which was shortening rapidly.

"What about the return trip?" Rodrigo asked. "I'll need to fill the balloon with lift gas again. The attacks are depleting it. Will there be enough gas left to fill the balloon *and* carry us to the *Sommerwind*?"

Miri glanced over her shoulder at the black ship and the attendant bat riders. The black ship had reached the cluster of islands and was having to negotiate its way through the narrow channel. This had slowed the ship's progress, but wouldn't slow the bat riders if they decided to come after them.

"We have to calculate the weight of the survivors, the amount of lift gas I've already put into the balloon, the amount we used traveling to the island, the amount we'll need to make the trip back . . ." Miri gave a little sigh.

"Well?" Rodrigo asked worriedly.

Miri smiled. "Rigo, no matter what happens, you are my hero. I'd give you a hug, but I can't leave the helm."

"What you are saying by not saying is that there won't be enough lift gas," said Rodrigo glumly. A thought occurred to him. "The refinery makes the liquid form of the gas! We can use that!"

Miri gave a noncommittal nod, not wanting to shatter his

hopes. The lift tank on the pinnace was constructed to carry only gas. She couldn't figure any possible way to fill the tank with liquid.

"One worry at a time," Miri told herself. "After all, we may not even live long enough to care."

The three bat riders were flying in for another attack. This time, when the green fire struck the magical shield, the blue glow was noticeably weaker. The balloon was shrinking. The bat riders must have grown frustrated. They veered off, flying back to the other side of the island.

Miri breathed a sigh of relief and fixed her sights on the refinery.

"The landing could be a little rough," she warned Rodrigo.

Stephano stood in the doorway of the storage room—the door through which he and Dag had entered—waiting for the signal. He couldn't see either Dag or Sir Henry from his vantage point, but he knew where they were. Sir Henry, armed with two pistols, one in each hand, stood at the main double doors located in the center of the building, facing the lab. The doors opened onto the only large patch of bare ground on the island. The workmen had planted grass and even a few flowers. They called it "the yard."

Dag was behind Sir Henry, pistol in hand. The sergeant stood nearby, holding the loaded rifle and several more pistols. Workmen with spyglasses were posted as lookouts, keeping watch on the enemy's approach and trying to determine the exact location of the second sharpshooter. Frau Aalder and her helpers were preparing the wounded for transport.

Across the yard was the laboratory in which the other sharpshooter had taken refuge. The lab was the second largest building after the living quarters and it, too, was made of stone. The building was rectangular in shape, with another, smaller building attached at the north end. Unlike the living quarters with their slit windows, the laboratory had been constructed with glass-paned windows on all sides to provide light for the workers.

Unfortunately, the windows gave the sharpshooter a variety of options. He could fire at the larger building directly across from him out of the east windows, at the scaffolding from the windows in the south, or at the pinnace, which would be coming in from the west.

Sir Henry wasn't certain, but he believed the second sharpshooter was concealed in an L-shaped building situated at right angles from the laboratory. This building housed the refinery offices; its windows faced north, west, and south, looking into the yard. If the sharpshooter was in that building, he and his comrade would catch anyone venturing into the yard in a deadly crossfire.

Exactly what Stephano needed for his plan to work.

"We're putting our lives into the hands of your sergeant," Sir Henry observed to Stephano. "Is Thorgrimson that good?"

"He's that good," said Stephano.

He was in the storage room near the door that led to the yard, holding a brick in one hand and Rodrigo's grenade-in-a-jar, as Dag termed it, in the other. He had stowed two loaded pistols in the pockets of his dragon coat.

Stephano waited impatiently. He hated these gut-twisting, palm-sweating moments before going into action.

Sir Henry shouted the signal, "For Freya!" and slammed his foot into the double doors, kicking them open. He and Dag burst out into the yard. Sir Henry fired his pistol at the Bottom Dweller in the lab, Dag shot at the windows of the office, then both men turned and ran, hoping to find cover before the sharpshooters could return fire.

Reaching the door, Dag took the rifle that the sergeant

held out to him, and positioned the weapon at his shoulder. Sir Henry was near the door when one of the blazing green bullets struck him in the back. He pitched forward onto the grass.

"Keep down!" Dag shouted. "Where did that shot come from, Sergeant?"

"The window in the office, sir."

Stephano waited until he heard gunfire, then shoved open the door of the storage room and ran to the window at the south end of the lab. He peered inside and saw long stone tables covered with glass bottles, coils of tubing, boxes, barrels, and the Bottom Dweller. He was in front of the east window, his back to Stephano, firing at Sir Henry and Dag.

Stephano smashed the window with the brick and tossed the grenade inside, hurling it as far into the room as he could. He made a mad dash to the storage room for cover and had managed to reach the door when the lab exploded in a shower of broken glass and splintered wood, smoke and flame.

Stephano dove for the open door as debris and cinders rained down. A chunk of stone hit him a bruising blow on the arm, knocking his pistol out of his hand. The magical constructs of the uniform coat protected him from serious harm and he was on his feet before the smoke cleared. Snatching up his pistol, he ran out into the yard to find Sir Henry lying facedown on the grass. He was swearing, so he was alive.

"Duck, sir!" Dag bellowed.

Stephano glimpsed the sharpshooter running out of the burning laboratory. Stephano swore and flattened himself, as Dag fired over his head. The bullet struck the Bottom Dweller in the helm, between the eyes. He pitched backward into the blazing rubble.

Stephano was on his feet again. They still had to deal with the sharpshooter holed up in the office. Stephano had hoped the smoke from the fire would provide cover for their movements, but the wind was out of the east, blowing the smoke away from them. He looked into the doors of the main building. Dag was nowhere in sight.

The sergeant pointed. "Look out! Office, sir! Lower floor!"

Stephano saw the glint of sun off the barrel of a pistol and fired at it, as he crouched down beside Sir Henry. He could see a smoldering bullet hole in the back of the man's coat, between the shoulder blades. Blood trickled out around the hole and was oozing from the wound, but wasn't pouring out in a torrent.

Sir Henry was twisting his head, trying to see.

"How bad is it? It hurts like bloody hell!"

"Thank your seamstress," Stephano answered. "Your magic-laced coat saved your life. Can you stand?"

"I don't plan to lie here the rest of the day," Sir Henry said through gritted teeth. "Give me my pistol."

Stephano shoved Henry's pistol into his hand, thrust his own discharged gun into his pocket, and drew his dragon pistol. Both men aimed and fired at the office window, then Stephano helped Sir Henry to his feet and they ran for the doorway. A bullet whizzed between the two of them.

"I'll keep him busy!" Stephano said. "You go get that wound treated."

Stephano tossed his empty pistols to one of the workmen for reloading and grabbed two loaded pistols in return. Sir Henry ignored Frau Aalder's horrified exclamations and picked up two more loaded pistols. He and Stephano fired from the doorway, neither of them hitting the Bottom Dweller, apparently, for another bullet smashed into the door.

A single shot rang out.

The Bottom Dweller's horse pistol tumbled out of the window and landed on the ground. While Sir Henry and Stephano had been keeping the sharpshooter's attention on them, Dag had slipped around to the rear of the building, entered, and shot the man from behind. Stephano left the safety of the living quarters and began running in that direction.

He had almost reached the office when he caught a glimpse of yet another Bottom Dweller darting out from the side of the building to shoot him in the back. Stephano tried to shift his stance, but he wasn't going to be fast enough.

The Bottom Dweller aimed . . .

A pistol went off. Sir Henry fired at the gunman from the doorway. The Bottom Dweller staggered, but stayed on his feet. Stephano fired into the mouth of the helm at point-blank range. The sharpshooter toppled over and lay still. Dag came running out the door of the office.

"The one in there is dead. I heard a shot—" Dag stopped to stare at the corpse in amazement. "Where did that bastard come from?"

"He was hiding around the side of the building," Stephano answered, mopping his face with his sleeve. He looked up overhead to see the pinnace bearing down on them.

"We need to be ready to load up the moment the pinnace lands."

He looked around, assessing their situation. The lab was still burning, smoke rolling into the sky. Beyond the living quarters, out in the Breath, the Bottom Dwellers had elected to split their forces. The black ship was sailing toward the *Sommerwind,* while the bat riders escorting it broke off, flying for the refinery.

"Going to be a tight fit, sir," Dag observed, looking at the pinnace and looking back at the small yard.

"If anyone can bring the boat down safely, it's Miri," said Stephano. "Guide her in for the landing."

He returned to the living quarters and found Sir Henry sitting on a chair, hunched over the back. He had removed his coat and shirt. Frau Aalder was probing the wound, washing it with soap and water.

"The bullet is still in there," she reported. "It's not deep. I can dig it out with a knife. I'm afraid it's going to hurt."

"Take it out," said Sir Henry, grimacing. "I don't want a damn contramagic bullet in my back doing God knows what to me! There's a knife in my boot."

He handed over the knife. Frau Aalder washed the blade, then leaned over Sir Henry.

"Miri's coming in for a landing," said Stephano. "We need everyone ready to go."

Sir Henry started to say something, then yelped in pain as Frau Aalder began digging with the knife. Sweat rolled down his face. He clenched his fists and said a few choice words in Freyan.

"Got it!" Frau Aalder held out her hand. A flattened piece of lead, glowing faintly green and covered in blood, lay in her palm.

"Drop it in my coat pocket," said Sir Henry. "I'll want to examine it."

Frau Aalder began to dress the wound, putting plaster over it and binding it with strips of cloth. Stephano noticed several other scars on Sir Henry's body, including a scar from another bullet.

"Hazards of the spy trade, I suppose," Stephano said to himself. He wondered, suddenly, if anyone had ever tried to kill his mother.

Grimacing in pain, Sir Henry drew his shirt over his head. Stephano helped him on with his coat.

"Miri . . . I look forward to seeing that fiery redhead again," Sir Henry remarked. "And her beautiful sister."

"I'm sure Miri will be pleased to see you," said Stephano, grinning. "You shot down her boat. You might have a difficult time persuading her to let you on board the pinnace."

"You could mention to her that I saved your life," said Sir Henry.

"I could," said Stephano. "Thank you, by the way."

"Don't take it personally, Captain," said Sir Henry, smiling. "You are still a damn Rosian. I look forward to the day when we meet on opposite sides of the battlefield."

"As do I, sir," said Stephano.

He went outside to watch the pinnace descend. Miri was handling the boat deftly. Dag was there to help, but Miri had waved him off.

"Get out of the way!" she yelled.

"We could sure use their help, sir," said Dag. He was gazing morosely at the three dragons, huddled on the small island, keeping watch, and keeping their distance.

"Why did they leave, sir?" Dag asked.

Stephano looked at the bodies on the ground, the smoke rising from the destroyed buildings. He looked down at the blood on his coat and at Dag, whose face was black from the gunpowder and smoke. He thought of Sir Henry, pale and tight-lipped, covered in blood and sweat, swearing as someone dug a bullet out of his back.

"It stopped being fun," said Stephano.

41

Diplomacy is always my first choice; negotiating saves lives and money. If diplomacy fails, I try blackmail and bribery. And if that fails, nothing beats a flotilla of heavily armed war ships.

—Sir Henry Wallace

The pinnace slowly drifted down as Miri controlled the ballast from the helm. Looking up, Stephano was astonished to see Rodrigo leaning over the rail.

"Rigo! What are you doing here?"

"I'm being a hero," Rodrigo called. He eyed Stephano anxiously. "What did you do to your face?"

Before he could answer, Miri yelled down, "I need to talk to you, Stephano! There's a problem."

"Of course. There's always a problem," Stephano muttered under his breath.

"Come find me!" he yelled and pointed to the living quarters. "I'll be in there."

"That's going to leave a scar unless you take care of it!" Rodrigo called as Stephano hurried off.

Inside the building, Dag and Sir Henry and the sergeant were portioning out weapons and the last of their supply of powder and ammunition. There were seven pistols, counting his two and Sir Henry's two. The sergeant had one, and Dag had two. The rifle was a different caliber than a musket and required specially sized bullets. Dag reported he had about a half dozen left.

Lord Bjorn sat near the table watching them load the pistols. He was pale and nervous, gulping and wiping his hand over his face. Frau Aalder and the workers stood ready to carry their wounded comrades on board as soon as the workers had tied down the pinnace.

Miri and Rodrigo entered the building, Rodrigo talking excitedly. Frau Aalder latched hold of Miri and the two began discussing the disposition of the wounded. Rodrigo hurried over to the table where Stephano and the others were loading the weapons.

"You should have seen me, my friend!" Rodrigo said exultantly. "My balloon saved the boat. I—"

He stopped talking and stood staring.

"Sir Henry!" Rodrigo gasped.

"Monsieur de Villeneuve," said Sir Henry, pouring powder into a pistol. He was moving stiffly, careful of his wound. "I am pleased to see you in good health."

"I regret to say that I cannot return the compliment," said Rodrigo, recovering himself. "I would be pleased to find you in the worst health possible."

Miri heard the name. Her cheeks flushed crimson. Her eyes flared.

"You bastard!" she cried. "You shot down my boat!"

She lunged at the table, snatched up one of the pistols, aimed and cocked the trigger. Dag caught hold of her and wrested the pistol from her grasp.

"Why did you stop me?" Miri cried furiously.

"We're letting bygones be bygones," said Stephano. He glanced at Sir Henry and added drily, "He saved my life."

"That's no reason," said Miri angrily.

Stephano looked at her, his eyebrows raised.

"You know what I meant," she muttered.

She was breathing hard, and her green eyes remained fixed on Sir Henry. Her hand lingered near the pistols.

"You said there was a problem," Stephano reminded her.

"We don't have enough lift gas to make it back to the *Sommerwind*," Miri replied, glowering at Sir Henry.

"My fault, I'm afraid," said Rodrigo.

"What did you do?" Stephano demanded.

"He saved our lives," Miri said. "But he used up the lift gas. Now we don't have enough."

"But there's the Blood," Rodrigo said eagerly. "These workers make the liquid form of the Breath here in the refinery. We can use that."

"No, we can't," said Miri.

Rodrigo stared at her in shocked dismay. "I don't understand. Back on board you said—"

"I didn't want to upset you, Rigo. The tank of the pinnace can only hold the gas." She shook her head. "It can't hold the liquid. I was thinking they might store spare lift tanks here. The ferries use them."

"We had spare tanks," said one of the workers. "They were stored in the laboratory."

"That's the building you see burning," said Stephano. He eyed Rodrigo grimly. "Explain to me how you used up the lift gas."

"Three Bottom Dwellers attacked us on the way here. Rigo saved us with a magical balloon. Yeah, I know it sounds crazy—"

"I used the same magical constructs Alcazar used on the pewter mug and Gythe used on the *Cloud Hopper*—only different," Rodrigo explained.

"Rigo's magic balloon requires lift gas," Miri added. "If you don't have any here, we're not leaving."

"Where are the bat riders now?" Stephano asked.

"The three that attacked us flew underneath this island," said Miri. "Probably waiting for reinforcements."

"They'll be here soon," said Stephano, with a glance out the window at the bat riders flying in their direction. "Apparently we're stranded. We need to prepare for an attack. We should move the furniture against those doors—"

"We're not stranded," said Frau Aalder.

Silence fell. The workers exchanged uneasy glances. Some looked away. Some shook their heads.

Lord Bjorn stiffend. "The work is secret, Frau Aalder. We have no authority—"

"Authority be damned!" Frau Aalder returned sternly. "What does it matter whether we tell them or not? As the captain said, the secret's going to be in the hands of the fiends soon enough anyway. Do you want to escape or do you want to die here?"

Lord Bjorn was sweating, gnawing his lip.

"Well, my lord?" said Frau Aalder.

"I suppose we have no choice," Lord Bjorn said bitterly.

"In the storage room are four barrels marked 'salt,'" said Frau Aalder. "Inside the barrels are large chunks of silvery white crystals. If you drop one of these crystals in the lift tank, you will have more than enough lift to sail back to the ship." Frau Aalder added with pride, "You would have enough to sail to Rosia and back."

"The Tears of God!" Sir Henry Wallace said, regarding Lord Bjorn with narrowed eyes.

Lord Bjorn looked at him, gave a ghastly smile, and looked away.

"What do you think?" Stephano asked Rodrigo, who was looking thoughtful. "Is it possible to make a crystalized form of the Breath?"

"No," said Miri, pursing her lips.

"Oh, most certainly," Rodrigo said. "The idea has been around for years. The cost of producing the crystal form was always considered prohibitive."

"The Tears of God," Sir Henry repeated in a low voice, still keeping his gaze fixed on Lord Bjorn. "So the reports I've been hearing are true."

Lord Bjorn cast Sir Henry an unhappy glance. "We discovered a method . . . needed Freyan funds for development . . . We were going to tell you—"

"*Were* you?" said Sir Henry in biting tones. "When were you going to tell me? After you transferred the crystals to that ship waiting out there? I wondered how you knew the name of that vessel. You called it the *Sommerwind.* You either have extremely good eyesight to be able to see that name from here or you knew the ship was coming."

"*Of course,*" Stephano said softly. "Leydecker's mysterious, valuable cargo. Money to buy the crystals. A lot of money."

He was glad the mystery was solved, but all this talk was wasting time.

"Miri, I know you are skeptical, but we have to try this. Go make the pinnace ready to sail. Frau Aalder, you supervise loading the wounded on board. Rigo, go with Miri and do whatever you need to do with your magic balloon. Dag, come with me."

Stephano searched the storage room and soon found, amid a jumble of lumber, tools, and crates, four barrels, each about the size of a large keg of wine, stacked in a corner. The four were labeled "Salt."

"I need a crowbar to pry off the lid," Stephano called over his shoulder.

A crowbar appeared, the hand holding it adorned with a lacy, bloodstained cuff. Stephano turned to find Sir Henry with Lord Bjorn hovering unhappily in the background.

"Where's Dag?" Stephano asked.

"Your sergeant's strong arms were required to help with the wounded," Sir Henry said.

Stephano grunted, but he didn't have time to argue. Taking the crowbar, he thrust it under the lid and pried it loose. The barrel was filled with white crystals, each of them about as long as his index finger.

"The most highly refined form of the Breath ever produced," said Sir Henry. He picked up one of the crystals. "More precious than diamonds. A barrel of these, magically enhanced, could lift a fortress off its foundation."

"A fortress . . . ," Stephano murmured. "That's how we take the fight to them!"

An idea came to him with such suddenness that he almost dropped the crowbar. He forgot where he was, forgot the danger, forgot everything except the vivid mental image of a floating fortress that for an instant was clearer, more real than his surroundings.

"Fight to who? What are you talking about?" Sir Henry asked.

"Nothing," said Stephano, returning to the grim reality of their situation. He replaced the lid and pushed it down with the crowbar, then tipped the barrel onto its side and began rolling it across the floor.

"Sir Henry, I need you to move those crates and hold the door—"

When Sir Henry did not reply, Stephano looked around to see him overturning another barrel.

"What are you doing?" Stephano demanded. "We need only one. There's not room—"

"We'll make room," said Sir Henry. "Or should we leave these for the fiends to use in their black ships? Lord Bjorn, take that third barrel."

Stephano had to admit Sir Henry was right. The Tears of God should not fall into the hands of the Bottom Dwellers.

He left his barrel and went to move the crates himself. Once the path was clear, he trundled the barrel out the door. Sir Henry with his barrel came behind. The pain of his wound must have been excruciating, for he grimaced and pressed his lips tightly together. Lord Bjorn followed, rolling his barrel awkwardly.

Stephano had taken only a few steps when he heard Dag yelling, "Look out, sir!"

Stephano looked up to see the three bat riders—now joined by two more—had flown out of hiding.

Dag was on board with his rifle, waiting for the enemy to come within range. Frau Aalder was waving her arms and shouting for Stephano and Sir Henry and Lord Bjorn to make haste. In the center of the pinnace was the improbable figure of Rodrigo tying a string around a red balloon.

Miri had been watching for him. Catching sight of him, she began to yell, "Stephano! Hurry up! We can't take off until we have the crystals!"

Stephano rolled the barrel over the uneven ground as fast as possible. The yard had a slight downhill grade, which made the task easier. One of the bat riders, spotting the three men out in the open without any cover, flew to attack.

Dag aimed his rifle and fired. The bat flipped over and crashed onto the ground right in front of Stephano, blocking his path to the gangplank. The barrel bumped up against the bat's carcass.

The dead bat's rider tried to crawl out from under the bat, but his leg was pinned. He had dropped his weapon, one of the cannonlike guns. He reached for his weapon, just as Stephano made a dive for it.

Stephano grabbed the gun first and tossed it aside. He drew his pistol, but didn't fire. The man was trapped and unarmed. His helm had been knocked askew, revealing his face. He was young, in his late teens.

This was the first time Stephano had ever seen the face of his foe. He had half expected the Bottom Dwellers to be hideous, evil, like their demonic masks. The young man looked like any other young man with the exception that his skin was milk white and his eyes were unusually large. He seemed bothered by the bright sunlight, for he blinked constantly and appeared to be having trouble seeing. He fixed Stephano with a hate-filled glance. His lips parted in a sneer. He spoke the Trundler language.

"Go ahead. Shoot me."

"I'm not like you," said Stephano. "I don't kill the helpless."

He thrust his pistol in his pocket and leaned down to try to examine the young man's leg. He saw Sir Henry Wallace out of the corner of his eye.

"Give me a hand," said Stephano, wrestling with the bat.

"Certainly," said Sir Henry.

He put his pistol to the young man's head and fired. The Bottom Dweller slumped onto his back, half his skull blown away.

Stephano gasped in shock. He stared at the corpse, then rounded on Sir Henry.

"What did you kill him for? He wasn't armed," said Stephano. "He wasn't a threat!"

"Not anymore, he's not," Sir Henry replied cooly. He pointed to the barrels. "Start rolling."

Stephano took one last look at the dead man, shook his head, then bent to his task. Dag shouted a warning. Green light flashed. A wave of heat washed over him. A horrible, gurgling scream came from behind him. He turned to see Lord Bjorn engulfed in a whirlwind of fire. He was screaming, staggering about in agony. His clothes were ablaze. His flesh was blackened, crackling and bubbling. His hair was on fire. His eyes bulging, he reached out to them.

Stephano took a step toward him. Sir Henry caught hold of his arm.

"Leave him. He's too far gone."

Lord Bjorn pitched to the ground, writhing. He gave a last, fearful cry and stopped moving.

"God save him," Stephano said, shaken.

"A little late for that," Sir Henry said caustically. He waved at the pinnace. "Some of you men! Come take these barrels!"

The workmen ran to help with the barrels. Dag remained at his post, firing at another Bottom Dweller. The bat rider flopped over sideways and hung limply from the saddle as his bat flew away. Another bat rider dove down on Stephano and Sir Henry.

Both men raised their pistols and fired. Sir Henry's shot struck the bat. The creature shrieked and kept coming. Stephano aimed and pulled the trigger. The hammer clicked, but nothing happened. He swore and thrust the useless gun in his belt. As he reached for another, a green fireball struck him in the legs, knocking his feet out from under him. The constructs on his coat saved him from exploding in flame like poor Lord Bjorn, but the heat generated by the green fire radiated through the coat, scorching his flesh. For a moment he could do nothing but grit his teeth and wait for the first wave of searing pain to pass.

When the pain subsided, he tried to push himself to his feet, only to fall down with a curse. He had twisted his leg when he fell and wrenched his right knee.

The fourth bat rider was circling around for another attack.

"I'm out of ammunition," Sir Henry called.

"Take mine!" Stephano tossed his last pistol to Sir Henry.

He took aim. Before he could fire, the bat and rider suddenly burst into flame and fell in a burning tangle to the ground.

Stephano looked up to see Viola pulling out of her dive, angling her body the way Stephano had taught her so that she avoided hitting the pinnace with her wings. Glimmers of flame flickered in her fangs.

Limping on his injured leg, Stephano shouted to draw her attention. Viola would not look at him. She stayed near the pinnace, flying in circles overhead. At the sight of the dragon, the remaining bat rider retreated, flying off to wait for reinforcements. The workmen were loading the three barrels onto the pinnace.

"Stephano, hurry!" Miri called.

"Can you walk on your own?" Sir Henry asked.

"Yes—" Stephano began.

Sir Henry thrust the pistol at him. "Cover me."

He turned and ran back to the shed.

"What the devil are you doing?" Stephano shouted.

"I'm not leaving without the last barrel," Sir Henry called over his shoulder.

"We don't have time— Damn it! Dag, cover us!"

Stephano hobbled after Sir Henry and reached the storage room in time to see him hauling the barrel out the door. He began rolling it across the yard toward the pinnace. Stephano gamely kept up, keeping watch for more attackers.

Reaching the pinnace, he yelled again at Viola.

"We need you! You and the others."

He pointed to the black ship.

Viola gazed at Stephano. She seemed to be trying desperately to communicate with him. He had no time to try to commune with her. "We need you!" he said again. She shook her head, made a final circle of the pinnace, then flew back to join the other two dragons on the distant island.

The workmen grabbed hold of the last barrel and hustled it on board. Stephano and Sir Henry hurried after them. Sir

Henry was pale, blood stained the back of his coat. Stephano stumbled going up the gangplank, favoring his injured knee. Frau Aalder came to his aid. Ignoring his protests, she put her arm around his waist to assist him to a place on one of the benches.

"I am sorry about the death of your friend," Stephano said.

"Lord Bjorn wasn't my friend," Frau Aalder said. "I barely knew him. I heard rumors he wasn't a very good man. Still," she added with a softened glance at the blackened remains, "no one should have to die like that."

Miri had already prized the lid off one barrel. Taking out a crystal, she regarded it skeptically.

"What do I do with it?" she asked.

"Place it in the lift tank," said one of the workmen. "When you activate the tank's magic, the crystal will release the gas."

Miri flattened herself on the deck and reached underneath the tank where the spout to fill the tank was located. She hurriedly thrust the crystal inside and closed the spout. Rising to her feet, she shook out her skirt and took her place at the helm.

"We'll see if this works," she muttered, her hands running over the brass plate.

Stephano looked out to the black ship crawling inexorably closer to the *Sommerwind*. He doubted if the Bottom Dwellers on the ship could see what was happening at the refinery, but they could hardly miss spotting the pinnace when it rose into the air. The swarm of bat riders would find them an easy target.

He turned his attention back to the pinnace to make certain all was secure. The wounded lay on mattresses that had been wedged between the benches. Frau Aalder and some of the workers were keeping them as comfortable as they could. Rodrigo was standing in the center of the boat, fiddling with his balloon, talking to himself, running his hands over the silk.

Stephano left the bench and limped over to the prow, where Dag was standing guard over the barrels of crystals. Sir Henry was seated on a bench nearby.

Sir Henry was no longer the elegant Freyan diplomat. His coat hung in charred strips from his shoulders, his fine shirt was filthy and stained with blood. His face was streaked with black powder residue. He had been shot in the back and yet he seemed as cool as though he were attending a game of lawn tennis. He greeted Stephano with a slight smile, as if he knew perfectly well what Stephano was thinking and found it amusing.

Stephano mopped his sweating face with his sleeve.

"Give me your pistols, sir. I'll reload them," Dag offered.

"Thank you," said Stephano.

He handed Dag the pistol and his dragon pistol.

"If you would be so good as to attend to my pistols, as well, Sergeant," said Sir Henry.

He drew the two empty pistols from his belt and placed them on top of one of the barrels.

Dag made no move to pick up the weapons. "Should we put a loaded gun in his hands, Captain? He wants those crystals."

"Given that I'm not likely to sprout wings and fly off with them, I believe the crystals are safe, Sergeant," said Sir Henry drily. "We don't even know if they work."

"I think we're about to find out," said Stephano.

Miri was watching the gauge that measured the amount of lift gas left in the tank. Stephano couldn't see the gauge from where he stood, but he could see Miri. Her brow creased. She shook her head.

"Nothing is happening," she said in a strained voice.

Stephano envisioned what they would do if they were trapped here. They would fight until they ran out of ammunition and after that they would fight with bricks and lead pipes. After that they would fight with their bare hands and after that, they would die.

Miri gasped. "I'll be damned!" She was staring at the gauge in amazement. "It works! It really works!"

Stephano felt the pinnace shudder beneath his feet. The ground began slowly to fall away, as the pinnace rose into the air. Miri activated the air screws. She set their course for the *Sommerwind*.

"And here they come, sir," said Dag.

He handed Stephano the dragon pistol, now loaded and ready to fire.

42

*In the most common variant of "punto banco" bac-
carat, the game requires a gambler to make just one
decision: whether to bet that the value of a "player"
or "banker" hand of two or three cards will end up
totaling closest to nine, with face cards counting as
zero and aces as one. Game outcomes are fixed by
the cards dealt, and players make no decisions after
the initial bet. There's no skill to it at all . . . unless a
person cheats.*

—*Guide to Baccarat*

"We may reach the *Sommerwind* only to find there's nothing
left," Sir Henry observed. "The black ship blew up the *Royal
Lion* with a single shot."

The bat riders were coming for them, but the black ship
was heading for the *Sommerwind*.

"The *Royal Lion* didn't have our Gythe!" Dag stated
proudly.

"What is a Gythe?" Sir Henry glanced quizzically at
Stephano, who was watching the bat riders through a spyglass.

"Miri's beautiful sister." Stephano lowered the glass. "I

count a dozen or more of the enemy. Dag, you're the best shot. Take the rifle and go over by the helm, guard Miri and Rigo."

"I've got just a few bullets left, sir," said Dag.

"Then make every shot count."

Dag detoured around the wounded when he could and carefully climbed over them when he couldn't. He took up a position beside Miri at the helm. A few feet from her, Rodrigo cradled the balloon in his hands. The constructs were starting to glow with a faint blue light. Sir Henry regarded the proceedings with twitching lips.

"Forgive me if I don't put much faith in Monsieur Rodrigo's magic balloon," Sir Henry said.

"Miri said it worked," Stephano returned.

"Women are softhearted," said Sir Henry.

Stephano smiled at the idea. "We are talking about the woman who was going to shoot you in the head. How are you feeling?"

"Like hell," said Sir Henry. "Yourself?"

"That about describes it," said Stephano. His skin burned. His knee throbbed. He leaned against the bench, keeping his weight on his good leg.

Sir Henry examined his pistols, making certain they were primed. Miri turned the air screws on full. The wispy mists of the Breath flitted past the boat in tattered rags. The sail billowed. The cool breeze was a welcome relief after the heat of the island. The bat riders were spreading out, coming to attack them from all sides.

"You'd better hurry, Rigo!" Miri told him.

"You cannot rush genius," said Rodrigo.

He lifted his balloon in the air, holding it above his head. A soft blue glow spread from the balloon to envelop the pinnace. Stephano raised the glass again, focusing on the

Sommerwind. As he watched, a similar silvery blue glow rimed the masts and rigging of the ship like hoarfrost and cast a blue sheen over the hull.

Sir Henry was watching the *Sommerwind,* as well. At the sight of the blue glow, he raised his eyebrows.

"What is that? Some sort of defensive magic? How does the spell encompass an entire ship?"

"That would be our Gythe," said Stephano.

"Amazing," Sir Henry murmured, awed. He glanced at Stephano. "I am impressed, Captain. You have some very talented friends."

He glanced at Rodrigo, talking to the balloon. "Odd, but talented."

The first bat riders were almost within range of the pinnace, taking aim with their long guns. Stephano drew his pistol, cocked it.

"Shoot the bats," he said. "They're not wearing armor."

A green fireball struck Rodrigo's blue shield and burst into a shower of sparks that rained down harmlessly around the pinnace.

"Did you see that, Stephano?" Rodrigo called out proudly.

He went back to talking to his balloon. Sir Henry drew his pistol.

"Too bad your dragon friends deserted you."

Stephano looked over his shoulder. The dragons were within sight. Perched on their island, they were keenly observing what was going on. They showed no signs of wanting to come anywhere near the Bottom Dwellers. Stephano turned away.

Dag fired at a bat rider flying overhead.

Sir Henry raised his pistol, aiming at another bat. "Your sergeant is very perceptive, Captain. He's right. I do want those crystals."

"The crystals belong to the Braffans," said Stephano. "Would you steal from your allies?"

He and Sir Henry both fired at a bat and its rider. At least one of them hit it, for the bat spiraled downward with a shriek. Sir Henry laid down his empty pistol and picked up another.

"If I have the crystals, Captain, I don't need my allies."

Stephano drew his second pistol. Green fire blazed around the pinnace. The blue protective glow was starting to dim. The boat was slowly closing the gap between them and the *Sommerwind*. Dag fired again and another bat dropped.

Stephano sighted in on a bat rider, fired, and missed. He swore briefly, and was about to draw another pistol when, from out of nowhere, a bat rider burst up from underneath the keel. Before either Stephano or Sir Henry could react, the bat rider fired and then veered off.

The green fireball hit the blue shield in a spattering burst of blinding light. The heat of the fireball seeped through the shield.

"I have one shot left," Sir Henry reported. "Then I have to reload."

"I have one shot. You fire, then reload," Stephano told Henry. "I'll cover you."

Sir Henry fired at another bat rider, then ducked down behind the gunwale and began to hurriedly reload his two pistols and Stephano's dragon pistol. The rifle went off behind them. The blue glow was fading. Stephano cast a glance over his shoulder to see Rodrigo frantically running his hand over the balloon, trying to strengthen the spell.

A bat rider flew toward him. Stephano fired and hit the bat, to judge by the hideous screech. The bat didn't fall, however, but kept coming.

"Hang on!" Stephano yelled.

The bat smashed into the hull, causing the pinnace to rock dangerously. For a sickening moment, Stephano feared the boat was going to capsize. People grabbed hold of whatever they could find. Rodrigo lost his footing and pitched forward, almost tumbling out of the pinnace. He grabbed the mast, saving himself, but losing the balloon. It floated up and away, taking the magic with it.

Miri was clinging to the helm with one hand and operating the controls with the other. After another terrifying lurch, the pinnace finally righted itself.

Stephano found himself standing back-to-back with Sir Henry, both firing. Stephano missed his bat, but hit the long gun, sending it spinning out of the fiend's hands. Sir Henry shot a rider in the throat.

"The powder's almost gone," Sir Henry said over his shoulder. "Not that this matters, since we have no more bullets."

"We just need to hold out a little longer," said Stephano.

The *Sommerwind* had taken up a defensive position in the middle of a channel at a narrow point between two islands, putting herself between the black ship and the pinnace. The *Sommerwind*'s gun bay doors were closed. Those six small cannons wouldn't do much damage anyway and Stephano had warned the captain about the risk of a blast of contra-magic causing the cannons to explode, which is what had sunk the *Royal Lion*.

Miri steered the pinnace toward the *Sommerwind*'s stern, where sailors were waiting to help catch the ropes and pull the boat on board.

More bat riders were coming. Stephano waited tensely for the next assault. He was ready to fire his last bullet when, as if acting on a signal, the bat riders broke off the fight. They veered, wheeled, and flew off toward the refinery.

"Why didn't they finish us?" Stephano wondered.

"They'll leave us to the black ship," said Sir Henry, shrugging. "The Bottom Dwellers now control all three Braffan refineries. Your King Alaric is going to be a very unhappy man."

King Alaric's new, modern navy had been designed to use the liquid form of the Breath. The larger, heavier ships were dependent on the Blood to provide the lift to carry a greater number of bigger cannons. Without the liquid filling their capacious lift tanks, Rosia's fleet could not sail. Refitting and modifying them would take months and during that time Rosia's vaunted navy would be out of action. Freya's ships, which operated on lift gas, were not as big as the Rosian ships and lacked the firepower. None of that would matter if the Rosian navy couldn't get off the ground. A war with Freya would be over without a shot being fired.

If, on the other hand, the Rosian navy had the Tears of God, they wouldn't need the Blood.

Sir Henry must have been thinking the same, because he leaned close to Stephano to say softly, "I want those crystals, Captain."

"You can want them all you like. You're not going to get them."

The pinnace hovered over the stern, where the dragons had been accustomed to sleeping.

Miri held the pinnace steady, while Dag threw down ropes to the sailors waiting below the black ship.

They caught the ropes and hauled on the pinnace, lowering it to the deck as Miri gradually reduced the flow of magic to the lift tanks.

Leutnant Baumann came running, shouting orders. "Haul away, lads!" He waved at Stephano. "Once the pinnace is down, we're going to try to outrun that thing."

He gestured at the black ship.

Gythe stood on the deck, eagerly waiting for them to

land. The blue magic glittered all around her, sparkling on the deck, glowing on the hull. The workers were lifting the mattresses bearing the wounded.

Stephano shifted his pistol to Sir Henry's midriff and said politely, "I would be obliged, sir, if you would relinquish your weapons. Otherwise I will be forced to kill you."

Behind him, Frau Aadler gave an outraged cry. "What are you doing, Captain? Put down that pistol! Sir Henry is a Freyan ambassador!"

Stephano didn't have time to explain that the esteemed ambassador was in truth a spy and a cold-blooded killer who would have no compunction about killing them all if it suited his purpose.

He ignored her and kept his pistol aimed at Sir Henry, who was divesting himself of his weapons.

"What do you intend to do with me, Captain?" Sir Henry asked, seeming not the least perturbed.

"The *Sommerwind* has a brig," Stephano said shortly. He gestured with the pistol. "Pocket gun, too. I know you have one."

Sir Henry reached into his coat, drew out a small pistol, and added it to the collection on top of a barrel. Stephano picked up the pistols and the pocket gun and stowed them away in his coat.

Sir Henry observed him, then said, with a casual air, "Do you know how a man cheats at baccarat, Captain?"

"Not my game," said Stephano. "And I don't cheat. Walk ahead of me."

Sir Henry tugged at his tattered lace cuff. "He holds the winning card up his sleeve. Fair warning, Captain. I am not above cheating, not when the stakes are high enough."

Before Stephano could respond, the pinnace came down for a hard landing, bumping several times on the deck as the sailors fought to keep hold of the boat long enough to tie it down.

"All secure!" Leutnant Baumann called.

Captain Leydecker gave the order. The air screws whirred. The *Sommerwind* began to glide forward.

The black ship opened fire.

The mists of the Breath sizzled and evaporated as the green beam shot through them. The green contramagic fire struck the magic of Gythe's shield. The two forces flared up in a dazzling burst that lit the sky as bright as the sun, bathing both ships in hot, brilliant green-blue light. The magicks warred, blazing fiercely until it seemed to the terrified observers that the battle must end in a fiery explosion that would destroy both ships.

And then, with a deafening thunderclap, the magic burned out. Green light and blue vanished, leaving behind only a blinding afterimage burned into the back of the eyes. The blue glow surrounding the ship was gone.

Stephano looked out at the black ship. Several Bottom Dwellers were gathered around the green beam weapon, splashing what appeared to be some sort of red liquid on the barrel. He assumed they were preparing it for firing.

The *Sommerwind* was the faster ship and she was rapidly drawing away—just not rapidly enough. She had to navigate her way slowly through the narrow channel between the tree-encrusted islands or risk crashing and foundering. The black ship would have another shot at them, maybe two before the *Sommerwind* could escape.

"Gythe!" Miri screamed.

As Stephano half turned to see Gythe collapse and fall to the deck, Sir Henry made a swift dive for his weapons.

"I wouldn't do that, sir," said Dag. He had his pistol aimed at Sir Henry's heart.

Sir Henry smiled and let his hand fall.

"Dag, take him to the brig!" Stephano ordered.

"My pleasure, sir," said Dag.

He grabbed hold of Sir Henry and shoved his pistol in the man's back. "Start walking."

Dag looked worriedly at Gythe. "I hope she's all right, sir. Let me know."

Stephano nodded and limped over to the gangplank. Frau Aalder cast him a furious glance and turned her back on him. He painfully hobbled down the gangplank and onto the main deck. Rodrigo was kneeling beside Gythe, as Miri cradled her sister in her arms.

Gythe was unconscious. Her face had lost its color. Blood was seeping from her eyes and ears and trailing out of the corner of her mouth.

"Rigo . . ." Stephano couldn't talk. He felt stifled. He had to force the words out. "Is she . . ."

"She's alive," said Rodrigo. "But she's badly hurt and I don't know what's wrong with her. I believe it has something to do with the concentrated force of the contramagic. If that weapon fires again, it will kill her."

"Don't just stand there!" Miri said frantically. "Shoot them! Do something!"

"There's nothing we can do except try to outrun them," said Stephano. "Take Gythe below. Rigo, you stay with her."

Rodrigo lifted Gythe in his arms. Her head lolled. Her fair hair was gummed with blood. He carried her below. Miri walked at his side, holding fast to Gythe's hand.

Stephano measured the distance between the *Sommerwind* and the black ship and shook his head.

"How is the young woman?"

Stephano turned to see Sir Henry with Dag right behind him. Stephano gave Dag a questioning look.

"I thought you were going to take him to the brig?"

"He said he wanted to talk to you, sir."

"I'd like to watch, Captain," said Sir Henry. "I've never seen one of the black ships this close. This may be my only chance."

"I can take him below, sir," Dag offered.

"He can stay," said Stephano.

"How is Gythe, sir?" Dag asked worriedly.

"She is very ill. Rigo's with her . . . Do you think you could get a shot with the rifle from here? Target that gun crew?"

He gestured to the black ship and the Bottom Dwellers working on the green beam weapon.

"I could, but I'm out of bullets," said Dag. He gave the rifle a fond pat and added wistfully, "She is a fine weapon."

"The rifle is yours, Sergeant," said Sir Henry. "In return for services rendered."

Dag regarded the rifle with longing, then shook his head. "I don't feel right taking it."

"Consider it a gift from an enemy, Sergeant," said Sir Henry. "With the hope we will someday meet on the field of battle."

"With that hope, I thank you, sir," said Dag.

The three stood watching the black ship. The *Sommerwind* was steadily moving away. But slowly, much too slowly.

"That ship is different from the ship that attacked West-firth, isn't it?" Stephano said. He had to do something to take his mind off the fact that the next blast of green fire was going to destroy them.

"You're right, sir," said Dag. "That was an Estaran hulk, built during the time of the Bishop's War. This is a refitted Guundaran freighter, probably forty years old."

"Ugly, isn't it?" Stephano said.

"Ugly as sin," Sir Henry replied grimly. "See those strips that look like leather nailed to the hull? That is human skin.

That liquid they're splashing on the gun is human blood. They are using blood magic in conjunction with the contra-magic. The fiends probably sacrificed some poor devil before they came after us."

"How do you know all this?" Stephano demanded.

"Because I was acquainted with a woman who is one of them," said Sir Henry. "She is known to you Rosians as 'the Sorceress.' She is skilled in the diabolical art of blood magic and contramagic. It might interest you to know she is now in the royal court of Rosia, masquerading as a duchess."

"What's she doing there?" Stephano asked, alarmed.

"I do not know," Sir Henry replied gravely. "But where she goes, she leaves bloody footprints behind. I sent a warning to your mother."

Stephano was startled. "You really do consider these people a threat to the world, don't you, sir?"

"The Bottom Dwellers believe all the nations of the world conspired to destroy them," Sir Henry replied. "They have waited and worked for five hundred years to exact their revenge."

The men who had been splashing blood on the green beam gun moved away, leaving only the two who were in charge of firing. They adjusted its aim.

"Ship off the port bow!" the lookout cried.

Everyone turned in amazement to see a ship emerge from the mist.

"By God, sir, it's a gunboat!" Dag stared at it and scrunched up his face in disgust. "At least, I think it's a gunboat . . ."

"I'm not sure what it is," said Stephano.

"The sergeant is right. That is a gunboat," said Sir Henry proudly. "*My* gunboat, Her Majesty's Ship *Terrapin*."

The strange-looking boat was aptly named. The hull was covered in steel plating. Steel plates protected the wings, making the gunboat appear to be encased in a shell. Usually gunboats carried only two air screws, but the *Terrapin* had four, the other two having been added to compensate for the weight of the armor. The *Terrapin* carried fourteen twelve-pound cannons, seven on each side, and sixteen swivel guns mounted behind protective steel plates. The guns had been run out, gunners at their posts. The green and silver Freyan flag flew bravely from the masthead as the *Terrapin* sailed directly into the path of the black ship.

The two men operating the green beam weapon shifted to fire at this new and more dangerous target. The *Terrapin* sailed on with impunity.

Stephano recognized the tactics of the *Terrapin*'s captain, and he had to say he admired the man's courage. The *Terrapin* was planning to come in close and fire a broadside that would sweep the deck, targeting the crew, the rigging, and the masts. To do that, the *Terrapin* would first have to endure punishing fire. Steel plating wouldn't protect her from a direct hit by the green beam weapon.

Unless the plates were not made of ordinary steel.

"Alcazar's invention! The one you stole!" Stephano exclaimed. He turned to Sir Henry. "The gunboat is plated with Alcazar's steel! Rigo said it could withstand contramagic."

"This will be the first real test."

Sir Henry spoke coolly and calmly, but Stephano noticed the knuckles on the elegant hands gripping the ship's rail were white. A touch of color burned in the thin, aristocratic face.

The captain of the *Terrapin,* whoever he was, must have had nerves made of the same steel. He stood in the open on the quarterdeck, watching the enemy through his spyglass. His deep voice carried clearly amid the tense hush that had fallen over the *Sommerwind.* Every man, no matter his duties, had stopped to watch the confrontation.

"Hold your fire, lads," the captain called.

The gunners aboard the black ship had the *Terrapin* in their sights. A beam of green light struck the steel plating. The *Terrapin* rocked beneath the blast and something belowdecks exploded. Stephano held his breath. Such a blast had been the doom of the *Royal Lion*. The fire was contained, however, and did not spread. The metal plates glowed red from the heat, but they held. When the smoke cleared, he saw that the *Terrapin* had survived and was sailing on.

Those on board the *Sommerwind* began cheering. Stephano shouted with the rest. Dag was pounding the rail with his fist and yelling. At the sound of the cheering, the captain of the *Terrapin* turned, swept off his hat, and made a rakish bow.

"Steady, lads," he called, putting on his hat and going back to business. *"Fire!"*

His gun crews were exceptionally well trained. All the guns fired simultaneously. Smoke swirled around the black ship. Stephano waited impatiently for the smoke to clear to see the damage.

The *Terrapin*'s gunners had double-loaded the cannons, using small balls and chains. The broadside had swept the deck of the black ship. The Bottom Dwellers who had been lining the rails were gone, blown to bloody bits. The main mast had crashed to the deck, dragging down much of the ship's rigging with it. The balloon sagged, air leaking out of it.

"Fire swivel guns!" the captain ordered. "A purse of ten silver griffins to the man who takes out that bloody green cannon!"

The swivel guns aboard the *Terrapin* opened fire on the Bottom Dwellers who were working feverishly to reload the weapon. A marksman on board the *Terrapin* earned the purse by hitting the swivel on which the gun was mounted, causing it to collapse. The two men who had been operating the gun vanished in a hail of bullets.

"You've got blood enough now, you bastards!" the captain called, laughing grimly.

The *Terrapin* began to tack, planning to swing around to rake the black ship with more devastating fire from her guns on the starboard side. Red smoke began rolling off the black ship, covering the *Terrapin* in a noxious fog. Stephano caught a whiff and coughed. He knew this tactic of old, when the *Cloud Hopper* had come under attack. The fumes were poisonous, disorienting.

The captain of the *Terrapin* covered his mouth and nose, choking in the fumes. His helmsman must have been adversely affected, for the *Terrapin* faltered, hanging in the air. Under cover of the poisonous smoke, the black ship disappeared, sinking down into the Breath, hiding in the mist.

The crew aboard the *Terrapin* were shouting and pointing, eager to pursue the foe. The captain wisely decided not to push his luck. He altered course to come within hailing distance of the *Sommerwind*.

Led by Captain Leydecker, the crew and passengers of the *Sommerwind* gave the captain and crew of the *Terrapin* three rousing cheers.

"You have saved us, sir!" Captain Leydecker called. "We are in your debt."

"I thank you, sir," said the captain of the *Terrapin* with a deep bow. "I do have a favor to ask. I observed your pinnace transporting people from the refinery. I seek information about one man in particular. He is Sir Henry Wallace—"

"You have found him, Alan!" Sir Henry yelled, waving. "I am glad you came looking for me."

"I heard all manner of strange rumors in Braffa and, when you didn't come back, I thought I had better go find you," the captain said, adding with a laugh, "I figured if anyone could go up against the devil and win, it would be you, Henry!"

"Our steel worked!" Sir Henry said, pleased. "I cannot wait to tell Randolph."

"The heat was intense. A few of the lads got a bit roasted. We must find a way to fix that. But, otherwise, I say 'God bless Alcazar'!"

"Alan . . . ," Stephano said, enlightened. "Captain Alan Northrop. The pirate!"

"Sir Alan Northrop, privateer," Sir Henry corrected. He made a show of adjusting his sleeve. "You see my winning card. Captain Leydecker, I'll take the crystals now."

Captain Leydecker stared at Sir Henry in scowling bewilderment. "What the devil is this? I don't understand . . ."

"It's quite simple, sir," said Stephano. "The man who just saved your ship is now planning to rob you."

"Aptly put, Captain," said Sir Henry. He shouted to his friend. "Alan, the *Sommerwind* is carrying cargo that I fear will slow her down. It would be charitable on our part to relieve her of the burden. Have your gun crews remain at their posts, will you?"

Sir Henry turned back to Captain Leydecker. "The *Terrapin*'s gun crews are excellent shots as you have witnessed, sir. Order your men to bring up the money chest that I have reason to believe is in your hold. I will also take charge of the four barrels of crystals—"

Captain Leydecker glowered, grim faced. "I could give orders to have you shot."

"I'll be glad to carry out that order," said Dag.

Sir Henry chuckled. "That would be ill advised, gentlemen. Killing me would make Captain Northrop extremely angry—so angry I fear he would blow up this vessel and everyone on it."

In response, Captain Northrop ordered the men manning the swivel guns to train them on the *Sommerwind*. Marine sharpshooters targeted the *Sommerwind*'s officers.

Captain Leydecker glared at Sir Henry, speechless with fury. Leutnant Baumann went down into the hold to fetch the money. He sent a midshipman to supervise the transfer of the barrels of crystals to the *Terrapin*.

Stephano fumed, seething with rage. Once more, just as he'd done in Westfirth, Sir Henry Wallace had outwitted him. He and his pirate friend were going to sail away with the crystals. With the Bottom Dwellers in control of the refineries, Rosia's navy would be languishing on the ground. Sir Henry could probably already taste victory.

Stephano glanced at him. Sir Henry was keeping a close watch on the barrels and on the sailors who came up from the hold carrying a large strongbox. Stephano surreptitiously slipped his hand inside his coat, grasped hold of the bosun's pipe, and drew it out slowly. Bringing the pipe to his lips, he blew the Summons.

Men jumped at the sound of the shrill whistle. Sir Henry whipped around. Stephano paid no heed to him. He was watching the dragons, willing them to obey him, even if it was for the last time.

The dragons heard the whistle. They raised their heads and stared intently in his direction. Petard jumped to his feet and extended his wings. Viola hissed at him and he hesitated. Stephano feared for a moment she was ordering them to stay. She was, however, only ordering Petard to wait his turn. She soared into the air first, taking the lead. Verdi and Petard followed, Verdi with his clumsy leap, Petard with a joyous bound.

Stephano watched the dragons flying toward him, the sunlight shining on their scales, and he turned to Sir Henry Wallace.

"I believe my three cards beat yours, sir," said Stephano.

43

I find it sad to contemplate being forced to teach my trusting little son that for the sake of his own survival he must learn to mistrust.

—Sir Henry Wallace,
in a letter to Captain Alan Northrop

Viola flew in wide circles above the *Sommerwind*. Verdi and Petard hovered in the air, riding the thermals, not far from the ship. Stephano walked over to Sir Henry, who stood with his arms folded, gazing up at the dragons, a slight smile twitching his lips.

"At my command, sir, the dragons will attack your gunboat," said Stephano.

Sir Henry glanced at him. "Are you certain, Captain? Your dragons haven't done anything at your command thus far."

"Would you care to test them?" Stephano asked, though he had to admit he was wondering about that himself. "We could perform an experiment. Your vaunted magical steel withstood contramagic. Will it stand up to dragon fire?"

"Alan, what is your opinion?" Sir Henry called.

Captain Northrop was also gazing up at the dragons.

"We will fight dragons, Henry, if you say the word," he called back jauntily.

Sir Henry considered, probably picturing in his mind the dragons diving down on his gunboat from above, breathing fire on the rigging, the masts, the balloons. The dragons didn't have to touch the steel plates. They could burn up the deck on which Captain Northrop was standing.

Sir Henry gave a philosophical shrug. "The gambler's adage: One can't win them all. The game is yours, Captain de Guichen—for today," he said with a bow.

Stephano gave a deep, inward sigh of relief. He kept his countenance stern, not about to let Sir Henry see that there had ever been any doubt.

"I am your prisoner, Captain," Sir Henry continued. "As I see it, you have three choices: You can either hang me, lock me up, or allow me to depart with my friend, Captain Northrop."

"The decision is not mine, unfortunately," Stephano replied. He went to talk to Captain Leydecker, who was being hounded by Frau Aalder. The captain drew Stephano aside for a conference.

"Will you tell me what the devil is going on, Captain? Who is this man, Wallace? The Braffans all claim he's a diplomat. They're in a furor because you held him at gunpoint! Frau Aalder wants me to arrest *you*."

"Wallace *is* a Freyan diplomat and he was on a mission to Braffa," said Stephano. "He's also a spy and an assassin, one of the most dangerous men on the seven continents. He was planning to plunder your ship, if you will remember."

"Be that as it may, Captain," said Captain Leydecker, "I have to do business with the Braffans and the Freyans. I don't want to have to tell the Travian cartel that I hanged a Freyan ambassador from the yardarm. They'd end up hanging *me*."

Stephano pondered the situation. The captain could lock Sir Henry in the brig, but locks could be picked, guards could be bribed. Sir Henry was expert at both.

"Did the cartel tell you the nature of the cargo you were supposed to pick up at the refinery? Do you know what is in those barrels?"

"No, and I don't want to," said Captain Leydecker. "When dealing with the Travians, the less one knows the better. All I know is that I was contracted to deliver the gold to a Braffan gentleman. His name was . . . let me think . . . Westhoven. Lord Bjorn Westhoven."

"Westhoven, of course!" Stephano remarked to himself. "That was why he didn't want to tell us."

He looked over at Sir Henry. That gentleman, seemingly careless of his fate, was leaning over the rail holding an animated conversation in Freyan with Captain Northrop. Stephano didn't speak Freyan, but he did recognize a few words—military terms common to both languages. Navy—*marine*. Attack—*attaquer*. And repeated references to Alcazar.

This was all starting to make sense.

"I say we let him go," Stephano advised Captain Leydecker. "So long as Wallace is on board this ship and the barrels are on board, he will stop at nothing to obtain them."

Captain Leydecker was pleased, only too happy to be rid of this most dangerous gentleman.

"I do have one question, sir," Stephano asked, as the captain was turning to leave, "do you know the name of the buyer for the cargo?"

"I wasn't told and I was paid well not to ask," said Captain Leydecker. "My orders were to give the money to Westhoven, pick up the cargo, and take it to Evreux. Someone would be waiting on the docks to accept delivery. Now if you'll excuse me, Captain, I intend to put as much distance between my ship and these accursed islands as I can."

The sailors readied the bosun's chair, which consisted of a short plank attached to a length of rope with canvas backing. A sailor was on hand to assist Sir Henry into the chair, which would be used to transfer him to the waiting *Terrapin*. Stephano sent the sailor away.

"I'll lower the chair myself," said Stephano.

"Planning to cut the rope?" Sir Henry asked, seating himself on the plank.

"Much as I'd like to, we need to talk," Stephano said in a low voice. "Do something to delay. Pretend you sat on a splinter."

Sir Henry raised an eyebrow, but he did as he was told. He bounded up from the chair with a curse and turned to glare at the plank seat. He and Stephano leaned over it, searching for imaginary wood slivers.

"You must have run investigations on all the Braffan council members. What did you find out about Lord Bjorn Westhoven?" Stephano asked softly.

"He had recently made some extremely bad investments," said Sir Henry. "He was heavily in debt, about to lose everything."

"He found a way to get out of debt," said Stephano.

"The crystals." Sir Henry cast Stephano a sharp glance. "Westhoven sold them."

"My guess is that he and the refinery workers were in on the deal together. They arranged to sell the crystals. The buyer sent the money on the *Sommerwind*. But they had a problem. When the crystals were discovered missing, they would be the first to be suspected. They needed a cat's-paw. What made you decide to tour that particular refinery?"

"Westhoven suggested it," said Sir Henry.

Stephano nodded. "So when the crystal came up missing—"

"They could blame the theft on me," said Sir Henry. "Clever fellow, Westhoven. He fooled me completely and I am not easily fooled. At least I got to watch the wretch go up in flames. The important question becomes: Who is the buyer? Does your captain know?"

"Leydecker is working for a Travian cartel. All he was told is that someone will be waiting to take delivery."

"Where, exactly?" Sir Henry asked with disarming casualness.

Stephano grinned. "The captain didn't say."

Sir Henry smiled. "Why are you telling me this, Captain? What's to stop me from following this ship, letting you lead me to the buyer?"

"Because you are playing for bigger stakes, judging by the conversation you were having with Captain Northrop. The *Terrapin* is planning to meet up with the Freyan navy and launch an attack against the Bottom Dwellers to try to take back the refineries. If you succeed, you will be able to produce all the crystals you want, not to mention corner the market on the Blood. For I doubt very much if you'll hand the refineries back to the Braffans."

Sir Henry threw back his head and laughed. He clapped Stephano on the shoulder. "I like you, Stephano de Guichen. You are your mother's son."

He settled himself once more in the bosun's chair.

"You realize, of course, that you can't allow those crystals to fall into the wrong hands," said Sir Henry.

Stephano made no comment. He swung the chair out over the rail. The sailors manned the winch, lowering the chair slowly down to the deck of the *Terrapin*.

Arriving safely on board the gunboat, Sir Henry eased himself out of the bosun's chair and sent it back up. Captain Alan Northrop fired off a gun in a jaunty salute and the *Terrapin* sailed away. Stephano watched until he lost sight of her in the mist.

Captain Leydecker was ready to depart, as well. The Bottom Dwellers were, for now, interested only in securing their island refinery and nursing the wounds inflicted on their black ship. They had no interest in the *Sommerwind*. The ship set sail safely for Braffa, where they planned to drop off the survivors.

Stephano went below to his quarters that he shared with Dag and Rodrigo. He was exhausted, drained. His burned legs felt as though he'd been baking them in an oven. His knee hurt and his cheek throbbed. He found Rodrigo there, waiting for him.

"How's Gythe?" Stephano asked, frowning at Rodrigo. "You were supposed to stay with her."

"Dag and Miri are both with her. The cabin was getting crowded. She's fine," said Rodrigo. "A little weak, but a day's rest will cure her."

"What happened to her?"

"The contramagic happened." Rodrigo shrugged. "I have no idea how or why. I can't explain it. Father Jacob experienced similar injuries when he was attacked. I therefore assume it has something to do with being a savant."

Stephano shook his head and scratched at the plaster on his cheek. He gave a deep sigh and sagged down in a chair.

"What's the matter now?" Rodrigo asked. "Dag tells me you outwitted our friend, Sir Henry Wallace. You should be jubilant."

"You'd think so, wouldn't you? I need a few moments to myself, Rigo. I'll meet you in Miri's cabin."

Rodrigo rested his hand lightly on Stephano's shoulder, then left. Stephano knew what he had to do, though he dreaded doing it. The decision wasn't going to be popular. He couldn't risk the lives of his people.

He sighed again and then washed the blood and gunpowder off his face and hands, changed his clothes, then went to meet his friends.

Gythe was sitting up in bed with Doctor Ellington curled up in her lap. Miri sat on the bed beside Gythe, fussing over her. Rodrigo was cross-legged on the floor. The cabin was small. Dag had to flatten himself against the door for Stephano to squeeze past.

"Rigo said you are feeling better, Gythe." Stephano bent down to kiss her on the forehead. "You saved the lives of everyone on board this ship. You are a hero."

Gythe flushed with pleasure, but she didn't want to talk about her heroics. She asked, with a worried look, her hands flashing, "How are the dragons? Dag said they were afraid, but they came back when you called them."

"They came back," said Stephano. "After the danger had passed."

Gythe heard the anger in his voice and she guessed what was coming. She gazed at Stephano with pleading eyes.

"I've made a decision," he said. "I won't permit anyone to ride the dragons."

As he had foreseen, no one was happy.

"The dragons froze under fire, sir!" Dag argued. "They're new recruits. That's to be expected."

"Viola saved your life at the refinery," Miri added, unexpectedly taking the side of the dragons.

"And they took the wind out of that pirate's sails," said Rodrigo. "Nautically speaking."

"We should give them another chance, sir," said Dag.

Stephano looked at Gythe. She gazed at him unhappily, not saying a word.

Stephano shook his head. "How can I trust these dragons after what happened today? I have to face the facts. If it hadn't been for Captain Northrop, we would be dead by now—all except the dragons."

Gythe startled everyone, including the Doctor, by dumping the irate cat on the floor, throwing aside the counterpane, and climbing out of bed. Miri and Rodrigo both hurried to stop her. Gythe flashed fierce looks at both of them and a fiercer look at Stephano.

"I'm going to talk to Petard," she signed. "There must be a reason the dragons didn't fight. I'm going to find out."

"Gythe, you're too weak. Stay in bed. You won't change my mind," said Stephano wearily. "The dragons can stay with us, if they want to, but no one is riding them."

Gythe ignored him. "Where are my shoes? I can't find my shoes."

"Gythe—" Stephano began, exasperated.

"You might as well let her go, Stephano," Miri said. She handed Gythe her slippers. "She won't rest until she talks to the dragon."

Stephano saw it would be useless to argue with her. No matter what the dragons said, he wasn't going to change his mind. But he would be interested to hear what the dragons had to say for themselves. He told Gythe she could go.

Holding on to Miri's hand, Gythe made her way slowly across the cabin to the door. She was too weak to climb the stairs that led to the main deck, so Dag carried her. Doctor Ellington ran up with them, only to turn tail and dash off when he caught sight of the dragons.

Stephano came last. Miri touched his arm. "Maybe you should give them another chance."

Stephano glanced coldly at her. "I thought you would be pleased. You never approved of any of this."

He didn't wait for an answer, but walked away. He could feel Miri staring after him.

Gythe came on deck to the cheers of the crew. She again flushed, and shyly kept hold of Dag's arm.

The dragons were flying behind the ship, keeping their distance, yet still following. Dag put the bosun's whistle to his lips and gave the signal for Petard.

Stephano watched the dragons a moment, then turned to Miri and Rodrigo.

"Do you think Gythe can truly communicate with the dragons? When she says Petard talks to her, does she hear his voice or does she imagine she hears him?"

"Gythe is a savant," said Rodrigo. "Her mind works so much differently from ours that we can't possibly understand what she is thinking or feeling or hearing. For myself, I believe she has found a way to communicate with those she loves—the dragons and Brother Barnaby."

The long day was finally coming to an end. The setting sun lit the mists with a pale golden glow and gleamed on the dragons' scales. Petard heard the whistle. He dipped his wings in response and flew to the ship.

The *Sommerwind*'s crew had hauled the pinnace from where Miri had landed it on the stern to its customary place, secured to the deck between the foremast and the mainmast. The stern where the dragons were accustomed to sleeping was clear. Petard landed on the deck. He was nervous, uncertain. He reared back his head, lifted his chest, shook his mane.

Gythe drew near him, gazing up at him. She began to sing. Perhaps the song had been suggested by their encounter with Captain Northrop, for she sang the old Trundler song about the Pirate King, one of the young dragon's favorites.

Slowly, little by little, Petard's head lowered until his chin touched the deck not far from Gythe, and he closed his eyes. Gythe walked over to the dragon. Resting her hands on his snout, she laid her head on the glittering green scales. Dragons could not cry; they couldn't shed tears. Stephano had the feeling that if they could cry, he would be seeing tears falling from the young dragon's eyes.

Gythe remained with him for long moments. There was

no longer any doubt in Stephano's mind that she and the dragon were talking. At last, she gave Petard a loving pat, then drew back from him. Petard hoisted himself up and raised his wings. He hovered just above the deck, letting the *Sommerwind* glide out from underneath him. His eyes were fixed on Gythe. Then he turned and flew off to join the others.

She walked slowly back to Stephano. Her head drooped. She was downcast, unhappy. She came to Stephano and raised her eyes to meet his. Her words were in her sorrow.

"The dragons are leaving us," she said.

"Why?" Stephano asked.

Gythe began to sign so rapidly that he couldn't follow her.

"The dragons know you are upset with them," said Miri. "They are sorry they fled the battle. They had made a promise to the elders that they would come back safely, but they didn't want to leave us. You see . . ."

"The elders?" Stephano recalled the elder dragon who had flown over their boat. "They said they ran away."

"They did not tell the truth." Gythe signed the words. "They are the last."

"The last what?" Stephano asked.

"The last young dragons," said Miri. "There are no more hatchlings. They have all died. The dragon magic is failing. They didn't know why. The elders thought perhaps the Bottom Dwellers came from our world, that we were the cause. They sent the young to find out. Now they know differently. They will take this information back to their elders."

"I had no idea," said Stephano remorsefully. "I wish I'd known. I wished they had trusted me."

He walked over to the rail and waved to Viola, giving her their private signal. She led the other two dragons close to the ship. She was troubled, regarding him with concern. She was uncertain how he would react.

Stephano could not communicate with dragons, not the

way Gythe could. But he knew what Viola was thinking. She wanted him to understand. She had not been afraid. She had made a promise to return with information and she needed to keep that promise. She needed him to understand and to forgive.

He looked at the three, the last of the young dragons, and there was nothing to forgive.

"Thank you, Lady Viola!" Stephano called. "Godspeed."

The dragons dipped their wings and bowed their heads. They turned as one unit, in formation, as Stephano had taught them, and flew to the west, toward their home.

Gythe wept bitterly, clinging to her sister. Rodrigo blew his nose. Dag cleared his throat and brushed his hand across his eyes. They watched in silence until long after the dragons were gone.

Twilight drifted into evening. The air was moist and soft. The *Sommerwind* sailed as rapidly as she dared through the darkness, with lookouts posted to keep watch for the floating buoys that marked the channel. The air screws whirred, the wind sang in the rigging.

Doctor Ellington came strolling up on deck, tail twitching. Coming to Dag, the cat twined about his ankles and gave a defiant "yeowl."

"At least the Doctor is happy to see the dragons go," said Stephano.

"He is that, sir," said Dag. He reached down to scoop up the cat and place him on his shoulder.

"Come, dear," he said to Gythe. "I'll take you back to your cabin."

"I'll come with you," said Rodrigo. "I need to make some notes on my magical balloon. I believe there is a way to expand the radius of the protective magic."

"And you, sir, need me to look at those wounds," Miri told Stephano sternly.

Stephano followed her below. She wrapped his injured knee and smeared him from head to toe in yellow goo. He stank to high heaven. Rodrigo took one sniff and banished him from their cabin. Even the Doctor shunned him.

Stephano went back on deck to stand by the rail, gazing out into the night, at the few stars that could be seen through the mists. He was surprised when Miri joined him. She wrapped her hands around his arm and leaned her cheek against his shoulder.

Stephano clasped her hand, grateful for her comfort.

"I was wrong, Stephano," said Miri. "The dragons didn't stay with us for the adventure. They stayed out of love."

"And they left out of love," said Stephano.

"Which means they'll be back," said Miri.

They stood in companionable silence, watching the Breath slip away beneath them.

"The young dragons listened to our stories and songs of glory," Stephano said. "I wonder if they will tell their own story when they reach home."

"Not if they know what's good for them," Miri said crisply. "The elders would *not* be pleased to hear stories of their young fighting human battles."

She glanced at Stephano. "You're in a good mood tonight. What's the reason?"

Stephano smiled. "Other than being roasted and shot at and losing the dragons, our own story ended well today."

"For a change," said Miri with a sniff.

44

Our tragedy lay in the fact that your father and I loved . . . but we could not trust.

—Countess Cecile de Marjolaine,
Last Will and Testament

The return voyage of the *Sommerwind* proved to be blessedly uneventful. The weather was delightful with sunny days, mild winds, and clear skies. The refinery survivors disembarked on Braffa. After talking with Stephano, Captain Leydecker agreed that the Braffans should receive payment for the crystals. He turned the money over to Frau Aalder, who left still firmly convinced that Stephano was a scoundrel and a vagabond.

Sailing through the Straits de Domcáido, they noted with interest that the Freyan navy had departed. The ships had vanished in the night, or so they heard when they stopped at an Estaran port to pick up a shipment of wine, bales of silk, and barrels of creosote used in the preservation of wood.

The Estarans were eager to relate how the Freya ambassador had told the Estaran king that the Braffan refineries had come under attack by the Guundaran mercenaries in the name of Travia. Freya had been asked by the Braffans to liberate them.

The Estaran king had sent an indignant letter to his Travian counterpart and withdrawn his ambassador. The Travians had responded by sending their own indignant letter denying the charge and withdrawing their ambassador.

King Alaric of Rosia was said to be on the verge of going to war against Freya and Estara. Queen Mary of Freya was said to be preparing her people for battle.

"I see Sir Henry's hand in all this," said Stephano. "He won't want to start a panic by revealing the truth about the Bottom Dwellers taking over the refineries and yet he *does* want everyone making preparations. The royal court of Rosia must be in chaos. My mother will be extremely busy these days."

The *Sommerwind,* with its hold filled, continued on to Rosia. The barrels containing the Tears of God resided safely in Stephano's cabin. He and Dag took turns guarding them, which proved to be unnecessary. None of the crew had the slightest interest in them. The casks of wine were in far more danger of being stolen than were the crystals.

Stephano's biggest concern was what to do with the Tears of God when they landed.

He gave that matter a great deal of thought and then called a meeting in the cabin, which was even more cramped than usual because the four barrels of crystals took up most of the space. Miri and Gythe sat in a hammock. Rodrigo was forced to sit on one of the barrels, which he dusted with his handkerchief. Dag and the Doctor guarded the door. Stephano remained standing.

"Sir Henry warned me that we can't let the crystals fall into the wrong hands," said Stephano. "We have to figure out who the buyer is. Judging from the amount of money the person paid for them, whoever bought them is very rich, very powerful—"

"And very dangerous," said Rodrigo in gloom-laden tones.

"Any ideas?" Stephano asked.

"A proxy for the Bottom Dwellers," Miri suggested. "Maybe that Sorceress woman Wallace told you about."

"Wallace himself," Dag said. "His plan to buy the crystals fell apart because he didn't expect the Bottom Dwellers to attack, so he feigned ignorance."

"The Travian cartel," said Rodrigo. "They would make a fortune selling these crystals on the black market."

Stephano nodded in agreement to each of these. He was silent a moment, then said with an embarrassed air, "The truth is I want those crystals myself. One barrel. Maybe two."

"While that would help our desperate financial situation," said Rodrigo, "I don't see—"

Stephano raised his hand. "Let me finish. Sir Henry was right in something else he said. Rosia and Freya, Travia and Estara—the nations of the world can no longer afford the luxury of being enemies. We have to stand together against this foe. The Bottom Dwellers are destroying our magic, knocking down our buildings, blowing up our ships. We have to find a way to stop them. And I think I've found it. The idea came to me back on the refinery, when I first heard about the Tears of God. The Bottom Dwellers have thus far attacked us with impunity. We should take the fight to them."

"That assumes we know where they are," said Miri.

"We could determine that easily enough from the last known position of the sunken island," said Stephano. He began pacing in his eagerness, forgot he was in a small cabin, and bumped his head smartly on a beam in the ceiling.

"My plan is only half thought out," he continued apologetically. "We could use that fortress, the one the navy shot down. Where Lady Cam died and Dag and I first met. What was the name?"

"Fortress de Ignacio Orales," said Dag. "Named after an Estaran hero or king or something. We called it Fort Ignacio."

"You said the fortress survived the crash in relatively good condition."

Dag grinned. "That was the only way *I* survived in relatively good condition. The fortress was well built. Our crafter, Master Antonius, who maintained the walls, knew his business. When the naval bombardment shot us down, he managed to lower the fortress in a controlled landing. The building is mostly intact."

"With Rodrigo's magical constructs, Alcazar's steel, and the crystals to give it lift, we could travel inside the fortress down through the Breath. We would catch the Bottom Dwellers completely by surprise!"

Dag was excited. "I think your plan would work, sir."

"I might even ask some of the noble dragons for help. Former members of the Dragon Brigade—"

Rodrigo cleared his throat. "I feel I should point out a serious flaw in the plan—the crystals don't belong to us. And while we may have on occasion bent the law, we've never actually broken it. We have not stooped to thievery. At least, most of us have not—"

He cast a glance at Dag.

"I did a lot of things I wasn't proud of, but I was never a thief!" Dag said angrily.

"I rest my case," said Rodrigo with a grave aspect. "None of us are thieves."

Gythe's hands flashed in a question. Miri translated.

"Gythe wants to know if stealing something that was stolen is really stealing."

"I'm afraid it is. Captain Leydecker has a contract to deliver the crystals to the person who paid for them. The Travian cartel would not look kindly on him if we walked off with the cargo." Stephano sighed and ran his hand through his hair. "He might even be suspected. Leydecker's been good to us. I won't put him in that situation."

"The only thing we can do is to see who comes to the docks to take delivery," said Dag.

"And then ask them nicely for the loan of a barrel of priceless crystals," said Rodrigo. "I'm sure *that* will work."

By the time the *Sommerwind* was heading toward the port of Evreux, Stephano had formed a plan.

"We'll see who arrives on the docks to purchase the crystals," said Stephano. "He'll be an errand boy, not the true buyer, who wouldn't risk being seen. We let the errand boy leave with the crystals. Miri and Gythe and Dag will follow him and he will lead them to the purchaser."

"While you three are on the trail, Rigo and I will go to my house, find out if it's still being watched. If it is, we'll go to the home of the Han brothers. I'll send Benoit to tell my mother I need to talk to her. I'll be honest with her, tell her the truth—"

"She may die of the shock," Rodrigo said.

Stephano cast him an annoyed glance. "Dag stays with the crystals. Miri and Gythe report back to me. Once we determine who has the Tears, we make our decision on what to do to try to obtain them."

"I hope the warrant for our arrest has been lifted," said Rodrigo. "I've already missed the summer season at court. I simply can't miss the fall."

The next day dawned with a crack of thunder and a steady rain. Water dripped from the masts and the rigging, rolled in sheets off the balloon, and drenched everyone on board, including the Doctor, who ventured out for his morning con-

stitutional without first checking the weather and came back
wet and irate.

Despite the fact that they were all soaked to the skin, passengers and crew on the *Sommerwind* were in good spirits.
The ship was going to be in port for several days, which
meant shore leave for the sailors. Stephano and his friends
were thankful to be home, and looking forward with impatience to reaching some resolution regarding the Tears of God.

Traffic was heavy around the Evreux dockyards. With no
further attacks by the Bottom Dwellers, merchants were
once more daring to set sail. The *Sommerwind* sent word of
her return to shore and messages to those expecting cargo.
The ship had to wait most of the morning for the pilot to
come guide her to her berth. Stephano paced the deck,
soaked to the skin, water dripping from the brim of his hat,
chafing at the delay.

When the harbor pilot finally came on board, he met with
the *Sommerwind*'s sailing master to guide the big ship safely
through the multitude of vessels to its designated berth.

The rain had let up slightly by the time the ship arrived
at the wharf, changing from a downpour to a desultory
drizzle. The dock came into sight, gray against a gray background of dingy warehouses. Stephano was on the deck with
a spyglass, hoping to catch a glimpse of the person waiting
to pick up the crystals.

Dag was down below to keep watch on the barrels. Miri
and Gythe, dressed as well-to-do passengers, were waiting
to disembark. Rodrigo was still packing.

The merchants had sent conveyances of various types to
pick up their cargo. Stephano noted several hansom cabs for
hire, their drivers hoping the *Sommerwind* might be carrying passengers who needed a ride to their destination. The
cabs' drivers lounged about on the dock, talking to each
other. The dockworkers waited resignedly in the rain for the

Sommerwind to land. A few idlers lounged about, hoping to pick up some extra money by offering to help load the wagons. Two men, both with umbrellas, which marked them as gentry, stood talking together. Stephano observed the two closely, then shook his head. Merchants—probably the owners of the wine, the silk, or the creosote.

The *Sommerwind* floated down to the dock. Captain Leydecker was on deck to supervise the landing, standing near his helmsman who had to reduce the lift enough, but not too much, to bring the ship down safely. When the ship was level with the wharf, the crew threw the mooring lines to the dockworkers, who tied the ship down.

Once the *Sommerwind* was secure, Leutnant Baumann appeared on deck carrying a large ledger, pen, and ink. Two crewmembers came behind lugging a writing desk and a chair. They placed the desk on the deck underneath a canvas awning, to protect it from the rain. Captain Leydecker and the lieutenant sat down at the desk and indicated they were ready to conduct business.

The *Sommerwind,* like most merchant ships, took on passengers. Miri and Gythe appeared in gowns and hats they had purchased in Estara. Rodrigo was attired as a traveling gentleman in a greatcoat and hat. Gythe carried a basket containing the Doctor, whose muffled growls expressed his objection to this mode of conveyance.

The three descended the gangplank and went ashore, where Rodrigo secured a cab for himself and Stephano and another for Miri and Gythe. Sailors brought their bags and Rodrigo's crate of books. Stephano saw them all secure in their cabs, then went back on board. The others settled back in the cabs to keep watch.

At a word from Captain Leydecker, Dag hauled the four barrels up on deck. He and Stephano stood near them, waiting for someone to board to claim them. The dockworkers and the crew of the *Sommerwind* unloaded the cargo, swinging the heavy bales and barrels up out of the hold. The two men Stephano had marked as merchants boarded the ship. They took charge of the silk and creosote, closed out their financial transactions with Captain Leydecker, and left with their cargo. Another merchant arrived to claim the wine.

The *Sommerwind*'s hold was now empty and no one had come to claim the crystals. Captain Leydecker was toting up numbers in his ledger. The lieutenant was counting out the money.

"Likely the buyer wouldn't want to come when there's a crowd here, sir," Dag pointed out.

Stephano agreed, but he was growing uneasy. What if the buyer didn't come? He hadn't made plans for that. Miri and Gythe and Rodrigo were still in the cabs. Stephano could hear the Doctor's howls from this distance.

A horse-drawn carriage rolled up to the wharf and stopped in front of the *Sommerwind*'s berth. Stephano relaxed, his pulse quickened.

"I think this is our man," he said to Dag.

The carriage was owned by a person of means, for it featured brass lamps and glass windows with fringed window shades that could be lowered to give the passengers privacy. The horses were expensive—a matched pair of dappled grays. The door bore no markings, no family coat of arms or insignia.

The driver dismounted and went to open the door. The passenger did not bother to wait, but impatiently opened the door himself. He descended, paused to look at the name of the ship, as though to ascertain he had the right vessel. Seeing that this was, indeed, the *Sommerwind,* the man strode up the gangplank.

Stephano couldn't see the man's face, for he wore a tricornered hat and a long cloak with a shoulder cape suitable to the inclement weather. He walked rapidly, giving every impression that he was in a hurry.

Captain Leydecker saw the man approach and cast a sharp glance at Stephano. Evidently the captain, too, thought that this was the buyer. Stephano motioned to Dag, who had been standing guard over the barrels of crystals. Dag casually strolled over to take his place beside Stephano.

As Dag did so, he twitched aside his coat, revealing a pistol in his belt. Stephano felt reassuringly for his own dragon pistol, concealed in the inner pocket of his coat. Hopefully there would be no need for firearms.

The man in the cloak walked up to Captain Leydecker, who greeted him pleasantly and asked his business. The man took off his hat and tucked it under his arm.

"I am to pick up four barrels—"

Dag gasped and elbowed Stephano in the ribs. "Sir! Isn't that—"

"It is!" Stephano stared in amazement. "D'argent!"

D'argent turned at the sound of his name. "Stephano?" he said, shocked. "What are you doing here?"

By way of answering, Stephano flung his arms around D'argent in a bear hug, much to D'argent's extreme astonishment.

"My dear D'argent!" Stephano exclaimed. "I was never so glad to see anyone in all my life. I said the person who bought the crystals would be rich, powerful, and dangerous—that exactly describes my mother!"

He laughed out loud and clapped D'argent on the shoulder. D'argent was not laughing.

"I am sorry, Stephano," he said, his brows coming together, "I do not understand—"

"No, of course you don't. I will explain. Allow Dag and me to load the crystals in your carriage. We'll take them to my house. I assume my mother will agree with that arrangement. She can hardly store them in the palace. I will keep close guard on them, you may be sure. Once we have dropped off the crystals, you will take a message to my mother that I need to speak with her on the matter of the utmost importance. Wait," Stephano said suddenly, "are the arrest warrants for us still out?"

"No, sir," said D'argent. "They were canceled. I am in great haste, Stephano, but I need to talk to you." He glanced at Dag. "In private. Perhaps you could leave your friend on board ship to guard the cargo. You and I could go to my carriage."

Stephano detected an odd tone in D'argent's voice. The thought occurred to him that his mother's confidential man of affairs was unusually grave, his expression somber.

"What have I done to anger my mother now?" Stephano demanded.

D'argent regarded him intently. "We need to talk."

Stephano shrugged. He asked Dag to stay with the barrels. D'argent settled with Captain Leydecker, who had been watching the reunion with the greatest astonishment. Stephano accompanied D'argent to the carriage. Rodrigo left his cab and hurried to join them.

"D'argent, why are you here?" Rodrigo asked, alarmed. "Am I being hauled off to smelt something?"

"Come with me," Stephano said, adding to D'argent, "You know I'll tell Rigo everything anyway."

D'argent gave a faint smile. "Perhaps that would be best, sir."

Stephano hurried over to hold a brief conversation with Miri and Gythe.

"Why is D'argent here?" Miri asked.

"I don't know. I'm about to find out. Unload the luggage and send away the cab. Go back on board and wait with Dag. I'll tell you everything."

"Damn right you will," said Miri.

Stephano walked back to the carriage. D'argent and Rodrigo were both inside waiting for him. The driver opened the door for Stephano. He climbed inside and sat down opposite D'argent.

"Drive around the block," D'argent ordered.

Shutting the carriage door, the driver climbed back onto the box. He clucked to the horses and the carriage rolled slowly out into the street.

"What is it?" Stephano demanded. "What's wrong?"

In answer, D'argent reached into his coat and drew out an envelope.

"I have been carrying this with me, hoping I would find you."

D'argent handed the envelope to Stephano, who recognized his mother's bold handwriting. Turning it over, he saw her bee insignia stamped on the back.

"You should read it at once, sir," D'argent said.

Stephano broke the seal and opened the letter. He scanned through it hurriedly, then stopped to look up at D'argent in shock.

"Is what she says here true?" he asked in a low voice.

"I fear it is, Captain," said D'argent.

Stephano handed the letter wordlessly to Rodrigo. He read it swiftly, gave a soft gasp. "Dear God! The princess! An elopement! The scandal . . ."

"This isn't an elopement," said D'argent grimly. "This is an abduction. The woman who took the princess hostage is not a duchess. She is—"

"In league with the Bottom Dwellers!" said Stephano. "She's a sorceress, skilled in blood magic. Sir Henry told me."

"Sir Henry Wallace?" D'argent was amazed.

"A long story," said Stephano. "You say my mother knew

this and she went after them? That was madness! Why didn't you stop her?"

"We are speaking of your lady mother, Stephano," said D'argent with a faint smile. "I could no more stop her than I can stop the sun from rising. If it is any comfort, she did not go alone. She is accompanied by Sir Conal O'Hairt, a Knight Protector, a friend of Sir Ander Martel, your godfather."

"D'argent, I'm going after my mother. I will meet you at the palace—"

"No!" said D'argent in a tone as sharp and chilling as a gunshot. "Do not go to the palace."

Stephano stared at the man. "I know the king hates me, but I have to do something—"

"Do not go to the palace, Stephano. Nor you, Monsieur de Villeneuve." D'argent was pale. A muscle in his jaw twitched.

"Why shouldn't we go to the palace?" Rodrigo asked.

"I cannot tell you why, monsieur," said D'argent in a low voice. "I have made a promise to His Majesty. I am sworn to secrecy. I should not have even told you that much. Stephano, I have something else to give you."

He drew out a packet, a formal legal document, and handed it to Stephano.

"The countess's will. You are your mother's sole heir."

Stephano didn't touch it. "I am a bastard," he said with a curl of his lip. "I can't inherit."

"The Countess de Marjolaine is your mother," said D'argent. "Sir Julian de Guichen is your father. You are their legitimate son."

"I don't understand," Stephano said, frowning. "The law requires my parents to be married at the time of my birth—"

"The law states only that the parents should be married, no matter when the marriage takes place. Your parents were married, Stephano. The explanation is here, in your mother's will. You are heir to the de Marjolaine fortune. You are now one of the wealthiest men in the kingdom."

Rodrigo sucked in a breath and stared at his friend. Stephano took the will and gazed at it in dazed bewilderment.

"They were married? But if that's true, why didn't she tell me?"

"Your mother has enemies, Stephano," said D'argent gently. "Her enemies would have become your enemies. She sought to protect you."

Stephano was startled to feel tears burn his eyes. He blinked them angrily away. He could see Rodrigo looking at him with concern. Stephano abruptly handed the will back to D'argent.

"You keep it. My mother's not dead. She's not going to die."

He sat listening to the rain, which had started up again. He could hear it drumming on the roof of the carriage. D'argent took the will and put it back into his pocket.

"You came to purchase those barrels, D'argent," said Stephano, changing the subject. "Do you know what they contain? Did my mother?"

"The Tears of God," D'argent replied. "The Countess received information from one of her agents that the crystals were being offered for sale to a select clientele. Although she doubted the claims being made about the crystals, she dared not take a chance of them falling into the wrong hands. She arranged to purchase them."

Falling into the wrong hands. Stephano smiled grimly to hear Sir Henry Wallace's words echoed by his mother.

"The Tears of God perform as claimed," he said. "As usual, my mother made an excellent bargain."

"A better bargain than she imagined," said D'argent, almost to himself. "You say they work, Stephano, they provide lift. Did you observe this for yourself?"

"I did, sir," said Stephano. He described briefly how they had used one of the crystals to sail the pinnace.

"Excellent news," said D'argent. "Truly excellent."

By this time, they had circled the block. The carriage rolled to a stop in front of the *Sommerwind*. Stephano opened the door and stepped out. Rodrigo followed, keeping close to his friend. D'argent remained inside.

Shutting the door, Stephano leaned in the window to ask, "How is Benoit? Have you heard from him?"

D'argent shook his head. "He has not been around."

Stephano wondered if Benoit knew about the marriage. He remembered how Benoit had always held the greatest respect for the countess. Stephano had assumed the old man had done that just to irritate him.

"What should we do with the crystals?" Stephano asked.

"I'll take charge of them," D'argent answered. "Have them placed in my carriage. What will you do?"

"I told you. I'm going to find my mother."

"You will need money," said D'argent. "I will bring the funds to you tonight. You must tell no one, Stephano. You must keep up the pretense that your mother has taken the princess to her estate."

"I will tell my friends, that is all. I'll need their help. Where is the *Cloud Hopper*? My mother had it impounded."

"Mistress Miri will find her houseboat restored to her, docked in its usual place. And now I must be going. I have been away too long already. I will see you tonight."

Stephano wondered why D'argent was in such haste. Why the constrained manner, the shadowed countenance? Why the warning to stay away from the palace? D'argent would have been left with the responsibility of keeping his mother's affairs in order, maintaining the falsehood that she was visiting her estate with the princess. He could manage that easily enough.

As D'argent was about to give the signal to the driver to leave, Stephano halted him. He reached through the window to shake hands. "We have had our differences in the past, D'argent. But I have always appreciated your loyalty to my mother."

"My loyalty extends to her son," said D'argent.

He reached out to clasp Stephano's hand in both of his own, then shouted orders to the driver. The carriage rolled away. Stephano stood staring after the carriage, though not really seeing it.

"Your mother is a very courageous woman," said Rodrigo.

"And she has a fool for a son," said Stephano in bitter tones. "I am not proud of myself, Rigo. The way I have treated her, the horrible things I have said to her—"

"You had no way of knowing," Rodrigo said. "Your mother wanted you to think as you did."

Stephano gave a deep sigh. "Don't tell our friends yet. I need time to think."

What he truly needed was to talk to his mother. The one time in his life he had ever longed to see her, she was gone, perhaps beyond his ability to find her.

"I won't say a word," Rodrigo promised.

Stephano held a meeting with his friends on the deck of the *Sommerwind*. He explained briefly that his mother was the one who had purchased the crystals, that D'argent had taken them to the palace. He told Miri that the *Cloud Hopper* was back in its usual place and that he had another job for them already lined up and he would explain the details when they were home. Before they could ask questions, he walked off, saying that he was going to bid farewell to Captain Ley-decker.

Miri and Gythe and Dag looked at Rodrigo.

"Do you know what's going on?" Miri asked.

"It's about his mother," said Rodrigo.

"Oh, Lord!" Miri said, groaning. "Here we go again."

Dag scouted out a small horse-drawn wagon and paid the owner for the use of it for an hour. They loaded the crate of Rodrigo's books in the wagon, along with their possessions. Gythe and Miri and Rodrigo rode in the back of the wagon. Stephano sat up front with Dag and the Doctor, who had been released from the basket and was once more riding proudly on Dag's shoulder.

"I'll drive," said Stephano, picking up the reins.

The traffic around the dockyard was heavy, with lorries and wagons, cabs and pedestrians crowding the streets, and he had to concentrate on where he was going. He was aware that the others were concerned, wondering what was going on, worried for him. He resolved to tell them everything when they got home.

Home . . . He pictured his friends gathered once more around the kitchen table. Benoit would have purchased a barrel of ale and perhaps even wine with the money his mother gave him. They would have a hot meal and Stephano would sleep in a bed that wasn't suspended from the ceiling, didn't swing back and forth. They would make plans tonight. Tomorrow they would leave again, set out in pursuit of his mother and the princess.

When they arrived at the Boulevard of Saints, the street on which Stephano and Rodrigo lived, Stephano was starting to turn the wagon into the alley behind the house, planning to unload the crate of books at the tradesman's entrance, which was in the rear. He gave the reins a jerk, brought the horse to a sudden stop.

"What's the matter?" Dag asked.

"Look at the house," said Stephano. "It's the middle of the afternoon and the curtains are still drawn."

He jumped off the wagon. Dag hobbled the horse and he and the others came to join him.

"Benoit opens the curtains first thing in the morning," Stephano explained.

"He does it purposefully to irritate me," said Rodrigo. "I have told him time and again that civilized men do not rise before noon. Instead he flings open the curtains at some ungodly hour, filling the room with eye-piercing sunlight . . ."

"He doesn't like a dark house," said Stephano. "He wouldn't leave the curtains closed."

"Maybe something's happened to him," said Miri anxiously. "Maybe he's fallen ill."

"That old man is never sick. I don't like this. Dag, drive the wagon down the alley. The rest of you wait with him."

Stephano started off. Hearing footsteps, he turned to see Rodrigo hurrying after him.

"I'm coming, too. If there are thieves, they may have absconded with my valuables. My handkerchief collection alone is worth a small fortune."

Stephano smiled. "You're a true friend, Rigo."

"I may not be good for much else," said Rodrigo. "But I do try to be good at that."

Stephano circled around the house to the backyard. The windows in the back were closed, the shades drawn.

An iron fence surrounded the yard. Stephano gave the gate a gentle push. The hinges screeched alarmingly. Stephano froze. Rodrigo ducked behind a hedge.

"I told Benoit time and again the damn gate needed to be oiled," Stephano whispered irritably.

He waited tensely, but there was no sign that anyone had heard. He and Rodrigo squeezed through the partially opened gate. Motioning Rodrigo to wait where he was, Stephano ran stealthily across the yard to the back wall. He searched the bricks a moment, found the one he wanted, and pried it loose. Inside the hollowed-out brick was a spare key to the back door. Stephano replaced the brick.

He drew his pistol and crept up to the back door. Rodrigo joined him.

"First assassins and now intruders," Rodrigo whispered. "I think we should move."

Stephano slid the key in the lock and turned it softly. He heard the lock click, felt the door give. He looked back at Rodrigo, who had picked up a rake as a weapon and was trying to look as though he was prepared to use it.

Stephano shoved open the door with a bang and jumped inside. He stopped to stare in astonishment. Rodrigo, rushing in behind, almost fell over him.

Benoit was sitting at the kitchen table with three monks in crimson robes, drinking tea. The teapot was in the center of the table along with a loaf of bread and Dag's favorite jam. The monks and Benoit turned to stare at Stephano, who flushed in embarrassment and lowered his pistol.

"Reverend Brothers, I beg your pardon—"

Benoit gave a howl and leaped to his feet.

"Run, Stephano!" Benoit cried. "Run, sir! It's a trap!"

Before Stephano could react, one of the monks extended his hand. Blue streaks of magical energy flared from the monk's fingers, striking Stephano in the chest. Every nerve in his body burst into flame. His muscles spasmed and his heart seized. He dropped the pistol and fell to the floor and lay there twitching and jerking, helpless. The other monk casually walked over and picked up the pistol.

Rodrigo flung away the rake to kneel beside Stephano.

"Stop the spell!" Rodrigo cried angrily. "You're killing him."

The monk ended the magical construct with a flick of his wrist. Stephano rolled over limply, groaning. He could still feel the magic sizzling in his body.

"Go fetch the coach," the monk told his fellow.

"Rigo, help me up," said Stephano. When he was on his feet, leaning against the back of a chair for support, he faced the monk. "Who the devil are you? What's going on?"

"They're from the Arcanum, sir!" Benoit said, his voice shaking. "They're here to arrest you and Master Rodrigo!"

"The Arcanum?" Stephano was stunned.

"There must be some mistake," said Rodrigo.

"Lord Captain Stephano de Guichen and Monsieur Rodrigo de Villeneuve," the monk said formally, "you are both hereby placed under Seal on the order of His Holiness, Grand Bishop de Montagne. You will be transported to the Citadel of the Voice where you will stand trial for heresy with your fellow conspirators, Father Jacob Northrop and Sir Ander Martel."

"Conspirators!" Stephano repeated, bewildered. "We barely know those gentlemen—"

"You were at the Abbey of Saint Agnes with the priest and the Knight Protector," said the monk. "Sir Ander is, I believe, your godfather. You met again in the city of West-firth."

"All that is true, but—"

"You will have a chance to defend yourself at your trial, Captain. Please turn around. Place your hands behind your back. We have a coach waiting."

Stephano refused to move. "Do not arrest Monsieur de Villeneuve. He had nothing to do with this."

"Monsieur de Villeneuve is wanted on the additional charge of conspiring with the enemy, Sir Henry Wallace," said the monk.

"Oh, God!" Rodrigo whispered. He had gone deathly pale.

"This is ludicrous!" Stephano said angrily. "Rigo was Sir Henry's hostage!"

"Please face the wall, Captain. We do not want to have to hurt you or your friend."

Stephano turned, his hands behind him. He felt Rodrigo shudder when they put on the manacles.

"I've told them who your mother is, sir," Benoit said fiercely. "I'll go to the palace. The countess won't stand for this!"

Stephano and Rodrigo exchanged glances.

"My mother isn't in the palace, Benoit," said Stephano steadily. "She's gone to her estate."

The monks took hold of Stephano by the arms and marched him through the kitchen, to the front door. The second monk had hold of Rodrigo, who was close to fainting. His feet dragged the floor.

A wyvern-drawn coach landed on the street in front of the house. The Arcanum wasn't wasting any time. Stephano had to get a message to Dag, let him know what was going on. And he had to do that without implicating his friends. Benoit was standing in the doorway, a stricken look on his face.

"Benoit, you're not well!" Stephano called urgently, struggling to look over his shoulder. "Remember your heart palpitations. You should go see Doctor Ellington! His office is across the alley. Our old family physician, *Doctor Ellington.*"

"My heart? Doctor . . ." Benoit blinked, then gasped in sudden understanding. "Ah, yes, Doctor Ellington! I do feel all of a flutter, sir. I'll go see him at once."

The coach door was open. Stephano recognized the black equipage of the Arcanum; the official seal—a sword and a staff and a flame. He caught a glimpse of his friends waiting with the wagon. They hadn't seen or heard anything, apparently. Fearing the monks might see them, he looked quickly away and climbed inside the coach.

Rodrigo collapsed on the seat, half senseless. The two monks entered the coach. A third was riding with the driver. He plied his whip. The wyverns rose into the air. The coach left the ground.

Stephano looked down on his house and the streets around it. His friends were in the alley, gathered around the wagon, now staring up in wonderment at the black coach flying over their heads. As he watched, Benoit emerged from the back of the house and ran to talk to them.

They looked up again, this time in shocked dismay. Miri started to cry out to him. Dag stopped her and she stood gazing up at him helplessly. She put her hand to her lips . . .

The monk closed the shutters, leaving Stephano in darkness.

Turn the page for a preview of

THE SEVENTH SIGIL

MARGARET WEIS
AND
ROBERT KRAMMES

Available in September 2014 from
Tom Doherty Associates

TOR® A TOR BOOK

1

The wyvern-drawn prison carriage transported Stephano de
Guichen and Rodrigo de Villeneuve to a makeshift wharf
located only God and the Arcanum knew where. The terrain
was isolated, rock-bound. A yacht painted black and marked
with the symbol of the Arcanum was the only boat docked
at the wharf. The rain had let up and now the sun shone
through gray, trailing mists. The time must be somewhere
near midafternoon. Only about an hour had passed since
Stephano and his friend were accosted by the monks of Saint
Klee, placed under arrest, and carried off in chains.

The carriage landed. The monks ordered Stephano and
Rodrigo, both still in chains, to descend, then escorted them
to the black yacht.

They had been charged with heresy. They would be taken
to the dungeons at the Citadel, the home of the Arcanum, the
priests who enforced Church laws. The Citadel was a fortress

located on a mountain surrounded by the waters of an inland sea. If anyone had escaped from the Citadel's dungeons they had not lived to tell the tale.

Two monks sat in the driver's box of the yacht. One was the driver, operating the helm and handling the two wyverns. The other rode along as guard.

"We're dangerous criminals," Stephano remarked bitterly to Rodrigo.

His friend said nothing, might not even have heard him. Stephano regarded him with concern. Rodrigo walked with his head bowed, seemingly oblivious to what was going on around him. He wasn't even watching where he was going. He stumbled blindly over the uneven ground.

"We'll prove our innocence, Rigo," Stephano said to him.

Rodrigo bleakly shook his head. He knew as well as Stephano that those who went into the dungeons of the Citadel never came out.

The monk who had accompanied Stephano and Rodrigo ordered them to the yacht. The entrance was located behind the driver, which meant they had to climb up on the box to make their way inside.

The driver stood to allow them to pass. Stephano hoisted himself up on the box—not easy to do with his hands shackled. Rodrigo followed more slowly, missed a step, and nearly fell. The monk caught him and assisted him through the door. Once his prisoners were safely inside, the monk entered, then shut and locked the door behind him.

Stephano had been in Father Jacob's black yacht. It was luxurious, homey with a table, comfortable chairs, and beds. The interior of this yacht was bare, stripped down. The only furnishings were benches built into the bulwarks, a table—bolted to the deck—a chair, and several storage lockers. The portholes were covered by iron bars. This yacht was designed for prisoner transport.

The driver shouted at the wyverns, and the black yacht rose smoothly into the air.

"If you give me your word as gentlemen that you will not cause trouble, I will remove the manacles," said the monk.

Rodrigo held out his hands. Stephano was about to tell the monk to go to hell.

Rodrigo, seeing Stephano's obdurate expression, said, "Don't be a fool. Look at your wrists."

Stephano looked down. His wrists were cut and rubbed raw from the manacles. And he had to admit he felt helpless without the use of his hands.

"You have my word," he muttered dourly.

A blue spark sizzled from the monk's fingers and the lock on the manacles clicked. The manacles popped open and fell to the floor. The monk did the same for Rodrigo, then pointed to the benches, silently indicating they were to sit there.

Stephano sat down and rubbed his wrists. Rodrigo eased himself down on the bench and lay motionless, staring up at the ceiling. He was deathly pale. Stephano rested his hand on his friend's shoulder.

"Everything's going to be all right, Rigo. These charges that we conspired with Father Jacob and Sir Ander are ludicrous. There's been some sort of mistake. We're innocent."

Stephano spoke loudly, aiming his words at the monk, who had taken a seat facing his prisoners in the yacht's only chair.

Rodrigo closed his eyes.

Stephano sat forward and continued his argument. "These charges make no sense! The idea that either Father Jacob or Sir Ander are heretics is absurd and the notion that we conspired with them against the Church is more absurd still! Sir Ander is a Knight Protector, a man of honor, a true knight, dedicated to his faith. We met him and Father Jacob at the

Abbey of Saint Agnes. They were there to investigate the murders of the nuns. When the Bottom Dwellers attacked them, their yacht was damaged and we towed them to West-firth for repairs. That's all there was to it."

The monk remained unmoving, seemingly deaf.

"You're wasting your breath, my friend," Rodrigo said in a listless tone. "The monks of Saint Klee are the guardians of the Citadel, sent to arrest us and deliver us safely to the inquisitors. They don't care if we are guilty or innocent."

"They *should* care," Stephano said angrily.

Rodrigo gave a wan smile and again closed his eyes. The monk sat upright in his chair, watching Stephano and Rodrigo without appearing to watch them. Stephano had heard stories about the monks of Saint Klee, the guardians of the Citadel.

Saint Klee had been a man who taught that life was sacred and that one should subdue a foe, if possible, rather than kill him. To this end, the monks of Saint Klee had, over the centuries, developed specialized magicks designed to subdue their victims. Stephano could attest to the magic's effectiveness. His body still tingled from the spell they had cast on him, which had left him twitching and writhing on the floor.

This monk was short, lean, and spare. He wore the traditional red robes of the monks of Saint Klee. His long curly black hair was tied in a knot at the back of his head. He spoke with an Estaran accent. The other two monks in the driver's box wore the same red robes. They were both built the same—all bone and muscle and gristle. The only difference was that one had sparse graying hair and one had brown.

Stephano, feeling the need to move about, started to stand up. The monk jumped to his feet. Stephano hurriedly raised his hands to show he meant no harm.

"I gave you my word, Brother!" said Stephano, annoyed. "I just want to walk around a little, stretch my legs."

The monk considered, then nodded and settled himself again.

Stephano paced aimlessly around the yacht's only room, then walked over to look out one of the iron-barred windows. He was aware of the monk's eyes on him the entire time and he was tempted to ask if the monk thought he was going to try to rip out the bars, smash the glass, and hurl himself to his death on the ground far below.

The yacht was flying just beneath cloud level. Below, Stephano could see a walled city and outlying homes and farm fields spread over lush hillsides. A large river meandered among the hills. By the sun's location, he could tell they were sailing south. There were no other walled cities in this part of the country. The city must be Eudaine, on the banks of the river Conce.

A flash of lightning followed quickly by a crack of thunder startled him; then came a deluge. Rain poured down in a gray curtain, drumming on the roof and rolling down the windowpanes. The yacht's interior grew dark as clouds closed in.

A lamp stood on the table. The monk apparently liked to sit in the gloom, however, because he did not light it. More thunder rumbled and the yacht rocked with the gusting wind. The storm was worsening.

Rodrigo had not moved and Stephano feared he might slip into melancholia and never recover. He needed some way to distract him, rouse him from his dark thoughts. Stephano went back to sit beside him.

"Rigo, we need to talk," he said. "It's about my mother."

Rodrigo opened his eyes and sat bolt upright to stare in astonishment. The subject of Stephano's mother was forbidden by Stephano, who disliked thinking about her, much less talking about her. He now was driven by recent events to do both.

"I'm listening, but just remember, so is our friend," Rodrigo said with a glance at the monk.

Stephano shrugged. "He probably knows everything anyway. D'argent showed me the will that states I am my mother's legitimate heir."

"I know," said Rodrigo. "I saw it. What about it?"

"I don't believe it. It's a fraud. To be my mother's heir, she and my father would have to have been married."

"Then that must be the case. My dear fellow, your mother's will was drawn up by lawyers, signed and attested with her signature and the signatures of witnesses. How could it be a fraud?"

"According to my grandfather, my father never saw or communicated with my mother after I was born. He never talked about her; never uttered her name."

"Your grandfather must have been wrong. You have to face facts my friend," said Rodrigo. "Upon your mother's death—which sad occasion we all hope will not happen for many years—you will become one of the wealthiest men in Rosia, maybe in all the world. The crown's riches are said to be nothing compared to those of your mother."

Stephano brushed wealth aside. "D'argent said that he told me about my mother's will on her orders, because she fears she might not return. I am worried about her, Rigo. Seems strange to say, since I have always hated her."

"You could ask Sir Ander—" Rodrigo began.

"—When we see him in prison?" Stephano said drily, forgetting that he was supposed to be keeping Rodrigo's mind off their current predicament.

Rodrigo paled a bit, but he rallied.

"What I was going to say is that *once we are freed*, you can ask Sir Ander if he knows anything about your parents being married. He was a good friend to both of them."

Stephano thought this over. "I think Sir Ander *does* know

something. He tried to tell me back at the abbey, but I wouldn't listen. I resented the fact that he was friends with my mother, and I accused him of being disloyal to my father's memory. But maybe—"

He was stopped in midsentence by the shrill shrieking of the wyverns. The next moment, a fiery blast hit the yacht, throwing Stephano and Rodrigo off the bench and dumping the monk out of his chair.

"Were we struck by lightning?" Rodrigo asked.

"Not unless lightning is green," said Stephano grimly. "That was contramagic! Keep down."

Rodrigo flattened himself on the deck.

The monk twisted catlike to his feet. He cast Stephano a warning look. "Stay where you are, sir," the monk ordered, finally speaking. "Don't move."

The monk hurried to the window. Stephano had no need to move. Looking past the monk's shoulder, he could see armed men riding gigantic bats flying out of the rain clouds.

"Bottom Dwellers," said Stephano.

"Dear God!" Rodrigo groaned. "First we're arrested and now demons are attacking us! Could this day *get* any worse?"

The riders appeared to be aiming their fire at the driver. The wyverns were shrieking in terror at the sight of the giant bats, and he was having difficulty controlling them. The yacht rocked and pitched, making it hard to stand. Stephano could see at least a dozen more bats emerging from the storm clouds. He doubted if even the legendary monks of Saint Klee could fight off such numbers.

The monk remained standing in front of the window, gazing out at the bat riders, who now had the yacht surrounded. Stephano waited tensely for another attack, which likely would send the yacht plunging to the ground. But nothing happened; no more blasts.

"They are trying to force us to land," Stephano said.

"Why?" Rodrigo asked in muffled tones. He lay face down on the deck with his arms covering his head. "Why not just blow us out of the sky?"

Stephano shook his head. He spoke to the monk's back. "Do you know why, Brother?"

"They want the yacht," the monk replied. "They don't want to damage it. And they want to capture us alive."

Stephano at first wondered why and then recalled what Father Jacob had told him about how the demons had tortured the nuns of the Abbey of Saint Agnes before they killed them. He started to say something, glanced at Rodrigo, and was silent.

The high-pitched screams of the wyverns were growing louder and more frantic. The Bottom Dwellers, wearing demonic looking helms, flew alongside the yacht—a strange and hideous escort. The monk walked over to a bench and reached underneath it to draw out what appeared to be an ordinary wooden walking staff. Stephano guessed it wasn't ordinary or a mere staff. The monk returned to the window.

"I can help you fight them, Brother," said Stephano. "Give me a pistol. I know you rely on your magic, but you must have weapons stored somewhere on board."

The monk made no answer.

"I gave you my word as a gentleman I won't try to escape," Stephano promised.

"Mine, too," said Rodrigo from the deck. "If you have some silk I can cover it with constructs to defend against contramagic—"

"Rigo!" Stephano said sharply. In a lower voice he added, "Don't talk about contramagic! You're in enough trouble already!"

The monk was keeping watch out the window. He smiled faintly. "We also know how to defend against contramagic, Monsieur Rodrigo. Father Jacob warned us to be prepared."

"Then why are they charging us with heresy?" Stephano asked. "None of this makes any sense."

The monks launched their own attack. Bright, fiery red light reflected off the gray clouds, then another blast of green contramagic shook the yacht. Bats screeched; the wyverns screamed. Stephano caught a glimpse of a bat and its rider tumbling out of the sky trailing smoke.

"Please stand back, Captain," the monk ordered.

Placing himself directly in front of the iron-barred window, the monk raised the staff. The wood began to glow. A blast of red light streaked from the staff and struck the porthole. The glass exploded. The iron bars glowed red hot. The bat riders saw their danger, but it was too late to flee before the fiery wave hit them, immolating the two bats and their riders, consuming them in white flame.

"Good thing we didn't try to escape," Rodrigo remarked, shuddering.

The wind gusted, sending rain rushing through the broken window. The monk glanced over his shoulder at Stephano.

"The pistols are stored in a compartment in the bulkhead just above your head, Captain."

Stephano looked, but he could not see a compartment. The monk spoke a word and blue magical light illuminated the wall, revealing a secret cabinet.

"The pistols are loaded," the monk continued. "I will have to remove the warding constructs—"

A bat rider appeared outside the shattered window, and another bat rider swooped down beside him.

"Brother, duck!" Stephano warned.

Green fire blasted through the window. The monk cried out and reeled backward. Blood and rain streamed down his face. He staggered and Stephano caught hold of him.

"Rigo, light the lamp!" Stephano ordered, lowering the

wounded monk to the deck. "Bring it over here. And keep your head down!"

Rodrigo activated the lamp's magic with a word. Crouching low, he brought the light to Stephano. Rodrigo took one look at the monk's face in the lamplight and sucked in a horrified breath.

"Oh, God!" he whispered.

One of the monk's eyes had been pierced by a large, jagged splinter of wood; the other was dark with blood.

"I can't see!" The monk started to raise his hands to his face.

"Lie still. Don't move," Stephano said to the monk. Taking hold of his hands, he gently lowered them. "I'll get help."

Green light flared, and Stephano could feel the yacht take another hit and make a stomach-dropping dive. Stephano and Rodrigo froze, helpless. Finally the driver managed to bring the yacht under control and they leveled out. Stephano breathed a sigh of relief.

"Rigo, stay with him. I'll go fetch the others."

Stephano started to stand up, but Rodrigo seized hold of his arm, dragging him back down.

"Look!" Rodrigo held the lamp over the monk.

A large stain, black against the red of the monk's robe, was slowly spreading over the monk's chest. Stephano tore open the monk's robes to examine the wound. The lantern wavered. The beam of light stabbed all around the yacht's interior.

"Stop shaking, Rigo. Hold the lamp steady," Stephano ordered curtly.

Rodrigo swallowed and made a valiant effort to hold still. A projectile of some sort had entered the monk's chest. The man's head lolled, and his body was limp.

"He's dead," said Stephano, as he sat back on his heels.

The gray clouds reflected the green and red of the flaring attacks as the yacht rolled despite the driver's struggles with the wyverns. His fellow monk was still alive, still fighting. Another flash of red light accompanied by an extremely loud explosion was followed by the sound of a bat screeching in its death throes.

"They won't be able to hold them off," said Stephano. He stood up, then staggered across the deck to the cabinet, nearly falling as the yacht took another hit. "Rigo, I need those pistols. Can you see the warding constructs he was talking about?"

Rodrigo lurched toward Stephano, stumbled, and crashed into him. "I can see them, but they're—"

"Good! Work your magic and get rid of them."

"I can't," said Rodrigo, keeping one arm braced against the bulkhead.

Stephano glared at him in frustration. "Damn it, Rigo, you have to!"

"You saw the kind of fancy magic these monks use!" Rodrigo protested. "It would take me a week to unravel—"

"Hush!" Stephano ordered.

Rodrigo froze. They could both hear the sounds of a desperate struggle right outside the door. They heard another blast, loud screams and the shrieking of fear-crazed wyverns. And then they could feel the yacht begin to descend. No more red flares of light. The fight was apparently over.

"What's happening now?" Rodrigo whispered. "Can you tell?"

Stephano could see through the hole the tops of trees rising up to meet them.

"They're going to try to land," said Stephano.

Rodrigo gulped. "What do we do?"

"I have an idea," said Stephano, thinking as he spoke. "Block the door with that crate!"

"Is that going to stop them?" Rodrigo asked. "The crate's not very heavy."

"No, but it will slow them down."

Rodrigo dragged the crate across the deck and pushed it against the door. Stephano retrieved the lamp. Holding it, he placed himself directly in front of the gun cabinet.

"Get behind me," he ordered Rodrigo. "Out of the line of fire."

"Meaning you're going to let them shoot at you. You can't be serious!"

"Not shoot at *me*. Shoot at the cabinet and destroy the magic. It's the only way to break those damn constructs. When the magic is gone, you yank open the cabinet and grab two pistols. One for you and one for me."

Rodrigo blanched. "Me! You know I can't hit anything!"

"You can hardly miss at this range," said Stephano grimly. "Just make sure to point the barrel at the bat rider, not at me. Or yourself."

Rodrigo groaned. "Oh, God!"

A bat rider tried to open the door, only to find it blocked. He struck the door with something, probably his foot. The first blow shifted the crate. The second knocked the door open.

From his vantage point, Stephano could see two Bottom Dwellers in the driver's box. One was driving the yacht, trying desperately to calm the wyverns and not having much luck. The other bat rider stood warily in the doorway. He wore demonic-looking armor and was carrying one of the short-range green fire weapons.

Stephano waved the lamp back and forth to draw the man's attention. He shouted, raised his hand as though he held a pistol, and took aim.

Startled, the Bottom Dweller shot at him.

Stephano leaped to one side. Fiery contramagic streaked past him and struck the cabinet right where he had been standing. The warding constructs flashed blue, then started to disappear as the green-glowing contramagic ate away at them.

Rodrigo desperately tried to open the cabinet. The magical constructs were broken, but he discovered a manual lock. Such locks were generally no problem for Rodrigo, who was accustomed to doing a little harmless snooping around the palace. Judging by his muttered imprecations, he was having difficulty with this one.

The Bottom Dweller drew a second weapon and aimed it at Rodrigo. Stephano flung the lamp and hit the soldier in the arm, disrupting his aim. The lamp broke, plunging the cabin into darkness.

"Rigo!" Stephano called urgently.

"Got it!" Rodrigo cried.

A small sizzle of blue electricity flared around the lock, sparks flew, and he pulled open the cabinet door. Several pistols were mounted on one of the cabinet walls, along with powder flasks and ammunition. Rodrigo took down a pistol and tossed it to Stephano, who caught it and dove for cover underneath the table. He hoped the monk had been right when he'd said the pistols were loaded.

Barely taking time to aim, Stephano pulled back the hammer of his pistol and fired, just as the bat rider fired his weapon at him.

The soldier grunted in pain and clutched his leg as green light flared, and a wave of heat washed over Stephano. The wooden tabletop went up in flames. Stephano beat a hurried retreat, crawling across the deck. He knew he had at least hit the Bottom Dweller, but unfortunately, not critically. Even as blood was running down the man's leg, he was reloading his weapon.

Rodrigo, white-faced, held a pistol in his shaking hands. "Don't make me kill you! Don't make me! Don't make me!"

The Bottom Dweller raised the weapon and aimed it.

"Rigo! Shoot!" Stephano yelled.

Rodrigo shuddered, closed his eyes, and pulled the trigger. The gun went off, Rodrigo fell over backward, and the Bottom Dweller staggered as the bullet slammed into him. Stephano dashed across the deck to the cabinet and grabbed another pistol. He turned to shoot, caught a glimpse of tree limbs flashing past the window and realized that the yacht was falling much too fast. With a horrific, wood-splintering crash, the yacht slammed into the trees, flipped over on its side, and went tumbling, rolling through the branches. Tree limbs snapped and cracked.

Stephano lost his grip on the pistol and crashed into what had once been the ceiling and was now the deck. The yacht continued to fall. Rodrigo slid on his belly past Stephano. The body of the dead monk tumbled past Rodrigo. The Bottom Dweller slammed into the table, which was bolted to the deck and was the only object in the yacht that wasn't in motion. Then the terrifying plunge through the trees suddenly ended. The yacht came to bone-jarring stop.

Stephano lay on his back, too shaken to move. Dim light filtered through the wreckage. He looked for the door and saw it hanging open above him. Through it he could see nothing but leaves and branches. The yacht shifted and shuddered and Stephano sucked in a breath, expecting another fall. The yacht was apparently only settling, for it stopped moving.

"Rigo," Stephano called softly.

"I'm here . . . I think . . ."

Stephano looked over his shoulder to see his friend lying on his belly, his arms outstretched, his feet against the blood-spattered wall.

"Are you all right?"

"I bit my lip," Rodrigo said plaintively. "And my arm hurts. What about you?"

"Bruises and cuts, nothing serious. Where are we?" Stephano asked, still whispering. "Can you see out the window?"

Rodrigo gingerly turned his head.

"I think we're on the ground. The yacht is tilted at an angle, leaning against a tree trunk."

Stephano was about to try to raise himself off the deck when he heard sounds coming from outside—a groan and someone moving about. Whoever had been flying the yacht—presumably a Bottom Dweller—was still out there.

"Lie still!" he hissed at Rodrigo.

Stephano shifted his head to locate the gun cabinet and silently swore. The pistols were there, mounted in the gun cabinet, but he couldn't reach them. The cabinet was now about twelve feet above his head.

"Odhran!" the driver—he assumed the man was the driver—called.

Stephano was startled. Gythe had claimed the Bottom Dwellers spoke to her in the language of the Trundlers, and this one had a Trundler name. He recognized it because one of Miri's innumerable cousins was called Odhran. Stephano cast a glance at the Bottom Dweller in the cabin. His body was wrapped, unmoving, around the table.

The driver called again more urgently, "*Odhran, cabru le!*"

Stephano knew a few words that he'd picked up from Miri. These words were among them, good words to know in any language: "I need help!"

Rodrigo's eyes were wide. "What do we do?" he mouthed.

"Play dead," whispered Stephano.

"I can do that," Rodrigo muttered. "I'm halfway dead from fright already."

Stephano kept looking at the door, his eyes half closed, peering out through his eyelashes.

The Bottom Dweller said something else, something about his legs. Stephano wasn't sure, but he thought the man was pinned inside the driver's box. A head appeared in the open doorway. The Bottom Dweller had removed his helm and his large eyes squinted in the dim light, trying to see. When he saw the body hooked on the table legs, he groaned and shook his head.

He called Ohdran's name for a third time, then muttered something and shifted his attention to Stephano and Rodrigo. Stephano closed his eyes and held his breath.

A flapping of bat wings came from outside the yacht. The Bottom Dweller drew back his head.

"Captaen! Thar anseo!"

Through the open door, Stephano could see a mounted bat rider hovering in the air above the yacht.

"There's another fiend outside," Stephano told Rodrigo softly. "Don't move!"

"Don't worry!" Rodrigo gasped.

The bat rider descended, out of Stephano's view. He could hear the man outside, talking to the driver. Stephano had trouble understanding, but he caught enough to gather that the driver was trapped inside the box and the captain was attempting to free him. The latter asked about Odhran, to which the driver said something Stephano couldn't hear due to the rustling of leaves and cracking of branches. After a lot more noise, the captain was successful in freeing his comrade, and the next thing Stephano knew, both men were peering inside the door.

Stephano closed his eyes. The captain called Odhran's name again, and Stephano waited tensely for him to climb into the yacht to investigate. After several heart-pounding moments, the captain backed away from the door and said something to the driver.

Stephano recognized the word, *marbh*. Dead.

The captain left the doorway.

"I can't stand this. I'm going to be sick," Rodrigo murmured.

"No, you're not," Stephano whispered savagely. "They're still out there." He waited a moment, listening. "I think they're leaving. Don't move yet."

Watching through the open door, he saw the bat rise from the ground, now carrying two riders. Stephano waited until the bat was out of sight, then took a breath. He didn't realize until then he had stopped breathing.

"Can I be sick now?" Rodrigo asked. He was in pitiful condition, his face smeared with soot and blood from where he'd bitten his lip, and his jaw swollen and bruised. He moved his left arm and winced.

Stephano felt a large lump growing on his forehead, and realized that a painful gash across his nose was bleeding profusely.

"Wait until we get out of here," he said, as he helped Rodrigo to his feet.

Kicking aside some broken boards, they crawled out of the wreckage. Once out in the open, Rodrigo ducked behind a tree, and shortly after, Stephano heard the sound of retching.

When Rodrigo returned, pale and disheveled, he was cradling his left arm.

"Is it broken?" Stephano asked, concerned.

"I don't think so. I'm going to have an unsightly bruise," he added.

He paused a moment, clearly distraught.

"Did I kill that wretched demon, Stephano?" he asked finally. "My eyes were closed. I couldn't see."

"I don't know, Rigo," said Stephano, who was fairly certain Rodrigo's shot had by some miracle actually hit the fiend. "Everything happened at once. If you did, you saved us. He would have killed us."

"I know," Rodrigo said softly. "But still . . . he was some demon mother's son."

He sighed deeply, wiped his face again and looked around.

"Do you have the faintest idea where we are? All I see are trees."

"The yacht flew over the city of Eudaine not long before we were attacked," said Stephano. "We can't be far from there. We were flying south, and we can tell by the position of the sun which way is west. So if we start walking that direction—"

"Stephano, look," said Rodrigo suddenly, pointing to a tangle of green leaves and gray branches and a splash of red.

The body of the Saint Klee monk lay in a heap a short distance away. The body must have been thrown from the yacht when it struck the trees.

"We need to do something for him. We can't leave him here. We should bury him," said Rodrigo, his voice breaking.

"We have no tools to dig a grave," said Stephano. He walked over to the corpse. Taking off his coat, he draped it over the monk's ravaged head. "God rest your soul, Brother, and give you peace."

"Amen," Rodrigo said softly.

He slumped against the trunk of the tree. Stephano eyed his friend with concern.

"Sit down and rest. I'll search the yacht. There must be food and water on board." He glanced at Rodrigo. "We don't want to spend the night here, I'm thinking."

Rodrigo shivered. "With two dead men? God forbid. But I've thought of a problem, Stephano. We gave the monk our word of honor as gentlemen we wouldn't escape."

"I think he would release us from that promise," said Stephano. He was silent a moment, then said somberly, "We will have to go to the monks, tell them where to find his body."

"That means they'll arrest us again!" said Rodrigo. He looked back at the corpse lying beneath Stephano's coat and sighed. "You're right, of course. The poor fellow must have a proper burial. I suppose the monks will bury the demon, as well. We should leave them a note, tell them his name was Odhran. Strange that his armor didn't go up in flames, like the first demons we encountered."

"Good thing for us it didn't," said Stephano grimly. "The same happened with the Bottom Dwellers that died on Braffa. Their armor didn't destroy the bodies. I wonder why."

"Maybe because they're not taking time to add the magical constructs that would make it catch fire," said Rodrigo, adding in thoughtful tones, "That could be significant."

"For what reason?" Stephano asked, trying to sound interested.

His mind was on other things, such as wandering about lost in the wildnerness without food or water. He was glad to see Rodrigo thinking about something else, taking his mind off their terrifying experience. "I'm going inside the yacht to look around. Keep talking."

Stephano made his way back to the wreckage of the yacht, shifted some tree branches, and climbed inside. Rodrigo's voice floated through the cracks.

"They went to great lengths to make us think they weren't human. They were fiends from hell with faces out of nightmares and bodies that were destroyed by magic fire. They wanted to demoralize, terrorize. But now they don't care. And maybe they've stopped caring because it doesn't matter anymore. The flaming corpses, the murder of the nuns, the attack on Westfirth, the destruction of the Crystal Market, the seizure of the Braffan islands and the attempt to bring down the palace—they are rushing headlong toward some dire ending."

Stephano considered this highly likely. "All the more reason I need to go ahead with my plan to take the fight to them," he muttered. "That assumes, of course, we're not languishing in some dungeon."

Rummaging about, he found blankets, a bag of dried

sardines, complete with the heads; dried fruits so shriveled up he couldn't recognize them; and bread that looked as if it had been baked sometime during the Dark Ages. If this was what the monks lived on, no wonder they were so thin.

He also found a water skin filled with tepid water. He hauled his finds out of the yacht, then walked over to where Rodrigo was sitting and handed him the water skin, figuring he'd tell him about the unappetizing looking food later.

Rodrigo took several sips of water and seemed to feel better. Some color returned to his face.

"Do you feel up to walking? We have about two hours before dark," Stephano said.

"I'm ready," said Rodrigo, rising a little unsteadily to his feet. He cast a gloomy look about. "There are certainly a *lot* of trees."

"I think that's why they call it a forest," said Stephano.

He and Rodrigo set out, gauging their direction by the sun that every so often would break through the clouds. Their progress was slow, for they had to make their way through the dense undergrowth, climbing over fallen logs, pushing through brush and bushes. Both of them were soon bruised, battered, and exhausted.

Stephano called a halt when they reached a small stream. Rodrigo built a fire, using his magic to light the kindling.

"Reminds me of being marooned on that damn island," he remarked.

He eyed the food with a shudder and said he wasn't hungry. Stephano persauded him to eat something, to keep up his strength. They huddled near the fire, for as the sun went down, the night was growing cold.

"How far do you think we are from Eudaine?" Rodrigo asked. "How long will it take to get there?"

"I don't know," said Stephano. "Several days? Maybe a week."

"What if we keep walking and walking and we never find our way out?"

"That's not going to happen," said Stephano.

Rodrigo pressed him. "You're certain?"

"Mostly certain," said Stephano with a smile.

Rodrigo sighed.

The woods were now dark outside the circle of firelight, filled with shadows and strange night noises. Stephano banked the fire. They wrapped themselves in the blankets and tried to burrow down among the leaves.

"Keep talking," said Rodrigo. "Whenever I close my eyes, I see that poor monk's face. What do you think our friends are doing now?"

Dag, Miri, and Gythe had been in the alley outside Stephano's house, waiting for him and Rodrigo, who had walked into their kitchen and straight into an ambush. Their friends had watched, helpless to save them, as the monks took them away.

"They will all be sitting around the kitchen table," said Stephano. "Dag will be forming schemes to break us out of the Citadel. Miri will be fuming, sweeping, cleaning like she always does when she's upset. Gythe will be trying to keep the doctor from licking the butter and Benoit will be telling them how he could have fought off the monks single-handed if it hadn't been for his lumbago."

Stephano smiled at the thought of the crotchety old steward.

"Maybe our friends will come looking for us," said Rodrigo, a tinge of hope of in his voice.

Stephano had to squelch it. "They won't try to find us, Rigo. Because no one knows we're lost."

ABOUT THE AUTHORS

Margaret Weis attended the University of Missouri, Columbia, graduating in 1970 with a B.A. in literature and creative writing. In 1983, she moved to Lake Geneva, Wisconsin, to work as a book editor at TSR, Inc., producers of the Dungeons & Dragons® role-playing game. Margaret Weis is the author or coauthor of a number of *New York Times* bestselling series, including The Dragonlance® Chronicles, Darksword, Rose of the Prophet, Star of the Guardians, The Death Gate Cycle, Sovereign Stone, and Dragonvarld. She lives in Wisconsin with her four dogs.

Discover more at www.margaretweis.com.

Robert Krammes lives in southwest Ohio with his wife Mary and their two cats. He is a longtime member of The Society for Creative Anachronism, an avid Cincinnati Bengals fan, and a backyard bird-watcher.

Storm Riders is their second collaboration; their first was *Shadow Raiders,* the first novel of the Dragon Brigade. Their third book, *The Seventh Sigil,* will complete the trilogy.